Special Tributes:

My gratitude goes to my co-author, Elf... help and devotion, this story could never have been written. I'm hopelessly lost when analyzing our combined efforts in bringing this amazing story to the world. It seems almost beyond imagination that two strangers could meet under the most bizarre of circumstances and produce this epic saga of love without ever coming face to face. I can only concur with one of the major messages from "The Meadow," and that is to accept that everything is connected in one way or the other. I wholeheartedly support the quotation of one our characters in the book when it is said that the *interconnectedness of multi-dimensional consciousness* is what supports our souls as we surf the cosmic waves of Truth. For that reason alone, my heartiest and warmest thanks go to Elfreda, who entered into this adventure with me.

Mike O'Hare

I would like to dedicate "The Meadow" to the man who invited me to co-author this wonderful novel with him and to all people who believe that there is much more to life than what "reality" suggests. A central theme of the book is the interconnectedness of the Universe and nothing else can explain how two strangers, who live an ocean apart, could collaborate to write a story of these dimensions *and* forge a life-long friendship as part of the bargain. My special gratitude goes to my own family for their unconditional love and support as they watched the progress of "The Meadow" and never complained about the many nights when writing progressed into the small hours of the morning.

Elfreda Pretorius

The authors want to express their gratitude and appreciation to Willem Pretorius who designed the cover of the book, title page and graphics.

Special mention: Louise Salton, Editor.

Endorsements:

There is a saying known by those on their path of enlightenment: Everything comes at the perfect time, in the perfect way. "The Meadow" is exactly the sort of work where if it somehow comes your way, it is a timely message and gift from the Universe to assist you in advancing your own spiritual evolution. "The Meadow" is a magical journey for the characters in the story and the reader alike. The lessons learned by the protagonists will shine a light on whatever issues a reader may be experiencing. The work is serendipity, synchronicity, and spirituality. Note to the Showtime Network: We expect to see "The Meadow" as a mini-series and/or trilogy of films. When this novel graced our presence, we had set aside a three week period to devour its contents. Little did we know how captivating it would be as we finished it—cover to cover, word for word, in three days! Do the same and treat yourself to a modern-day literary masterpiece.

Veronica Grey
Philanthropist, Actress, Novelist
Founder of Eternal Youth Empire

When Mike first approached us to read "The Meadow" in the early stages of development, we found it hard to believe that as a young boy visiting the Forum during the Billingham International Folklore Festival, on hearing the International music, an idea was born. From this idea, came this outstanding book of love, re-incarnation, espionage, and deceit. A powerful thought provoking read, you will not be able to put down.

Joe Maloney
Director
Billingham International Folklore Festival

What a fantastic book; couldn't put it down. Tel Aviv to England had my heart in my mouth! I wish the authors only the greatest success. Readers should know that they will not be able to get any work done. I read two hundred pages in one go. It is thrilling, encapsulating, sad and heart warming.

Gillian Scott, M.A.T.A.
Reflexologist and Amatsu Teacher

"The Meadow" is a sensational and captivating account of two people's lives as they meet again and again over many centuries. It weaves a path of wisdom through the ages, and awakens our curiosity, enriching our lives as we become involved with its wonderful characters.

Judy Suke
Motivational Humorist
President, Triangle Seminars
Professor, Sheridan College

Get ready for a consciousness shift! "The Meadow" is the most intriguing, mysterious, beautiful love story I've ever had the pleasure of reading. I am still amazed that the authors could have brought this masterpiece to life while living an ocean apart. The gamut of emotions they dare the reader to experience makes for a wild, but thrilling ride. "The Meadow" touched the very core of my being and gave me a whole new perspective on all those who have come and gone in my life, the ones that shared beauty with me as well as the ones who caused me pain.

Susan Nicholas
Reiki Master

"The Meadow" takes you along on a captivating journey connecting powerful characters through time. This engrossing journey, through many eras and parts of the world, is suspenseful, emotional, riveting and insightful. The magical MEADOW—fascinating! The authors are well deserving of "Top Ten" recognition.

Mary Hanna
Psychoeducational Consultant

"The Meadow" is a poignant story of eternal love that transcends the boundaries of time, age and gender. Interwoven through the intrigue, passion and drama of the many lifetimes of the protagonists, is a deep spiritual thread. A profoundly moving story—written with the emotion and subjectivity of two authors whose intimate awareness of the lives of the various characters suggests first-hand familiarity.

Louise Salton
Retired Editor
Oakville, Canada

This book of multiple lives and other dimensions has challenged me to look beyond the words on the pages and contemplate if I have indeed visited the Meadow in between previous existences. "The Meadow" is cleverly thought-out and construes a path of development for the characters through each life. The book is intriguing, enlightening and superbly written! I hope a sequel has been planned for this very advanced work.

Susan Bridges
Childcare Specialist
Mississauga, Ontario

"The Meadow" is simply one of the most engrossing books I have read in years. It grabbed hold of me on the opening page and did not let go. I cannot recommend it highly enough.

Lesley Lomon
Avid reader of approximately 100 books annually
Toronto, Canada

Copyright © 2009 by Mike O'Hare and Elfreda Pretorius

All rights reserved. No part of this book may be used or reproduced by any means, graphic, electronic, or mechanical, including photocopying, recording, taping or by any information storage retrieval system without the written permission of the publisher except in the case of brief quotations embodied in critical articles and reviews.

This is a work of fiction. All of the characters, names, incidents, organizations, and dialogue in this novel are either the products of the authors' imagination or are used fictitiously.

iUniverse books may be ordered through booksellers or by contacting:

iUniverse
1663 Liberty Drive
Bloomington, IN 47403
www.iuniverse.com
1-800-Authors (1-800-288-4677)

Because of the dynamic nature of the Internet, any Web addresses or links contained in this book may have changed since publication and may no longer be valid. The views expressed in this work are solely those of the authors and do not necessarily reflect the views of the publisher, and the publisher hereby disclaims any responsibility for them.

ISBN: 978-1-4401-4581-0 (sc)
ISBN: 978-1-4401-4583-4 (hc)
ISBN: 978-1-4401-4582-7 (ebook)

Library of Congress Control Number: 2009929216

Printed in the United States of America

iUniverse rev. date: 08/18/2009

To Jean.
Best wishes,
Mike O'Hare
Nov. 12th 2009.

THE MEADOW

Mike O'Hare
Elfreda Pretorius

iUniverse, Inc.
New York   Bloomington

Every Native American has heard the story and dreams of one day finding the feathers. It is said that following a night of the full moon, when the mountain snows have disappeared and the buffalo finally return, the most wondrous crossing of two sacred birds takes place in the skies above the open plains.

Cloaked in the gloom of early dawn, the eagle leaves its lofty nest and approaches the forest where it circles silently, waiting with piercing eyes for the owl to rise from the wooded darkness. Before the sun illuminates the outer rim of the world, the king of the day and lord of the night rapidly ascend into the heavens where, in a sight to behold, they initiate a spectacular aerial display.

But when daylight creeps stealthily across the prairie, the birds unexpectedly drop from the sky and plunge toward a seemingly inevitable, but senseless death. Shrieking with talons extended, on an apparent collision course with the earth, they abruptly pull out of the free fall and silently glide past each other. It is rumored that just as a glimpse of the rising sun is captured in the eye of the owl, and when the fading moon shimmers in the glare of the eagle, a tail feather is dropped by each bird.

Legend has it that the feathers will bring their finder true love and bless him with wisdom. Every young brave dreams of wearing a headdress proudly displaying these feathers. But there's one more sacred promise; to live forever with the one that you love.

Rachel

The eagle saw her first. It puffed out its neck feathers in warning and opened its beak slightly where it sat on the nest. Without moving its head, the huge bird glared intensely at the girl. Rachel stood quite still and returned the unwavering look, but her young heart sang. If the eagle didn't fly off, it meant that it was brooding and protecting eggs. She stifled the giggle that bubbled up, thrilled at what was so blatantly obvious. She and the bird had something big in common; the eagle expected to hatch eaglets and she was ready to hatch a dream.

After the long Canadian winter on the island of Cape Breton, Rachel couldn't wait to scale the cliffs behind their home again. The secret route to her favorite hideout still had some icy patches, but she knew how to navigate these and was impatient to reach the pinnacle, from where she could sit and gaze at the ocean, while nurturing her dream. The eagle kept her vigilantly in sight; the thought of her dream sent a tremendous rush through her body. She leaned forward and, taking care not to make sudden movements, she softly addressed the bird.

"Mrs. Eagle, keep your eggs warm so that your babies can hatch when the time is right." She smiled conspiringly. "I will tell you when my dream comes true. I promise." Then she retreated cautiously. It was time to check the mail again! Her excitement was boundless.

Rachel's mother noticed her new routine and asked her husband what the daily scaling of the cliffs meant and why their sixteen-year-old daughter was keeping a vigil at the mailbox. She raised a curious eyebrow at his reply.

"She wrote a love story for a magazine in Toronto?" She pursed her lips in a distinctive habit that accentuated her high cheekbones, which made her appear hard. Then she added with the faintest tinge of cynicism. "What does she know about love?" She had long become used to Rachel confiding in her father, rather than her.

Editor to the local Cape Breton Post, Rachel's father didn't reply, but watched the object of his love rush in through the backdoor and strip off her parka and boots. Taller than the average girl, her slender limbs and long chestnut hair defied family genes on both sides, as did her sunny disposition, portraying none of the dullness so characteristic of other relatives. It was still cold on the higher elevations and he noticed her rosy cheeks and the bright light in her hazel eyes.

"How much longer before they hatch?" he whispered softly in her ear, hugging her.

"Not long, Daddy. I think she minds my presence less and less. We have a bond now." She smiled and kissed his cheek, holding up her hands and shaking her head in playful protest. "Don't ask—nothing yet in the mailbox! But soon, I think." His heart contracted on her behalf, wishing he could scoop up all the hurt and disappointment scheduled to cross her path now and in the future and protect her from it. He admired her courage but, paradoxically, it also exposed her vulnerability. His girl had written her story first in longhand and then carefully typed it before sending it off. Only once had he asked her about it.

"What kind of love story is it, Rachel?" She sat next to him on the dock where he had cast a leisurely line, resting her head against his shoulder. Like her, he was lost in the reflection of the clouds on the water. She answered without hesitation.

"The kind that makes your bones ache, Daddy; even if you have not yet had a chance to love anyone like that." He tugged at the line, overwhelmed with her ability to express at such a deep level.

"How do you know, Rachel? You're sixteen." When she didn't answer he turned his head to look at her. Her eyes were filled with tears and she looked straight ahead. But her expression was serene and accepting, as if she felt the weight of the load and was used to carrying it.

"I don't know, Daddy. It just feels like a very old memory."

Sixteen weeks since she had first come across the brooding eagle, she crept closer to the nest again. The mother was nowhere in sight and Rachel looked forward to admiring the reflection of the sun on the young birds, and listening to the excited squeaking that her presence evoked. But the eaglets were gone. Rachel stared at the empty nest in shock and then she knew that this was the sign that she had been waiting for. She turned and dashed along the path which led down the cliff, running and jumping over rocks and dried tree stumps; her heart thundering in her chest. This had to be the day!

She was right. The long awaited letter was in the mailbox, but she was not prepared for the cold, businesslike rejection. Her father found her in her bedroom curled into the fetal position and read the letter on her dresser with a wistful expression on his face. Then he sat down next to her and softly stroked her hair. What else was there to do?

Jake

"Stop being silly! Now get off the floor and climb back into bed!" Little Jake could do nothing else; he was so frightened. Not daring to look at the window, he scrambled back into bed and hid under the covers; his heart thundering in his ears. Had that owl really spoken to him? The next minute he flew out of bed and ran downstairs into his mother's arms. She smiled and ruffled his fair hair, placing a reassuring kiss on his crown.

"You must have been dreaming, Jake. Owls don't speak, dear."

Whether it was the fantastic interlude with the owl that triggered the interest in birds, he didn't know. The image of that wise old barn owl perched on his windowsill and ordering him about when he was only four was etched into his memory forever. By age twelve he amazed everyone with his knowledge of birds, but it was the owl species that had captivated his imagination. At every opportunity in school he wrote fantasy stories about owls. His teachers thought these odd, but they merely checked his grammar and awarded his imagination with good grades. Only Jake knew that the scrapbook in which he scribbled all his short stories had been inspired by the interlude with the owl in his dream.

Living on the rural boundaries of Tees Valley in North East England provided easy access to the countryside; a favorite place he visited frequently to pursue his writing. Mr. Borthwick's barn backed onto his village and he had permission to use this cool dark shelter freely. The magic of the barn was its smell. Lying on a bale of sweet smelling hay, he deeply inhaled the familiarity of the old wooden building. It was infused with odors of grease and gas emanating from farm implements cooling down after a hard day's work; mingled with the musky smell of Fred, the old horse that his owner couldn't bear to have put down. The idea came to him for the first time in the barn, confusing and bewildering his young mind. He knew *nothing* of love;

where did these images and thoughts come from? He had no idea; he was only sixteen.

The presence of the pair of barn owls nesting in the roof was an unexpected and pleasant surprise and Jake quickly realized that as long as he kept quiet, he and the birds could go about their business undisturbed. Now and again he looked up into the rafters and wondered if the magic of so many years ago would repeat itself, and one of the owls would begin to speak. But under the scrutiny of their unwavering solemn stares, absurd thoughts like that quickly vanished. Yet he was convinced that his love of writing had been inspired by that strange visitation of a member of their species. Jake could no more explain the episode with the owl at that young and tender age, than account for the origins of the love story that had begun to take root in his mind and which was growing in stature every day.

For many years his heart remained his own and no one had moved him as deeply as the story in his head had suggested was possible. The memory of the fire in the barn, when he was but a boy, was the catalyst which put him in touch with his deepest feelings. The birds and their young hadn't stood a chance and Jake wept as he watched the burning embers fall to the ground. And then he heard a familiar voice inside his head. *Stop being silly! Now go and write that story.* He smiled through his tears and gave his head a shake; amazed that he had never forgotten that dream.

Jake didn't write it then or the next year, or the year after that. In fact, he didn't write it until he came across Rachel's website almost thirty years later. Theirs is another story, but *this* is the tale that she helped him to write. It is about the dream he had as a young boy that became real.

Before recorded time, in the ancient land of Mexica, the day of reckoning had arrived. A battle was about to commence.

Chapter 1
The Pact

The trained eye of the archer expertly focused on the *quah*, eagle emblem of his illustrious target. His muscles were relaxed, yet stealthily supported his body in the perfect posture for the execution. In absolute stillness he waited for the precise moment to release the first arrow. He was in no hurry; death was a certainty.

History paused briefly, without judgment, ready to record a single death or a bloodbath, the same way it would a birth or a victory celebration. As it waited, an aberrant quietness descended upon the valley. The heavy stillness infiltrated the consciousness of the target, obscuring the imminent violence which was to follow. The strike of the first arrow would, as always, invoke involuntary, but brief astonishment at the ambush. Notwithstanding the surprise, the life of the target would be smothered anyway and, in this instance, change the balance of power and dictate a new course for history to follow.

The uneasy alliance of the two rulers, Zolton and Atonal, was about to be extinguished. For Zolton, the *Cuhtli,* lord and ruler of Fentztohl, thirty years of peace was sufficient. Impatience was etched in deep furrows on his forehead; testimony to his quick temper and smoldering antagonism. For too long had he begrudgingly shared a coalition with Atonal, the tall soft-spoken ruler from the south who, given normal circumstances, would be a natural adversary. But now, under the influence of his jealous and scheming son, Zolton had recognized a way to claim supremacy of both regions. He was no longer prepared to see his power neutralized.

Prior to their coalition, both Zolton and Atonal were forced to keep a watchful eye on the Cautzpal Empire which had dominated the Mexicas for hundreds of years. Zolton, who ruled Fentztohl and Atonal, lord of Amustopl, were thorns in the side of the imperialistic Cautz rulers who desired to annex these fringe regions.

Topographically, mountain and river buffers that were difficult to breach offered protection, but the Cautz were experienced and very patient in conquering new land. They knew that vulnerabilities eventually would be exposed and soon, borders could be penetrated. It didn't take long before they identified the first chink in the armor of the Fentztohl region in the north and strategically deployed their garrisons to exploit this weakness. At the same time, scouts from the area of Amustopl in the south returned with reports of sightings of smoke signals, typical of the Cautz, which convinced Atonal that without help, his beloved Amustopl would soon be swallowed by the Cautzpal Empire.

Mightier combined, but at risk on their own, both Zolton and Atonal knew that only an alliance of their economic and military forces would prevent annexation by the Cautz. Temporarily, sovereign rule for either leader was no longer a viable option. In its own right, each territory contributed strength and value to the coalition. Amustopl, under Atonal, had tremendous mineral wealth around the lower river regions. Fentztohl, under Zolton, had the military strength, along with the frontier mountains that protected both of these areas. They needed each other, albeit begrudgingly, but in the face of the Cautz threat, Zolton and Atonal agreed to bury their differences and became integrated. The region was finally stabilized.

Zolton took his strategic move to strengthen the coalition one step further and offered his hand in marriage to Hautlaeh, who ruled on the other side of the Pocas Mountains in the east. Hautlaeh, raven-haired and gaunt, disguised her vulnerability behind an athletic body acquired from frequent trips to lookout points in the mountains. Her physique deceptively suggested a fierce independence. Both her parents had died in quick succession and she was forced to assume the duties of leadership which were not a natural trait to her. Zolton's offer came as a great relief personally, but strategically it offered security to her region, known as Chimalstol.

Despite his arrogant nature, Zolton, brooding and stout with unruly flaming curls, was not a warmonger, yet he reveled in his ability to control that which was under his domain. In his marriage to Hautlaeh, an arrangement of convenience rather than choice, his demeanor was distant and cold and he only occasionally physically united with her. It was the birth of their daughter, Anacaona, which changed many things, including Zolton's unforgiving manner.

The baby girl, born with dark hair and delicate olive skin, emerged into this world with an arresting quality about her, noticeable from the beginning. She seemed illuminated with a light from within and from the earliest times could hold her ground in eye contact with others, a characteristic which earned Zolton's immediate respect and admiration.

As Anacaona progressed through infancy into a young girl, she exhibited traits unlike any of her peers. Fascinated with nature, she had a quietness about her that suggested instinctive knowledge beyond the level of most others. Every quality of this beautiful dark-haired girl emphasized her uniqueness and, whereas her friends gave way to many lighthearted flirtations, Anacaona seemed unmoved by the lavish attention bestowed upon her. Her best friend, Teuch, a tall and fair young warrior with penetrating light gray eyes, came from the south and was the son of her father's co-ruler, Atonal.

On the surface both leaders were pleased with the easy relationship that existed between their young children. After all, it served its purpose for the *tiacapan,* firstborn of each ruler, to be united in marriage, plans of which lay firmly in their future. And in the absence of other siblings, Teuch, son of Atonal and Rahltaeah, found it easy, even natural to bond with the golden-limbed girl with the waist length black hair.

Neither Teuch nor Anacaona had any idea that just prior to incarnating, somewhere, somehow in the cosmic heavens two energies had converged ecstatically, if only briefly. Earthbound for the prehistoric Mexicas, they were destined to start a journey together of which enactment on the worldly stage would result in deep reward as well as personal devastation. They had no idea either, that their story would not reach its final conclusion for many thousands of years.

When Anacaona was five years old her mother, Hautlaeh, finally gave birth to the long awaited son that Zolton would have preferred to be his firstborn. Mautotl's entry into this world prophetically foretold the way he would live his life. In his zeal to be born, he forced his way so violently that his mother's desperate screams reduced the experienced midwife to a nervous bundle of hysterical incompetence. She had clasped a hand in horror over her mouth, powerless to console or assist the distressed woman, whose writhing body was imprisoned by never-ending waves of excruciating contractions.

After what seemed a very long time, Hautlaeh ceased all movement and appeared to stop breathing. The midwife leaned forward and urgently whispered her name although she had already recognized the eerie quiet as an ominous signal. Hautlaeh did not answer, as the midwife knew she wouldn't. Squatting beside the reed mat, she waited helplessly for the uncontrollable shaking to start; a fatal sign of the body's loss of rhythm and power to control the birthing of the infant. Soon, she knew, Hautlaeh would begin to hemorrhage.

Minutes later, covered in Hautlaeh's blood, the big burly midwife looked away when her patient's body finally went limp. Death had come to claim its victim and defeated, she straightened to fetch the customary mourners who would adequately wail the loss of a brave woman. But it was *his* first cry that stopped her in her tracks and she glanced back in utter shock. Somehow the child had survived the birthing nightmare and she stared transfixed at the screaming, scrawny baby boy that had been deposited between Hautlaeh's legs. His mouth was wide open and he loudly yelled his demand for immediate attention, and while his mother steadily inched her way into permanent darkness, he kept up his frantic squeals to be noticed. Only then did she become aware of Anacaona, crouched frightened in the corner of the room.

"What are you doing here, child?" she asked exasperated and out of breath.

"Why is my mother so quiet?" The midwife noticed the wet patch on the soil where the little girl was sitting, and realized that she had witnessed the entire ordeal. Her heart sank.

"Anacaona, please go outside!" She didn't know what else to say.

"Why is she not breathing?" The girl's voice was soft, but insistent. "Please! *Please!* Help my mother!"

"I cannot, child." Her voice sounded old and resigned; not because she hadn't encountered scenarios like this before, but because the child stared so distraughtly at the screaming baby. She was as unnerved by his relentless squeals as Anacaona seemed to be by his presence. The newborn appeared unconscionably strong and healthy for having caused his mother's end; like it had won a battle and was proud of it.

"Is my mother dead?" Her little face contorted in anguish.

"Yes," the midwife whispered hoarsely, wringing her hands together. She was incapable of explaining why. Anacaona slowly approached the big sweating woman and stood trembling at her side, refusing to look at her mother's face. Her voice was barely audible.

"Is it a boy?"

"It is a boy, child." The midwife suddenly remembered that she was addressing the offspring of one of the rulers and tried to appease the young girl's anxiety. "And by his relentless screaming, I would say that he is healthy and well."

"No he is not! He is *evil*." The little girl's gaze was transfixed on the baby. "Look at him!" Her eyes filled with tears and she choked on her words. "He knows not that my mother is dead!" Anacaona turned and fled from the room as quickly as she could.

"Come back, child!" But she kept on running. The reality of her new brother's presence filled her little heart with despair. And she knew not why.

On this day a keen observer would have known that Mautotl had established his life's pattern very early on. Years later when told of his mother's death, the possibility of Hautlaeh surviving instead of him struck him as completely absurd. It never crossed his mind that perhaps both could have lived. Mautotl was born selfish and from the very beginning his consciousness was devoid of empathy and the ability to share. Death was always an easy choice for him; the preferred punishment he meted out for his opponents or adversaries.

At the tender age of ten Anacaona was assigned the difficult task of assisting in raising Mautotl. Cursed with his father's wild red curls, the selfish and violent child demanded constant attention and had uncontrollable anger outbursts when his wishes were not fulfilled. As a toddler he hung around her legs and insisted on attention every moment of the day which tried his sister's patient nature. As he grew older, Anacaona found it increasingly difficult to obey her father's wishes in showing the belligerent child the way. His energy seemed low and sluggish and she often caught his brooding stare on her, following her every move. Mautotl rarely smiled or laughed and Anacaona learned to disassociate from his negative nature. Whilst still attending to his needs, she consciously placed emotional distance between herself and her younger brother, as though she understood that his influence was detrimental to all who came in contact with him.

In time Mautotl earned the reputation of the "evil one." For every friend he made, he added ten disgruntled enemies, all of whom had to bow to every ludicrous wish and whim of the spoilt boy, because of who his father was. Mautotl had learned quickly to take shelter under the protective wing of his father. Zolton, in turn, was utterly blind to his son's shortcomings and indulged his mean-spirited behavior as attempts to assert his power as the offspring of one of the rulers. But in truth, the boy stimulated Zolton's arrogant nature and he secretly enjoyed Mautotl's obvious desire to win at any cost. As the years went by, the young boy's anger and frustration at not being the natural heir to his father, shaped into an evil plan to steal the power, not only from his unsuspecting sister, but also from Zolton.

As if nature kept a watchful eye, it endowed Mautotl with squatness and introversion to match his angry and disgruntled manner, while it blessed Anacaona with beauty and elegance to reflect her sunny disposition. Teuch too, made an effort to sympathize with his best friend's younger brother and helped wherever he could, but Mautotl angrily repudiated any efforts to establish a bond of familiarity with him. Instead, he relished the close relationship with his father, constantly pandering to his sympathy and attention by alleging victimization, thus establishing his trademark of lies and deceit in an effort to obscure his personal shortcomings.

In stark contrast with how Mautotl carried himself, the relationship between Teuch and Anacaona was based on true friendship, familiarity and complete trust. From those playful vineyard encounters when the rulers met on a regular basis, to the later respectful duties of subservience to their lords, they delighted in the liaisons that play, and eventual responsibility, gave them.

As Teuch grew older, Atonal took great pride in his accomplishments, yet couldn't help but admire the tall and muscular stature of his son, so similar to his own. But his mother's secret pride was undoubtedly the gray eyes and fair hair, a mysterious throwback from their southern ancestors. At the age of fifteen, as a symbol of his love and admiration, Atonal presented him with a young black stallion. Teuch stood outside in the bright sunlight when the horse was brought to him and astounded Atonal with his behavior. For a long time the boy and the stallion stared at each other and then Teuch lifted his arm, saluting the horse.

"Spethla! Your name is Spethla. I dreamt of you, and here you are!" Atonal remained quiet and watched the interaction between his son and the horse with great interest. He had never heard about the dream that Teuch had mentioned but he had long learned to trust his unusual son and just let him be. Yet, from that day on Atonal observed the special bond between Teuch and the pitch black stallion and was constantly amazed at their communication.

Spethla and Teuch seemed to understand each other on a level that transcended the normal barriers between man and beast. Only once did Teuch mention in passing that he and Spethla were old companions; that they had made their acquaintance somewhere else before. As always, Atonal listened but made no comment. He did not understand how that was possible, but coming from Teuch, the likelihood of the statement at least intrigued him.

During this time, and with Zolton's approval, Atonal had enrolled Teuch into the army to ensure that he would serve his military responsibilities appropriately in the alliance between the regions of Fentztohl and Amustopl. This became one of the first major turning points in the life of the heir apparent to Amustopl when the young warrior began to discover some amazing aspects about his physical being.

Early one morning, he was summoned to his father's quarters. Teuch knew immediately why his father wanted to see him and expected that some kind of punishment would be in store. Atonal beckoned him to approach and handed back the sword that he had presented to him upon his enlistment into the army. His father spoke very softly.

"It appears that one of my officers has been reduced to a humble and nervous wreck. He is being treated by one of my healers." Teuch anxiously interrupted and dropped to one knee.

"Forgive me father. Your captain would not accept my explanation that I was simply an enlisted foot soldier. He saw only his authority being threatened by my presence as your son. Will you please pardon my actions?" Atonal took his son's arm and pulled him to his feet.

"My men witnessed what had happened yesterday and you are exonerated." His voice dropped to a soft whisper. "But tell me where have you learned to use a sword with such agility and stealth that you were able to avoid the lethal blows from your opponent? I am told that your skill exceeds our regular training." They sat together and Atonal listened proudly to how his son dealt with the bullying tactics from one of his officers.

"The man pulled the sword from my belt and thrust it into my hand." Teuch's voice shook with emotion as he confided in his father. "He said that he was going to teach me a lesson and that no prince would assume authority without proving his worth." Teuch paused for breath, obviously distraught by the necessary action that he had taken. "I am sorry for wounding one of your able and trusted men father." Atonal simply smiled and placed an assuring arm around the shoulders of his only offspring.

"It was but a scratch my son, but enough to disarm him with the least injury. His arm will soon heal and I have already learned of this man's admiration and willingness to follow you anywhere in battle." Teuch bowed his head in appreciation of his father's words and bade his permission to carry on with his duties. He stood tall and proud, and as he was leaving the quarters, he turned to face his father. His voice was suddenly solemn.

"All I can say, father, is that I was infused with a sense of truth and justice and I had to defend myself because of those I love and who love me. It felt right and what I did came to me as though I have always had this ability. I hope you will accept this explanation." Atonal remained silent but intrigued. Teuch's words confirmed his suspicions about the special abilities his son seemed to possess from a very early age. As word traveled, both the armies of Amustopl and Fentztohl eventually adopted this unique means of self defense based on concentration, stealth and speed into all of their military training.

The unusual bond that existed between the *tiacapan* of the rulers was a constant source of inspiration to all who saw them together. To the untrained eye they were best friends who shared playgrounds as the two regions interacted commercially and socially. But as they grew older it became apparent that theirs was a union made in heaven. The transformation from innocent childhood interaction to the first stirring of adult feelings occurred unexpectedly when Teuch was in his seventeenth year and Anacaona, in her sixteenth.

As with all celebratory events, Zolton and Atonal came together to present a united front to their subjects on this day, the festival of *Quecholli*, also known as the day of the Precious Feather. *Quecholli* was characterized by a ritualistic hunt that followed a fast, after which the priests sacrificed game, and everyone was invited to join in the ceremonial feasting. Heaps of *tlaxcallis,* a thin cornmeal pancake, were stacked on sturdy wooden tables everywhere. The villagers used these to scoop up the wonderful aromatic fillings made of wild duck, various types of game and goat's cheese.

Celebrations were in full swing in the town square and court musicians mingled freely with the villagers who danced merrily to the catching flute tunes that filled the air and mixed with the fragrant smoke of the sacrificial fires. Teuch sat contentedly next to Anacaona on a low stone wall in the blazing hot sun. With most of the eating done, the dancing was in full swing and from the corner of his eye he watched her joyful expression as she looked upon the happy villagers twirling around and clapping their hands. He leaned over to her and whispered in her ear.

"Come with me." Anacaona looked away from the festive crowd and turned her gaze on him; his words had raised an unfamiliar stir in the pit of her stomach.

"Where to?" The expression in her eyes was soft and curious. For the longest time Atonal's only son had occupied a very special place in her heart.

"To the forest where it is cool. We will go on horseback." He grinned at her. "I will race you there!" She looked down at her hands in her lap and smiled secretively as if contemplating his suggestion, but the next instant she was up and away. For a few moments Teuch didn't move. He watched her long black hair streaming behind her as she ran, weaving her way through the colorful stalls and dancing people.

He wanted to give her a head start, so he waited patiently until he saw her mounting her horse that had been tied to a stake in the shade of a huge fig tree. Then he followed her and soon the people and the music faded away as they sped across the open field toward the dark green edge of the forest where they had spent many happy hours as young children.

He purposely held Spethla back and listened to her beautiful laugh as she clung tightly to the mane of her horse, urging it to go faster. Then, unexpectedly, her steed stumbled and Teuch watched in shock as Anacaona lost her grip and went flying and screaming through the air. She hit the earth with a dull thud and rolled away ending face down in the grass; suddenly eerily quiet.

With his heart thundering in his chest, he reined Spethla in beside her and in one movement dismounted and fell onto his knees next to her still body. Fear gripped his heart as he carefully reached out to roll her onto her back. Her eyes were closed and she appeared very pale. An ominous feeling of incredible loss filled his entire being as he carefully put his hands behind her head and lifted her slightly.

"Anacaona?" he asked in a hoarse whisper, but when she didn't respond he tried again, this time with more urgency. "Anacaona? Please, talk to me!" Still, she didn't move and he stared at her motionless body, stunned and powerless to deal with the dreadful reality of what had happened. Then his eyes filled with frustrated angry tears. "No!" he called in desperation, squeezing his eyes shut. "This cannot be happening! Not to this girl! Not to the most important person in my life!"

But then miraculously, she opened her eyes and looked straight at him. Teuch froze, speechless at the sudden happy turn of events and stared in wonderment at her. He had never been this close to her and lost himself momentarily in the beauty and intensity of the direct gaze that was so characteristic of her.

"Teuch." She whispered his name softly and lifted a trembling hand to his face. "I am not hurt." And seeing his distress, her eyes filled with tears and she pleaded with him. "Do not be concerned for me, please?"

Teuch caught the wrist of the hand she had placed against his cheek and without thinking, turned his head and pressed his lips passionately into her open palm, closing his eyes. Anacaona held her breath but didn't pull her hand away, overwhelmed by his intimate gesture and surprised at how spontaneously she had consented to it. But for Teuch the realization of what was happening between them was so exciting that he was temporarily confused and the next step was not immediately clear to him. He was intensely aware of her body in such close proximity to his own and felt an urgency to know what the mysterious expression in her eyes meant. He reached a tentative hand to her face and without a word, tenderly explored the contours of her jaw, her eyebrows and nose, still amazed that she was not hurt by the fall and that it had brought them together in this way. His gaze fixed upon her mouth and he traced the outline of her lower lip with his thumb, bewildered by his own feelings, but overcome with the powerful way in which his beautiful childhood friend stirred him.

Then Teuch lifted his eyes to meet hers and realized that she had been waiting for him to notice her in this way. Time stood still. They were both inexperienced, but her nearness was incredibly stimulating and his instincts at once took over. Without taking his eyes away from hers, he pressed his thumb down on her lower lip, subtly increasing the pressure and when she didn't offer any resistance, he parted her lips slightly.

Under the spell of his touch, Anacaona closed her eyes and felt his warm breath on her cheek. In her chest, her heart fluttered like a little bird and the anticipation was almost too much to bear before, at last, his mouth closed warmly over hers. For a moment her excitement turned to uncertainty and she instinctively held back, deeply aware of how their relationship was changing, but he sensed her hesitation and withdrew his mouth long enough only to thickly whisper her name.

"Anacaona." What was left of her defenses crumbled and she ecstatically wove her arms around his neck to pull him closer. And thus, with their arms tightly about each other, they surrendered into the wonder and miracle of their first intimate kiss. Safely cocooned within the intoxicating bliss of his physical closeness, she knew with great certainty that she would carry the warmth and sweetness of this moment with Teuch to the end of her days, and into eternity.

Anacaona's sensitive spiritual nature felt their bond on a very different level. The love she had for Atonal's only son seemed destined from beyond the stars and she held tightly onto him, savoring the intimacy of his mouth trailing all over her face and silencing, at least for the moment, any words between them. And yet, despite the joy of their closeness, Anacaona could not suppress the ominous feeling that their happiness would be short lived.

The relationship between Teuch and Anacaona blossomed with little interference from her father, Zolton, the more tiresome of the two rulers. If anything, this bonding helped to sustain the coalition and three years later Teuch and Anacaona were married in an elaborate wedding ceremony celebrated, as tradition dictated, at night in the groom's house.

That afternoon Anacaona participated in a ritual bath and washed her hair with sweet smelling herbs, after which she had her arms and legs decorated with red feathers and her face painted with yellow pigment. Atonal and Teuch arrived shortly after on her doorstep to declare that she was welcome in their house and showered her with ceremonial gifts of finely woven garments and gold coins before guiding her with blazing torches to her new home. The exchange of incense between the bride and the groom symbolized their mutual respect for each other and when the old women, the *cihuatlanque,* tied the bride and groom's blouses together, the marriage ceremony was complete and the real festivities could begin.

They were a particularly handsome couple and their devotion to each other and spiritual behavior reflected in their appearance. Anacaona was taller than most women. Her strong and beautiful features were often hidden behind her long black hair and with her olive skin and her gift to see things others could neither understand nor articulate, Teuch lovingly called her his mysterious *dream catcher*. By contrast, he was very tall and his skin was paler; his fair features bore the hallmark of the southerly tribes who came from the colder regions of the South American continent.

In response to Teuch referring to her as a catcher of dreams, Anacaona gave him the title of *Quah Atowahl*, Eagle Man. His ancestry was steeped in warrior tradition and his genetic inheritance gave him the foundations for what was beset before him. But he was mercifully oblivious that his path to glory and happiness would not be an easy one.

As Teuch matured, he distinguished himself as a natural leader and those who came in contact with him witnessed a fair man whose actions were founded in his dedication to discipline and duty. He used his position of authority to lead, instead of manipulating others which, by contrast, was Mautotl's preferred way. Teuch promised himself and his beloved Anacaona that he would use and develop his skill to always favor defense. Neither soldier nor civilian could match his fine horsemanship or his mental and physical agility and strength. Within Teuch the knowledge and execution of martial arts rose to a level of such mastery that it became encrypted in his soul. At this time he had no idea yet just how important these skills would be and how many times in the future he would have to call on these gifts.

Anacaona instead had an ability to pre-empt events, and her sensitivity to nature and understanding of its natural laws sharpened her senses and endowed her with the ability to feel very deeply. She was intensely curious about spirit and soul, whereas Teuch's inner world bowed to the more immediate needs of the physical. His attention was drawn to the requirements of day-to-day life which created a barrier to achieving greater knowledge in this regard. Anacaona sensed a path of destiny for her and Teuch but also intuitively felt that its fulfillment would be fraught with danger and difficulty. Their initial attraction to each other was only the first manifestation of Universal Law, which provided the stage for a partnership where they could assist in each other's growth—physically, spiritually and mentally. Anacaona's awareness and subtle understanding of the uniqueness of their relationship would be her strength in times to come, but her knowledge was not complete.

On regular trading missions, Teuch covered the rear of the caravans; a position that provided him with the opportunity to observe nature more closely. On this day they were returning from a two-day mission carrying raw material and salt from the lower regions to trade in the markets of Amustopl. To reach their destination by midday, they had broken camp very early and were making good progress across the bushy terrain still veiled in semi darkness of the night. The waning moon adequately lit their path.

Teuch noticed the outline of the approaching eagle first and lifted his gaze to the star strewn heavens, dumbfounded by the unusual sight of an eagle in this pre-dawn hour. But it was the nervous jerk of Spethla's head that drew his attention to the owl that had spread its wings to soundlessly rise from nearby trees and then whooshed past them.

"Steady, Spethla!" he said under his breath as he reined in the horse slightly and watched in astonishment as the owl seemed to head straight toward the circling eagle. "What have we here?" he mused surprised as he witnessed this very strange interaction. "These two birds of prey *together*? One from the night and one from the day?" He spoke softly to himself. "I must be dreaming." But he waited quietly; utterly mesmerized by the unusual aerial fly-past display in the darkened heavens.

They glided past each other for a few more sweeping turns, and then suddenly, as the sun began to rise, the birds seemed to fall from the sky, shrieking frantically as they tumbled helplessly toward earth. Transfixed, Teuch watched in astonishment as they rapidly pulled out of the free fall, and glided past each other; the eagle disappearing into the vastness of the sky while the owl returned to the canopy of the woods.

It was only when he resumed his easy canter that he came across the two feathers lying in the dry sandy soil and dismounted to pick them up. The tail feathers were still warm to the touch, and it instantly reminded him of his beloved Anacaona and how she had enchanted him at *Quecholli*, the Festival of the Precious Feather. He slowly brought them to his nose and smelled the wide open plains where the birds lived.

Then a profound thought entered his consciousness, prompting an instant need to share this experience with the woman he loved. Having left his escort post for a short while, he mounted Spethla and quickly caught up with the caravans moving swiftly on to Amustopl. As they entered the market place in a cloud of dust, he pulled off to the side to feed and water Spethla and then leapt right into the quarters he now shared with Anacaona.

"I have brought these for you my love," he said as he stood eye-to-eye with the beautiful woman who was first his friend and now his wife. He handed her the two feathers, one with gray patterns and the other with brown. "At the festival of the Precious Feather, I kissed you for the first time. That day I knew my life without you would be incomplete. When you look upon these feathers, always know that I will be close. Never be blinded by what you see, instead feel beyond and you will always find me." Anacaona trembled as she stared at the feathers, deeply touched by the gesture.

"I know why you have done this, my gray-eyed eagle man," she whispered softly, holding back the tears. "It is obvious that the brown one is for me, to match the color of my eyes, but the gray one is to remind me of you." Overcome by the extraordinary meaning of the special gift, she reached her slender hands out to enfold his strong face, drawing him close.

Neither of them knew that the feathers would become a symbol of their love and would remain so as earthly time marked thousands of years in the cosmic heavens. But as she held him to her heart, Anacaona had a foreboding of impending doom that filled her with despair. She stared at the feathers in her hand and couldn't find the words to express her fear. In vain she tried to shut off the inner knowledge that suggested to her time and again that her presence on this earth would be cut short. How could she burden Teuch with this knowledge? But as she contemplated her deep feelings for this wonderful man to whom she felt so bonded in mind and in spirit, a profound feeling of such proportions came over her that it quieted her entire being.

Anacaona's sensitive awareness detected the presence of a great force with an intensity and clarity she had not previously encountered. She closed her eyes and waited breathlessly for something to unfold. Then wondrous shapes and colors appeared on the screen of her imagination that were so real she could reach out and touch them with her hands. She had no idea what it possibly could mean, but it dawned on her consciousness that she was witnessing a key to a mystery, something that she was meant to unravel. But the meaning escaped her yet.

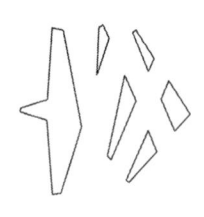

Zolton had underestimated how convenience would give way to permanence. After thirty years of trading with Amustopl, his military strength had gained momentum and, unobtrusively, the time had arrived where he no longer needed the arrangement with Atonal.

Consumed by civil war, the Cautzpal Empire was no longer a threat and under the influence of Mautotl he became convinced that Fentztohl, with his leadership and that of Mautotl, could rise again to become the sole power of the region. His biggest problem now was his daughter's love and devotion for Teuch and their natural, combined ascension to leadership by birth.

Gradually Zolton had begun to share Mautotl's resentment for the cruel act of nature that chose Anacaona to be the firstborn. In the close but unhealthy relationship that festered between him and his father, Mautotl finally convinced Zolton that Fentztohl stood to lose its identity and disappear into obscurity, unless absolute power was taken back again. The goal required a sacrifice, and the sacrificial lamb would be his sister and Teuch. The seed of corruption was planted and the fate of Anacaona and Teuch was sealed. What Zolton did not know was that what he had consented to for his daughter and her husband, would become his fate also; meted out by the evil hand of his own son.

Mautotl was perversely obsessed by supreme rule and the fate he had planned for the region of Amustopl would become legend. Resulting devastation would eventually permeate throughout the Native American nations, leaving its legacy to the day, centuries later, when the Spanish would change things for ever. The beginning of the murderous campaign was marked by Mautotl's plan to have his sister secretly assassinated.

The deed proved to be easier than anticipated and was committed when Teuch was away on a trading mission in the north. The final act was swift as the blade of one of her brother's henchmen severed the life from Anacaona while she slept. With Mautotl's cowardly deed done, Zolton had his excuse to turn against Amustopl. It was only a matter of time before Atonal's inferior army would capitulate regardless of Teuch's prowess and exceptional skill.

But neither Zolton nor Mautotl knew of the incredible cosmic journey and events which the taking of Anacaona's life would set into motion. Despite the physical slaying, her soul had remained untouched by the evil of her brother. Even before Teuch and Anacaona were born, a pact had been made in the cosmic heavens that would not reach its completion and fulfillment for many thousands of years.

Teuch was not as receptive as his wife about these matters and found it impossible to accept her death; he remained inconsolable and there was no end to his grief. He had no doubt that the wicked hand of Mautotl was behind Anacaona's assassination; that the family of Atonal would be blamed and that war between the regions was inevitable. Emotionally devastated and having lost his reason to live, he vowed to take revenge against Mautotl.

But it was Zolton who seized the moment and ruthlessly stoked the fires of hatred. He openly blamed Atonal for his daughter's death, knowing that the divide between Amustopl and Fentztohl was now inevitable and that the battle would have to be fought to the bitter end.

Teuch felt Anacaona's presence constantly and it was as real to him as the last time they had embraced. Knowing her spirit was present, life held little value as he fought proudly in battle by his father's side. His soul reached out to her, distraught in the knowledge that their union would never be consecrated on the holiest of grounds; that of parenthood.

Then inexplicably, an eerie quiet descended upon the battlefield. Teuch looked at the feathers that he had taken from her lifeless body and closed his eyes in pain, momentarily losing his concentration. This was the moment Mautotl, his executioner, had been waiting for and he did not hesitate. His arrow was swift and accurate as it penetrated the quah crest, proudly emblazoned on Teuch's chest. Three more hit Spethla, fatally wounding him as they fell together alongside his already slain father.

"You are coming too, my friend?" It was an incoherent painful whisper to his trusted horse as his consciousness began to slip. "Anacaona!" He cried her name with his dying breath and mustering his last ounce of strength, he leaned over weakly and kissed his father's brow. As his spirit began to leave his body, Teuch caught his first glimpse of an incredible cosmic journey, and this is when he forgave Mautotl, knowing he would rise from the strength gained from his forgiveness. He would find Anacaona again, with Spethla by his side.

But shedding the blood of his sister and her husband only spurred Mautotl on to dispose of his father in a similar fashion, to become the most merciless and cruel leader of the region. He did not anticipate that the many enemies he had made in his life were also waiting for their opportune moment to rise to power. No one remembered the cruel squat man who maimed and killed to take what he wanted, but in years to come the memory of Teuch and Anacaona had been passed on to the Native American people and the story became etched into folklore. Their tale of love was shared over and over again and cosmic winds magically carried the symbolism of the feathers to become a cherished legend amongst many indigenous tribes.

In the countless times the story was retold, no one realized that a doorway would open to future meetings between these two, for a union made in heaven could not be complete without its earthly counterpart. The pact they had made would call them back again and again.

Chapter 2
Brief Acquaintance

On the open plains of ancient Mexica, Anacaona's sensitive nature afforded her tiny glimpses into the mysteries of creation. Her boundless joy, so characteristic of her soul composition, was noticeable in her uncomplicated childhood friendship with Teuch and as she grew older it stirred a much deeper knowing in the consciousness of the young girl. Although vague and undefined at first, her receptive spirit recognized faint traces of a calling or a mission within the warmth and camaraderie of their bond.

From the night the handsome young warrior took her as his bride, their forces began to flow as one and her romantic heart was overwhelmed the day he lay the tail feathers of the eagle and the owl in the palm of her hand. To him it was a perfect symbol of their love, and although Anacaona was filled with infinite affection for Atonal's only son, her heart at once contracted and quivered with inexplicable trepidation.

Despite their intense devotion to each other, she was unable to ward off the constant feeling of impending doom, and her only consolation was to creep deeper into his embrace. Cradled in the circle of his arm, she shut out the fear and shared with him intriguing experiences of strange colors and shapes that constantly flashed across the screen of her mind. And whilst he loved her dreamy quality and cherished the depth of the intimacy between them, he was equally mystified by the meaning of her dreams and visions.

When their lives ended prematurely and their spirits left the earth plane, they were carried into the next dimension and suspended above earthly time in the afterlife where the Cosmos holds multiple realities in a location described by some as the Middle Place. Here the seeds of cause and effect reach across the boundaries of life and death into this domain where good, bad, innocent and indifferent souls collectively exist with their agendas set according to their own evolutionary path.

But within the Middle Place there exists a special heavenly region known as the Meadow and it is from here that souls on a spiritual path await their time for re-emergence onto the earth plane for another chance to continue learning. It is to this celestial rendezvous that Teuch and Anacaona arrived joyfully for the first time as evolving souls and it is to this same place that they would return again and again, in an effort to find each other and unite in body, mind and spirit. Unbeknownst to them, the tender and beautiful memories of their earthly encounter had been encrypted in the ethereal bodies of their souls, and powerful laws were set in motion that would repeatedly draw them together.

Then somewhere in the celestial heavens the energy increased; the wind changed direction and purposely rippled the grass in the Meadow. The stir was felt by all, and those for whom the time had come, felt a strong desire to once again take mortal form. And so it was that hundreds of years later, two souls held safely within the Cosmos outside of time and space, were about to be released onto the open plains of North America. But in the first of their many challenges to reunite, the Cosmos cruelly, yet deliberately, released them ten years apart, setting the stage for a pattern in which their struggles to bond would become legion.

In the middle of the 4th Century a son was born to Matoska and Watnehma of the Ukula brethren, which centuries later became known as the mighty Sioux. Matoska's lineage descended from a great line of trackers of whom he was by far the most experienced scout, not only within the Ukula nation, but throughout the tribes of the open plains where they whispered around campfires of his skill and superior knowledge of nature and its creatures.

He and Watnehma named their son Chaska, meaning firstborn. They poured all their love and devotion into raising their only offspring, after an illness rendered Watnehma's womb barren. Matoska's heart overflowed with joy for his handsome child, and he carefully initiated him into the secrets of listening to silence and feeling the vibrations of the earth. On long excursions into the wild, Matoska, lanky and weather-beaten, took pride in teaching his sinewy, but strapping child how to be at one with nature and respect its manifold expressions. His characteristic sleek braid, lovingly arranged by Watnehma's nimble fingers, reflected the bright sunlight where he sat alongside his son in the scorching heat of the day. His hawk eyes missed nothing. The expression within the young boy's finely chiseled features was evidence of serenity far beyond his years.

"I have shown you how to read the direction of the wind before you could walk." He smiled, keeping his eyes on the dancing shimmers above the horizon. "But to survive on the prairies, there are far greater secrets to know. Not everyone can learn them." Like his father, Chaska stared at the horizon and dropped his voice to a whisper.

"When will the earth show me its mysteries, father?"

"When you know how to listen." Matoska gently pushed his son to the ground and stretched out alongside him. Then he pressed an ear to the soil, and waited with his eyes closed while Chaska curiously looked on. Matoska spoke softly. "Follow my lead, young brave." But it took many attempts for Chaska to know what his father was listening for. It took time to learn to relax his body and tune into the vibrations of the sun-baked earth. And when least expected, he finally heard it. Matoska smiled. "That is the sound of many hooves, Chaska, and the herd is kicking up vast clouds of dust across the open plains; a three day journey away from here." This breakthrough brought great delight to both father and son.

Later that day, laying flat on their backs, he pointed to gigantic caverns of gray and white clouds stacked across the wide expanse of the sky. Then he showed him how to tell that from its depths would pour life-giving rain, or if the rumble would dissipate into nothingness over the distant horizon. Chaska learned from his father how to feel moisture in the air by combining smell and taste and breathing deeply through his nose, even when the clouds were reluctant to share their intention to make rain, or just blow away in the wind.

The boy's keen intelligence and sensitive soul effortlessly opened the ways of nature, and his unusual ability to learn surprised many, except his parents, particularly Matoska. A proud and devoted father, he was also a very wise and spiritual man, and treading a path very close to the boy, he became aware of how unique his son was. Not only did the young brave learn his father's skills, but he perfected them. He noticed Chaska's searching spirit and wondered if the child was being groomed for greatness. Then one night he had a vivid dream in which his son tracked a deer that kept eluding him and he returned after days, devastated and heartbroken that he had not succeeded in his mission.

Much later, when he contemplated the dream while smoking his pipe on the low hill behind his tepee, he knew with great clarity that the deer was symbolic of something else. But Matoska knew not what and therefore became more vigilant and watched his son even more closely. He was thus not surprised when the boy came to tell him about the vision that had come to him in the darkness of night.

Chaska's first initiation into the mysteries of the future came on the evening before his tenth birthday when he fell into a deep slumber and had a profound experience. Suddenly a young woman with waist-length black hair stood inside his dream and he half awoke, staring confused at the beautiful vision in his tepee. Keeping eye contact with the bewildered boy, she approached quietly, clasping two feathers in her hand. He stared at them, one brown and one gray, and suddenly his entire being was inexplicably filled with great sadness. Stifling a sob, he felt an overpowering urge to weep. But the expression on the face of the vision was soft and tender and closing her eyes momentarily, she raised a finger to her mouth, shaking her head slightly. When she opened her eyes, he noticed the glint of tears although her smile remained angelic and reassuring.

The boy sat up confused, a shiver running down his spine and he had difficulty breathing. Caught between the netherworld of reality and a dream, his consciousness was sluggish and unprepared for what he was witnessing and he desperately looked for an explanation. But he was unable to comprehend the full meaning with the awareness of a young boy and became bewildered with the strange feelings that stirred so suddenly and urgently in him.

Overwhelmed with joy that sprung from his inner being, he wanted to reach out and touch the beautiful creature in front of him. But those same feelings also stimulated guilt as he remembered the only form of love he was familiar with, that of his parents. At this tender age he was not ready for the intensity of emotion that washed through him and the only solution he could think of was to find shelter in the comfort of his parents' bed, a place where he had not been for a long time.

Acknowledging the consternation she read on his face, the beautiful vision kissed her fingers and leaning over him affectionately, she gently placed them on his lips. To his astonishment, he felt the physical sensation of her light touch, but was unable to move in any direction. Then she lifted her hand holding the feathers and touched them delicately to her own lips.

Chaska's body had gone into light shock and he involuntarily began to tremble. Fascinated by the magic of her presence, he was beset with the thought that he somehow knew who she was. Yet, no matter how hard he tried, his efforts were thwarted by his heightened emotional state and lack of skill to bridge the gap between her and his memory banks.

Then she retreated slowly, keeping her eyes on the stunned boy as she took her leave, never once turning her back on him, honoring an age-old promise still slumbering in his consciousness at this time, and disappeared from his dream. He awoke abruptly and hid for a while in the blankets of soft skin that was his bed. Then he picked up and ran to the safety and comfort of his parents' tepee pitched a short distance away from his. Matoska had been awake for a while and when he saw the silhouette etched in the moonlight, he spoke first.

"The flap is not tied. Come in, Chaska." His voice was soft and reassuring. "What brings you here at this hour, son?" When he felt the warmth of his son's body against his own, Matoska turned a loving eye to Watnehma, who lay on her side facing away from them; only the delicate snoring revealed the depth of her slumber. Then he gave his attention to his only child and listened with great interest to the dream which he, Matoska, knew was not really a dream. He was convinced that Chaska's nightly visitor came from the outer realms, and whoever the vision was, had come to alert him to something very important. He smiled and remembered the dream of his son and he was glad the darkness hid his surprise when he learned about the woman.

"All dreams have meanings my son," said his father, stroking his moist brow tenderly, remembering his earliest thoughts that Chaska was unusual in some way. "If you listen to your heart you will always get an answer." For Matoska, insight and understanding slowly began to dawn and he felt the dampness in his own eyes as he continued softly. "You will not know the meaning of this dream today, or even years from now. But if you remain attentive, it will be revealed to you. Just as we must be enduring when we track the buffalo for days and sometimes weeks, you must be patient also. Over centuries we have learned to outwait the herds and let them come to us, and the meaning of your dream will find you in the same way, if you can be patient, my son."

Chaska never forgot the words of his father and the vision remained fresh in his memory. But it would be ten years before he gained his first understanding of it, and even a longer time before he knew that it coincided with the birth of a little girl to the nomadic tribe of the Kawahi, on the day he celebrated his tenth year.

The next day Chaska was out with his father and other tracker braves eagerly searching for new breeding stock. The day was unforgiving in its heat and they were glad to find some shelter and refresh themselves after corralling a herd of wild horses. Chaska gratefully took the goatskin pouch, which held his water, to the cool side of a rock and sat down. Then he heard the rustling movement behind him and was startled by the cold nose of a very young stallion nudging him in the back.

"Hello my friend. Where did *you* come from?" The young boy's eyes lit up with delight and surprise at such an easy catch. "Are you thirsty?" He didn't want to scare the horse away and, rising slowly, he poured water from the pouch into the palm of his hand and watched the stallion drink. It was barely ten hands high, white in color and looked to be only a few weeks old. An incredible feeling of familiarity entered Chaska's being as he stared at the beautiful animal which seemed in no hurry to move on. Instead, it allowed the boy to take in the beauty and fine proportions of its striking body, as if begging for recognition. Without taking his eyes off the horse, he beckoned his father in the hope that he would be allowed to adopt his newfound friend. "See how easily he drank from my hand father! Will he be mine?" Chaska gripped his toes in anticipation of a positive response.

"Find his mother and bring her also. From this celebrated day of your birth, the two of you will grow together as true Ukula warrior braves," said Matoska looking on proudly at how Chaska and the young horse seemed to instantly take to one another.

Before he could reply, a black mare approached cautiously and, watching her offspring closely, she snorted softly, waiting to reunite with it. His prayers had been answered and he remembered the wonderful stories his mother used to tell when he was very young of a horse named Nwaptoah. Chaska's heart overflowed with joy as he slowly approached his newfound friend, whistling softly and calling him by this name for the first time. The young stallion did not move until the boy stood in front of him and lay his open palm on his forehead. Watching from a distance, Matoska remained very quiet. Never before had he witnessed an instant bond like this between a man and a beast.

Unbeknownst to Chaska and Nwaptoah, in that very moment of sweet reverie between them a special soul was being brought back into the world as the new daughter to the mighty Kawahi.

As Nahiossi, the old medicine man, stood outside the tepee, his body writhed and contorted to the rhythm of the drums until he finally brought his enthralling chant under control. His activity was aimed at distracting attention inside the tepee to drown out Cahota's screams as she gave birth to a healthy daughter. To her this was a royal occasion as her husband, Wuti, was lord and master of the Kawahi nation. Nahiossi crouched at the entrance of the tepee at the infant's first cry and waited for the midwife to stick her head out, but he already knew the gender of the baby before he heard the rustling at the flap.

"It is a girl." The tall crow-faced woman sounded impatient. "Now be gone!"

"I know." Nahiossi smiled. "Name her Tiva. A daughter gifted with great enlightenment and wisdom has been given to the Kawahi people." He knew the midwife wasn't listening any more, but he didn't care as he slowly walked away, nodding his head. *It has begun!*

Weayaya, firstborn to Wuti and Cahota, now had a sister whom he could love and take care of, relieving his parents of a task that would conflict with their tribal responsibilities. Weayaya's path was that of the spirit and at first Wuti had passionately objected to his only son breaking the traditional warrior line. The lineage was proudly carried from one generation to the next, the sons honoring the fathers by following in their footsteps. And it was only the intervention of Nahiossi, also known as Three Fingers, which finally swayed Wuti's resolve.

The medicine man was leather faced and resplendent in a headdress comprising of feathers and small animal skulls covering his long white hair. He explained to the ruler that the continuation of the spirit line was vital to the future of the tribe. Wuti eventually yielded to Nahiossi's relentless chanting to persuade him, and the old man was finally given the responsibility of Weayaya's development as a holy man.

The spiritual aspect of the American Indian nation was ingrained deep within its culture. On the wide expanses of these plains, all the tribes respected family traditions; they passed down love and respect as codes of honor by which to live, ensuring that the young, the fragile and the old alike were nurtured. To them, the physical plane was only a means to an end, whereby progress in mind, body and spirit could be achieved through experiencing the polarities that existed between great love and intense fear.

Nahiossi realized the importance of this tradition and that it be maintained. One day as a young man on his many walks around the furthest perimeter of the village, he had encountered a scouting party from the nomadic Sapeti. Rivalry usually manifested between tribes during periods of severe drought, when unreasonable claims on hunting grounds were made and intolerable temperaments amongst the rivals became apparent.

The men of his tribe had been gone for days in search of the buffalo and apart from a few inexperienced youngsters, there was no real protection. On that day he realized the fate of his people was in his hands and he wanted to protect them by the most peaceful of means possible. Nahiossi also knew that he would have only one opportunity to make a lasting impression to avoid confrontation. He waited until they were almost upon him and, in an act of extreme bravery, Nahiossi demonstrated to the young Sapeti warriors how his tribe would deal with unreasonable demands by swiftly cutting off the two little fingers of his left hand. They stopped dead in their tracks and stared at him in astonishment and horror.

"Pain and hardship mean nothing to my people!" he called out through his agony, holding up his bloodied hand for all to see. "We live with it every day! And let this be a display of our resolve to protect our own!" Nahiossi could barely hold himself upright while he stood there challenging the incredulous members of the Sapeti tribe. But his plan had worked and they turned their horses around in awe and left in peace.

From that day Nahiossi was given holy status. Affectionately known as Three Fingers, he was carefully initiated into the secrets of the Universe through the traditions and hidden mysteries of his tribe and now it was time to pass on this knowledge to his pupil Weayaya, who in turn would entrust it to his beloved sister, Tiva.

The years gently rolled by in dreamlike monotony and then one day Tiva, now ten years old, was playing at the fringes of the village with her imaginary friends. To onlookers it appeared that she was expecting someone or that she was planning some kind of reception. Members of her tribe thought nothing of seeing her play seemingly alone. They had come to love this unusual child with the piercing stare whose clarity of mind and spirit moved them all. Serious in nature, the small doll-like face didn't laugh as often as others of her age, yet she seemed filled with an inner joy which frequently resulted in the presence of a tiny secretive smile. She appeared to live in a place where the silver cord of the world beyond easily reeled her in, as if she had never lost contact with her origins, and she moved effortlessly between these two dimensions.

Weayaya saw himself as the keeper of his little sister's dreams and her destiny. He also could visit the places Tiva spoke of, but kept his knowledge secret. Therefore he was not surprised by her gift to turn within and speak in what seemed like riddles to others. He mentioned to Nahiossi once that he knew who she was but the old man only squeezed his eyes shut and carried on chanting. It seemed that all communication with Three Fingers took place during a chant, for he never stopped.

Weayaya watched his little sister closely and realized that she was looking for someone and that there was both a sadness and expectancy present in her all the time. She constantly told stories of a man and his faithful horse, and while others imagined she was fantasizing, her brother knew that she in fact was remembering. Weayaya was the only one who knew that Tiva had keys to a cosmic memory bank that not even she understood.

She often spoke to Weayaya of two feathers, at which he only smiled, for her mind brought forth fantasies in all shapes and sizes. To him they were harmless but he sat up and took notice when she insisted that she had dreamt of a prominent shape the night before and that she could not forget it. She spoke of strange sounds and colors emanating from the shape which kept changing and pausing, as if daring her to unravel its mystery. Her brother could not explain his interest in her dream but, to his own surprise, afterwards found himself drawing patterns in the sand to imitate what she had described. He had no idea what it meant, neither had he an inkling that this mystery would impact his whole being in a far distant future.

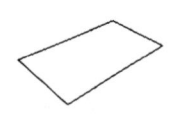

But on this day she insisted that an important visitor would come, and brought out the feathers from her small bundle of personal possessions that she had been hiding for a long time. She told Weayaya that she was expecting an honored guest and that one of the feathers was for him. When she held them up for him to see, he went very quiet, a little taken aback that they were real.

"Where did you get the eagle's feather, Tiva?" he asked startled.

"Nahiossi gave it to me. It fell from his headpiece during one of his wild chants and when I picked it up, he said to keep it. He traveled very far north before he became our medicine man. And this is one of three eagle feathers he collected on his journeys." He nodded his head slowly, his eyes still on the feathers which he had recognized instantly. Nahiossi had painstakingly initiated his protégé into the mysteries of herbs, medicinal roots of trees and wild berries, but he also had a great love of birds. And feathers were sacred, especially those of predator birds not indigenous to the wide open plains. Weayaya had no trouble recognizing the feathers of the two kings; one of the day and one of the night.

"And what about the owl's feather?" he asked softly.

"The midwife who took care of our mother when I was born gave it to me." Little Tiva smiled sweetly. "She chased me away when I wanted to watch her tending to another birth." She whispered behind her hand as if sharing a secret. "The feather was sewn into the flap of her tepee. Our father, Wuti, gave it to her when I was born to thank her for helping mother. The midwife said father had received it from one of the nomadic tribes in the north as a gift when he was a young brave."

"And you took it?" Her brother sounded astonished. She didn't waver and met his inquiring stare without blinking.

"Yes, brother. She said the feather should be with us. It belongs to me now." Then she calmly resumed her imaginative game as if nothing had happened and Weayaya left her in peace to play.

She did not notice the young Ukula warrior right away as he entered the perimeter of their village on a magnificent white horse. His four companions remained at a respectful distance behind him, waiting for his return as he cautiously approached the child so engrossed in play. As he drew closer he heard her voice and wondered who she was talking to, for he could not see anyone nearby. Then Chaska counted three protective braves in the shadows of the trees behind the child and realized that they were guarding her. This could only be the daughter of the legendary nomadic Chief Wuti.

He steered his horse in their direction, but his progress was slow for he could not tear his gaze away from the girl. Suddenly the braves were around him and, protective of their ward, inquired harshly about the purpose of his visit. Chaska kept his composure and replied that he had been given the honor of representing his village and offering a hand of friendship to Chief Wuti and the Kawahi people.

Unlike other tribes, the Ukula welcomed nomadics and their way of life. The buffalo herds were thin on the ground and co-operation and a spirit of sharing was in the best interest of survival for all. He was about to be taken to Chief Wuti when suddenly the little girl stepped closer. In her outstretched hand she clasped two feathers, one gray and one brown.

"This is for you." She held out the gray owl's feather whilst keeping the eagle one close to her heart as if to indicate that it belonged to her. She stood quite still, staring intently at him. Long black hair enfolded her tiny shoulders like the mighty wings of a bird, but it was the unfathomable expression in her eyes that drew him in. Her murmur was barely audible and for a moment the braves knew not what to do. It seemed as though the daughter of their chief was familiar with this stranger although the brave on the white stallion appeared taken aback and hesitant to take the feather from her. "Please." It was a soft plea and as Chaska leaned down to accept the strange gift, his eyes met briefly with the direct stare of the child. The moment froze in time as his memory involuntarily grappled with a unknown past, a strange, nameless yearning while the child held his gaze fearlessly. Then the guarding braves became impatient and urged him quickly to follow them.

"This is my friend!" Her urgent voice stopped the whole procession when they were a short distance away and they all looked back at her, surprised by her intervention. Tiva walked slowly up to the men and placed herself between the handsome young warrior with the shoulder length raven hair, and the guarding braves. "Please do not hurt him!" she urged. "He comes in peace." She wanted to reach out and lay a hand against his face to make him feel welcome, but remained rooted to where she stood, noticing that his eyes were as dark as the night was black in a starless sky.

"I am Chaska, son of Matoska and Watnehma of the Ukula tribe," he politely introduced himself, still overcome with the boldness and the beauty of the child.

"I am Tiva, daughter of Wuti and Cahota, and sister to Weayaya," she said, watching him closely. Her young heart was filled with joy and she secretly reveled in the realization of who her visitor was. She had expected him and he had come! And now she had given him his feather. She had no doubt that he had emerged from her dreams and visions and that was more than enough for her.

Chaska felt her eyes on him as they finally took their leave and was aware of her essence reaching right into his soul. It was a feeling such as he had never experienced and as he glanced back over his shoulder he was deeply under the impression of the beauty of the girl and her confident manner. Looking at the feather in his hand, he was suddenly overcome by a strange melancholy; completely at a loss to understand how a young child could influence him in this way. As a young man and a warrior who had not yet succumbed to the beauty or the need for a woman, he was surprised at how disturbed he was. He silently admitted to his own confusion as he fastened the feather to his lance, still incapable of erasing the girl from his memory.

Chaska did his village proud and convinced Wuti to enter into an agreement that would ensure the future of the buffalo. After refreshing himself he sat for a while in the shade of a big tree fingering the new gray feather on his lance, lost in thought.

"Do you recognize this feather, Nwaptoah?" he asked of his faithful steed. "The girl kept the brown one; there are two and I know they mean something. So help me, my friend." But the horse only dug his hoofs into the ground and grunted softly, nudging his wet nose against his master's shoulder. When the escorting braves appeared, they left together and galloped to the same place where he had met Tiva earlier that day. She was waiting for him and he reigned in Nwaptoah beside her. Then he respectfully raised his lance to her which displayed the newly attached feather.

"Nehanupti little one, and thank you. Perhaps we shall meet again one day." She stared at him strangely, retreating a few steps as if somehow registering a great loss, but said nothing as he turned his horse. He did not expect a response from her as he lifted an arm to bid farewell to the braves.

"Nehanupti, Eagle Man." The words came from her very soul and she spoke them without thinking. "Yes, we shall meet again." Her voice reached him barely as a whisper but something very old grabbed hold of his being, and every part of his nervous system reacted to the neural commands, ordering every muscle to lock. An invisible hand fleetingly drew back the veil to an ancient time of which he had no knowledge, and revealed the deadly strike of an assassin's blade, and a marksman's poisonous arrow finding its target. And in that moment his entire body inexplicably registered tremendous physical pain.

As it did so his heels dug into Nwaptoah's belly and it obeyed as always by rearing proudly into the air. Caught off guard, Chaska fell backwards, still holding his lance as his head crashed hard against a rock. His last haunting grasp of reality was a strange name that filled him with love and sadness as it echoed through his confused mind. *Anacaona, Anacaona.*

Chaska's companions took him back to the Ukula people where his wound took much longer to heal than he had anticipated. In fitful sleep, the same beautiful name resurfaced repeatedly, interspersed with clear visions of Tiva handing him the feather. By the time Chaska had regained his strength he had only one thing on his mind, and that was to find Wuti's daughter. Perhaps *she* could help make sense of all his confusion.

But when he arrived in the valley where they had pitched their tepees for so many moons, he was too late, for the Kawahi, in true nomadic nature, had moved on. Chaska felt strangely empty inside, a nameless longing made him feel uncomfortable and out of sorts with himself as he stared at the deserted plane where they had made their temporary home. She was only a girl, but he knew he had to find her again.

For the next fifteen years Chaska did not take a bride and fulfilled his obligation to the Ukula by taking care of the crops and continuously scouting for new hunting grounds. Eligible young girls, eager to find his favor, quickly became discouraged by his indifference and gave up on winning his heart. From his father he had learned respect for the womenfolk who bore the children and prepared their meals, but although he enjoyed their dancing and singing, he felt no depth of commitment to anyone. He was always thankful to leave on the next hunting expedition, wondering if this time he would come across the Kawahi and see Tiva again.

Matoska silently watched his son's lonely path. From the time the braves had brought him back after he had fallen from his horse, he had gained deeper insight into Chaska's destiny. Respectful of his privacy, he never gave word that it was he who had squatted at his side and poured cool water on his head while Chaska slurred odd names in his delirium.

But the braves who had escorted him to the Kawahi had told Matoska of the strange encounter with the girl. Patiently awaiting his son's recovery, he stared at the lance with the feather and knew without doubt that Tiva was the vision in Chaska's dream of so long ago. And his heart became very heavy for he felt that not only was Wuti's daughter too young, but he knew that the Kawahi seldom returned to the same place and, once they had left, he would never see her again.

Chaska's searching heart became Matoska's pain, but he could do nothing but pray to the gods that his son would find another more suitable woman worthy of warming his bed and bearing his children. Musing about his own dream and Chaska's vision, he realized that Tiva had reached to his son across other worlds shortly before she was born. Then Matoska knew that her pain was as deep as that of his son and that they had a history together. Where the old man sat in the opening of Chaska's tepee, he sighed and looked up at the stars where he had given up hope a long time ago of finding answers.

Chaska searched for Tiva on all his hunting expeditions and travels. Every time he encountered a nomadic tribe his heart rejoiced in anticipation that he had stumbled upon the Kawahi, but to no avail. He knew that she would no longer be a child, and with the years that had gone by since their first encounter, imagined that she had been given to someone as a wife. His mind had made the calculation over time, but his heart held out hope and he wondered at the source of this fire that could not be extinguished within his soul.

The severe drought that swept across the American plains ravaged the Ukula nation and forced them to fold their tepees and move on again. Chaska's experience as a hunter and explorer stood his people in good stead and they trusted his judgment implicitly. They felt safe following his lead as they stayed on the move, week after week. When he stretched out on the barren soil to feel for the vibration of buffalo, they stood back and waited in silence for him to signal if they should change course.

Then, six weeks to the day of changing course for the third time, the Ukula found new buffalo ground and they finally set up camp. Soon scouting groups were sent out to acquaint themselves with their neighbors and alert them to potential foe. One of the braves that had accompanied him to meet Chief Wuti years before brought tidings that the Kawahi were camped one day's journey to the east. Chaska remained quiet for a long time and then he nodded his head and gave orders for the official greeting party to prepare. He knew with great certainty that he would come face to face with Tiva again.

The unwritten code for tribe leaders was to confront each other and come to an agreement on hunting rights. Chaska had taken this task over from his father, who took pleasure in witnessing the leadership of his son. But on this day, Matoska's heart reached out in silence to his only offspring. The gods had given Chaska another rare chance to see Tiva again and he, Matoska, quietly despaired about the outcome.

As they entered the village, Chaska knew that she was there. Children ran over to wave and stare at the impressive party of Ukula representatives slowly entering their perimeters. Amongst the curious children a young boy separated from the group and, walking toward the approaching party, he fixed his gaze on the tall man riding the white horse. Chaska reigned in Nwaptoah and lifted his lance in greeting at the child whose eyes had strayed to the ceremonial weapon as it rose in the air. Then the boy abruptly turned and ran to the tepee where his mother was. Chaska sat very still on his horse; all eyes were on him waiting for the signal to proceed. But he was not quite ready. The boy was hers, of that he was sure. The eyes were the same.

Tiva stepped from her tepee to appease her son's excitement. She was accustomed to visitors but it was her husband, Akecheta's responsibility to meet strangers. At his discretion they were invited to the inner circle and only then did she prepare a peace meal and offer them a small cup of beer brewed from wild fruit. Shielding her eyes from the blinding hot sun, she fixed her gaze on the commotion of milling children surrounding the man on the white horse. Then her heart stopped as she recognized a single, gray-feathered lance in his right hand. *Chaska! Could it be? After all this time?* Her heart pounded loudly in her chest as her husband stepped closer to take control.

Akecheta was the village leader, second only to Wuti, Tiva's father. He was a great admirer of the Ukula and was even named after one of their warriors in honor of a debt paid to them. Now he was married to Tiva and he held out his hand inviting her to join him in welcoming the Ukula party. Tiva stood erect next to her tall and graceful husband who was equal in height to this visiting stranger. She faced Chaska with her heart in her throat as he dismounted and walked up to them.

As was the custom, the men made their acquaintance first by putting their hands over their hearts and then bowing their heads to each other. When they had finished exchanging their official greetings and respects, only then did Chaska trust himself to look at Akecheta's wife. *Tiva.* Time stood still as two souls briefly connected like the wingtips of two eagles in flight. Their hearts fluttered anxiously, painfully and fifteen years of wondering evaporated in a single moment as Chaska and

Tiva agonizingly faced each other. Together again, yet still apart, the enchanting child he remembered and had searched for after only one fateful meeting, had grown into a beautiful serene woman who now belonged to Akecheta. The gray streaks on Chaska's temples accentuated his chiseled features, but she kept her eyes averted. She would know him even if a thousand moons passed in time. In the company of so many others neither gave an outward sign of recognition and amidst all the activity they remained quiet, whilst inside, a dull ache began to throb telling of the misfortune that had been their fate; an unkindly and cruel act designed by the great unknown that kept them apart.

That evening, as the two tribes celebrated uniting again after fifteen years, fires were lit everywhere and while the dancing and chanting captivated the attention of the young children, many fell asleep in the laps of their mothers. And at last Chaska and Tiva found an opportunity to speak. As they walked quietly amongst the horses, the air was filled with great sadness. When they stood opposite each other in the pale moonlight, he spoke first.

"I made my acquaintance with you on the evening before my tenth birthday. I know that now." Her eyes shone with unshed tears, but she remained quiet. He wanted to reach out and run the back of his hand over the soft skin of her face but he refrained from moving and dropped his voice to a low whisper. "That was you."

"As a little girl, I dreamed often of a young boy alone in his tepee and a woman who brought him two beautiful feathers. I did not understand that dream until today." She spoke very quietly, but didn't take her eyes off him; it was still that direct stare he remembered from their first encounter. "That was us." Her voice grew stronger. "We do not have much time and we should soon join the others at the festive fires."

"I have no knowledge of you other than my dream and our first meeting, but I only want your happiness." His voice was filled with respect and honor. "Tell me that you are happy."

"I was young when I found the only true love in my life, Chaska." The tears were flowing freely now, but she persevered bravely. "Then you were gone and left me with no choice but for my elders to choose me a husband; a good one. He too is on his path and gave me the great honor to help guide him along his way. One day he will find his own chosen one, as we found each other so many years ago. Even though we spent no time together, we still recognized each other. You know that."

"The feathers?" He could barely get the words out.

"Yes, Chaska. The feathers from the birds of prey. One from the night and one from the day. One is yours and the other belongs to me." Tiva's voice was tinged with regret and she wept quietly as she laid her soul bare to him.

Chaska tried to swallow the lump in his throat, overcome by his own aching heart and her pain. His soul reached out to her as he listened to the words of the woman he loved but could not have; yet his head told him to be patient. The embrace that followed was unplanned and spontaneous as they renewed their pact of centuries ago in secrecy, holding onto each other briefly, desperately. And in this moment of their physical touch, understanding dawned for them together. Teuch and Anacaona knew themselves as Chaska and Tiva, and this knowledge was enough to carry them through into the future, on every journey they would make.

Chaska bade a quiet and resigned farewell to Tiva and honorably paid his respects to Akecheta, her husband by law, and their son. He valiantly followed his companions to the village perimeter, turned one last time and gave her a final glance of devotion. This time he purposely dug his heels into Nwaptoah's belly. He proudly looked upon his lance as it silhouetted against the setting sun and again the symbolism of the two feathers registered deep within his soul. He secretly vowed to carry the memory of their significance into eternity. He and Tiva would meet again.

Chaska's highest homage to his father, Matoska, was to become one of the greatest scouts in the Indian Nation. He tracked and found buffalo herds when no one else could and acted as intermediary for his tribe many times in disputes, thus endearing him into Sioux folklore of later years. After meeting Tiva and knowing with certainty that their journey would continue in another time and place, he finally took a bride and married a cousin to his beloved. Without mentioning it to each other on the night they had recognized who they were, their resolve was equally strong to live their lives with as much purpose as possible. They were certain that their paths would cross again.

Four years later when Chaska was bringing new scouts through their training, he felt the familiar cold nose of his horse pushing him in the back. As he turned, Nwaptoah bowed before him on his front legs. But Chaska knew his wonderful friend had become old and tired. Snorting quietly and shaking uncontrollably, Nwaptoah's back legs at last gave way and he lay before his master in a heap of obedience and subservience. Chaska cradled his head lovingly, understanding in his heart that it was Nwaptoah's time. Then he sent the others away indicating he wanted to be alone with his trusted steed and that night lay with his body pressed close to his old companion. As he slept, he had a vision of himself and Tiva mounted on a young black stallion. They each held a feather in their hands and were bathed in brilliant light.

"Teuch." Her breath was sweet and warm against his face as she whispered in his ear. "Spethla, or Nwaptoah as you now know him, has gone before us and is waiting on the open plains of the Cosmos for you to join him when the time comes." Chaska awoke feverishly, startled by the dream.

"*Anacaona!*" He unconsciously called her ancient name in distress, but was met only with the sight of his dead companion. Then he slowly leaned over and placed an open palm on the head of his old friend, sending him off the same way that he had welcomed him into his life. "Goodbye, Nwaptoah." The big white body under his hand was already cold and he could barely speak. "I remember now. You are Spethla and we shall meet again."

Both Chaska and Tiva lived into their seventies. The news of Chaska's death reached Tiva within days and her heart contracted as she physically registered his loss. That evening the rain came down hard and she slipped away to the nearest hill. Here she stood for a long time with her face lifted toward the dark skies and allowed the rain to mingle with the salt of her tears.

"Until we meet again, Chaska." Her face contorted in pain. And when she had no more tears left, the heavens cried on her behalf.

Ten years later when Tiva died peacefully in her sleep, it was Akecheta who negotiated a special place of burial with the Ukula elders for his beloved wife to rest alongside their legendary leader whom she had loved all her life. He stood a short distance away next to Chaska's widow who helped to mediate this unusual arrangement. Silhouetted against the blood red skyline of the setting sun as a gentle breeze ushered a dusty trail over the open plains, they stood in absolute silence and bowed their heads in honor and acknowledgment of Chaska and Tiva's sacrifice. Before them, on the highest hill, was a ceremonial lance impaled into the roots of a large tree, proudly holding two preserved feathers—one brown and one gray.

Chapter 3
THE REUNION

Two souls had dissolved back into universal consciousness, imperceptibly rippling the ether like dewdrops merging into the surface of the ocean, eternally striving to unite with the vastness of their Source. Temporarily liberated from the physical in their lives as Chaska and Tiva, they were blissfully unaware of their next worldly adventure. With all the pain and suffering of separation now only a dim soul memory, the root personalities of Teuch and Anacaona were powerfully attracted back to the celestial halfway house of the Meadow to continue the journey.

Drawn together by higher levels of conscious understanding, they joyfully came across their old friend, Spethla, trotting the open fields in the Meadow, impatient for their return and eager for the crossing. Powerful images of Africa manifested and Spethla reared excitedly on to his hind legs, sensing a wild, untamed world beckoning them all. This choice would test them profoundly as Teuch and Anacaona were forcefully attracted to Africa in the 12th century to integrate the experience of unconditional love between father and daughter.

The handcrafted mallet hammered the last wedge firmly into the lock on the high channel of the sophisticated irrigation system. Sekayi straightened his agile body, eyeing his handiwork with pleasure, and he felt good; he was undoubtedly a master of his craft. Much more than just a stonemason, Sekayi was also a skilled toolmaker, a creative carpenter and, to the delight of his family, a gifted yarn weaver and garment maker. Sekayi had instinctive knowledge of farming and hunting which, as the village leader, he freely shared with all. Yet none of his skills or his advanced knowledge could match the devotion he felt for his beautiful bright-eyed daughter, Nyasha.

From the moment she had emerged into this world, his heart filled with joy, as naturally as his lungs filled with air; she was significant to his existence, a part of his reason to live. For twenty four moons he had toiled night and day, using his vast skills and talents, turning his hand masterfully and, to the astonishment of all, Sekayi had created a livable and working environment out of the low grounds just below the wet periphery of the awe-inspiring river Kariba. His happiness came from the knowledge that his Nyasha would now grow up safely, sheltered and well fed.

To escape the inevitable hardships and instability that a nomadic lifestyle brought, a constant supply of water was the key to securing a habitat that would support life in a cruel, hot and exceptionally dangerous land. Since the death of his beloved wife, Japera, Sekayi had long grappled with the idea of changing their lifestyle for the better. Japera's death was a direct result of the inhospitable terrain in which they lived, subjected to immense heat and infestations of flies and mosquitoes. Until only a few moons ago, their way was to constantly traverse the grasslands below the mountains, following the phenomenon of shifting lava sand, which carried the fertile soil necessary for sustaining life and limb.

But this was a treacherous and unsuitable existence for one who felt an affinity to the land, and understood its ways as a farmer and member of the Lemba tribe. Finally, Sekayi had conquered the elusive problem of continuous water supply in order to grow his crops, water his herds and protect his people. At last, settling down in one place and sheltering against the unforgiving heat became a reality with the life-giving source of water nearby and in such abundant supply.

Hundreds of years ago this land, now known as Zimbabwe, was home to the Bantu-speaking people, and consisted of indigenous tribes such as the Hamisi and Aquaara ethnic groups from the southern part of Africa. Despite the raw, unspoiled beauty of the landscape, it was a hostile and warring terrain for dwellers of this wild paradise. Just beneath the surface of the intoxicating natural splendor, raging rivers of hate, lust and greed coursed through the hearts of men, and the land was stained red with the blood of the innocent and defenseless.

Here man had learned to kill instinctively rather than as a means of self-preservation. But Sekayi's tribe had elevated itself to a place of uniqueness from the very beginning, bearing the unusual characteristics of non-indigenous genes. Their features were unusual and striking, as somewhere in their lineage a pertinent Jewish component had been added by a nomadic wave of settlers that had reached these southernmost parts of Africa and lived with them long enough to leave behind a legacy.

Sekayi's people were attractive and pale-skinned. They had aquiline noses and lips clearly reminiscent of their Jewish heredity. Wherever they went they were always noticed, but just as often they were resented by those who felt lesser in their presence. Sekayi was oblivious to any of this. He felt endless gratitude toward Japera for blessing him with a child as beautiful as Nyasha when it seemed that his wife's belly would never swell with child. Tall and regal, Sekayi's face was etched with permanent laugh lines from doting on his only offspring whose eyes and skin were as golden as the shifting sands. In awe of their physical beauty and unusual sand-colored hair, some admired them but many more, by comparison, felt rage and envy. It was Sekayi's decision to build a fortress and settle himself and his people deep within the dry-stone walls that he had crafted by his own hand from the lava rock that abounded in the region.

Along with his peaceful villagers he created a perimeter wall that buffered a deep ravine, which curved and surrounded the enclosure—now home to a rural community. It was not unlike a castle with a moat, only in this instance, the moat was on the inside, also serving as a channeled irrigation system, bringing life-giving water into the village from the river Kariba. Its Achilles heel was at the northern end where Sekayi had created a small lake to act as a feeder reservoir. And it was from this end that the Lemba tribe was vulnerable.

A proud and disciplined people, blessed with a keen intellect, they were known for their industriousness and strength. Sekayi's body spoke of unusual agility and athleticism, coupled with a mysterious skill, great speed and precision, which helped to protect him from his enemies. He was greatly admired for his capabilities and was a natural choice to become leader to his people, all of whom recognized this special gift. Sekayi freely shared his talent, training his compatriots to defend themselves with equal skill and effectiveness.

The ability of the tribe to create defensive weapons, as taught to them by their wise leader, secured their position in this wild, open land. Eventually, as the result of many retaliatory encounters, they became feared and envied amongst the surrounding indigenous tribes. Their reputation paved the way to secure their position and acted as a deterrent for many who contemplated hostility toward them. Sekayi's real genius surfaced with the design of the reservoir and the natural way in which it attracted wildlife right to their doorstep. This made long and dangerous hunting excursions into the wild unnecessary and Sekayi thus constructed high observation walls, keeping wild animals out, but allowing the villagers to observe them in their natural habitat.

But in the building of his masterpiece, Sekayi lost sight of the envy of men—neighboring tribes who came and stared with open amazement at the technological wonder in front of their eyes. He was aware of the greed and envy of his fellow man, but unprepared for the dark forces slowly encroaching on them from the north. To ensure the continuous flow of water from the reservoir into the irrigation system, Sekayi trained a permanent lookout; guards to watch over the safety of their property and people day and night.

Sekayi had always sensed that he had a special mission to help protect his people. He believed that he was guided from beyond the stars by a force he couldn't name but whose presence he very powerfully felt, and by the time Nyasha was four years old, he began to see evidence of her exhibiting the same tendencies. Story telling, an ancient and much loved way of teaching the young ones, suddenly took on a whole new meaning when Nyasha, with her natural openness and charm began to tell stories that filled him with wonder. She would speak of a warrior-like man of heavenly appearance who came looking for her on a horse of great strength.

"He loves me father, like I love you." She'd stare him straight in the eye, quietly demanding confirmation.

"Nyasha, little one, what do you know of love?" Sekayi tried to reason with his headstrong offspring, but the light in her golden eyes and the small hand on his arm silenced him.

"He loves me, father." The determination in her voice brooked no resistance. Sekayi would sit by the fire and watch the flames dance over her beautiful face, casting her in shadow and then illuminating her fine features as the wind softly moved over their warm bodies. Her words resonated in a place deep within him that he couldn't mentally fathom, but his heart felt her and every sinew of his being tightened in fatherly protection, drawing him even closer to his beloved and treasured daughter. How could she know so much for someone so young? His strength grew through his need to protect Nyasha and he vowed silently never to leave her vulnerable side.

The Lembas, meticulous in their planning and organization, killed game only for consumption equal to the needs of the people. Their grazing herds, kept inside the fortress, provided them with milk, and the emphasis here was on breeding animals, rather than slaughtering them, especially since the impala herds were plentiful on the other side of the ravine.

One day, as the sun anchored itself maliciously in the center of the blue sky and relentlessly scorched down on the dry grass and dusty plains, Sekayi and his fellow hunters were returning with their kill from the outskirts of the surrounding ravine to the safety of the fortress. With a dead impala draped around his shoulders as they trod silently through the tall grass, Sekayi's sensitive nature suddenly became aware of an unusual presence. He stopped dead in his tracks and held up a warning hand. Behind him, like one man, the hunting party froze in their footsteps. Then he expertly scanned their surroundings, not making a move in any direction; his senses were highly alert and primed for signs of an ambush.

On this day, Sekayi felt the danger, but he also felt another presence, which he could not explain. His eyes roamed expertly over the bushy terrain and tall grass trying to identify the source of the unnatural quietness, the familiar suspension in sound to which nature submits, just prior to a kill. Then he heard a muffled snort, and a shiver of ancient recognition ran down his spine, instantly bewildering him. At last his eyes locked onto the source of the sound as he stared in shock at the long-haired, golden mane of a stallion, masterfully camouflaged in the tall grass, backed up against a dense thorn bush. Front legs apart and head down, it leaned slightly forward. Poised to flee, it did nothing but flare its nostrils anxiously. The stallion was cornered, with no way out.

"Hau!" A stifled gasp of panic and then the hand behind him pointed urgently to the shorter grass in front of them where the shoulder blades of a lioness showed briefly as she came out of the stalking position, preparing to attack. Then Sekayi knew there would be more than one, that the stallion was surrounded and that the frightened animal sensed this.

His next move was instinctive and very dangerous, but with a growl that tore from his very gut, he reached for the impala on his shoulders and with a mighty effort thrust the dead animal toward the lion closest to him. It flew through the air and flopped noisily into the grass a few feet away from the lioness, kicking up a cloud of dust. The sudden distraction interrupted the ritual of the kill as two more lions stood ominously in the tall grass, disturbed and irritated. Drawn irresistibly to the smell of blood and a meal, they hesitated only briefly and then pounced ferociously on the carcass. Sekayi and his warriors knew not to move or to blink. He lifted his eyes carefully toward the stallion and sent it a silent message. *Don't move, my friend. Be very quiet.*

The horse seemed to understand, as if it had been waiting for him to show up. As soon as the wild cats were immersed in the feeding frenzy, Sekayi and his group slowly retreated, never taking their eyes off the lions and carefully circled away from them to the north, moving slowly toward the stallion that still seemed to be waiting. Sekayi hooked a long piece of dried skin worked into leather over the head of the horse and noticed the deep gashes in its flanks where the animal had pushed itself into the thorn bush in an effort to retreat.

A very strange feeling came over Sekayi as he led the stallion away from danger and into the safety of the compound. He remembered Nyasha's dreams and stories of a golden horse similar to this one; a horse, she had said, that would one day grace their presence. Sekayi shook his head in disbelief, grappling with inexplicable feelings of familiarity toward the horse, and amazement at his beautiful daughter. He couldn't wait to see her face when he showed her who they had rescued from the jaws of death.

Sekayi allowed the villagers to lead and tether the nervous horse into the sheltered enclosure that they used for the herd, so as to tend to its superficial wounds. He stood a few feet away from the commotion as some of the other livestock scrambled to one side, and watched the rippling of strong muscles play under the skin of the stallion as he was being tended to. The wild, fearful look in his eyes had been replaced with a look of contentment and he hardly winced as cool water was applied to his wounds to wash them down, removing some of the dried blood from his shiny coat.

Locking eyes with the stallion again, Sekayi's mind reached vacantly into a void of the past. Naturally of a joyful disposition, he was perturbed by an emotion he couldn't fathom and stirred by a dull nagging ache, the origin of which fit nowhere into his memory banks. Hardship and struggle in this unforgiving land was one thing that he had to deal with, and losing Japera so many years ago had left an empty space he had learned to live with. But this strange reaction to a wild horse was not anchored to anyone or any thing and it left him feeling strangely empty.

Then the horse looked away, snorting gently and fixed his stare on someone or something behind Sekayi. It let out a soft neighing sound, rearing its head a little and Sekayi turned to see a wide-eyed Nyasha behind him, clasping her hands to her mouth in astonishment. She was older now and much taller. Sekayi had been silently watching her gentle but unmistakable advancement into womanhood. At fifteen years of age, Nyasha was tall and graceful in her movements, filled with the promise of passion and warmth still slumbering and veiled in the darkness of her eyes. In this moment Sekayi again witnessed the childlike excitement of his beloved little girl.

"Zuka!" The cry of utter joy bubbled up from her innermost core as she took off and ran toward her father almost knocking him over as she heavily collided with his chest. She threw her arms around him in wild abandonment, unable to hide her joy. Sekayi encircled her waist instinctively to steady them both, but she impatiently wiggled free of him, her eyes shining with intense emotion. "Where did you *find* him? *Where?*" Nyasha's heart was filled with indescribable happiness.

A wondrous thing was happening in front of her eyes and she could hardly believe she was looking at the flight-footed messenger of her dreams. She had awoken this morning with feelings of anticipation, an inner knowing that the day would somehow be special. She had become used to the sensations in her mind and body that told her secrets of the past and hinted of things to come. At her tender age, Nyasha sensed experiences of a time long ago that would equip her to endure many things of which her present life showed no evidence. She comprehended pain and loss on a level of which she had no actual knowledge, but she seemed to instinctively know the meaning of things, as if somehow, somewhere, she'd been down many distant roads before.

These feelings troubled her from time to time, causing deep frustration and she now briefly felt a resurgence of the niggling void she had experienced so many times before, suggesting that the future was unclear; that events would unfold for which she would need much courage and strength. As before, this void was strangely overlaid with a mysterious but simple shape, emitting patterns, numbers, sounds and colors, flowing into one another so fast that even her mental eye could not take hold of it long enough to unravel its meaning. Sometimes the shape would change, but the feeling it gave her was always the same, that of something she instinctively knew, but the final solution always eluded her.

"Nyasha, my sweet little one." Sekayi's voice brimmed over with excitement at her obvious joy and enthusiasm. "You came before I could surprise you. Can I hide *nothing* from you?" He tilted his head to one side and regarded her quizzically. "Is this *the one,* Nyasha?" he asked softly, watching her closely as her eyes went from him to the horse and then back to him again. Nyasha did not hesitate for a single moment; she had already seen visions of this magnificent animal the previous evening in her dreams and had felt that the reunion was inevitable and at hand.

This knowing had started earlier that day, when she was returning from the outskirts of the compound after her long daily walk. The experience she had had in the center of the wooded area where she waited for the sun to relent from the dead aim it had taken in the middle of the day, still deeply perplexed her. She hadn't told her father anything yet of the strange occurrence that had occupied her mind since the day before. Now, as she looked at him, she knew she still couldn't tell him about the feathers.

She had no idea why the feathers she had picked up seemed so unusual or why they evoked such confusing emotion. *How did the eagle's feather end up under the canopy of the trees?* Where she stood, she had looked up toward the leafy roof and remembered that these big winged hunters often sat atop the highest trees from where they scanned the ravine and surrounding areas for prey. The feather seemed as if it had been lost recently and had drifted down from the branches and leaves to find a resting place in the shade of the short grass and shrubs at her feet.

Bending down to pick it up, she caught sight of another just a few feet away; this was from an owl. Nyasha knew the origin of the feathers instantly for Sekayi had taught her to love and respect the animals and the birds. As she held both of these feathers, a great sadness came over her. She brought them slowly to her nose and delicately smelled them, scenting the wind and the wild. But the feeling of despair wouldn't pass; she seemed immobilized by the power it had over her and was incapable of stemming the tears. *What is wrong with me?*

The answer didn't come and Nyasha held the feathers close to her heart as she made her way through the dry grass on her way home, convinced that she would find the answer. In the coolness of the hut, she put them under the cushion of soft skin that was her pillow, and then the incredible vision had come while she was sleeping. In her dream she saw the silhouette of a tall, handsome man on a magnificent stallion galloping across an open plane. He held two feathers in his hand, one of an eagle and one of an owl. Nyasha's heart could not stand the anticipation, for she had been waiting for him and he was coming to fetch her; she would know him and his unusual horse amongst thousands.

Now she looked at the big creature in front of her and saw its trembling muscles and the guarded look of recognition in its eyes. Then she realized the glorious animal of her vivid vision was standing in her presence. She glanced from the horse to her father and she spoke softly, clearly.

"You ask if this is the one, father?" Her voice quivered with pent-up emotion. "This is the *only* one."

When they reached the enclosure together, holding hands, the horse turned away from the villagers tending it and walked straight to the pair, using his nose to gently separate them. Sekayi laughed uncontrollably, the joy coming from a source that he could not determine, but he was happy in the knowledge that his new-found friend was not seriously injured. Nyasha and her father both felt the strange energy that was present as they embraced its powerful neck, admiring the beautiful golden mane and making sure to avoid the open wounds.

"It appears that our friend is happy to be here, Little One." He found it difficult to dispense with the endearing term that he had used ever since she was so small. "You want to call him Zuka?" he asked curiously.

"Yes. This is Zuka of my dreams, father. I told you he would come!" She laughed as she pressed her face into the side of the stallion's neck. "You came, as I knew you would, Zuka!" Her joy was contagious and Sekayi laughed too, filled with wonder as he remembered how the horse had come to him earlier that day.

Zuka had found his place within the village, first as a treasured and beloved member of the family and community, and secondly as a practical *and* symbolic worker in the furtherance of the village's future and its protection. Sekayi realized that Zuka had to have other members of its herd nearby, as the waterhole surely attracted them away from the more hostile area around the river Kariba. Luring and catching more of the herd heralded a new era for him and his people, who now had the means to hunt with more safety, on horseback.

But another change had come to their land, a change that no one could have foreseen. The sophistication of their dwelling in a land so wild and untamed drew predators of another kind. Arab traders from the north had caught wind of their success and lay an evil plan to steal away Sekayi's most treasured possessions. And while he basked in the freedom of their lifestyle for which they had worked so hard, and lived for the happiness of his daughter, Sekayi was completely unprepared for the menacing presence that had been tracking his good fortune; just as wild dogs never lose the scent of blood.

Chapter 4
Awareness

The setting sun cast long dark shadows from the nearby mountains over the village and, as the day slowly ground to a halt, it turned the day by degrees into night, marking the end of a long and arduous task for Sekayi—repairing the irrigation channel. He straightened his weary body and stretched stiffly as he stood a few steps back to inspect his handiwork. He had replaced the rotten wooden gates in the final lock system, a job that required constant attention. His creative ability as a master carpenter was paying dividends. Maintenance was a high but necessary price to pay for the abundant supply of fresh water, which also brought extra responsibilities for the villagers; that of cultivating and harvesting their plentiful crops.

His years of sweat and toil in the creation of such a technological feat was now bearing fruit and his people enjoyed abundance and a high quality of life, of which the rumors and legends reached far beyond the protected walls of the compound. Their good fortune had become the envy of those who were eager to harvest what they had not sown but more significantly, word had spread of a beautiful woman who sometimes accompanied the hunting parties on horseback. Those who had spotted her told tales of an excellent rider on a golden haired stallion, a slender-limbed woman with a melodic laugh that echoed merrily across the open plains.

It was said she was always in the company of an older man, rumored to be her father and the leader of the tribe. Those who were plotting to steal Sekayi's triumphs and success secretly watched him with his daughter and realized that she would be the key to disarming the leader. But for now, on his way back to his hut, Sekayi was oblivious to the envy and greed lurking in the shadows beyond the ravine. As always, he was looking forward to the end of the day, to spending time with his beloved offspring, of whose stories and enthusiasm he never seemed to tire.

She was a dreamer, this one; a ball of energy and passion who had grown into eighteen years of beauty and grace. His love for his only child had no end, but Sekayi was wise and he realized that her life could not indefinitely be a part of his. He knew that one day, as a woman, she would have to turn to a man to become complete. He forced himself to accept the inevitable and waited patiently for Nyasha to notice the young men who seemed to lose their tongues in her presence or couldn't keep their eyes off her when she moved about the village.

He stopped by the hut where they stored their mallets and other hand-made tools, a favorite resting place of his, and sat for a while. Taking the weight off his tired feet, he took a grateful drink of water from the skin pouch hanging in the shade of a tree, and shut his eyes. Then he felt the familiar presence of a close friend and high elder of the village and looked up as Farai approached to sit down beside him. It had been three years now since that eventful day when Zuka had become a part of their lives. In this time all manner of change had taken place that had altered the way they performed many tasks, both inside and outside the walls of the village.

Having captured and tamed more of Zuka's herd that regularly came to drink from the reservoir, they became mobile and could travel faster, all of which considerably changed the capabilities of the tribe. In a way they were now on equal footing with the nomadic Arabs, who had trekked down south as far as their home alongside the river Kariba. Sekayi and his people had not seen any of the nomads but the accounts of burnt down villages three days away on foot made everyone uncomfortable. And then there were the trading posts that had sprung up all around them, the purpose of which remained unknown to Sekayi's people.

"Your hard work over the years has brought great rewards, Sekayi." Farai spoke calmly to his most loyal and trusted friend while chomping on a piece of grass between his front teeth. "And tomorrow will be another adventure for us. I look forward to these excursions, but sometimes I forget that even on horseback we are still fair game for predators when we leave the compound." He smiled crookedly. "You have given us such admirable training. I am sure that you do not feel nervous anymore."

Sekayi didn't reply immediately; he was apprehensive about the task for the next day. He knew that Farai referred to four-legged predators that killed to eat, but he couldn't escape the troublesome foreboding that there were predators that also killed viciously to hurt, and that these were far more dangerous and unpredictable. The sun had dipped behind the mountains on its journey to the other side of the world, erasing the long shadows it cast in its final glory, and left them sitting in the half-light of early dusk. Sekayi smiled distractedly.

"Could we ever say we are not nervous anymore, Farai?" He didn't address his fears with his friend, but he was much more concerned than he let on. Of course he cared about the safety of the scouting group, but he feared for the wellbeing of the village, particularly Nyasha. Of late, the village hunting parties had returned with disturbing stories of being secretly tracked and followed by figures on horseback when venturing beyond the community perimeter. The Arab travelers had not only secured certain trading posts within the vicinity of the reservoir, but they were ostensibly using the plentiful supply of water as a reason for securing the land for the purpose of commercial bartering.

Although none of his tribe had actually run into any of the newcomers, all knew they were there. Their presence hung like a stench in the air, but the nomads themselves were conspicuously absent. In his wisdom Sekayi understood that the water drew them close and was a major drive for their immediate presence, but he was filled with doubt about the intentions of these mysterious travelers who purportedly were very skilled equestrians. *Who do they want to trade with and why?* There were not enough villagers within the community to warrant regular trading and besides, his people were self-sufficient and they hardly traded with any of the surrounding tribes in a land where survival of the fittest dictated self-preservation to be the first law.

Their sudden presence was a deep source of concern for Sekayi and all the far-flung tribes of the area. From past experience he knew that nomads usually moved on swiftly when they realized there was little profit to be gained. Deep within however, he feared that it wasn't trade they were interested in but that the comfort of the compound and the bountiful lifestyle of the Lembas community was the sought-after prize. Along with Farai and a few other village elders, he had decided to investigate the trading posts further, to see if they could come face to face with the unwelcome intruders to their world. At least they'd have the advantage of being on horseback, meeting them as equals.

In the meantime he would spend his evening enjoying the company of his beloved Nyasha and some close friends. They would sit by the fire together after a satisfying meal and he would listen to her stories of the day; he would hear her carefree laugh and share in her joy of living. Sekayi had no idea that in a few short hours, paradise would be lost forever and that in obscurity outside the walls of the compound, death was being contemplated in a fate so unthinkable, so cruel that it would tear the heart from his very body.

As Sekayi and his party left the village the next day to investigate the strangers, his heart was heavy and he tried in vain to shut out thoughts of the village and his beloved Nyasha whom he had left tending to her inseparable companion, Zuka. In the coolness of her hut Nyasha waited nervously on her father's homecoming. She had taken the feathers from under the soft skin of her pillow and stared at them intently for a long time. Something was different today, she didn't know what it was but she had a nagging feeling of looming fate; an uneasiness she couldn't shake off.

Again she smelled the feathers and closed her eyes, like she had done so many times in the past, willing herself to make the connection with the aching sadness she always felt when she held them. But it was not yet time and Nyasha was met with only darkness and frustration. Then the image of Sekayi drifted clearly into her mind, as if he stood in front of her and her eyes flew wide open in apprehension. *Where are they? What was taking them so long?* But then she heard his voice and without thinking Nyasha tucked the feathers where she always hid them—under the soft fabric of the tunic covering her bosom, and ran outside to meet her father.

She sat quietly beside him staring into the flames and listened to his account of their visit when earlier that day the party had entered the strangers' enclosure and was met by the Arab chief, Bahar. Using the universal ancient Arhaaht language of the moon, the eagle and the eye, Sekayi had learned that the traders were keen to set up an agreement where protection would be offered to the Lembas in return for a share in the wealth of their prosperous community. Sekayi looked around the fire at his trusted elders and advisors.

"What do we need to be protected against?" he asked. "For years we have toiled to make a life for ourselves and even the natural predators of the open plains and grass fields respect us as we do them. What danger are they speaking of, if not themselves?" He looked around the circle slowly, deliberately, making eye contact with each and every one of them, except Nyasha, who sat so close to him he could hear her soft, uneasy breathing.

"I said no." It was a statement of finality, met by a solemn silence. Then he reached out and put his hand over hers. "Quiet now, Little One." He dropped his voice down low so only she could hear him. "I have made my plans. You will be safe." She looked up into his eyes and for a brief, unguarded moment father and daughter both recognized the fear in each other's faces. She instinctively leaned toward him and put her head on his shoulder, comforting him and being comforted. But as Sekayi spoke he felt a heavy weight on his heart. "You will be escorted tomorrow together with the women and children to a place of safety." He would remember his words to her for years to come, an earnest promise made by the fire that would torment and haunt him in his darkest hours of despair.

The next day, as preparations were being made for the evacuation, Nyasha went to the animal enclosure to attend to Zuka, seeking his company and the comfort of his presence. She looked proudly upon the horse; he was every inch the warrior with elevated head and quivering muscles, ready to do battle. She took a step closer and pressed her face into his neck whispering softly.

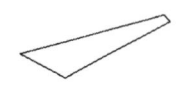

"Zuka, why is my heart so heavy for this day?" The horse stared straight ahead and flared his nostrils lightly, his fixed gaze suggesting that he sensed danger. He let out an anxious little snort as if to indicate he didn't like what he saw, but Nyasha watched him carefully and felt it too. "And what about the visions I see so often, Zuka?" She spoke softly into his face as she gently stroked his strong neck. "What do I make of all the patterns and sounds? And those delicate colors, Zuka, *what do they mean?*" Nyasha's voice dropped to barely above a whisper as she closed her eyes and recalled the perplexing recurrence of the strange shapes. One of these shapes suddenly entered into her mind sending out its usual scrambled message, that so haunted her dreams. "And why do they always appear when I feel anxious and afraid, as if to comfort me? I knew a long time ago that you and I would meet and I recognized you the instant I saw you, but why does the meaning of the visions keep escaping me?" But Zuka didn't answer, for he too, did not know.

The first attack came without warning. The evacuation effort to the caves in the mountains two days to the south of the compound was not yet in full swing when the northern wall was suddenly breached. With an earth-shattering battle cry, countless Arab warriors spilled over it in quick succession. Sekayi's reaction was instinctive as he turned on his heel and rushed back to Nyasha.

"Take Zuka and go with the women and children. Now!" Their eyes met briefly and he saw the hesitation in hers but Sekayi knew that there was no other way. He stepped forward anxiously, desperately and pulled her close to him, if only briefly. "Go swiftly, Little One! I will send for you when it is safe. Farai's escort is leaving through the southern exit. Go *now!*" He dropped a kiss on her head, lifting her in a swift movement onto Zuka. "Hurry, Nyasha!"

Nyasha's voice strangled in her throat in a fatal premonition; she kept looking at him with her heart in her eyes and let out an anxious "Father!" as he slapped Zuka hard on the hind quarters and the horse took off like a bolt of lightning. She looked over her shoulder one last time as they sped away, tears streaming down her face, but Sekayi stood frozen for a moment in time. He didn't know he would never see his beloved daughter alive again.

Inside the compound the Arab warriors quickly began to retreat in the face of the skill of the Lemba leader who expertly led his people. The tall, agile man and his villagers were trained to swiftly disarm and dispose of them. The moment he picked up a discarded sword, an ancient shiver of recognition ran down his spine as he cut expertly with it through the air and aimed it in deadly precision to the chest of the terrified man in front of him. The Arab died instantly as Sekayi leaned forward with his whole body weight and pierced his heart while keeping eye contact, honoring the villain's life like a true soldier.

They were quickly gaining the upper hand and as the enemy inexplicably, suddenly gave up and began to flee, Sekayi realized for the first time that something was amiss. "Nyasha!" Her name tore in agony from his lips as he grasped the cunning plot in paralyzing horror. He had sent her right into their trap and he now knew with deadly certainty that it was the women and children they wanted. They were *slave traders* and he had made their wicked task easy for them!

The realization of the magnitude of his error sent his mind reeling and he stood nailed to the ground, immobilized by the weight of guilt and remorse; bitter tears stinging behind his eyes. Then his heart sank like lead as Zuka stormed wildly into the compound, wounded and bleeding from his left flank and without his usual companion. Something very old and very painful manifested in his chest that made it hard to breathe and Sekayi knew that there was no alternative; he had to find her or lose his sanity. In a rapid movement he mounted the wounded horse, turned it around and thundered out of the compound in a cloud of dust, leaving the elders to take care of the village and its damage.

Nyasha looked at the man in front of her and knew she was staring death in the face. Bahar had expertly cornered her away from the rest of the fleeing women and children by wounding her horse first. An experienced and excellent equestrian, he had grabbed her skillfully from behind, lifting her from the stumbling animal and thrown her roughly over his legs as he took off toward the nearest trading post. Looking at her supple body now before him, he remembered the look of the leader as he refused their offer, and recognized the same expression in the eyes of the woman only a few feet away from him.

Rage and wild desire coursed insanely through his veins and his breath came in shallow, acrid gasps as he lunged forward to grab her. Trapped inside the unfamiliar, foul smelling tent, Nyasha instinctively moved aside to escape his rough hands but misjudged the size of the man as Bahar caught her in flight and spun her around. For a brief moment their eyes met and the big Arab, filled anew with anger as he saw the contempt in her look, slammed her mercilessly to the ground, grabbing her tunic and ripping it open to expose her young, firm breasts.

The brutality of the assault knocked her out as she violently hit the dried animal skins beneath her. When she finally came to, the heavy weight of the big Arab was on her, impatiently waiting for her to regain consciousness, cruelly sensing that the violation would be that much more intense if she understood what was happening to her. He was going to abuse her so he could punish her arrogant father; that was part of his evil plan. She opened her eyes slowly and saw the feathers he held in his coarse hands.

"What is this?" he demanded gruffly in his own language. "These fell from your bosom. Are you a *witch*?" As he spoke the words, he pinned her hands behind her head and forced himself brutally into her, dropping his face into the hollow of her neck and bit down hard into the soft flesh of her shoulder. Still dazed from the physical attack, Nyasha struggled in vain against his crushing weight. Her consciousness mercifully began to slip again just as the immense pain of his violent invasion seared like a hot knife through her body. On the brink of oblivion, she reached weakly for the feathers and in that instant, hundreds of years rolled back and she finally made the breakthrough that had escaped her memory for so long.

"Teuch!" she screamed, before darkness again enveloped her. The Arab lifted his head, momentarily ceasing his ferocious movements and stared confused at her closed eyes and the pain etched on her face.

"Whore!" he uttered in frustration and clasped a dirty hand over her mouth and nose to stifle any further sound, and then continued his barbaric assault on her. *A witch and a virgin!* He lost himself completely in his thousandth act of mindless violation and didn't even feel her body go limp beneath him before he slumped in final climactic release. His big hand still blocked her airways, but the beast was temporarily impotent.

When she opened her eyes she was standing in a field of grass blowing gently in the wind. It was all so familiar and her heart filled with indescribable joy. Time was of no consequence here, and soon, she knew, he would come. She smiled and closed her eyes against the brightness of the sun; content to wait.

That was when she breathed her last breath as Nyasha, and the body the Arab had violated didn't matter at all any more. The hand that held the feathers, unconsciously torn from the Arab's grasp while he tore her apart, opened slowly and she let them go as she quietly surrendered to death. She was safe at last.

With Bahar long gone, Sekayi stood in the opening of the tent and his stomach lurched violently. Mute, and beyond physical movement his mind tried to make sense of her still, naked body. Then his muscles moved involuntarily and he crept closer to his dead child and froze in confused agony as he crouched over her and saw the feathers in the palm of her limp hand. Sekayi's mind went blank and incredible emotion rushed through his heart threatening to destroy it, but he reached blindly, angrily for understanding as he looked upon her peaceful expression. Then he picked up the feathers and brought them slowly to his lips; tears streaming down his face. A door into the past opened fleetingly at just a crack and what he glimpsed dropped him instantly to his knees.

"*Anacaona?*" The hoarse whisper spilled brokenly from his trembling lips, while his bewildered heart panicked and strained desperately under the immensity of the unbearable, baffling realization of her true identity. Sekayi's tortured mind reeled dangerously out of control and swayed mercifully toward insanity but he held on agonizingly, and fought his way back with every ounce of strength he had left. "Nyasha, Nyasha, my sweet little one, *how could I not have known?*" There was no end to his despair and Sekayi wept uncontrollably as he held her lifeless body to his aching heart.

Every step of the journey back to the compound was pure torture as he walked beside Zuka, who limped painfully from his injuries. At first Sekayi carried her in his arms but her dead weight became too much even for his strong body and he finally put her over his shoulder, still walking beside Zuka, holding onto him lightly as they made their way home. It was a solemn, mechanical walk and for the first time in his life here on the banks of the river Kariba, Sekayi lost his focus and concentration as he gave himself over to the grief of a loss too enormous to contemplate. His mind thrashed about wildly, trying to grasp all the pieces that didn't yet fit. He had brought the feathers with him but couldn't bear to think of them. He moved forward taking every step in a void of pain and guilt, trying to understand how this day could have turned out differently, but there was only darkness.

Zuka suddenly stopped in his tracks and reared his head, neighing anxiously. Sekayi instinctively followed suit and realized too late that they were defenseless targets as he noticed the lioness standing openly in the tall grass in front of them. Then he saw two more on either side of her. They were easy prey and there was no need for disguise or stalking, something the wild predators sensed immediately. Sekayi's mind reached feebly for a solution but he could think of none. And then Zuka pressed his head close to him, sniffed one last time at Nyasha's limp frame and took off in a wild gallop toward the lions offering his already broken body in exchange for Sekayi's.

The wild cats didn't hesitate for a second; they smelled the blood from his open wounds and took him down in swift, ferocious movements growling their call of death as they skillfully went for his jugular vein. Zuka didn't put up any fight and Sekayi listened in horror as they closed off his airways and slowly suffocated every ounce of life from his big, golden body. He waited in absolute torture for them to start feeding before he slowly shuffled his way back to the compound and the years of emptiness that stretched forlornly ahead of him.

Farai had become an even closer companion. There were days that Sekayi's words sounded like mindless babble, but he, Farai, had never witnessed utter torment like this in another human and he let Sekayi speak of places and names no one had ever heard of. This came after the terrible revenge and hunting expeditions he organized at night to eradicate every trading post in the vicinity, but nothing could take away his pain. With the Arabs finally gone and their former life style restored, Sekayi was still a haunted man.

Even the grotesque sight of Bahar's body outside the compound where Sekayi had pinned him to a tree with his own sword and dispassionately watched his agonizing slow death, only deepened his pain. The void Nyasha had left threatened to swallow him wholly and he carried the feathers he took from her lifeless body everywhere with him. The magnitude of her loss hit him the day he found her but the impact of her absence kept reverberating through his body and mind in relentless anguish that only escaped him in fitful sleep. Farai saw Sekayi's struggle but was powerless and silent in the face of so much suffering; all he could do was listen as his old friend spoke.

"I will see her again." Farai looked up from his reverie hearing Sekayi's voice; he had heard that statement before. He knew what to do, and he wanted to aid his old friend. They were warriors together and he wanted to help ease his emotional pain.

"In the Meadow?" he inquired softly, politely.

"In the Meadow, Farai. Zuka is there too, with her, and they are waiting for me." He stared into the setting sun where they sat at their favorite resting place and then he closed his eyes and spoke barely above a whisper, feeling a wave of incredible emotion well up from his innermost being, drowning the words. "This time she came as Nyasha." His voice quivered uncontrollably. "But she and Zuka have other names." He struggled today more than in the past, his voice faltering as his consciousness drifted disjointedly between two worlds. Farai's gaze rested on him, sensing every ounce of his anguish, understanding nothing, but feeling a real concern as he looked at his friend. Something was different today, but he didn't know what that was.

"Tell me about the feathers again, Sekayi," he prompted softly. But Sekayi no longer heard his friend. An immense pain rose from his chest that instantly smothered his words. The hand clasping the feathers reached weakly to his upper body in a feeble attempt to ward off the terrible ache, but then he glimpsed the Meadow of which he always spoke and his hand dropped without further resistance to his side. An expression of wonder slowly erased the lines of anguish that had been there for ten long years as he recognized her beside the magnificent stallion.

"Nyasha, Anacaona. Spethla…" His lips barely moved. Farai didn't stir or make a sound. Nothing could stop his old friend now.

"Go to them," he whispered through joyful tears as Sekayi's hand slowly opened and the feathers slipped silently to the ground. Farai sat there for a long time beside his dead friend and felt the peace that Sekayi had finally found as he left the pain of this world behind. Then he leaned over and with two fingers gently closed his old friend's eyes. "What did you mean when you said that only the names were different and that you would continue your journey until all the pieces finally fit?"

But Sekayi didn't answer for he was striding through the Meadow with the sun on his face.

Chapter 5
Harsh Reality

The Meadow is a regular staging post or point of departure from whence the Cosmos expertly directs souls as they are appropriately delivered to their next earthly stage. It is here that Teuch, Anacaona and Spethla readily awaited their opportunity to continue their learning in the 17th Century during the English reign of Charles I. Endlessly inquisitive and mighty curious, it appears the Absolute has the ability to lace huge strands of energy through the Universe connecting souls from anywhere and everywhere for the purpose of weaving the delicate and fine tapestry of life.

In the manifold expressions of individual essence across the great expanse of endless space, it leaves no stone unturned in its efforts to experience itself. It is here in the Meadow that mind, body and soul manifest yet again to take up the challenges of life and conquer the unknown in the earthly fires of compassion, lust, violence and above all—love. But evolution requires the integration of both sexes. Ready once again to make the crossing, neither Teuch nor Anacaona had an inkling of the gender reversal in this life or the immense learning curve that awaited them in the challenging circumstances into which they were about to be born.

It was a memorable day in the year 1634 when Ann Connelly married the Reverend Henry Bettsford. Although many years her senior, Ann had at long last found peace and refuge with a kindly man, a Methodist who was determined to make a better life for his family. In times of upheaval and uncertainty he held on to his ideals of stability and visions of love that would eventually result in children and sustained happiness. With the encouragement of his devoted wife Ann, Reverend Bettsford made plans to soon leave behind the damp shores of England for good and settle in the New World across the Atlantic.

Ann was born and raised in the primitive Lancashire town of Haslingden in 1612; a place deeply entrenched in the traditions of quarrying fine stones, a legacy that has stood the test of time even to this day. The original primitive cottage industries where many managed to eke out a meager living were supportive to this harsh enterprise, which in later years became the backbone of the future prosperity of the town and its surrounding neighbors. Work was plentiful but very hard and laborious. It took its terrible toll on the human body in endless disease and suffering but it was the soul that struggled most to endure the mindlessness of it all. It was especially hard for someone as sensitively strung as Ann, whose tendencies toward spiritual insight were more pronounced than most others.

In those days of merciless sweat and toil to keep body and soul together, it was not unusual for the women to work in the quarries with the men, but Ann intuitively sensed early on that her calling was elsewhere. It was through her helping as a soothsayer that she first met Henry, a practicing Methodist whose business it was to gather lost souls as he traversed the country in his quest to preach the gospel. But Ann had experiences in her dreams and visions she could reveal to a precious few, including the thoughtful man to whom she was bonded in marriage.

Feminine and soft in nature, she nonetheless had many confusing but vivid male recollections in these exciting spiritual adventures. Henry not only loved his much younger attractive wife but found her unusual interests very stimulating and endearing. The independence she displayed as a woman was unequaled for these times but the Reverend was much taken with her active mind and colorful imagination, and he loved her more for her courage to express herself so openly with him. It was after all, the source of his initial attraction to the soft-spoken woman with the golden brown curls and soulful blue eyes.

Four years later marked the birth of their son, Nathaniel. It was an extremely difficult birth. The midwives struggled for hours to relieve her tortured body of its human cargo and were frightful that neither mother nor child would ultimately weather such intense hardship. His birth left Ann very weak and exhausted and gifted little Nathaniel with the undesirable legacy of being crippled for life.

Times were very hard in England and political tension and economic adversity mounted by the day and finally manifested in palpable unrest when Charles I audaciously decided to act against Parliament. With so much uncertainty in the air and before full scale war could break out in 1642, Henry, Ann and Nathaniel had their passages booked for the New World, and were ready to leave the bleak English shores before the Royalists and Roundheads decided they could not settle their differences.

The crossing was eventful and dangerous as was to be expected with a boat full of Puritans, managed by a motley crew made up mainly of angry ex-convicts and rowdy navy deserters. Together they were a loud, disorderly bunch, grateful for the wages they were earning, but with so many women on board they were out on the prowl. Henry had his work cut out for him protecting his family. He noticed the stares his wife's fine features attracted, but as a minister there was a grudging respect that afforded him the opportunity and freedom to become acquainted with his new son and get to know Ann in her tender role as a mother.

It was on this trip across the Atlantic that he gained deeper insight into Ann's most special qualities. He watched her face in wonderment as she shared with him her knowledge of worlds unknown. Henry was astounded with his wife's natural wisdom and ability to reach into the past, and in her soft voice, confidently relay stories of extraordinary times and places. When he looked into her eyes he was convinced of her sincerity, but felt helpless to assist her to overcome her frustration at not knowing enough to complete her insight.

Her biggest struggle was to understand the strong masculine undertone of her thoughts and for one as feminine as Ann it was a perplexing aspect that troubled her deeply. Her saving grace was the wonderful presence of little Nathaniel with his mop of pitch black hair with whom she bonded the moment she laid eyes on him after their grueling ordeal of physical separation. In every waking moment whilst she carried him she *felt* him and in later years it came as no surprise that he would be the one to bring light into her darkness. Only then did Ann know how the bond, first created and later severed through the umbilical cord, continued through emotional and spiritual roots that reached into distant antiquity.

By the time it was Nathaniel's fifth birthday, they were happily settled on the shores of Massachusetts Bay in a place called Cambridge which had recently changed its name from Newtowne. It had been built on the Charles River at the entrance to a small creek just upstream from the main town of Boston. Cambridge was a paradise in comparison to the cluttered and cold living quarters they had been accustomed to and each new family owned a separate house lot in the village. As a community they worked well together, planting their fields just outside the perimeters of their homes and all had a common share in the land.

Five glorious and happy years had passed, and Nathaniel had serenely adjusted to his handicap, which would have crippled another not only in body but also in spirit. His affliction allowed him to walk only with the aid of a crutch since his right leg was completely withered and, due to grave injury during birth, his spine cruelly curved to the point where he could comfortably see only the ground in front of him. Yet this brave little boy never complained; it soon became apparent that he was no ordinary child and that he shared in the same unusual gifts as his wonderful mother.

He too felt a strange uneasiness in his heart when he watched her move about. His love for her was as boundless and deep as the confusion and conflict he experienced with his gender. Still too young to fully understand, he curiously felt as though he belonged in a female body and oddly sensed powerful male energy within this soft-spoken woman. The mystery intensified as he noticed the light in her eyes when she looked at his father or the way in which she held her body close to him in conversation. Nathaniel had no doubt his mother *wanted* to be with his father, but hoped the answers would reveal themselves when he was older

A school sprang up to teach the young in the bustling little community of Cambridge. A busy marketplace drew the villagers into its sweet smelling squares where they heartily ate and drank together and to Henry's delight, the steeple of a church soon completed their sanctity and his bliss. Life inside the village was busy and full of neighborly activity and as the days rolled on, for the most part, the villagers were oblivious of events that took place outside the comfort of their smoking chimneys and robustly growing crops. A frontier war with the Indian Nation loomed menacingly and the reality of it would creep ever closer and change the course of their lives.

Mary and William Wainthorp were the first of the settlers to this little 'New England' who had bravely set sail with seven hundred other hopeful passengers in a fleet of eleven ships in the year 1630. They settled down swiftly in their new surroundings and Mary's services as an experienced schoolteacher were soon in big demand. Her rather unrefined husband, William, was a butcher by profession, who unceremoniously reassigned the brutal ways of his trade to his fellow man. Of medium height, but stocky, he had an unsavory reputation for being a bigot and a bully, and those who knew where to look for signs of abuse quickly noticed the telling bruises on his defenseless wife. They were an odd pair, the violent butcher and his kindhearted mousy wife.

Mary had, however, learnt long ago to find her solace in other ways and by the time Henry, Ann and Nathaniel settled in the Cambridge community some nine years later, she was overjoyed at meeting the sensitive Nathaniel and took him to her bosom like one of her own. The sweet, handicapped child became the object of her love and devotion and she took pains to teach him over and above what was required. Nathaniel was in seventh heaven. He reveled in the attention that Mary gave him and, as a consequence, his education blossomed.

The love he received from this poor abused woman was in stark contrast with the brutality he suffered at the cruel hands of his peers. As the son of a Methodist minister, he was fortunate to have some kind of education, but this privilege diminished into insignificance when the judgment of his peers took over the same way animals reject abnormality in the wild by casting out the different ones. Blameless for his own physical condition, they still punished him in their ignorance for being so painfully dissimilar and beat him, tied and ridiculed him, whipped him mercilessly and spat in his face.

Their verbal abuse was, in reality, a declaration of their fear, a sadly misplaced glee for having had the good fortune of escaping his terrible lot. As always, Nathaniel's inner strength was the anchor onto which he held through the most difficult of situations. He dreamed often and vividly, remembering his dreams well. Sometimes he just heard comforting voices in his head that soothed him and made him feel better, but on many occasions he'd awaken from a brilliant dream where an impressive knight on horseback would be at his side. It was this constant image of great comfort that helped to make the crippled boy's life bearable, for when he was distressed, the knight always came and stayed until he was peaceful again. Nathaniel kept his secret within his heart and shared it only with his parents, but it was especially Ann whose eyes filled with tears as she listened to his stories.

"Do not be sad, mother," he said solemnly, noticing the emotion so easily stirred within her. "I am quite safe when the knight comes. I promise you." But Ann knew not from whence the melancholy came.

"I know, dear Nathaniel. I know," she whispered, bewildered by the confusing emotion his words evoked.

By the time he was twelve years old his father had established himself as a leading and respected figure within the Puritan community. As the population grew and the area expanded, so did Henry's exploits and his time spent away from home increased steadily. Most of the community's leading figures were men of a professional nature who contributed to improvement and progress on many levels. But there was also William Wainthorp who, alas, had made many enemies with his dogmatic and undemocratic ways.

William was self-serving and intolerant of those who would try to change law and order for the better of the community. He was especially inflexible in religious matters, which could possibly allow some of the indigenous people of the area to be taken into the Puritanical way of life, a thought that filled him with blind rage. He had no tolerance for the Indian tribes who went about their lives peacefully and mostly minded their own business.

Driven by an inexplicable rage toward the innocent and a general insufferable nature, William looked upon these people as inferior, only fit to wipe his boots on and would regularly publicly demonstrate his contempt. His hatred was legendary and it wasn't left at the doorstep of these red-skinned, peaceful people, but reached into the dark corners of his evil heart and lashed out indiscriminately to anyone who didn't serve his purpose. Anyone or anything that didn't add to his already substantial coffers, he abused in word and deed. Naturally, William had only contempt for Nathaniel, and the youngster avoided him like the plague.

During a break in his schooling, Henry decided to take Nathaniel with him to one of the Indian villages a few miles inland where he had spent much of his time becoming acquainted with the people. He had made good progress establishing effective communication and commercial trading. These friendly people felt akin to him and he enjoyed learning from them. Henry and his crippled son packed their one-horse-drawn buggy, proudly made by Wilfred, master carpenter of the town, and set off with enough provisions for about five days.

No one in this peaceful town with its cheerful lifestyle could have foreseen that soon Wilfred would be forced to exchange his ingenious trade from the practical buggy-making to manufacturing coffins in numbers out of proportion to regular village life. The day was cloudy and very gray and after a few damp miles and traveling with limited visibility, they realized they were finally leaving behind the mists that clung so possessively to the Massachusetts coastline. They at last were out of the fog and emerged into the bright sunlight, relieved and pleasantly surprised with the vibrancy of all that met the eye.

The mist and fog had an eerie quality, which was disquieting to most, especially in uncharted territory. Then out of the blue, before they could accustom themselves to their new breathtaking surroundings, a large black dog appeared seemingly out of nowhere and jumped onto the back of their buggy. Father and son were both taken by surprise and momentarily undecided about their uninvited but friendly, tail-wagging visitor.

Henry watched with wonderment as the dog crouched underneath Nathaniel's arched body to find his face and began to lick it enthusiastically until the young boy shrieked with laughter. So enthralled were they with their newfound friend that neither noticed its quiet, watchful keeper high on the ridge, following their movements with interest. Henry felt his presence first and looked up, recognizing young Sakhota, son of the Indian chief of the village they were approaching.

Sakhota stood silently for a while, his gaze wandering intentionally from father to son, and then he acknowledged Henry by lifting his lance high in recognition, offering greetings and respect in the customary Indian way. After a brief exchange of pleasantries, Sakhota tethered his horse to the buggy and said he would travel to the village with them. He sat between Henry and Nathaniel, much to the youngster's chagrin. His discomfort lasted only a few minutes as Sakhota easily fell into the tongue that Henry had taught him.

"So this is the young brave that you have been telling me about, Gospel Man?" He used the respectful term having learned of Henry's dedication to his holy book. "We have much to talk about when we arrive at my village." Sakhota was unusual in his proud, erect stature and an extremely aware young man. He was finely tuned into his surroundings and understood nuances and meanings, which made him suitable to act as a spiritual leader, something his father granted him willingly, for Sakhota naturally knew the needs of his people.

This meant that he would maintain his warrior responsibilities as son of the chief but would act as adviser, soothsayer and healer, a role he proudly undertook. Sensitive and extremely spiritual in nature, he had many intense visions, but the most vivid of all was that of the spirit of a striking woman who had regularly visited him until his tenth birthday. Her presence did not alarm him, for by this time Sakhota was familiar with his nightly visitor and her soft but firm assertions of unfinished business.

She also spoke of a male companion and made clear reference to a trusted animal spirit and that one day they would reappear to participate in their journey toward fulfillment. She said for his pains and consideration in the meantime he would be gifted with a special dog, which would house the spirit of their animal companion. Then her visitations suddenly inexplicably ceased. And so by the time he turned eighteen, Sakhota received confirmation of his dreams and visions when a young puppy was presented to him from a trusted village elder.

"You choose the name, young brave." Her soft, persuasive voice echoed from his visions straight into his mind, convincing him of the urgency of this mission. The young warrior carried the most important part of her message in his head constantly and became vigilant and watchful in his efforts to do as requested. He relied on his intuition to inform him when the time approached for him to act. She had said: "I want you to remember that one day you must gift the dog to another, just as he was gifted to you, Sakhota. All the pieces have to fit for these souls to continue." He thought he heard a deep sadness in her voice.

Then his consciousness became highly alert and he instinctively joined the loose ends together and knew in his heart that the spirit lady now walked the earth somewhere in physical body and that she wouldn't rest until she had found her perfect mate. He secretly felt honored to be instrumental in a heavenly design of this scale. Inexperienced in matters of love he wondered at the power of this emotion. *Does it really reach across all boundaries?* But even Sakhota, with his natural wisdom, would not comprehend the full meaning of this vision for many hundreds of years.

He thus named his dog appropriately, Wyomah, Spirit Wind. When he reached the age of twenty-two, he became aware that her promises were about to be fulfilled. On this day, as he stood high on the ridge and watched the buggy approach from afar, Wyomah suddenly stirred beside him and moaned softly. Sakhota quietly bent down to crouch beside his friend and stroked his shiny, black coat lovingly. Never taking his eyes off the approaching horse-drawn cart, he whispered softly in his ear.

"Is it time, Wyomah? I feel it in your quivering muscles," he said in a soothing voice. "You recognize someone, my friend?" A joyful smile spread slowly over his face. "Yes, I feel it too." Many years later the tale of this wonderful experience became legend amongst his people. The events that unfolded as a result of Sakhota's intervention embedded itself in time in the tribe memory as folklore.

But on this day he welcomed Henry and his son into their midst, and as he spoke with Nathaniel, he knew the time had finally come. When they reached the village, the boy strained suddenly, feeling a strong energy run down his painfully curved spine; something was familiar but he couldn't place it. He instantly felt comfortable and at home and in a short time bonded effortlessly with these wonderful people, who would soon take him in as one of their own. Sakhota became his guide and teacher. He explained many wonderful things to Nathaniel, as Henry set about his mission with the Indian elders.

Nathaniel eagerly soaked up the knowledge that his Indian guide imparted to him. Deep in his heart he felt as though he was being prepared for an unknown event of great proportions. But it was only on the last day of their stay that he got another glimpse into the future, one that simultaneously excited him and made him very fearful.

Sakhota approached him solemnly just as they were about to leave and took both of his hands into his own.

"These are for you," he said and placed two feathers into the palm of Nathaniel's hand, one gray and one brown. "These were left to me by two gracious birds of prey. I have been asked to keep them safe until a spirit who would know the meaning of it would come to claim them. I now give them to you." Where he sat beside his father on the buggy, ready to leave, Nathaniel's breath suddenly caught in his throat and his heart lurched violently. He stared bewildered at the feathers, unable to speak or cry. Sakhota watched him silently. "You know, do you not, brave heart?" Henry knew not what to say but understood that the moment was important for his son.

"Nathaniel?" he inquired softly after a long silence in which no one dared to speak. Then finally he heard his son's tortured voice.

"We must leave now, father. I must go to mother." He sounded as though he was having difficulty breathing and his voice broke as he looked up at Sakhota, pleading for help. "She needs me." It came out agonizingly. His Indian teacher looked at him for a long time. There was endless compassion in his eyes as the silence stretched eerily, and then lifted his lance in respectful parting and took a step back.

"Yes, she needs you, brave heart. Go swiftly and take Wyomah with you." As he spoke the words, the dog jumped onto the back of the buggy and pressed his body close to Nathaniel, sniffing excitedly over his curved spine. He too, sensed an old bond, an ancient journey and a companion who would really need him.

Chapter 6

Persecution

The crippled boy had grown into a horribly deformed young man. At eighteen years of age, Nathaniel's body seemed more contorted than ever before as he sat in his favorite spot in the town square with his beloved Wyomah at his feet. His strong features and prominent hazel eyes were seldom noticed; his physical discomfort being such a deterrent for onlookers. With its head resting on its front paws, the dog curiously eyed the passing human traffic as some mumbled quick greetings but then hastened their pace, anxious not to prolong the embarrassment of finding appropriate words. Others noticed his painfully curved body under the shadow of the big oak tree and looked the other way to avoid close contact. Nathaniel knew this but didn't care.

Those who were in need of his considerable talents as a soothsayer to calm their fears, knew where to find him. The discomfort others felt with his physical presence was something they had to deal with, for Nathaniel was often not present in his material body. Sakhota's tutoring years ago when he had visited the village with his father, had led him into wonderful, unknown worlds of color and sound of such immense intensity that even he thought at times he couldn't stand the vibrancy and the frustration of not knowing the meaning of it all.

Color and sound often converged into magnificent patterns, which both mesmerized and confused him. Deep within, Nathaniel understood that these endless, recurring patterns and sounds that haunted his visions and dreams had some profound meaning and he strained tirelessly to put all the pieces together. A very keen intellect, ingeniously hidden in a twisted body, painstakingly began to glimpse its immense significance. Town folk who pitied his tortured frame knew nothing of the ecstasy the crippled young man felt as his agile mind traversed these heavenly realms and occasionally was rewarded with fleeting visions of people whom he was sure he knew.

At these times his body would contort as if gripped by agonizing seizures. Nathaniel desperately tried to hold onto the fading laugh of a woman with long black hair. She streaked like the wind across an open plane on a beautiful black stallion in the arms of a man whose face escaped him every time. So intense were these visions that he would utter involuntary sounds and reach out a fraught hand in a feeble effort to catch the dream, but he always missed and would end up trembling uncontrollably.

The shattering disappointment drove him to despair as these familiar images and feelings disappeared again to merge back into patterns of sound and light. Then they would finally converge into a single shape which seemed to represent all these patterns. Passers-by thought he was losing his mind and watched at a distance as Wyomah reacted to these wretched emotional displays and would jump up moaning softly to lick Nathaniel's face until the shaking finally subsided.

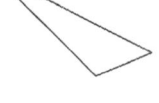

The bond between the crippled young man and his dog was obvious to even the most ignorant, but it was William Wainthorp who was immensely troubled by the presence of the imperfect human being and his constant companion in the town square. He had great difficulty coming to terms with Nathaniel's affliction, but he was more obsessed with Ann. He saw how Nathaniel turned his head and accurately sensed her draw near amongst so many others. With mounting intolerance William watched her slender body and her graceful walk, and an insane jealousy took hold of his dark irate heart as he irrationally compared her to his Mary, to whom the years had not been as kind.

Stout and clumsy in many ways, Mary was subservient from years of abuse and had transformed into a mindless, frightened woman who had fallen out of his favor a very long time ago. He used her body to release his unbearable anger only, forcing his way with her, or punishing her defenseless frame with that fist his employees feared so much. He had always secretly admired Ann's handsome stature but it was the look in her eyes that so tested his patience and hardened his fanatically religious beliefs.

He was deeply troubled with her and her son's spiritual endeavors and the rumors that they were performing miracles, helping people to become relaxed and calm by whispering ungodly things to them. He openly blamed Henry and held him responsible for not keeping a tighter reign on his blasphemous family. In his expert opinion, the blessing and continued wellbeing of the people of New England were at stake. Something would have to be done—and soon.

"Nathaniel, my dearest." It was a simple declaration of complete devotion as she sat down beside him in her usual spot, shielding his body from curious onlookers as they passed, pretending not to see them. The pair was known to most in this town of New England but they remained an oddity so openly visible in the market square. Where they sat together, neither Ann nor Nathaniel cared about the outside world; they were strangely complete when they were together. He stretched out a withered hand, which she immediately took into both of hers and kissed tenderly. "It is hot today, Nathaniel," she said. "You should retire earlier." He listened to his mother's soft voice and as always his heart skipped a little beat at her concern and unconditional love for him.

The day Sakhota had given him the feathers, his mother's image had come vividly into his mind and he had remained wretched and anxious until he saw her at long last. He didn't understand why she had been crying when they returned, but he instinctively hid the feathers from her as she wrapped her arms around his body.

"Oh, Nathaniel," she whispered tearfully, "do not ever go away for so long. I do not know why my heart is so heavy for the future, but it is, my child." Nathaniel remembered the look on his father's face hearing her words. Henry tried to discourage such discussions, warning them that no one knew the future and that those who claimed they did were inviting the wrath of the authorities.

On this day, William stood at a distance and witnessed the closeness between mother and son, becoming unreasonably enraged at the bond between the striking woman and her grotesquely disabled offspring. Somewhere in the murky soil of his irrational mind the seed began to ferment that she was an accomplice of the devil, in some way responsible for this abomination of nature. He was certain nothing good and Christian could come from this unholy combination. He had already decided they needed to be punished for causing him so much mental anguish, and knew it would not be long before he found a reason to publicly disgrace them.

As the thought of chastising the infidel took root deeply within his mind, William salivated involuntarily; few knew that he secretly looked upon himself as a savior of the people of New England. His frequent visits to other far-off towns where sinners against God were cruelly castigated for their disobediences, only fed his frenzied need to eradicate everything that was unholy. But it did much more; the murderous campaign brooding under his feverishly sweating brow, prepared the ground for the atrocities of an outright witch-hunt in nearby Salem in later years that forever guaranteed it a place in the history books.

If ungodliness was not tolerated in other places, neither could he allow it here. He vividly pictured the torture they had so self-righteously inflicted upon those they had branded as witches in obscure locations, the early testing ground for their brutality. William's huge body began trembling uncontrollably with anticipation in his wild desire to see the same fear in Ann's face. He would give anything to hear her plead for mercy! Of course he would callously lead her to believe that she had been successful in seeking a pardon, but then he would mercilessly smite her deformed son before her eyes. William swallowed thickly and slowly forced himself out of his self-induced trance as he watched Ann lead her son home.

Your time has come, treacherous witch! You and your miserable offspring will pay the price for your sins. I will see to that.

Putting down roots in New England tested the endurance of the early settlers in every respect. The thin, rocky soil and harsh winters did nothing to welcome immigrants to their new homeland, but the Puritans soon demonstrated their industrious heritage and engaged in the commercial activities of fishing, shipbuilding and lumbering. Although most New Englanders continued to live on small family farms, the constant need for expansion and growth rapidly encroached on the borders of the nearby native Indians and trouble erupted in the form of land disputes, amplified by a deep misunderstanding of the ancient spiritual practices of these indigenous people.

Border altercations at first resulted in the odd death here and there on either side, but soon intolerance and anger blossomed into full-scale skirmishes that frequently left several dead bodies in their wake. In Cambridge, Wilfred watched anxiously as his prize buggies began to bring back more and more lifeless bodies from combat and before long, inevitably, coffin making boomed alongside his master craft. Nathaniel's frequent visits to the village where Sakhota lived became more and more dangerous as the distrust between the Puritans and native Indians grew.

In an effort to alleviate the unnecessary concern of their respective communities, and as devoted friends, they agreed to meet half way in an open field on the banks of the Charles River, adjacent to the nearby woods. Every month when the moon was full and rose above the edge of the trees, these two kindred spirits came together to share their knowledge and experiences with each other, while Wyomah lay at their feet, keeping an ever watchful eye.

Over the years William Wainthorp had strong-armed his way into a position of power within the community, through his considerable financial means and ruthless manipulation of the less fortunate. He bought and sold businesses as easily as he decided upon the life and death of the innocent, during short clandestine trips taken from time to time with a few of his cohorts. Mary was one of the few who knew the truth about these nocturnal visits. She had long ago learned to feign sleep when William returned under the cover of darkness from these furtive expeditions, having prostrated himself before his personal demons yet again.

She knew the pact he had made with the evil masters who lived inside his head. His pledge was to eradicate the infidel in vicious killing sprees and they would, in turn, allow him to keep the appearance of sanity, enough at least, to fool and manipulate the people of Cambridge. She once caught a glimpse of his face in the flickering light of the candle as he undressed after an absence of three days. She could smell the unwashed body from a distance but it was the glazed look in his eyes that frightened her most; he was still dangerously intoxicated with the illusion of his power to take human life and she knew instinctively that the wrong move would make her his next victim.

Mercifully, William had begun to lose interest in her sexually. He achieved his perverse satisfaction through the use of excessive force and violence, necessitated by the unbearable pressures within his body and mind. His sadistic pleasure came from witnessing the fear of his victims and inhumanly ordering them to fight back, forcing them into a match they could never win. Final release for William never came until he used his monstrous power to thwart his victim's feeble attempt at self-defense. Mary's compliance and willingness to serve his every demand resulted in shameful impotency on his part and he angrily scorned her hapless, unattractive body and finally rejected it with utter contempt.

Mary had thus learned how to survive but she suspected the prostitutes whose quarters were near the lumberyard would not be that fortunate. Moreover, her heart was anxious and heavy for her friend, Ann, and her beloved Nathaniel. She had seen the look on William's face as his gaze followed Ann's every move in the town square. Courteous, but disinterested in his covert, sly attempts to impress or win her favor, Ann had no idea that William irrationally construed this as dismissal of his otherwise feared persona or that his wicked plan for retribution was beginning to take shape.

Help in executing his ghastly plan to punish Ann for her indifference, Nathaniel for his deformity and their mutual defiance of church dogma, came unexpectedly in his butcher shop on the day of the full moon. William hardly noticed the protective hands some of his more refined customers held in front of their noses in his store that permanently reeked of dried blood and animal entrails. Having forcibly created a monopoly to provide fresh meat to the growing Cambridge population, William did not care that the place swarmed with flies; for it was here that he overheard many things that he could use to his advantage, personally and professionally.

And it was here, hidden behind the dirty curtain of the back room, that he overheard Ann in her soft voice tell Mary, who worked in his shop when she wasn't teaching, about Nathaniel's visit with Sakhota scheduled for that evening. Fuelled by his hate for the Indian nation and their unholy spiritual practices, William was instantly enraged by this news but he strained with all his might to contain himself in order to hear all the details of this nocturnal call which this time would include Ann. William knew then that her time and that of her horribly deformed son had finally come.

The mere thought of the brutal justice he would inflict upon them resulted in his usual physical arousal and, armed with the information of the location of the rendezvous, William left abruptly to find his regular murderous accomplices. He never heard Mary catch her breath in shock and revulsion as she noticed his hasty departure. Having shared a bed with the devil for so long, she knew that tonight he would be absent from hers and that he wouldn't be back until he had shed more innocent blood, that of Ann and Nathaniel.

Mary's heart contracted with immense fear as she hastily discarded the blood-smeared apron and turned on her heel. Then she fled the store, hurrying to find her doomed friend. Emerging from the dimness and familiar nauseating smell inside the butcher shop, her eyes took a few minutes to adjust to the bright sunshine. The market square was bustling with its usual activity and many people went about their business as she frantically tried to locate Ann who had been here only a few minutes ago.

Where she stood on the dirt road, Mary suddenly froze in horror. In the distance and out of earshot, she recognized Ann's slim upright posture next to Nathaniel's crouched form as their buggy disappeared around the corner of the road leading out of town. Mary stood there for a long time, unable to move or make a sound, clearly knowing she had been defeated. Then she began to cry softly, her body shaking with powerlessness and pain at what she knew with certainty would transpire in the full moon of this night. It was the forlorn cry of one who already mourned the dead while they were still fleetingly alive.

With Henry gone on another one of his long evangelical trips to the north, Ann couldn't explain why she felt such an urgent need to go with her son this time. She only knew she wanted to be near him and Nathaniel eventually gave in, knowing and loving his mother's sensitive and persistent nature. Upon their arrival, Ann offered to leave him and Sakhota alone for a while as she wandered in the full moonlight down to the river with Wyomah at her side. The night had a strange quality, as if a stage was set for a big event to occur, but when she looked around her, the terrain looked peaceful and quiet.

It was Wyomah that noticed it first. He stopped in his tracks and sniffed the air suspiciously, then froze as every muscle in his body tightened like rods of steel and the hair rose threateningly on his back. Ann heard the deep snarl as it rose from his stomach and her heart caught in her throat as she too suddenly felt the presence of indescribable danger and evil. Wyomah had pressed his body up close to her as if wanting to protect her and then the growl exploded into a vicious bark. Ann's eye caught a movement to her right and in front of her and she knew instantly that they were surrounded.

She counted at least five shadows. As the first one stepped out from behind a tree, Ann recognized his huge frame, as Wyomah purposely took off in giant strides and lunged through the air in a gallant effort to take the first assailant down. But Ann caught the glint of a long butcher's knife in the reflecting moonlight and closed her eyes in fright as William plunged the long steel blade deep into Wyomah's chest, dropping him with a pitiful yelp and dull thud instantly to the ground. The big man was an experienced killer.

Ann didn't move; she kept her arms straight at her side and averted her eyes. She knew resistance would be futile and waited with an unnatural calmness for William to come closer; listening to his heavy boots as they flattened the short grass in his approach. She was hoping to distract the beast in front of her long enough to give Nathaniel and Sakhota time to flee, but somehow Ann knew that hope to be in vain.

They must have heard the noise, and they wouldn't flee; they would come to investigate. He halted his approach a foot away from her and Ann got her first glimpse of the stage that was set for this night as she smelled his pungent breath in a silence that seemed to stretch forever. *Where are Nathaniel and Sakhota?* Standing so defenselessly before him, she had never felt the presence of anything so cold or so evil and, not wanting to look at him, she kept her eyes averted and attempted to reason with him.

"William, if it is me that you want, then let—"

"Look at me!" He abruptly cut her off, his voice thick and slurring. He had not lifted a hand to touch her yet but William's body shook with wild anticipation. His breath came in spasms and as he stared intently at her it took all of his self control not to immediately fell her to the ground with his big fist. Ann lifted her eyes slowly and looked into the darkness of his black soul. There was no mercy, no reason, and her body went ice cold.

"What can we do—" But the coarse hand that shot out and closed around her throat silenced the rest of her words. William squeezed with all his might and felt the euphoria of a kill coming on coupled, as usual, with painful sexual arousal. He wanted to finish her off there and then, but he realized that it would never be enough for him. Maintaining his murderous grip on her neck, he yanked her closer, touching his parched lips to the delicate curve of her ear.

"You want to strike a *bargain* with me?" he bit out through clenched teeth, incredulous of what she had begun to say. She was actually thinking she could *negotiate* with him, like an equal! That filled him with even more rage for he wanted to hear her plead and beg for her life and that of her miserable son; he wanted to destroy that look of dismissal in her eyes and replace it with insane fear. To alleviate his terrible mental anguish at having felt so insignificant in her presence all these years, he needed her to suffer. William suddenly caught himself and let go of her just as Ann approached the edge of the abyss and began to lean toward the merciful oblivion it offered. His rapid release dropped her to the ground and she blacked out.

When she came to, and looked at her surroundings, Ann knew this night would be endless and that only death could cut it short. She and Nathaniel had no chance. For Sakhota the struggle was already over. She closed her eyes to the sight of his decapitated head. It was grotesquely planted on his lance propped in the ground between them where they somberly waited under the tree with ropes around their necks; feet touching the ground. Ann had not said a word to Nathaniel and he too was very quiet. He kept his head angled so that he could see his mother at all times and Ann had a strange sensation that he had accepted their fate and was at peace with himself. In their eerie surroundings, with the full moon high in the velvet sky, a witness to the execution about to take place, Ann had an unfathomable realization of strange familiarity. Then Nathaniel spoke for the first time in a subdued voice so as not to attract the attention of their five executioners a little distance away from them, contemplating a seemingly important matter.

"I have always loved you." He said it simply, but his voice trembled with pent-up emotion. "Always." He repeated the word softly, keeping his eyes on Ann as if he wanted her to understand something. She looked into her crippled son's face and saw something that silenced her words but her body understood, for it translated her intense emotion into uncontrollable trembling. Seeing her distress and knowing that their time together was short, he gestured with his eyes toward Sakhota's head between them. "Look down, please," he implored softly. "One of them took those off me when they surprised us. William stuck them in the ground under Sakhota's head. I know you will understand. Do not look at his head; look at the ground beneath."

Ann could barely breathe as she listened to his calm voice and slowly cast her eyes to the ground underneath the head with its open staring eyes, still dripping occasional sticky drops of blood. When she saw the feathers, she frowned as her heart contracted agonizingly, stopping for a painful moment to weigh the magnitude of what she saw, as if waiting for a decision to live or to die.

"*Oh, God—No!*" She spoke the words weakly, her face twisted in pain, then a tortured sob escaped her constricted lungs and every muscle in her body locked painfully. As the tears began to stream down her face, the veil of the past fell back and before her stood, not her crippled son, but a beautiful young woman with long black hair blowing gently in the wind. "*Anacaona?*" The strange name spilled unwittingly, barely audible, from her lips as Ann's tortured heart faltered once more but she held on with every ounce of her strength, fighting through tears to bring Nathaniel's face into focus.

"*Teuch.*" Nathaniel whispered Ann's ancient name softly. He had known for so long, but couldn't bear to share this knowledge with her. As a cripple he had no real future with another woman and he had discovered their past through techniques that Sakhota had taught him. Since his discovery, he could live in his fantasies of times gone by, but she belonged to another in this life.

Nathaniel had tried to gain deeper insight into the patterns and colors he always saw in his visions and dreams, and intuitively knew that their story was not yet complete. His heart reached out to Ann, feeling the raw agony so deeply etched in bewildered confusion on her face. With the ropes around their necks there was no time to explain his visions. All he could do for her right now, as Nathaniel, was to surround her with his love.

Ann kept her eyes closed and allowed the endless tears to wash over her face, whilst her body shook with the onslaught of the memory of a love as great as the one Teuch and Anacaona had shared. She prayed for the end to come quickly for she knew that they could never be in this present life as they were before.

The murderous conference of William and his cohorts ended suddenly as a dark figure emerged from over the hill bringing word of a search party of Indians approaching in the night, by far outnumbering them. William made his decision in haste and anger. He felt cheated for not having had the opportunity to torture his two captives as planned, but he had no choice. He walked over to Ann and stood in front of her tear-streaked face. He looked coldly at her, and then purposely drew his hand back and slapped her hard across the face. Ann involuntarily cried out in pain but kept her eyes closed, unable to face so much evil in one person.

"You are a filthy witch and you and your deformed son are an abomination to our way of life! Tonight you will both die for it." With these words he pulled forcefully on the loose end of the rope hanging over the branch above them and hoisted her body a foot off the ground. William heard her gag but didn't even turn to look at her. Then he grabbed Nathaniel's rope and duplicated his murderous action, yet strangely, Nathaniel made no sound. William had no idea that his second victim knew how to leave his body, and while he was securing the ropes, Nathaniel's spirit had freed itself permanently from its crippled, pitiful prison and hovered over Ann, encouraging her to let go.

For Nathaniel, the Meadow was already in sight, but he waited patiently, lovingly for Ann to leave her tortured body. He drifted effortlessly between the delicate separation of two worlds, one called Reality and the other, Illusion. He had heard Spethla's soft call and saw the magnificent stallion standing in the Meadow, waiting impatiently upon their return. But Ann took much longer to die than he had. Her spirit had been trained over centuries to be strong and enduring and her body instinctively fought death.

Then from the darkness of the woods an owl approached silently and suddenly changed direction, swooping in under the canopy of the tree. It quietly perched itself in the soft light of the full moon on the branch from which their motionless bodies hung. Nathaniel watched as the huge bird of prey stretched its massive wings and let out a muted hoot. Then it dropped a feather from its tail and took off as quickly as it had come to disappear into the darkness of the sky. As the single gray feather drifted soundlessly to the ground it lightly brushed Ann's pale cheek and, at that moment, her body finally released her spirit.

Anacaona felt Teuch's strong arms lift her off the ground as he leaned down from Spethla to gather her to his heart.

"Teuch." She breathed his name into his loving face as he pulled her body close to his own. They were back once again in the Meadow; they were safe and they were home.

Mary heard William come in and pretended to be in deep sleep. She had been waiting all night long and took pains to keep her breathing normal. When he stepped into their sleeping quarters, she smelled him as always and had great difficulty suppressing the nausea that welled from her stomach as he undressed carelessly, dropping his stinking clothes where he stood. Naked, he walked to the bed and fell noisily into it, unconcerned about waking her. For a terrifying moment he reached a rough hand out to her, as if his day's business was not yet over, but then he let out a muffled curse, rolled onto his back and quickly sank into a deep dreamless sleep, his body shaking as he snored.

Mary waited until she was certain that he was fast asleep, and then crept carefully from under the covers. She reached beneath the bed and slowly pulled out the axe from where she had hidden it earlier that day. It was the same axe that William used to behead poultry and it was stained with the blood of thousands of hapless creatures whose lives he had expertly ended, swinging and striking with cold precision in the same place every time. Mary stealthily crept around to his side of the bed and for a few seconds stood looking dispassionately at him. She knew it was his life or hers.

There was no other choice and there was no room for error as she leaned forward and carefully pulled the covers off his naked body. Mary drew in her breath and lifted the axe high above her head. The first blow carried her full body weight and struck him hard across the pelvic area, the sharp blade cutting deeply into his groin and thighs, instantly severing his genitals. Thus, Mary leveled a long overdue score with William in one clean swoop. The immense pain caused his body to shoot up in astonished reflex and doubled him forward and over as he blindly reached toward his groin, roaring like an animal.

With his head still bent down and moaning incoherently, Mary knew she had only one more chance as she raised the axe again. Weakened by the impact of what she had already done, there was less power this time as she brought the axe down on the back of his neck. That was the fatal blow, although Mary didn't wait long enough to know that William took hours to die and agonizingly bled his body dry in the same bed in which he had so often abused her.

She left that night in the buggy and a week later bought her passage back to cold, dreary England with the money she had taken from the metal box he kept under the bed. Her plan was to find work in an orphanage, or make good in some way for the indescribable heartache she had suffered on the shores of New England. More than anything, she wanted to erase the memory of a life so futile and utterly wasted.

The Reverend Henry Bettsford no longer preached the gospel. Following the death of Ann and Nathaniel, some said he had lost faith in his God while others suspected Henry had lost his mind. He wandered around aimlessly in the town square talking incessantly to himself, and he had also stopped eating. One full moon after their passing, a lonely traveler discovered his lifeless body hanging from the same tree on which Nathaniel and Ann had closed the chapter of this life together.

Introduction To The New World

Upon release from its Source, the celestial journey of the soul is a mystery to most. It has been and will remain for many more centuries a lively topic of discussion in the debate halls of myriad philosophers. Precisely how it is molded over eons into a sentient being with the ability to feel and experience is a closely guarded secret of Creation; one that has intrigued inquiring minds since the dawn of time. But there are instances of refined consciousness, capable of traversing heavenly realms, which have discovered the Meadow ingeniously hidden in the astral level or Middle Place.

They report this to be a celestial waterhole from whence developing souls are directed in acquiring new experiences that could assist them in their quest for growth and better understanding. To aid this growth, a limitless gamut of emotions are available for each incarnation in which the soul could potentially walk through fire as it learns to make better choices by experiencing the polarities of each emotion.

In their first acquaintance, the Cosmos freed Teuch and Anacaona onto the earth plane with a great capacity to love and be loved. The deep feelings they had for each other however, remained mostly unfulfilled in physical form and their lives were cut short by the envy and jealousy of others. In its infinite intelligence, Creation allowed this love to linger on and buried the memory of it in their ethereal bodies as the heavens beckoned their return to the Meadow.

And so, time after time they were released onto the earth plane in conditions and circumstances that would test their endurance and devotion to each other down a long and arduous road, filled with passion, fear, extreme pain and unimaginable exhilaration. As their love grew in intensity over thousands of years, the desire increased to find each other and demonstrate to a disillusioned world how unconditional love, in its many forms, could also manifest as the undying love between a man and woman.

As the firstborn children to their respective parents, the stage selected for the root personalities of Teuch and Anacaona afforded them the opportunity to learn the significance of *duty*. But as the bond between them solidified and grew, what started out as a precious friendship in the playful vineyard encounters of their childhood, blossomed into love as they discovered a deeper attraction and meaning in their need to be together. In the short time in which they shared a marital bed, they were disallowed the pleasure of parenthood, yet both souls departed from the physical world with a clear understanding of *duty, friendship and devotion*.

Next, the Heavenly Architect chose to release Teuch as Chaska, back into the earthly environment ten years before it repeated the role with Anacaona as Tiva. Born into different tribes, where family tradition and honor preceded personal choice, and in the absence of opportunity for fulfillment, their love intensified. With Tiva already belonging to another man, their mutual *devotion* was enriched with *endurance*, as their spirits recognized each other but remained unable to act on their burning desire to be together.

Teuch struggled through his life in Africa as Sekayi. This time Anacaona was given to him as Nyasha, his beloved daughter. In the harsh setting of 12th Century Zimbabwe, Sekayi learned to apply skills and knowledge from other lives to assist and lead his tribe, the Lembas, in the most coveted skill of Africa, namely that of *survival*. Although the specific nuance of the love they shared had adjusted from romance to that of father and daughter, Sekayi's obsession with his beautiful, vulnerable offspring resulted in indescribable pain. In this life, *devotion* and *endurance* led to understanding and integrating *sacrifice through loss*.

Drawn together life after life, Teuch finally found himself in a female body in the 16th Century as Ann, wife to the Reverend Henry Bettsford, when Anacaona made her appearance as their gifted but crippled son, Nathaniel. In a time that preceded the terrible witch-hunt period, Ann hardly noticed Nathaniel's pitiful body as she cared for and loved her deformed son. Equipped with *devotion, endurance* and *sacrifice through loss*, the important lesson of *unconditional love* added another vital aspect to their characters and the love they had for each other.

There were many other earthly rendezvous, all of which had added dimensions of growth and understanding that shaped their insight and prepared them over thousands of years for taking on the challenge and responsibility of modern times. Teuch and Anacaona also briefly met in ancient Egypt around the 4th Century BC. Anacaona, again in the body of a male, this time came as Kahotep who worked side-by-side with the High priest, Ashai, in contributing to the hieroglyphically colorful language of this unusual race.

Kahotep's purpose in his life in Egypt was to learn *focus* and *concentration*, traits he integrated through the development and interpretation of signs and symbols. But he had great admiration for the skill and patience of their camel master, Akhom, whose name meant eagle. He was the tolerant and humble guide who led their caravans on vast expeditions into the mountains to gather clay for their tablets and herbs for the color mixtures. Kahotep knew the old guide wasn't well, and he was strangely, deeply upset when he heard of Akhom's sudden death one night in his sleep. Unaware of their true identities, both souls added experience and depth from interacting with others. Teuch's gain, as he left the sick body of Akhom behind, was *humility* and *dedication*.

There were many more lives; some lived separately and others simultaneously. But these were seemingly always orchestrated into roles in which recognition of their root personalities was obscured by interfacing with other souls, from whom they also had important things to learn.

However, their re-emergence in the 21st Century would test the strength of all the lessons learned combined. Thrown onto a stage where they were finally capable of mature love, their paths would be obstructed by invisible players who seemed intent on keeping them apart and stealing the fruits of their knowledge and experience gained over centuries, to serve their selfish needs and sinister ends. As with each prior incarnation, the veil of the past drew down upon birth, and neither Teuch nor Anacaona had an inkling of how vigorously this life would test their devotion and endurance. Neither did they know of the sacrifices they would have to make to experience the deep love they had nurtured for thousands of years.

Chapter 7
Responsibilities

"Damn these wretched flies!" In the confined space in which he sat, Dmitri could barely wave a hand over his face to chase away the irritating pests that seemed to creep in from everywhere. His movements were severely restricted by all the technological clutter that surrounded him in the cramped area in which he had to do his job. "How on earth am I expected to maintain one hundred percent surveillance with all this heat and these cursed, blasted obstacles in my way?" he grumbled, mostly to himself.

He shuffled awkwardly on his narrow swivel stool, taking great pains not to touch his partner, Tomer, who sat in close proximity to him. He wasn't a tactile person at the best of times, but to be in the vicinity of another male in the confines of a heavily equipped surveillance vehicle was really testing his limits and patience. The monitor screens caused even greater discomfort as they spewed out another ten degrees of heat into the cramped rear cab of the white van, discreetly parked a few hundred yards from their target's home.

A single bead of sweat hung precariously from the end of Dmitri's nose and as it dropped on to his surveillance schedule, he realized that his entire body was overheated and he was perspiring profusely. For a moment he stared at the tiny, wet blotch spreading and intermingling with other stains on the well-worn piece of paper in his hand, and then he looked up and spoke over his shoulder.

"Soon I'll not be able to read a thing on this stupid chart. Look at it! It's one big mess of sweat and ice tea stains! How does anyone stay sane in conditions such as these and what's so important about this woman and her bloody son anyway?" He didn't care whether Tomer was listening but the mention of ice tea made him reach for his flask.

"Shut up, Dmitri." Tomer didn't bother to conceal his annoyance with the self-absorbed man who was his partner. "And stop these crazy questions; you get damned well paid to endure the flies and the heat. I've heard enough for one night, and we have an important job to do, so just give it a rest." He was in no mood for Dmitri's outbursts today as they sat cramped in the back of the van behind the school, waiting for any kind of movement within the house. "Tomorrow's your day off again, so you can take that silly little fishing rod and go about your silly little business, pretending you don't have to work for a living like the rest of us."

He let out his breath slowly, watching Dmitri through the dim lighting in the hot, sticky van. Dmitri had bought himself a small fishing dinghy that he kept conveniently down at the municipal harbor in Tel Aviv. Tomer knew from Dmitri's persistent talking about his hobby that he regularly took off from there and went straight to the port of Jaffa, only a short distance away by boat or road. Tomer shook his head almost imperceptibly as he watched his partner's broad, sweaty back.

Dmitri was very rough around the edges and Tomer knew that the historical and beautiful places in Jaffa with its many tourist attractions did not interest this coarse man at all. As a native Israeli, Tomer continued to enjoy the colorful artists' quarters, studios, galleries, archaeology and the specialty shops of Judaica in his free time. His partner, instead, having graduated from the stinking Moscow River to the commercial fishing waters of the Mediterranean, was only interested in fishing. The bulky man with beady black eyes incessantly blabbed to anyone who would listen, complaining about Moscow where you could only eat your catch if you fished in special inlets or visited paid areas like the restaurant Rybatskaya Derevnya, also known as the Fisherman's Village.

That pond was stocked with very many different fish, but the tight fisted Russian was vehemently opposed to paying five hundred rubles for a day's admission plus another hundred and fifty to seven hundred and fifty rubles per kilogram, depending on whether you caught pike or sturgeon. He intensely disliked the municipal areas of Moscow and although these were relatively clean, they were unbearably overcrowded. Each time he went there it was as if more and more sweaty bodies were scampering for a spot from which to cast off a line.

Thus, to be offshore and fishing in the beautiful Mediterranean was confirmation to him that the move from Moscow to this part of the world was every bit worth the sacrifice of leaving his homeland. But as Tomer stared at the big Russian, he suspected that there were aspects to Dmitri's personality that he kept carefully hidden from the scrutiny of others, and he was sure that these same aspects would make him very dangerous.

"What the…! Can you believe this?" Dmitri spat out angrily, pouring out what he thought to be ice tea into a plastic cup. "This is not *ice tea*!" He was fuming, whereupon he carelessly threw the contents at one of the monitors, short-circuiting it immediately, sending sparks flying everywhere, accompanied by the synthetic smell of burning electricity. Wisps of thin, white smoke hung in the thick air of the cluttered space in which they sat, making the atmosphere even more oppressive. Tomer, a local Jew from Tel Aviv, observed the outburst with his normal detachment as he noticed the manufacturer's label under the flask. His voice was cold.

"Your thermos is *Soviet made*, Dmitri. What else can I say? If you weren't so hopelessly frugal and didn't spend all your money maintaining your boat, maybe you'd consider investing some of it in equipment that would actually keep your beverage cold. Welcome to the West, where things actually work." Tomer's voice was heavy with sarcasm as he realized that Dmitri would now have to take up manual surveillance at the rear of the house. "Your fairy godmother has granted your wish." He smiled, but his eyes remained emotionless. "Now you can step outside and taste the wind."

Dmitri cursed under his breath at Tomer's deliberate goading, knowing that his carelessness and bad temper could easily jeopardize this covert operation, but he was nonetheless glad to get away from him. He collected his field glasses and left the van at the rear without a word to Tomer. Once outside in the fresh air he quickly turned back, reopened the door and stood there until Tomer finally looked at him. Neither showed any humor as they eyed each other.

"Don't wait up, comrade; this could be a long night." Dmitri turned his head slightly to the left and spat on the ground. "I'll have the stars to sleep under, while you instead can stew in this shit hole. Lucky you! You should pray to your gods, friend," he advised dryly, "and maybe

Josh will let you have aircon in your next surveillance vehicle. I hear the flies don't like cold air either." Driven by his malicious nature to always have the last say, Dmitri quickly slammed the door shut before Tomer could respond, as he ran for cover at the rear of the school.

As an ex-KGB agent, having tasted the Soviet way of life for so many years, Dmitri was relieved a year ago when the American, Josh Goldberg, chief of the Israeli branch of Azvaalder Electronics, approached him one cloudy and dreary day in Moscow just as he was fetching his customary ham sandwich from the street vendor at the corner in front of his office. Josh was a shrewd and experienced operator who knew how to choose new recruits and Dmitri's profile fitted his needs perfectly. Not only was he a disgruntled Russian about to lose his job, but he was also a meticulous creature of habit, the kind that would move heaven and earth not to have his routine disturbed. He knew them to be the best workers.

Locating Dmitri was thus no problem as Josh waited patiently for him to put in his twelve o'clock appearance. He offered the Russian a way out from under the crumbling administration that had supported the Kremlin so well over the years and Dmitri eagerly jumped at the chance to make a new life for himself in the West.

Since the Soviet collapse in 1991, the impression deliberately portrayed to the world was one of transparency and, as a result, Dmitri Anchov had lost his usefulness to them in many respects. He knew it would not be long before they found a way to get rid of him, and not being much of a planner, he had not yet decided what his next move would be. He was a large, overweight man in his forties, who had never learned how to win the favor of a woman and he was still single. In fact, Dmitri felt contempt for women that grew stronger as the years went by. He did not know the source of his own grievances, and neither was he interested in finding the origin of his harsh nature.

Deep matters such as these could not hold the attention of a Soviet spy who was used to snaring the enemy and then brutally punishing them first before passing them over to his handlers. It was much easier for him to project his lack of self-esteem onto anyone who crossed his path by hammering on their shortcomings. Tomer was a good example of this; the imperfections of the balding humorless Jew with whom Azvaalder had chosen to partner him, occupied his mind almost obsessively and he constantly tried to show him up as an incompetent fool, but completely overlooked the brilliance of his partner.

Right now, Dmitri had to make sure he reached the rear of the school where Azvaalder's hidden camera had been rendered obsolete by his foul temper. After scuffling around a little, he found a suitable place in the nearby bushes facing the same direction as the hidden camera and begrudgingly settled down for what he expected would be a long and uneventful night. Lying on his stomach, he lifted the binoculars to his eyes to scan the target's house; his elbows boring into the hard soil as he strained to support the considerable weight of his upper body in this uncomfortable position. He suddenly saw her walking into her bedroom as he made a slow, sweeping movement to cover the house from side to side.

"Promudobliadskaja pizdoprojebina" he mumbled. It was a pet phrase he had concocted himself and often used, meaning *fucking bitch*. "You could have taken it off before you closed the bloody curtains!" He laughed joylessly, for a moment not caring if he was overheard. "Who am I kidding? I don't give a shit." Dmitri sighed heavily, rolled onto his back and closed his eyes for a few minutes. The night was going to be much longer and a lot harder than he had anticipated, and he couldn't even smoke out here. He prayed inwardly that his fishing trip for the next day would not be jeopardized. It was part of his routine and Dmitri hated an upset of any kind in his schedule.

Tomer checked his cell phone to make sure there was ample battery power, hoping that Dmitri had had the sense to do the same before he left in his usual irresponsible and somewhat immature way. Dmitri's spiteful reminder of the lack of an air conditioner in the Azvaalder vehicle made the surroundings all the more unbearable and he made a note to himself to convince Josh to supply a suitable vehicle next time, large enough to take all the equipment *and* the aircon. Tomer settled his tall and sinewy body into the newly acquired space vacated by Dmitri and concentrated on the two remaining working monitors, focusing on the front and side windows of the corner dwelling.

It was more difficult to position their covert cameras at the front of the house, as the only building that could be used was a busy and well-lit sports complex, which was in regular use. Azvaalder was used to this kind of covert business, working in tandem with the Israeli government and any third party that could afford to employ the electronics specialists.

They were now into their third week of surveillance after having discovered that Eva was no longer prepared to co-operate with Azvaalder, after catching wind of their unusual and unhealthy interest in her son, Hugo. The suggested change of location for his education plus her inability to contact her British diplomat husband, Tom Norman, made Eva very uneasy. All of this was due to the hyped interest around Hugo's talents, which Josh Goldberg tried to play down. She had been part of the secretive world of diplomacy long enough to know that changes are subtly felt before they hit you in the face, and by the time altered behavior reached a level of being openly visible, it was usually too late to counteract.

Hugo was now eleven years old and the school, which had catered to his considerable intellectual demands despite his communication handicap, had reached a saturation point. It could no longer provide the expertise for which Azvaalder's grant was paying, and a suitable college or university had to be found, or so they claimed. The only practical purpose the school still served was to act as a means of cover for the surveillance cameras that Azvaalder had secretly installed around the house on a Saturday morning when no one was home, to monitor Eva's every move as she went about her business in her mother's house.

But it would have paid them to do a little research about this very astute woman, who fooled them with her quiet demeanor. Until recently they were only interested in the capabilities of her exceptionally gifted son, and overlooked the intelligence in her eyes, and the confident, unassuming way she maintained eye contact. Above average height and blessed with a well-proportioned and naturally slim frame, her stride was gracious and feminine. Eva kept her shoulder length thick black hair pulled away from her face, which accentuated her high cheekbones and soft full mouth. Her beauty was evident and complimented her unpretentious persona. Azvaalder had gravely underestimated her potential in every respect, especially her ability and determination to protect her vulnerable son.

Whilst they had her under surveillance in the privacy of her mother's home, secretly following her every move, Eva was well aware of their activity but went about her daily routine pretending to be oblivious to their intrusion. They were playing a dangerous game but she was ready to meet them every step of the way. She arranged to get her and her son's possessions together in preparation for leaving Israel with the help of the secret service department of MI6 within the British government.

Eva's heart was heavy as she hastened to put the finishing touches to her packing. It wasn't easy to leave an entire life behind with all its memories. Her heart was anxious and troubled; she had no idea what the future held, but she was overwhelmingly aware of the peril she and Hugo were in if they remained in Israel. Then her eye caught the gilded frame atop the dresser holding the photograph of herself and her husband, Tom. She reached out for it with both hands and held the picture at arms length, staring intently at the joyful expression on their faces. In the picture he had his arm protectively around her shoulders. They stood together, laughing, on the steps leading to the foyer of the British Embassy in Tel Aviv, where she had first met the sandy-haired man with the square jaw. A little frown creased her forehead. Tom was gone *again*. In years gone by, his official duties had taken him away often, but at this critical time it was hard not to feel some disappointment that such important decisions had to be made without him.

She understood the world of diplomacy very well; she herself had scripted some of the finer nuances in communicating with foreigners, but where Tom was concerned Eva was mystified at the constant level of secrecy he maintained around his responsibilities, even with her. There were times she could not reach him on a cell phone, and all messages had to be relayed through the Embassy. Today was one of those occasions and she wished with all her heart she could just speak to him. How long had he been gone this time, six weeks, eight weeks? She was beginning to lose track. And yet, their relationship hadn't started out this way.

As a twenty-two-year-old, all who made her acquaintance in the busy reception area where she established a reputation for tact and diplomacy quickly noticed the talents of the young attractive Eva. A gifted linguist, she could change gears and languages at the drop of a hat and she was as comfortable with royalty as she was with other heads of state and of course, the ubiquitous diplomat who frequented this building.

The attraction between Eva and Tom was instant when he first entered her domain. He was quite a bit older than the vibrant young Eva who, in fluent English, was tending to the needs of an elderly gentleman by her side. Tom noticed the undivided attention she gave him; the gentle hand on his elbow and the polite way she bent her head toward him to better hear his words. The elderly man finally left and respectfully touched his hand to his hat as he strode toward the exit doors. Then she looked up at Tom, still smiling, and extended a hand to the tall, distinguished-looking man.

"Good morning. I am Eva Cohen, communication specialist here at the Embassy, and welcome to Tel Aviv. We haven't met before, Mister…?" Her voice was soft but confident and carried a very slight trace of Hebrew accent, which gave it an attractive lilt.

"Tom Norman." He was briefly taken aback by the directness of the look in her clear, hazel eyes and he held her hand longer than was necessary. "Special emissary from Her Majesty," he smiled warmly. "Oh, never mind! I'm British." He finished his sentence a little lamely, still looking into her eyes and thought that he would enjoy getting to know this striking woman better. After that first introduction, he had left the Embassy unable to erase Eva from his thoughts. At twenty-two she was more mature than most people he knew. He was surprised by his uncharacteristic interest in a complete stranger, albeit a very charming one, especially after the numerous failed attempts of other women to snare him into a permanent commitment.

Within a month Tom knew that for him the attraction ran very deep and that his heart was truly captivated. After so many years, and for the first time, he was willing to consider sacrificing his valued bachelor status and share his life with this beautiful, intelligent woman in whose company he felt both stimulated and appreciated. Deeply feminine, she instinctively understood the art of putting him first without sacrificing a fraction of her worth as a partner.

Sometimes, when he looked at her, Tom was conscious of a depth of feeling and emotion within her that she had not shared with him. He wondered about that often in the beginning of their relationship but never tried to probe, for he was convinced Eva would never intentionally shut him out. There was a distinct mystery that surrounded this unusual woman, which he found exciting, although the invisible limits it set were very hard to move beyond. When they were together, she was warm and giving and he couldn't fault her devotion or her concern for his happiness.

Yet, as time went by, Tom knew the woman he held in his arms had never once lost her composure with him. She had never shown wild abandonment in their lovemaking although he was convinced of a compelling and deep passion running through her veins. Occasionally he wondered what it would take to bring that passion to the surface. He fantasized about lighting that fire within to match the light in her eyes; he wanted to see her melt in the intensity of it and lose her identity with him. But that never happened. Even if he lost himself in her, Eva remained always Eva; attentive, content to bring him pleasure, perfect in her role.

"Does anyone really know you, Eva?" He didn't mean to voice his insecurity but it slipped out in an unguarded moment after making love to her. She lay in the circle of his arm already drifting off into sleep and he regretted asking the question the moment it hung in the air between them. She opened her eyes and looked directly at him.

"Of course not." She smiled a half smile and closed her eyes again with a little sigh, ending the discussion. "What woman would allow that?" His busy schedule took him away from her frequently and often for long periods of time. The dream he had of them truly finding each other eventually suffocated into a superficial closeness, which became commonplace between them, an obstacle that was harder to overcome each time he returned from a long absence.

Those who knew Eva admired her character and strength, but her extraordinary intuitive ability was not known to anyone but her. The day she met Tom she felt the attraction like he did, but she also sensed something that she shared with no one else. Without being able to explain why, she had the bizarre feeling that their paths would not lead together into old age. She found this thought disturbing and consciously suppressed it as much as she could, but to no avail. When he proposed, Eva accepted without hesitation. Tom was charming and experienced; she enjoyed being in his presence and she thought that was enough.

The marriage was initially happy and pleasing to them both, but it was Tom in particular who was ecstatic with his striking wife. True to her nature, Eva devoted all her love and attention to the handsome man she had met that day in the foyer of the British Embassy. In her exposure to the complicated and hectic diplomatic world and its varied players from across the globe, Eva often wondered about Tom's specific role as a British diplomat.

At the time of their marriage, they had made an agreement to continue with their respective careers, as the nature of his job dictated that there would be times when they would be separated from each other. Her services at the Embassy were in demand by personnel as well as many visitors from across the world, which meant she would be stationed in the Tel Aviv area for quite a while. The British government had been very helpful in finding Tom suitable accommodation right in the middle of town and his apartment was conveniently located only a few blocks away from the Embassy.

This close proximity to buildings and people made it easier for them to spend as much time together as possible as they went about their busy schedules. Although familiar with the secrecy that surrounded most of the diplomatic core, Eva did not understand why special concessions could not be made in her case; she was after all committed to Israel through birth and to Great Britain through marriage. But every time his long absences became untenable, Tom would return as if on cue and the discontent would temporarily be forgotten.

It was after one of Tom's brief homecomings that Eva's life changed dramatically. After he had left, her monthly cycle disappeared and she didn't need a doctor to confirm that she was pregnant. Her heart overflowed with joy at this new life that had begun to grow within her and as her body slowly began to change, Eva powerfully sensed the spiritual bond between her and the growing fetus. She felt it in the intensity of her dreams and visions, which had become more vivid than ever before, and a strange awareness that she did not understand stirred within her. Despite the joy and anticipation of the child's birth, a nagging, nameless melancholy had taken hold of her, which she intuitively knew had nothing to do with Tom.

Even before she began nurturing the new life within her, an invisible hand had once again rolled the dice. This time all the players would be on board, poised and ready to play. As Eva contentedly waited for the pregnancy to reach full term, she had no idea yet of how drastically her life would change in the months to come.

Chapter 8
A Born Genius

Eva resigned from the Embassy and began to direct all her attention to the new life she had to take care of. She felt alive and wonderful and a fresh awareness stirred within her consciousness that filled her with great anticipation, not only for the arrival of the baby, but there was something more, something very subtle that she couldn't define. Its presence hovered like a shadow in the outskirts of her peripheral vision, but every time she tried to identify what it was, it disappeared and she was left wondering if her active imagination was running away with her.

With Tom's extended periods of absence during the pregnancy, Eva turned within and became highly sensitive to the growing fetus. Not only did she feel its physical presence as her body began to change, but she was convinced of its sex and communicated with it constantly. In the beginning of her fifth month she felt the first butterfly movements under her hands and the bond between her and her unborn son intensified immeasurably. She regularly sat in her favorite rocking chair where the late afternoon sun bathed them both blissfully in its golden light, and Eva would tell the baby about the visions she was having.

"It is quite extraordinary, little one," she whispered softly with her eyes closed, "and I don't understand what any of it means, but there are these beautiful colors and the most extraordinary shapes." She'd stroke her stomach lightly and smile. "Somehow, you're a part of this. I don't know how, but you are." Cocooned in the warmth of the sun, sleep would overtake her as she and the baby drifted off together. During these wonderfully intimate times she shared with her unborn child, Eva felt his physical presence in her body, but her heart was filled with him on a level so deep that she had no words for it.

In diplomatic circles Tom was respected and held in high regard for his academic accomplishments at Cambridge University and the years he had served as a commissioned officer in Her Majesty's Services. Eva smiled to herself, lightly hugging her stomach. It was during these times of deep reverie and sharing of information with the baby, that she knew Tom's impressive intellectual capacity had been handed down to their son.

"I'll call you Hugo." She liked the sound of the name. "You will have your father's intellect, but I will share with you my ability to dream. We were destined to be together, you and I. These visions I see are significant, they *mean something* and I know that you know. Who is going to teach whom I wonder, Hugo?" After Hugo's birth, the subtle changes became more visible and Eva's priorities shifted as her maternal duties took hold and Tom's regular absence became more tolerable. In a short time her entire life began to revolve around her newborn son, and happiness took on a whole new meaning in her life as she immersed herself completely into motherhood.

The remarkable progress of the baby astonished everyone except his adoring mother. Hugo's physical development was rivaled only by his mental advancement. Alert and attentive, his eyes had begun to follow her every move when he was only six weeks old. At six months, no place was inaccessible to his agile little body. He crawled all over at the speed of lightning and soon his caretakers noticed an unusual, but unmistakable responsiveness to sound and color as he moved about seeking out objects and shapes of particular interest. The only thing that seemed very odd was his lack of communication with others, save his own mother.

His activities grew with intensity almost by the day and Eva took early note of how typical children's toys were quickly discarded in favor of any game or plaything that represented a challenge or required an elementary degree of reasoning. She marveled at the ease with which he mastered the ability to place the customary squares of his play set into the square holes; the round ones into the round holes and the stars into their respective orifices.

At nine months he pulled himself up against the leg of the dining room table as he had done so many times before, but this time he let go and with outstretched arms walked his first ten unsteady steps right into his mother's waiting arms. Eva caught him just before his balance gave way and swung him excitedly, laughingly into the air. She covered his wet face with kisses, and hugged him closely against her, hearing his little heart beating as he breathlessly babbled the pleasure of his accomplishment into her neck.

Hugo was three years old when Eva's earliest notions of his potential were confirmed by Mrs. Bartholomew, a teacher of twenty five years, now retired, at whose house he attended a playgroup twice a week. Hugo seemed to have an internal clock as to when the day's activities would draw to an end, and at this time he usually hovered around Martha in the kitchen. He was his usual silent self, something his caretaker was used to by now, as he patiently waited for his mother to arrive. But on this particular day, everything was different and Martha opened the door just as Eva reached for the doorbell. Eva's eyes automatically looked down to locate Hugo, but when she didn't see him, she was instantly alarmed.

"Hello Martha." The small woman in her late sixties had wiry gray hair kept short for the sake of convenience and she wore no make-up; no one taking care of toddlers had time to titivate. "This is a surprise! Is everything okay? Hugo—?" The older woman smiled gently, her clear blue eyes mirroring the deep love and endless patience she had with young children.

"Oh, your little man is just fine, Eva. Relax, dear. And please, won't you come inside?" Eva's eyes roamed over the entrance hall and part of the living room that she could see from where she was standing. There was still no sign of Hugo, but as requested, she stepped inside and closed the door behind her. Martha Bartholomew hadn't moved and was still looking at her, but the expression on her face had undergone a subtle change and she stared at Eva, as if trying to find the most appropriate way to say something important.

"Martha?" This time she felt a faint anxiety and put a hand up to cover her heart. "What is it? Where is Hugo?"

"He's in the playroom, Eva," she said softly, "and we can go there in a minute, but first I would like to ask you something." Eva looked at the older woman and waited with baited breath for her to continue. "Have you ever noticed anything unusual about Hugo? And I don't mean that he mostly only speaks to you." She asked the question evenly, watching the younger woman carefully. But then she saw the light in Eva's eyes and she smiled. "You *do know*, don't you? Mothers are always the first to notice special traits as quickly as they are aware of shortcomings. Some need outside validation for their beliefs, but I don't think you do, Eva. You have known for some time, haven't you?"

"Yes," she said softly. Eva felt her body relax and the anxiety subsided. "I knew while I was still carrying him, Martha. Don't ask me how I knew, I just did." She took the older woman's arm. "But please, won't you take me to him? What has he done to impress you in this manner?" Martha silently led the way and held up a hand as they stood in the entrance to the playroom. Amidst the noise and chaos of four other toddlers running around and creating the normal screaming havoc that signified the end of a busy day, Hugo sat quietly at a table in the corner with Meccano pieces spread all over the surface; he seemed to be lost in a world of his own. "Oh, he likes to build things, Martha," Eva whispered, watching the concentration on his face as he leaned over the table, clearly looking for a missing piece.

"Does he?" Martha looked at her and then back to the child who still seemed oblivious of their presence. "He found the set in the toy cupboard, Eva. It belonged to my son, Aaron. It was a favorite of his when he was about ten years old and this particular set was designed to promote mental stimulation with the assistance of robotics and science, of which at least an elementary understanding is required." She looked penetratingly at the woman beside her and her voice grew a little more intense.

"Hugo is three years old, Eva. We bought the set years ago because my late husband, an engineer by profession, had hoped that Aaron, he's our eldest, would develop a taste for design and construction and follow in his father's footsteps. My husband also believed that playing with these more complicated pieces would stimulate creativity and develop entrepreneurial skills in a child. He saw the potential with this kit to promote a career in science, teach problem solving, and out-of-the-box thinking; not to mention dexterity of mind and muscle. What business do you think a three-year-old has in building *that?*" She pointed to a structure partially hidden behind the empty Meccano box lying askew on the table.

"What is it?" Eva asked apprehensively, taking a step closer. A strange feeling took hold of her as if she was about to come face to face with something with which she was not equipped to deal. Then, before she could analyze her feelings any further, she identified the structure he had built and froze in shock as she recognized its outline as one of the recurring shapes that so haunted her dreams. She stood motionless and held her breath.

"It's a bird, isn't it?" Martha inquired softly behind her. They were both silent as they watched the child in wonder. When Eva finally spoke, her voice was barely audible.

"No, Martha, that isn't just any bird. It represents an eagle. And the piece he has been looking for since we have been standing here is a wingtip. Look! He has just attached it." She was astounded at how the asymmetry of Hugo's design precisely matched the recurring vision to which she was now so accustomed. Hugo suddenly looked up and the sight of his mother brightened his face with a broad smile and, jumping off the chair, he came running at her. She always looked forward to the warmth of his hug for it was the greeting that she was used to.

"Are you sure of that?" Martha frowned, still staring at his baffling handiwork.

"I have no doubt," Eva said without hesitation as she caught him expertly, hugging him closely and smelling his hair and his skin as she dropped a kiss on his forehead. But she had no idea yet of how drastically life would change for them all after this day. While she still carried Hugo under her heart, it was only a faint knowing, but the experience in Martha's house created a certainty, an urgency to provide her son with all the possible means to develop his extraordinary talents despite his handicap.

During one of his irregular visits home, Eva discussed the matter with Tom, who seemed pleased to learn about his son's abilities but felt that Hugo was still too young for any special tutoring. For the next three years Eva kept a close watch on Hugo's rapid development and was amazed at the expansion of his creative talents. Her little boy began to draw shapes and designs every time he met with someone with whom he had had a meaningful interaction.

In time she began to realize that his substantial capability to create these shapes and designs was triggered by a connection or association he felt with such a person, or in rare cases, a special animal. She never interfered but watched quietly how meticulously he went about interpreting his impressions of people through these. Eva marveled at how the expression on his face would change, from complete serenity as he sat down in front of a blank piece of paper, to intense concentration as the shapes began to take form. That's when Eva understood that Hugo was *receiving* information and that the shapes were not random, but had significance. She had no idea what any of this meant, but was nevertheless convinced there was a definite connection between Hugo's gift and her dreams and visions and that, in time, all would be revealed.

Just after his sixth birthday Eva noticed a new dimension to Hugo's designs as he began to introduce colors into the equation and although he was still incapable of verbalizing what he felt, she realized that the shapes and colors had a definitive meaning to him. Her quiet smile at his creations confirmed her unconditional support for him. It was rooted in an unshaken belief, *a knowing*, that in his innocence, Hugo was extraordinarily talented but as yet she was uncertain how this would unfold as he grew older. In the protracted absence of his father, the bond between Eva and Hugo intensified and she was the first to notice Hugo's uncanny ability to read or to feel an event before it took place, and despite being familiar with the unusual behavior of her son, she was nevertheless taken aback when it happened for the first time.

It was early on a Saturday morning and Eva was baking blintzes for lunch, a traditional Jewish crepe filled with mash potatoes and onions, a favorite of Hugo's. He was particularly fond of the dessert, which was another crepe, but this time filled with cherries and sour cream. She turned to look at him and immediately noticed the serious expression on his face. He stood in the doorway, looking nervous and distracted, holding a piece of paper with a symbolic design that she had seen before.

"Holly?" she asked softly, sensing rather than knowing the source of his distress. "Is something wrong with her?" Holly was Martha's pet Labrador that had accidentally been run over by a car. It was Hugo who helped nurse it back to health and sat with the dog for hours every day, holding its head in his lap and making soothing sounds in its ears. A bond developed between them and they became almost inseparable. After outgrowing the nursery, little could stop Hugo from seeing his favorite animal. He visited Martha and Holly regularly before official schooling made it impossible to see them often. Eva dropped everything and walked over to him. "Hugo, my darling." His eyes were filled with tears as she put her arms around him but he squirmed and strained to be free of her embrace. He pulled at her hand and understanding the urgency in her child, she took his design from him. "Holly is not well?" He kept his eyes on the picture as tears began to gather in the corners. Knowing how old Holly was, Eva didn't hesitate any further. "Let's go."

Martha wasn't in the least bit surprised to see them arrive shortly after breakfast as she had been up most of the night with her ailing dog. Martha and Eva had become good friends since the early days of the nursery and the continuing visits between Hugo and Holly helped create a very special relationship between them.

"I was about to phone you, Eva. And here you are!"

"What's wrong with Holly?" Eva asked as Hugo took off and ran to the kitchen to find the Labrador in her usual place, lying in her basket.

"She's just old, Eva. And much as we love our pets, they too reach the end of the road." Her eyes shone with tears. "She's old and very tired, but your little man seems to know this. What a marvelous child you have!" They stayed for lunch and went home in the late afternoon. Holly died shortly after they arrived home but the news of her death didn't seem to upset Hugo as much as when he had first sensed the graveness of her condition.

It was what happened afterwards that stunned Eva completely. Hugo disappeared into his bedroom to draw his customary shapes and designs and stayed away for a very long time. When she became concerned and went looking for him she found him sound asleep, curled up on his bed. Then her eye caught the paper on his desk and she moved closer to inspect the drawing. The design was in three colors. It was the first time that she had seen him produce anything that totally comprised curves and connected swirls. It resembled a distorted circle and the colors that graduated from the left were of red, purple and gold. Eva had never seen him use colors as boldly as this, neither had she ever seen him use gold in any of his designs. She was looking at a schematic representation of some very important information regarding Holly. That much she knew. *But what?* She looked again at his peaceful face as he slept. *Some day we will all know, won't we, my darling? But for now, the secret sleeps with you.*

After this experience Eva would not be deterred any longer and without consulting Tom, she made an appointment at the offices of the British Embassy, her former employer, to visit James Stanway who was an expert in intelligence and related matters. Nicknamed "Silver Fox," Eva had had limited personal dealings with him during her tenure at the Embassy, but his reputation was spiked with colorful tales of great expertise and a very short fuse. He was a man of few words who didn't suffer fools gladly and those who knew him, steered clear of his bad temper. But his presence, like so many others at the Embassy, was as a direct result of the Gulf War.

This war had considerably changed the situation for Israel. Although the Americans finally managed to keep the Israeli involvement at arm's length from the Iraqi onslaught, it brought home some pertinent questions as to its position in the Middle East, particularly its vulnerability—politically, geographically and strategically. Intelligence was thin on the ground and communications, particularly access to satellite data, was limited. Much of the technology used in the war was of British design and, as usual, the inevitable parallel commercial conflicts were won by those organizations with the biggest clout. Many British companies could not directly compete against their American counterparts and, as a consequence, they sold their ideas to the highest bidder. This was not the same as having representation on the ground, so the British saw their opportunity in increasing their involvement in the country.

Soon, the British Embassy at Tel Aviv was brimming with personnel who were capable of introducing technology that could be safeguarded and maintained at a local level. In turn, this brought in opportunities for specialist British companies who could delegate their employees to the highest level. One such person was James Stanway, an electronics and communications expert who was soon to hold office in the most influential department of the British Embassy. At fifty five he was a bachelor who appeared to live only for his profession. Having turned completely gray before the age of forty, he sported a brush cut, shaven very close to the scalp. He rarely smiled. Small black eyes and a pointed nose gave him almost a comical look, but those who crossed his path knew the man was shrewd and ruthless. The Silver fox had earned his stripes.

He watched her closely as she explained the nature of her visit and even though Tom's wife was probably entitled to special treatment, at this time he didn't think that what she was asking for was warranted.

He nevertheless concluded that Tom Norman was a very lucky man. He steepled his fingers and, through habit, scrutinized her body language and voice intonation, while she shared the information about Hugo. James Stanway knew a genuine article when he saw one. He of all people understood Tom's prolonged absences, but he still wondered how the man could tolerate being away from her so often. He cautiously calculated the length of his pause after she had finished speaking to create the impression of careful consideration and then looked her directly in the eye.

"Well then, I'm sure the boy takes after his father, Eva? Tom is nobody's fool. We all know that." His words were delivered in apparent good humor and he was smiling, but Eva could sense his impatience. "And they tell me we have never been able to replace you either! Young… Hugo…is it? Well, he seems to have *two* gifted parents. Perhaps you want to consider coming back to us, now that this clever young man has started school." Eva easily picked up on his faintly dismissive tone and knew she wasn't making any real progress. Yet, she knew that if anyone could give her advice regarding Hugo's extraordinary talents, James Stanway would either know the answer or at least be able to point her in the right direction.

"James, if it were your child—" But before she could finish her sentence, he got up and held his hand out in greeting, indicating the conversation was over.

"I will make a few inquiries and get back to you. How about that?" His eyes narrowed as he suddenly remembered an important point. "I know your son is fluent in Hebrew and English, even though he does not speak to anyone. But does he have a preferred nationality?" Eva met his stare evenly.

"Hugo's father is British and I am Israeli. At six years of age, he may be gifted, but he does not yet have judgments such as the one you are suggesting. His handicap is called Asperger's syndrome, which amongst a whole bunch of variables, also means he is highly selective with whom he interacts. We would nevertheless appreciate your recommendation of any avenues worthy of pursuit."

Two weeks later she opened her front door to Josh Goldberg. His accent was unmistakably from the Bronx area of New York, and she recognized it instantly as he held out his card. His dress was immaculate, complimented by the tall frame of a lean and trim body. His eyes were very dark.

"Mrs. Norman? I represent Azvaalder Electronics. James Stanway from the British Embassy referred us to you. I believe you're acquainted?" His smile was overly friendly and he didn't wait for her reply. "I am told you have a very gifted son and our company regularly sponsors exceptional children to assist their growth and further development. I think you might want to talk to me?" He waited until he had finished his delivery before he allowed himself to casually run his eyes over her, shaking his head imperceptibly. *My God! What a gorgeous woman!*

"You're American, Mr. Goldberg?" Eva inquired, not stepping aside for him to enter yet. Josh Goldberg immediately detected her skepticism and gathered himself. Still smiling, he brushed a hand through his dark brown hair and moved back a pace. Eva Norman had no idea who he was and she wasn't going to let a stranger into her house.

"My apologies," he offered smoothly. "How inconsiderate of me! Azvaalder, Mrs. Norman, is an Israeli-based company with diverse interests in the vast field of electronics. I was recruited by the company's American chiefs to head up this organization a few years ago and we recognize the urgent need to identify talent at a very young age. Once they graduate from our own rigorous testing program, protégés of Azvaalder have a bright and guaranteed future ahead of them. And I am led to believe your son could very well fit this description."

Chapter 9
An Unquestionable Void

The Papagaio Restaurant on Har'arba'a Street in Tel Aviv bustled with its customary clientele of regulars and tourists from all over the world who had come to taste the exquisite variety of meat in this internationally renowned paradise for meat lovers. A favorite of Josh Goldberg, The Papagaio specialized in American and Caribbean cuisine and Eva sat quietly looking over the impressive interior with its array of delicately flower-shaped lamps adorning the walls and the sizzling grand barbeque, in full view of the guests.

The very public preparation of the food was not only intended to demonstrate the extraordinary culinary skills of the chefs, but aimed at arousing the senses of the guests. Tom was home again on one of his rare visits, and her gaze wandered back to their table where he and Josh were engrossed in a detailed discussion about some exciting, technological development in electronics. Eva had not participated much in the conversation and speculated about the reason she had been invited to join them; she felt out of sorts with both men tonight.

Despite the generosity demonstrated by Azvaalder toward Hugo, she had never much liked Josh as a person and was very surprised to learn that he and Tom had been meeting regularly for a while. What interest could Tom possibly have as a diplomat in the advancement of electronics? She meant to raise the matter with him in the privacy of their home. While she picked at her food, the conversation inevitably turned to Hugo and how pleased Azvaalder was with his progress.

"He is definitely in a class of his own." Josh spoke to Tom but kept his eyes on Eva. She was more beautiful than when he had first met her four years ago and he always found contact with this striking, dark-haired woman stimulating and challenging. The diffused light in the restaurant highlighted her classic features, and the expression in her eyes, which seemed darker than usual in the dim lighting, was tranquil and undisturbed like the surface of a still lake. With Tom away so frequently, Josh had in the past tried to invent reasons to meet with her under the guise of discussing an aspect of Hugo's education. And clearly, where her son was concerned, Eva was always attentive and interested, but the woman in her remained unfathomable, distant and inaccessible.

Josh kept his observations to himself but as an expert in neuro-linguistic programming, he was highly aware of her distraction at the dinner table and this concerned him. One of the first things they had established at Azvaalder was the exceptional bond that existed between Hugo and his mother. With the boy now ten years old, nothing in this regard had changed and Josh knew their link had to remain undisturbed, especially with the new project they had in mind. He looked directly at her, taking pains to control his voice and not sound over excited.

"We have barely scraped the tip of the iceberg with Hugo," he said evenly. "The boy is exceptional in many respects." Goldberg was assured of their attention, but knew that he had to play his cards carefully, especially where Eva was concerned. *If only you knew the true brilliance of your son. You don't know that he is a savant and I will not tell you!* He looked from Eva to Tom and waited for his words to sink in, smiling. *It takes a genius to recognize a genius, and talent like his belongs in the circles of the great. The boy is mine.* "As the parents of this gifted child," he continued smoothly, "you should know that I have not seen *his* capability to reason and calculate, in any other. Your son has an extraordinary talent to concentrate which is greatly enhanced by his reluctance to speak. He is capable of almost complete exclusion of distractions, both physical and mental, and given the right circumstances he can access the Zen state without much difficulty. This is something many adults have trouble with, all of which makes him extremely suitable for psychic development. His mind is unblemished and objective and that is a huge asset in this particular field." Eva met the penetrating stare in Josh's eyes.

"What is the Zen state?" She felt uncomfortable with the way he was looking at her and looked to Tom for support, aware of a slight anxiousness at the terms being used in relation to her beloved Hugo. "He is only a child, Josh! And what is this field you mentioned where he is supposed to be so valuable?" The discussion around Hugo had drawn her into the conversation and seeing the alarm in her eyes, Josh Goldberg wondered if he had gone too far but then thankfully, Tom stepped in. He put a reassuring hand on his wife's arm and smiled at her.

"There is no reason for concern, Eva. Josh has explained everything to me in detail. The Zen state is best described by 'what it is not.' It is devoid of ideas, metaphysics and religion, and Hugo's entire mind in this regard is virgin territory. To be in the state of Zen is to be an empty vessel. Such unusual clarity, combined with objectivity and reason is very rare and could be developed into something quite extraordinary." Tom leaned forward and dropped his voice. "Do you remember last year when you asked him what he wanted as a birthday gift? Josh was amazed when I told him that Hugo already knew what you wanted to get him because he had somehow read your mind! Remember how he demonstrated that he just thought of you and then he knew?"

Eva stared at her husband, a cold hand closing around her heart. *You told this man about that day? How can you ask me if I remember any of these events when you are never here to experience anything first hand?* Her discomfort intensified on account of the direction the conversation had taken and she was overwhelmingly aware of how distant she felt from Tom. In twelve years of marriage his frequent absence had resulted in a part-time relationship. Now her loyalty and devotion could no longer bridge the huge chasm that had opened up between them; a direct consequence of lack of physical and emotional closeness. Through devoting most of her attention to raising their only child, Eva had managed to find creative ways of not addressing the unquestionable void she felt as a woman.

Tom had become a phantom husband and father, who affirmed the reality of his presence in their lives with his generous financial support and by putting in predictable appearances around holidays and birthdays. But as the years went by, intimacy was less and less practiced and rarely discussed. What had started out as a loving relationship with the potential to grow into a significant bond, gradually transformed into polite exchanges of pleasantries with very little or no physical contact. Eva's sensitive nature required nurturing, familiarity and closeness but she found herself struggling, each time Tom returned after a long absence, to get to know the stranger whom he had become.

The dinner engagement with Josh had ended on rather stilted terms, and with Hugo staying over at his grandmother's for the evening, Eva and Tom went home to the privacy of their Tel Aviv apartment. Josh had taken his leave fairly quickly when he noticed how concerned Eva was with the new developments, and he only hoped that Tom could take care of his wife's noticeable apprehensions. He did, in fact, depend on Tom to smooth things over; their future plans had colossal potential for the Israeli government and any disturbance in the sensitive bond between Hugo and his mother, could upset the boy and cause unnecessary delays, which he did not want to see happen.

Face to face in the intimacy of their bedroom, Tom looked at his beautiful, distant wife and felt a sharp stab of regret. Earlier, at the restaurant he had felt his control beginning to slip as he watched her in her ever-perfect role as his mate. She never put a foot wrong and even though she was upset about Hugo, she had controlled her responses and waited until this moment to talk to him. He wasn't looking forward to this conversation and paused for her to broach the subject first.

"You're a diplomat, Tom." She spoke calmly, without accusation. "What is the nature of your business with Azvaalder?" Tom took a step closer to her and was suddenly so intensely annoyed that he found it difficult to speak. She was so gorgeous, so desirable and yet so remote. He clenched his fists in frustration. *Why can I never reach you, Eva? In the past you had dutifully given me your body, but you have always kept your heart. Who do you need? Because it sure as hell isn't me!* He took a deep breath and composed himself as he ran his eyes over her attractive frame from head to toe.

"No need to worry, Eva. Hugo is in good hands. And he truly is exceptionally gifted; there isn't any doubt about that." He smiled distractedly, surprised that these old feelings of frustration around his wife had surfaced again in this way. "As for Josh Goldberg, we met a few years ago at a symposium in Bern, Switzerland where Azvaalder demonstrated to a number of European countries some new developments in the field of electronics. I thought it would be a good idea to meet the man whose company was footing the bill for our son's very expensive education. Don't you think that was a good idea?" The diplomat had taken over again, and he waited politely, poised for her reply.

"I don't want Hugo involved in politics, Tom. Stanway told me that Josh Goldberg used to be in the CIA, and I know old habits die hard." She put a hand out and touched his arm lightly; her gesture was a plea for his understanding, not an invitation to intimacy, but Tom already knew that.

"Never, Eva." He looked her straight in the eye and put his hand over hers. "I promise."

A year later that promise still rang in her ears when a representative from Azvaalder showed up on her doorstep with an official letter informing her and Tom, who was on another mission abroad, that the grant for Hugo's education had been increased substantially. But Eva was instantly alarmed, for the letter also stated that the venue of his education would be changed from the special school comfortably located near her mother's home in Herzliya, to the University of Tel Aviv. It alleged that Hugo had outgrown the capabilities of the school to educate him sufficiently and that a specialist from Austria, Herr Muller, would take over once Hugo arrived on campus.

Insisting on more detailed information as well as doing her own research, Eva established that Herr Muller's expertise was mathematics and advanced physics. Hugo was further designated to participate in a very exclusive project in the heart of the physics department, located in a part of the building that was subject to a high level of security and offered very limited access to outsiders. Josh had assured her that she could see her son whenever she wanted; the only stipulation was for her to pass through security every time she came back into the facility.

Eva was troubled at the elaborate precautions prescribed for a program with which her innocent 11-year-old son would be associated, and requested that Hugo be tutored by Herr Muller at home. Josh pretended to understand her concerns but denied her request on grounds of logistics and the fact that an expert in Asperger's syndrome would be on hand to assist Hugo. He said it would be too difficult to conduct their training off campus and purposely neglected to tell her of their progress in helping Hugo to communicate verbally what he otherwise understood. Knowing that the boy associated this new skill with the work being done in the lab, he didn't think Eva was yet privy to the new development. Goldberg assured her again that Hugo would be safe; that she had no need for concern and that they were looking forward to a speedy reply.

Eva didn't hesitate for a second and immediately contacted James Stanway, who had written an official letter of support shortly after he had learned from their Israeli counterparts about the extraordinary capabilities of the young Hugo Norman. This time he assured the boy's parents that Great Britain would also be honored to aid in the development of such a talent, and since Tom was a British subject, no stone would be left unturned should an occasion for assistance ever present itself.

When the letter from Azvaalder arrived, Eva knew it was time. She simply could not allow Josh and his specialists to separate Hugo from her at this young age. After this sudden turn of events, she attempted to contact Tom but, as so often in the past, she had to leave a message with the Embassy in the hope that they would know where he was.

Azvaalder was waiting for her official reply, and except for a brief message left with a secretary that she was considering the offer, she had neither written nor called to inform them of her final decision. She was anxious to hear from the British Embassy and decided to take up residence with her widowed mother, Carmela, who lived in Herzliya, opposite Hugo's present school. Carmela welcomed their presence as a bonus and accepted that Hugo had to be on hand for more testing. Eva realized that her mother could not be privy to the truth at this point.

Three weeks had gone by when Eva noticed the presence of a plain white delivery van that seemed to follow her around and this amplified her suspicions that something was amiss. Reluctant to involve her mother in matters which she knew would only cause her more strain and unnecessary concern, she called her brother, Uri, in whom she had always placed a great deal of trust. He was well-traveled and had campaigned for many years against conformist politics, a characteristic she admired.

"Nothing is as it seems." He often jested with Eva about her and Tom's roles at the Embassy. "Very few people know what is really going on. And if the rest of the world were told the true state of affairs, even fewer would believe what they were told. The beast depends on the ignorance of the people. It relies on the fact that the masses trust blindly and question nothing." Eva didn't always understand what he was talking about, but she let him be. If anything, she enjoyed his investigative mind and if anyone could give her guidance with the apparent menace parked outside in the plain white van, Uri could. They agreed to meet in The Carmel Market, known as "Shuk Ha'Carmel", the city's biggest marketplace, on the first Friday after she contacted him.

"Why here?" she asked as they wandered through the outdoor market; a crowded, narrow alley with long lines of colorful stalls on either side. A number of vendors tried to get their attention, holding up their goods and loudly chastising them for the bargains that they were forgoing. Eva had always loved this market and had often brought Hugo here as a toddler and just browsed around this fascinating place where almost anything imaginable could be found for the lowest prices in the city, from different kinds of bread and pastry to delicious olives, dried fruits and exotic spices.

"If you are under surveillance, Eva, then it is my guess that mum's house will also be bugged." He spoke under his breath and caught her arm when he saw the fright in her eyes. "Don't," he whispered, lifting a finger to his mouth and shaking his head almost imperceptibly. Then he wove his arm through hers and strolled purposely ahead, keeping his voice low. "I'll come and check tomorrow in broad daylight. When you get home today, call me about the computer. Invent some kind of software problem you're having. If I'm right, then they will be expecting my visit tomorrow. Ask any questions you may have now, not when I'm there." She nodded, uncertain what to make of this new development, but she felt a tightness take hold of her stomach that made her feel very uncomfortable. The next day Uri found a bug under the unit which housed the computer and also one in the house phone.

"There will be more, Eva, of that I am certain. Bloody Azvaalder! I've never trusted that bunch." She was seeing him off at his car and fought hard to keep her composure. *Tom? Azvaalder?* The implications were just too overwhelming.

"I don't understand, Uri." She tried to keep her voice under control. "If this is about Hugo, what could they possibly want with him? He is only a child!"

"They know something we don't, and it doesn't look good to me. By their behavior, they sure as hell are laying claim to you and Hugo.

You will have to weigh all your options carefully, and you might have to take very drastic steps to protect yourselves." He looked at her earnestly and addressed the question he saw in her eyes. "Don't ask me what that means right now. I'll help you wherever I can, you know that." He smiled cynically. "His father isn't around right now, so someone has to step up to the plate. Let me know what you decide." For the first time in her life, Eva felt fearful about what the future held for her and Hugo, and her heart was filled with great uncertainty about Tom and the promises he had made about their son's safety.

Hereafter she returned briefly to their apartment to gather a few more necessary things for her and Hugo's stay at Carmela's. She left a note for Tom in the apartment as well as a message at the Embassy as to their whereabouts. In Hugo's room she looked through some of his more recent designs, drawings and symbols and, as always, a strange feeling stirred in her. *What do these mean? And how is he capable of capturing my visions?*

These designs had been haunting her dreams for years, but her young son saw them simply as equations, numbers and colors, all of which had mathematical relevance. Eva knew that Josh Goldberg had also seen some of these designs and she suspected that the offer to further educate Hugo away from her at Tel Aviv University had something to do with these. They wanted control of her son. *But why? How could a young boy be of such interest to a company whose business was electronics?*

She quickly gathered the designs and drawings together and stored them in a file folder to take with her. She had never felt the presence of danger before, but she sensed it clearly as she prepared to leave the apartment. She didn't know why, but it seemed as though time was running out and that she and Hugo would have to leave soon. On some very deep level, Eva knew her life was about to change drastically and this thought filled her with both fear and anticipation. As she locked the apartment door behind her, an even stranger realization rooted in her mind. *I have been down this road before. But how?*

On her way back to her mother's house Eva decided to pay Martha a quick, but long overdue visit. She wasn't in the habit of confiding in others but Martha had always had a special place in her heart and that of Hugo, and she needed to lighten the burden of all these frightening and unexpected developments. Martha had a strange expression on her face as she listened quietly to Eva's account of recent events. Her gaze was fixed somewhere in the distance and she only realized that Eva was waiting for her reply when the silence between them began to stretch. Then she took both Eva's hands in her own.

"You are in danger." She sounded distressed and appeared to have difficulty speaking. "What are you going to do?" Martha's eyes glistened with tears. She shook her head slowly and looked away from Eva. "Oh, my God! I don't know what to say."

"Martha, please—" Eva felt sudden regret at having involved her friend in this matter. She seemed unduly disturbed by the news and Eva was a little perplexed at the very emotional response. "Don't be so upset, Martha." She stood and tried to make light of it. "I've spoken to my brother, Uri. He has promised to look into this for me. It's going to be alright, I promise." Eva put her arms around her and hugged her closely. "Don't be concerned for us, please?" She left a short while later wondering about the wisdom of having spoken to Martha. After all, what could she do to help? She had probably only upset this dear woman and caused her unnecessary worry.

That night Martha had great difficulty falling asleep. She read for hours but found it hard to concentrate; her eyes kept going to the few pages of Hugo's drawings that Eva had left as a gift for her. She picked them up again and again, straining to fathom the meaning of the intricate designs. She remembered the shape of the eagle he had built when he was only three years old, and as her eyes wandered curiously over the extraordinary shapes he had created on these papers, she was still no closer to understanding this unusual child.

In the small hours of the morning, with the light still on, she eventually fell into a restless sleep and drifted straight into the barren landscape of a very old and eerie world inhabited by faceless shadows. Her presence seemed to go unnoticed and she pressed her body nervously against the outer wall of a building that emanated a horrible smell and instantly nauseated her. Her mind groped anxiously to make the connection until she heard the deadly squeal of animals being slaughtered. Martha stood frozen as the horror of an ancient memory crept into every fiber of her being. Then a big man stood in front of her and cast a menacing shadow. She stared, petrified, into the black sockets of his dead eyes, unable to utter a sound or make a movement.

She looked in terror into the dark hole that was his mouth and the hollow echo paralyzed her.

Martha put her hands up to her face and tried to hide from his evil towering presence. *It's too late! I can't save them!* Her throat felt parched and dry and she strained with every ounce of her strength to scream the warning. "Ann! Please don't go! Ann!" In her bed, Martha rolled over and vomited violently as her conscious mind mercifully rescued her from the nightmare and she sat up, sweating profusely. She put a shaky hand to her mouth and felt the stickiness surrounding it and then she began to weep. It was the cry of one who desperately wanted to right a wrong from a very long time ago. *But who on earth is Ann?*

The next day she wrote the note and addressed it "To whom it may concern." It was the only solution she could think of. Years before, Benjamin had given her this address and said that if she ever needed help to find him or needed assistance of any kind that had to do with his "other" occupation, she should write to this address. Martha didn't know if this would help her friend, but she knew she had to try. She carefully made photocopies of Hugo's drawings and included them in the letter. Then she drove to the British Embassy in Tel Aviv and went to the reception area as Benjamin had instructed her to do so many years ago. She asked for the letter to be delivered to the diplomatic bag leaving Tel Aviv that day.

"Please identify the sender." It was a polite request from the young interpreter who kept her distance and didn't touch the letter. Martha leaned forward and whispered Benjamin's code name softly to the woman.

The next day in London, England, Mrs. Hogan opened the envelope from Martha Bartholomew. She identified the code name and checked it against their records before she logged the origin of the message as the spouse of an agent who had died in 1992 in Gaza. Then she pulled Benjamin Bartholomew's file. She knew Colonel Appleyard was going to ask for it.

Chapter 10

A Soldier First

It would be hard to detect anything out of the ordinary in the opulent and comfortable office of David Appleyard. Hidden from the casual eye was technology capable of putting him in touch with the highest office in Her Majesty's Government, or tracking skirmishes in obscure parts of the world at the touch of a button. Balding, overweight, and of average height, the Colonel was approaching his sixtieth birthday. Working behind a desk had transformed his once trim military physique into an uncomfortable shape squeezed into expensive suits he wore in the position he now held. Years before, Sir Ronald Patterson, the Regiment's Commander-in-Chief, was the first to notice Appleyard's considerable diplomatic potential. Upon his recommendation, the Colonel was promoted from the Royal Corps of Signals, where he excelled as a linguist and communicator, to his present position as head of the Foreign Section.

The department had come a long way since those early pioneering days in 1909 when the Committee of Imperial Defense had established the Secret Service Bureau. Operating out of their Vauxhall Cross building in London, MI6 was now a formidable force presumably aiming not only to protect the international interests of the British people, but also liaising with all its global counterparts in helping to counteract terrorism and bring stability to a very unpredictable and volatile world. He was about to leave for his usual business luncheon at his Gentleman's Club in Trafalgar Square when his secretary unceremoniously buzzed through.

"I have Mr. Adams, the attaché from the Embassy in Tel Aviv on the line, Colonel. He says it's quite important and he apologizes for contacting you at this time. Shall I put him through?" The Colonel's military training was irreversibly a part of him and his penchant for routine and discipline made him feel irritated and annoyed that a call, important as it was, should come through at such an inconvenient time. However, duty was always his first priority, although it did nothing to promote his congeniality.

"It's alright Mrs. Hogan. Yes, I'll take it." He sat back in his chair, glancing at his watch and impatiently waited for the indicator to show green on his private telephone. Then his eye caught the closed file with Eva Norman's name on top of the pending stack, and he impatiently began to tap his pencil on the desk, as if in a countdown. His eyes narrowed as he waited for the connection to be made. Then the green light flickered. "Hello Adams. Is everything okay? I don't want any trouble with the Israeli government."

Peter Adams was not a typical civil servant but he certainly looked and portrayed the part. Colonel Appleyard could spot the military type with a flair for undercover operations a mile away, but it was the extent of the young man's military training that had ultimately grabbed the attention of the Colonel. His impressive career as a soldier engaged him in hot spots around the world, including being a member of the SAS. Appleyard had a special interest in recruiting experienced members with unique skills to his undercover operation.

In some of the reports he had read before contacting Peter Adams, it was abundantly clear that he had a natural instinct to kill and Appleyard knew the worth of a fearless soldier with not much of a conscience. He didn't doubt that Adams would be an asset to his department. In his highly specialized line of work, Appleyard required only one chief but lots of Indians. The exception to his own rule was Tom Norman.

Adams was a skilled soldier with special electronics training, but blending him into a diplomatic landscape required some refinement. The British Embassy in Tel Aviv was just the right training field and before long, Adams justly earned his stripes as a valuable asset at both ends of the spectrum. The Colonel intended for Adams to be part of the ongoing operation supported by the West in this region. But in the interim, as standard protection of a diplomat's family, Peter Adams had the unenviable task of reporting directly to Colonel Appleyard's department on the whereabouts of Mrs. Norman and her son. He was soon to find out that everything had a price and that the master negotiator in the person of Colonel David Appleyard, was about to call in his marker. Peter Adams didn't know that soon he would be heading back directly into the fold of MI6 for a deadly assignment to kill one of his own.

"Hello, sir. I'm terribly sorry to interrupt your regular luncheon appointment, but this is important." He got right to the point. "It's about Captain Norman." Peter Adams was glad he had got that part out. There was no escaping the wrath of Appleyard's short temper and as someone had to bear the brunt of it, the messenger was always in the line of fire. But the Colonel sounded taken aback, even shocked.

"Tom Norman? What about him, Adams?" The Colonel groaned inwardly to himself and his tone changed quickly as he fetched one of his favorite cigars from the top drawer of his desk and guillotined the tip. "Get on with it man!" He was relieved to hear the call wasn't about the other two Normans and the delicate operation MI6 was planning, but he was nevertheless surprised to hear the message was about Tom. "Adams!" Appleyard barked.

"He's gone missing, sir." Peter Adams braced himself for the onslaught of verbal abuse he knew was coming. He was beginning to regret being a part of James Stanway's department, now that he had the job of also having to report to MI6 on Tom Norman's whereabouts.

"What do you mean he's gone missing? Tom is in Pakistan working on the Toresh deal."

"No, sir. Apparently he finished early. The Lahore office said they received his reports and that he had left word about taking a brief vacation."

"*What!*" Appleyard rose halfway out of his chair, slamming his hand on the desk. "A vacation? He was supposed to get back to us right away!" he shouted, outraged by the turn of events. "Where the hell is he taking this holiday? Are you tracking him?"

"I can't, sir." Adams made an effort to hide the irritation in his voice, knowing full well that none of this was his fault. Mrs. Hogan decided it an appropriate time to leave when she heard the Colonel's outburst. Diverting all calls to the main office, she left in a hurry. Right now her boss wanted someone's hide and she was determined it wasn't going to be hers. Adams pressed on, trying to ignore the unwarranted accusations. "I have the last satellite fix, sir. And that was at the High Commission in Lahore." He dropped his voice. "It appears that Captain Norman is in breach of departmental agreement and has his communication equipment switched off. Either that, or he is in danger." Adams kept his voice even. "We know he is still in Pakistan because he has not crossed any official borders. We put out the standard worldwide border alert, sir." Peter completed his doodle of a tracking micro chip that he wished someone had surgically implanted in Tom Norman as he spoke with the Colonel. *And if it were my job to implant the fucking device, Norman, I know exactly where I'd put it!*

"Jesus Christ!" Appleyard muttered to himself, resorting to his customary profanity. He felt momentarily defeated; neither he nor his department could afford the slightest mishap. Bringing Eva Norman and her son onto British soil without causing an international incident was not only a priority, but also a difficult operation to execute. They were two legitimate citizens of a country with friendly ties to Great Britain and according to Stanway it offered this Goldberg character the perfect opportunity to create an international scandal. But the state of affairs was far more delicate. This was a potential political quagmire; one Adams was not yet privy to. The Colonel understood that Stanway's raising hell about Tom's absence was a smoke screen. He and Stanway both needed to get in touch with Tom and their business had nothing to do with the Toresh deal.

"I'm sorry, sir." Adams knew someone had to be the punch bag, and he resented that in this instance, it was him.

"Oh, shut up, Adams! Let me think." Colonel Appleyard was at his wit's end with Tom's disappearance. It had taken time to bring Tom Norman into the exclusive fold of false flag operations. Not everybody understood the cause. Tom did, or so the Colonel thought. But this was not the first time that Tom had been unaccounted for, and Appleyard's instincts told him that something was amiss. He would have to get to the bottom of this matter, and quickly. *Damn you Tom! Why the hell are you avoiding us? I need that information!* In the meantime, he would have to ensure that Stanway, who knew the score, created a diversion to allay suspicions at his department regarding Tom's recent activities. He composed himself with effort and softened his approach. "Mr. Adams, there's no need for concern. Give James my fond regards and tell him I'm onto this. I think I know why Tom is lying low at the moment. You'll be hearing from me." Having realized that Mrs. Hogan had taken an opportune and early lunch, he rang down to reception to order his car to take him to his club. Then he reached out and picked up the folder he had requested after receiving those strange drawings from Israel. It was the file for Eva and Hugo Norman.

He stared at the pictures. The boy resembled his mother and they were a handsome pair; dark-haired with classic features, although the son's were still reminiscent of a growing child. Eva Norman had an arresting smile and projected openness, a sincerity that he thought exceptionally attractive. Then he reached behind the picture and once again looked at the handwritten note, together with a photocopy of some very unusual drawings which had reached him from the wife of a deceased undercover operative in Israel. *My name is Martha Bartholomew, wife of Benjamin Bartholomew, deceased in 1992 on a mission in the Gaza strip. Enclosed are copies of drawings made by the son of a British subject who is presently under surveillance. I have tutored this child and know his talent to be unparalleled. His father is Tom Norman. I thought this might be of interest to you.*

Appleyard put the note back and glanced at the photocopies Martha had sent before closing the file. He couldn't interpret a single thing, but his experts insisted they were highly unusual. He wasn't personally acquainted with Benjamin Bartholomew and had to ask for his file after he received his widow's note. He learned that MI6 had sent Benjamin in as an undercover international observer following the massacre of seven Palestinian workers from Gaza in the summer of 1990.

They were killed by an Israeli gunman near Tel Aviv, after which Yasser Arafat had called for the deployment of a United Nations emergency force. He demanded international protection for the Palestinian people to safeguard their lives, properties and holy places. But the United States vetoed this motion and a fact-finding mission was then sent to the area. In light of the strained US relationship with Palestine, it was deemed necessary to send a local into these troubled areas, someone inconspicuous who could speak Hebrew and Arabic, namely Benjamin Bartholomew. Two years later Bartholomew's body was found in his car just outside the city of Asquelon in the Gaza strip. The coroner's report stated it was a heart attack, but all his documents and identification papers were missing, and the case went cold.

Shortly after receiving this unusual message from Benjamin's widow, James Stanway contacted the Colonel to let him know that Eva Norman, unable to reach her husband, had requested their aid. Much of Appleyard's success in heading MI6 was based in his ability to make quick judgments and act accordingly. In light of the uncertainty around his prized soldier, Eva's plea for assistance was just the leverage he had been looking for. A red flag had been raised about the Azvaalder operation, and Appleyard was curious to know why the benefactor of the Normans had put them under surveillance. However, this was Tom Norman's child and with the stakes as high as they were, keeping Tom in his debt could only benefit him. Therefore, the decision to bring Eva and her son on to British soil was an easy one to make.

On the short journey to his club, Appleyard reminisced about Tom's meteoric rise in the department. After graduating with honors from Cambridge University, with a commission of lieutenant, he enrolled into The Department of Communications and Management Studies at Sandhurst where he excelled as a leader. Soon he was traveling the world representing his country with the Signals regiment and was rapidly promoted to Captain. As his superior officer, he quickly recognized Tom's potential and made his move before the rest of his peers could lay their claim. As expected, politicians and other government officials soon became interested, envisaging a diplomatic role for Tom in the Foreign Office. But the Colonel was an astute negotiator who knew his man was a soldier first. Thus, Appleyard outsmarted everyone by securing a solution that would see the Foreign Section at SIS as one of the main beneficiaries of Tom's activities, but still allow him to retain his military commission.

David Appleyard was more than aware that Tom might be forced to choose between being a diplomat, a military strategist or an international economic manipulator, the latter of which his man had already graduated to. It was a game without rules that relied heavily on cunning diplomacy, a role that Tom had perfected.

Chapter 11

Painful Admission

The strong Tibetan tea was beginning to appeal to Tom's pallet as he spoke with his host at the modest dwelling, located in the lower Himalayan Mountains close to Gujrat. He had thought his riding days were well behind him but his aching back and sore inner thighs painfully reminded him of the half day's mule ride and steep climb he had had to endure to finally reach this beautiful plateau.

He had left his car in Gujrat the previous day after completing the Toresh Earthquake deal. Managing to finish those delicate negotiations seven days sooner than planned, he had left brief word at Lahore's British High Commission that he'd be taking a well-earned break and would collect his car later. Tom hoped this would be enough to stop wagging tongues as he set about his 'other business,' justifying his position on the Azvaalder payroll, a position that Colonel Appleyard was oblivious to. He purposely avoided contacting Stanway or Appleyard, gambling on the grace that the extra seven days offered. But now it was time to change diplomatic hats and unofficially meet with his guide for the journey ahead. He estimated that a week should be enough. It wasn't easy to convince the sinewy Sherpa that his business with Chong-ba was of a spiritual nature, but Josh was a meticulous planner and had briefed him well.

"Your problem is not the monk, Tom," Josh had told him. "The challenge will be to convince his custodians at the foot of the mountain to take you to him. He does receive visitors, but as far as I can tell, you have to be in some spiritual need. So be creative, and fake it." He laughed. "Not a difficult thing for us Godless people to do!" Tom ignored that statement.

"Considering this man's spiritual reputation, what makes you think he will be open to your plans?"

"Ah, but you should know! Every man has his price. The right offer can undermine the strongest conviction. Our little monk needs a platform in the West, and I know how to provide it." Goldberg sneered openly. "I have a hunch that we will not be negotiating about money. The currency is power." Tom decided not to pursue the matter any further. After that conversation he purposely dropped his cell phone in the trunk of his car; it would be useless in the mountains.

Despite the significant resources available to Azvaalder as communications specialists, Josh still had to go through his old CIA network to find the expert most suited to his needs. Recent records regarding the Tibetan and Chinese conflict proved to be very helpful, even though it meant that establishing contact would send Tom on a perilous trip into the mountains. The next day Tom bought a copy of the Baghivad Gita, a Sanskrit poem about the Hindu path to spiritual wisdom and unity with God, and kept it tucked under his arm while talking to the guide. Tom wondered about the kind of reception he could anticipate from a monk who was not expecting him to show up on his doorstep.

Locating the base camp was the easy part. Convincing one of the trusted guides to accompany him was quite another. But that was the least of Goldberg's concerns. Tom Norman could sell ice to an Eskimo; he would find a way. He was right. Tom kept the name of Chong-ba's appointed guide supplied by CIA sources under his hat until the last minute. When he asked for Da-nu by name, the locals were impressed and the deal was done. And as they slowly made their way toward the hidden dwelling, he realized that he was troubled by his deception to gain an audience. He wondered why. It had never bothered him before.

Unlike his Sherpa, Da-nu, Tom found the going tough, but after five hours they finally reached the cliff upon which the modest cabin was perched. The simple dwelling sat just below one of the summits of the mountain, hugging the thin trunk of a leafless tree. Da-nu pointed to the cabin, nodding his head before turning his mule and unceremoniously beginning the journey back. He had told Tom earlier that Chong-ba would know how to contact him when his services were required for the return journey.

Tom took in the solitary picture and surmised that growing

anything in this inhospitable terrain had to be a challenge. Then he made his way to the door but before he could knock, it opened and Tom looked down on the slight figure of a Tibetan monk. Despite the fact that he towered over the smaller man, the monk showed no sign of being intimidated. He stared Tom straight in the eye, wearing only a trace of a smile.

"I have been waiting for you." He looked at the Holy book in Tom's hands. "You will not need that, sir. That is not why you are here."

Tom made a space for his delicate teacup, the only sign of luxury in an otherwise sparsely furnished cabin, amongst the papers spread carelessly on the floor between them. He re-crossed his legs to find a more comfortable position on the cushions that were made available to him.

"My knowledge of your language is extremely limited Chong-ba, thus I'm very grateful that your English is so good. Are you quite sure that there are no means of locating me up here?" Tom knew the answer to his question, but thought of his British colleagues and looked over toward one of the bags that he'd carried up to the cabin which housed his satellite communication equipment. He felt relieved that he was temporarily out of reach from those who demanded explanations.

Chong-ba was a small, delicately-built man with pale yellow skin offset by the brightness of his orange robe. His shaven head and wrinkled face made it difficult to gauge his age, but the look in his eye was piercing and direct. He was very different to the rest of his Sherpa brethren who were originally from Kham in eastern Tibet. They now all had to get used to living in the mountainous regions of Northern Pakistan. Chong-ba was a devoted monk, who had spent many years studying in Tibet, but due to the Chinese occupation, he had become an outcast and had to tend to his own needs and carve out an existence in any way possible. If it weren't for his high profile and the considerable number of Western followers that traveled from all corners of the world to hear his teachings, the Chinese would have found a way to dispose of him together with many of his hapless peers.

"If you are trying to avoid contact with your colleagues, you are quite safe here for the time being, Mr. Norman. As long as your equipment is switched off. However, they are very astute and it will only be a matter of time before they locate you. It would seem that you have gone to a lot of trouble to find me, and your very brief proposal suggests some substantial consideration on my part, so I would like to know a little more about it, if you please. How exactly can I help you and your colleagues?"

Tom found the monk's mannerisms uplifting. Of late he had had to tolerate vicious verbal attacks from all angles due to his covert actions and it was becoming more difficult by the day to explain his extended absences. Tom was in fact a man at war on all fronts. In the past he had kept in touch with Colonel Appleyard as a matter of priority, but of late had begun to question the morality of the secret missions known only to himself, the Colonel and Stanway. But in light of his additional underground involvement with Azvaalder, his life had become extremely complicated. And then there was Eva.

Hugo's phenomenal potential had transformed Tom into a very valuable asset to Josh Goldberg. His existing diplomatic and political contacts and the many locations he visited offered ample opportunity to buy and sell information, which could benefit Azvaalder's intelligence. Industrial espionage was a dangerous but lucrative occupation. Tom grappled with the ethics of his side operations from time to time but managed to convince himself that it provided a financially secure future for his family. The irony of not being a part of that future was not lost on him.

He thought of Eva and his heart contracted painfully. She was his Achilles' heel; beautiful, mysterious and despite being the woman who had borne their only child, she was out of his reach. He knew this with certainty and the paradox of it pained his very soul. Tom had taken a very long time to admit to himself that his long absences from home were not motivated by money, but driven by the pain he felt in losing the only woman he had ever loved. The new role Appleyard had devised for him prolonged his absences and intensified the growing distance between them.

Eva tried very hard to please him, but he had known for years that despite being his wife, this gorgeous woman was inexplicably beyond his reach. And thus, the opportunity offered by Appleyard complemented the work he did for Josh, for he traveled almost constantly. It provided the escape he needed, but dug a hole so deep that he could no longer see his way out. Tom glanced up to find the scrutinizing look of the monk fixed upon him.

"I can only tell you so much Chong-ba, because I'm not qualified to explain the intricacies of the proposal. My colleague in this matter would be more suited to this. After all, it was he who found you and I'm amazed at how he managed to do it." Tom tried to keep the conversation at his level, dealing with more practical matters surrounding the topic as he waited for the monk's response.

"If your colleague has connections with the CIA as you mention then surely, with his resources, the matter of finding a renegade monk, listed on all Chinese records, should be quite easy. And I believe you have a wife and a son?" Chong-ba sat back and noisily sipped at his tea, deliberately staring at Tom.

"Josh told you about my private life?" Tom felt slightly disturbed. Why on earth would Josh share personal details about him with a total stranger? But he composed himself and met the blunt stare of his mountain companion evenly. "Josh Goldberg is head of the Israeli branch of Azvaalder and is ex-CIA, unless I have been misinformed." He spoke firmly, putting down his cup. "What else has he told you?" Tom's feeling of discomfort was growing and he tried his best not to appear as agitated as he felt. Chong-ba's face broke into a huge, sympathetic smile.

"You forget the reasons you were asked to contact me in the first place. Did I say Mr. Goldberg *told* me about your wife and child? On the contrary, Mr. Norman, it was *you* who told me." The monk stood up and walked toward the window of the small, but warm room of the cabin. There was a fire ablaze and enough fuel outside to last for months. It appeared Chong-ba was prepared to wait here for the right opportunity to arise.

Tom stared at the monk's back as the little man gazed out over the mountains, and his mind scrambled to make sense of his last statement. Chong-ba's small body was clearly silhouetted against the bright daylight streaming in through the window. It was difficult to read the expression on his face as he turned to face Tom, but he nevertheless felt the monk's unwavering stare. Chong-ba was in no hurry to help and waited quietly, but then as the answer dawned on Tom, he opened his mouth to speak but his rational mind immediately rejected it.

"You—" Tom hesitated, unsure and somewhat nervous as he suddenly found himself in unfamiliar territory. "You mean you knew this *through me?*" Chong-ba neither confirmed nor refuted the statement, but kept watching Tom. Finally he pushed away from the window and walked toward the fireplace to put on more firewood. Tom watched the relaxed way of the monk and a smile crept slowly around his mouth. *Oh, my God, of course!* "My apologies, Chong-ba. Please forgive me." His voice dropped down low. "Of course you knew. In the West we know so little of your secrets. May I ask how you receive this information?" He joined the monk as they both sat back down on the cushions.

"It is no secret, Mr. Norman. The information, as you put it, that I receive is freely available. Your civilization chose to take a different road with their materialistic obsessions and lust for control and power. What is available to me is available to you also. Now you must learn to release the *conditioning* that has ruled your life for so many years. There are those in your society who control these so-called secrets, as you call them. They use this to influence the masses to pass on their responsibilities to others. Once this has been established, it is easy to take control. Planted fear is what encapsulates the Western world and people have lost their ability to truly think for themselves and, instead, look to others to tell them what is right and what is wrong. Are you following me, Mr. Norman?" Tom evaluated the monk's words carefully in true diplomatic fashion and replied with as much sincerity as he was allowed under the circumstances.

"It's hard to say that I agree with everything you said, Chong-ba. But it is as you say, in the West there are many physical, mental and spiritual shackles, and I am a part of that world. However, your line of thought is intriguing and I would like to know more." Tom couldn't believe what was happening to him, but felt comfortable and almost at peace in the presence of this strange monk.

"What a tangled web you weave, Mr. Norman." Chong-ba's statement was without judgment. "Your path is very intricate and you have many allegiances in your attempt to fulfill your life. Do you really know what you require in return? In fact, do you understand your own life? Pray, tell me exactly what you expected from your very hard journey to locate me?" Tom didn't know how to answer him and turned to the reasons for his visit.

"As I mentioned earlier, Mr. Goldberg has asked me to make you an offer to come and join him in Israel. He guarantees that you will be comfortable for the rest of your life. He is involved with developing an intricate mind game. He has briefly explained to me what it's about and he believes it will benefit the national security of Israel. You've seen the documentation. Is this offer something that you will consider?"

In the silence that followed, Tom was astounded that he had actually got that sentence out. It at once sounded silly and completely ridiculous that this man, staring at him with that serious look, would even think about coming down this mountain, much less serve the selfish needs of Josh Goldberg. He looked into the flames of the fire for a long time, still feeling the eyes of the monk on him. Then, without his usual diplomatic touch, he took a deep breath and spontaneously answered his own question.

"What a stupid thing to ask, Chong-ba. Did I really have to travel thousands of miles to realize that? I see that it is out of the question. I know that in the past, many people from all walks of life have sought out your guidance and now I come with a selfish proposal, which is quite preposterous. Again, please forgive me." His statement was not a request for redemption, but a sober observation that at once troubled him and he waited for Chong-ba to make the next move. The fire crackled energetically in the long ensuing silence between them. Then, finally, the monk spoke.

"You have both misjudged me, Mr. Norman. I have no interest in material comfort, other than that which sustains physical life, which is nothing more than a plateau where I can experience my mind in the quest to serve my fellow man. What I would share with you and Mr. Goldberg is nothing less than what I would share with the whole of mankind. The mind games you speak of are doomed to failure because they serve only the negative aspects of human nature. With your permission, I would like to ask something of you." By now, Tom felt as if he was an open book to the astute man opposite him, and he was almost willing to answer anything that would sooth his unsettled mind. Not for a long time had he felt so relaxed and at peace with his surroundings and, more importantly, himself.

"Go ahead, Chong-ba, I'm listening."

"Forgive me, Mr. Norman, I am not asking you to reveal your innermost secrets. On the contrary, I am just interested to know how you perceive the world and its complexities. I feel that you are a man of great intellectual learning. Would I be accurate in this assumption?" Chong-ba communicated using simple questions. Through experience he knew that asking was often the best method of teaching. Whatever doubts Tom had had about this mild-mannered man earlier were no longer present. Despite the polite inquiries, he knew this monk could *feel* him in all respects and it was no use trying to play any of Josh's psychological games here. He had had this feeling before, but always in the presence of Eva.

"I have certain knowledge of academic matters. Is that what you are asking?"

"You have studied mathematics?"

"Yes, extensively."

"You have some knowledge of physics and its components?" Chong-ba offered him some of the vegetable broth that had been simmering in an iron cast pot since he first entered the cabin. Without thinking, Tom gratefully received the soup and began sipping at it. "Science has come a long way over the last two centuries, Mr. Norman. This is just another road of discovery when seeking truth and there are many more. It is not important which road you take as long as you tread it sincerely with your heart and not your head. Interestingly, all roads lead home. Some just have many detours and it might take you longer to get there. How is your broth?" Tom had no idea where this was heading, but he responded with a nod and a grunt of approval, not realizing how hungry he was. "Have you ever really studied the atom, Mr. Norman? Oh I know you are aware of its constituents, but have you ever considered its significance?"

"Pardon? You mean other than electrons revolving around a positively charged nucleus, or it being the smallest physical particle and so on? Physics was not my specialty although I do have a good mathematical brain." Chong-ba added more dry sticks to the fire and turned to warm his rear. He seemed to be engrossed in his own conversation and didn't answer Tom's question directly.

"Everything that is physical stems from the atom. Would you agree?"

"Yes. Everything is made up of atoms." He waited for the monk to continue. He was beginning to enjoy this meeting and inwardly hoped something positive would come of it.

"So, we are both composed of atoms?" Tom nodded again. He smiled at the repetitive question while watching the fire cast its dancing shadows on the face of the man opposite him. "In this world of matter, you hardly exist, Mr. Norman, as the atom constitutes less than one per cent of physical mass. Put another way, your body is almost devoid of matter." The two men stared at each other. Both were familiar with this knowledge, but one was interpreting it rationally whilst the other dealt exclusively with it in spirit.

"Perhaps we should be floating in thin air or something, Chong-ba? Or maybe we should be invisible?" Tom was tired, but Chong-ba had roped him firmly into this discussion and he sensed this was leading somewhere. The monk was not making small talk with him.

"We have all this space within us and around us, Mr. Norman, because the ground beneath you, even our atmosphere and our oceans, constitute those same atoms. Is all this space simply fresh air?" Chong-ba had launched into a monologue where he both asked and answered the questions, and Tom just let him be. "No, Mr. Norman." He still stubbornly insisted on his formal, courteous way of addressing Tom. "This is not fresh air, but a gateway to inner knowledge and it is at *your* disposal. It is simply one of many countless different dimensions and the equipment that you have in your bag works on a frequency that relies on one of these dimensions to carry its signal."

Tom had a sudden, painful vision of Eva. She would *love* a discussion such as this. Indescribable regret mixed with an enormous feeling of loss suddenly filled his heart and he remained silent as he listened to the monk's explanations of other worlds and dimensions. There was an unexpected lump in his throat and he found it hard to swallow. In just a short period of time he had allowed a complete stranger to look into his heart and know everything about him. Strangely, he didn't feel at all bothered by this. He was much more aware of two important things.

He knew that Josh Goldberg had made a grave error in assuming this man was there for the taking, in *any* capacity.

But sitting here in the presence of Chong-ba, Tom Norman also knew without a doubt that Eva was lost to him forever. The thought filled him with immense sadness, and for some reason he was overwhelmingly convinced that destiny had selected separate paths for them, and that no matter how much he loved her, Eva's heart had never belonged to him. He forcibly ended his sad reverie, knowing it was time for him to reconnect with the outside world. He intended to do just that as soon as he had enjoyed a good night's sleep. He owed many people explanations, not least of all Colonel Appleyard. He had always valued the trust the Colonel had placed in him and it was time to come clean, but he had not spoken to him for weeks.

"Chong-ba, I need some sleep. Perhaps we can carry on this conversation in the morning?" He met the stare of the monk, who had not taken his eyes off him, as he pulled out one of his bags and unrolled a blanket. "Would that be okay? My weary body needs rest after this strenuous day." But the monk sat motionless and appeared to be in a trance. "Chong-ba?" Finally the little man spoke; his voice was barely above a whisper, but Tom could hear every word.

"The secrets you speak of, Mr. Norman lie within this space—*your* space. And your colleague Mr. Goldberg is seeking to use this knowledge to selfishly secure his own future. As you sleep and your active mind rests, there will be information available to you, and if you train yourself away from your thoughts, as your son does—" The monk paused and Tom sat up, suddenly wide awake. Chong-ba leaned forward as if to make sure no one else could overhear the last part of his sentence.

"If you could do this you would see—you would *know* that your very capable wife is going through great change. She is no stranger to these worlds that we spoke of. She knows." Chong-ba held Tom's gaze. "What does your heart tell you now, Mr. Norman?"

Chapter 12
QUADRAQUEST

The early morning sun wrapped the farmhouse and surrounding meadows in blissful warmth. North East England was showcasing one of its glorious summer's days and at barely seven in the morning, all was quiet and the air smelled sweet. The day was full of promise. Then, incessant banging on the large old oak front door abruptly disturbed the peace.

"Are you there, Steve?" Brad Weston cocked his head to one side and listened for any movement inside the house. He glanced briefly at the papers in his hand and could barely contain his excitement. "Steve!" This time he yelled his friend's name with more vigor and forced his normally impatient nature to remain as composed as possible. *Darn! If he knew what I have in my hand, he'd fly out of that bed!* Brad suspected Steve would be completely exhausted from the previous day's activities. *Imagine punishing yourself the way he did.* "Steve! Come on buddy, open this bloody door!" A few more times he banged hard. *Jesus, he sleeps like the dead.* "Steve!" *I don't care if I wake up the entire bloody neighborhood for this.* Brad looked around and noticed the mail flap in the door. He opened it quickly and hollered loudly through the opening. "Steve Ballantire, drag your tired ass out of that bed. Right now!"

Steve moved reluctantly in his sleep, annoyed by the intrusion of the persistent banging and calling of his name. His mind vaguely identified Brad's voice, but his body demanded more rest and tried unsuccessfully to override the interruption and go back to sleep. However, the racket continued and he finally gave in. He opened his eyes slowly and tried to orient himself as the room swam hazily into focus. Then he dropped a tired leg out of bed and winced in pain as his foot hit the floor. *Oh, my God, what have I done? Maybe I'm getting too old for this.* He smiled wryly to himself. *Nah! I won, didn't I? Stop the banging!*

"I'm coming, Brad! Hold on!" He sat up in bed, feeling his body protest even simple movements. His thoughts reached back to a couple of days ago when the competition had started and almost instantly the physical pain was replaced with satisfaction and pleasure at the success of his accomplishment. Planning the Quadraquest had taken months out of his busy schedule but the competition was *his* brainchild, and Steve did nothing in half measures. Not only did he meticulously plan every challenging aspect of the contest, but he also personally participated, thus demonstrating the discipline required to successfully complete an event of this nature.

Steve's athletic ability was complemented by an illustrious academic career, excelling in both from a young age. Born into a family of farmers, the lineage of the Ballantires could be traced back hundreds of years. He was anchored in generations of men who loved the land and understood the delicate ecosystem that allowed them to learn from it, but also make a good living. The farm was surrounded by the large estate of Bernard Harringdon, the local landowner with whom George Ballantire, Steve's father, had a very good relationship. Mr. Harringdon also grasped the importance of ecological balance. Like his ancestors, he made untended pastures available to trusted farmers at a reasonable price, thus making it unnecessary to purchase expensive land.

This quaint and attractive part of North East England was the ideal place to raise livestock and, more importantly, carry on the famous tradition of horse training that had made Ballantire a household name in the area. The picturesque village of Elwick is nestled in this world of beauty and charm that draws potential equestrians from all regions of the UK and indeed, parts of Europe and North America. A wave of excitement washed over the exclusive horse riding community when the competitive and generally aloof Arab fraternity expressed an interest to invest. They wanted to see their great thoroughbreds submitted to the rigorous training offered by experts to enhance their already formidable reputation as horse breeders.

As a child, Steve had the run of the land and he knew every hill, every trail, all the secret hideouts where they had played as children, and he used this area extensively to do the grueling training the Quadraquest required. George was openly proud of his only offspring who, despite his vigorous intellectual pursuits, had shown a keen interest in maintaining the farm. With a demanding academic load, Steve employed a few experts to help him run the farming operation, and the older Ballantires could retire satisfied that Steve had it all under control.

When Steve was a youngster, George keenly watched his son's natural ability to work with horses and marveled at his capacity to read behavior patterns in animals that came to the farm for training. As Steve grew older, he and Janet often stood at a distance and watched him tear over the open meadows as his body moved in harmony with the strength of the animal beneath him.

"*That* is equestrian poetry, the union between a man and his horse." Janet would whisper in awe. It was a favorite expression of hers and each time it made him smile for he knew her love for their handsome child was boundless. Over the years his parents had become used to his athletic and equestrian accomplishments, but it was his interest in martial arts that they did not understand. Neither of them had a history of athletic prowess, and they were mystified with the origins of his love of physical activity, especially the dedication he exhibited in mastering skills, from *Akido* to *Zui Han Chuan*.

George was enamored with his son's diversity and relentless pursuit of mastery. Descending from a long line of devout farmers, he was immensely proud when the school of Physics and Applied Mathematics at Newcastle University had honored Steve with professorship to lead and chair this prestigious department. Through the years he had seen many beautiful women on his son's arm but they were rarely brought home to meet the parents, and every so often George wondered why his son had not yet found a woman to share his life. But Janet was convinced that she knew.

"He's waiting for someone, George. Steve won't settle for anyone less than the right woman." George looked at his wife of forty five years and chuckled. She was an incurable romantic and her still finely tuned female instincts noticed things others easily missed.

"He's waiting for the right one you say, Janet? Well, he had better hurry! At forty one our Steve is not getting any younger. Besides," he said with a twinkle in his eye, "I didn't have any trouble spotting a winner when I snagged you, did I? And as I understand there is no shortage of attractive contenders to be the new Mrs. Ballantire. Could it be that hard then?"

She didn't respond immediately. Through the panoramic window of their spacious downtown apartment, to which they had now retired, her eyes wandered over the bay area at the prestigious marina of Hartlepool. She caught a glimpse of a beautiful yacht negotiating the marina lock gates. Janet knew that George was referring to the inevitable rumors amongst staff members at the farm, of women who stayed over for the night.

"He's a grown man and no one expects him to be celibate!" she sighed with exasperation, knowing full well he was teasing. "And you won't understand anyway. He is not like you or me. Come to think of it, he's not like *anyone* I know."

George considered himself and his family fortunate that they had such a wealth of experienced trainers to employ as the area had entrenched itself with a colorful history molded around horse training. Only a few miles away was the site of the former world-famous racehorse training camp at Bishop Auckland, where multiple winners had been produced over the years. As a child, Steve had spent a great deal of his time there studying horses and their habits. He instinctively knew the tone of voice to use for commands; he could read and interpret expressions in their eyes and intuitively understood that the first and most crucial approach was always eye contact.

Steve knew that once this was established, a skillful master could gently coax any horse into a lifelong partnership. Having been in the presence of horses since his childhood, Steve had a great affinity for these magnificent animals, yet in his subconscious mind the feeling persisted that his kinship with them was not rooted in his present day memory. As a child he had often had dreams and visions of the perfect horse and every time he mounted a new steed, he automatically compared his dream to the horse he sat upon, but they always came up short. He once described to Brad exactly what he was looking for whilst his friend, and local veterinarian, did a routine check on the stable horses. But Brad just smiled and shook his head in good humor as he ran his hand expertly over the underbelly of the mare standing between them, feeling for lumps, the early telltale signs of a cyst or a growth.

"Perfection is hard to come by." Steve looked up and caught his eye.

"Is this advice for the women in my life or the horse I want you to find?"

Brad did not respond immediately and continued with his examination. They had grown up together and as adults, the bond between them had solidified. Yet, he had never seen Steve taken with any woman. He had courted many but had chosen none, and he remained an enigma to females who endeavored to establish a permanent closeness with him. Brad smiled, finally relenting.

"How will you know when you find her? So far, in over twenty years, you have excelled in physical training and academics but you have not dedicated the same attention to a female. Sometimes I think women are just not important enough to you and that you prefer to be alone."

"No one wants to be alone." He looked back at the horse they were examining and stroked its strong neck with a firm hand. "I know the right woman is around and when I see her, I will know." His resolve to remain single was more than skin deep. It was hard to explain that he had felt the presence of a woman who sometimes haunted his dreams but, upon awakening, the vision of her always dissolved into the brightness of day.

But right now, Brad was impatiently waiting outside the front door, about to break it down. Steve's tired body was still reluctant to move. He grinned boyishly, running a hand over the day-old stubble on his chin. *I really showed them, didn't I?* He relished the success of the event he had worked so hard to put together, after his disappointing age disqualification for the Olympic Modern Pentathlon. After this setback, he devised the Quadraquest, a competition much better suited to the English climate; one which he hoped would become a major event on the collegiate calendar. The absence of well-equipped swimming pools at international standards was no longer a deterrent, for this grueling contest was to be fought all on dry land, unlike the Modern Pentathlon, and required endurance and skill in its most refined forms.

Steve was extremely pleased that the competition had already worked its charm and permeated down through the educational faculties, to be accepted on the official student-teacher calendar of his own University. This was exactly the kind of recognition he needed to introduce the event into the international arena. He could barely contain his excitement at his personal participation in the two-day event of pistol shooting, fencing, cross country on horseback and cross-country running; all geared toward testing endurance.

Brad's contribution to the Quadraquest was invaluable; they had been working together on this athletic dream contest for a long time. A few inches shorter than Steve, Brad was slightly stockier in build with thick blonde hair. His jovial personality attracted women like a magnet and years later he convinced Caroline, the vivacious and outgoing darling of their schooldays, to become his wife.

While Steve maintained his level of participation in all sporting events, Brad had eventually toned his down to that of a great supporter and spectator to become an enthusiastic sideline specialist. A dedicated and disciplined athlete, Steve was nevertheless prepared for stiff competition in the six mile cross-country race of the first day. He knew his determination and years of training would be measured against the youthfulness of the majority of the competitors. Others of his age might have thought twice about participation, but he loved a challenge and looked forward to the contest, to be held in the beautiful Northumberland countryside, just north of the University of Newcastle.

As could be expected, quite a few of his students showed up to support their popular and well respected professor. Halfway into the race, Steve heard their screams and shouts that Morrison, a much younger athlete and former graduate student, was only slightly ahead of him. His legs were already beginning to hurt but, like all committed athletes, he felt a tremendous adrenalin surge at their encouragement and pushed himself even harder. The muscles in his body obeyed the determination in his mind and he slowly started gaining on the younger man.

As they rose to the summit of the next hill and started the grueling descent that so taxed and strained the quadriceps in the thighs, Steve suddenly saw them. His mathematical mind was alert and trained to notice inconsistencies and the two men dressed in suits observing his race from a distance, stood out starkly amongst the crowd of casually dressed supporters. With his attention focused on the race, these characters nevertheless bothered him subconsciously and he felt a fleeting, but real discomfort at their presence.

With only two hundred meters to the finish line and Morrison still ahead of him, he purposely pushed the strangers to the back of his mind and focused all his attention on the final effort of winning. The closing attempt would require him to increase his steady, strong run to the excruciating and almost impossible level of a sprint. Steve dug into a now almost empty reservoir of power and endurance, determined to locate a final burst of energy to maintain his aching lungs at maximum capacity for a few seconds longer.

The mammoth effort rewarded him with sudden force and vigor; a small grace, which he knew would be short-lived, if not used instantly. He surged forward, carried on this brief explosion of energy, surprising himself and the spectators as he swiftly caught up to a few feet behind Morrison. His daring move whipped the crowd into an instant frenzy as they realized that the younger man had been expecting to win the race and was oblivious of the six foot four mass of willpower about to pass him.

Morrison realized too late that he had been outwitted and outrun as he desperately hurled his body toward the finish line, but it was too late. Steve Ballantire's heart thundered loudly in his chest and he gasped for air but he got there first and almost instantly the track began swarming with elated well-wishers, astonished at his athleticism and physical accomplishment.

"You old son-of-a-gun!" Brad slapped his back and laughed, amazed at the final effort Steve had put forth. "What can I say? This race should go down in the history books. My God, you won like a thoroughbred!" Steve grimaced at the comparison, too tired to laugh.

"Thanks Brad. Did I earn that steak you are buying me tonight?"

"You sure did, but I can't stay. I have a vet call to make. I'll see you tonight after you have put them all to shame with your sharp shooting skills." Brad grinned. "That's what you're going to do, right?" Steve enjoyed the light banter with his good friend even in his state of physical exhaustion.

"Before you go, did you notice those guys in the suits?" He was still breathing heavily, endeavoring to regain his composure. "You have any idea who they were?"

"Yes, I saw them; they weren't exactly inconspicuous or subtle. I have no idea who they are. They were definitely not scouting for athletic talent." But later that day the same two men showed up at the shooting range where the second part of the competition was held. Through years of training, his marksmanship was unequaled and Steve won without exerting a great deal of effort. Yet, he felt distracted and concerned with the unusual presence of the well-dressed strangers, especially when he noticed one grabbing his ear and angling his head to the side. *Well, I'll be damned! He's talking to someone! Who the hell are these guys?*

Over dinner the suited strangers were temporarily forgotten as Brad enlightened Steve about his research and long-standing assignment to find a horse that met with Steve's requirements.

"You're a hard man to please. And right now I can't make any promises about it being the perfect horse. All I'm willing to say is that we're making headway."

"That is good enough for me, Brad."

"So, it is fencing tomorrow morning then?"

"One of my favorites."

"Your competitors will need all their skill and wits about them." He smiled. "But back to my mission again; I'm going to need about two days to put everything together. Delivery has been guaranteed, and you'll be amazed at the reasons, but before we get too excited, I have to check out some final x-rays. Good luck for tomorrow." He stood to leave. "Not that you need it. I'll be there. Get some rest."

Gray skies greeted the second day of the Quadraquest as Steve made his way down to the auditorium. His legs still felt somewhat shaky from the previous day's grueling running event and he knew he would have to rely greatly on his refined expertise and intuition to read his opponent. But he had looked forward to this entire day, for both fencing and show jumping evoked feelings and memories in him that he couldn't quite place. They brought an excitement and awareness into his physical body and aroused a familiarity that perplexed him. His favorite weapon was the foil for it represented the dueling implement used over centuries for defense and offense.

The great expertise and agility acquired through years of martial arts training set him in a class of his own, and he sent Morrison packing for the second time in two days. The final was to be decided between Steve and a French champion who was on a research assignment in England. With each hit he made, his memory banks registered a shock of recognition, and adrenalin poured into his system, brilliantly heightening his senses and leaving his opponent defeated and exhausted.

"I wouldn't want to be your enemy, Professor Ballantire. I am truly impressed!" said the French student as they shook hands. Steve smiled in good humor, puzzled again with the images that fencing always induced of an ancient soldier disarming his opponent.

The equestrian number had been purposely modified by Steve to cover extra cross-country activity, making it more hazardous. Fuelled by his success thus far, he was excited and could barely wait to get on horseback. After the fencing event, all participants were given time to acquaint themselves with the horses to partner them. Steve stood in front of the sturdy steed to be his companion and waited patiently until the horse looked at him. He didn't blink.

He waited quietly for a sign of acknowledgment from the big animal. It stood there for a long time eyeing him curiously, and then the horse neighed softly, snorted in submission and dug his front hooves into the soft soil. Steve nodded his head. *We have a deal. Great!* Then he mounted the big beast, and as he leaned forward to whisper in its ear, he felt every muscle of the horse underneath him tighten and quiver. When it was their turn they took off as one. Steve felt the huge animal stir beneath him and he was instantly transported to his childhood as they moved together in unison.

His desires and thoughts translated into just the right tone of voice as they flowed in gracious movements of harmony and precision, a man and his horse taking the field as if they had known each other forever. When he held the winning cup, Steve turned to the horse at his side, acknowledging its contribution by patting its neck. But while the cheering crowd was still overwhelmed with his performance over two days, Steve was already planning to upgrade his training program for the next year. *How else will an old guy like me be able to do this again?*

Steve finally gathered himself sufficiently to make it to the front door. He wrenched it open with irritation and immediately lifted a protective arm to his eyes as the bright sunlight assaulted him. Brad stood up from the wooden bench on the front porch and eyed Steve with disgust.

"Jesus! You look like shit," he said unceremoniously, his patience worn thin. "And that's a compliment, by the way."

"And a very good morning to you too, Bradley." With his eyes slowly adjusting to the glaring light, Steve folded his arms over his chest and leaned heavily against the doorpost, scrutinizing his friend. "This had better be very good." Brad's outgoing and impatient nature was at once irritated with the delay and excited with the news he couldn't wait to share.

"What's taken you so long? *Christ!* You have a woman back there?" Steve looked him over calmly and ignored the last question.

"What have you got, Brad? It looks like official papers."

"I've found him, Steve!" His impatience was momentarily forgotten and he could hardly contain himself. "I swear I have found him!" He waved the papers in the air. "These are all in order. And he is magnificent! He is a beaut, a real beaut—and he's as black as ebony."

Chapter 13
A Man And His Horse

Steve was filled with excitement and in high spirits as he drove down the winding country road toward The Spotted Cow, the local pub in the quaint, historic village of Elwick. Located on the outskirts of bustling Hartlepool, and dating back to the nineteenth century, the village had a proud history of training and breeding racehorses. It housed two traditional English Pubs of which one, The McOrville Inn, was named after a famous racehorse champion. The owner of the horse that Brad had found, hailed from the Doncaster area some hundred odd miles south of Elwick, and he was about to meet him in the other traditional pub, named The Spotted Cow. His trusted friend's assurances still rang clearly in his ears and he remembered Brad's enthusiasm the day after the Quadraquest when he had come to inform him of his find. In the spacious and comfortable kitchen he had finally heard more details over a steaming cup of coffee.

"The horse comes from Wroot, near Doncaster?" Steve had asked, leaning back in his chair. He stretched his long legs in front of him and grimaced with pain. After what he had put his body through, he expected recovery to be slow. "What were you doing in the Doncaster area?"

"Location of the Quarterly Veterinarian meeting. I might have mentioned it to you in passing, but I don't quite remember. As you know, injuries are a specialty of mine." Steve nodded but waited for Brad to continue. "The local vet approached me to take a look at an injured horse belonging to one of his clients. The injury occurred recently, and with a bunch of experts on his doorstep, he wanted a second opinion." Brad put down his cup and leaned forward. "I couldn't believe my eyes when I saw him. He's injured alright, but his stature completely overshadows the wound and I immediately thought of you. But of course, I was there to give my medical opinion and it was only after I received a copy of the x-rays and did a full examination that the owner, Mr. Emerson, revealed that he had changed his mind about surgery." He leaned back and scratched his head absentmindedly.

"Emerson said he didn't want to go through with such expensive treatment. He had bought the horse from an Arabian acquaintance, intending to race it, but it was injured shortly after its arrival here in England. I suggested that corrective surgery could very well put him back on the racetrack, but he seemed reluctant to take a chance on something that couldn't be guaranteed. That's when he mentioned that he should perhaps cut his losses and sell. And thinking of you, I immediately asked for the first option to purchase. There is just something about this horse, Steve." Brad stared at him. "When you see him, you will know what I mean; I can't imagine many of *his* caliber around!"

After having searched for so long, Brad was adamant the sum asked for this steed would not only be well spent, but also a real bargain, and his enthusiasm was wholly contagious. Steve had smiled quietly at his fervor, confident that if anyone understood the qualities he was looking for, Brad did. They were both excellent riders, educated from a young age to identify spirited horses with a strong sense of independence.

These horses were more difficult to train but once a bond had been established, they handled beautifully and took pride in executing commands. Steve had not yet laid eyes on the stallion he was about to sign a deal for, but he trusted Brad's skill and knowledge implicitly. Earlier that day he had gone over the official papers with a fine tooth comb and he could hardly wait to meet Mr. Emerson, as he found a parking space beside the village green opposite the solid wood front door of The Spotted Cow.

With its whitewashed walls and black-slated roof, the two storied building extended a friendly welcome to visitors and locals. The window baskets were overflowing with lush greenery and the handwritten specials on the pavement blackboard invited passers-by to partake in the hearty food and affability of a gracious owner and jovial guests. Steve particularly enjoyed the ambiance; he had spent many happy hours with friends and family inside the walls of this quaint country pub.

At the entrance he was immediately welcomed by a warm buzz of activity and laughter; the aroma of wonderful English cooking infused the air. Almost immediately the pain and discomfort he had endured during the Quadraquest was forgotten as he scanned the faces of some of the locals around him. Steve was glad that this comfortable, relaxing place was to be the venue for signing the documents and securing the deal for the stud he had spent so much time looking for.

From his seat, he kept an eye on the front door, and Steve recognized Jack Emerson from Brad's description as soon as he entered the busy pub with a little girl in tow. Brad had told him that the locals in Wroot gossiped jokingly that Emerson went nowhere without his boater, a traditional English hat woven from straw, and his pipe hanging from the corner of his mouth. The deceiving casual look obscured a wealthy horse trainer. But although Mr. Emerson hailed from the sizeable horse training fraternity, Steve was not personally acquainted with the middle-aged, portly gentleman approaching him. He had heard that he descended from a long chain of South Yorkshire breeders. Steve stood politely to identify himself.

"Mr. Emerson." He was greeted with a warm smile and before he could continue, the older man clasped two firm hands around his outstretched hand.

"Jack. Please, call me Jack. The only Mr. Emerson I know is my father and he's long gone. And you must be Steve Ballantire?" The soft-spoken man exuded kindness.

"I am very pleased to meet you." Then Steve looked down to where a little hand was visible from behind the older man's legs, holding onto his pants, and said loud enough for the child to hear. "Mr. Emerson—Jack, thank you for making the trip to our neck of the woods. Now, won't the two of you join me for a bite to eat?" The two men's eyes met briefly and then Steve looked around searchingly as Jack quickly picked up on his game. "But where did *the girl* disappear? I could have sworn I saw the most beautiful child follow you in here?" Still hiding, she could hardly contain herself and quickly stuck her head around her grandfather's legs.

"I'm here!" she laughed elfishly and tilted her head sideways, partially hiding her pretty face behind tumbling, golden curls. Then she drew back again to conceal herself behind Jack, obviously thrilled that she had tricked Steve.

"Ah! And please meet the lovely Natalie, Steve. She is my wonderful granddaughter and only six years old, but much cleverer than you or I. Sometimes we can't see her because she can make herself disappear and then no one can find her!" Unable to contain her excitement any longer, she jumped out to reveal all of herself, enchanting the two men with her contagious laugh and playful antics. With the formalities now out of the way, Steve bent down to her, inquiring kindly.

"Would you care to have lunch with us, young lady?" Her response was another soft, bubbly giggle. She was entirely thrilled with the attention and tucked closely under Jack's wing as they took their seats in the privacy of a more secluded corner.

With the official papers spread over the solid wooden table, Jack scrutinized them once again. Natalie briefly glanced at the documents and realized her grandfather's attention was diverted to business matters. Without a word, she turned her gaze directly onto Steve and studied him openly with the characteristic candor of a young child. Then her face turned more serious and a tiny frown creased her smooth forehead. Steve watched the changing expressions with interest.

She was a very attractive child. Dressed in denim overalls with a pretty blue and red plaid shirt underneath, her beauty was highlighted by the careless innocence of her age. He had noticed the lively and animated interaction with her grandfather. Her conversation with the older man was characterized with frequent spontaneous laughs, embellished by energetic hand and head gestures which occasionally caused her big blue eyes to disappear behind an unruly mass of soft, yellow curls. But now, as she stared at him, she kept quite still and seemed a little more tense than a minute before.

"Bullet is my friend." The words came out simply, with just a trace of sadness. She kept watching him. "Is he going to live with you now?" Steve looked at the little face and realized that a bond had been established between her and the horse and the thought of losing him most likely caused her some pain. He was suddenly eerily aware of a strange quality around the gorgeous child so earnestly talking to him. With no experience of young children, he was at a loss to answer her question, or appease the anxiety of losing something seemingly so special to her. Nevertheless, he didn't want to encourage a discussion that might spoil the business deal going down between her grandfather and himself.

"Is *that* his name, Natalie?" He pretended not to know what the pitch-black stallion was called, even though it was clearly stated on all the official papers. "My goodness, who would think of giving a horse such a wonderful name?"

"My grandpa did," she said without hesitation, still staring at Steve. "He runs very fast, that's why." She uttered a little sigh, obviously exasperated at having to educate him on such a simple matter. Steve couldn't help but smile at the little woman he noticed in the child in front of him; she was surely going to break a few hearts down the road. "But now his foot is sore, and he can't run far anymore." She dropped her voice and looked away as if she had a secret to share but wasn't ready to tell.

"Now just look at my little representative here, Steve!" Jack had overheard her comments and he turned to Natalie, speaking confidentially. "I should take you everywhere with me, then you can do all the talking! Isn't that right, Miss Natalie?" She smiled shyly at Jack. She was a little embarrassed but said nothing. In response to her grandfather's light reprimand she hid her face in the comfort of his sleeve and snuggled closer to him.

Steve knew about as much of the injury as Brad had told him, but Natalie had unexpectedly opened the door to explore more of the detail and he was curious as to the exact circumstances that had led to the transaction they were about to conclude. When Brad had first shown him a picture of the horse that day, he was slightly taken aback and confused at the instant shock that ran through his body, but he put it down to his interest in exceptional horses and then forgot about it. He had no personal interest in horse racing and planned to use Bullet as a stud.

In the short summary of the horse's history and background, the documents stated that Bullet had been bought from Azzam, an Arabian owner who, from time to time, had stabled at Bishop Auckland, the former training camp further to the west. All Jack now needed was for Natalie to confuse the buyer sitting opposite him by disseminating unnecessary information in her "advisory role" as Bullet's most loyal supporter.

"How did it happen, Jack? The injury, I mean." Steve sensed Jack's discomfort and tried to put him at ease. "Oh, I'm not planning to race him at all, so the injury is not of particular importance to me. But I'd be interested to know more, regardless." He had been scouting for a suitable stud for many years and finding the right thoroughbred was a bigger task than anticipated. He had acquired three mares over the past few months with good lineage, and now he was about to obtain a thoroughbred from Arabian stock, which meant he was in a position to produce a breed suitable for some of his new Arab customers.

"If it wasn't for his high temperament, the accident would probably never have happened." Jack spoke softly. "He is not the easiest horse to mount and ride. I've never seen so much independence; it's almost as if he's aware of himself, but in a different way than any other horse I've seen. Bullet seems to know what he can and can't do and he is very selective about who he allows to mount him." Jack looked away and smiled down at Natalie who was still nestled close to him, listening attentively as her grandfather spoke. He lifted a hand and tenderly tucked a wild curl behind her ear. "We'll both miss him, won't we, Natalie?"

"He doesn't want to race, Grandpa." She looked up at Jack, intensity shining in her blue eyes. "He's a special horse, Grandpa; I told you." Jack smiled warmly, catching Steve's eye again.

"This is where I become helpless, Steve. How can I argue with my grandchild's ability to speak horse language? If she says he doesn't want to race, then I should listen. Right?" Steve quietly watched their intimate interaction with each other and realized that love was not in short supply between the older man and his delightful grandchild.

"How do you know he doesn't want to race, Natalie?" he inquired of the blonde, nymph-like child sitting across the table. But she had suddenly become very quiet, averting her eyes and hanging her head.

"I just know," she said barely above a whisper, fidgeting with a button on her overalls, still refusing to make eye contact.

"Well, Steve, Bullet hadn't been in the country very long when I bought him from his previous owners, who neglected to inform us of his headstrong nature. We discovered after his injury that whilst in their possession he had been equally selective of whom he would allow to straddle him. In retrospect, I realize that that was the reason they couldn't keep him." Jack put his arm protectively around his granddaughter and hugged her lightly, confirming his support for her convictions. "So Natalie is right. With his first training session the trouble started. We made an effort to use different riders to see if he would take to any of them, but his temperamental nature made it very difficult to establish a routine or preference. It was impossible to know if it was merely the damp weather he didn't like, or if we were simply unable to supply a suitable rider who would understand his unusual traits."

"Bullet has only one rider." She said the words under her breath, but Steve heard them and his body registered a shock wave similar to the one he had felt the day he saw a picture of the horse, only this time it was stronger. He stared at the child but she kept toying with her buttons, refusing to look at him. He turned to Jack.

"What does she mean?" he asked, mystified by her words, and a little perturbed as to where the child's participation in this conversation may lead.

"See? That's it, Steve! She knows better because she talks to Bullet!" Jack let out a deep belly laugh, gathering her tiny body for a brief moment close to him. "Natalie knows because she saw it all. If you had been there the day he finally allowed a rider from a neighboring farm to mount him, you would know what I mean. After the second round, he suddenly began to balk and tried to shake the young boy at every turn. Then he rose onto his hind legs, flared his nostrils like one possessed and veered off the course into the open fields where we had barbed wire laid out to repair some fencing. It snagged his left front hoof just as he finally launched the desperate rider from his back, fiercely tugging and pulling at the wire until it caused part of his hoof to separate. It has never healed properly and still grows inward." He slowly let out a sigh and continued.

"So there you go—the glorious animal's history and hence, our meeting today. He'd be a great stud, I'm sure, as long as you don't want to ride or race him." Jack's cell phone suddenly rang in one of his pockets and after fishing around to silence the persistent ringing, he finally extricated it from the breast pocket of his jacket. "Pardon me," he excused himself, "I have to take this, but I'll be right back. Steve, will you keep an eye on my precious girl here?" He picked up his hat and pipe, and made his way to the front door. Natalie quietly watched her grandfather leave. Then she turned her head and caught Steve's eye. She spoke softly under her breath.

"Bullet isn't his real name." She didn't blink, calmly waiting for his response.

"Oh?" Steve was intrigued with the child's unusual behavior. "Do you know his real name?" he asked politely.

"Yes, Grandpa showed me. But he liked Bullet better." Her voice sounded tentative at first but then it grew stronger. "I like his real name, so I copied it when I learned to write and I always keep it with me." She appeared a little anxious and nervous and Steve wasn't sure if she had already felt the effect of separating with this horse, or if there was something amiss that he didn't understand, or to which he wasn't privy. Then she stuck her hand into the top pocket of her plaid shirt and pulled out a small piece of paper. She held it between the thumb and forefinger of her right hand and watched him closely. Steve noticed it was a bigger piece folded into a tiny square; it looked worn and tattered. Somehow he sensed that he should not interrupt this child, so he let her speak, watching her beautiful, expressive face. "We always went for long walks around the farm." Her voice dropped to a murmur and it became soft and sweet, like one remembering a dream. "He never tried to run away, so Grandpa didn't tether him. When his foot was still very sore, we walked slowly." She smiled secretively. "I didn't know he was looking for something." Steve was completely caught up in the delicate, childlike spell she had cast over him.

"Bullet was looking for something?" he inquired softly. He didn't know if he was unintentionally playing her game or if he really needed to know the answer.

"Yes." She suddenly grew very intense. "It was hidden in the grass and I didn't see it until he wouldn't walk any further. He kept sniffing and when I looked, there it was!" Her big blue eyes were fixed on his face.

"*What*, Natalie?" A strange feeling stirred in him, a vague urgency he had not felt before. He didn't know what to make of the girl's strange behavior. He was partially confused as to whether she was fibbing or merely fantasizing, but either way, he couldn't tear his eyes away from her.

"The owl's feather," she whispered softly, not moving her gaze from his face. "It was a gray tail feather. When I picked it up and tickled his nose, Bullet made very funny noises. I think he cried, but I don't know why." The last statement was barely audible; she leaned forward in confidence as if to make sure no one else heard a word of what she was sharing with him. "I saved the feather, because it belongs to Bullet. But if he is going to live with you…"

Steve didn't move. He watched spellbound as she unfolded the tiny square of paper and placed it between them on the table. He leaned forward to read the two words scrawled in the unsteady hand of a six-year-old and, drawn like a moth to a flame, he turned the paper to decipher the words more easily. *Quah Dreamer.* He read the name with his mind, but without warning his heart caught painfully in his throat.

"His real name is Quah Dreamer?" he asked hoarsely, confused and bewildered at his own reaction. He had never heard this name and yet the sound of it awakened something incredibly confusing, a faint pleasure or a forgotten pain that set his heart racing.

"Yes." Natalie reached into the deep side pocket of her overalls. "And if you take him, then this belongs to you." She laid the single gray tail feather alongside the crumpled piece of paper with Bullet's authentic name written in her handwriting. "Quah Dreamer and the feather go together." She finally sat back; relieved that she had at last got it all out.

Steve stared at the feather and every muscle in his body tensed and ached in fleeting recognition of something he still couldn't place. What felt like an ancient memory, struggled to reach his conscious mind, but vanished each time as quickly as it came. He wanted to speak but his mouth was dry; he just kept looking at the little girl. *Who is this child?* Finally his voice returned and he managed a crooked smile.

"Thank you, Natalie." Then he reached out and placed his hand over the feather and piece of paper. He lowered his voice, pretending to conspire with her so only she could hear him. "Do you want to know what I think?" The man and the child looked intently at each other.

"What?" she whispered back.

"I think Quah Dreamer will let me ride him. And I think you should come to visit when he lives on my farm as often as you like." Her face lit up with boundless joy at his words and she jumped excitedly out of her chair to share the news with her grandfather who was strolling back down the isle. Steve looked at the feather in his hand and a shiver of great anticipation ran down his spine. "Quah Dreamer," he repeated softly. "Why does your name so tug at my heart?"

For the next two days Steve's attention was diverted to professional matters at the University. The day after his meeting with Jack Emerson and the enchanting Natalie, he learned at a faculty meeting that his department was to accommodate a special guest somewhere in the near future. The specific time of arrival was yet undefined and subject to a host of factors not under the direct control of the school. The only sketchy, but rather intriguing detail was that an exceptionally gifted child would become his protégé for an unknown period of time. He was expected to prepare a set of papers and programs to stimulate the growth and development of a young boy who allegedly was in the ranks of a genius. What made his task even more challenging was that he had also been informed that the child suffered from Asperger's syndrome, a form of autism. Steve found the circumstances unusual and slightly suspect.

"Why not Oxford or Cambridge? And what do I know of handicapped children?" He directed his question to Henry O'Malley, the Vice Chancellor, who rarely attended any of these meetings but now acted as the spokesperson.

"You have been selected as Hugo Norman's tutor. My only other information is that the boy has been educated in your subject matter at a very high level in Tel Aviv. You are expected to continue along the same lines," O'Malley said evenly, without blinking. "But regarding you specifically? Well, your reputation reaches beyond the boundaries of the North East it seems, Steve. Perhaps they have heard of the professor who not only won his own grueling Quadraquest, but has a reputation for befriending his students?"

O'Malley attempted to circumvent the answer by making light of the question, but knew he wasn't fooling the man in front of him. He relied on the fact that Steve would not press for more information in the presence of other faculty members but he nevertheless fully expected him to pursue more detail at an appropriate time. The meeting was finally adjourned and he met O'Malley at the door as they prepared to leave.

"Who will be responsible for the supervision of this special child, Henry?" The older man made brief eye contact, but looked away quickly.

"His mother. And they will not be living on campus." Henry had a healthy respect for Steve's impressive accomplishments, both athletically and academically but he unconsciously avoided that direct stare, which he found unnerving.

"I'm not concerned with their living arrangements, Henry. But I am relieved to hear we are not expected to be nurse maids for a child within the demanding curriculum we have for our own students." And with those words, he was gone. He could barely wait to get on the road the following day to finally meet Bullet and bring him back to his new home.

The scenic drive to Wroot took about an hour and a half, after which he finally entered through the farm gates and drove onto the rough cinder track. Steve spotted Natalie's golden hair immediately where she sat atop a much smaller horse. He slowed his vehicle and came to a complete halt, waiting for Natalie to approach him on what he assumed to be Razzle, the pony Jack had told him about earlier that week. Steve couldn't help but admire the ability of the six-year-old to handle an animal so much bigger than herself.

"Hello, Steve!" She leaned down from Razzle and reached a small hand to the one he had stretched out in greeting. "We've been waiting all morning!" Her eyes were dancing and she smiled brightly. "And Bullet is waiting too." She pointed to the field behind her. "But you'll have to walk."

"Are you coming, Natalie?" he asked as he got out of his SUV. She shook her head and stroked Razzle's neck, smiling softly.

"No, we'll wait for you at the house. But hurry up! He is impatient!" And with that she expertly turned her pony around. "I'll go tell Grandpa you're here," she called over her shoulder as she took off in a light gallop toward the farmhouse; her playful giggle disappearing into the wind.

Steve closed the gate behind him and stood motionless. The warm summer's day had become very quiet, as if it too, was waiting.

He carefully looked around the soft green field and the hills nearby and although he could not see the horse anywhere, its presence was unmistakable. He could *feel* it. Then a strange and irrational idea surfaced. *Have I been here before?* He tried to dismiss the thought but it persisted and returned, each time with more urgency. *Why does this feel so familiar?* His rational mind grappled in frustration with the recurring, bewildering notion, the nagging call for recognition.

Then he heard the approaching gallop. It came from behind the nearest hill and Steve's heart tightened with excitement and anticipation, making it hard to breathe and near impossible to move. He stood riveted as the magnificent black stallion finally appeared. With its mane flying wildly in the wind, it headed straight for him, thundering its way down the hill.

Somewhere deep inside of him, the scab of a very old wound sloughed off and his body began shaking, but he took a deep breath and forcibly steadied himself as the horse drew nearer. *Oh, my God!* He watched in awe as the big animal came to a sudden halt a few feet away from him. His shiny coat reflected the sunlight brilliantly as he reared onto his hind legs to greet him but the wild, uncontrolled neigh the horse let out sounded more like a tormented cry. Steve instantly reached out to touch and comfort him and as they stood face to face, the kinship was unmistakable and very disturbing, for it was not anchored in conscious memory.

"We know each other, Quah Dreamer. Don't we?" he whispered into the horse's ear, overcome with emotion. "But how?"

At the gate to the field neither Jack nor Natalie moved. After a long wait at the house, they had come to find Steve, but found themselves quietly admiring the skill and the grace of the man so effortlessly riding the black stallion without a saddle. Then Natalie turned to Jack.

"See, I told you, Grandpa. Bullet is a special horse."

"Yes, you were right, sweetheart," he said under his breath, still appreciating the magnificent demonstration of harmony between a man and his horse. "And you were right about something else too." Jack put an arm around her shoulders and drew her close. "Bullet has only one rider. And he has finally found him."

Chapter 14
Point Of No Return

When Eva had left word at the British Embassy for Tom regarding her whereabouts, she also met with, and informed James Stanway that her mother's house was under surveillance and that the phones were bugged. This news disturbed him greatly and he looked at her with more than a touch of concern.

"How do you know this?" His voice concealed his alarm for the implications of this new development. With Tom missing and his family in apparent danger, the tables were suddenly turned and Stanway cunningly recognized his chance to manipulate the situation. Placing the Normans under British protection would surely lure Tom back, which was a matter of urgency. While Eva explained about the white van and Uri's help in discovering the listening devices, James remained guarded and silent. Eva was no one's fool either—he would have to weigh his options carefully. Then he spoke solemnly.

"This is a drastic turn of events." She nodded, but said nothing, and he continued without blinking. The Silver Fox had his eye securely fixed on the target. "Our authority in a foreign country, understandably, is limited. If you want us to help you, then you must understand that we cannot protect you or Hugo effectively unless you are on British soil. Offering our assistance means that you and Hugo will have to relocate; at least temporarily, to the United Kingdom. That could take some time. Do you realize this?" She nodded apprehensively, but he waited for his words to sink in before continuing. James was a skillful observer and he didn't miss the flicker of hesitation that crossed her face.

"You are both Israeli citizens and spiriting you from this country could cause a huge international scandal, one Britain can ill afford at this time. I'm going to ask you not to contact the Embassy again until we get in touch with you. And you can leave it to us to find a way. We will get our people on to this immediately, and if the facts check out, we will have to find a way to move fast." He walked her to the door and somehow his demeanor seemed softer, more sympathetic than before. However, his departing words sent a shiver of apprehension down her spine. "Eva, if you know where Tom is, you must tell me, please." Her soft reply was without any hesitation.

"I have no idea where my husband is, James. You have my word on that." Eva's heart was heavy as she left James Stanway's office. *Why doesn't James know where Tom is?* Then an absurd thought struck her and she remembered the awkward dinner she and Tom had had with Josh Goldberg. *Azvaalder and Tom? Could there be a connection?* The implication was too sinister to consider and she put it forcibly out of her mind.

Before the door had closed behind her, Stanway was dialing Appleyard. They had just been handed a trump card and they couldn't afford to make a mistake. Maintaining support for the Norman child's gifts would be an important part of the façade, and he relied on Appleyard to identify an unobtrusive spot to place Hugo on short notice. Despite Tom's frequent absences, everyone in the department knew how important his family was to him. As yet, Stanway didn't know what Josh Goldberg was up to, but he would find out real quick and beat him to the post. Eva and Hugo was the only bait Tom Norman would take.

Two days later Eva did her usual midweek shopping in the local market and, as always, made her final stop at the flower shop. Isaac Halevi, who had occupied the same stall for more than ten years, greeted her with his wrinkled face and customary smile.

"I kept some yellow roses for you. Just in case." He grinned. "I know how much you love them." He held up a fresh bunch of yellow roses to her face and she laughed joyfully, closing her eyes as she smelled the delicate fragrance.

"They're lovely, Isaac. Thank you, I'll take them. Better hurry though; I've more errands to run." She paid for the flowers and watched as he expertly wrapped them. Eva waved as she exited the store and made her way toward the crowded parking lot.

Unwrapping the flowers in the kitchen at Carmela's house, she noticed two plastic packets taped to the stems of the roses. One was the standard preserving crystals that came with fresh cut flowers, but the other one had her name on it. She hesitated only briefly, and then slipped the packet with her name unobtrusively into her pocket. Eva took her time to trim the stems and arrange the sweet smelling roses into a wide mouthed glass vase filled with lukewarm water and a tinge of sugar. Then she quickly grabbed her car keys and headed for the front door without telling Carmela where she was going. She needed to get away from any hidden surveillance equipment in the house before she opened the little white packet. *Isaac? Is he involved?* Her head was spinning. She had no idea, and she probably would never know the answer to this question.

At the first red light, she fished it out of her pocket and tore off the plastic cover, realizing for the first time how fast her heart was beating. The message was cryptic and brief. *Columbus Restaurant tomorrow, noon. Bring Hugo. Table reserved. Contact is Robert McGahan. Do not mention this to anyone. Destroy this note. J.S.* Eva's heart filled with fear as she put a shaky hand over her chest, feeling its erratic beat. The words of James Stanway echoed in her ears. *You will have to relocate to the United Kingdom. We cannot protect you unless you are on British soil.* For one incredible, mitigating moment her conscious mind rejected what was happening, and she contemplated the possibility of being trapped in a nightmare, fervently hoping that she would wake up and none of this would be real.

But then she looked at the note again and knew it was all true. She and Hugo were both in danger, and the most frustrating part was that she still didn't know what Azvaalder wanted with her child. In the midst of her anguish, Tom's face drifted into her mind, and years of repressed frustration and anger spontaneously welled to the surface. Her eyes stung with bitter tears. *We shouldn't have to go through this alone, Tom! It isn't fair!* Eva dropped her forehead briefly on the steering wheel and stifled a sob. *I'm scared, and I'm lonely. What happened to our love?* She dried her eyes with the back of her hand. *I don't even know who you are anymore.*

When the light turned green she was composed and her mind made up. *Do not mention this to anyone.* The words in the note echoed hollowly in her head, driving a painful wedge between loyalty to her family and the necessity of trusting a stranger. She had no intention of telling anyone about the scheduled meeting the next day, but trusting her mother implicitly, Carmela had a right to know if she and Hugo were temporarily leaving Israel.

"Where have you been, Eva?" Carmela was waiting on the porch, a concerned expression on her face. "Hugo has speech lessons today, so I know—"

"It is nothing to do with Hugo, Mum." She walked up to her mother and put an arm around her shoulders, whispering in her ear. "He won't be home for a while. Let's go for a walk." Aware that something strange was indeed going on, Carmela obeyed and fell into step beside her daughter. Eva steered her mother up the road in the opposite direction from where she had previously noticed the parked van. They casually strolled toward the park with the big outdoor fishpond where they fed the fishes as children; it was three blocks away from the house. Carmela listened in stunned silence as Eva filled her in on everything she knew in their native Hebrew tongue. Eva had inherited her mother's dark good looks and as Carmela had aged well, she was often mistaken for Eva's older sibling.

She ended her talk with Carmela by stressing the urgency for them to leave the country temporarily. A long silence followed after Eva had finished speaking. The day was very hot and the sun beat down ruthlessly as they slowly made their way up the road. Finally Carmela broke the silence. Her voice was shaky and she halted to take both Eva's hands in hers, her eyes mirroring the fear in her heart.

"This is very extreme. *Oh, my God!* Is there really no other way?"

"Hugo is all I have, Mum." Carmela heard the tremor in her voice and looked into her eldest daughter's tear-filled eyes, acknowledging the sad truth of that statement. Eva had been alone for a very long time and even though Carmela had always liked Tom, his wife had virtually raised their son on her own. Tom was a part-time husband and father and she understood why Eva couldn't risk Hugo's safety in any way. She had suspected for quite a while that Tom had lost his significance as a man, but never pried or tried to discuss the matter with her fiercely private daughter.

"Who else knows, Eva?" Carmela asked softly.

"Uri knows. He confirmed the camera surveillance in the house when you were away on one of your regular bridge days. Come, let us keep walking." She took her mother gently by the arm and steered her into the park entrance.

"When is this going to happen?" Carmela's voice sounded faint. She was struggling to understand the full implication of what she was hearing. Her daughter and grandchild were about to leave the shores of Israel, their country of birth, and the realization of this shattering news made it hard to maintain her composure. All she could think of was when she would see them again. She had no answers to all the questions flooding into her mind and felt utterly bewildered.

"I don't know; I'm waiting to hear." Eva held herself together for her mother's sake. "Everything seems to be on a need-to-know basis, I don't quite understand why."

"What about Margalit? Will you tell her?" Carmela's question drew Eva's thoughts to her younger sister, but she remained silent. Margalit, fair skinned and flaxen-haired, was married to Oren Steiner, a technical sales representative for an electronics components manufacturer. That fact alone bothered Eva, for she knew that in an industry such as his, everyone knew each other. Moreover, Oren's company operated on the components side of the industry and it was not inconceivable that they could have supplied parts for Azvaalder. She had no idea what the real circumstances were. She only knew that Azvaalder had become a poisonous snake, ready to strike, and she and Hugo had to get away as soon as possible.

Oren had always troubled her more than she let on to Margalit, who seemed very much in love with her street-wise husband of five years. Eva had learned to refrain from comment when Margalit endlessly regaled them with how Oren had worked his way from dismal poverty to affluence. The swagger of the skinny man with the sunken cheeks and dirty blonde hair belied his humble beginnings. Even before they were married, Eva had noticed Oren's foul temper and how a particular look from him in Margalit's direction had the power to instantly silence her customary, happy chatter. She had no doubt that her sweet younger sister constantly had to earn the favor of her rather superficial and domineering husband.

"Are you going to leave without telling Margalit?" Carmela broke quietly into her reverie, repeating her earlier question.

"I cannot tell her. I don't trust Oren, and I never have. I'm sorry that it has to be this way, but we cannot take any chances." Eva still remembered the day the news broke within the family that Azvaalder was going to take Hugo on as their protégé. Oren and Margalit were only newlyweds then but on that day his behavior was completely out of character. Whereas he ordinarily limited contact with his attractive sister-in-law, he inundated her with endless questions of what the implications were for them and for Hugo. Even Tom, home on one of his rare visits, wondered what had possessed his brother-in-law. Eva couldn't help but be apprehensive in Oren's company. "I will go and see her and it might as well be today when Hugo returns from speech lessons. I want to see her before we leave, but Margalit does not have to know what is going on. She won't understand anyway."

The next day Eva fetched Hugo early from school and they headed together into Herzliya Pituach, a neighborhood of Herzliya. Only ten kilometers north of Tel Aviv, pocketed amongst an on-going building construction program, are some of the finest beaches in Israel; a paradise to holidaymakers and sun worshippers alike.

Herzliya Pituach is the epicenter of Israel's high tech industry, locally known as Silicon Coast. Scattered around the many high rise buildings are countless restaurants catering to mass-market tastes with international cuisine to match. As stipulated by James Stanway, Eva and Hugo were on their way to the popular Columbus restaurant in the Sh'ar HaYam Building. Specializing in American food, it was a favorite with both the American and British Embassy personnel, offering open and convivial surroundings; an appropriate place for exchanging anecdotes or any other business.

Navigating the ever-busy Tel Aviv traffic, Eva's thoughts drifted back to her visit with Margalit the day before and the surprise to find Oren at home upon their arrival. Her sister explained that he worked from home once or twice a week. Although he stayed in the background, Eva was aware of his presence all the time and she cut the visit short with an excuse of another appointment later that evening. She left rather awkwardly, her eyes tearing up as she hugged Margalit and glimpsed Oren's curious expression as they left. She was unaware that before they turned the first corner, Oren had locked his office door and deftly keyed in a number on his cell phone. His call was answered without a greeting.

"What have you got?" The voice sounded bored. Josh Goldberg found Oren distasteful, but a necessary nuisance to keep around. As a member of Hugo's family, he was in a position to provide inside information on Azvaalder's star pupil and his mother, and for that he was handsomely rewarded.

"The goddess came down from the mountain today and paid us a visit."

"You mean Eva?" Josh inquired coldly. He was instantly irritated by this description of a woman whom he found very attractive. Oren's constant demeaning comments about Eva annoyed him and he thought of him as a sniveling dog, not worthy of standing in her shadow. "Is that unusual, Steiner?" Josh waited.

"Yes. She hasn't bothered to do that for more than a year. She showed up out of the blue with the crown prince in tow and stayed for less than a half hour. Margalit doesn't know what is going on, because I asked her. Eva was crying when she left." That got Josh's attention.

"Well, well, Steiner. Finally something useful." He had been waiting for this. As an ex-CIA agent, he knew that any behavior out of the ordinary was a cue that something was going down that required his attention. Eva had not yet responded to their offer of many weeks ago, to educate Hugo on a higher level. Apparently she was aware of the surveillance team and electronic equipment in her mother's house since not a single word had been said over the phone to lead them in any significant direction. Eva Norman was a lot more astute than she had let on and he was convinced she was negotiating with someone else. Josh suspected the British because of Tom, but he needed confirmation of this and there was no time to lose. He had invested a lot of time and money in Hugo and, more than anyone else, he understood the boy's real potential. Josh Goldberg was not about to have his prize pupil taken away from him.

Anyone who thought they could rob him of his chance to greatness had no idea with whom they were dealing. He regarded Hugo as his property and he was determined to protect his investment. The fact that Eva was a necessary part of the deal where Hugo was concerned excited him and he looked upon her distant attitude as an alluring personal challenge.

"Cancel everything for the next few days, Steiner. I'll be in touch."

Josh put down the phone and leaned back in his chair, anticipating the exhilaration of a chase. Then he muttered softly. "You beautiful witch! You want to play games with me? Ah, but you should be more careful who you choose to spar with, madam! I play to the bitter end and I don't like losing." He glanced at his watch and rose slowly to his feet. It was time to pay Martha Bartholomew a visit.

Looking around the busy restaurant, Robert McGahan spotted them almost immediately. James had told him to look out for a beautiful, dark-haired woman accompanied by a young boy of around eleven years of age. His eyes came to rest on a gorgeous woman leaning in conversation toward a child who fitted the description. He instantly knew that had to be Eva Norman and acknowledged that Stanway's graphic appraisal of her was indeed accurate. Even from where he stood, he could tell that she was classically beautiful.

He didn't, however, approach her immediately. Years of experience had taught McGahan not to enter any place without first doing a thorough visual scan. He stood casually aside and ran his eyes over the bustling eating area, checking for familiar faces or unusual behavior. When he was satisfied that nothing seemed out of place, he approached the table where Eva and her son were seated and waited for her to notice him. She looked up almost immediately and he held out his hand.

"Mrs. Norman? Robert McGahan, I believe you are expecting me?" Eva brushed a curtain of silky black hair aside and produced that arresting open smile, taking his outstretched hand.

"Hello, Mr. McGahan. Pleased to meet you. And this is Hugo." She nodded in her son's direction and pointed to a vacant chair. "Please, won't you have a seat? I hope you don't mind, we got tucked into the lovely fresh bread that was delivered as we sat down."

"Not at all. This place is known for its specialty bread." McGahan pulled out a chair and caught Hugo's stare on him. The similarities between mother and son were striking. He had her dark eyes and hair, but a paler skin, obviously inherited from his father. The young boy seemed withdrawn and was watching him oddly. McGahan decided to get right to the point. He reached into his pocket and laid a small package on the table, smiling. "Hello Hugo. You like solving problems?" Hugo's gaze wandered from the package to Eva and then back to McGahan. Then he nodded, but made no effort to pick it up.

"Is it a game of some sort, Mr. McGahan?" Eva inquired.

"It is. I've had it for a while and I'm damned if I can figure it out." He smiled at Hugo and pushed the package across the table. "Here, son. You are welcome to keep it. It has baffled everyone in my office, but I'm told you're quite a whiz at these things! What do you say? You want to have a go at it?" He had purposely brought the electronic game to occupy Hugo while he briefed Eva on plans for the next twenty four hours. Hugo nodded. He finally accepted the gift and was soon lost in a world of his own as his fingers flew nimbly over the small keypad. "Are you comfortable with your son being privy to our conversation?" He lowered his voice, glancing at Hugo who seemed oblivious of his surroundings and engrossed in his task of unraveling the problem.

"Of course." Eva smiled. The food they had ordered earlier was being served and she waited until the waiter had left their table before she continued. "It's alright Mr. McGahan; you can talk freely in front of Hugo. I keep no secrets from him." Her words were unpretentious and genuine and confirmed the bond that existed between her and her son.

"In that case—" Just then Hugo leaned over the table and pushed the device toward his mother. Capable of communicating inside the field of his brilliance, he spoke softly to her.

"There are twenty three variables, each with one root and one secondary number. The binary and carrier…" McGahan didn't pay attention to the rest of the answer and tried to hide his astonishment behind a laugh. Eva smiled, familiar with her son's gift.

"Was this the answer you were looking for, Mr. McGahan?" she asked.

"So they weren't kidding back at Division when they told me how sharp you were. Excellent, Hugo! I'm very impressed, young man." But for the boy, the quest was over and he turned his attention to his food and resumed his controlled meticulous eating. While they finished their meals, McGahan attempted to make small talk, but Eva noticed that he constantly ran his gaze over the crowded and noisy restaurant. He seemed on edge. Then he pushed his plate back and spoke deliberately.

"It is tomorrow." The shock of his statement was openly visible on her face.

"*Tomorrow?*" Eva stared at him, confused and alarmed. "Why tomorrow? We won't have enough time to get ready—" McGahan didn't miss a beat.

"We looked into Goldberg's background, Mrs. Norman. As an ex-CIA operative, he is a very dangerous man and there is no telling what his motives could be. So as a precaution to protect the family of one of our very best, you are being removed immediately." The smile didn't reach his eyes. "With your permission, of course." She opened her mouth to speak, but he held up a hand to stop her. "We'll take care of the details. That is not your concern."

"I see," she managed faintly. She struggled to digest the full impact of what was happening to her, but Eva realized that to protect Hugo she would have to go along with their plans. "What do you want us to do?"

"Are you familiar with the Al haMaim restaurant on the Sharon Beach?"

"Yes. Tom and I have been there a few times. They specialize in seafood." Eva kept her voice down, but she knew Hugo was listening. Glancing at him, she leaned over to put a comforting arm around him. "Don't worry, darling." The boy looked at her but didn't reply. McGahan watched the brief interaction between mother and son and then continued; his demeanor serious and businesslike. He kept his voice even.

"Find a way to leave your house unobtrusively tomorrow. Hugo should go to school like every other day, because his absence will be noticed immediately. Pack nothing. You'll be provided with the necessities at your destination; we'll send for your belongings at a later date. Be on the seaside patio of the Al haMaim restaurant on the Sharon Beach promptly at eight o'clock tomorrow evening. You are scheduled to leave at 2300 hours with El-Al from Tel Aviv. That is all you need to know right now." Robert McGahan finished his sentence, aware that Hugo had stopped eating and was staring strangely at him.

Eva sat very still. It was hard to believe that any of this was real and that they were about to leave their homeland and embark on this wild journey into the unknown. She had thought that she would have a thousand questions, but as it were, there were none. The wheels were in motion and there was no turning back. Her young son had felt her fear and there was no denying it. But something else had caught her attention; a mannerism quite different from his stereotyped math and physics dialogue. It was in the protective way that he looked at her. Was it possible that Hugo was ready to engage in normal conversation? She reached out and took his hand.

"Hugo, darling. What do you want to say?" He remained silent but the tiny squeeze he gave her hand belied the look of frustration on his face. The unknown lay ahead of them like a vast body of uncharted water, but despite the tremendous challenge that faced them, Eva felt a faint excitement that she couldn't explain.

"You'll be met by a colleague who will provide you with further details. Please be on time." McGahan stood and held out his hand. "I wish you a safe journey, Mrs. Norman. It was a pleasure meeting you." He nodded his head to Hugo. "Keep up the good work, son!" And then to Eva, "I'll settle the bill on my way out." And with those words, he strode away swiftly. After lunch, as Eva and Hugo were making their way to the parking lot, her eye caught a man hastily jumping into a taxi.

"Isn't that your uncle Oren?" Eva asked, pointing at the car speeding away. Hugo nodded, staring at the disappearing vehicle. Surprised to see her brother-in-law in the same area in which she had met with Robert McGahan, she recalled Margalit mentioning that Oren would be out of town on a business trip for a few days. Something was definitely amiss. *Could this be co-incidence?*

It was past eight o'clock when Martha heard the knock at her front door. Puzzled as to who her late visitor could be, she hurried down the hall and flicked the porch light switch at the same time as she unlocked the door and opened it. But only darkness greeted her; the light was out and there was no sign of anybody. She wondered what had happened since it had worked fine earlier that evening.

"Hello, Martha." The voice was soft and menacing and then she saw a figure rise from the chair beside the potted rubber plant.

A scream rose from her lungs but became inexplicably muted as she opened her mouth to let it out. She stood frozen as the big imposing man deliberately approached and halted right in front of her. Then he held up the light bulb he had unscrewed earlier and leaned forward, dropping his voice to a terrifying whisper. "You and I have unfinished business. I suggest we get on with it." The next moment he roughly pushed her back into the house and locked the door behind them. "Now then, Martha. The time for games is over. Who is Eva talking to?"

"Eva? Who are you?" Martha had found her voice again but something strange was happening inside of her. "Why are you asking me about Eva? *Who are you?*" She looked at the tall, angry man in front of her and although she had never seen him before, she was instantly panic-stricken, making it hard to breathe. There was a part of her that wanted to run and another part that knew it would be futile. She was trapped, that much she was sure of. He ignored her questions and continued to stare at the fragile gray-haired woman in the semi-darkness of the living room, relishing the fright in her eyes. Martha nervously tried again. "I don't know what you want with her. I can't tell you anything because I don't know anything—" But before she could finish her sentence, his big hands had closed around her throat and he pushed her hard up against the dining room table, forcing her to bend backwards until her upper body collapsed on top of it. He increased the pressure on her neck, holding her down firmly so she couldn't move.

"Think harder, Martha! You're not doing your best here! She's going to steal my star pupil, isn't she? That kid is worth a fucking fortune and she thinks she can pull a fast one on Josh Goldberg, after everything I've done for them? No fucking way!" He screamed the words in her face, vaguely realizing in the back of his mind that he was losing self control.

"What do you want with Hugo?" Her words became a painful splutter as the big man choking her, swam in and out of focus. A cold hand closed around her heart. Martha had no illusions about how this would end. "Please! He is only a boy…"

"Yes! That's what they all believe." He laughed without any joy and squeezed harder. Then he leaned closer to her and pressed his face right up to hers. "You also think he's just a little autistic boy with a special flair for mathematics, don't you? Well he is much more than that, Martha. Hugo is a *savant* and they don't come dispatched any more brilliant than that!" His voice had dropped dangerously low, and despite his overpowering closeness, she had to strain to hear him. "And this one has the ability to communicate! Not even his parents know this, *but I found out!*" She didn't reply because she could no longer speak. She had known about Hugo's gift for a long time, but she didn't realize that he was a savant or that he had potential to communicate normally. And suddenly it was all crystal clear to her. Little Hugo and the eagle… *Oh God, Eva! He is coming after you and Hugo!*

Goldberg had begun to sweat profusely and for some reason, none of his sophisticated neuro-linguistic experience mattered and he only felt blind rage as he deftly closed off her airways. He had big plans to use Hugo's unusual talents in building his own business to become a market leader and possibly also scoring some significant political points. The mere thought that Eva had the temerity to cross him, drove him insane and he wanted to punish someone. The defenseless woman under his hands was the perfect target. Through the haze of his fury he stared into the older woman's face and realized that he was about to snuff the life out of her without getting an answer.

"Bitch!" he yelled. "Don't you die on me!" Josh released his grip on her neck and shook her violently so that she would regain consciousness, but Martha's eyes rolled in her head and she did not respond. In utter frustration he suddenly released her and watched her body slide down the table and hit the floor, while he sat down in a nearby chair to keep an eye on her. "Talk to me, Martha! It's my business to know who she kept in touch with, and you're it! Speak to me!"

But Martha was beyond responding. The nightmare of a few nights ago had returned and she was re-living every awful moment of it on the floor of her dining room when, with frightening insight, she suddenly realized the real identity of her assailant. Her nostrils were filled with the stench of the back room where he killed poultry with such precision so many centuries ago, and she wanted to vomit. And then his name came to her, as if she was still Mary, the pathetic abused wife that cowered before his relentless cruel beatings.

"*William*, please…" Her lips moved and she tried feebly to raise a protective hand to her face but her body had gone into severe shock, clearly recognizing Josh Goldberg as William in her horrible nightmare. "Oh, Jesus, it's *you*! You're going to kill them!" Her eyes flew wide open and for one agonizing moment she met his ice-cold stare, and then her body convulsed violently as a massive blood clot entered her brain, silencing her forever.

Josh Goldberg dispassionately watched Martha Bartholomew die. When the body tremors finally stopped, he got up and stood over her where she lay on her side. He poked a foot at her chest, rolling her onto her back. For a long time he stared at her dead eyes, wondering why *his* being the cause of this woman's death, a virtual stranger, filled him with so much satisfaction. Then he shrugged and made his way to her bedroom and expertly began ransacking it in search of his answer. He finally found the manila envelope in one of her drawers and sat down on the overturned bed to open it. Inside were some of Hugo's drawings, which he had not seen before. There was also a photocopy of a letter that started with "To whom it may concern."

"Bingo," he said softly when he had finished reading it.

Once outside the front door, he pulled off the surgical gloves and jammed them into his pocket. He had to try and stop Eva before she left the country. He still had a trump card to play, but he needed her to be within reach when he forced her to choose between her husband and her son. To do that, he would have to foil her plans of leaving the shores of Israel. There was no time to waste.

Chapter 15
A Race Against Time

The next morning the white van was gone and the apprehension Eva had felt the previous day intensified. It was still early morning as she stood barefoot in front of the window holding the brown manila envelope that had been pushed through Carmela's letterbox some time after she and Hugo had returned from their lunch meeting with Robert McGahan the previous day.

Carmela had found the envelope on the floor and handed it to Eva as she walked in the door. It had Eva's name on it and was marked "private and confidential" but she held onto it until after Hugo had gone to bed. When he was safely tucked in, she curled up in a chair in the living room and tore it open. Carmela gave her daughter privacy and went into the kitchen to make some coffee.

Upon her return she found Eva with her arms wrapped around her slim body staring into space; a concerned expression on her face. The contents of the envelope were back in its cover and Carmela waited until Eva was ready to talk. The hollow feeling in the pit of Eva's stomach was very real and when she lifted a hand to brush a loose strand of hair from her face, Carmela noticed the nervous tremble. Eva felt frustration and fear simultaneously welling to the surface, and she swallowed hard to disguise the sob rising in the back of her throat.

"Mum, I'd rather not involve you any further in this mess. The less you know, the better for you, I think. It is about Tom. That is all I can say." If they were listening in to her conversation with her mother, then she wanted them to know that Carmela was not privy to any information.

Later, in the privacy of her bedroom, she spilled the contents of the envelope onto her bed. There were four pictures of Tom talking to different individuals. The handwritten inscriptions beneath each photo alleged the various locations as Tehran in Iran, Caracas in Venezuela, Riyadh in Saudi Arabia and Rabat in Morocco. A single attached note read: *Where has your husband been all this time, Eva?*

The note wasn't signed, but Eva had no doubt that it originated from Josh Goldberg. She stared at the pictures laid out on the bed and felt completely numb. Had Tom been working for Josh Goldberg? Did Goldberg arrange to have Tom followed to blackmail him at some point? And was he now threatening her? She had no idea what to believe anymore and it was very hard to remain objective, especially in the light of Tom's long absences and the complete secrecy he constantly maintained around his work. She wondered if this was an effort to stall her and why the envelope had only just arrived. Intuitively, she knew there was some validity to the evidence staring her in the face, but her diminished role in Tom's life made it near impossible to help him. She had to make sure Hugo was safe; that was her first priority.

Then Eva froze. Of course! Josh must have caught wind of their plans for the next day and wanted to force her hand by using pictures of Tom in potentially compromising situations. She sat down shakily on the bed. *That must be it! He knows!* It was too late for her to contact James Stanway, and besides, the house phone was bugged and she knew Azvaalder had the technology to intercept her cell phone calls as well. She needed rest, but knew that the night would be very long and that sleep would not come easily. When day finally broke, she was exhausted and fatigued from a restless night drifting feverishly in and out of dreams and visions. She was sure some of it had meaning, but in her tired state of mind she couldn't remember any detail, yet felt deeply unsettled.

"Mum." She turned around, stunned at how Hugo had addressed her. He was standing in her doorway, still in his pajamas but his eyes were clear as though he had been up for a while.

"Hugo, darling?" Eva approached her son with wonder in her voice. In all of his eleven years he had shown affection only by staying close to her, hugging her or squeezing her hand in response to questions; his use of language was exclusively assigned to the world of math and physics. Amidst the great uncertainty that surrounded their future, her eyes stung with tears of joy. Were the barriers to ordinary communication finally crumbling? She hoped and prayed that it was really happening.

She held her arms out and he came readily into her embrace; another very encouraging sign. Overwhelmed by the new development, she tried to keep the conversation as normal as possible. Then she dropped a kiss on his head and whispered in his hair. "Why are you up so early, sweetheart? We have a long day ahead of us. And there is still school." He freed himself from her arms, shaking his head.

"No school." He spoke barely above a whisper and, moving closer to the window, he lifted the voile curtain slightly and pointed outside. "No van." He tilted his head backwards as if in deep thought and looked curiously at his mother.

"Of course, Hugo!" Eva suddenly remembered the listening devices, but she could scarcely contain her excitement. Her little boy was communicating in short sentences, but he was talking to her! She held a finger in front of her mouth and whispered. "You're right. They think you are going to school today, but I think we should surprise them!" Then she bent down and leaned in closer, keeping her voice very low. "I could never do this on my own, but now I see that you are going to help me." Eva was accustomed to her son only seeing and feeling things. He had limited ability to verbally express any of it. Hugo's gift was the world of mathematics and physics; languages in which he was very proficient, but few could speak. But their immediate danger apparently was the catalyst to a whole new world beckoning her handicapped child. She smiled lovingly. "We had better hurry, hadn't we?" He watched her closely.

"Green, yellow, red..." He had changed his focus slightly and was looking past her. Eva felt a chill run down her spine.

"Where do you see the colors?" He waved his hand in a circular movement, identifying her auric field. Whereas she normally let him be, on this day she felt an urgency to understand the full implication. "Tell me what you see or feel, Hugo! What do you mean? I know that you relate to numbers and equations, but can you tell me in simple terms, *what* do you see?"

"Changes..." Then his demeanor altered and, reverting back to the only language that he could comfortably speak, he said softly. "The fifth quadrant—" He had no choice but to slide back into his world of describing things in numbers and more numbers. For the first time, the look of consternation on her face stopped him abruptly. They stared at each other; aware of the transformation. "Changes...more colors..." Eva smiled at her son, knowing that they both felt the tension of the day ahead, but he was incapable of verbalizing the significance. Eva didn't hesitate; her mind was made up. The word "changes" was enough.

"You love museums and art galleries as much as I do, right?" He nodded. She leaned closer to him and spoke softly in his ear. "I am going to listen to you today, young man. Get dressed and we'll have breakfast with grandma, and then take off for a day of adventure. We are leaving right away, so let us make this as interesting as possible." Hugo drew his head away to find her eyes. For a moment he seemed undecided but then nodded his head almost imperceptibly.

"Yes, Mum."

Josh Goldberg was in a cold rage. He stood at the window of his office and watched the busy traffic outside, his knuckles white as he gripped his cell phone.

"What do you mean she gave you the slip, Mendel?" His eyes narrowed and despite his best effort to remain calm, his voice rose to the level of a scream. "Are you a fucking imbecile? We withdrew the surveillance because Oren Steiner suggested it would put her at ease. And the kid was supposed to come to school today! Does that mean you are completely off duty? She ignored the mail drop we did yesterday and the kid never showed up. And now you tell me there is no sign of her!" Tomer tried to get a word in but Josh ignored him. "And where the hell is Steiner?"

He was yelling, feeling the same anger beginning to rise as when he had visited Martha Bartholomew. His free hand cramped painfully as he opened and closed his fingers in aggravation. He could not believe that Eva had ignored the photos he had sent to her mother's home. Surely she understood that her husband's career, their future, was on the line? But he had misjudged her yet again. She clearly didn't fall for his scheme and God knows where she was now. They could have changed their plans altogether; she and Hugo could very well already be on their way to Britain.

Then a completely irrational thought crossed his mind and,

drowning out Tomer's voice, Josh drifted off into a silent psychological rant. *You don't know who you are dealing with, Eva! I've had enough of your off-hand treatment and I'm going to expose your husband for the hired hand that he is. Neither my attention nor my anger moves you, and that pisses me off! You think I am insignificant? We'll see, we'll see. I make people pay for their sins, and you will be no exception.* He heard another beep in his ear and unceremoniously put Tomer on hold to take the latest call.

"*What!*" He reserved a special kind of contempt for Oren.

"I am following her, Mr. Goldberg!" Oren Steiner could hardly contain his excitement. "And it looks like she is on her way to Jaffa."

"Jaffa? Are you sure it is her?" Josh's spirits lifted immediately as he felt the excitement of another chase.

"It's her, alright. And she has Hugo with her. They are traveling south along the Herbert Samuel Esplanade."

"Don't lose her, Steiner! If you know what is good for you, you'll stay on her tail. I'm on my way." Oren listened to the usual orders barked at him, watching the electronic device blipping away on his instrument panel. *Fuck you, Goldberg. I'm going to beat you at your own bloody game!*

"No, sir, I'll keep her in sight," he said compliantly, but pulled a face as he watched the device tracking Eva at a distance. *Screw you, Goldberg.* Relying on the electronic apparatus, he stayed well back of her. The last thing he needed was for her or Hugo to recognize his vehicle, but it was Josh who didn't miss a beat.

"Call me when you know where she's heading and don't let her see you. I don't want to lose her again. Stay in touch and that is an order!" He switched back to Tomer. "Steiner has her in sight. She is on the road to Jaffa. I have no idea what the bitch is up to, but I want a word with her before she shakes the soil of this country from her feet. I wonder if she will still be so high and mighty when I tell her that Tom has lost his value to me, now that she is stealing my prize pupil. Let's see how much she really cares! Call Steiner and follow him. I'll do the same. And remember, I want to *speak* to her, so tell Anchov to keep his bloody hands off her! Use your discretion, if you know the meaning of the word. The whole bloody area is probably swarming with fucking agents. I don't want a scene or an incident!" He snapped his phone closed and grabbed his car keys, determined not to fail.

Hugo stared out of the window, his gaze focused on the ocean and the activity of sailboats, motorboats and other sea traffic that characterized the ever-busy Mediterranean. Eva threw him a sideways glance, finding strength and reassurance in the presence of her young son.

"We are going to Jaffa, Hugo. We have quite a bit of time to kill so we're going into the artists' quarters with all those studios and galleries. I want us to be amongst lots of people, because I am not sure we have shaken our pursuers. I don't think they will give up so easily." Despite the excitement, Eva sounded distracted; her thoughts were still with her mother and the difficult parting earlier in the day. Carmela barely spoke a word as they said their final goodbyes. She held her hand over her mouth and allowed the tears to stream freely down her cheeks. Eva had put her arms around the distraught older woman and buried her face briefly in her mother's shoulder.

"I'll contact you soon, I promise. I called Uri to say goodbye, and he agreed to be the contact between us while we're in England." She too was choked up and had difficulty speaking. Hugo stood aside and watched the two women with a curious expression on his face. When the time came to say goodbye to his grandmother he gave her his signature stare and hugged her without saying a word. Then he ran out to the car parked in the driveway and waited for his mother.

Eva found a space in the parking lot of the Simtat HaZchoochit, a French restaurant named after King Lear's daughter, located on the corner of Yefet Road, not far away from the sprawling cacophonic Shuq Hapishpeshim, Jaffa's flea market.

"Come, Hugo. Time to go!" She looked around carefully as they strode away together but didn't notice anything that seemed out of place.

There was no sign of them when Oren parked a short distance away from her car. He slammed his door shut, feeling frantically for his cell phone. The sooner Josh and the others got here the better. *Shit! How the hell did Eva and Hugo disappear so fast?* In the market square Eva and Hugo joined the growing throng of tourists and locals enjoying the sights and scenery of one of Israel's favorite tourist attractions, making their way to the narrow alleyways named after the signs of the Zodiac.

She thought if they kept a low profile and visited the obscure shops and galleries, locating them would be like finding a needle in a haystack.

The air was already filled with the aroma of kebabs and fresh fish being prepared to feed the constant hunger and curiosity of visitors who were always ready to eat, and she marveled at the traditional smells that hung thickly in the air, even at this time of day. Eva knew that she would miss the familiarity of this place but quickly banished the thought as she and Hugo entered the quaint store of a jewelry maker who specialized in birth stones. Named Bull's Eye, it was located in the alleyway of Taurus. On the spur of the moment she decided to buy Carmela a delicate chain with a beautifully polished garnet as a pendant. Her mother's birthday was in January and she would send the gift with whomever she was to meet later that day and ask them to deliver it to her.

They had already been on their feet for more than two hours when they cautiously entered the Museum of Antiquities of Tel Aviv-Jaffa. Eva found a pamphlet advertising daily tours conducted at the Ilana Goor Museum, pinned to a bulletin board whilst browsing around the crowded chambers with other tourists. It stated that the museum, located just outside the old city walls, offered special educational programs for children of all ages. Eva didn't hesitate and walked up to the counter where a young girl was in charge of selling copies of artifacts.

"Could you call us a taxi please? Unfortunately, my cell phone battery is dead." Eva and Hugo waited unobtrusively inside the building and five minutes later they were in the safety of the taxi making their way slowly toward Mazal Dagim Street, just outside the old city walls of Jaffa, where the Ilana Goor Museum was located. She looked at Hugo and noticed that he was tired, although he had not once complained. At that moment she recognized Oren on the opposite sidewalk amongst the throng of people. He was in conversation with Josh Goldberg who had a scowl on his face and looked angry. Pleased that they had managed to elude their pursuers thus far, she turned her head away quickly, confident that they had not been noticed.

This day and its demands were beginning to tell on her. She was tired and anxious and she suddenly felt very weepy. For the first time, as they approached the museum, Eva candidly admitted to herself that her marriage to Tom was over. She leaned her head against the back seat of the taxi and closed her eyes. There were no tears anymore; only sadness that they could not salvage their relationship, even if only for the sake of their son.

Annoyed and defeated, Josh and Oren were back in the parking lot where Eva had left her car hours before. Josh stood quite still and eyed Oren coldly.

"So, you were clever enough to pay a waiter to deposit a bug under the serviette in the bread basket when they were having lunch. And you were smart enough to track her with an electronic device you hid underneath the fender of her car. But where are they now?" He spoke softly, menacingly, watching the other man squirm as he tried to explain to his outraged boss how he had lost the Normans.

"I thought they would have to come back to her car—" But Josh interrupted him.

"I see. Did you forget that her kid is a fucking genius? Did you also forget that his mother had outsmarted all of you by ensuring that we got absolutely no information through any of the surveillance equipment? What does that say, Steiner? I'll tell you. That she *knew* we were onto her, that's what!" He took a step closer to Oren and dropped his voice dangerously low.

"What use have you been to me? Tell me why I paid you many thousands of shekels when all you did was to feed me bullshit about a woman you pretended to know. You alleged you could be my inside source, but you apparently know her as well as any man in the street, which is not at all! Weren't you the one who suggested yesterday that you knew her and that the photographs would persuade her to stay, that we should call off the surveillance?"

Josh knew he was losing control again, and that someone would have to pay for this failure. There was no other way that he could relieve the tremendous pressure he felt in his head, or stop the painful stir in his groin, similar to the sensations he had watching Martha die. He breathed heavily into Oren's face, realizing that he had most probably lost Eva and Hugo. He wanted to kill Oren there and then, but they were in a public place and he tried to restrain himself.

"She ignored the report!" His scream was out of control. Horrified, Oren didn't move. But then Josh gathered himself. "That much is clear, don't you think?" He sounded almost pleasant. "We'll have to stake out their original meeting place tonight, but I won't be surprised if they have already changed their plans." A vein on his forehead bulged, and his face turned red as he suddenly lost control again. "And you thought she would come back to her car! *Jesus Christ!*" He slammed his hand violently into the door of Eva's vehicle, leaving a huge dent in it. "You're coming with me now." He turned on his heel and strode away, not looking back once.

Oren followed, anxious and distressed. He had never seen Josh this angry and he was uncertain what was expected of him, regretting that he didn't pay more heed to the warning he had overheard in the Columbus restaurant about how dangerous Goldberg was. That day he had decided to find a way to sever his ties with this volatile man, but not before showing off his own brilliance and beating the arrogant Jew at his own game. However, with losing Eva and Hugo, things had gone horribly wrong. He realized with growing concern that he was in way over his head and knew that cutting loose wouldn't be easy. Josh was already in the car when Oren opened the door to get in.

The next movement was so swift that Oren never saw it coming. Neither did he have time to respond; even if he did see the needle plunged expertly into his aorta. Josh withdrew the thin spike swiftly and felt enormous satisfaction spread throughout his entire body as he watched Oren grab his chest and open his mouth, gasping desperately for air. The drug was Corazol, produced in Bolivia to develop seizures in rats. The pain in his chest was so enormous that he couldn't muster the power to even cast an astonished look at his executioner.

He took nearly three minutes to die, during which time Josh experienced an intense orgasm. When the convulsion of Oren's body ceased, Josh looked around the parking lot carefully. There was no one in sight. Then he opened the passenger door and edged Oren's body out of the car with his foot. He made sure not to accidentally drive over the hapless form and pulled away calmly to catch up with Dmitri Anchov. He had a task that he knew the big Russian would enjoy.

After she had signed him up for the tour, Eva left Hugo in the care of a guide who eyed his small group of seven children enthusiastically. He had encouraged her to take a walk through the various chambers and waved her off good-heartedly, promising that he was going to educate the children about the rich history of the past.

Eva wandered through the main atrium, admiring the displays of times gone by, and realized just how tired she was. Hugo would be fed with the rest of the children and she made her way to the roof garden where there was a magnificent view of the port of Jaffa on the Mediterranean. She sat down, ordered tea and tuna on rye bread and leaned back in her chair to close her eyes. Within a few minutes she drifted off into light sleep, exhausted from all the tension.

The cool breeze from the ocean washed over her, but Eva was already standing in the Meadow, a familiar blissful place her subconscious mind seemed to find easily in the dream state. It was very quiet as she slowly looked around in all directions but like always, there was no one in sight. The breeze was fresh and invigorating and she took a deep breath and closed her eyes, allowing the unusual energy of her surroundings to permeate every pore of her body. Then she heard it. A soft giggle came from behind the large leafy tree just ahead and her curiosity deepened. She had never come across anyone in this sanctuary of peace and harmony. Who was there? Was that the laugh of a child?

"Hello? Who are you? Please don't be afraid!" Eva had never felt as exhilarated as in this moment. The thought that this mysterious place was inhabited filled her with indescribable joy. Just then, a head of bright golden curls peeked out from behind the tree and Eva stared mesmerized at the child of about six years of age. The little girl's hand was clasped tightly over her mouth, playfully struggling to muffle the laughter. But when she couldn't contain herself any more, the golden-haired child turned on her heel and ran away, no longer restraining that elfish giggle. Just in that moment, the breeze changed direction and the waving grass was the last thing that Eva saw.

"Pardon me, madam, your lunch is ready." The young man stood aside politely as he put her food down on the circular table. "The fresh air is wonderful and the view is absolutely intoxicating, is it not?" He smiled. "Enjoy your lunch." Eva felt a little embarrassed and put a hand to her forehead.

"Thank you. And yes, you're right. This is almost too much to take in." It was the same dream she had had the previous night; she now remembered it clearly. But she had never seen the child. *Who was that little girl?* Unable to solve the riddle, she composed herself and remembered that she had not yet spoken to James Stanway about the contents of the envelope. She decided to give it to her contact later that evening, knowing it would reach Stanway. If anyone could help Tom, Stanway could.

Her gaze wandered over the magnificent panorama of blue sea and the old port of Jaffa with its huge rocks, and suddenly she knew clearly that she would never return to live in this country again. The certainty of the thought upset her tremendously and she didn't try to stop the tears that began to run freely. She was not only leaving her country of birth, but her husband and their marriage. Nothing would ever be the same again.

In the back of a taxi taking them to the Al haMaim restaurant on the Sharon Beach, Hugo leaned against her shoulder, overwhelmed by the activity of the day. Still absorbing the events of his interesting experiences in the museum, he remained quiet, but Eva was distracted and kept looking at her watch. It was 7.30pm and they had about thirty minutes to reach their rendezvous.

She wondered what had happened to Josh, and cringed at the thought that her suspicions about Oren were right. Poor Margalit. This would have to come out, one way or the other, but she resigned herself to the fact that she couldn't do anything about it right now. She thought of Tom again and realized that Hugo had virtually no contact with his father. He seemed reconciled to the fact that he had only one parent who played an active role in his life. On one occasion, some months ago, she had asked him if he was bothered by the absence of his father, to which he only shook his head. She didn't pry any further.

The cab pulled up to the well-lit front porch of the restaurant, and Hugo waited for his mother to pay the driver before they both stepped out. Walking up the steps, she looked around the crowded foyer and wondered whom she was meeting. Robert McGahan indicated the contact would know her. Then she saw him. It was no other than James Stanway. He caught her eye and immediately began walking away, heading toward the busy patio area where the night air was abuzz with laughter and the aroma of seafood. A young waiter carrying a tray with empty glasses suddenly bumped into her. Leaning forward apologetically, he spoke softly, but clearly.

"Follow your contact down to the beach. Hurry! The others are here." With that he lifted the tray above his head and wove his way back to the bar in the far corner. Eva grabbed Hugo's hand and pushed forward, following Stanway who was briskly crossing the patio and heading toward the stairs leading down to the beach. Eva and Hugo caught up with him as their feet sank into the sand coming off the last step. He spoke under his breath.

"Hurry, Eva! Just walk beside me and don't look back. There is a dinghy on the beach. I will escort you myself to the motorboat waiting for us in deeper water."

"We're not flying from Ben Gurion any more?" She felt her heart thundering in her chest.

"You are not flying with El-Al. Come," he said as they arrived on the wet sand and came upon a dark object just beyond the reach of the incoming tide, "I'll explain when we're under way. Here, put this on." He threw them each a life jacket, donned one himself and pushed the dinghy into the shallow water. "I'm sorry, but you are going to get a little wet. You have your British passports?" She nodded as he helped her into the small rubber boat. He lifted Hugo in, jumped aboard and instantly pulled the starter cord of the outboard motor. It fired at once and a whiff of gasoline mingled briefly with the salty smell of the ocean. In the semi darkness, she realized that Stanway was wearing a tracksuit and sneakers; very unusual attire for the man known as the Silver Fox.

"Hold on," he cautioned as they began to splash their way across the ocean. "Getting over the breakers can be somewhat tricky." When they had finally cleared the last big waves rolling onto the shore, he turned and looked back at the silhouetted figure standing on the beach. Eva followed his gaze.

"Goldberg?" she asked, openly scared.

"No. He is too clever to show his face when the heat is on. It's one of his goons." Stanway turned away from the beach and began navigating the dinghy under the night sky as they bumped their way over the dark ocean, speeding off into the night.

"Where are you sending us, James?" In the frantic rush to get away, it suddenly struck her that she had no idea of where they were heading in England. Her stomach contracted nervously; it was very hard to be so completely at the mercy of others.

"We are geared for emergencies like this." Stanway kept his eyes on the water. "Suffice to say that we have our own esteemed instructors in Hugo's field, and the needs of your child will be taken care of." Then he abruptly changed the subject.

"I am afraid I have some bad news for you, Eva." He didn't look at her but kept his concentration on steering the little boat. She had no idea what to expect and waited stoically for him to continue. "We found Martha Bartholomew today. She seemed to have died from a blood clot to the brain, but the bruises on her neck and the rest of her body tell another story. There were no fingerprints." Stanway had to shout over the roaring engine and glancing briefly back at her, he noticed her distress. Eva stared at him in horror, unable to make a sound as she and Hugo held on tightly to stay in the small craft. She caught the look of shock and anguish on Hugo's face but could do nothing to comfort him as they clung to the side of the boat. "That is not the end of it." This time he slowed the dinghy down slightly, holding onto the rudder. "Your brother-in-law is also dead. We found him in the parking lot where you had left your car. The cause of death appears to be a heart attack, but it is very suspect." He didn't ask how or why Oren was involved; he would find out later. This was not a time for explanations.

"A heart attack? James, he was only thirty!" Eva felt physically sick, and Hugo's face was without any expression. The death of a human was a frightening new experience for the boy, and she knew that he had retreated behind his wall of seclusion. Then Eva pulled her son closer to her. She couldn't believe what she was hearing, but felt her world beginning to cave in. "Oren is *dead?* But how?" She kept perfectly still and held Hugo's trembling body whilst listening to Stanway's voice; unable to process the ghastly news.

"If we did an autopsy, we probably wouldn't find the answer either. A professional killer knows exactly what to add to the blood stream that would make it look like a heart attack. It is usually administered by punching a needle into the neck that leaves a hole so small, that it cannot be detected. I can't speculate about that now, but we had reason to believe your life and Hugo's were in danger—hence the change in plans."

They skidded over the dark surface of the ocean in silence and James Stanway let her be, expertly maneuvering his way into deeper water. He knew this would come as a very big shock to her. He didn't go into the details of how Colonel Appleyard had asked to be put in touch with Martha after the note she sent and the subsequent discovery of her body. Neither did he tell Eva that one of his own agents had followed her the whole day. The agent didn't witness the suspected assault on Oren, but found his body when he realized she and Hugo were finally heading back into the city by taxi after the hours they had spent at the Ilana Goor Museum. Stanway sympathized with her, but couldn't do anything to help ease her anxiety. The rest of the journey passed in a complete haze. When they reached the waiting motorboat, Robert McGahan was there and helped them aboard. He winked at Hugo, but the boy just stared at him.

"One more thing, James." Eva barely recognized her own voice. "Please take this." She handed him the brown envelope containing Tom's pictures. "This was delivered to me last night; it can only come from Josh Goldberg. I think Tom needs help." Eva reached into her bag and pulled out another small packet. "This is for my mother. I'm concerned for my family's safety, and from what you have told me, Goldberg will stop at nothing." Stanway nodded.

"I'll see to everything, Eva. Don't worry." He waved as McGahan turned the boat and quickly sped away into the night, heading back to the port of Jaffa. From there they would be taken by car to Bert Linnigan's farm, a thirty minute drive away. Linnigan was an ex-RAF pilot who made his living as a crop duster and his four-seater was fuelled and ready to fly them to Cyprus. The scheduled flight connection would be made from there. Within ten hours, Eva and Hugo would be winging their way to a new life.

James Stanway hadn't looked at the content of the envelope yet, but he had a suspicion that the shit was about to hit the fan. He had no doubt that Eva was unaware of the true lay of the land. He would have to get in touch with Appleyard—and soon.

Chapter 16
From A Distance

The English summer was breaking its tradition of intermittent rain and shifting temperatures by offering a few weeks of resplendent sunshine where one glorious day just effortlessly rolled into the next. High clouds, which often characterized the North East landscape were burnt away quickly, providing that feel-good factor as all went about their daily business under the clear blue sky with an extra spring in their step.

The farmhouse kitchen was awash this Monday morning with brilliant light and Steve basked in the pleasant heat of the early morning sun streaming through the window. *So, they have arrived.* He absentmindedly stirred the cup of coffee in his hand, his mind occupied with the email he had read a few minutes ago. Henry O'Malley's message explained that the guests from Israel were moving into their off-campus apartment later that day and that he had arranged an informal dinner at his house the following evening for Steve to meet with his new protégé and his mother. Steve scratched his rough unshaven chin. He imagined dinner with a strange woman and her young son to be somewhat awkward.

He couldn't help wondering what they could possibly talk about, except perhaps the gifts that the child apparently possessed. The brief communication mentioned that he was welcome to invite a companion, but Steve had already decided not to bring anyone. The meeting would be cordial, but short. He intended to focus on the child to determine his specific needs, and then as soon as he could, beg his leave to prepare the midterm paper for his final year students.

He sipped on his coffee and thought of the young boy that was to become his special project. O'Malley had made it clear that curriculum development would be left up to him, but grimaced slightly at the thought. What did he know of kids? He was forty one years old and had mostly been around the children of his friends. He never came closer than the odd hug or wet kiss placed on his cheek by one of the younger ones.

He wondered what an eleven-year-old genius with a handicap would be like. In the back of his mind he was aware of an irritation at having been chosen for this task. His usual drive and focus was aimed at training the minds of his students to be razor sharp and alert in identifying logical thinking patterns and then looking for the next level at which this information could be applied.

His success and popularity as a professor in applied mathematics was ascribed to the fact that he treated his students as adults. He was known for his keen sense of humor and the exceptionally high standard he demonstrated and demanded. What would the protocol be for a child with such an unusual talent? Was this boy really a child? He didn't know and temporarily banished all thoughts about the newcomers as he began to prepare his breakfast.

He sat on the kitchen stool facing the window and enjoyed his usual bowl of oatmeal followed by a slice of rye bread with a thin layer of goat's butter and marmalade. He watched the early morning activity outside as the trainers were beginning their day, bringing out their latest stock of clients' horses for the grueling adventures of trying to break old habits and introducing new disciplines. His gaze wandered to the paddock next to the training field where he noticed Bullet being led out for his early morning trot. Some of the staff still referred to him as 'Bullet' but Steve wanted the horse to be known as Quah Dreamer.

He smiled and chuckled to himself as he saw three fillies following his jet-black companion. The horse's beauty and superior stride was an obvious attraction as they eagerly vied for his attention. Steve watched as Quah Dreamer increased his pace, forcing the fillies to keep up with him. It would not be long before his offspring were added to their existing stock, satisfying the needs of a growing clientele and enhancing the popularity of the training camp.

His gaze followed Quah Dreamer around the paddock and he noticed how the brisk trot had become a gallop and the proud way in which the horse swung his head from side to side. He and Quah Dreamer had a bond that still gave him shivers, and he thought fondly of how he and this magnificent horse were rediscovering the local countryside. Now and again Quah Dreamer would pull up unexpectedly and dig into the earth with his injured leg and, dropping his head down low, removed deep divots from the field in an attempt to relieve the irritation in his injured hoof.

Steve kept an eye on this behavior when they were out riding, but knew that the horse was comfortable. Quah Dreamer was working in his first set of special shoes provided by the hot shoe blacksmith at the nearby market town of Yarm. Thanks to Brad's intervention, this two-year program of regular re-shoeing would finally get the horse's hoof back on the road to recovery. He had explained that it was like fitting braces to teeth. Regular adjustments encourage the teeth to move and eventually settle down, and the same thing was expected to happen with the injured hoof.

Steve arrived at the campus with minutes to spare before his first class. As he entered the lecture hall, he glanced over to the large blackboard spanning the length of one of the walls and then looked over the waiting students.

"No attempt at greatness yet?" He feigned surprise that no one had added the next step to his brainteaser. "No?" They pretended boredom; waiting for the deep laugh, which they knew would come when he couldn't keep his face straight any longer. "Are there really no geniuses in this class?" Then he relented and laughed. The brainteaser on the blackboard had become a habit with which Steve challenged his students. Mind benders were provided by astute mathematicians such as Robert Muller and each morning someone would attempt the next link until the equation was complete. But this time, even by his standards, the problem was a whopper and he wasn't surprised that it hadn't been solved. "This one stays until someone cracks it." His eyes wandered over the students. "Agreed? There are still forty-two stages left. Six jars of Mrs. Shepherd's home-made jam to the bright spark who comes up with the answer." The students already knew that Mrs. Shepherd was a neighbor who was an expert in home-made produce.

"Did you remember to bring your lunch today, Professor?" Amy, an attractive redhead, asked at the end of class as she and her best friend, Megan, were about to leave the lecture hall. They had booked him for a short session in preparation for midterms which was around the corner. "We'll wait for you on the grassy slope outside the main entrance."

"I didn't forget, ladies. I'll meet you there in a few minutes." Steve looked over the remaining group as they began to file out for the lunch break. "Anyone for squash at six?" His regular companion, Anthony Stockton, raised a hand and looked at him with a crooked smile. "You *again*, Stocker?" Steve asked, switching to his nickname. "You have not had enough punishment yet, I take it?" Anthony held his gaze.

"No, sir. But one of these days…" he laughed, gathering his books.

"Was that a threat, Stocker?" Steve's tone sounded serious, but the younger man knew it was all a game.

"No." He lifted his hand in mock salute, laughing. "That was a promise. Six it is then. This time I'm going to give you a run for your money!" When Steve caught up with the female students, they were stretched out on the grass, already engrossed in unraveling their problem. He sat down next to them and listened to their reasoning without interrupting.

"Not bad," he remarked. "Now, remind me again why you needed me?"

"Perhaps we only have to be in the presence of greatness?" Amy ventured. She and Megan burst out laughing. "There is a bright side to this equation, Professor. Even if we solve the problem ourselves, you still get to enjoy this glorious sunshine instead of being in a stuffy cafeteria. That must be a bonus."

"Right," he agreed dryly. "But next time you want to date me, just say so, girls." The atmosphere was light and filled with their banter. Steve unwrapped his home-made sandwich with tuna and cucumber and began tucking in. He intended to soak up every moment of unremitting sunshine that this unusual summer was bestowing upon them, allowing for plenty of outdoor time to enjoy the fresh air.

At this time of day the campus was abuzz with activity and Steve took pleasure in observing the unhurried routine of academic life as students moved about. He watched as the executive campus vehicle turned into the main gates followed by an unmarked, but official-looking car with tinted windows. Both vehicles pulled up to the front entrance and then Henry O'Malley alighted from the first car. Intrigued by the second vehicle, Steve waited for its occupants to emerge, barely aware of the incessant chatter of the girls.

Then the front doors of the second vehicle opened and Steve immediately recognized the two suited men as the out-of-place visitors at the Quadraquest. Their presence immediately piqued his curiosity and he wondered what the connection between O'Malley and these two men could be. He watched their interaction for a while and then lost interest and decided to continue the pleasant experience of picnicking with his two students on the lawn. Just then the back doors of the second vehicle opened and a woman and a young boy emerged into the bright sunlight. Steve's eyes fastened onto the woman who stood waiting for the boy to come around the back of the vehicle to join her. Then she gracefully approached O'Malley and held her hand out in greeting.

The sandwich in Steve's hand froze in midair as he stared at the woman in conversation with Henry. Her raven black hair gloriously reflected the bright sunlight and something urged him to pay attention. *Who on earth is this?* He was utterly captivated and only vaguely aware that his subconscious mind was scrambling to locate a place where he could have seen this woman before. Then he relaxed, realizing that these were the expected visitors from Israel.

Just as Steve made an effort to gather himself, the warm summer breeze carried her joyful, melodic laugh across the short distance. He listened spellbound. Amidst the on-campus buzz, a strange feeling stirred in him. He found himself eerily in a space in which he was aware of nothing except the attractive stranger some fifty meters away. *Where have I heard that laugh?* But before he could deliberate the thought, she turned her head and for a brief moment made eye contact with him. He thought he saw her stiffen slightly, but O'Malley's hand on her arm, ended the interlude as he led her toward the main entrance.

Henry O'Malley closed the door to his office behind his guests and politely gestured for them to sit. A formal and courteous man, his habit was to make small talk before getting down to business. Eva answered his questions about their trip mechanically. She and Hugo were tired and she found it hard to concentrate on what their host was saying. Her mind kept wandering back to the startling experience of a few minutes ago when she had made eye contact with the man on the grassy slope.

She was slightly uncomfortable with a stranger occupying her thoughts, especially when meeting with the head of the department responsible for Hugo's education. She had felt his presence before seeing him and wondered who he was. Confused with her irrational behavior, she put it down to the exhaustion and tension of their sudden departure from Israel. But her thoughts involuntarily drifted back to him. He seemed much older than his female companions and she wondered if he was a mature student.

Curiously, and despite the brevity of the interlude, Eva was inexplicably unnerved. Her conscious mind searched for explanations, but to no avail and she forced herself to concentrate on O'Malley's voice. He was asking if they had found the furnished apartment comfortable, and said something about it being located within walking distance of the campus. *Who are you? Why do I think I know you?* She thought of the tall stranger again and had trouble staying with the conversation.

"Why don't we go on a quick tour of the campus after we have had some refreshments?" Henry finally managed to break into her reverie. "I think young Hugo would like to see Professor Ballantire's class room." While his secretary poured tea for everyone and offered a tray of cookies, Henry continued. "Professor Ballantire will be in the annex this afternoon with the science project for undergraduates, but I've arranged for us all to meet over dinner tomorrow evening, at my house, if that's alright with you, Mrs. Norman?" He smiled warmly. "I thought to introduce you to some really good English cooking. I can personally vouch for my wife's culinary skills and we'd like you and Hugo both to feel at home here with us." Eva nodded politely.

"Thank you." She smiled and realized for the first time how utterly exhausted she felt. "We accept. Hugo and I will both enjoy meeting your wife and spending some time with you. But I believe that a short shopping trip has been planned for us later today?" She nodded her head to one of the agents a few feet away. "Mr. Rowlands here tells me we are going to the Metro Center to buy some necessities while we wait for our belongings to be forwarded from Tel Aviv."

"Ah, yes, the Metro Center. I'm sure that you will thoroughly enjoy the experience of this shopping complex. It has about three hundred and fifty shops and more than fifty restaurants." He looked at Hugo, but the boy returned his stare without showing emotion. He had already finished his tea and cookies and appeared tired. "Shall we go on that brief campus visit?" O'Malley stood and held the door for Eva. He looked at the two agents. "Please feel free to wait in the front office, gentlemen. Mrs. Norman and Hugo will be back shortly for their trip to the Metro Center."

They entered Steve Ballantire's lecture room whilst Eva listened to Henry's voice drone on about all the campus facilities, and she was relieved when they had finally reached Hugo's future classroom. They walked into the empty room and she sat down thankfully in one of the benches in the front row. Eva looked around. The place felt incredibly academic. It seemed filled with knowledge that hung tangibly in the air and yet it had a friendly touch to it. She imagined what it would be like when it was filled with the students and their teacher. The front podium sported a single plant with an exotic flower on it. O'Malley caught her eye.

"An orchid. He is quite an unusual man, I assure you." He looked over to Hugo, standing in front of the blackboard which spanned the length of the room with a long and complicated problem written on it. The boy pointed to a message above the unsolved equation. *Finish this if you can!*

"Mum?" Eva smiled, thrilled with her son's ability to communicate where mathematics were concerned.

"It's for the students, Hugo." But he was already holding a piece of chalk.

"Please?" he asked softly as he walked the length of the blackboard, already engaged in the problem.

"Another time, Hugo. We have to go."

"And why not?" Henry placed a gentle hand on her arm. "Go ahead, Hugo, while your mother and I continue our conversation. Why don't you see if you can solve Steve's problem?" The boy needed no further encouragement. Stepping back, he rolled the chalk between his palms and silently began reading the equation from the beginning. When he was confident that he grasped the essence of the problem, he ceased his fidgety movements and became very still, as if deep in thought. Then he came forward and slowly began writing. Hugo systematically moved along the blackboard, gradually revealing the solution that had befuddled Steve's students for more than a week.

Eva and O'Malley watched in silent fascination as Hugo finally arrived at the answer, signed his name and put the chalk down. O'Malley was speechless. An eleven-year-old boy had just solved one of Steve's brain teasers in the most unusual, creative way. Henry had noticed that Hugo did a lot of the calculations in his head and communicated minimally, which meant he was processing raw data at a very high level. In lieu of the briefing that he had received of the boy's handicap, he imagined that Hugo would find it difficult to verbalize how he had arrived at the answer.

Henry was eager to discuss the phenomenon he had just witnessed with Steve and immensely excited by the potential of the child that had been brought to them through very unusual circumstances. He could barely contain himself and couldn't wait to see Steve's face when he discovered that his brain teaser had been cracked.

Steve arrived a few minutes late for his next assignment of assisting Mike Burley in the science lab. His presence was not immediately required and he stood in the doorway leaning against the post, still trying to process the experience of a few minutes ago outside the administrative building. A very strange feeling had taken hold of him that stubbornly persisted and he was somewhat annoyed with the way he felt. Who was that woman? She came from another part of the world so she had to be a stranger, and yet his entire system screamed recognition. But how? Logically, it was simply not possible. He decided to make a quick stop at Henry's office before the day was over. He needed more information.

"Ah, Steve!" Henry waved him into his office. "I'm glad you are here. Our guests have arrived." Henry looked very pleased with himself, as if he was privy to some special information. "I know you were in the science lab the whole afternoon, but have you been back to your classroom?" Steve noticed the unusual excitement in Henry's demeanor.

"Why would you ask that?" He kept his voice even. Neither midterms nor work were on his mind, and he didn't quite know how to broach the subject of his real curiosity. Henry supplied the answer without him having to probe.

"I took Mrs. Norman and her son on a short tour of the campus. I showed them the lair where we tutor geniuses, since this is where Hugo, the boy, will spend most of his time." He smiled, watching the younger man closely, noticing that his quip did not cause the surface to ripple. "The child is everything and more than they have claimed. You'll see." Steve listened to every word and became very quiet. He took a deep breath and ignored the last part of Henry's statement.

"I see." He suddenly felt somewhat foolish and wanted to get out of Henry's office, but despite his best intentions, found himself asking the next question anyway. "Where is Mr. Norman?"

"Well, curiously, he is one of us, Steve; an Englishman and a diplomat, but Mrs. Norman is Israeli. I understand her husband is presently on assignment somewhere abroad." Henry's thoughts went back to what he had witnessed earlier in Steve's lecture hall. "Give me a call tonight." He smiled, gathering some papers on his desk. "You'll understand later." Steve's eyes narrowed, but he decided not to probe any further. When he made for the door, he was impatient to get away and engage in that game of squash with Stocker. He was angry and frustrated with himself and intended to punish that little rubber ball when he stepped onto the court. Stocker should not be expecting any mercy.

He left Henry's office and strode down the corridor. Despite his best efforts to forget the striking dark-haired woman, the inexplicable hollow feeling in the pit of his stomach persisted. *What in God's name is the matter with me? I haven't even met her!* But then he remembered her laugh, and realized that he was looking forward to meeting her. Glad to reach his lecture room, he wrenched open the door and headed straight to the locker in the back corner where he stored his sports gear. He glanced briefly at his watch and noticed that it was already close to six o'clock and if he were late for his appointment, he would never hear the end of it from Stocker. From the corner of his eye he caught the writing on the blackboard and then froze in his steps as he turned to look at it head on.

"Well, what do you know!" He spoke softly under his breath. "I had better get hold of Mrs. Shepherd to buy some jam." Just then his eye caught the name signed at the end. *Hugo.* "Jesus!" The profanity exploded softly from his lips. He took a step closer and stared in amazement at the work on the blackboard. Not only was another link added, but the whole equation had been completed. Underneath, another teaser had been started. What he was witnessing was the beginning of an illogical formula, which related more to theory physics than conventional mathematics. It concerned string theories and their dimensional impact when brought into line with advanced mathematics. He smiled wryly, remembering Henry's request for a phone call. Small wonder the man could not conceal his excitement. Steve took his sports bag and headed for the door, where he stopped to look one more time at the blackboard.

"Who's going to teach whom, Hugo? I wonder."

Dinner at Henry's house the following evening was both surprising and challenging. Young Hugo turned out to be very interesting and, contrary to expectation, Steve connected with the boy from the moment he bent down to shake his hand and compliment his work on the blackboard. He liked the direct stare of the child and throughout the evening Steve was aware that he was being carefully scrutinized. Although he talked about nothing else, the young boy's intelligence shone through in short but stimulating statements about the equation he had solved.

Eva listened in astonishment to the way in which Hugo not only articulated his particular genius to his new professor, but she was overwhelmed at the way he strung sentence after sentence together, seemingly becoming more proficient by the minute. Steve caught Hugo's eyes on him a few times but he didn't mind being examined by one with such great mental agility and was thrilled at the prospect of working with the boy. He couldn't help wondering about Hugo's handicap and how it affected him. He could see very little amiss.

But meeting Hugo's mother had completely shaken him up. Driving along the country road back to the farm, he recalled the attractive lilt in her voice when they shook hands and she introduced herself as Eva. Outwardly he was composed as he returned her polite greeting, but being face to face with her had stunned him. She was taller than average, but well proportioned and slender. Steve registered the totality of the woman in front of him with one look and quite irrationally, knew he would never forget her for as long as he lived. Throughout the evening the conversation shifted from Hugo's academic needs to the events leading up to their sudden departure from Tel Aviv as Steve learned of their harrowing flight from Israel.

He was captivated by her charm and easy manner and watched in silence how she used her hands when she spoke, or how easily she laughed. And while she seemed relaxed and at ease, he felt an unbearable tension beginning to build. Her smooth olive skin and hazel eyes were brilliantly offset by high cheekbones and a shiny curtain of black hair, and Steve had trouble not openly staring at the captivating Mediterranean woman across the table. Then the confusion of the day before when he first saw her, returned and there was no sign of his hallmark confidence when it came to the opposite sex. On the contrary, he was torn between making an excuse to leave early or to draw the evening out for as long as possible.

At a loss as how to deal with the effect she was having on him, he suddenly looked up from his reverie and met with her open stare. Their eyes locked and for an instant there was no one in the room but them. Her poise and ease was temporarily gone and he knew that she was aware of the moment between them. Steve's heart beat loudly in his chest, and his mouth felt dry, but she withdrew at once and smiled faintly, raising a trembling hand to her hair. When she looked away, the moment was gone, but it left him in a peculiar void and at a loss of explaining the nagging familiarity her presence summoned.

The arrival of the MI6 agents automatically signaled the end of the meeting. They were going to escort Eva and Hugo home before making the journey back to London. The evening ended with formal greetings between them and Steve left first, thanking his hosts for dinner and shaking the hands of Eva and Hugo again. Steve noticed that the boy made no effort to hide his curiosity and interest, but the mother avoided looking at him. Despite the handicap, he had no doubt that he and Hugo would understand each other. After all, mathematics was their shared language.

Steve stood beside his car in the dark. The farm was quiet and peaceful. At eleven o'clock there was barely any activity, save the sounds of the night. Suspended high in a velvet sky, the full moon was ample light for the trained eye. He surveyed the quiet landscape bathed in its muted glow and knew sleep would not come easily. Then he heard Quah Dreamer's soft call and his mind was instantly made up.

He had lost all track of time as he led the black stallion up the cinder track to the training course where he rode for hours. Quah Dreamer seemed to feel his mood and interpreted his master's intentions even before commands were given. They sailed through the night together in bursts of neck-breaking speed and only toned it down to a gentle gallop when both rider and horse were gasping for breath. When Steve finally led Quah Dreamer back into his stable, he took pains to brush his companion down thoroughly, all the time whispering in his ear and making soothing sounds. The horse snorted softly and responded by pressing his nose up against his master's shoulder.

Oblivious to the restless movements of the other horses, Steve sat down on a bale of hay and began feeding his steed by hand. For a long time he was lost in thought as his mind grappled with the events of the last two days. Past rationalizing his feelings and reactions, he was incapable of explaining the turmoil that this woman had caused; a stranger to him only a few days before. In fact, turmoil was not a word he had ever used to describe his feelings for a woman.

He had been briefly attracted to many and ended up bedding a fair deal. In one or two cases he was even mildly interested in pursuing a relationship but somehow always opted for his safe, solitary existence. But meeting Eva Norman had completely taken the wind out of his sails and he was at a loss to explain his feelings. Quah Dreamer bent his head and Steve scratched the horse absentmindedly on his forehead, speaking softly.

"Quah Dreamer," he whispered. The horse lifted his head abruptly and flared his nostrils, staring straight ahead, as if remembering something very important. Steve stood and through the high window behind them, caught the glint of the moon in the horse's eye. "What the hell am I going to do? I have been waiting for this woman all my life. But she is spoken for."

Chapter 17
Pangs Of Remorse

It was a day like any other when Chong-ba stepped from his cabin into the thin mountain air. His humble abode was craftily hidden in the shadows of the snow-capped peaks and only a few special guides knew how to avoid the dangerous cliffs along the way to reach him. He slowly filled his lungs with the cold air and sensed something extraordinary in his surroundings. He carefully scrutinized his immediate environment and allowed his gaze to travel far below to the sparse woodlands faintly hemming the foot of the mountain. He knew that terrain to be as inhospitable as where he lived amongst the creatures of this area. But nothing seemed out of place.

It was early but the rays of the sun cut through the thin wisps of moisture of a few lingering clouds and penetrated his weather-beaten skin to warm his very soul. He smiled. In all its harshness and generosity, nature occasionally bestowed small favors upon remote corners of the world and its grateful inhabitants. On this day it had surprised him with unexpected warmth in the same place where bitter cold is etched into the bleak rocks, as evidenced by the bristly, meager plant life.

Chong-ba's awareness was heightened as he started out on the narrow footpath to gather firewood. Years of meditation had taught him great patience. In time his persistence had been rewarded with the privilege of witnessing many wonderful manifestations of what often began as an intuitive feeling leading to an imminent event. But the monk was infinitely capable of more. Dedication and experience had blessed him with a talent to interpret meaning also, and on this unusually warm day, he felt the familiar stirrings of excitement.

It was the eagle that broke his rhythmic stride and stopped him in his tracks. He had noticed the bird on the first day he came to live in the mountains and from the very beginning they had struck a strange bond, a silent rapport that enchanted and surprised the monk. Leaning in against the wind, he held up a thin arm to shield his eyes against the brightness of the sun and stared in wonder at his rare, but welcome visitor.

The powerful body of a golden eagle sat motionless atop a barren tree, about thirty meters away from where his orange robe billowed slightly in the ubiquitous mountain breeze. Its head turned away, the bird scanned the valleys below for signs of life. Laser-sharp eyes were trained to catch every scuttle or nervous movement which could alert the hunter to the presence of prey. Like Chong-ba, the eagle was basking in the unusual warmth that this day had so unexpectedly bequeathed on them.

On the narrow footpath, the monk slowly went down on his haunches and waited while he stared at the magnificent bird of prey quietly scouting the mountainside. Time was suspended. The eagle was aware of Chong-ba's presence, but neither the bird nor the monk broke the spell. A small distance apart from each other, the early morning sun had wrapped them warmly together in time and space. Within an interconnected Universe, man and creature were one. Then suddenly, without making a sound, the bird spread its massive wings and lifted off from the treetop. Its rise into the blue sky took it precariously close to Chong-ba and as the eagle flew past him he noticed the bird's gaze fixed somewhere in the distance. The monk closed his eyes, convinced of the magic and mystery of the silent encounter. Then the eagle masterfully caught the undercurrents in the thin mountain air and maneuvered itself to higher elevations where it could ride the winds to soar above the mountains and the valleys far below.

When it was no longer visible, Chong-ba resumed his task of gathering firewood. Under the tree where the eagle had sat, he picked up a single brown tail feather that had been released from its body. He studied the intricate weave of the pattern in the reflecting sunlight and curiously lifted it to his nose to smell it. And then he knew.

"A visitor comes," he said softly. When Tom showed up the next day, Chong-ba had been waiting for him.

But now the two men sat quietly together. Their modest breakfast of bread spread with a thin layer of ghee and jam, washed down with a hot cup of tea, was long over. The only sound was the crackling fire which left a thin smoke trail in the cold air outside the cabin. Chong-ba knew that Tom had much on his mind, but he waited, allowing the Englishman to formulate his thoughts in his own time.

"I have a lot to answer for, Chong-ba," he finally said, moving his gaze from the dancing flames to meet the benevolent expression in the eyes of his host. "And I am in trouble." The monk nodded his head slightly in agreement. He briefly looked at the small compact case alongside his visitor, but refrained from comment. Tom caught his glance. "My communication equipment. It has to be turned on at all times, but I deliberately disabled it in Lahore with my last visit to the British High Commission."

"Your mission to me is on behalf of Mr. Goldberg. Surely he knows where you are?" Chong-ba watched him closely.

"None of this concerns Josh Goldberg." Tom nodded his head in the direction of the compact container beside him. "This is so that Colonel Appleyard, whom I also work for, can know where I am at all times. Turning it off represents a signal of distress. They will immediately start looking for me by using their last set of co-ordinates."

"I see." The monk stared into the flames, while the silence between them stretched. "You serve two masters," he remarked softly at last. The blatant truth of the statement hung in the air between them. Finally Chong-ba looked away from the flames and focused his stare on Tom. "How would you explain your transgression to this Colonel when you leave the mountain?" he asked quietly.

"Chong-ba," Tom smiled half-heartedly, "I can talk myself out of almost anything. I didn't think it would pose a real problem. I told Appleyard's people that I was taking a small vacation and I thought I'd be able to come up with—"

"You have had a change of heart about the purpose of your life." His words were barely audible, but Tom caught every one syllable. He nodded, impressed with the monk's perception.

"Appleyard is a very persuasive man, Chong-ba. He convinced me that our work was for the good of mankind; that certain undeveloped people were expendable and that common sense dictated that we lessen the burden on the planet by eliminating excessive demands on natural resources and food supplies. That would ensure the survival of the rest." He looked at the monk, but his thoughts were far away. "That was until you began talking about the interconnectedness of our world. Now I know it is no more than the slaughter of the innocent." His voice trailed off. "How could I have been so blind?" The monk didn't answer his question.

"What is your biggest urgency, Mr. Norman? Is it to contact your wife; is it Mr. Goldberg, or Colonel Appleyard?"

"My first responsibility is toward Eva. She and Hugo deserve better than the constant darkness in which they have been kept. She deserves a full explanation and I mean to give her exactly that. Straightening out my life starts with Eva. I want to set her free, Chong-ba. My wife is entitled to happiness, and her loyalty is keeping her bound to me. No matter how much I love her, I am not the man she needs."

"Then you should leave as soon as possible, Mr. Norman. We don't have to wait for a guide; I will accompany you down the mountain at the break of day." The tone of the monk was decisive.

"I'm afraid it is not that simple, Chong-ba," Tom said. "Because of the breach in communication policy, all border posts will be on the look out for me. They will pick me up long before I can get to Eva." Tom's voice had grown stronger. "I assure you that Colonel Appleyard will exact his pound of flesh before he allows me to see Eva. He wants the information I had been gathering over the last thirty days, and he will not let me go before he gets what he wants. Now that I see the error of my ways, I cannot reveal to him in good conscience what I know." The monk remained quiet for a long time. Then he leaned over and carefully placed more wood on the fire.

"That means you cannot leave the mountain at this time," he said, drawing his own conclusions. "It seems that presently the Colonel is a bigger threat than the man who sent you here." When he caught Tom's inquiring look, he continued. "But I also sense great danger from Mr. Goldberg, especially if he is crossed." Tom ran a fatigued hand over the stubble on his face, nodding in agreement.

"I'm afraid that we're at an impasse," he whispered in utter frustration. "I need to reach Eva, but Appleyard will prohibit contact until I meet with his demands."

"There is one more alternative." The monk reached his hand to his chest inside his robe. He stared intently at Tom. "If you write your wife a letter, I will take it to her." He said it simply, quietly while holding Tom's gaze. Tom didn't move, caught off guard by the extraordinary offer. Finally he spoke.

"You would leave the mountain and go to Tel Aviv for me?" He sounded incredulous. "*Why?*"

"Well, Mr. Norman, one part is not so difficult to understand. From what you have told me, if you tried to enter Israel or any other country, you would be intercepted at the airport. Either that or Mr. Goldberg would get to you first and rob you of the chance to put things right with your wife. Wild dogs rarely lose the scent, Mr. Norman. And you have two after you."

"How do you know these things?"

"On some level everything is known," the monk said quietly. Tom waited. He knew the little man wasn't done yet. Then Chong-ba withdrew his hand from inside his robe and held up a large brown feather. He placed it on the floor between them. "The second part requires a leap of faith on your behalf. A golden eagle dropped this here the day before you came. I knew that you were coming before you showed up, Mr. Norman." He picked up the feather and studied its patterns in the flickering light of the flames. For a long time neither said a word. Then the monk looked at Tom. "This feather is part of an enigma, a riddle, Mr. Norman. I cannot solve it, but your wife can. I told you the first day we met that your wife knows things." Tom nodded, still mesmerized. "My part is to make sure she gets this." Again Chong-ba inhaled deeply as he smelled the scent of the wild in the feather. "I will take your letter to her, Mr. Norman." Tom sat very quietly. For the longest time he just stared at the feather in Chong-ba's hand. When he finally spoke, he was still confused and his lips barely moved.

"Why can't it be mailed at the foot of the mountain?"

"Two reasons. The post is very unreliable from here. But even if the letter is mailed safely, that does not mean it will reach its destination. The CIA keeps a close watch on me for reasons we can discuss later, and they might intercept it. They have seized communication of mine before, which is why I rarely send anything by mail. Just a precaution."

Tom listened spellbound, surprised to learn of the CIA's interest in the monk.

"I have a question." Chong-ba waited motionlessly. "Is there such a thing as destiny?" Tom stared at his bald head as he posed the burning question. It all just seemed too easy, too obvious. And he didn't understand any of it. The monk smiled and shook his head almost imperceptibly.

"Universal Law can unlock many mysteries, Mr. Norman, but it harbors a special responsibility. Knowledge of these laws requires application of instinct as well as common sense."

"What universal laws are you talking about?"

"It will take time to explain, Mr. Norman. An obvious law at work here is the Law of Attraction. Incidentally, it is a law that is widely misunderstood in the world you come from, but more about this at an appropriate time, as it works in unison with some other important laws." The monk looked straight at him. "We have more pressing matters to deal with. Suffice to say that my bond with the eagle is certain. I had not understood it for a long time, but my desire to know had been very strong. The day I found the tail feather, I knew some answers were about to be revealed. Then you showed up and much of our conversation has been about your wife. That is how I know that the feather is for her, and I must find a way to deliver it." The monk smiled. "This is where logic and faith blend. You have to get a letter to her, and I have a feather in my possession that I sense she will understand the meaning of. You cannot leave here, so I will go." Tom nodded his head slowly, astounded at Chong-ba's explanation.

"We have one more challenge," the monk said quietly. Tom met his level gaze and waited. "The CIA might still have an interest in my movements, although they have not bothered me as long as I stay in this area." When he saw Tom's curious look, he continued. "It has to do with the Dalai Lama. The West has a vested interest in upholding the status quo. They have reasons for promoting all forms of organized religion, and the Dalai Lama is a favorite of theirs. Most people do not even know about the Penchant Lama, whom I support. But as I said, this is a discussion for another day." He smiled. "I have a hunch your stay will be extended here." Tom sat back and relaxed a little.

"You are a very interesting man, Chong-ba. And I would like to learn a lot more. But as for you crossing borders, I might know how to deal with the CIA. It is really quite simple." Tom chuckled. "Colonel Appleyard can arrange for your safe passage. He gives me what I want, and I reciprocate."

"We both know the Colonel is going to be disappointed with what you have to say. More lies, Mr. Norman?" The monk was serious again. "Your motives are already suspect. Why will he agree to this arrangement?"

"David Appleyard wants the information I have more than he cares about a letter being delivered to Eva. He will let you go to her and deal with me later." Tom stood and stretched his long legs. "But you will have to call him on a secure line and only I have that number." He locked eyes with the monk. "I will give it to you. That alone will convince the Colonel of the significance of our mission. Believe me, he will co-operate. The stakes are very high."

Colonel Appleyard stared with narrowed eyes over steepled fingers at Peter Adams. The agent had been flown in from Tel Aviv and was explaining the challenges of the mountainous terrain in which Tom supposedly found himself, in terms of electronic surveillance or communication. Even though he was rightfully an expert in his field, Adams was nevertheless annoyed at the volatile man glaring at him as he meticulously went over the technical difficulty of locating an agent whose equipment was turned off. It wasn't his fault that Norman had broken the rules. He sort of wished that the golden boy was dead somewhere in a ditch and if not, he would be picked up real soon anyway. Not even Norman could slip by a global alert if he dared to cross international borders.

He was tempted to advise Colonel Appleyard that locating Tom Norman without any hard evidence of his whereabouts would be equal to finding a needle in a haystack, but he refrained from using metaphor. He had a feeling the Colonel did not want to be reminded just how complicated matters had become. Appleyard remained silent for a long time. He still could not believe the extent of the mess staring him in the face. Then he spoke.

"This is a diplomatic disaster, Adams." Colonel Appleyard's voice was dangerously soft. He didn't blink. "Without Tom Norman's perspective I am feeling my way around in the dark and in the process we have already managed to trip over two corpses. These dead people showed up in Tel Aviv, *your* neck of the woods, and have understandably transformed your boss into a raving lunatic because a trail of death seems to be following the Norman family. Our Foreign Office and the Israeli government want answers, Adams. Answers that we simply don't have yet! Unless, of course, I can talk to our prize diplomat who, judging from those incriminating pictures your boss sent, has someone on his tail recording his every move!"

Appleyard eyed the man in front of him. Adams didn't know how high the stakes were, although his time for initiation into the real game was not far off. His composure was suddenly gone and he slammed his big fist violently onto his desk.

"Jesus Christ!" he shouted. "I can't believe this! I can't fathom that the man I had handpicked and groomed—" He left off in the middle of his sentence and cocked his head to one side, listening to something. The Colonel wrenched his top left drawer open and then Adams could also hear it. There was a clear buzz that sounded like a phone ringing, but the tone was a lot more subdued. Colonel Appleyard regained his composure and stared at the red phone buzzing away in the drawer. It was Tom.

"*Jesus!* Speaking of the devil—" He grabbed the phone as fast as he could and yelled at the top of his voice. "My God, Norman!" His rant was suddenly interrupted. "What? Yes, yes, of course, we'll accept the charges." His stride was only momentarily broken by the international operator with the heavy Indian accent. Then he heard the connection being made. "Where the hell have you been, Tom?" His outburst was met with a short silence.

"Colonel Appleyard?" The voice on the other end of the line was soft and composed. Appleyard froze in his chair, frowning. His control returned instantly and he was once again the head of MI6, aloof and on guard.

"Who is this?"

"A friend of Tom Norman's, Colonel, sir."

Appleyard considered the answer and realized that insisting on identity would be pointless; there was no way to establish the truth of any claim right this minute. If Tom had entrusted another to call him at this number, he could only surmise the reason to be a good one. At least there was some form of contact and he was determined to make the most of it. He took a deep breath and exhaled noisily through his nose.

"Tom is in trouble?" he asked evenly. The voice on the other end hesitated for a moment and then ignored the question.

"He wants to contact his wife, sir." Appleyard was momentarily confused and very angry.

"*What?*" Then he gathered himself. "Why doesn't he simply go to her? We've been waiting to hear from him—"

"Colonel, things have changed, sir. Mr. Norman is in some difficulty which cannot be divulged at this time."

"Who the hell are you? I want to talk to him!" Again the monk only answered part of the question.

"My name is Chong-ba. I am a monk from Tibet." Appleyard's brow furrowed heavily. He didn't reply immediately and leaned forward to scribble the name on a yellow legal pad on his desk. Something about that name instantly bothered him but, in his confusion, his mind wouldn't focus properly. He tore the sheet from the pad and passed it to Adams, indicating for him to check it out straight away. What was going on? A Tibetan monk is Tom's personal messenger?

"Where is Tom? I said I want to talk to him!" He glanced at Adams frantically checking international files on his laptop. It took only seconds to make the connection between the mystery caller and his name and he quickly scribbled a few key words down and passed them back to Appleyard who stared at the paper, raising his eyebrows only slightly. A big fish like this was speaking on behalf of Tom, one of his own? Appleyard closed his eyes in concentration to make sure he heard every word the monk spoke. Chong-ba remained courteous.

"Yes, sir. But after the delivery is made."

"What are you talking about? What delivery?" Appleyard's voice had gone deadly quiet.

"Mr. Norman wants to send his wife a personal letter. I am to take it to her in Tel Aviv." Appleyard immediately sensed his advantage. Obviously, Tom did not know that Eva was no longer in Israel.

"Absolutely not! First I speak to Tom and then we will arrange for him—"

"Then we have nothing further to discuss, Colonel," the monk said firmly. Appleyard hesitated and that was enough for Chong-ba to know that Tom had been right. The Colonel wanted to be privy to Tom's information. He pressed on. "That is the condition. Mr. Norman will answer all your questions after his wife gets the letter. He is quite anxious to speak to you also." David Appleyard tried once more.

"The letter could be couriered. I can make arrangements—" He was playing for time.

"No, sir." Colonel Appleyard wavered only briefly. He glanced again at the information from Adams.

"You're in Lahore?"

"I am in that area, sir. It would be foolish to try to locate Mr. Norman without my help, Colonel. You have my word on that." Appleyard's tactical mind was working ferociously. He was busy piecing together what he could remember from the past and checking it against the information that had just been handed to him. He could not let the opportunity to make contact with Tom slip through his fingers, but he also could not blindly trust a complete stranger, especially not *this* one.

"This is rather sudden. I will need to give the matter some thought. Is there a number where we may reach you?"

"No, Colonel."

"You have a passport?" It was a perfunctory question for he knew the answer. He noticed Adams' information stated that the monk was inactive and that he had retreated into the Himalaya Mountains to avoid capture and consequent incarceration. Appleyard's senses were highly alert as he listened to the voice on the other end. What an interesting, but dangerous turn of events!

"Yes."

"What is the name on it?"

"Chong-ba Chong." *Of course.* The Colonel smiled.

"Very well then. Call back tomorrow. I will give you my decision then."

"You have one hour, sir." The monk didn't hesitate and wasn't deterred. "Mr. Norman said you would try to trace the call, but your people will not be able to get here in less than two hours. If in one hour there is no decision, the deal is off. Good day, Colonel." Chong-ba replaced the phone and slowly backed away from the wooden table on which it sat, until he felt the flames of the open fire warm his backside.

He smiled at his old friend who owned the dilapidated convenience store in the rural outskirts of Lahore. The store was an extension of his house and mostly served the mountain dwellers. The luxury of a telephone was added a few years ago to hasten orders placed to far-off suppliers in Lahore. It was a simple piece of equipment and still operated through an exchange, which had made the collect call to the Colonel somewhat easier and a lot cheaper. He bowed his head gratefully when a bowl of broth was handed to him.

The two men didn't speak as they sat side by side scooping the steaming hot curried dhal into their mouths with pieces of sourdough bread. For now, they both waited. Without the need to fill time and space with unnecessary words, an hour between two old friends would pass very quickly. When Chong-ba called back, it was the monk's turn to pay attention. Colonel Appleyard got right to the point.

"You must listen carefully. You will not be traveling to Tel Aviv. Tom's wife and son are under our protection in England. His clandestine dealings with Mr. Goldberg necessitated that."

"England?" Chong-ba sounded shocked and Appleyard, enjoying the monk's surprise, deliberately refrained from elaborating. He too knew how to play this game.

"You can tell Mr. Norman that I look forward to talking to him at his earliest convenience." The sarcasm did not escape the monk. "If Tom is unwilling or unable to enlighten me as to the details of his circumstances, then Mrs. Norman can explain to you and her husband why she is in the United Kingdom."

"She is safe, sir?" Chong-ba couldn't help himself, but it was the Colonel's turn to play his cards close to his chest.

"Your ticket and all relevant documents will be waiting for you at the information desk of Pakistan Airlines at the airport in Lahore. We used the address and phone number of a local colleague in the city for identification purposes. You leave the day after tomorrow at 11.45am local time which should give us enough room to organize your visa.

Upon arrival in Newcastle, go to the British Airways information desk where a driver will be waiting to take you to your hotel. You are staying at the Royal Station Hotel in the center of the city where you will meet Peter Adams of my department. He will accompany you to Mrs. Norman whom you are meeting at the world-famous Beamish open air museum for 1pm. We chose a public place for security reasons. She'll be in the ladies' waiting room at the old railway station. You will both be protected; I'm sending a few of my men ahead to keep a watchful eye."

"Thank you, sir." He would have been surprised if they didn't put a tail on him. But Appleyard's impatience was growing.

"Tell Tom that I will be waiting. Adams will return with you to Pakistan the following day to interview Tom on my behalf. Tom Norman has much to explain." There was a short silence. "No tricks, Chong-ba. I am overextending myself here. If either you or Tom tries to—"

"I see. Mr. Adams is traveling back to Pakistan with me." He didn't wait for confirmation. "Thank you, Colonel. No need for threats. I will not miss my flight. Good-bye." His voice was respectful, but firm. Appleyard heard the muted click in his ear and for a long time he just sat staring at the phone in his top drawer. Then he closed it slowly and caught Peter Adams' eye.

"Stanway tells me this Goldberg character of Azvaalder was fired by the board of directors in New York. He gave me sketchy details only, enough to be able to negotiate with the monk." His stare was dispassionate. "Frankly, I was only concerned with reaching Tom Norman until he made his wife my business also. You had better fill me in."

"Yes, sir. He has two accomplices, Dmitri Anchov, an ex-KGB agent recruited by Goldberg some two years ago, and Tomer Mendel, a local Jew from Tel Aviv. Mendel is a communications expert and a wizard on a computer. Anchov is just a goon, but a very dangerous one. He kills first and then asks questions. We checked his background in Moscow where he has left a bloodied trail. It was all in the line of duty and service, but it really wasn't pretty."

"Go on." Appleyard listened intently.

"Azvaalder is headquartered in New York. They are leaders in the field of electronic surveillance and Josh Goldberg headed up their Tel Aviv organization. He is ex-CIA and still has many contacts in the field. I think it will be safe to assume that his employers found his particular background and experience enticing. Azvaalder sponsors gifted children with the aim of recruiting them at some point into the business.

"The Norman child was one of their protégés, but Eva Norman was uncomfortable with the interest in their son, especially when Goldberg wanted to transfer him to a location at the University of Tel Aviv where she would have had limited access to him during the day. That was when she contacted Mr. Stanway and asked for advice. Shortly after, she discovered that her house was under surveillance and, with Tom unavailable, she requested our help. Tom had previously left instructions with us that if his wife ever needed help, it be given to her. We hastily changed our plans from flying them out on a scheduled flight from Tel Aviv to quite an unconventional route, after Martha Bartholomew's strangled body was discovered and Eva's brother-in-law turned up dead in a parking lot. Martha Bartholomew's slaying was exposed only after you saw the drawings of the child and requested to speak to her."

"I remember." Colonel Appleyard steepled his fingers again, staring at Adams as he listened.

"Goldberg tried to create an international incident by suggesting to the Israeli government that Eva Norman had been sprung from Israel without her consent and that we had ulterior motives in bringing her and the boy onto British soil. James Stanway retaliated immediately by contacting Azvaalder in New York, accusing them of unethical practices as far as having Eva and her son under surveillance.

"We have proof of that. We found hidden microphones and cameras in her mother's house after Eva and the child had left; all of it Azvaalder equipment. As a precaution, Mrs. Norman's mother was then taken to a safe house, to give us time to put all the pieces together. Mr. Stanway stated in his letter to Azvaalder that, due to Tom's diplomatic status, the Normans were removed at the request of Mrs. Norman after she had complained of feeling unsafe. My boss also copied the Ministry of Foreign Affairs as well as the Ministry of Public Security of Israel in his letter. I'm sure you can imagine the upheaval this caused.

"Azvaalder was in the middle of negotiating some very big contracts with the Israeli government, but these were unceremoniously put on hold even though Goldberg and his cohorts were summarily fired. As you can imagine, the Americans are demanding Tom Norman's role in the whole affair be revealed. Apparently those pictures of him also showed up at Azvaalder headquarters. They are not willing to take the fall alone and they are demanding answers as to his connection with the disgraced Josh Goldberg. Someone has to pay the piper and they have their sights securely set on Tom and, of course, the Embassy, us." Adams stood. "Goldberg, Anchov and Mendel have since disappeared, sir. No one knows where they are."

"This does not look good, Adams." Only Appleyard and Stanway knew the real lay of the land. "I realize that. That's why we have to get to Tom first and hear his side of the story. Why was a perfectly good operative of ours involved with the likes of Goldberg? Was it only to make extra money on the side, or are there other reasons? That is what we don't know and what we must find out. You're just the man to handle this project. That's why I brought you back here." Appleyard rose from his chair and walked over to the window overlooking the Thames River. Adams looked at his bulky figure silhouetted against the gray skies outside.

"I'm curious, sir. Why would you allow a letter to be delivered to Mrs. Norman? We have no idea what Tom might say to her and I'm wondering if—"

"Mr. Adams, I cannot even begin to guess what circumstances Tom Norman finds himself in at this time. But this I know: he would never be so reckless as to involve his wife in any of his activities. Besides, we need that information!" He turned and stared at Adams. "The monk gets the go-ahead from us and the CIA. Is that clear?"

"Yes, sir."

"Mrs. Hogan has booked your flight and hotel accommodation along with that of the monk. You will accompany him to Eva Norman and give him the chance to deliver Tom's confession, or whatever the hell it is he needs to get off his chest. Then you and the monk will board the first plane to get his holy ass together with your not-so-holy-ass into bloody Pakistan so we can get some closure to this mess. I need to know all about those extended visits Norman made from Tehran to

Rabat and find out what else in God's name he had been up to whilst he was over there." He turned and stared directly at Adams. "He's been incommunicado for too long and now it looks as though we may lose him permanently! Why else has he disappeared and the monk is acting as his spokesperson?

"That information is crucial and you are my man. You will travel on a need-to-know basis, and you will receive your final orders once you are in Pakistan with the monk." He lowered his voice. "I hand picked you. I know you are up to the task. Right now, the Israeli's are foaming at the mouth. If they had their way, our prized diplomat, presently freezing his balls off somewhere in the bloody mountains of Pakistan, if he's under the monk's protection, would be dragged back here to be court-martialed. Let's face it, no matter how you look at it, Tom Norman is not in an enviable position." Appleyard turned around. He didn't smile. "And who can blame the Israeli's for all their anger and fury? This has made all of us look like a bunch of incompetent fools."

Appleyard felt a stab of regret. Something had gone wrong and Tom needed help, and it was the kind of help only he, Appleyard, could provide. He just wasn't sure if Tom was still on board or not. Politics was, after all, a selfish game, a game that richly rewarded the winners and dearly punished the losers. There was only limited space for friendship and loyalty; qualities usually ascribed to the highest bidder. And it was a genuine problem if you liked or preferred one who couldn't pay. Tom Norman had once fitted that description, but he changed the goalposts and had become a loose cannon. The situation had become highly unpredictable and the balance of power could shift at any moment. And that he couldn't allow.

"Bingo!" Tomer Mendel exhaled slowly and wiped the sweat from his brow. Tracking the activity in and out of Pakistan was not difficult if you could hack into government computers. The rush of excitement that had coursed through his body when he broke the first code was almost worth the punishment that would follow if he was exposed. He was disappointed that the challenge was over so quickly. The booking was actually made under the monk's own name. He laughed softly. *Now that was a real blunder.*

Josh had given him a bunch of variables to work with, and Chong-ba and Tom's names were the most important ones to watch for. Norman was in Pakistan, and if there was going to be activity, it would be generated from this location. Mendel had hacked into the immigration network of Pakistan and constantly monitored who was entering or leaving the country. With a smirk on his face, he printed the details of the flight and the hotel booking in England, all handled through the same company. Then he picked up his cell phone and didn't bother to greet the person when the call was answered.

"It is the monk. He is scheduled to leave Pakistan tomorrow. I will email the details to you." He snapped his phone shut. He had to work for Goldberg because his options were somewhat limited after the scandal in Tel Aviv. But that didn't mean he had to like the bastard.

When Chong-ba reached the cabin early the next day, he found Tom much refreshed and more relaxed than he had been so far. In a way, Tom was glad that he had found a place which would provide the seclusion that he required. On the other hand, he had no idea how long he would have to remain here. Chong-ba found him outside, pacing around the cabin's perimeter and taking in the breathtaking beauty of the mountainous regions. Soft white clouds had rolled into the side of the mountain beneath the cabin; they reflected the light from the sun and transformed the whole area into a brilliantly lit paradise.

"Come inside, Mr. Norman." Chong-ba stood at the door. He had been traveling all day and yet didn't appear tired at all. "You wrote your letter?" he asked when they were seated and each holding a cup of steaming hot tea. Tom pointed to a sealed envelope lying on the mat which also served as his bed.

"Yes. And I know it is inadequate, but it is at least a start. This is Eva." He held out a picture of his wife, which Chong-ba took and placed in the palm of his hand. Chong-ba stared for a long time at the smiling face of the beautiful dark-haired woman and then looked up to meet Tom's gaze. He didn't tell him that he already had seen her in a vision and knew what she looked like.

"I can understand your pain, Mr. Norman." Tom nodded, distraught and unable to speak. He quickly put the picture away and leaned back against the dirt wall of the cabin. He was shocked to hear his family had been taken to England but assumed that Stanway had acted on his request for protection in case of an emergency. Tom wished he could leave the mountain, but knew it was too dangerous and that he would have to count on Chong-ba to bring him news of his family; the wait would be excruciating. He looked at the slight frame of the man sitting opposite him.

"Adams is Colonel Appleyard's insurance policy. That is why he is sending him back with you." The monk nodded silently. "You will need some sleep, Chong-ba. Tomorrow you have to go back down the mountain again and stay overnight somewhere." Chong-ba smiled and answered the unasked question.

"I will find a bed with the local store owner in the furthest outpost from Lahore. We made arrangements yesterday to catch a ride to the airport with a delivery van that comes to his place occasionally. Do not be concerned, Mr. Norman. I will be fine. And I have brought enough supplies for you to last about ten days, but I will be back before then."

"Will you tell her how sorry I am?" Tom couldn't help himself. The finality of their separation weighed heavily on his mind, and he found himself tripping down memory lane constantly, feeling the sharp pangs of remorse at losing such an unusual woman. But it was too late for that and he hoped the letter would explain to her some of his difficulties over the years. He wanted her forgiveness and he wanted her to be happy. He also wanted to set her free before he had to answer for his past. Chong-ba nodded his head imperceptibly.

"I will, Mr. Norman. Now let us prepare a meal together and get some sleep." He leaned forward and took Tom's letter. "I will put this where I keep the feather; inside my robe where my heart beats."

The next morning when Tom awoke, he was alone in the cabin and his body shook with cold. He had not heard the stealthy movements of the monk, who had risen at 4am to start his long and dangerous journey to the foot of the mountain. Tom sucked in his breath as he stepped into the cold air outside to fetch more firewood. Trundling along the narrow mountain path, he was suddenly met with the unexpected sight of a magnificent bird perched atop the high branches of a leafless tree.

The air was freezing but Tom held perfectly still as he watched the bird silhouetted so clearly against the gray sky. Could this be Chong-ba's visitor of the other day? Then the eagle expertly lifted itself into the wind and spread its wings, skillfully ascending to higher elevations. Tom watched the powerful movement of the bird in the wind and his heart was suddenly filled with indescribable joy. Chong-ba had said that the tail feather would mean something to Eva. Warm tears stung behind his eyes. *I think he was right, Eva, my darling. I hope with all my heart that the monk was right.*

Chong-ba was a light traveler and insisted on carrying his single piece of luggage to his room. The porter was annoyed. If the monk could afford the rates of the Royal Station Hotel, he could afford the expected gratuity fee. But Chong-ba hardly noticed. It was 9am and the desk clerk informed him that Mr. Adams had checked in the previous day and was awaiting his arrival in room 409.

Instead of using the elevator, he chose the stairs and mounted them two by two as he made his way to the fourth floor. He was excited about the meeting with Eva, scheduled for 1pm that day and he was more convinced than ever that his intuition had been directing him accurately. In front of room 409 the monk suddenly froze, instantly aware of a very strange presence. He looked around him but there was no sign of movement and the corridor was completely deserted. Then he slid the card key through the narrow slot and a green light alongside flashed briefly. Chong-ba opened the door and stepped inside. In the dimly lit room he identified the silhouette of a man sitting in a chair in front of the window. He didn't acknowledge the monk, nor move.

"Mr. Adams, I am Chong-ba." He walked up to the man and respectfully bowed his head. Then the monk's entire body went rigid and he clasped his hands together as his eyes adjusted to the twilight conditions in the room. The man in the chair was clearly dead, strangled with his own tie. Chong-ba looked around the room carefully, but it seemed devoid of any life or movement.

He did not have a lot of time to make decisions, but knew that alerting the authorities to his find would not only delay his meeting with Eva, but possibly prevent it altogether. He would have to take a calculated gamble and proceed to the meeting place on his own. His hand automatically reached inside his robe where he kept the five hundred pounds he had discovered inside the envelope that held his flight ticket to England. Colonel Appleyard had thought of everything. He closed the door behind him again and stepped into the corridor. Then he noticed the stairs to the fire escape.

At the back of the hotel Chong-ba took a few moments to orient himself. Then he casually walked around the building to the front and stepped onto the curb to hail a taxi. Inside the cab he caught the curious eye of the cabby.

"Please take me to your world-famous museum, Beamish." When he saw the slight hesitation of the driver, he pulled out a few ten pound notes and waved them so the cabby could see them in the rear view mirror, and continued. "I'd like to brush up on a bit of culture, sir. I believe this museum has won many prizes? I can't wait." The cabby nodded and pulled into the traffic. He reminded himself to never again say that he had seen and heard everything.

Josh Goldberg started the rented car on the opposite side of the road.

"Beautiful!" he said as he quickly merged into the traffic. He was exuberant. "Thank you, your fucking holiness! If I had the time to be humble I'd get out of the car to kiss the goddamned ground. But you're just a stupid little monk in a frumpy, outrageous orange dress. Who cares?" He laughed without any joy. "You are going to lead me straight to Eva. And if you were really close to that God of yours, he'd be warning you that I will make her pay dearly for all the humiliation and for stealing my opportunity to greatness by taking Hugo from me!"

Josh followed at a safe distance behind the taxi carrying Chong-ba. For a fleeting moment he thought back to the incident in the hotel. Posing as a technician checking television equipment, Adams had surprised him by showing up in advance of the monk. He obviously had to kill him; there was no alternative, although he did not enjoy it as much as meticulously planning an execution. And he had surmised that discovering the body would send the monk running. He was right.

As Josh thought of Eva, his breathing became labored and he began to sweat profusely. The anticipated kill would not happen for quite a while, but his body responded with the usual sexual arousal as he imagined squeezing the life from her. He clenched his teeth in an effort to stay the pain rising from his groin.

It is not long now, bitch! I made a pact with the devil some time ago, and he promised to make the excruciating wait every bit worth my while!

Chapter 18
Electrifying Experience

Steve watched Hugo carefully from where he stood at the podium. Eva Norman's brilliant child, with whose education he was entrusted, was back before the blackboard with a piece of chalk in his hand. Steve observed as the young boy effortlessly wrote out an equation which involved complicated angles and trajectories.

He was captivated with the way Hugo's mind worked and could only surmise that the new equation was somehow linked to theoretical physics, a most unusual pathway for any mind to explore, let alone a child of his age. Steve did not interfere. He looked at the intense concentration on the child's face, took a deep breath and grappled once again with his emotions that had been in such disarray from the moment he met Hugo's striking mother.

Eva Norman. Steve's gaze traveled from Hugo to the exquisite orchid adorning the podium. Like this delicate plant that he had nurtured for so long, she was very unusual. He had made a concerted effort to consciously exclude her from his thoughts, but to no avail. In the few short weeks since he had met her, he had become used to encountering her image in his mind's eye upon awakening, or imagining hearing her beautiful laugh. But he was still no closer to explaining why a virtual stranger almost constantly filled his thoughts.

He grinned a little to himself, transferring his attention again to her son writing away on the blackboard. He had absolutely no idea what the future held, but somehow Eva's son had become his protégé and he had been assigned to helping this highly gifted child develop his talents and skills. He forcibly put the image of the boy's mother out of his mind. Hugo took a step away from the blackboard and scanned the brainteaser from start to finish. Steve smiled at the boy's seriousness.

"Very impressive, young man," he said softly. "Tell me, Hugo. Do you expect any of my students to solve this one?" Hugo tilted his head to one side.

"I can make my mind still. That is how answers come. It is the Zen state." He stopped, suddenly unsure of what to say next. He felt relaxed in the company of his new teacher and liked how easy it was to talk to him. Steve laughed as he walked around from the podium to join the boy at the blackboard. He and Hugo had established a bond that first night at Henry's house where they had met for dinner.

"So you think they're up to it? Firstly, I don't think many of my students know what the Zen state is. This equation of yours will challenge even *me*, let alone my class, who puzzled for weeks over the problem that you solved in a half hour or less." Steve casually lifted himself onto one of the desks, looking at Hugo, whose attention was back to the blackboard. He imagined the upbringing Hugo had had so far to be vastly different from his own. Although the child was not exuberant in nature, Steve could not detect his handicap, and made a mental note to discuss the issue with Henry O'Malley.

The farm on which Steve had grown up held a special place in his heart. It was an intriguing setting which held many mysteries that had fascinated him for years. Some time ago he had learnt from local historical documents that his homestead was situated on ancient ley lines. These were well-trodden routes left by early travelers of times gone by; denoted by energy spots.

Eventually these routes became energized from so much regular activity where sensitized topographical blueprints evolved over time, which could easily be detected and read by an insightful observer. Despite the speculation about the existence of these lines, Steve had a feeling that his interest ran deeper than anything that history books or blueprints could satisfy. He was sufficiently intrigued and endeavored to construct a theory that would give him some answers. So far it had resulted in frustration every time. His gaze wandered back to what Hugo had written on the blackboard, quite in awe of the boy's potential.

"Do you know what ley lines are, Hugo?" The boy briefly glanced at him.

"Very old energy markings." Steve hesitated for a moment, marveling at the extent of the child's knowledge. Hugo's serious and innocent exterior was quite deceiving and he tremendously enjoyed the company of the young boy. Completely unpretentious, it made the depth of his knowledge and untapped talent that much more stimulating to work with. The child's ability to communicate seemed to be unfolding on a daily basis, although his speech was restricted to math or science. Hugo didn't know how to make small talk. Steve couldn't help wondering what his students would make of the serious, gifted child from Israel who had come to join them midterm.

"That is correct," Steve said evenly. "It is an energy print of times gone by." Then he launched into a discussion of the intricacies of energy lines and mentioned that there were some on his farm he wished to understand better. As he spoke he noticed how the boy's expression began to change. Then without another word Hugo entered some quick calculations on the board.

"If we use leading trajectories, keeping quantum numbers—" Hugo stopped abruptly and looked at Steve. The Professor was smiling as he arched his back to scratch it with a ruler.

"What are you thinking, Hugo?"

"Have you tried to use parts of your farm and triangulating them with the stars?"

"Not quite, young man. I've tried other methods, but please, tell me more." He was suddenly enormously excited by Hugo's suggestion. The child had an incredible mind!

"Could I see these on your farm?"

"Of course, Hugo. That would be the best way to do it, wouldn't it? Then we could examine these together." Steve hesitated again. "You could come with me, or you might want to bring your mother along and visit for a day or so."

"Ask her." The boy said it simply, calmly, before turning back to the blackboard again, instantly immersed in his latest train of thought. Steve smiled at the back of Hugo's head.

"It is settled then," he said softly. "I will call your mother and invite the two of you to visit on Saturday, if you don't have other plans." The feeling of anticipation that filled his heart was very hard to suppress. He was genuinely interested in Hugo's contribution in solving the mystery of the ley lines on his farm, but he could not deny the excitement he felt at the prospect of seeing Eva Norman. One way or another he had to deal with his emotions. Perhaps if he saw her again, it would all dissipate and he would feel quite the fool for having entertained thoughts about a woman he had only once met. His resolve was not very convincing, but he chose not to analyze it any further.

Earlier that morning Eva answered Henry O'Malley's phone call and listened with her heart in her throat. MI6 had word about Tom and wanted to meet with her. She was instantly unnerved and fearful that the meeting was once again shrouded in secrecy. It was scheduled to take place at a museum in the area, known as Beamish. She had difficulty speaking.

"If it is bad news about my husband, Professor, why don't they just tell me?" As she spoke, she realized that O'Malley would not be privy to anything of a personal nature nor any security issues. In her short acquaintance with the clandestine world of secret organizations, she knew that they would not involve an outsider without good reason. Henry O'Malley was nothing more than a messenger. The short silence with which she was met confirmed her suspicion. "Pardon my ignorance," Eva apologized softly. "What is Beamish, Professor, and when is this meeting to be scheduled?"

"I'm sorry that I don't have more information, Eva." He sounded genuinely regretful. "I really wish I could be of more help." He made an effort to change his tone to a more optimistic one and found himself rattling off the information. "But I can at least enlighten you about Beamish. It is world-famous and is quite different from your conventional museum. It is a huge outdoor complex, and is concentrated on buildings and artifacts from the year 1913. You are to meet the representatives in the ladies' waiting room at the old railway station within the museum."

"What time and when?" she asked faintly. "And how do I get there?"

"Monday at 1pm. I will send the campus vehicle to pick you up at noon. That should make matters easier for you." Eva didn't ask any more questions. She thanked O'Malley and put down the phone. Tears of frustration blurred her vision. *When will this end?* She realized that the meeting place was chosen because it was public and relatively safe and they probably wanted to keep Hugo out of the picture as much as possible. Although she had managed to bring their child to his father's country of birth, she had not been able to escape the nagging concern she felt for Tom. The uncertainty about him had been eating away at her; she knew he was in trouble but she was powerless to help. All she could do was to wait. Now, suddenly, out of the blue, there was word about Tom, but she had no idea what to expect. Her husband's movements had been a mystery to her for most of their married life and it was responsible for the emotional distance between them.

Lost in thought, Eva stood at the window and allowed memories of Tom to wash over her. Still the handsome man of years ago, she loved him in her way but had known for years that the essential passion needed to keep the flame of intimacy ablaze had never burned intensely; instead, with his constant absences, it had finally flickered out. She had tried to keep it alive, but after so many lonely nights she had resigned herself to circumstances and concentrated her energy and attention on the needs of their growing son. As the years went by, the sharp pangs of regret she occasionally felt were gradually replaced with acceptance and a simple need to know that Tom was safe. She no longer had to be the caretaker. And now suddenly, after escaping Josh Goldberg and coming to England, there was word from him. *Why now?*

Then she saw the campus vehicle pull up to the curb outside their apartment. Hugo got out of the car and ran as fast as his legs would carry him toward the front entrance of the building. He appeared very excited and she wondered what might have caused her son to behave so out of character. When he came through the front door he threw his arms around her waist and pressed his face tightly into her body.

"I want to go!" Eva laughed at his unusual display of emotion and enthusiasm.

"Where do you want to go, Hugo?" She was still so overwhelmed with the new doors of communication that had opened between them. It didn't matter that he only used short sentences.

"The Professor's farm. Tomorrow. He will call." He abruptly let go of her and began talking about solving mysteries on Steve's farm using the constellation of the stars. He mentioned ley lines and some other terms she did not understand. But her thoughts were captured by the mental image of Steve Ballantire; the tall fair man on the grassy slope outside of the administrative building and whom she later met at O'Malley's dinner.

"Tomorrow?" But Hugo was already making his way to the safe

haven of his bedroom. Then the phone rang in the hallway. Long after Eva had replaced the receiver on its cradle, she stood in the same spot, lost in thought and confused at feeling excited and apprehensive about his gracious invitation to spend the day at his farm. Steve Ballantire had offered to fetch them early in the morning and return her and Hugo after dinner. Eva put a hand to her throat and closed her eyes. *What is the matter with me? I hardly know you.* She was not aware of Hugo in the doorway or of his curious expression. He saw his mother brilliantly silhouetted against the light streaming in through the glass panel in the front door.

"Are we going?" he asked, staring at the colors clearly visible in her energy field.

"Yes, Hugo." She felt flustered and didn't know why.

"You know my teacher?" he whispered.

"Only from meeting him at Professor O'Malley's. Why?"

"Nothing." He couldn't explain it either. He had only seen her aura lit with colors like that when she was very emotional. He did not understand any of it; the Professor was a stranger to her.

The next day the mystery intensified. From the moment he stood in her doorway and politely held out his hand, Eva was intensely aware of the man in her presence. Even the breathtaking journey along the green pastures and winding roads around Elwick did little to distract from her engaging company until they turned into the gates of his farm, Ocean View. She tried to ignore aspects about his physical persona, but while Hugo leaned his arms on the back of her seat and soaked in his surroundings, she noticed things that she had not paid attention to in a man for ages. She saw how the sun glinted on the tiny hairs on the back of Steve's hands and listened to his deep voice as he entertained Hugo's carefully constructed questions about the farm, ley lines, star constellations, the horses he trained and many, many more. A whole new side of her boy was opening up and she was thrilled. It was her own reactions that she did not understand.

She marveled at the way Steve included her in every discussion. He was clearly socially skilled and she caught his casual glance resting on her a few times. Eva struggled to analyze her feelings. The man sitting next to her was visibly comfortable with members of the opposite sex and although she hadn't noticed a ring on his left hand, she knew that to be meaningless. Steve Ballantire was every inch the comfortable, polite host intent on entertaining his guests. Every time he looked at her, his manner was reserved but friendly. She chastised herself that she had imagined that short interlude with him during dinner at O'Malley's house. There was no trace of personal interest as he easily shifted his attention between Hugo and her.

For the first time in her life, Eva was faced with feelings that she could not control and it unnerved her. She was relieved that the attention would be on Hugo and resolved to make sure his needs were met. But the introduction to the horse changed that decision instantly. Pulling up to the front of the farmhouse, Steve explained that his elderly neighbor, Mrs. Shepherd, had packed a picnic and that the plan was to visit the wooded areas to investigate the ley lines. He wanted to leave right away and bring his favorite horse, after confirming that neither of them feared these big animals.

Hugo brimmed over with enthusiasm as he waited beside his mother for Steve to return with the horse. Eva had rarely seen her son so openly excited and felt a little sad that his biological father had never seemed to be able to stimulate his interest the way Steve had captured his attention. But neither of them was prepared for what was to follow as Steve led his beautiful black stallion through the gates of the paddock from the training camp. Eva watched the horse from a distance and felt her mouth go dry. Twenty feet away from her the horse suddenly halted and refused to move. Steve urged him along and tugged at his reins.

"Come on, boy!" But the horse would not budge. He held his head high and seemed to look at Eva. In the bright sunlight his muscles rippled nervously under his shiny, ebony skin all the way from his head to his tail. The huge animal was clearly distraught and Steve was momentarily concerned about the strange behavior. He looked at Quah Dreamer's big head and spoke softly to him, but the animal just flared his nostrils and snorted nervously.

"Why is he crying, mum?" Hugo stood beside Eva, tense and in awe of the quivering animal. He was incapable of explaining to his mother that the numerical pattern of the horse indicated its discomfort. It appeared upset and he didn't understand why. Eva could barely speak.

"I don't know, Hugo." She stared transfixed at the gorgeous animal. "How do you know he is crying?" But Hugo didn't answer, and her voice trailed off as she felt her heart thundering in her chest. The horse maintained eye contact and she felt the emotion build like rising floodwater. She put a shaky hand up to her throat and began to tremble uncontrollably.

When the horse broke free from Steve's grasp, it happened so fast that Eva barely had time to move. Taking a few huge strides, he halted right in front of her in a cloud of dust. Then he spread his front legs and dropped his head so that she could reach out and touch him. Steve stifled the urge to restrain the horse and stood riveted as his prize animal allowed Eva to stroke his powerful neck. Her other hand covered her mouth and by the time he had reached them, he noticed that her eyes were filled with tears. Steve firmly took hold of the reins and looked at her, unable to explain the behavior of the horse or to apologize.

"I'm sorry," she whispered awkwardly. "I have no idea what has come over me. I have always admired horses, but this one—what is its name?" She looked from Steve back to the horse, unable to find the right words. She desperately tried to prevent her body from trembling so noticeably.

"He was sold to me as Bullet, but he has another name. Please accept my apology. I didn't mean for him to scare you." He retained his hold on the horse, but he really wanted to reach out and comfort her. She looked so vulnerable and lost and he felt responsible for having upset her. "I'll take him back. He can do his walk later on. I'll get one of the farm hands—"

"No!" She reached out a hand, but refrained from touching him. "I'm sorry." She was suddenly flustered and nervous. "I mean, it is fine. *Please.* He could come with us if that was your original plan. I know you and Hugo are going to be busy and I'd be happy to walk him." She held out her hand, asking for the reins from Steve but in that moment the black stallion put his head down and gently sniffed her hair. Eva laughed spontaneously and stroked his face, aware of something very strange happening. Steve stared at her. There was that beautiful laugh again, the one he remembered from their first meeting, and the same laugh that had been haunting his dreams. He was mesmerized with the instant bonding of his trusted steed with this dark-haired woman. Then he gathered himself and smiled at Eva as he handed her the reins and took a step back. He couldn't help wondering what he was getting into. Regardless of her charm, this woman was not available.

"As you please, Eva," he said softly. "He is usually apprehensive of strangers but he seems to have instantly taken to you." Then he looked over at Hugo who had been quietly observing the emotionally charged exchange. He watched intently as the big animal and his mother seemed to recognize each other, but he was more intrigued when he noticed how the energy patterns around her intermingled with Steve as she moved closer to him to take the reins. He had never seen that happen with his father.

"Can you help me with the picnic basket, Hugo?" Steve made his way to the back of his SUV to fetch the lunch that Mrs. Shepherd had packed for them. Eva and Quah Dreamer followed behind, but Hugo remained stationary. Then the boy smiled, took a deep breath and inhaled the invigorating fresh air of the farm. He was thrilled to be in Steve's company and he was utterly fascinated with the energy patterns he had just observed. He had only ever seen them around his mother in those colors and shapes. He wondered how they could have affected Steve. Hugo increased his pace to catch up with them.

"Ready."

The rest of the day passed as if in a dream. Steve and Hugo were constantly off on little trips into the woods. Eva heard them laugh and talk while she walked Steve's magnificent stallion around and explored the farm. At first she held onto his reins, but as they spent more time together, she realized the horse wasn't about to run off. It did in fact follow her footsteps as they wandered about and stayed close.

Lunch was a delightful experience of fresh fruits and dainty triangular sandwiches filled with all sorts of delicacies from Mrs. Shepherd's kitchen. There was juice for Hugo and a bottle of ice cold white wine for them. Steve smiled at the sophisticated touch of his neighbor. Eva declined the wine and opted for the juice in the heat of the day and he joined her.

Throughout the meal Hugo spoke mainly about new theories and different applications of old ones. But most of all, he seemed excited about the energies that he said he could feel in the exact spots where the ley lines were supposed to be. Steve was intrigued by this statement and knew the boy wasn't merely making this up, but at that moment he did not know how to verify any of it, so he let him be. On a few occasions he caught Eva's eye, but she looked away every time, as if not wanting to intrude in their conversation. After lunch they slowly made their way back to the farmhouse, and Steve explained that his horse had to be walked as well as ridden every day because of a hoof injury.

"Do you ride, Eva?" he inquired politely.

"No." She smiled at the horse who was still tagging along behind her. "Never learnt that as a child. There were no farms around us." Then a thought struck her. "Don't you want to ride him today? We could wait for you and perhaps watch?"

"I will, but much later tonight. I don't think we will have time while you're here. Don't worry about him. Even though my days are often long, he always waits." He looked up at the horse's face close by. "You don't mind that, Quah Dreamer, do you?" Eva stumbled without warning as a shock ran through her entire body. She froze in her steps.

"What did you call him?" she whispered, pale-faced, staring at Steve. Trailing some distance behind them, Hugo was not in earshot, but for once she was not aware of where he was.

"His other name is Quah Dreamer." Steve's voice had dropped to a low whisper. "Look." He stuck his hand in the top pocket of his shirt and fished out a tiny square of paper and held it out to her. "I bought Bullet from Jack Emerson and his granddaughter, Natalie. I meant to show you and Hugo earlier. Natalie gave this to me for safekeeping." Without touching it, Eva looked at the piece of paper with *Quah Dreamer* written in the unsteady hand of a child. She was inexplicably rooted to the spot and felt disoriented and speechless. "Eva?" He took a step closer to her. "Are you alright?" Eva closed her eyes for a second and tried to regain her equilibrium. She didn't dare to make eye contact with him.

"I'm fine," she whispered inaudibly, putting a hand to her forehead. "It must be the heat. There is no need to be concerned." And with that she strode slowly ahead with Quah Dreamer in tow. Steve watched silently as she walked away, deeply perturbed at her response to Bullet's real name. She seemed to have had the same reaction he had had when he learned about Quah Dreamer. But how was this possible? She had not grown up with horses, and knew nothing about them. He wondered who this beautiful creature was who had entered his life so unplanned, wreaking havoc in his tranquil inner space. *Where is her husband? What man in his right mind would let her out of his sight for so long?*

"My God, I'm actually jealous!" he admitted softly, envious that she belonged to another man. Then he felt Hugo beside him and pulled himself together again. "Come, Hugo," he said, still focusing on the boy's mother as she led Quah Dreamer home. "There is more work to do in my study."

But the day had one more shock in store that neither Steve nor Eva was prepared to handle. They didn't see it coming, but long afterwards they both knew that they had been touched in a very unusual way and that nothing would ever be the same. Shortly before dinner, with Hugo busily working away on some new theory in his study, Steve sought the company of the boy's mother whom he had not been able to erase from his thoughts the entire day. Eva Norman seemed to fill every space, every thought he had. He found her in the living room in front of the mantle piece holding the feather that Natalie had given him.

"I see you found it," he said quietly from the doorway, looking at her bowed head. He came closer to stand right beside her. "That is the second piece of the puzzle around Quah Dreamer. Little Natalie said—" But she didn't look at him, nor did she move. Then he noticed how the hand trembled that held the gray feather of the owl. "Eva?" He strained to get her name out and put his hand on her arm in an effort to help, but she remained rigid and refused to look at him. Instead she handed the feather to him and turned away as he took it.

"I am so embarrassed, Steve." She choked in an attempt to get the words out. "I wish I knew what was happening to me. I'm sorry. I have never—"

"Eva, please look at me." He let go of her arm and dropped his hand to his side. She turned slowly to meet the intense look in his eyes. "Who *are* you?" he whispered hoarsely, as their eyes met. For an agonizing moment they just stared at each other but then she turned away to escape the confusion she read on his face and to stay her own bewilderment.

"I don't know," she answered softly, unsteadily, not trusting herself to look at him. "Please forgive me. I am not normally this emotional. I have absolutely no idea what any of this means."

Through the delicious dinner Mrs. Shepherd had prepared, Eva kept her eyes averted and barely spoke. Hugo noticed that his mother was very quiet and that Steve's concerned gaze rested on her continuously throughout the meal. But the boy kept his observations to himself while he talked about his theories, their application and the possibilities these held for discovering the real meaning of the ley lines. Steve listened distractedly and found his mind consumed with the still figure opposite him who barely touched her food and spoke minimally.

By the time he finally drove them home, Hugo had keeled over on the back seat, overwhelmed and exhausted with a day of intense learning and packed with excitement. Eva smiled at her offspring when he awoke bleary eyed and stumbled off to his bed after saying goodbye to Steve at the front door.

"Thank you for a wonderful day." She looked up and extended her hand. Steve took hold of it.

"Come with me to the International Folklore Festival at Billingham next week?" He saw her hesitate, but something would not allow him to let go. "It is quite spectacular and I'm sure it will help to make you feel at home here in this part of the world. It would be my pleasure to demonstrate some of the festivities of the North East." Eva looked into his gray eyes and her mind warned her to decline but her heart urged her to say yes.

"Thank you, Steve. I'd like to come." She smiled faintly; amazed at how easily she had accepted an invitation she would certainly have refused had it come from anyone else.

"I'll call you nearer the time." Then he lifted her hand to his mouth and lightly brushed his lips over her fingers. "Get some sleep, Eva. This has been a long day," he murmured softly. Then he turned on his heel and walked away into the night.

Chong-ba paid the taxi driver and asked him to stay around for about an hour. Obviously his plans were now somewhat uncertain. He had no idea how long it would take for the discovery of Adams' body, but he surmised that the long arm of the law would kick into high gear once the support staff of the hotel opened the door to suite 409. As he stepped out of the taxi, he admitted that he was rather nervous. He looked around carefully but noticed nothing that seemed out of place. At twenty minutes before the hour, Chong-ba decided that he had time to kill and entered the premises after paying the entrance fee and was handed a map of all the exhibits and their specific locations.

He wandered around for a while without much interest and then easily located the ladies' waiting room in the old railway station. The sign plaque on the station platform clearly showed that it was 'Beamish' so that everything fell upon the Beamish banner, depicting the year of 1913. However, the station, which was demolished brick by brick in 1973/74 and rebuilt on the museum site, was originally built at Rowley, a small community only fourteen miles down the road from Beamish. In 1867, Rowley consisted of only twenty people. The station served the community and its surroundings and was closed to passengers in 1939. It wasn't until 1966 when the station closed for good that a decision was made to preserve it for posterity and transport it to the world-famous open air museum. The monk found the information interesting, but he was here to meet an important person and his mind was preoccupied with her.

Upon opening the door, he found the interior deserted but decided to wait outside on the platform. He sat on the bench opposite some old fashioned luggage, obviously awaiting a porter's attention for transportation on the steam train of the British 1913 era. From here he had a good vantage point of all the visitors coming in and leaving.

He noticed her immediately. The shapely dark-haired woman approaching in a pair of jeans and elegant white blouse was unmistakably Tom Norman's wife. Chong-ba watched her draw near. They made brief eye contact but she casually dismissed him as another tourist and he realized that she was even more beautiful than her picture suggested. Then she reached for the door to the waiting room.

"Mrs. Norman?" Chong-ba stood and waited respectfully for Eva to turn around before approaching her. Eva's hand froze on the door handle. She had not noticed anyone except the monk as she entered the building. "Please do not be alarmed. I am the person whom you are to meet with." He placed his hands inside his wide cuffs, courteously bowed and stood back as Eva turned to face him. She stared at him in shock and caught his sharp, clear, almost colorless eyes. Then he took a step closer to her and brought his hands into full view; his fingertips were lightly pressed together, like one in constant prayer. "I have a very important message for you from your husband." Eva was speechless and afraid. What was MI6 up to and why would they disguise their agent as a monk? Chong-ba read the question in her eyes.

"I do not represent the government, Mrs. Norman. I am sure that whole story will reach you in due course. My only purpose is to deliver two packages to you. Then I must take my leave. I have a plane to catch to Pakistan."

"Is that where Tom is...Sir?" In her confusion they were the first words she could think of and she blurted them out.

"Chong-ba. Yes, and he is safe." His tone was soft, but clear. "I cannot stay very long." Chong-ba reached inside his robe and pulled out two envelopes. One had her name written in Tom's handwriting and the other one was blank. The monk stepped forward and held both out to her. Eva took the envelopes and felt the emotion well up again.

"Thank you for helping Tom, Chong-ba." Eva tried to swallow the tears that rose so quickly to the surface. In spite of everything it was a relief to know that Tom was safe. She looked up to find the monk's curious expression focused on her. Then he spoke.

"The letter is from Mr. Norman, and I am honored to be his messenger. But I was more honored to bring you the second package. I know that you will understand when you open it. Or soon after." He smiled, looking into the sun. "I have a personal message from your husband." He bowed his head again respectfully. "He wants you to know how sorry he is about everything. He said you would understand." Chong-ba's voice dropped to a whisper. "It is time I took my leave, Mrs. Norman. Peace be with you." Before she could say another word, he turned and quietly walked away. Appleyard's two undercover agents watched the monk's departure with some consternation. Where was Peter Adams? They had watched the brief interlude with Eva Norman, but when the robed man left shortly after, there was no time to waste. They decided that one of them would tail the monk whilst the other kept an eye until Mrs. Norman reached the safety of the campus vehicle. Something was definitely wrong. Their boss would not be pleased.

Eva sat down on the bench as the monk's orange robe disappeared around the corner. The shape of the second envelope intrigued her for it seemed light and almost empty. She looked at both and decided to read Tom's letter in the privacy of her home. Then she tore the second one open and caught her breath at the large, single brown feather that silently fell to the ground. As if in a dream she reached down to pick it up and slowly brought it to her nose. As she inhaled deeply she caught a whiff of the wild open expanses where this creature lived. She thought she felt something else strain to reach her conscious mind, but no matter how hard she tried, it sank back into the nebulous world of dreams and imagination. The sun brilliantly reflected the metallic colors of the brown eagle feather and Eva squeezed her eyes shut as her whole body began to shake with pent-up emotion.

"What does this mean?" she whispered agonizingly. "Who are you, Steve? And why do you have a gray feather and why do I think it means something? Why do I think I know you and your beautiful horse? Why did a monk bring a single feather to me all the way from Pakistan?" So many questions and not a single answer. Eva stood slowly and pulled herself together before meeting the campus vehicle and its waiting driver. She would read Tom's letter once she was home. Neither she, nor the agents noticed the man who watered the day lilies and daffodils alongside the train tracks.

Josh Goldberg could hardly contain himself. He kept his head averted as she walked past him. He smiled at how easy it had been to pay off the old geezer tending the gardens at the front entrance to loan him a pair of overalls. For now, he was not concerned about the monk, who had left first. His time would come. It was the thought of having traced Eva that stimulated his usual sexual arousal, his agonizing physical response to contemplating a kill.

"Didn't I warn you not to play games with me, Eva?" He stuck his hands deep into the soil and dug up the flowers in frustration. Inside of him the pressure was almost unbearable and he grabbed a handful of the plants and crushed them violently in his big hands. "If only you knew what I have in store for you, you beautiful bitch," he muttered, clenching his teeth and straining with all his might not to speak the words out loud. Then he shook the soil from his hands and took a deep breath. "Let me thank you again, your holiness," he said almost piously, "for leading me straight to her." Josh Goldberg stepped onto the pavement and made his way to his car. "Of course, you'll have to die for that. But you wouldn't mind that, you unselfish bastard, now would you?"

Chapter 19
A Moment In Time

With their son sound asleep, Eva finally read Tom's letter in the glow of the lamp beside her chair. Almost ten pages long, it was written in Tom's familiar longhand and told of his regret for not being able to live the life they had promised each other so many years ago. She couldn't stop the tears; something valuable had been lost. His continuous absences had transformed them into strangers. Between the lines, she understood the depth of his political quagmire and it overwhelmed her.

She wished she could help but knew that she was powerless in a game where the stakes were so high and one she didn't know how to play anyway. Still, the frankness of his letter left her torn and wondering if the separation between them had been caused by his activities or whether they would have drifted apart regardless. She read his last two paragraphs again and then put the letter beside the feather that the monk had given her earlier that day.

Eva stared at the feather and although she did not pick it up this time, she felt the emotion surging to the surface again. *Two feathers. One gray and one brown.* She was convinced it had meaning. *But what? Is this destiny?* She put her head back and closed her eyes. The final request in Tom's letter was unexpected and had deepened her state of confusion. She tried to recall his image, rummaging through her memory banks to remember the last time she had seen him, but her subconscious mind would not co-operate.

The man who appeared in her mind's eye was tall and fair. She vividly recalled his deep voice as he invited her to the festival and she remembered his touch as he lightly kissed her fingers and then straightened to meet her eyes. Then a strange thought entered her mind. His eyes were the same deep gray color as the owl's feather. The thought disturbed her deeply. She didn't know why.

The call from Jack Emerson solved Steve's problem about accommodating Hugo while he accompanied Eva to the festival. In his usual jovial voice, Jack inquired after Quah Dreamer's welfare and mentioned that Natalie would like to see the horse again. He had business in Newcastle and said he could stop by the farm with Natalie. Steve promptly invited her to stay over on the Saturday evening and told Jack that he planned to have company on the farm for his delightful granddaughter; he promised to confirm as soon as he had heard from his guests.

Steve wanted the Normans to stay over Saturday evening so he and Eva could attend the festival in Billingham and he would have more time to explore the ley line theories with Hugo. But he knew that there was much more to this arrangement and that he was in deep trouble. Eva Norman's image filled his mind almost constantly and no matter how hard he tried to remain rational, he could not ignore that he was smitten with a woman who was beyond his reach.

He grimaced at the thought, fleetingly remembering some of his attractive companions of the past. None had had the power to affect him like this dark-haired woman with the attractive lilt in her voice. Then he dismissed the matter and picked up the phone to call Eva. He hoped that she would accept the invitation to stay over if Hugo was included, and had the company of another child while they were at the festival.

Janet Ballantire had noticed the subtle changes in her son with the acquisition of Quah Dreamer some months ago. She asked George if Steve was unusually engrossed with the new horse, but her husband disagreed. He figured that her colorful imagination was off with her again, but Janet would not be deterred. She had never seen him bond with any animal the way he had taken to Quah Dreamer.

And then came this strange request for her and George to keep an eye on two children visiting Ocean View while he accompanied the mother of the boy to the festival in Billingham. Janet was more than just a little intrigued by this arrangement. She knew Steve was tutoring a young boy who had recently come from Israel but he had not mentioned the mother until now. She did not need a crystal ball; something was going on. The older Ballantires arrived early Saturday and witnessed a flurry of activity as three guest bedrooms were being prepared by the housekeeper. Steve left shortly after to fetch his guests from their apartment near the university.

"Please keep an eye out for Natalie, Mum," he said as he left by the back door. "She is a little blonde scrap of about six and she'll be arriving with her grandfather, Jack Emerson. I bought Quah Dreamer from Jack, but it was Natalie's permission I needed to conclude the deal." He laughed. "You'll see what I mean when you meet her." Janet smiled and remained silent. She was more certain than ever that her son had an interest that he had not discussed with anyone thus far.

Two hours later Jack Emerson pulled up in the driveway. She watched from the big kitchen window as the passenger door flew open and a mop of golden curls bundled out and ran toward the back of the car waving enthusiastically at Steve's SUV coming down the driveway with his guests. Natalie bounced up and down like a rubber ball, impatiently waiting for Steve to come to a complete stop. Then he opened his door and scooped her up in his arms as he stepped out of the vehicle. Delighted to see his little visitor, he carried her to the passenger door and opened it.

When the dark-haired woman emerged into the sunlight to take the little girl's hand, Janet became very quiet. Nothing had escaped her. As the older man with the boater and pipe caught up with them and introductions were being made, Janet noticed that her son had barely taken his eyes off the woman by his side. Warm tears welled up as she watched the small party approach. Natalie was talking up a storm to the older boy, who eyed her expressive antics with a shy smile, not willing to be drawn in that quickly. But it was the woman that held her attention. Taller than average, she was well proportioned and slim and seemed gracious and elegant beside Steve. Then she felt her husband's hand on her arm.

"Well, our Steve knows how to pick 'em," he said approvingly.

"He has found her, George." Janet said softly, drying her eyes with the back of her hand.

"How do you know?" His tone was incredulous.

"A mother *knows*." She squeezed his hand but the determined whisper brooked no resistance. "Don't argue with me, George."

The fifteen minute drive on the A19 dual carriageway to Billingham led them along picturesque farm fields toward their destination. Before they left, Steve had given permission for Quah Dreamer to be brought out so that Hugo and Natalie could walk him on the farm while George promised to keep a watchful eye on the youngsters.

By the time they had finished the light lunch of shepherd's pie and fresh garden salad that Janet had prepared, and Jack had left for Newcastle, Natalie had shamelessly stolen hearts around the table. Even Hugo sat on the edge of his chair studying her every move. Despite the age difference between them he was mesmerized with her cheerful chatter and contagious giggle and he surprised Eva a few times by laughing out loud at Natalie's quirks. Eva was the first to break the pleasant silence in the vehicle as they neared their destination.

"Natalie gave you the owl's feather?" She hesitated to ask the question but couldn't stop herself. The mystery and intrigue around the feathers had deepened and something drove her to investigate. Steve smiled distractedly as he pulled into the parking lot of the festival grounds.

"Yes. But she insists Quah Dreamer found it." He looked sideways at her. "She speaks horse language, you know."

"Then she and Hugo will get on like a house on fire, Steve." She laughed softly. "He also talks to animals." She was equally taken with the spirited child keeping her son company for the day. She and Steve had noticed Natalie's immediate interest when Hugo mentioned the ley lines on the farm. She had an odd expression on her face and tilted her head to one side; the girl seemed anxious to go with Hugo. Eva didn't tell Steve about her experience in the Meadow before they left Israel. How would she explain this place to him, or the little girl who resembled Natalie? Even the giggle was the same! It was all too bizarre.

"Here we are. I hope the performances are as good as the reviews. I have chosen two of the best for us to watch. The first is the Indian

Panghat Dance Troupe whose colorful display has received rave reviews, and the second is from a group in Africa, called the Imababwa Dancers from Zimbabwe."

"I don't know why, but I'm very attracted to that part of the world, even though I've never been there." Eva said it simply. "Africa, I mean," she explained when she caught his inquiring glance.

"Then this was the right choice, I hope? I am told they have brought their own African soil to dance on, so this particular event is held indoors and will be performed in the Forum Theater." For a brief moment he looked into her eyes. "Ready, Eva?" Afterwards she remembered saying yes, but was oblivious that the wind had picked up in the Meadow she so often visited in her dreams, or that the changing energy signified by this gentle breeze, was about to open a doorway into the past.

Faint flute tunes of the Indian Panghat group preparing for their first show drifted on the warm summer air toward them, when suddenly their path was blocked by a young girl dressed in a colorful Mexican outfit. She wore a striped ankle length dress with matching headband and broad pink waistband. Her eyes sparkled and big hoop earrings swung from her ears as she looked from Eva to Steve and then back to Eva again.

"You're perfect!" she exclaimed softly with an attractive Spanish accent, fixing her gaze on Eva. "You are just what we are looking for!" Then she looked at Steve who was somewhat taken aback with the unexpected interlude and didn't quite know what to make of the young girl still blocking their way. "Please, sir, we have a competition this year amongst the participating countries. The most authentic act involving guests wins a big prize which goes toward a favorite charity of the group. There are many abused young girls on the streets in our country and this money would be a great help. Please? We are portraying an ancient Aztec wedding ceremony during the musical numbers. We would be honored if you would be our guests." She finished somewhat breathlessly, but was grateful that she had got it all out, eyeing them expectantly. Steve looked at Eva.

"We have tickets to the show that starts shortly. Eva—?" But the expression in her eyes said that she was spellbound by the suggestion.

"I have read about the plight of so many young women in your country. What would be required of us?" she asked softly.

"Not much at all!" the girl exclaimed excitedly. "Except allowing us to dress and decorate you in the traditional costumes of the time and perform the ceremony while the singing ensemble gives their performance in the background. Don't worry," she added hastily, "the audience will be focusing on the dancers and singers." Eva looked at Steve and was met with an unfathomable expression. She was suddenly unnerved and not so sure anymore that she wanted to proceed with the plan.

"Steve?" Her voice shook a little.

"Why not? We only live once, don't we?" he said softly, his gaze still fixed on her face. "And we have the whole afternoon to take in the rest of the show." Then he looked at the excited girl in front of him and cleared his throat. "What is your name, young lady?"

"Conchita." She blushed openly under his direct scrutiny.

"Well, Conchita, my companion here seems agreeable to your suggestion." He smiled arrestingly, focusing all his attention on the nervous young girl. "If we're going to help you win a prize, you had better tell us what to do."

"Wonderful!" she breathed ecstatically. "This way to our tent." Overjoyed with her find she grabbed Eva's hand and pointed to a striped, medium-sized marquee pitched some fifty meters away in the open John Whitehead Park. Then she looked over her shoulder at Steve as she briskly walked away with Eva. "We need a half hour, no more. And you sir," she said breathlessly, "in great Aztec tradition, can only see the bride at the ceremony. Fernando!" she yelled loudly at the young man watching her from a distance. "You prepare the groom!"

Only they knew that this money would come in handy to rescue their little sister who had been on the streets of Monterrey for more than six months at the mercy of an uncle who had found a way to profit from the physical beauty of a needy family member. This money would go to a charity which in turn would buy the favors of a corrupt police force that held the power to rescue their sister.

The tent smelled of sweet incense and was littered with colorful costumes, trays of make-up and big, soft cushions. An older woman rose from a chair beside a dressing screen and came over to stand in front of Eva. For a few moments she just looked at her and said nothing. Then she smiled.

"You are beautiful," she said with genuine admiration, noticing her hazel eyes and high cheek bones. "But you are nervous. Why?" Eva looked into the older woman's face and realized that she had read her correctly. She was about to participate in an ancient ritual to help the fundraising effort of the Mexican group and instead of this being the fun event she had imagined when she first agreed, she felt emotionally highly strung and on edge.

"I don't know," she said softly. "Perhaps you need a younger couple to help you do this."

"No." She smiled as she kept her eyes on Eva's face. "Conchita is right. We've not seen many English beauties with your eyes, complexion and hair color, but you're not English, are you?" She suddenly stopped and dropped her voice, acquiring almost a chanting quality. "Come on, dear. It will be fun, I promise. And you will never forget this day. There is nothing to be concerned about. Besides, I will be on stage with you. There is a role for the old women in this too. We are called the *cihuatlanque*, and I'm one of them."

By the time the transformation was complete, Eva knew something extraordinary was occurring, of which she understood very little. She stared stunned at her image in the mirror while Conchita wound strings of delicate red feathers around her arms and legs and painted her face with yellow pigment. The garment she had on was made of soft white fabric that reached down to her knees with a sleeveless, loose fitting blouse overtop.

"This yellow pigment will wash off easily," said Conchita, as she pulled Eva's hair back to fit a soft leather band over her forehead with a red feather sticking out at the side. Then she stood back to admire her handiwork. "Breathtaking!" she whispered, staring at the extraordinary image of the Aztec bride she had dressed up. "Are you a couple?" she asked inquisitively remembering Eva's handsome companion.

"We barely know each other." Eva had difficulty speaking. She suddenly had an overwhelming desire to quit the ceremony and turn the clock back to where she could refuse the invitation to participate in what now felt like madness. What had started off as an outrageous, spur-of-the-moment desire to help, suddenly seemed ludicrous and she could not understand why she felt so on edge or why the tears were so close to the surface.

"Nonsense!" cooed the old woman, clucking her tongue, as she took Eva's hand to lead her out of the tent. "We have never performed this ceremony with anyone in the past that was not deeply in love with each other. Somehow we always make the right choice."

Eva did not remember walking to the theater with the small party of women around her, nor did she notice how many heads her exotic appearance turned as they slowly made their way to the back entrance. Overwhelmingly aware of the persistent rhythm of drums beating softly in the background as they approached the stage door, she seemed lost in the middle of a dream. The luring sound of the drums drew her in and filled her head so that it became hard to think coherently and, as the tension in her body began to build, she placed a tentative hand over her heart in an effort to still the dull ache.

She willed herself to calm down but she was powerless to stay the sudden rush of emotion as her subconscious mind unexpectedly made a shocking breakthrough. Standing outside the circle of performers on stage, Eva knew clearly that she was no longer under the spell of some ancient ritual, but that she was in fact *remembering* it. Her heart caught in her throat, making it hard to breathe.

Inside the building the lights were low and a ring of Aztec singers were chanting in perfect harmony and rhythm with the drums and pan flutes. And then from the opposite side, she saw him enter the circle. He was much taller than the two companions that flanked him and he was draped in a colorful cloak, illuminated brilliantly by the light of the burning torches in their hands. One of the men by his side gestured to where she waited outside the circle of light and then the dancers broke ranks to let her in.

The eerily beautiful creature waiting quivering a short distance away stunned Steve, and his bewildered mind grappled to comprehend what he was witnessing. *Could this be Eva?* At a distance he registered the shimmering vision of exquisite sensual femininity in a single glance and his mind reeled as the totality of her dawned on him. He saw the shyness in her eyes, but instinctively knew that the exotic woman decorated in red feathers was also warm-blooded and passionate. Captivated by her appearance, he was temporarily immobilized by an urgent need to remember. *But what?* Then his memory finally broke through a barrier that was thousands of years old and led him precariously down the uncharted road of ancient history. And suddenly, as the boundaries of time fleetingly fell away, he knew. He at once understood her apprehension and hesitation and in that moment he was dead certain that they knew each other. And he had no doubt that in the hands of the right man, Eva was capable of reckless abandonment.

Neither he nor Eva remembered any of the dancing and singing that completed the ritual. They had no recollection of their effect on the crowd who, caught in the magic of the moment, waited spellbound for them to finally come together. He wondered afterwards how he had reached the center of the circle where older women with wild long gray hair were performing an entrancing dance, swaying and bending with the rhythm of the music as a prelude to the ceremony of marital bonding.

He only remembered Eva's hauntingly beautiful eyes, highlighted by the glimmer of yellow pigment on her face, as they stood toe to toe. Then a *cihuatlanque,* old woman, took the corners of his cloak and her blouse and tied them together whilst muttering some incomprehensible syllables. Somewhere in the back of his mind a faint voice called out a warning, but Steve smothered it as he leaned closer to her.

"I know you," he said, his breath warm against her forehead. "It is so hard to explain how, but even harder to deny." Then he turned his head and touched his lips lightly to her ear. "You also remember, Eva. I can see it in your eyes."

When the dance was finally over, everything blurred into a sea of color and shapes that made it difficult for her to know what was real or what her imagination was inventing. She remembered vaguely seeing some flash lights going off toward the end of the show as the highlights of the dance were captured for the local newspaper. She also remembered being back in the tent, embraced by the soft bosomed woman who had tied her shirt to Steve's cloak. When Eva was dressed again and the pigment removed from her face, the old woman spoke.

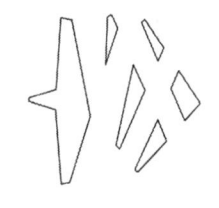

"We have never been wrong." She took hold of the long gray hair hanging in disarray over her back and combed it with her fingers.

She watched Eva closely while she nimbly began to plait it over her shoulder. "Never," she said deliberately.

They had left the show abruptly, overwhelmed with the immensity of facing emotions so raw in their intensity, and yet, rationally, seemed completely baseless and absurd. There were no words to describe what had transpired between them on that stage, but the tangible silence in the vehicle heightened the impression of unfinished business. It was not until Steve had turned his vehicle off the main A19 dual carriageway and they were headed for Elwick that he managed to bridge the silence between them. He glanced briefly at her averted profile and then fixed his attention on the road.

"When I was only a young boy," he said quietly, "I remember my folks taking me to the higher ground above the Tees Valley to the source of the river. From this vantage point I would watch the salmon battling the forces of nature, defying gravity in their attempts to reach the upstream breeding grounds where they could spawn. As a youngster I wondered why the fish chose this difficult feat to accomplish, and how or why they returned to the same place each year. I did not have the answers, but I was mesmerized with nature and all things wonderful. It was by observing life in all its wonderful manifestations that I realized that I would have to discover things for myself."

Eva sat quietly beside him realizing that she was becoming slowly undone as a distant forgotten past relentlessly cast confusing images and events on the screen of her mind. She listened to his beautiful deep voice, as he spoke of his childhood and how his interest in physics had demonstrated that magnificent forces were at work, the likes of which he said Man is nowhere near to understanding.

His voice and mannerisms were so painfully familiar that she wanted to reach out and touch him, but their intimate exchange during the wedding ceremony suddenly seemed surreal and fantastical, as if it had never happened, and she remained mute and bundled up in her seat. He was Hugo's professor and belonged to another world, a world of farms and race horses, beautiful meadows and picturesque castles. Her life in Tel Aviv had been nothing like that.

"There are no coincidences. Do you believe that?" His quiet voice brought her back to the present moment.

"Yes," she said softly. "But I don't understand—"

"Don't try." He reached out a sympathetic hand and touched hers briefly. "And here we are," he said as he turned into the gates of Ocean View. "I'd be interested to know how the two youngsters got along with each other. I am convinced that Hugo will need a break from that little chatterbox."

Eva smiled distractedly. She was relieved to be back on the farm and she desperately needed to alleviate the pent-up emotion. Still dangerously close to crying, she did not wait for Steve to open her door when he brought the vehicle to a stop.

"Thank you for inviting me today, Steve." Her voice was barely audible. Steve stood outside the vehicle and watched her closely.

"This day turned out much differently than we expected, Eva." He did not know which one of them was more confused or upset. And as he watched her walk away he was still no closer to a reasonable answer than when he had looked into the mysterious eyes of the beautiful Aztec bride.

At the dinner table the children were quiet. Natalie sat uncharacteristically demure beside Hugo, looking as though she was going to drop her face into her dinner plate and go to sleep in her chair. Janet and George noticed the tension between Steve and Eva and elected to keep the conversation light by focusing on the activities of the children. George looked at Natalie's drooping eyes and turned a wistful eye on Hugo.

"Seems to me the discoveries the two of you made today have worn out our little girl, Hugo? Now, wasn't she the one who said some really clever things when you were in the woods with Steve's horse?" Hugo nodded but turned his attention to Steve.

"Natalie helped find those energy spots. She did it differently." He glanced at his mother, whose aura was a brilliant array of colors that he had never seen before. He wondered why she and the Professor hardly spoke at the dinner table.

"Natalie helped you, Hugo?" Steve looked from Hugo to the girl. She had propped her head up sideways in the palm of her little hand and her mouth was slightly open as she watched Hugo relaying their experiences to the grownups. She had hardly touched the food on her plate, and he thought she might keel over any second. "I see you've had an exhausting day, Natalie. But I am so glad you could help Hugo. You sure are talented, girl." The tone of his voice was soft and appreciative. "What with talking to horses *and* understanding mathematics, I wonder what other surprises you have up your sleeve, young lady."

"What is mathema…?" She gave up trying to pronounce the word, and sat back in her chair, folding her hands in her lap. The shyness of the first day when he had met her in the Spotted Cow with Jack was suddenly back and she averted her eyes. "I just told Hugo where the fairies live and he followed me." Hugo moved in his chair, uncomfortable with her revelation about fairies, even though her discovery somehow corresponded with his calculations. But Eva, seated on the other side of Natalie, was intrigued with the child's behavior and she put a reassuring hand on Natalie's head and smiled at her.

"I too saw the little people when I was a child, Natalie." Her voice was soft and endearing. "Did you show them to Hugo?"

"No." Hugo became impatient. "They showed her a hidden stream. They told her the name of the place. It is very old." He looked at Steve. "She found the spot with the highest level of energy. I do not know how. My calculations showed another place. I think the running water underground reconfigured my numbers." Steve knew of the stream that ran through the farm, but Hugo's spot had indicated there was another one, underground. This information surprised him and he intended to investigate it as soon as he could, but Natalie's demeanor had caught his attention again. She was behaving in the same way as the day she had told him Bullet's real name. He leaned across the table.

"What is the name of this old place you found Natalie?"

"Thorp Pelkington," she whispered. "They said Thorp Pelkington. The fairies said that the woods are where everyone went to do their shopping."

"Yes," Steve answered under his breath. "It was called a market place." Then he looked around the table and noticed that dinner was over. The day clearly had had its share of excitement for all. Two tired children had to be packed off to bed, and he realized that his parents were probably ready to make their way back to their apartment.

Steve watched their tail lights disappear in the thick mist that had pushed in from the ocean after the warm muggy heat of the day. He stuck his hands into his pockets and breathed deeply. The smell and taste of the ocean was very distinct and he could see his breath as he exhaled slowly. The night was still young but his confusion about Eva was threatening to overwhelm him and he closed his eyes wondering what the next step could possibly be. A crooked smile crept around his mouth as he wryly admitted his frustrating indecision. He lacked no experience with women. Why was he hesitating now?

"They are both in bed, Steve." Her soft voice startled him. "Natalie was in dreamland before her head hit the pillow." He turned to her in the fading light and noticed that she was as tense as when they had returned from Billingham.

"Come with me," he said on the spur of the moment.

"Where to?" Eva could hardly breathe. His simple request caused her to hesitate. Everything seemed so familiar, but she wasn't sure if her imagination was running amok again. She shivered and took a step back, suddenly afraid of where this might lead.

"Quah Dreamer has not had his run for today. I'm sure you will enjoy watching him. He is quite spectacular when he stretches his legs. You requested this the other day, remember?" He kept his eyes on her. "It's still early."

"It's been a long day, Steve." She looked away, her indecision was obvious. He nodded slowly, considering her response.

"Will you be able to sleep?" he asked softly as he took a step closer. "Eva, if you really want to—"

"No, no...I'll come with you." She pulled herself together with great effort and forced an indifferent tone as she came to stand beside him. "I would like to see Quah Dreamer run." They walked in silence to the paddock and adjoining stable and without thinking, she blurted it out. "I heard from Hugo's father this week." Inwardly Steve froze, but he didn't break his stride.

"Oh?" He avoided looking at her as he opened the gate of the paddock and let her in ahead of him. "When will he be returning to England?"

"He is not coming back." Eva looked toward the stable where she could hear Quah Dreamer snorting lightly, amazed at how easily the admission had slipped out. Steve wanted to ask why her husband would not be returning to claim this gorgeous woman but he waited for her to continue, acutely aware of the unbearable tension that coursed its way through his body. "Tom has asked me to start divorce proceedings." Her voice faded and she looked away purposely, as if she wanted to discourage further discussion.

"I'm sorry to hear that, Eva." He didn't know what else to say and although he knew nothing of the circumstances between her and Hugo's father, he felt an immense sense of relief. But then he thought of her and took a deep breath to steady himself. "Are you okay?"

"Yes." She smiled faintly. "We should have separated a long time ago."

Quah Dreamer was bareback and he appeared huge and imposing in the thick mist as Steve led him from the stable. Soft cloud vapors of moisture billowed from his nose as he swung his head from side to side and stomped his hooves on the thick turf, displaying his sense of discipline as he remained a step behind his master.

"I can't ride." Her protest was unconvincing as he held out his hand.

"I'll show you," he said firmly as he mounted Quah Dreamer in one lithe movement and then looked down to where she was standing. "Use my foot as a step and give me your hand." He pulled her up so fast that before she knew it, she sat astride Quah Dreamer in front of Steve.

"Relax, Eva." He spoke close to her ear with his arms on either side of her body, holding the reins tightly. "You won't fall, you have my word. Just hold on lightly to his mane. Can you do that?" She nodded, and excitement crept into her veins as they took off on a gentle gallop around the training arena. She felt the power of the horse beneath her increase as they gathered speed and she strained hard to hold onto Quah Dreamer's mane. But Steve immediately felt her insecurity and transferred the reins expertly into one hand and circled her waist with his free arm.

"Calm down, Eva." He pulled her more closely into his body. "The horse can sense every emotion, especially fear." As they moved in and out of the fog, the magical ride on Quah Dreamer took on the appearance and feel of a dream. She wanted to speak, but the words to tell him that they had been together like this many times in other worlds, wouldn't come. The incredible feeling of familiarity that had so haunted her from the beginning was now a certainty as they sailed together through the night on the black stallion they both knew so well. The burden of this knowledge weighed heavily on her mind and was so overwhelming, so massive in its implication, that she could not bear it any longer.

"Please take me back!" It was a muffled cry as she turned her face into his neck so he could hear her. "I'm sorry to spoil your enjoyment, but I want to go back." Her entire body had become rigid and she could barely speak. Steve felt her distress and tightened his grip on her waist as he reined in Quah Dreamer and began to walk him back to the stable.

"No need to apologize." His voice was gentle and understanding. "It has been a very trying day for us both." In front of the stable he dismounted swiftly and threw the reins over Quah Dreamer's head. "Come on," he said with a smile, "why don't I walk you and the horse inside?" The interior of the stable was dimly lit and Steve tied the reins loosely to a hook in the wall and then turned to her. "Here, let me help you dismount," he said, holding out a hand. "Just swing your leg over the side." But she lost her balance and let out a frantic cry as she slid off the side of the horse and collided heavily with Steve. His arms locked instinctively around her waist and as he tried to stay her fall, he felt her arms behind his back as she struggled to keep her footing.

"Steady, Eva," he whispered as he found his balance, but forgot everything else as he looked upon her anxious face. She tried to push away from him to hide the tears streaking down her cheeks, but he refused to let her go and felt his heart thundering. They were back on that stage in Billingham and he was staring into the eyes of his beautiful, make-believe Aztec bride.

"That's why you wanted to come back!" he said hoarsely.

"Steve, please..."

"No!" he said in a tortured tone. "None of this is a fantasy, Eva." Then he pulled her hard up against him and buried his face in her neck, sounding lost. "It is all very real! When I saw you on stage today, I remembered. I remembered...Oh, God, Eva!" He smelled her skin and the delicate fragrance of her hair and felt her heart beating wildly against his own. She offered no resistance when he trailed his mouth from the warmth in her neck along her jaw to find her lips. He tasted the salt of her tears in his mouth and, incapable of finding the right words, he desperately held her closer to his heart, sensing that he had done this before, only to lose her every time. Nothing could fill the void left by a past that was still distant and unclear.

But in this moment of sweet discovery, she was neither a vision nor a dream. The woman he held in his arms, was warm and very real. And he was never going to let her go again.

Chapter 20
Haunting Memories

He could hear her sniffling and it infuriated him even further. His eyes had become used to the darkness of the room and the sliver of light shining in through the torn voile curtain silhouetted her starkly against the barren white wall of the motel room.

She was naked and crouched in terror on the floor after he had tossed her like a rag doll away from him. She had hit the wall with flailing arms and legs and a dull thud, before collapsing into a pathetic bundle, terrified and convinced that she was trapped and would die in this room if she didn't find a way to escape this madman. But to get to the door of the seedy motel room she would have to pass him where he lay on the bed watching her like a snake that had cornered its prey and was stealthily waiting for the right moment to strike. She swallowed hard and tried again; relying on the years she had been on the street and appealed furtively to what she thought his needs were.

"I'm sorry—what do you want me to do? I'll do anything you want." Her trembling voice belied her words. She was deathly afraid of him, but didn't know that fear and subservience made him impotent. It was violence he wanted.

"Shut your mouth," he muttered, closing his eyes for a moment to the unbearable pain in his groin. Her relentless pleading from the moment he had started roughing her up had severely depleted his capability and he was left having to deal with the pressures of a need that would not be satisfied unless she fought back. He saw the thin line of blood trickling from the corner of her mouth and remembered that it had occurred as he struck her the first time hard across the face when she mentioned that she did not get to service many clients as good looking as him.

"Clients?" he had asked softly, locking the door and stepping closer as if he had not heard her correctly the first time. She had retreated in the direction of the bed and smiled seductively when she noticed him following her. She felt in control then, thinking that she would be disappointed if he turned out to be a pussy that was into vanilla sex. He had looked damned promising as he took the unlit cigarette from her hands in the street and put it in his mouth to light it for her, but not before he dragged on it himself while watching her closely. That had excited her, for the deal was concluded without a single word and right at that moment she could have cared less what he wanted to call himself, as long as she was rewarded handsomely for whatever his fancy was. Josh Goldberg stood face to face with her and purposely lifted a hand to run his fingers through his hair, but before she could say another word he dropped his arm forcibly and struck her violently with his elbow full in the mouth.

"Don't you mean *customers?*" he hissed. The brutal impact of the blow jerked her head backwards and he chased in anger after her body as she flopped in utter shock onto the bed. "Whores have *customers*, don't they?" He deliberately planted his big hands on either side of her head and stared down into her frightened face, laboring to control his breathing and the nauseating pressure building inside his skull.

For one terrifying moment Justine gaped into the dark eyes of the good looking man she had picked up outside Harpers, a place that offered basic massages and other more explicit services not openly advertised. She didn't work there, but slyly stole some of the passing traffic in all sorts of creative ways, sometimes just by asking for a light for her cigarette, which always dangled readily between her fingers with the long painted nails.

The deal was usually halfway done, once she smiled into the eyes of her target and put a protective hand over the flame; sucking the nicotine back into her lungs to blow a thin line of smoke past his face. Justine had a fleeting, confused thought of the overweight woman who ran the brothel, and despite this man's unexpected display of brutality, she still had no intention of sharing her hard earned money with someone who was not worthy of the term "madam."

In its own right, Newcastle was a busy city on the commercial sex front, but she longed for the bright lights of London where she hoped to hit the big time and possibly even employ a few young girls to bring in some extra money. She had been planning to move south as soon as she could save enough dough to buy her ticket into the busy and profitable area of Soho while supporting her crack cocaine habit.

But his immediate, vicious assault had put her on shaky ground where the rules were not at all clear. Trying to ignore the salty taste of blood in her mouth and the monstrous way in which her face throbbed, she decided to play it coy and feigned interest and surprise in her customer's apparent taste for violence. She did not have much experience with aggressive men and reverted in desperation back to the only thing she knew, which was to put her wares on display and furtively appeal to what she thought was his kinky preference for lust. So she apologized profusely for misunderstanding his needs and in a few quick movements slipped out of the see-through top and unclipped her bra, realizing as she did so, that the man towering over her had not blinked once.

Justine Oliver could not have known that Josh Goldberg wanted her to put up a fight. She also could not have known what had set the man off that stared at her with so much contempt and hatred. She did not know that her large breasts and her pleading voice reminded him of his mother and the brutal way in which his father had regularly abused her. That was before the day he had beaten her into a coma and simply disappeared, never to return. She also knew nothing of the newspaper in which he had seen the picture of Eva Norman and an unknown man, staring at each other in apparent rapture. In truth, fate was not on Justine's side, and she had nothing going for her but her street smarts, which was no match for the man whose eyes had not left her face for a moment.

Eager to satisfy his every need, stay alive and still get paid, she was unaware that his mind was drifting between her and another woman. Josh Goldberg had been scanning the papers religiously to determine whether the English authorities had traced him. He was anxious to know if they had picked up his scent after he had killed the man at the Royal Station Hotel; if they knew he was in the country or that he was in hot pursuit of Eva Norman. Until this day, nothing significant had showed up and he was relatively confident that he was in the clear and that they had not caught onto him or the alias he was using. He had entered the United Kingdom fairly easily as David Weinberg with a US passport cleverly forged by the usual contacts with whom he had dealt during his service with the CIA.

As the pressure in his head continued to build, Josh Goldberg knew he was losing control. The signs were all too obvious and his rage became boundless when he felt every muscle in his body strain and tremble with unbearable tension, but his manhood remained embarrassingly flaccid. He had come here to find his own form of retribution and hoped that the immediate assault would anger her and encourage retaliation. But the whore with the big blue eyes was subservient and, instead, had quickly slithered out of all her clothing whilst nimbly undressing him with equal haste. He didn't stop her. The rueful smile on her face indicated that she was prepared to go to any lengths to please him, but lacking the right stimulus of violence and force, his groin just continued to ache and throbbed inexorably.

It was when she pulled him onto the bed and kneeled beside him, moving her lips from his cold mouth all the way down to his crotch that he suddenly erupted. A mortifying shameful growl rose from his gut when she caught her breath in surprise at the sight of his limp penis. Without thinking, he picked her up in one swift movement and flung her away from him in utter revulsion. From the corner of his eye he saw her violently hit the wall and crumple down into a pathetic heap, whimpering like a lost animal. He tried to ignore her but her constant sniveling drove him crazy and it took every ounce of his self control not to go after her and throttle her into complete silence.

"Shut the fuck up," he muttered wearily. Somewhere in his confused state, reason had crept in and he realized that he could not afford another killing at this point. "If you value your miserable low life, you had better put a sock in it." Then he flung an arm over his eyes, knowing that she was too afraid to go anywhere. He tried to make sense of the rage he had felt when he saw the picture of Eva Norman and her companion in the events page of the Northern Echo, a morning regional newspaper.

He was completely taken aback when he recognized her. Who was this man with whom she seemed so familiar? He read about the arts festival and how their participation as guests furthered the cause of the Mexican group, who then went on to win the competition. He stared at their picture and reflected angrily on how she had never once responded in the slightest way to his efforts to impress her. Attentive and polite where her child was concerned, Eva never reciprocated his interest and always declined closer contact no matter how cleverly it was concealed. *Who then, is this man?* How had he managed to get so close to her in such a short period of time, when his constant efforts to impress her in Tel Aviv had borne no fruit? And what about Tom? Had she forgotten about her husband?

Josh remembered staring at the picture of the man and feeling some strange, unfathomable familiarity that he could not account for. The uncertainty drove him to investigate the caption below the picture and it wasn't long before he knew that Steve Ballantire was a professor in applied mathematics and physics at Newcastle University. The rest was easy to assume. Hugo's talent would not be left unattended, so this man was his replacement! Shortly after seeing the picture, the dreams and troubling nightmares began and his confusion and annoyance increased.

It started with Martha, who was just a crazy bitch he had killed in Tel Aviv because she had refused to tell him where Eva and Hugo were going. Josh admitted to himself that he had been unduly disturbed since he had watched her die that day. Ordinarily detached from his hapless victims, he could not understand the satisfaction he had derived from snuffing the life out of her, or why it felt like payback. She was nothing to him! He remembered her shock when she had discovered him on her doorstep and although she didn't know who he was, she seemed to recognize him just before she died, and called him "William." He had been plagued by that name. He wondered who the hell William was and if she was only hallucinating and confused, struggling to stay alive as the darkness of death began to swallow her. He had tried to convince himself repeatedly that she was just a lonely old cow who was probably remembering someone from her recent past, but he could not forget the terror in her eyes or her desperate rasp.

"Oh, Jesus, it's *you*! You're going to kill them!" she had cried. *Kill who? Eva and Hugo?* Somehow Josh did not think she meant them. Since her death, Martha had become a frightening and unwelcome intruder in his sleep that transformed his dreams into agonizing nightmares. Sometimes she just stood laughing at him, and other times he saw her fleeing in terror, but from *what*, he did not know.

He began to dread going to bed. Martha's image chillingly interchanged with that of a stout woman, a stranger, who showed up subserviently wearing a dirty, blood-smeared apron. Once he thought he saw the glint of an axe blade as she quickly hid her hands behind her back, laughing hysterically. Josh woke up sweating profusely, incoherently screaming the name "Mary" and thought he was losing his mind. He feared Martha more than he was willing to admit because he could not understand the relevance, especially since he had killed her routinely for the nerve of standing in his way. He had taken many lives in the past but none of his victims had insisted on hounding him the way this woman did and that alone bothered him immensely.

And then more visitors began showing up in his bewildered dream state that disturbed him even more. The graceful woman with the horribly disabled child that quietly watched him from a distance caused him to wake up continuously throughout the night, gasping for breath. Who were they?

"You don't have to pay me anything. Can I go, please?" The pathetic plea was barely audible. He didn't open his eyes, nor move. Recalling his terrible dreams had put him into a morbid state.

"No." His mind was thrashing about and he thought he was close to a breakthrough; he didn't want to be disturbed. "We're not done yet. And stop whining!" His voice was ice cold. "You're a fucking slow learner, aren't you?" There was silence in the room again and he ignored her cowardly form on the floor the same way one would disregarded a dog that had just been kicked.

He opened his eyes and stared at the ceiling. Sometimes he could not believe the size of the calamity that had struck when Eva decided to take Hugo away from him. The boy was his ticket to personal greatness and he had had him in the palm of his hand until his mother interfered. What had he done that had not been to her liking anymore? What had set her off? *Nothing!* She was just a bitch who had used him. She had discarded him and his services like a dirty rag after he had determined Hugo's incredible ability to still his mind and enter the Zen state. She did not even know the real potential of a mind as young as Hugo's that could so effectively calm itself. Moreover, he had just begun to unlock the door to Hugo's communication when she stole him!

He was fuming all over again and recalled the picture of Eva and the man he now knew was Steve Ballantire. His years of neuro-linguistic training and a general psychic ability convinced him that very little of the intimacy and closeness the picture portrayed was an act. He sensed that Eva was somehow personally associated with her companion and that was more than enough to push him over the brink. He had no doubt that this person had to meet the same fate that he had in store for her.

Josh Goldberg had become a man possessed, who surreptitiously floated between the boundaries of his conscious mind and the nebulous worlds of ancient memory, which as yet, he could not confirm either way. For now, he was acting on the instinct of a wild dog that picked up the smell of blood and was closing in for the kill, not because of a vicious past, but because he hated losing. He pulled himself together forcibly. He could not let these uncorroborated feelings and memories of incomprehensible events interfere with the wicked and evil agenda which had become his entire focus. And yet, the image of Martha would not leave him. He even imagined her trailing him during the day, hiding somewhere in the shadows of his peripheral vision, taunting and teasing him. She challenged him to make the breakthrough and discover who she was, but he remained frustratingly incapable.

Moreover she stimulated unwanted memories of his childhood and he found himself returning again and again to the forlorn sight of a very small infant, an only child, left to cry alone on the sofa in the small living room of their apartment in the Bronx area of New York. As he grew older he became used to his mother cautioning him to remain quiet as his father made her pay for his inadequacies as a man. The beatings became commonplace and he learned very quickly that his father had no regard for, nor did he respect the Jewish morals and ethics that had been passed to him from generations before.

Eventually, mercifully, the older Goldberg had deserted them. It was a blessing and a relief to his mother, but opened the door for him into the murky world of crime and drug lords. Josh was glad to see the back of the man that had sired him, but held a grudge against his mother for suffering his presence for as long as she had. Most of all, he detested her for taking his father's abuse without fighting back.

He believed that his fetish for violence stemmed from his childhood and by the time he reached his teenage years, his mother could barely hide the revulsion she felt for his brutal behavior and the reflection she saw of her husband in her only son. And then she did an incredible thing, for which he had never forgiven her. She simply left him to the thugs of the neighborhood. To this day he still had the note she had left behind: *Like father, like son. The two of you are one. Eileen Silberstein.* The final insult was disassociating from the family name and reverting to her maiden name of Silberstein. Clearly, she was never coming back.

Josh didn't mourn for very long. His streetwise nature took advantage of the considerable entrepreneurial ability that lay dormant beneath his hard outer shell and for five years he managed to stay one step ahead of the law while he honed his budding negotiating talents, acting as middle man in small drug deals where he alternately blackmailed the sellers and the buyers. Pleased with his ingenuity at outsmarting both sides, Josh Goldberg was also intelligent enough to know when to quit. In the competitive underworld one could easily end up as very dead and *that* he could not allow. He sensed there was still unfinished business to take care of and that is when he had set his sights on the US Military.

Much to his surprise, a world opened up which combined the skills he had learnt on the street, with sophisticated instruments of communication and intelligence, and suddenly Josh identified grand possibilities for fame and fortune. He found a niche in the United States Military Intelligence and Security Command, known as INSCOM, headquartered in Arlington Hall Station, Virginia. The formation of INSCOM provided the Military with a single instrument to conduct multi-disciplined intelligence and security operations involving electronic warfare. Josh took to communications data and intelligence like a duck to water and very quickly recognized brilliant opportunities to express his darker side through manipulating and controlling others. His general disregard for human life had found an avenue whereby he could legally kill in the name of duty; he was in his element.

A tall and imposing man with dark hair, Josh took advantage of the rigorous physical training programs provided by the Army to bring his physical body to a level of fitness that provided him with an impressive personal armory, cleverly concealed beneath his smooth and polished exterior. But it was the CIA that identified his unusual talents and it wasn't long before they had lured him into their camp and he began dreaming of glory. Josh Goldberg believed in his own greatness and imagined himself to be unstoppable. He suddenly remembered the girl and opened his eyes to where she sat naked and huddled on the carpet.

"Come here." He was emotionless and disinterested, but as she immediately stood and walked over to the bed, he knew that she was still acquiescent and very afraid of him. He didn't care anymore. He wanted relief from the dreadful tension in his groin, which meant that he would have to con her into thinking she could win in a fight with him. He had changed his mind about not killing her. It was imperative that he got his physical needs met and that would probably result in her death anyway. He now saw her demise as inevitable, but entirely necessary for his requirements. He smiled coldly at her, wondering if she knew just how unattractive he found her. He thought of Eva again, and quite irrationally decided to punish this whore for being so unlike the dark-haired beauty that had stolen his prize pupil and made him feel so insignificant.

"Entertain me," he said arrogantly and closed his eyes, waiting for her to produce her repertoire of tricks before he struck her down again. He almost couldn't wait.

His brief lapse in attention was Justine Oliver's desperate cue to the only chance she had to escape this imposing but impotent animal sprawled naked on the bed. Without thinking, she instinctively grabbed the heavy, solid glass ashtray on the bedside table and smashed it with all her might into his face, instantly breaking his nose and knocking him semi-conscious with a single blow. He reached with a growl toward the blinding pain in his face and turned his head to locate her, but his vision was already blurring as she jumped backwards in horror of what she had done. Josh tasted a lot of blood in his mouth and moaned unintelligibly. He made a feeble effort to take hold of her leg, but she was just outside his reach. A cruel laugh distorted into a horrible gurgle as he struggled to clear the blood streaming into his airways. He was actually getting an erection! *Bitch! Oh, you fucking bitch.* But the words remained unspoken as he sank away into brief, blissful darkness.

"Well, I never! And here was I thinking you couldn't get it up!" Justine could tell that he was out of it. She was smart enough to know when she was ahead of the game and quickly threw her clothes back on. Then she rummaged through his pockets, found his wallet and opened it. For a few moments she stared dumbfounded and speechless at the content. Justine counted four thousand pounds and for good measure, stuck his credit card between her breasts. The irony of it all was priceless but the outcome was *so* worth it! Her body shook with hysterical laughter. At the door she turned once more and looked at his motionless figure on the bed. She knew he would be coming around very soon. Her face still throbbed dreadfully where he had hit her earlier but she couldn't resist a cynical smirk as she watched him with glee.

"I guess we're even now, you bastard!" she said when the laughing subsided. She threw her hair back defiantly and lit a cigarette with trembling hands. "You have just bought my ticket to Soho, you pig." She blew a thin line of smoke into the air, eyeing him nervously from where she stood in the doorway. "But I have earned it, don't you think?" He grunted incoherently but she ignored him. "And if I ever see you again, it will surely be in hell. Count on that." Justine had no idea how prophetic those words would turn out to be.

Josh inspected his face carefully in the vanity mirror of his bachelor's apartment. His nose was definitely broken, and he was badly bruised around his eyes and mouth. Then he purposely placed his hands alongside his nose and closed his eyes. He stilled his mind and began breathing deeply, intentionally inducing a light state of trance. Then he snapped his nose back into position and leaned over the basin as the waves of pain washed over him. When he straightened up again, he was met with his wary reflection in the mirror.

"The game is on." He spoke with difficulty, holding his throbbing face. "And there aren't any rules. Just like there will be no mercy." In his tiny living room he opened his laptop and revisited the official website of Newcastle University, staring at the picture of the tall athletic man smiling into the sun. The photograph was obviously taken at the sports event this man had designed, called Quadraquest, and was followed by a lengthy article about his athletic abilities, his role as the chair of Applied Mathematics and Physics, as well as his accomplishments in breeding and training horses. Josh congratulated himself on the ease with which he had located Eva and Hugo. *Did MI6 really think they could hide her from me?*

His neuro-linguistic training, courtesy of the CIA, had always served him, even in the most difficult of circumstances. Josh was a communications expert with an expressed ability to accurately read the behaviors and intentions of others. But he was hell bent on refining this talent even further by combining it with his considerable psychic ability to take him into relatively uncharted psychological territory, which could potentially deliver huge payoffs in terms of money and power.

This required tremendous effort and concentration but after the Azvaalder debacle, Josh Goldberg had nothing but time and patience. He would not be robbed again. He closed his eyes and concentrated on the picture of Steve Ballantire. For a long time nothing happened, but he persisted while the pain in his face faded into the background and he waited quietly for his mind to go blank.

The Josh Goldberg who was fired after the intelligence scandal in Tel Aviv was very different to the promising candidate Azvaalder had courted years ago to launch them into the big league of electronic surveillance. He had been ideal in most respects; talented, slick and a relentless go-getter with powerful connections in science and the political field. The offer Azvaalder had made was near impossible to resist, and Josh jumped at the opportunity to enter the world of free enterprise where he could make some of his own rules.

With his insatiable drive for knowledge and control, he continued to conduct his own research and discovered two scientists who had a serious dollar interest in flogging their unusual discovery to the highest bidder instead of turning it over to the department that funded their work at the Cellutrac Bio Academy, a research facility based just outside of New York. As a master negotiator, Josh strung them along for three months, greasing their palms liberally, while he devoted time to digesting their findings. He made an effort to corroborate their information with many other sources that explained and introduced the New Biology Era.

Josh could hardly believe his good fortune when he first discovered them quite by chance through an online chat room, ready to exchange information for money. Most modern molecular technology is concerned with the development of cellular and intercellular activity. But these rogue scientists had discovered that instead of stimulating messages to the brain from the compound eye of the human being, they could harness this signal at the photoreceptor level which meant that the transmission could be halted.

Their discovery excited and amazed them. Instead of expecting curtailment of information, they found that quite the opposite occurred. Somehow DNA was capable of naturally finding an alternate route and allowed non-physical interceptors to acquire data from a totally external source. They had discovered a means of acquiring information at a remote mental level and it was only through the changes in DNA activity that they had accidentally stumbled upon this incredible possibility.

Josh was willing to pay a hefty price for them to continue their research while he became obsessed with the idea of how previously learned behavior within the human psyche could be reprogrammed at a conscious level. This meant capitalizing on the findings of quantum physics that connect energy and thought whilst totally bypassing the physical aspects of vision recognition. His years of service with the CIA had taught him how control of individuals was a major criterion in accumulating power.

He believed that he had found the possible means to introduce technology that could also help him to see what others were thinking. He had come across similar programs that interested the CIA and their overseas counterparts, but he believed he had found a missing piece that no one else had; one which allowed the conscious mind to overrule the subconscious at a universal or collective level. This would break down the individual physical and mental obstruction that usually meant information stayed with its host. That information could then become available to anyone who developed the ability to tune in spiritually or, in his favorite term, inter-dimensionally.

Azvaalder's top management was not only intrigued with his findings but immediately saw the economic viability of the project in terms of market dominance and appointed him to set up a branch in Israel, hinting at Government officials that this brand new product could help keep them ahead of their enemies and warring neighbors. Israel was the perfect country for a first test run; it would save millions in export fees and taxes and at least safeguard the industrial secret temporarily. They chose Josh to head up the entire operation and recruit his own team to complement the new technology.

Azvaalder was sure that they had bought Goldberg lock stock and barrel, but they had seriously underestimated the loyalties of a man who was only capable of serving himself. Those who knew him were unaware of how dangerous Josh Goldberg was. Instead of acting out of control, his anger and need for revenge enhanced his psychopathic tendencies, and provided him with an eerie ability to become deadly calm. His mind was his most lethal weapon and he had trained it meticulously to serve his evil purposes. Lacking emotion and compassion for others, he was entirely capable of blocking out anything that could interfere with his end goal, including physical pain.

When he was finally completely drained of all thought and feeling, Josh opened his mental eye and looked upon the blank screen of his mind. He didn't strain and he felt no desire to see any particular image. He was the observer and he waited. She showed up first in the body of the disabled child. Josh did not react, nor move. Then a woman approached gracefully from afar and walked up to the pitiful body of her son and embraced him. That is when Josh knew without a doubt who Eva was and it filled him with revulsion. The first stirrings of emotion interfered with the fragile mental images in his mind just like one tiny pebble ripples the calm surface of a lake, but not before he recognized Steve as the woman and knew why Martha haunted him so. Martha was his wife, Mary, from a distant past and her unfinished business was to drive him stark raving mad.

He grimaced, realizing that she was out of his reach. But the fate of Steve and Eva was a foregone conclusion. He was thrilled at the unfair advantage which access to this knowledge provided. But his rage was back and it had intensified. He could now punish them for transgressing against him for more than just this lifetime, and they would never know unless he told them.

Tomer listened carefully to Josh Goldberg. He still needed the man to tide him over, while he investigated other possibilities. He was of the opinion that the man had completely lost his balance, but Tomer admitted that the money was still good and the assignments remained challenging and interesting.

"What is the name on the credit card did you say?"

"David Weinberg." Josh waited and then spoke deliberately. "I know her type. She is stupid. She would not have taken the card if she did not intend to use it. I am going to let her do that, for obvious reasons." He gave a joyless laugh. "Let her make a few transactions, and then call me. I want to know where she is."

"Is Anchov in England?" It was a dispassionate question, but Tomer knew what was coming.

"No, but he will be. Just as soon as we know in which hole the little whore crept into. I'm sure he will enjoy sharing the company of a willing woman." He didn't wait for an answer and hung up. Again he recalled the picture in the newspaper that so troubled him and felt his entire body trembling. His obsession with Eva and Steve caused him physical discomfort.

Josh was aware that of late his thoughts regularly crossed into the hinterland of the insane. He didn't care. He had only revenge on his agenda. Through his remarkable psychic ability, he felt Tom's presence with the monk in Pakistan, sensing that something significant had changed. An incredibly evil plan had begun to take shape in his mind. It would be his masterpiece, but he needed all the players to be on board and he couldn't afford a single mistake.

The details and specifics were crucial for its success, and he needed Tomer and Dmitri to assist him in taking Eva out of the United Kingdom into the mountains of Pakistan to meet her husband, and her death. He felt feverish with anticipation as more and more realizations about Steve began floating to the surface. He sensed that the tall athletic man would be a dangerous opponent of considerable skill and talent.

That is when another idea hit him like a ton of bricks. He wouldn't kill Eva straight away. He would wait for Steve to come and get her and then he would dispose of them together. Josh Goldberg could hardly wait.

Chapter 21
Road To Nowhere

Chong-ba waited patiently at the designated pick-up point beside the busy and colorful road. Time was of little consequence to the almost nine million people who lived in this crowded city and he didn't expect his ride to show up for quite a while. Life in Lahore was vastly different from the highly sophisticated metropolis of London from which he had just returned. A light traveler by nature, he folded his small bundle into his lap and went down on his haunches to let his gaze wander over the buzzing beehive of activity.

Across the road a merchant was selling off the leftovers of his colorful kite collection, unique to the *Basant* festival of spring, now long gone. Chong-ba watched him marketing his wares to passing-by tourists and noticed the demonstrative antics designed to attract buyers and persuade them to part with their money. The merchant spoke Punjabi, the language of Lahore, and used excessive hand gestures to reveal his indignation at the great bargains which ignorant tourists would not see for another year, and only resorted to broken English once he had snagged sufficient interest to get serious negotiations under way. He was a tenacious and experienced businessman who typically smelled profit when exasperated tourists could no longer distinguish between the details of the deal and how refusal to buy would contribute to the starvation of his family.

Chong-ba smiled distractedly. Where he sat beside the road in his striking orange robe, nobody paid him undue attention. He too, was another prop, a player in the daily circus of life on the streets of Lahore where all were welcome as long as it did not interfere with the profitability of your neighbor. The air was thick with spices from street vendors selling whole rotisserie chickens and Nihari, a beef dish saturated in spices and simmered for hours, mingled with delectable variations of bread, like Chapatti and Nan. Accustomed to a sparse diet in the mountains, his senses reacted to the tempting aromas of delicious foods wafting toward him from every direction and he felt his stomach contracting.

Tom Norman had been on his mind constantly since his meeting with Colonel Appleyard the previous day and he was anxious to get back to his cabin in the mountains. He took a deep calming breath. Life in this part of the world had a different rhythm, as dictated by the vibrant but idiosyncratic culture of a people who lived their lives sandwiched between the borders of Iran, Afghanistan, China and India. It was only the southern part of Pakistan which had a welcome watery outlet into the Arabian Sea that was not suffocated by people.

Then Chong-ba caught a glimpse of his ride behind the colorful Rawalpindi truck coming down the road. The driver of the beaten up pickup with the rickety wooden sporting that had brought him into Lahore a few days ago was unsuccessfully trying to pass the richly painted vehicle blaring out Hindi love songs to the tourists it was carrying. Chong-ba admired the extraordinary sight of the art on wheels approaching him. The truck was beautifully decorated and richly painted with miniature works of art of animals, birds, flowers and historic buildings. As the moving kaleidoscope of color noisily rambled past him, Chong-ba noticed the photo of Ayub Khan on the back of the truck, the first Pakistani military general to seize political power through a coup in the fifties. Below the picture was the traditional slogan, *Pak fauj ko salam*, which meant "Salute to the Pakistan Army."

"What else can one expect," Chong-ba murmured softly, "from a country that is almost constantly at war." He greeted his ride respectfully and jumped on the back of the gray pickup truck of indistinguishable make and year and took his seat on a hard wooden bench littered with goats' hair and prepared for the long and uncomfortable ride on the Grand Trunk Road. This road began its long and tiresome journey in Peshawar, Pakistan and worked an arduous route through Islamabad to Lahore, before entering India at Wagah, the only Indo-Pak road crossing between Amritsar, India and Lahore, Pakistan.

Soon they would leave the colorful scenery of the city behind and sputter along into the sparse, rural outskirts of Lahore. From here he would veer off course and travel on foot to the base of the Himalaya

Mountains in the vicinity of Gujrat, arduously working his way higher to the cabin where Tom Norman waited. He sat back as the shaky and uncomfortable journey began and remembered the day before.

It was mid afternoon by the time Chong-ba had caught his flight from Newcastle to Heathrow Airport. His connecting flight to Lahore included a wait of three hours and this thought unsettled him. From the moment he left Eva at Beamish Museum, his mind became ablaze with many different images. Eva Norman had left a lasting impression on him and he found himself constantly mentally placing her alongside her husband waiting at his cabin in the mountains, trying to see the connection between two such different people, but to no avail. Tom Norman was desperately looking for answers, whereas the monk sensed that, on some level, Eva already knew them. Even though his acquaintance with her was brief, Chong-ba was skilled at reading people and the moment he saw Tom Norman's wife approaching, he knew she was a kindred spirit.

By his own standards, he was pleased with the way nature and its creative influences had imposed on him such duties that would result in so much accomplishment. He did not need to know everything since he operated in close accordance with what his feelings dictated, and since his main purpose was to be of service, he had little concern for personal satisfaction. He was often surprised with the tasks laid before him, but rarely questioned why his participation was required. Instead, he trusted that all would be revealed in time. The mission into the United Kingdom to deliver Tom's letter and hand Eva the feather still filled him with a measure of wonder. He felt that there was much more still to be revealed.

Then he recalled his unpleasant discovery of Peter Adams' body in that darkened guest room of the Royal Station Hotel in Newcastle and knew that the authorities would be far less complacent and would demand real answers. If they lacked evidence in pointing a finger at the real culprit, Chong-ba suspected that they would be looking to him to cast light on their problem. And for as long as he remained on English soil, he expected to be stopped at every turn. Each event had its significance and, as a sensitive, wise student of life he consciously endeavored to connect the dots leading to deeper insight and understanding. The killing was just such an occurrence and he was curious to know how his undertaking to contact Eva Norman could lead to another man's death. Chong-ba was thus fully prepared when he felt the hand on his shoulder as he entered Terminal Three at Heathrow Airport where he was scheduled to catch his connecting flight to Lahore.

"Chong-ba Chong?" The monk froze in his footsteps, realizing too late that breaking his stride was enough to confirm his identity. "Please step aside, sir." He was almost relieved to hear the official sounding voice. The sooner he dealt with the inevitable, the quicker he could make his way back to his cabin in the mountains. He turned to face the tall, overweight middle-aged man who had reached inside the pocket of his immaculate gray pin-striped suit and was holding up an official looking identity wallet.

Ignoring the odd curious look of passers-by, Colonel Appleyard watched his unusual target like a hawk and did not blink. For a few seconds they stared at each other; East assessing West, before they silently reached a parallel conclusion of being evenly matched, if not in stature, then surely in determination. David Appleyard's assessment of the monk didn't take long. Without any difficulty, he identified stealth and a stony, quiet resolve in the little man's unassuming manner.

"Colonel Appleyard?" Chong-ba recognized the voice he had spoken to on the phone as they fearlessly held eye contact. Then he slowly lowered his gaze to the wallet and identified the crest and stamp of an officer of Her Majesty's Government. "You came alone?" he asked softly, sweeping his eyes over the busy terminal but failing to notice any sign of an official entourage. "A personal mission then." Chong-ba kept his voice low and respectful. Appleyard ignored the monk's observations and instant recognition. He spoke curtly.

"I understand that your flight is a few hours away. I'd like you to accompany me to the VIP lounge on the second floor. It will be easier to talk there." There was no discernible compromise in the Colonel's voice and Chong-ba knew that although much of this was posturing, it would be pointless to resist or object in any way without drawing undue attention. He graciously nodded and allowed the Colonel to lead the way. They rode the elevator in silence and remained quiet until they approached the mall leading to the VIP lounge. Then Colonel Appleyard spoke. "You seem anxious to leave England." Chong-ba recognized the bait as it was thrown out. He smiled, but purposely refrained from comment, waiting for the Colonel to continue. "The police at Newcastle notified my office earlier this afternoon after discovering a body. It was Mr. Adams; a member of my department. This was the man I had arranged to meet you earlier today. As you can see sir, this is a matter of extreme urgency and national security. Our man was strangled with his own tie."

"May I sit?" Chong-ba politely pointed to one of the VIP sofas scattered around the lavishly furnished room. He glanced over the cabinets filled with drinks, the elaborate pool tables, countless computers offering Internet access and large screen televisions before coming to rest on the Colonel. Chong-ba stood his ground and waited respectfully for permission.

Appleyard observed the monk silently. He already knew that the slight man dressed in the bright orange robe was not intimidated by him and found that slightly infuriating, yet he instinctively understood that aggression would not help his case. Since their first encounter on the phone, he had learned the monk was a formidable opponent and for many years had been a thorn in the side of the Tibetan authorities. Surprisingly, the CIA was also tracking his movements. Chong-ba was allowed to make this trip because the Colonel vouched that the mission was not religious in nature and involved an important operative of MI6. Appleyard was not at all interested in spiritual matters, but was intrigued that anyone could go to the lengths this man apparently had done in the past to disseminate truth, as he saw it. The significance of his past history was that the Colonel could use this information against him to further his own cause. He nodded his head curtly.

"Please." He gestured toward the sofa. "Make yourself comfortable, sir." Appleyard remained standing. Inwardly, he marveled at how the monk displayed no fear and seemed willing to go the distance with him. He knew that his small frame was no indication of his mental propensity and that Chong-ba was every bit as vigilant. The slightest misstep would immediately be noticed by the other party and provide an advantage. "We have a problem, sir. I'm sure that you know what I am talking about." He looked Chong-ba straight in the eye.

"Please, call me Chong-ba." The monk smiled at him. "Yes, Colonel. You have a dead body that needs explaining. Are you suggesting that I had anything to do with this poor man's demise?"

"Chong-ba, I'm afraid your outfit and background will not be convincing to the authorities. They know the room was booked in your and Adams' name and they lifted fingerprints in the room that they are anxious to match with yours. The fact that you are a monk will mean precious little to them once they can tie the evidence to a person who seems ready to skip out of the country without telling anyone what he knows." He took a deep breath. "Presently it is all purely circumstantial, but right now there are no other suspects. They have surmised that, given your background, you are probably trained in martial arts and on those grounds—"

"You do not believe I killed Mr. Adams, Colonel. And that is not why you came without any visual backup."

"This is not about what I believe, Chong-ba. I'm afraid I might have to detain you."

"I see. And to what end, Colonel? Will you not just be delaying getting what you really want?" Chong-ba spoke softly, looking straight at Appleyard. "I am sure you know that silence is second nature to a dedicated monk. What purpose will detention serve if you and I both know that the killer is somewhere out there, while your prize person waits in the mountains of Pakistan on my return?"

"That sounds like blackmail, Chong-ba. Or perhaps a veiled threat?" Appleyard's voice was ice cold.

"No, Colonel. It was just an observation. I have nothing to say to the authorities about the unfortunate death of Mr. Adams, but proving that might be complicated. And you cannot afford to lose unnecessary time. Your purpose and goal is to speak with Tom Norman, and that will not happen without my co-operation. You know that." Appleyard felt the frustration rising. He knew the monk was right, but he sensed that he was losing control and that was not a feeling he liked.

"I have checked out your background and I see that the Chinese, to mention only one group, are not too happy with you. You're regarded as a subversive; a dissident." He waited to see if the monk would react to this, but he didn't move, nor blink. "Without our assistance, life could be made very uncomfortable for you." Chong-ba dropped his voice even lower, but his gaze never wavered.

"I think we understand each other, Colonel." But Appleyard was not quite done yet.

"The Newcastle police have the authority to detain you indefinitely."

"And you have the power to override their decisions. Detaining me serves no purpose for I cannot help them, Colonel. I know as much as they do."

Colonel Appleyard watched the monk closely. The slight man sitting erect in front of him had given him no reason to doubt or disbelieve him. But only he and Stanway knew how big the conundrum was in which they had found themselves. Under the guise of doing work for the Foreign Office, the real activities with which they were involved were top secret. Tom had been entrusted with this information and his absence had put the entire operation into jeopardy.

Secretly he had hoped that Tom had confided in the monk and that he would be able to extract some answers from him, but looking at the small composed figure sitting on the sofa, Appleyard knew that it would be a fruitless exercise; Chong-ba's track record was impressive and spoke volumes. Even if the monk knew anything significant, he would not speak. Silence was his second nature, and Appleyard had every reason to believe that. Narrowing his eyes, the Colonel dropped his voice.

"Humor me, Chong-ba. Peter Adams is dead. You have accomplished your mission, but I am still empty handed! Your part of the deal is yet unfulfilled! That is why I am here." Chong-ba met Appleyard's fury calmly. He didn't blink.

"What does that mean, sir?"

"In place of the now deceased Mr. Adams, I will be accompanying you to Tom Norman. That's what this means."

"No, sir." He sat motionless, watching the veins bulge on David Appleyard's forehead.

"You are not in a position to dictate to me!" Appleyard hissed. "Need I remind you who made this trip possible?" He squared his jaw. "I'm coming with you. And you are going to take me to Tom."

"Too dangerous. I will not agree to it." Chong-ba didn't wait for a response. "Mr. Adams is dead because I assume the killer was really after me. That puts Mr. Norman's life in danger also. I will not risk the sanctity of my dwelling in the mountains by taking you or anyone else there under these circumstances. Instead, I will arrange for Tom to meet you in Lahore three days from now."

"Another change of plans, Chong-ba? Don't you think this is pushing the envelope?" The Colonel stuck his hands deep into his pockets. "I'm afraid this time you have no choice. We're leaving together to see Tom." The monk looked away from the Colonel and stared at his sandaled feet, as if he had lost interest in the conversation. Then he looked up.

"You said that you have studied my background, Colonel?" Appleyard nodded, watching him closely. "Then you should know that you cannot threaten me. I am leaving in a few hours. Without you. I will deliver Tom Norman to you in Lahore three days from today at the Pak Teahouse on Mall Road, near the Anarkali bazaar at 12pm." The monk stood and scooped up his tiny bundle of traveling gear and tucked it underarm. "Good-bye, Colonel. If you put a tail on me, I will lose it in the mountains. And you will never see Tom again." He took two steps forward and stood toe to toe with Appleyard. Then he folded his hands together and bowed his head. "Thank you for making this trip possible, Colonel. The gods are smiling." He kept his head bowed. "You have no reason to mistrust me." Then he turned and strode silently away.

Appleyard watched him leave, realizing that Chong-ba had once again managed to get his way. For a moment he wondered what exactly could have motivated him to come all the way to the UK to deliver a message for Captain Norman. It was beyond him, but he could not waste a single moment longer speculating about something that did not interest him anyway. When the monk's slight figure disappeared in the crowd, David Appleyard had made up his mind.

"Let him go." Colonel Appleyard spoke into the microphone under his lapel. "Change my booking to the next flight to Lahore. Get a hold of Bobby Naidoo and book him on the same flight. We're going to Pakistan." He had known all along who killed Peter Adams and he spoke decisively. "Put a national CCTV alert out for Josh Goldberg. And circulate his picture to all units. He's in the country and he is our man." He thought of the crafty little monk who had so cleverly manipulated him.

"You should have been in politics, Chong-ba," he murmured. "If you were, you would know that my promise to you means nothing. I'll find my own way to Tom when you least expect to see me. And I might just have to kill you also."

Dmitri Anchov reeled in the last of his quota for the day. He was fishing south of the harbor in the port of Jaffa in a small inlet used by local fishermen. The spoils were insignificant for the day and not enough to feast on, but his thoughts were elsewhere. He kept seeing her face and his hatred intensified. Josh Goldberg's email had rekindled the loathing he felt for women, but today it excited him. It concerned Eva Norman, the "juicy Jewish bitch," on whom they had done the surveillance. Dmitri could barely wait and he swallowed hard.

From the first day Eva's composed and elegant posture had drawn a stark contrast between her and the loose women with whom he had grown up. He didn't know what to make of someone who looked and acted like royalty; she simply fitted nowhere into his depraved memory or experience of the opposite sex. Even at a distance, watching her during the failed surveillance attempt, the grace and ease with which she moved reminded him vividly of his own clumsiness and shortcomings around females and he hated her for that. Dmitri was incapable of understanding his own reactions, but believed irrationally that if he could punish or hurt her, the tables would be turned and he would feel better. And now Josh needed him again and part of his duty would be to watch over her.

After the Azvaalder catastrophe, his remaining funds were tight and he had just enough shekels to pay for a couple of hour's fishing in shallow waters and what was left would give him his last night out on the town on Israeli soil. He had finally managed to sell his small boat to a Hungarian peddler who dealt in ironmongery and Dmitri was more than happy to get half his money back.

Tomorrow would be the start of a new adventure and he would be off to the UK, once again on the payroll of Josh Goldberg. His dismissal from Azvaalder had ruined his chances of having his work permit renewed and without Josh Goldberg around, Dmitri saw himself making his way back to dreary, dull Russia in very short order. That thought alone infuriated him and he irrationally blamed Eva for his predicament. If she had not fled the country none of this would have happened; he was still furious at her departure.

But tonight he planned to go to his favorite night spot, the sleazy Jolly Sailor, aptly named, as most of the foreign visiting seamen frequented this unlicensed strip club for unadvertised wild sex and some heavy drinking. Accustomed to regular police raids, the rundown joint was experienced at instantly transforming back into just a local drinking hole at the slightest whiff of a raid. Dmitri felt the excitement stirring. He had been there many times when the police had kicked down the front doors but he had never been caught in an uncompromising position with a woman.

Dmitri *wanted* sex but couldn't bring himself to participate in any relationship. Every time the sexual act came to mind it automatically transported him back to his childhood days and he would be reminded of where he used to live and that he didn't know his parents. He was sure it was not the gays of either sex that frequented the building, nor the so-called law enforcers who would leave the place intact once their palms had been crossed with silver so that 'business' could carry on as usual. The apartment where he lived was one of many in a block of flats on the outskirts of Moscow, built in the late 50's and early 60's during the Khrushchev era.

Known locally as "Kruschobas," these filthy establishments housed all manner of folk, including those who worked hard in menial government jobs and accepted the crumbs offered by the state but also made no effort to supplement their income. Dmitri lived here too, but in his home things were very different. Tatiana, the madam, who ran her establishment on ground level, took it upon herself to look after his everyday needs and he called her "mother."

He only hoped and prayed that Bogdan, the aging pimp to five of Tatiana's girls, was not his father. The bully hung around their joint like a plague and beat the young boy often for no reason other than being in his presence. Dmitri eventually developed a hatred which ran so deep that it completely consumed his thoughts. He detested the women around him for their subservience to the pimps, their loose morals and carelessness about his welfare. Bogdan, he simply wanted to kill.

His chance came much later when, after finishing military service with questionable honors and joining the KGB, he was able to nail a few accusations of drug trafficking on the unsuspecting head of Bogdan. His style of killing was grotesque and accompanied by excessive violence, earning him the unbecoming nickname in the KGB of the "mad killer," one who executed his victims first and asked questions later. When Bogdan's body was discovered in the alleyway between two rundown buildings, the whores who worked for him vomited at the gross sight, but the KGB officer on duty looked at the pulp that was once Bogdan's head, and whispered, "Anchov."

But tonight Dmitri had promised himself that things would be different. He planned to reward himself with a sexual interlude and he chose Isabella to satisfy his needs. He had no idea whether this was her real name or not, nor did he care. The bitch owed him a favor or two for all the drinks and cheap meals he had bought her. To date he had never asked for a return on his investment, contented only to offload his hatred for women on her in the way of insults and innuendos.

Isabella thought the deal to be sweet. After a hard, underpaid session of cavorting as a stripper to satisfy the vulgarity and lust of her all-male audience, she couldn't care less that the awkward Russian's fancy was verbal abuse. It wasn't her business if he got off on *that*! In fact, she was secretly convinced the man was impotent and that suited her even better.

They finished their pita wraps filled with spicy beef, chick peas and traditional hummus while walking back to her apartment. Isabella was slightly miffed that she didn't get to sit down and eat, but shrugged off the thought as she resolved to getting rid of him quickly, taking a quick shower and going straight to bed to rest her tired body. But when Dmitri fished a hipflask from his trousers' pocket and offered her some straight vodka, she was suddenly intrigued and wondered if he had it in him after all.

"You're coming in tonight?" she asked, genuinely surprised, eyeing him sideways as she threw her head back and took a big swig from the sleek, silver container.

"I will be leaving Israel in the morning for quite some time," he said. He was not particularly interested in her reaction but saw her eyes widen as she lowered the flask and unceremoniously wiped her dripping mouth with the back of her hand.

"Is my baby coming back?" she cooed unconvincingly in his face, flinging an arm around his sweaty body. But Dmitri became instantly rigid as images of Tatiana's girls floated into his mind and the way they shamelessly flaunted themselves to the highest bidder. He strained to control himself on the dimly lit sidewalk and brusquely pushed her up against the wall of the nearest building.

"I want something special," he breathed heavily in her face, "a going away gift." But Isabella misread his intentions completely. She had no idea that Dmitri's deepest desire was to be mothered and that he was confusing this with sex. To her, intercourse with him was nothing but an opportunity to help him offload his remaining currency, and for that she only had to be the whore she already was. She laughed in his face, smelling the vodka on his breath and reached an experienced hand toward his crotch. Dmitri caught her wrist and held it in an iron grip, furious that her vulgar groping at him had ruined his fantasies and destroyed the potential of it being "special." The realization that he was just another cheap customer instantly enraged him. His face was in her hair and he bit the words out through clenched teeth.

"Not yet, Isabella…" He felt the heat in his body rising and he almost choked. "Not yet." They climbed the stairs together to the third floor of the shabby establishment above the rundown pawn shop, and Isabella was more than just a little intrigued. The clumsy Russian was turning out to be quite a surprise and her tiredness was suddenly gone as they reached the door to her apartment. She could hardly believe that her meal ticket of so many months actually had sex on his mind!

She stuck the key into the latch but before she had time to turn the lock, Dmitri's shaky self-control suddenly snapped and he kicked the door down from behind her. In the same movement he shoved Isabella into the room and pounced heavily on her, fumbling and tearing at her clothes, leaving no doubt that she was about to be viciously assaulted and that the currency for tonight's transaction would be brutality, not money.

But Isabella was a tough customer herself and she was used to the violence of men in the strip joint where she made her living. She reached her long nails toward his face and fiercely scratched and clawed until she felt warm blood on her fingers. It was when he moaned and turned his face away in self protection that she saw her only chance and rolled out from under him while skillfully shooting her knee right into his groin.

"Promudobliadskaja pizdoprojebina!" *Fucking bitch,* he roared at the top of his voice as he doubled over through the paralyzing pain and feebly attempted to get to his feet. The stripper swam like a ghost in and out of his vision and watched him dispassionately from a distance while he gasped frantically for breath. When he finally was able to straighten, she was still standing in the same place and he looked up to the sound of her cynical laughter. Dmitri became dead quiet and stared coldly at her before speaking matter-of-factly. "For this you will die." Then he lunged at her throat.

Through his blinding rage he saw her bulging eyes and heard her wheezing for air. He vaguely remembered that Josh had cautioned him not to cause an incident in celebration of his departure from Israel before getting over to England. Dmitri reluctantly released his grip on her throat and crashed his right fist in frustration into her jaw, knocking her unconscious. She was nothing but a whore, just like the 'mother' he so hated. He really needed to punish his mother and the stripper tonight, but the latter lay unconscious on the floor and her limp body was useless to him now.

When he reached the road outside, Isabella and his disappointment were already forgotten. He stood under a street lamp and retrieved Josh Goldberg's email from his pocket. He was scheduled to fly to the UK the following day to be the minder of an 'old friend.' The message told Dmitri to keep his hands off his charge and he surmised that this person could only be Eva Norman. Within a short time, they were to take their 'guest' to Pakistan. He had no idea why they were going to that part of the world, but he was pleased to be included in Josh's plans again.

Josh ended the email with some interesting news. He had a score to settle with a woman named Justine and he wanted Dmitri to locate her with the help of Tomer and take care of her. Dmitri smiled. There were no instructions to keep his hands off this one. Perhaps Tatiana would be punished after all! If things didn't work out the way he planned, then maybe Eva could be returned to Josh's keeping as slightly damaged goods. Dmitri laughed cruelly and grimaced instantly from the pain in his face.

"Better get these cuts disinfected," he muttered as he made his way back to his dilapidated one-bedroom apartment behind the local bus station. "Dirty whore." He touched a tentative hand to the deep gash on his right cheek. "You could have fucking poisoned me!"

Tom sat beside the ice cold mountain stream that ran close by Chong-ba's cabin. He had washed his clothes and draped them over some sparse, thorny bushes to dry in the sunshine that felt infinitely colder in the constant presence of the wind. He had also used the opportunity to bathe in the frigid water but couldn't get out of the bitterly cold stream soon enough. Tom shivered and suppressed a smile as he looked down to where Chong-ba's only spare robe barely covered his knees. It was too short and uncomfortably tight, but as his only option while his own clothes dried in the inhospitable wind, he had to endure the outrageous fashion faux pas.

He was in a peaceful mood today and he felt much better than when he had arrived here in the mountains. Perhaps it was the fresh air, or the lack of worldly trappings, but he thought he could think much clearer about his life than even a week ago. Although he was completely alone, save the mountain-dwelling animals, he never felt lonely. At times when the wind let up, there was even a pleasant heat that penetrated his skin and allowed him to drift away in thought. For Tom, the feeling was quite extraordinary and in stark contrast with the frantically paced life he had lived in the fast lane of cities around the world. But here in the mountains, surrounded by so much serenity and peace, images of Eva constantly filled his mind.

He was anxious for Chong-ba to return and bring news of how she and Hugo were doing in his homeland. In the last few days he had been able to bring many aspects of his wife into perspective and despite their marital bond, Tom was convinced that Eva had never really belonged to him. There was a part of her that had been inaccessible from the very beginning, notwithstanding his most dedicated attempts to unite with her on this intimate level. Eva somehow seemed comfortable with loneliness. It was a feeling she was accustomed to, even welcomed, and she frequently disappeared into its embrace, like that of an old companion who had returned after a very long absence.

Tom mused about when they started growing apart, but the exact time the bond began to dissolve was hard to determine. Every time he was away for an extended period of time, it was harder to come close, especially since she never shut him out or refused him in any way. Eva was driven by loyalty and duty and despite her physical beauty, Tom never doubted her or imagined she would develop another love interest.

With Hugo in her life, Eva had begun to focus all her love and attention on their only child and while he remained incapable of bridging the growing distance between them, Tom's overseas missions and long absences became a blessing in disguise. He reasoned that it was easier not to be around than holding her in his arms knowing that the deep feelings he had for her were not reciprocated equally.

On a few occasions Tom visited high class establishments overseas where sex was for sale, but ultimately always left without crossing that line, haunted by Eva's clear hazel eyes and enduring freshness. His last interlude with a beautiful blonde girl in Caracas, Venezuela almost crumbled his defenses but when she dropped her negligee to reveal a voluptuous tanned body, Tom agonizingly thought of Eva who always waited for him to undress her.

It took him a while to gently coax his gorgeous wife into more exciting adventures with him, but there was never anything brash about her. She was the ultimate woman and he was enormously attracted to the sensual shyness she never lost. He dropped his face in his hands and didn't care that the girl nearby was visibly impatient with his lack of response.

"God, Eva…" The tortured whisper reached only his ears. "You've spoilt me for all other women. I'm damned if I do and damned if I don't." He never went back. Traveling for extended periods of time became his escape clause. At that first exhibition in Bern, Switzerland, Josh Goldberg had presented him with the perfect opportunity not only to bury his frustrations, but to also handsomely supplement his salary as a servant of Her Majesty's Government. Incapable of being with Eva, or bearing the thought of being without her, Tom found a way to channel his frustrations and became hooked on the adrenalin rush of the shady deals that Josh provided. However it was the unusual challenges that Appleyard laid before his door that tested every aspect of his experience and intelligence.

Josh Goldberg could not believe his good fortune. Industrial espionage required very high connections and an agile mind, and Tom Norman fitted the description perfectly. Not only was Azvaalder educating his exceptionally gifted child, but Tom was busy weaving a web so intricate that he would have to sell his soul to buy his freedom.

It all started in Istanbul, Turkey when, whilst on official business for the British Government, Tom learned about the employee of a large oil company who had been dismissed for embezzlement. Strangely, it was one of his regular conversations with Roger McPherson, his accountant in London, which alerted him to the fact that the same man was also sought by Interpol. He was selling trade secrets via sophisticated electronic means, using very advanced technology only available to large corporate financial institutions. That's when Tom knew that Josh would be interested and the race was on. He would have to make contact with the target before Interpol did. This was his first big deal and Josh Goldberg rewarded his efforts very generously; the trend for the future was set. Tom Norman had started collecting his thirty pieces of silver.

"The robe does not fit, but it suits you." Tom awoke from his reverie to find the slightly built monk eyeing him with interest. He looked tired, but there was a smile on his face and Tom was very happy to see him.

"Chong-ba!" He rose to his feet, momentarily oblivious of how comical he looked. "You move like a shadow. It is so good to have you back!" Hours later, after their simple dinner of broth and chapatti bread which the monk had brought from Lahore, they sat in front of the fire, staring into the flames. Tom was very quiet and Chong-ba knew that the news of Peter Adams' murder had shaken him and that he was extremely anxious about the safety of Eva and Hugo.

"There is still the matter of your meeting with Colonel Appleyard." Chong-ba spoke softly.

"I will meet with him as agreed. I think he expects my resignation, but he won't be happy with my refusal to divulge the names of contacts." The monk nodded, not taking his eyes off Tom.

"Yes." There was nothing more to say.

"How is Eva, really?" Tom asked, barely audibly.

"She looks well enough. We did not speak for long, as you know. Your wife is very unusual, Mr. Norman and I am sure your letter was of great comfort to her." Tom said nothing. He was not in a position to protect Eva and Hugo and he knew for sure that he couldn't rely on MI6 any longer after the blatant killing of Peter Adams. But he was more concerned with David Appleyard and his private agenda apart from MI6. Tom stared into the hypnotic flames and spoke deliberately.

"The Colonel wants to know what went down in Caracas, Riyadh and a few other places. He won't like the answers. I obviously disclosed no detail to my wife, but Eva is intelligent. She will read between the lines." He took a deep breath, reluctant to discuss the topic any further and looked directly at the monk. "I set her free, Chong-ba." His companion nodded his head slowly but didn't comment for a long time. Then finally he spoke.

"You know your reasons better than I, Tom." Tom looked up in surprise as Chong-ba used his given name for the first time, but the monk didn't waver. "Your wife knows what very few people know. We own nothing here, Tom. We can claim neither possession nor person. Eva knows we are all merely passing through. I saw that in her eyes." Then he reached a friendly hand toward his English visitor. "If you are not planning to leave the mountain, Tom, we will have to order you a robe of your own." Tom took his hand in wonder.

"How did you know?"

"I saw it in *your* eyes."

Chapter 22
Thor Hesp Elkin Ton

It had been a cool, overcast day and the night air had drawn in very chilly around the farm. Steve had kept the lights off in the living room but turned up the dial on the gas fire so the room began to warm up. As much as he would have preferred the burning of natural wood or bracken, it was not practical in this part of North East England where sparse woodlands did not warrant the costly service of forestry management.

The quietness inside the house matched the stillness outside and yet he was deeply aware of the presence of the other two people, now under his roof. He still could not believe the events of the past two days and how quickly circumstances had changed to bring Eva and Hugo into his home. It had all started when James Stanway showed up at Eva's front door.

He had learned that Stanway headed up the British Embassy in Tel Aviv and that he was a colleague of her husband, who had been missing for several weeks. Eva immediately assumed bad news and was in shock when she opened the door to her unexpected visitor. James Stanway was, however, the bearer of more sinister tidings that had nothing to do with her husband who had gone astray. He said that he had come to speak personally with her because he felt directly responsible for recommending Azvaalder's services when, years ago, she sought assistance for their gifted child. He went on to say they had no idea who Goldberg was then, and didn't have any reason to investigate his background until the surveillance order had been given. Then he told Eva that MI6 had reason to believe the man was on British soil and there was every indication that he meant to harm her and Hugo.

Stanway mentioned that the head of MI6, Colonel Appleyard, wanted them immediately moved to a more secure location where a closer eye could be kept, but this news upset Eva even more. Every move was hard for Hugo to handle and her heart sank at having to upset his routine once again when he had just begun to settle in. He liked the apartment and he was very comfortable with Steve and his predictable life on campus. Being taken from Israel to escape Goldberg's surveillance was a drastic measure that Eva had hoped would end the danger, but the news that he was in hot pursuit of her and Hugo and could hurt them, came as a genuine shock. Clearly, a very unstable element was present and it frightened her.

Stanway indicated that they had agents posted in the vicinity of the apartment and that he would be in touch the following day to discuss next steps. He told her of the death of Peter Adams, but not how drastically his demise had changed their plans; that his real reason for coming to England was to put together an emergency plan with David Appleyard. While it was important that a façade around the Normans' safety be maintained, Tom Norman had to be found as a matter of supreme urgency. They had no idea if the pictures that Goldberg sent to Eva were an indication that he had caught wind of the work Tom was doing for them, or whether these were simply taken routinely to maintain pressure on those who worked for him. Either way, they couldn't afford to take any chances.

As soon as he left, Eva called Steve. The anxiety in her voice forced him to contain his own apprehension. The thought of Eva and Hugo leaving, or going to an unknown location, unsettled him.

"Why don't you and Hugo come here?" He kept his voice even. "There are a lot of people on the farm and you will feel much safer being around so many others." Neither he nor Eva actually spoke to Colonel Appleyard, but Stanway informed them two days later that the Colonel had agreed to the new arrangement after he had convinced him that there was safety in numbers and that Goldberg was not likely to risk involvement in their presence. The only condition was that they be moved immediately, and that agents be placed strategically at the farm.

Unbeknownst to them the new arrangement came as a blessing in disguise for Appleyard and Stanway who could now focus their efforts on tracking down Eva's elusive husband. With the Israeli authorities, the British police and MI5 interested in his hide, the notoriety of Josh

Goldberg had reached international status. MI5 was itching to get involved due to the murder of Peter Adams on British soil, and only the highest authority had swayed them to temporarily sacrifice the glory of catching a villain. Appleyard knew he could only stem the tide for so long.

Their personal belongings from Tel Aviv were thus redirected to the farm and, under the watchful eye of a few agents, delivered during the afternoon. Hugo's apprehension about the move was overshadowed by his excitement at receiving his drawings and other belongings, and knowing how important these were to him, Eva had spent the entire afternoon helping him to organize his room and get everything in just the right place. When he dismantled everything and started over again no less than three times, she just let him be. Hugo organized information like no one else and she knew his physical environment had to reflect what he saw in his head, no matter how long that would take.

Steve spent the majority of the day tidying up matters at the university and preparing for the summer holiday which would commence in a few days. He was filled with strange feelings of excitement and concern around the new developments. He could not deny the joy he felt at having Eva so close to him, but he had a troublesome feeling of unrest that he simply could not attribute to anything in particular. He admitted that he knew precious little about the life of the woman and her child whom he had brought so spontaneously into his home. His reaction was simply instinctive; he only knew that when she mentioned that they had to move, he could not bare the thought of possibly losing contact with Eva.

Later that evening when he returned from the university and took Quah Dreamer out for his usual ride, his mind was still filled with Eva and her son. What had begun as an instant attraction from a distance as this dark-haired beauty stepped from the campus vehicle that day, in short order had blossomed into a feeling that filled his heart and thoughts constantly. It didn't seem to matter whether he was sparring with the minds of his students or tearing up the ground on Quah Dreamer's back; he was relentlessly aware of her presence. It seemed like she had been ingrained in his memory for ever and every thought of her filled him with a boundless joy that he had never felt in the presence of any other woman. Steve was in no doubt that he was deeply in love with Eva.

Knowing how important it would be for Hugo to settle down again in new surroundings, he had offered to get out of the way early that day to allow her to make Hugo's landing as soft as possible. It was well past nine o'clock when he finally entered the house where everything seemed quiet and peaceful. A timely phone call to his neighbor, Mrs. Shepherd, took care of dinner arrangements for a few days since he knew how important it was that Hugo's routine, including his 6pm dinner, should not be disturbed.

In the dimly-lit living room he warmed his hands in front of the glass doors of the gas fire to ward off the chill of the ocean air that had reached inside the house, despite it being summertime. Steve decided to head into the kitchen where he knew his dinner would be kept, when he suddenly became aware of Eva curled up in his favorite armchair in the darkness of the room. Startled that he had not noticed before, he hesitated, not sure if he should disturb her. He approached quietly. Her eyes were closed and she seemed very relaxed.

"Why don't you go to bed?" he inquired softly. As she came out of light sleep, a little shock jolted her body, but she instinctively reached for his extended hand. When she stood, he drew her close to him and without thinking, slipped his arms around her waist. She came readily into his embrace without any unnecessary protest as if it was the most natural thing for them to do. He could tell from the tension in her body that she was exhausted from the strain of the day and on impulse dropped a light kiss on her hair, smelling its fresh fragrance. He closed his eyes and had trouble resisting the urge to deepen the embrace with this woman who felt so familiar in his arms and so much a part of him.

Steve wanted to ask about her and Hugo's day, to make sure the boy was comfortable. He wanted to ask about so many other things that would explain how she had managed to erase the memory of every other woman he had been with or how she could make him believe that there had only ever been her and him. But the words remained unspoken and he took simple pleasure in her nearness, deeply enchanted that she made no effort to end the moment. Their closeness was impelled by a force that neither understood; prolonged by a mounting urge to remember. But they did not remember. Holding onto each other made the moment tender and sweet. And that was enough.

After she had gone to bed, he chose to remain in the dark and sat in front of the fire watching the flames dance behind the glass doors, his dinner forgotten beside him on the tray. No matter how he tried to rationalize the presence of MI6 agents around the farm, he sensed a danger that he could not explain. And although she had not discussed this with him, he felt that Eva was more perturbed about the reason for them having to move than she would let on and he admitted in frustration that there was a great deal that he simply knew nothing of.

It was well after eleven o'clock when he passed her bedroom door and noticed that it had been left ajar. Unsure whether this was an indication that something was amiss, he hesitated in the corridor, not wanting to intrude if she was sleeping but also not willing to walk away unless he confirmed that all was well.

"I left it open for Hugo." She spoke softly from the darkness of the room. "I don't want him to wonder where I am in case he wakes up. The last time we were here, he shared my room. But now he has to get used to a new environment."

"Are you okay?" he inquired gently from the corridor, but his question was met with silence. "Eva?"

"I'm fine." It didn't sound very convincing.

"Would you mind if I came in?" The question was out before he could evaluate the wisdom of asking.

"I don't mind." When he pushed the door open he found her sitting cross-legged wrapped in a blanket in the middle of the bed. "I can't sleep." She sounded very tired. "I have no idea how our lives became so complicated and I am beginning to question the wisdom of involving you in a plot that I don't understand." Steve crossed the floor to where she was, and sat in the armchair beside her bed.

"I wanted you and Hugo to come here. It was entirely my choice." He leaned forward, trying to find her eyes in the dark. "Please tell me about this Goldberg character and why he is so hell bent on coming after you. Is it you or Hugo that he wants?" His eyes had adjusted to the darkness of the room, but she had averted her head and her expression remained hidden behind a curtain of hair.

"I don't know." Her voice had dropped to a whisper. "I think it is Hugo he wants, but he knows that he cannot get his co-operation without my help. As you know, Hugo cannot concentrate at all when he is disturbed. He wanted to separate my son from me for long periods of time in his new program, and that made me suspicious of his intentions. Then we discovered that our home was under surveillance."

"You mentioned that Tom was involved with Goldberg. How is that possible? Surely he would not agree to anything that could harm his own child?" His tone was polite, as if to help her think everything through.

"It is all very confusing, Steve. I know a little bit from his letter, but I don't understand why MI6 is so concerned, and why they are showing such interest in us. I think there is a lot more at stake than controlling the mind of a gifted child." Her voice had dropped to barely above a whisper and she let out a muffled sob. "No one knows better than Josh Goldberg that Hugo is useless to him now, so what is he doing in England? Why does he want to harm us?"

"Eva—" But she kept talking as if she hadn't heard him.

"Who did we become involved with? Stanway told me two days ago that they had positively linked Josh Goldberg with the deaths of Martha Bartholomew and my brother-in-law, Oren. He said that forensics had found DNA fingerprints, apparently recorded from his days serving the military. This profile was matched in his office, and Oren's cell phone had Goldberg's number keyed in. Despite how careful he had been, the rest isn't hard to imagine. But it doesn't end there! Another killing in Newcastle is also being credited to him. Oh, my God, Steve!" Her voice shook, but she kept her head down. Steve stood and took a few steps to where she sat huddled on the bed. Then he sat down beside her and gently put his arm around her shoulders.

"Come here." He no longer questioned his actions and felt the enormous tension in her body as she briefly held back before relaxing against him. He locked her in a gentle embrace. "I won't let anything happen to you or Hugo," he said softly with his mouth in her hair, meaning every word. "You're safe here, I promise." And realizing how long she had kept everything pent up inside, he just let her talk while he listened.

She told him of her mother and sister and how they had found comfort in each other after her brother-in-law's death. But much of Stanway's information around MI6 and Josh Goldberg sounded incoherent and he just let it go, understanding how tired she was. He never questioned or interrupted; he just listened and held her. At last she fell silent and for a long time they sat quietly, and just when he began to wonder if she had fallen asleep, she spoke softly against his chest.

"Remember the festival?"

"How can I forget?" His voice was heavy with emotion. His beautiful Aztec bride haunted his dreams. He had not told her since that day how his mind had gone off in search of a name to match the mysterious creature he encountered on that stage.

"I think about that often." She spoke slowly, like one losing touch with reality and drifting off into sleep. "What really happened that day?" She didn't wait for him to answer, but continued her dreamy monologue. "Where does recognition come from, if not from us? But how is that possible? How much of it is conjecture, or simply derived from our subconscious minds because we feel a void and we need to fill it with something—*anything*? What if this were nothing but our fertile imaginations at work?"

Steve remained silent and listened to her voice fading in and out. He tried to follow her train of thought but despite the constraints of his rational mind, he was curiously at a point of acceptance, knowing that there were certain things he simply did not understand. His recognition of Eva and the bond he felt with her fell into this category and for the first time, instead of insisting on a rational explanation, he was willing to accept that he had an inexplicable prior association of some kind with this beautiful woman who was slowly falling asleep. When her breathing became regular, he lifted a hand and carefully tucked her hair behind her ear to reveal her profile, taking pains not to wake her. He immensely enjoyed the feeling of her sleeping against him and was loathe letting go of her warm body, but finally he gently eased her away until her head touched the pillow.

The skies had cleared and the pale moonlight partially illuminated her face through the window. He just stared at her, captivated by a feeling of indescribable acquaintance that unnerved him. Unable to resist, he reached out and gently brushed a few strands of hair from her face, but this time his hand lingered; lightly tracing the arch of her brow and caressing the smooth skin along her cheekbone. He dropped his thumb to her mouth and felt her warm breath, but she didn't move, despite the agonizing tension that gripped his body.

He knew that he should leave but couldn't, and kept struggling with the intense desire to further explore the contours of her lovely face. He watched in rapture as her peaceful sleeping expression appeared to interchange with the mesmerizing creature at the festival, and *again* felt the desperate urge to find a name to attach to the shimmering dream. But it was as elusive as the vision and kept escaping him until he finally let go. He closed his eyes in deep disappointment, at a loss as to how to solve the mystery, and decided to wait until her sleep became deeper before retiring to his room.

Hours later he awoke, startled and confused in the middle of what felt like a dream. When he turned his head, he encountered the beautiful face of a sleeping woman and his heart faltered painfully when suddenly her name surged with great clarity into his memory.

"Anacaona!" he whispered hoarsely, staring at her face. "Ana...*Oh, my God*!" His heart was racing wildly and he couldn't get out the last part of the strange name. He tried to move but every part of his nervous system reacted to the neural commands, ordering every muscle to lock and forcing him to remember. He sat frozen beside her on the bed while his memory banks opened and allowed him to traverse thousands of years and affirm unequivocally what was otherwise impossible to prove. At last he was able to awkwardly reach for the hand that lay relaxed by her side and he raised it slowly to his lips. "Anacaona," he repeated her ancient name softly, feeling the tears sting behind his eyes. *How could we have forgotten?*

He carefully rose from the bed and walked over to the armchair where he sat down, overwhelmed and weak with the knowledge his subconscious mind had so effortlessly revealed. Finally, he gave up the frantic search for answers. Then he leaned back, unable to take his eyes off the sleeping woman until exhaustion finally took its toll and he surrendered into a fitful sleep. When the first light of dawn crept through the window he opened his eyes, and this time his surroundings were familiar. She was still sleeping soundly as he carefully stood and walked silently to the door where he turned and looked at her.

"Anacaona," he repeated softly, reverently. "How long has it been?"

But she didn't hear him and he left quietly, walking down the semi darkness of the corridor toward the main bedroom. His mind was filled with warmth and wonder for the woman he had left sleeping so peacefully, realizing that *in this life* they had just spent their first night together. Despite the lack of a good night's sleep, Steve barely felt tired. He was still overwhelmed with his discovery of the previous night and, although his reasoning faculty begged him to reconsider the sanity of the breakthrough, he knew that it was equally impossible to refute the powerful feelings of identification when his subconscious mind had so effortlessly produced her name.

Taking a cold shower and allowing the water to run over his body to stimulate his senses, he wondered if he was losing his mind. But he knew the answer to that question was relatively simple. Eva's response to the name was the only confirmation he needed, but in the meantime he had to look in on Hugo. He found the boy fully dressed, sitting in the middle of the floor systematically arranging some of his precious charts, which had arrived the day before, along with the rest of his belongings from Israel. He waited until Hugo looked up and made eye contact.

"Hello." He gave Steve a wistful look, but said no more.

"Good morning, Hugo." He glanced at the charts and then waited until he caught Hugo's eye again. "I am looking forward to our expedition today, young man. But first you have to tell me what these mean?" He pointed to the stack of papers with different designs and noticed that the bed was already neatly made. Everything was organized and meticulously put in place. "Mind if I sit?" Hugo hesitated, but nodded and then directed his attention to the complicated designs surrounding him.

"These are blueprints. I use them to know what is happening," he said quietly. That sounded like Greek to Steve but he refrained from comment. He had already witnessed the child's extraordinary ability to work with mathematical equations and was fascinated to learn how designs on paper could assist the child to know what he was claiming. Moreover, Hugo's capacity to express thoughts and concepts in mathematical terms astounded him and Professor O'Malley. And it appeared that Steve's presence, like a magical key, helped the boy to articulate. He nodded his head in agreement, encouraging him to continue. "I sometimes use the stars," he announced unceremoniously without looking at Steve. He was already wrapped up in his explanation. "I got these from calculations I have made of constellations that I know. These constellations have patterns and designs. They relate to the position of those stars." He looked up and met Steve's attentive expression, and then continued. "If the constellation is close, I use my eyes and my mind. If it is too far, I use the telescope. Mum bought it for my birthday."

Steve realized that to an astronomer, they probably meant no more than already well documented fixed positions of stars from which various measurements and calculations could be made regarding the origins and evolvement of the Universe. But he suspected that to Hugo these represented different worlds and dimensions from which he could receive a form of communication; far beyond the comprehension of an orthodox astronomer.

He felt his excitement beginning to build. Hugo was not only the child of the woman he loved, but he had a brilliant mind, which to a great extent was still lying dormant. He had learned confidentially from O'Malley that Hugo was a high functioning autistic child, but that his condition was undefined in many ways. A few experts thought that he had Asperger's syndrome, which would account for the speech problem, but many things about this unusual child remained an enigma. The mind-boggling mathematical calculations he could master put him on par with a savant, but unlike other savants who could perform similar feats, Hugo was very proficient in describing his own genius.

Steve had done some personal investigations regarding the phenomenon and had discovered that there were more theories than facts. Some alleged that brain damage of some sort was what created a savant, but as far as he could tell, there was no sign of that in Hugo. The boy seemed to fit no definite description, which reminded Steve of a television program, featuring a young man in England with similar extraordinary talents and abilities; only Hugo seemed to surpass even that. In the short time that he had known the boy, he had demonstrated that he was capable of charting new ways of thought and application of information, and in the absence of labeling his specific condition, he was simply in awe of what Hugo could do.

"And are we using this particular method to uncover the secrets of the ley lines later tonight?" he asked softly and attentively, fascinated with every word.

"Yes. To see the mysteries of the hot spots, we must triangulate the stars and make a pattern from our calculations. The pattern holds the answer."

"Are there other ways in which we may determine these meanings, Hugo?"

"I do not know. The stars' positions are just one of many ways that we can use mathematics to make patterns. Patterns are what I understand and they have helped me to know things that others do not. I think that is because they do not see what I see."

Steve contemplated Hugo's words quietly. Although only a boy, he was determined to help fathom the ley lines which passed through and merged at certain points on the farm where there had been much activity from the past. Without being able to prove it, Steve suspected that the Cosmos would give up its secrets if the right connection was made by charting the positions of the stars, resulting in a design that Hugo could comprehend. He recalled a favorite statement to his students when he reminded them every so often that everything in the Universe was simply information and that if the codes of how it was organized could be deciphered, many mysteries would be solved.

Listening to the boy, he realized that once Hugo could determine a shape or pattern by calculation, a definite energy signature could be determined from which information would follow. This, potentially, could be interpreted by a sensitive individual with an extraordinary mind.

"The Universe communicates with you, Hugo?" he asked softly.

"Yes. With anyone." The expression in his eyes was serious. "If they do the math."

"I think there may not be many who have the patience to identify those shapes."

"I only know what I can see. It is very hard for me to imagine that other people do not see what I see. Mr. Goldberg taught me how to see much more." The innocent mention of Josh Goldberg's name jolted Steve and he made an effort to restrain himself.

"How is that, Hugo?"

"He told me that I used my feelings. He said the other students had never done that and we were going to try and find the relationship between designs and their meanings. But I would have had to be away from mum for too long and I do not like that."

"I see. What is the most important thing he taught you, Hugo?"

"His secret; to make my mind go quiet."

"And did he?"

"Yes. Once I had the pattern fixed in my mind and entered the Zen state, it would fade, leaving information and answers behind. Mr. Goldberg said that happened because I had the ability to leave physical matters to the subconscious. I am not sure what the subconscious means because to me there is only one mind and that is the one I see and feel. But he also said that if there was no interference from any source, all things could be read or known. Because of this, Mr. Goldberg knew that I could already speak normally and only had to remember." Steve looked at the collection of designs depicted on the many papers surrounding the young boy.

"I don't see two designs that look the same. You must have worked very hard at this, Hugo?"

"They cannot be the same." He rubbed his right ear and Steve recognized this as a familiar gesture that he was becoming tired. "It is not difficult for me to form a calculation around a certain pattern and transform it into a living schematic. I did not know what that meant until Mr. Goldberg told me. He was very excited about what we could do together. But I do not know why everyone cannot do this because all shapes and designs, from a pattern on the wall to a cloud cluster, produce a way for energy to be channeled. Mr. Goldberg called this the interconnectedness of multi-dimensional consciousness. He said that I could apply my mind in any way I choose. We are always able to see and know anything when we open up ourselves, especially if we can process data through mathematics first. That is what would make it an exact science, but not many people know this."

Steve's mind went back to the day when he had found the equation on the blackboard completed by Hugo. He knew the child had to be unusual but until today he had not quite realized the extent of Hugo Norman's talent and all his idiosyncrasies and strange behaviors paled in comparison to his gargantuan gift. Listening to the calm but mind-boggling explanations from this young boy, he was aware that his own mind was trying to connect some of the dots that orthodox physics have not yet made. He knew psychics worked through earthly vibrations and this was how clairvoyants relied on higher energies, like that of the aura, or the body's electromagnetic field, to retrieve information.

In some of the research he had read about these people, which was mostly aimed at discrediting them, he had come to the conclusion that even though they often produced accurate answers, they seldom had any awareness of the origins of the phenomenon that was presented to them, other than their own interpretation. Thus, it was very difficult not to dismiss their work simply as sophisticated guessing.

But he suspected that something else was at work where Hugo was concerned, and that the boy, in essence, was a psychic *and* a clairvoyant, albeit a calculating one. The advanced level at which he operated, that seemed so natural to him, was totally alien to others; except to Josh Goldberg and his mother, and now Steve also had gained a glimpse into Hugo's strange and wonderful world.

Whether by design or accident, it appears that brain development of some handicapped individuals is quite out of the ordinary and that the range of variance in autistic subjects in particular, is quite high. He had read that a few psychics, obviously from non scientific backgrounds, alleged that the dysfunction of autism can be ascribed to being stranded between two realities. He wondered about that. Steve was convinced that the spiritual aspect of the human composition was greatly underestimated, but as yet he had no real experience of what another reality would look or feel like. Studying Hugo was almost impossible and in the light of his extraordinary abilities, it hugely complicated any definition of him.

He was beginning to believe that Hugo was working from a higher vibrational level of coherence, gaining multi-dimensional access and giving credit to theory physics which was only just beginning to be understood by certain specialized institutions, such as Azvaalder. He also surmised that if Azvaalder was so intensely interested in Hugo's talents, they would have jumped on this same bandwagon due to Josh Goldberg's intervention. Then the fuller implication dawned on him and he realized why Goldberg must be a man possessed, after Eva had taken Hugo away from him.

From papers that had recently been published, Steve was aware that research had already confirmed how human DNA could re-route itself after conscious recognition had been halted and non-physical interceptors would switch on to take the mind to another level of cohesion and insight. Hugo, with his extraordinary talent, was thus the perfect specimen. His DNA and brain frequencies were probably a match with the extensive research that had been so costly to implement. Small wonder Josh wanted to protect his investment, or mete out revenge for having been thwarted. Hugo was still rubbing his ear and Steve knew it was time to end the discussion.

"Natalie's coming to stay with us for a week or more; her grandpa is bringing her tomorrow. Did your mum tell you?" Hugo nodded and Steve was glad to see the shy smile on Hugo's face. The two children had a strange bond and Natalie followed Hugo around like his shadow. Eva had been quick to notice this and commented that for the first time her son did not seem to interpret another child's presence as an intrusion. "Come, it is time we fed you breakfast, young man! We have a busy day ahead of us. Natalie is bringing Razzle, so there will be lots to keep the two of you busy." He stood and carefully straightened out the bed while Hugo watched him, before walking to the door. "I can't wait for our excursion under the stars tonight, Hugo!" He smiled warmly. "I'll be taking notes. You can be sure of that. I want to learn from the master."

"Can I draw pictures too?" She was leaning on her elbows and watching him intently through the unruly blonde curls that tumbled over her forehead, as he concentrated on the design.

"These are not pictures." He didn't look directly at her because she was standing very close to him and he could smell the candy she was noisily sucking. He didn't want to encourage her to put her sticky hands anywhere on his work. "These are charts and designs."

"I can do this too," she declared, leaning even closer to the chart in front of him. Hugo finished the last of his calculations, and gently pushed his elbow out to increase the distance between her and his handiwork. Then he sat back and looked at her for the first time.

"No, you cannot. Do you know what these calculations mean?"

He pointed to the numbers he had written alongside the triangles and squares. She shook her head.

"What is it for?"

"For that special place your fairies told you about. The Professor and I went there last night. I found the right cluster of stars and that is how I got those shapes. Then I did the math."

"Oh!" she said and nodded her head as though it was all suddenly crystal clear to her. "I could have shown you again, Hugo! You didn't have to make all these pictures! I still know where it is." He eyed her carefully.

"What are you eating?" he asked, not knowing how to answer her and no longer able to contain his curiosity about the fresh smell on her breath.

"Mint humbugs. You can have one if you want to. I have saved you some." She reached inside the little fluffy pink purse that she had strapped to her wrist and took out a roll of candy. Then she tore off the paper wrapping and handed him a piece. Hugo took it before she could put it down on the chart, and popped it into his mouth. He had an important question to ask her. He glanced at the open door to make sure that no grownups were around and then he looked at her, keeping his voice low.

"How did your fairies know about Thorp Pelkington?"

"Can we go back there?" she asked excitedly, as if she had forgotten his question. But then she noticed the frustration on his face and unceremoniously plopped down on his bed. Hugo got up and straightened the bedding around her before sitting down again, unable to hide the scowl on his face. "You're funny!" she exclaimed. "Why do you do that?" When he didn't answer, she pulled a face and kept her eyes on her feet, which were swinging vigorously off the bed. "Don't be cross, Hugo. You look just like the medicine man when you frown."

"What medicine man?" he asked, intrigued by the strange direction she had suddenly taken. "Is he from Thorp Pelkington?"

"Maybe," she whispered conspiringly, not looking at him.

"Who says?" he asked incredulously. "The fairies?" But she was unperturbed and too young to catch the sarcasm.

"Everyone," she insisted, "in Thorp Pelkington, went to the Meadow. Dead people go to the Meadow and when I dream I always visit the Meadow." Suddenly she fell right into what he thought was a fantasy. In one quick movement she turned onto her stomach and rested her right cheek on the bed while her left arm hung down freely. Then she began humming softly, dreamily while tracing patterns on the hardwood floor with her index finger. Hugo suppressed the urge to straighten the bedding again and stared mesmerized at his little friend as she began to speak almost in a sing-song tone with her eyes half closed. "A long, long time ago I saw a horse in the Meadow." She shut her eyes completely and remained silent as if she was trying to remember something important. He watched her closely, wholly caught up in her fairy tale or dream. He wasn't sure which one it was.

"Razzle?" he asked. She didn't open her eyes.

"No, a big black horse. Like Bullet."

"You mean Quah Dreamer. Why would he be in a meadow of your dream?" he asked baffled.

"Quah Dreamer is his special name. He was waiting for someone."

"Who?" But she didn't answer and resumed her humming again. Hugo stared at her, unsure what to do next. He was frustrated with her lack of response and the confusion she was creating. "Natalie…"

"The medicine man is very clever, Hugo. And he knows about the stars too. Just like you. I know his name."

"The fairies told you his name?" The tale was almost becoming too tall, even for him, but he found himself pursuing it further, almost against his will.

"The fairies don't live in the Meadow. Only here." Her voice had become very soft and he leaned forward to hear every word.

"*What* medicine man?" She opened her eyes and looked directly at him and then fixed her gaze somewhere behind him.

"You," she said still staring past him. "They called you Sakhota. And you also lived in Thorp Pelkington long ago." Hugo could barely speak and he no longer wondered if she was fantasizing or relaying a dream. The name "Sakhota" had sent shivers down his spine and he tried to make sense of this completely new feeling that upset his intense desire to slot knowledge into places where his mind could categorize it. Then he looked at his little friend and asked earnestly.

"*And who are you?*" A delightful giggle bubbled from her mouth and she suddenly jumped up from the bed.

"I'm Natalie, you silly! You can ask my grandpa Jack. He says there is only one Natalie, and that is me!"

"I talked to Dave Sanderson, our history expert at the campus, about the origins of Thorp Pelkington." Eva watched him from where she sat on a bale of hay in Quah Dreamer's stable. The lantern cast him and the horse in a soft yellow light and she marveled at the unquestionable communication between him and his steed as the horse grunted and snorted his pleasure at Steve's touch.

Their day had been filled with activities with the children and, amidst Hugo and Natalie's excitement around Thorp Pelkington, they had not seen much of each other. There was a definite air of secrecy around the youngsters and she was surprised to see Hugo participate in it with Natalie, but was nevertheless happy to notice the uncharacteristic childlike aspect to him. Steve washed his hands from the tap that filled Quah Dreamer's water trough and then walked over to sit down beside her, continuing where he left off.

"At first he couldn't find anything until he decided to search the Scottish records. Our neck of the woods here in the North East was once a regular battleground between the Scots and the English. I won't bore you with the history of it all," he smiled and took her hand, "but there was indeed a small village built here which was regarded as one of the first safe havens between the two countries, south of the heavily-guarded border fortresses based in Northumberland." Eva rested her head against his shoulder and just enjoyed being close to him in the intimacy of the stable, listening to the marvelous way he paid attention to detail.

"The name he found for the village based approximately in this area was Thor Hesp Elkin. 'Thor' is of Viking origin meaning lonely or isolated farm. Dave reckoned that 'Hesp Elkin' was a Viking family name and when the 'ton' was added, it would signify the title of a place derived from the family name. When you pronounce 'Thor Hesp Elkin Ton' quickly and in the regional accent of this area, it sounds very much like Thorp Pelkington and this would have been the more modern equivalent name given to this place.

"Yesterday, when I was in town, I looked in on my parents and I mentioned this to my father. Can you imagine my surprise when he immediately recognized the name of Hesp Elkin and showed me the genealogy search of the family, which he had done as a young man? From the subsequent family tree he created, it seems I'm of Viking descent and my genes can be traced all the way back to the Hesp Elkin family period. So you see Eva, everything fits. Natalie really did come up with some information from a source that we can't even begin to imagine and Hugo's abilities are beyond what society is willing to accept."

"I know," she concurred softly, "but I wish I had a better understanding of all of these confusing images and feelings of recognition. They are so hard to ignore." He rose abruptly and pulled her up so that she stood in front of him while he rested his hands lightly on her shoulders. The look in his eyes was serious but his voice remained gentle and comforting.

"When science finally discovered the quantum theory, all the goalposts had to be moved. It is estimated that there are eleven or more parallel universes to ours. I'm not sure just how many, because theory is not my strong suit. What this means, Eva, is that consciousness exists beyond what we regard as the third dimension, or our physical Universe. In my work, the world of discovered physics is evolving at an enormous pace. Physics, in any expression, does not recognize coincidence and for the first time in my life I'm beginning to realize that I'm a specialist in this subject for a reason. And so is Hugo, even though there is much about his condition and abilities that we don't understand." She leaned forward and rested her forehead lightly against his chest.

"Then it seems that between you and Hugo we will discover many wonderful things." He dropped his arms behind her back and purposely pulled her closer to him.

"I already have." His voice was suddenly thick with emotion and she looked up, instantly aware of the change in his tone. Then he lifted his hand and tenderly placed it against her cheek. Neither of them spoke and she closed her eyes when his thumb began to explore the outline of her mouth and lingered on her lower lip. "Wasn't it right here in this stable," he said as he parted her lips and drew his mouth nearer to hers, "where I kissed you the first time...*in this life?*" Her eyes flew open in astonishment and she stared at him, unable to move or make a sound, yet she clung to every belabored word. "But I found you last night in *another world* that I had been searching for since that day of the festival." He struggled to speak, sounding like one in pain. "Eva, my darling..." His voice faltered. "Dear God, you are *Anacaona!*"

"Anacaona?" she asked faintly, as the wedding ceremony in Billingham swam into focus and it all became clear. "Steve...*you remember!*" Her legs couldn't hold the weight of her body any longer and she clung helplessly to him.

"Yes!" It was a hoarse whisper, but his eyes burnt like coals in his head. "*You are Anacaona!* I finally remembered!" When his mouth closed over hers it was because he desperately needed to anchor the overwhelming emotion that surged through his body in some form of physical contact with her. But when she returned the kiss with the same intensity, it was like a switch had been thrown on the hands of time and they slowly became undone, helpless and stunned by the raw passion laid bare after so many eons. He tasted the salt of her tears in his mouth and it mingled with his own, but he didn't care about anything except the quivering woman he held in his arms.

When the shaking in her body finally subsided, she slowly pulled away from him and through her tears she took his hand and placed it over her heart. Then she laid her hand where his heart beat loudly and while their bodies and minds flooded with the memory of a love so old and so beautiful, she whispered against his mouth.

"How long has it been, *Teuch?*" His heart strained mightily in his chest. That was *his* name. She knew! "*Quah Atowahl!* My eagle man." It was all the confirmation he needed.

Chapter 23
Retribution

Dmitri walked up the four steps to the base of the statue of Eros in Piccadilly Circus and surveyed his surroundings dolefully. When Josh mentioned Soho, he had envisaged a seedy place with cheap food and rowdy drinking holes filled with easy women; much like the Jolly Sailor in Tel Aviv, where he had hung out with Isabel. But that place didn't seem to exist and he was very disappointed.

He had rambled through Soho earlier in the day in search of sleazy bars where he could have his needs satisfied before his encounter with Justine, but ended up in Soho Square with its mock-Tudor cottage that served as a resting place for gardeners who took care of the lawns and flowers. *Where the hell are the bloody whores?*

He stared frustrated at the wide collection of locals sprawled out on the benches and grass; from tired waiters taking a smoke break from nearby restaurants, to the Hari Krishnas with their robes and drums from the temple on Soho Street. *Fucking religious freaks!* He scowled angrily and spat into the base of the fountain beneath the wings of Eros. Dmitri was not at all in a friendly mood.

All day he had been looking to find a street corner call girl touting her wares, but was oblivious that he was searching for a place from the past. He didn't know that it was the Soho of the fifties that had sported unlicensed sex shops, cinemas and clip joints. At the time the area was lavishly filled with illegal bars and squalid brothels which supported many freelance prostitutes luridly soliciting beneath flickering neon signs, or offering their services from staircases with open doors to the street. But by the eighties the City of Westminster and the police purged the area of its unlicensed and shady inhabitants and the creatures of the underworld took shelter in hideouts around Brewer Street and Berwick Street, where prostitution and drug dealing were still the main trades.

Elegant Soho, where Dmitri felt so out of place, was situated between major thoroughfares; Regent and Oxford Streets to the north west with their stores and displays, Charing Cross Road with its bookshops to the east, and Shaftsbury Avenue and Leicester Square to the south, boasting theaters, cinemas and shows. It is to *this* Soho that thousands of visitors come day and night as they have for countless years, hunting its good food and drink and hearing its siren songs of excitement and brief company.

With the help of a co-operative London taxi driver and a healthy tip into the bargain, Dmitri eventually found himself outside an old but stylish-looking Victorian terraced apartment building opposite some high-class boutiques and a few coffee bars. He smirked as he stood on the sidewalk and eyed the building contemptuously. *Ah! The little rat seems to have acquired expensive taste after relieving Josh of four thousand pounds.* Even though he disliked Tomer so much, he was still in awe of his sophisticated electronic infiltration methods and that he had the ability to trace Justine Oliver through a few stolen credit card transactions.

She was in for the shock of her life, and he felt the excitement beginning to build. Killing came easily to him, but the deed itself held little pleasure. Surprising and shocking the victim is what provided the ultimate thrill and this one was as unprepared as a lamb being led to the slaughter. From across the street where he loitered around a coffee shop, he recognized her instantly from Josh's detailed description as she entered the building, laden with packages from a shopping trip. Her time had come, but Justine Oliver didn't know. She had no idea that Josh Goldberg was about to make good on his promise and that he had sent the Angel of Death to settle the score.

Dmitri slowly approached the building, cracking the knuckles of each hand with anticipation and cricking his neck both ways. Today he had no weapon other than brute force on which to rely. The doorway had a coded entry, so he patiently waited for the next person to show up. It didn't take long.

She was a small, petite girl and Dmitri forced a smile, holding a folded twenty pound note discreetly between his index and middle fingers as he leaned amiably against the front door. She stood a few feet away from him and listened as he explained that his date was Justine

Oliver but that he had forgotten the floor and number to her apartment. His eyes traveled deliberately over her body, completely unconcerned that in future she would easily be able to identify him. By the time Justine's body was discovered, he would be long gone.

"Oh! The Geordie girl from Newcastle!" The platinum blonde in the short tight skirt was from Egton, Yorkshire and the Russian could barely understand a word as she prattled on about how fortunate Justine was to be able to afford the top floor apartment. He kept his eyes blatantly on her breasts, well aware that all prostitutes understood the universal language of visual assault; even welcomed it. And if he were interested in her, this would be foreplay. When he indolently made eye contact with her she held his gaze without flinching. "Okay, lover boy," she crooned, acknowledging his unabashed appraisal with a promising little smile, "but only if you agree to come see me also."

"Of course—what is your name?" *God, just another cheap fucking whore.*

"Patti Norris. Number 12. Second floor." With that the deal was done; she grabbed the money and let him in.

He knocked gently on the door, hoping not to arouse any suspicion on the floors below. It opened with the security chain still attached and a nervous-looking face appeared in the small gap.

"Justine?" Dmitri forced a smile as she acknowledged him and he peered discretely over her head to see if anyone was inside. "A colleague of yours downstairs had double booked, but recommended you. She saw you coming in and thought you were free. I pay rather well."

"Who did?" she asked hesitantly, still hiding behind the safety chain and forgetting that no prostitute sends business away.

"Patti in room 12, on the second floor." Dmitri appeared calm but inwardly he was shaking with excitement and anticipation.

"Not if I have to share the money with her." *Of course not, bitch! You'll be as dead as a doornail.*

"And so you shouldn't. How about it, can I come in?" She never knew what hit her. When she came to she was lying naked, face down on the bed groaning from intense pain in her stomach where he had launched his big fist with all his might as soon as she opened the door. Doubled over and winded, he had caught her before she hit the floor and then quietly locked the door behind them.

While she strained to catch her breath behind the big hand covering her mouth, he skillfully applied pressure with his other hand to the carotid arteries on either side of her neck, instantly stemming the blood flow to her brain. It was an old and dangerous technique used in erotic asphyxia that often led to death, but Dmitri was experienced enough not to kill her just yet. Within seconds her body went limp and he quickly duct-taped her mouth before roughly stripping her down. Then he took her pantyhose and wound the legs into a tight nylon rope and sat in a chair waiting for her to open her eyes.

Justine agonizingly lifted her head and met with his cold stare. Looking at him she knew there would be no mercy and no way out. With her mouth taped she could neither negotiate with him nor plead for her life, and while she waited stoically for his next move, he stood and walked around the bed to stand at her feet. Her hands were tied behind her back with her shirt and she kept still, weakly bracing against a brutality the shape of which she didn't dare to imagine.

"It seems you have a way with men, you fucking bitch. Do you usually club them senseless when you've finished with them? Well, not with this one you won't." Then he slid Josh's credit card, which he had taken from her purse while she was briefly unconscious, beside her onto the bed. "Remember this man?" he whispered in her ear as he leaned over. Justine stared transfixed at the card, instantly reminded of the horror of that day, but the frantic scream that rose from the pit of her stomach was muffled by the duct tape.

"That man has a message for you, *sukka* or is *slut* better?" He grinned at the Russian slur. "He says you will be in hell before him, but to wait for him there." She heard him undoing his pants and waited motionlessly with dry, staring eyes. Her mind was frozen, yet she sensed that he was going to sodomize her and all her muscles locked rigidly while she braced for the violent encounter. Then he flung the nylon rope around her neck and simultaneously forced brutal anal entry. And there was not a single thing in the whole wide world that could have prepared Justine for the unspeakable violence which was to follow. "Seems to me, *sukka*, that dead or alive, you're *fucked!*" She didn't hear his words through his frenzied grunting or feel the saliva dripping from his mouth onto her back. She was already hurtling down a harrowing black hole infinitely more terrifying than the monster wasting her life.

Afterwards he had no recollection of when he had squeezed the last bit of breath from her. Beneath him, her body was still warm, but he was too drunk with ecstasy and couldn't tell if the satisfaction came from the rape, or the kill, or both. He didn't care. Josh would be pleased and he was already thinking about his next assignment, Eva Norman.

When two days had passed without Hugo being delivered to the campus, Josh knew something big was amiss, but he didn't panic. He smiled grimly, nodding his head slowly as he surveyed the closed up apartment where there was no sign of activity. He lowered the powerful binoculars and spoke softly under his breath.

"You sense the danger, don't you, Eva? Ah, but that makes the hunt exciting, didn't you know? As long as you fear me, I will never lose your scent." He closed his eyes in concentration. "Now where would they have taken you?" He sat still for a long time, and then slowly opened his eyes. "To your lover? Would they be that stupid? I hope so."

Scouting the area around Ocean View at dusk he discovered a small private woodland perched on a hill above the farm. Early the following morning, he drove the rental car off the road and hid it in nearby bushes, covering it with branches and leaves to make it inconspicuous to passing traffic. He had come equipped for a few days, with food, water, a sleeping bag and weapons he had obtained without difficulty through his CIA connections in the underground black market that exists in every country around the world. He hid the handgun under the backseat but took the binoculars and his cell phone with him. The glass surfaces of the binoculars were multi-coated, ensuring that his presence would not be revealed by chance reflection of light.

Dressed in army fatigues, he moved stealthily around the perimeter of the woodland, scouting for a vantage point from where he would have a better view of the acreage of the farm. It took Josh about an hour to find the right spot, but by 7am he was sitting high up in a tree, after breaking away the foliage in front of him. With the help of the binoculars he could see the roof of the farmhouse, a fair deal of the horse training facility, as well as a large part of the wooded area east of the house. He settled in to wait.

All his senses affirmed that he was on the right trail and that he was closing in on his target. Years of experience had taught him endurance and patience, but cold-blooded anger and a burning need for retribution simmered just beneath the surface of his otherwise unruffled exterior. Only he knew that his bitterness was many thousands of years old. He laughed without pleasure. *Or have I really lost my fucking mind?*

He spotted Hugo first and sat up, straining to get a better view and wondered about the presence of the little girl who was leading him around on a pony. Then he noticed the man on the huge black horse, camouflaged in the shade of the wooded area where he sat quietly, observing the activities of the children. *Horse riding lessons for Hugo?* Josh Goldberg wanted to laugh out loud. *My Hugo with his brilliant mind and his fetish for order and symmetry riding a horse?* But that was clearly what was happening when the man emerged into the sunlight and drew closer to the pony, lifting the boy easily off the smaller animal to sit in front of him on the black stallion. Josh watched with mounting fury as the man, whom he recognized as Steve Ballantire, kept his arms protectively around Hugo and took him on a gentle gallop around the clearing; the girl trotting behind them on the pony.

"You have figured that out, you bastard, haven't you? Eva is a package deal which includes Hugo." He spoke softly to himself as he followed their movements. "I wonder if you know the true potential of that child." He lowered the binoculars and stared off into the distance. It didn't matter anymore. Hugo would never trust him again and the boy's potential was lost to his cause.

He looked over at the horse riding activity again. *You and that Jewish bitch you're shacked up with will pay for this, Ballantire. No one crosses Josh Goldberg. No one!* He slammed his knuckles violently into a branch of the tree and only registered the pain when he felt the blood trickling over the back of his hand. A grim smile crept around his mouth. *What a pity Justine Oliver couldn't be here to testify to this.* He thought of Dmitri's call the day before when he had learned of the prostitute's demise.

"*Jesus*, Anchov! Could it have been any messier?" He didn't wait for an answer. "Get that Russian ass of yours onto a train to Newcastle and lie low. You know where to go and what to do; my contact is waiting for you. And don't kill a fucking fly on your way here!" He would have to keep a close watch on that killing machine around Eva. Josh wanted her dead, but that privilege was his and his alone.

By the end of the second day his instincts and common sense told him he was observing a pattern. Steve and the children were probably making the most of the remaining summer days and engaged in riding lessons around 8am, presumably after breakfast. During this time he had the opportunity to scout out the positions of the agents posted at the farmhouse. There were two of them. One was placed at the inner perimeter of the farm near the house, but not close enough to cause an intrusion, and the second agent was posted near the entrance, from where he could see all traffic entering and leaving. The agents were not in visual range of each other. Josh knew they would be in cell phone contact as well as a command post of some sort.

His senses were highly alert and he knew his assessment was not far off the mark but that he would have to act fast. The success of a delicate operation such as this one depended on swiftness and zero hesitation in order to keep the surprise element high and working in his favor. The obvious target was the guard at the gates who parked his car at the side of the road about two hundred meters from the entrance. Shift changes occurred around 7am and on the morning of the third day he was ready. He had not seen any sign of Eva, but intuition told him she was in the house.

After stripping down beside his vehicle and dressing in a business suit, he carefully trimmed and groomed the three day old beard that he had been purposely growing and dusted it down with a silvery white powder. Then he fit a curly gray wig over his head to hide his dark hair. He rounded his headgear off with a Kangol Tweed Peeble cap and stuck a pipe in his upper pocket. The finishing touch was the dull gray contact lens he slipped over his right eye, creating the illusion of blindness.

Josh felt a potent adrenalin rush as he prepared for the day. The hunter was moving in for the kill and there could be no mistakes. He cleaned the branches and leaves off the vehicle and hid all his equipment and fatigues in the trunk. Then he checked his cell phone battery power, put the spare in his pocket and placed his briefcase on the passenger seat. He retrieved the gun and stuck it loosely in his pocket; there was no room for error. Backing out of the brush and low growing shrubs and heading in the direction of Ocean View, he marveled at how his ability to adopt a foreign accent had served him many times in the past. For his encounter with the agent, he chose his favorite London, Cockney accent, one he had used many times before with great effect. Today he was a traveling salesman from Herd-wise Farm Foods as he lowered his window and smiled at the agent who approached him, immediately holding up his hand.

"'Ello to you, sir!" Josh called out dropping the "h" in customary Cockney fashion. "I'm Wallace from 'Erd-wise Farm Foods and I 'ave an appoi'ment wif Mista Ballantiya at eight firty." He pointed to the winding driveway leading to the house. The man behind the sunglasses frowned but didn't move.

"He's expecting you?"

"Sure is!" Josh wore a wide smile and touched a hand to his cap, appearing relaxed and relieved to have found the place.

"I'll call the house. Wait." With that he reached for his cell phone, but Josh needed only that split second's loss of concentration to produce his gun and point it at the agent's head.

"Give me that phone, and don't move." The Cockney accent was gone and, completely taken aback, the agent stared down the barrel of the gun as he snapped the phone shut and gave it to Josh. "Now, step away from the vehicle and keep your hands where I can see them." With his weapon trained on the man, Josh got out of the car and checked both ways for oncoming traffic. "Put your hands on the vehicle and spread your legs." Josh expertly frisked the man and disarmed him by removing his shoulder holster containing his only weapon. "Jesus," he remarked sardonically, "you fresh out of college, Officer? This was easier than deflowering an underage prostitute in the back streets of Mexico City." The agent didn't reply and Josh looked at him with disdain. "Get back to your guarding position. Now."

"Fuck you!" Agent Barrie McNeil had found his voice again.

"Yeah, trooper?" Josh was ice cold. "You want to know what someone looks like who's been fucked by me?" Then he reached for the binoculars on the backseat, not taking his eyes off McNeil.

"What the—?" The agent stared bewildered at Josh.

"Take them! And shut up! I'll do the talking, and you'll do as you're told. You are going to train the binoculars on Steve Ballantire and the children and do some running commentary when I tell you. To passing traffic we will just be observing something in the distance, but my gun will be pointing unobtrusively at your back. One unexpected move, or one wrong word and you'll be a paraplegic for life, or dead." He glanced briefly at his watch. "They should be there by now. Pick up the binoculars and tell me what you see."

As Steve and the children came into focus, McNeil told Goldberg that a horse riding lesson was in progress, while Josh used his free hand to dial Eva's cell number, which he had acquired from Tomer. He always knew that the man was brilliant and extremely well connected in communications.

"Steve?" Eva answered her phone, surprised and a little anxious. Only a few people had this number. "Is something wrong?" Josh did not try to disguise his voice.

"Listen carefully, Eva. And do *not* hang up." The shocked silence on the other end spoke volumes. "I have a gun pointed at this agent's balls and he in turn has a telescopic lens trained at your boyfriend's head. Be very quiet." He stepped closer to McNeil and pressed the phone to his ear while ramming the gun into his back. "Tell Mrs. Norman," he said loudly enough for her to hear, "what clothes her precious son is wearing; just in case she imagines I'm bluffing." McNeil swallowed hard, his voice sounded hollow.

"The boy is wearing khaki shorts and a black T-shirt with a pair of running shoes and a red baseball cap." Josh brought the phone back to his own ear.

"You get that, Eva? Is that how mummy dressed our precious boy today?" She didn't answer his question.

"What do you want?" She was paralyzed with fear and her heart was racing. In her entire life she had never felt so helpless or so afraid. *How could this have happened?*

"Pay attention," he spoke deliberately. "I want you to come to me. One wrong move and Ballantire and the children die instantly. Write a note to your boyfriend and tell him that if you and I are apprehended within the next forty eight hours, you will die and so will your mother and sister in Israel. A sharp shooter will kill them if he does not hear from me during this time. Bring your passport; nothing else. Then get the hell out of there. How you do that is not my concern. You have exactly fifteen minutes. And one more thing. Leave your phone open at all times and talk to me. If you break contact, Steve dies first."

"Please don't harm them! I'll do as you ask!" She was shaking uncontrollably and her legs could barely carry her as she ran to her room and grabbed a piece of stationery off her dresser and started writing the note to Steve. She thought of her mother and sister and wondered if Stanway and MI6 had arranged the protection for her family that she had requested. She had no illusions about Josh Goldberg's resourcefulness; he had found her with little difficulty, so getting past the authorities in Israel to locate her mother's safe house would be child's play to him.

At the last minute she noticed the eagle's feather Chong-ba had brought from the Himalayas and took it. She had no doubt that Josh was very capable of carrying out his threats, and the tears were streaming down her face when she left the note on the kitchen table and placed the feather on top of it. She knew that Steve would understand.

"The note is written. How do I—" Her voice broke.

"I don't give a shit. Find a way and you had better hurry! I'm itching to kill. You have ten minutes."

With her passport in hand, Eva left by the back door and quickly made her way to the stables. The trainers had been out since seven o'clock working the horses and there was a flurry of activity in the open arena. No one seemed to notice her and she kept her head down, slipping into the stables through a side door that led directly to the grooming area. With no one in sight she grabbed the nearest pair of overalls and threw them over her jeans and T-shirt. On her way out she took a baseball cap sitting on the counter and pulled it low over her eyes, and then made her way toward the three farm trucks parked next to each other sporting the Ocean View livery. Without thinking, she opened the driver's door of the nearest one and got in, shaking with fear and barely able to breathe. The keys were in the ignition and the engine was still warm. She bent low over the steering wheel to fish her open cell phone out of her pocket.

"Where do you want me to go?" she choked.

"The Spotted Cow in the village. Ah! Good girl! I can see you. Now back out slowly and get into the driveway and don't speed. Pretend you are running a normal errand into Elwick and go to the car park behind the Spotted Cow. Do not get out of the vehicle or signal anyone. Keep your phone line open at all times and talk to me. If you try to cross me, Eva, your mother and sister will die today. And then I will come after your boyfriend and Hugo." He heard a stifled sob and refrained from comment. The last thing he needed was for her to become hysterical; he had to push harder. "Two minutes, Eva! This is not a school concert rehearsal. I'm getting impatient, so get the fuck out of there!"

When she had cleared the gates of Ocean View, he ordered McNeil at gunpoint into the driver's seat of his vehicle and told him to drive up to his own car a few hundred meters away.

"Ready for an adventure, Officer? Hand me your keys."

"You won't get away with this, Goldberg. You're a marked man." Josh smirked.

"I wouldn't bet on that, Officer. Mrs. Norman seems to have less confidence than you that I can be stopped, but then again, she's smarter than you." He lifted his cell phone to his mouth. "You hear that, Eva?"

"I'm here…" She was on her way to Elwick.

"We're switching vehicles," he said to McNeil, waiting for the road to become clear of any traffic. "It will take them a while to identify my abandoned rental, but your car sitting beside the road will be noticed straight away especially if you are missing." He opened the door and stood outside pointing the gun at McNeil's head. "Get all my gear out of the trunk and load it into your car and hurry!" When the agent slammed the trunk shut, Josh bundled him into the passenger seat and ordered him to secure himself to the grab handle above the door with his own handcuffs. Then he got into the back seat and secured the agent's body with a rope from behind.

"If you make one suspicious move, I'll shoot your kneecap off." He felt around in McNeil's pocket for his cell phone and flipped it open without looking at him. "What is the contact number? I will dial and you will confirm that a farmhand left the premises but that all is clear." With a gun pressing painfully beneath his earlobe, McNeil made the call, wondering how he would ever be able to explain any of this. He had a sick feeling in his stomach that it wouldn't be necessary.

Then Josh drove the rental off the road and parked it under a tree, an appropriate distance away so as not to attract immediate attention. Two minutes later they were on the road to Elwick.

She sat waiting, petrified, in the truck and Josh reveled in the fact that he had never seen her so nervous. He parked next to her and calmly got out to open her door.

"Give me your phone." He snapped it shut and slipped it into his pocket. Then he gestured toward the vehicle with McNeil in it. "You're driving. Get in." Eva got in and kept her head down.

"Where are we going?" she whispered hoarsely.

"Head for the A19 highway just west of Elwick. We're going north. I have a gun trained on both of you. Do not try to be brave." He dialed a number on his cell phone and waited for Dmitri to answer. "We're on our way. Be ready in about two hours." When they approached the outskirts of Newcastle, Josh picked up the agent's phone again.

"Time to say hello to your buddies one more time, trooper. Make up an excuse for why you had to leave in a hurry so they can send a replacement for you. Your absence will be missed and we can't have that, can we?" He dialed the number and held the phone to McNeil's ear. Josh smiled as he listened to the indignant explanation of a sudden, violent diarrhea attack and asking for a replacement to immediately take over for him.

"No! I can't wait until he gets here!" McNeil yelled into the phone, red in the face. "Are you an imbecile?"

"Nice," Josh said, deliberately closing the phone and leaning back. "Amazing how creativity blossoms with a gun in your neck." Then he casually reached into his briefcase and pulled out a syringe. Eva saw the jab to the side of the agent's neck and let out a terrified scream as his eyes bulged in shock and he lurched forward, violently straining against the rope securing his body. Thirty seconds later Barrie McNeil was dead.

"Pull yourself together." She was crying openly and he watched her distress emotionlessly from the back seat. "And keep your eyes on the road. He was in my way, that's all." Fifteen minutes later he directed a shaken Eva into an underground parking garage and while she kept the car idling on his instructions, he untied McNeil's body and released the handcuffs. Then he dragged him from the passenger seat and bundled his hapless form into the trunk. "Let's go!" He pointed toward the exit, ignoring her anxious shallow breathing. "We're going to the Caledonian Hotel where Dmitri is waiting. We have no time to waste. The ferry leaves at 5.30 and we have to be on it."

The real show was about to begin. It was time to become respectable again.

When she was dressed in the long black abaya with its matching head scarf, known as a hijab, Eva began to realize the extent of Josh Goldberg's connections and influence. The three men in the room had ignored her for the past hour as they worked on falsifying the rest of the travel documents. The stranger with the distinct American accent took head shots of her, Josh and his Russian accomplice against a white wall.

From their conversations, she surmised that forgery was his forte and that Josh had paid the man handsomely to portray him as a Cultural Attaché from Jordan, traveling under diplomatic immunity to Europe with his wife and personal secretary. She also realized that her passport was nothing but a decoy to throw pursuers off their trail. Josh never intended for her to use it legitimately.

She had not touched the food Dmitri had delivered to the room and sat rigidly in a corner, paralyzed with fear for the safety of her loved ones. Only a few hours in his company had convinced her of Josh Goldberg's ruthlessness. He would stop at nothing.

She imagined the third man also had some secret service ties and heard him mention that the vehicle they needed for reservation purposes on the ferry was parked at the front of the hotel. Their passage had been booked a few days before and they were traveling as Mr. and Mrs. Ishmael Khaznawi. She glanced in the mirror opposite from where she sat and had to admit that the disguise was effective. The birthmark they had attached to the right side of her face stung while the glue was being applied but subsided after a while.

Her olive skin and hazel eyes complimented the black outfit and her hair was completely hidden beneath the hijab, secured tightly under her chin to leave only the contours of her face visible. She did look Middle Eastern, and with a first name like Zada, Eva knew that she would not be easily recognized. She found it hard to breathe. Once they were outside the borders of Britain, she knew the chances of her rescue were dismally small. She had to find a way to leave Steve and MI6 a clue as to her whereabouts, but she was terrified that Josh would find out and engage in his killing spree.

The rest of the afternoon passed like a lucid dream in which she was an unwilling participant, but completely unable to change the course of events. Standing two steps behind him and with her head down she listened, stunned, as the customs officer scanned their documents only briefly and actually had them escorted to their cabins. They were some of the first people on board. When he closed the door behind him and leaned against it, she spoke for the first time, looking him straight in the eye.

"How did you do that? It could not have been easy to forge diplomatic immunity." He looked at her and felt his anger rise again as she calmly confronted him. He took a step closer to her and balled his fists behind his back, ignoring her question.

"Everyone in this world has a price, Eva," he said softly, menacingly. "And before long I will know yours too." She remained silent and just looked at him, incapable of hiding the contempt she felt. He noticed it instantly and covered the distance between them in two long strides. It took all of his self control not to hurt her as he grabbed hold of her shoulders and shoved her hard up against his chest. "Look at me!" he demanded fiercely as she closed her eyes and tried to turn her head away. An eerie feeling of remembrance crept into her consciousness. Finally she opened her eyes and stared into his dark face. *Who is this animal and why does this feel so familiar?*

"Why, you *bitch*!" He let go of her and took a step back, still staring at her, groping wildly at making a connection between the contempt he read in her face and the defiance in her manner. But he was too overwhelmed by his anger to find answers and he retreated in better judgment to the door. "Dmitri is outside and he will make sure you do not attempt to leave this cabin." His gaze traveled the length of her body; even hidden behind the folds of the Middle Eastern outfit, she was as beautiful as ever. "A word of advice. Don't anger the Russian. He hates women." And with that he was gone.

It was long after twelve o'clock when she drifted off into a restless sleep from pure exhaustion and fell right into a nightmare where she was fleeing on horseback with a group of women and children. She kept looking over her shoulder for someone but she didn't know whom, overwhelmed by a tremendous feeling of impending catastrophe. Unaware that she was crying in her sleep she strained to awaken from the unpleasant experience, tossing and turning as the ferry bumped its way along on the dark choppy North Sea.

And then she smelled him and her eyes flew wide open. Josh Goldberg's face was inches away from hers, but that was not whom she saw. She felt his presence, but she was still caught in the hinterland of the nightmare and was briefly unable to identify him as Josh. Instead, what she saw was a tall acrid smelling Arab with murder in his eyes as he felled her mercilessly to the ground, tearing away her tunic. He shouted something to her in a language she did not understand as he grabbed the feathers she had hidden in her bosom. And then Eva recognized her tormentor from hundreds of years ago.

"It's you!" she screamed terrified as she feebly tried to scramble away from him, confusing him with the Arab in her nightmare. But Josh only leaned closer, perplexed at her words. He had obviously not yet made the same breakthrough.

Josh had stayed in the lounge all night because he could not trust himself around Eva. Posing as a Muslim, he purposely did not drink and finally, around two o'clock, decided to get some sleep. Dmitri was still in front of the door and he waved him off to his cabin. His head was filled with murder and punishment although he knew that it wasn't yet time. Her tossing and turning attracted his attention and he walked over to watch her. Somehow her discomfort, even in sleep, gave him great satisfaction.

The whole evening his thoughts had been filled with Eva. He knew instinctively that she would fight him with everything if he tried to take her, and the thought of that excited him enormously. Out of deep desire to defend herself, she would inadvertently provide the violence he so desperately needed to set him off. But that is also why he stayed away. Raping her was one thing, but he knew he might just kill her in the spur of the moment and that would defeat his whole plan. He had much more suffering in store for Eva and her lover.

He noticed her frightened expression, and sensing the hidden contempt beneath the fear, he deliberately ignored her. He took a deep breath to calm down and closed his eyes as if she wasn't even there. His purpose was to blank the screen of his mind entirely and this took several minutes, during which time Eva did not know what to think or what to do. She was caught in the cabin with him at least until the next morning and she waited breathlessly for his next move.

And then he saw her too. They were on the open plains of Africa and she stood trapped and cornered in his tent where he had taken her after wounding the golden stallion. She had nowhere to go, and yet he saw nothing but defiance in the expression on her face. It was the *same* look that her father, the leader of the ancient Lemba tribe, had given him when he refused to accept their offer of protection. And for *that* he had taken her life, but her father came after him and repaid him in turn. It was all suddenly crystal clear to him and he began laughing softly.

"*Jesus Christ!* No wonder I hate you and your lover so much! You've been a thorn in my side for thousands of years!" The howl that came from his mouth bordered on insanity and Eva curled terrified into the corner, trying not to look at him.

"You're evil," she whispered, overwhelmingly aware of the magnitude of their individual revelations.

"Yes." The laughing had subsided. "I can't wait for your lover to show up, as we both know he will." His eyes pierced through her. "Who comes up with all these different roles, I wonder." His voice dropped dangerously low. "Damned creative—father, lover. What else is around the corner?" Then he pulled himself together. "I think we've been spoiling for this meeting for millennia, but *this* time I will annihilate you both *and for good!* Better get some sleep, Eva." He stood and walked over to the other bunk bed. "I thought it would be a pleasure to visit retribution upon your heads for what you had done to me before *without* you knowing what you're being punished for. But now I realize the game has become fascinatingly dangerous, even for me. And I love danger! It makes me cruel *and* creative. Who knows *what* we may remember next?" He fell onto the bed and threw his arm across his eyes and kept talking, not caring if she was listening or not. "But first they have to find us. Either way, I can't lose. If they track us down within forty eight hours, your mother and sister will be dead. And I will personally kill you before I let them take you from me. You think my promises are meaningless, Eva? You can count on that one."

She didn't reply. She knew by now that their immediate destination was Amsterdam, but had no idea where they were heading from there. She also knew with overwhelming certainty that Steve would follow her and that the mission she had always sensed but could never identify, was about to be revealed. If what Josh said was true, then she had a part to play in leaving Steve a clue to find her, and she was determined to do so. Knowing who her adversary was, the moment would have to be chosen well. There was no room for error.

Chapter 24
The Meadow

Steve's gaze went from Natalie where she sat in front of him on Quah Dreamer to Hugo, who was riding Razzle. The children were uncharacteristically quiet. There was a very strange quality in the air that made Quah Dreamer ripple his muscles nervously. He chomped impatiently at the bit, shaking his head from side to side. Natalie leaned forward and threw her arms around the horse's neck; she rested her cheek against his mane and closed her eyes. The walk home was not far, but Steve could not shake the uneasy feeling in his chest. Natalie suddenly sat up and reached toward him.

"*Steve,*" she whispered urgently as he bent his ear toward her mouth, "why is Hugo sad?" He lifted his head and looked at Hugo with new eyes. The boy was sitting rigidly on the horse and barely held the reigns. His stare was fixed on the ground and he seemed unaware of his surroundings.

"Hugo?" But the boy didn't move or acknowledge hearing him. An ice cold hand locked around his heart and suddenly the eerie quality of the day, the aberrant and deafening silence around them, took on a whole new meaning. Hugo had an almost unnatural bond with his mother and something was definitely wrong. *Eva!* Steve's heart began racing wildly as he hurried the children and the horses along, eager to get home.

At the paddock he handed Quah Dreamer and Razzle to one of the trainers and quickly began to make his way home with the children. He was sure of it now and had to restrain himself from breaking into a run to reach the house. Somewhere inside he felt the sickening feeling of impending disaster, the unmistakable threat of something evil that could ruin the rest of his life. With every step the feeling grew in intensity and then he knew with certainty that he had traveled down this road before, but that he had lost every time. His heart felt like lead. Natalie slipped her little hand into his as if she wanted to take shelter against something unholy that had furtively forged a presence in the tranquil surroundings of Ocean View.

"I'm scared, Steve." She sounded lost and pressed herself closer to his legs.

"Come here, Natalie." Without thinking he picked her up and turned his attention to Hugo who kept walking faster and faster. The boy's behavior was the only confirmation Steve needed and he was absolutely convinced something big was amiss. He had become used to Hugo's uniqueness and knew that if anything was out of place, the boy would withdraw into his world and try to deal with it in his own way. Hugo was clearly heading in this direction and Steve increased his pace to keep up with Eva's son.

Hugo suddenly stopped at the open door to the kitchen and refused to go inside. Steve noticed the note and the feather immediately from where he stood. It was *her* brown feather! He put Natalie down and she instantly scrambled over to Hugo's side, squatting on the ground beside him whilst looking anxiously at Steve as he entered the kitchen and picked up the note.

They had placed the feathers on the mantel piece in the lounge to remind them of the mystery they had to unravel of why each had one from a bird of prey. Together, they seemed to symbolize an ancient bond, or a very old promise; a piece of history or a prophecy waiting to run its course. But separated, they appeared forlorn and suggested tragic loss and pain and he felt the warning of an old, but terrible hurt on the verge of repeating itself. There was a sick feeling in the pit of his stomach as he opened the note with trembling hands.

Goldberg came for me and threatened your lives. If you contact anyone within 48 hours my mother and sister will die. He's mad and very dangerous. I dreamt that a very long time ago you made a promise to always be near. Here is my feather. I know it means something. Please take care of yourself and the children. Eva.

He was completely numb and stood frozen with the note still in his hand, finding it hard to breathe. *Oh, God!* His mind refused to co-operate in determining the next step. *Eva, Eva...* He squeezed his eyes shut, trying to force coherent thought, but he was completely stunned and for the first time in his life he felt utterly powerless. The impact of what had happened registered in his body before his mind could accept the implication of her absence and he began trembling, struggling with a nauseating feeling that this scenario had played itself out before, in another time, another life.

He tried to organize his thoughts logically but his mind could only come up with images of her. He remembered his bewilderment at the sight of the elegant raven-haired beauty when he had first laid eyes on her. He shook his head to clear his mind but they only kept coming. One moment the shimmering vision of his beautiful Aztec bride stood waiting inside the circle of dancers. The next moment she was sailing with him through the night on the back of Quah Dreamer, willingly molded into his frame as he drew her close to him. No other woman had ever inspired possessiveness in him, but the combination of her vulnerability and strength was so seductive and charming that he wanted to be the man who had the right to love her.

Everywhere he turned, Eva was before him. How she had become engraved in his memory, in his soul, was a stubborn secret the Cosmos was still keeping, but her unmistakable presence was everywhere. Since that night when her sleeping image had unlocked a door into the far distant past, he had rarely spoken her ancient name, as if it was somehow sacred. But now it spilled into his consciousness. *Anacaona, Anacaona!* The name begged him to end the maddening confusion.

And then he felt a blind rage rising. *Who is Josh Goldberg? How could he have taken her so easily? What if he harms her?* The last thought cruelly tore the scab off a very old wound and something in his center snapped, forcing him to bridge the gaping abyss between antiquity and the present. His consciousness filled with the image of a large bearded man in strange Middle Eastern garb, staring menacingly at him and he took an involuntary step backwards, reeling in horror. *Oh, Jesus!* His stomach lurched violently and he held onto the table to steady himself. *Goldberg? Could this be Goldberg?* And then suddenly he knew with great clarity that he had uncovered the truth. He did not have all the pieces, but in this moment of great need, his subconscious mind had begun to unravel some of the mystery. *Eva! Oh, my God, Eva...If it takes my last ounce of strength, my last breath...I have to find you!*

"Steve! What is wrong with Hugo?" He heard Natalie's anxious cry and the spell was instantly broken as he turned his attention to the children still standing in the doorway. Natalie pointed to Hugo; her big blue eyes were filled with tears as she stared transfixed at the boy. His expression was vacant and his stony gaze was riveted onto the note and the feather in Steve's hand. Then the boy began to rock his body to and fro and with alarm Steve recognized the first signs of Hugo withdrawing back into his world.

Hugo was visibly distressed and had apparently sensed his mother's absence on their way back from the early morning riding lesson, but looking at the child, Steve noticed symptoms he had not seen before. Hugo's face had lost all color, his pupils were dilated and there were strange twitches around his mouth; his whole body had begun to tremble lightly.

"Hugo!" He crossed the space between them in two large steps, but the boy didn't move and Steve was temporarily at a loss of what to do. Then he put his hands on Hugo's shoulders and carefully directed him to the sofa beside the kitchen table where he helped him to lie down. The phone began to ring incessantly and he tried to ignore it while fretting over Eva's son who was behaving very strangely. But the persistent ringing forced him to finally answer. It was the security guard at the gate, still entirely unaware that Eva had been taken from under their noses.

"Brad Weston says he is your vet and the black stallion is due for a check-up."

"Who—*Brad?*" He kept his eyes on Hugo. The tremors had increased and his eyes were rolling in his head. "Yes, yes! Ask him to come straight to the house and tell him to hurry!" Steve slammed the receiver down. "Natalie, get some water, please!" He didn't know if that was the right thing to do but he was grateful that his old friend had shown up at this opportune time. Moments later he heard the car door slam, followed by running footsteps.

"Steve—" Brad hesitated in the doorway, taking in the scene with a single glance. "Who are these children?" But then he noticed Steve's anxious look as he waved him over.

"Later, Brad. I need your help with the boy." Brad pushed Steve out of the way and put his hands on either side of Hugo's head, gently forcing it back.

"He's having a seizure! Help me to roll him onto his side. Sometimes they vomit and we have to make sure he doesn't swallow any of it or that it doesn't block his airways."

"Should we try to hold him down?"

"No. We shouldn't restrain him in any way; we just want to make sure his airways remain open. It doesn't seem very severe." He looked up at Steve. "Does he have medication for this?"

"I don't know, but I don't think so. His mother has never mentioned seizures before. He is mildly autistic."

"Who is his mother?"

"Eva Norman. Brad, we haven't spoken for a few weeks, but some significant things have happened since our last meeting." Brad's gaze traveled from Steve to Natalie who had come to stand close to Steve, then back to Hugo again.

"Evidently." He spoke softly, remembering their conversation many weeks ago at the stables. "You have found her? *The* one?" A tiny smile played around his mouth.

"Yes," Steve said simply, "the boy is hers. And this little nymph here," he said as he ruffled his hand through Natalie's hair, "is Jack Emerson's granddaughter, Natalie. I'm sure you met her when you found the horse for me?" Brad nodded and Steve directed his attention to Hugo again. "How is he doing?" Steve looked at Hugo, still anxious about the seizure and wondered what it meant. He was sure that if the boy was prone to attacks like this, Eva would have told him. This was something new and he was convinced that it had meaning. In the short time he had known this gifted child, nothing appeared to be coincidence.

"He's okay for now; it looks like the shaking is subsiding. I think he is coming out of it. We should give him a chance to recover completely and don't be surprised if he falls asleep after he comes around. It is quite normal behavior after a seizure." When Hugo settled down, Brad sat back on the sofa and looked Steve straight in the eye. "We've been friends for as long as I can remember. So tell me, what is going on here?" But the revelation had to wait, for Hugo suddenly sat up and looked around the room.

"Hugo?" Steve reached a hand toward him, but the boy appeared oblivious. He stood and reached for his folder of drawings that accompanied him everywhere. Then he sat down at the kitchen table and began to sketch on a blank piece of paper. The two grownups and the little girl stared at him in astonishment, but it was Natalie who, after a few minutes, made the first move.

"Steve!" she whispered urgently, tugging at his hand. Steve held his finger in front of his mouth to keep her quiet, but when she wouldn't quit he bent down and picked her up. She cupped her hands together and spoke delicately into his ear. "He has made other pictures like that." She pointed a finger at Hugo's drawing, but the boy still seemed non-responsive. Steve drew his head away and looked imploringly into her big blue eyes.

"Like *that*?" he asked softly, as his gaze wandered over to the complexity of what Hugo was sketching. "Are you sure? When did you see this?"

"The day after you and Hugo looked at the stars." She didn't blink. "He showed me his special drawings and I told him about the medicine man in the Meadow." Steve's head jerked back.

"Natalie, sweetheart, what are you *talking* about? What meadow? What medicine man?" he asked imploringly, trying to keep his voice down.

"Sakhota." She seemed to lose sudden interest in the conversation with him and wiggled her way out of his arms.

"*What?*" The strange name jarred him, but he didn't know why. "Natalie!" There was an odd hollow feeling in his solar plexus and he wanted to know more, but her attention had moved on to Hugo and she was already standing at the boy's side. She put an elbow on the table and rested her head in the palm of her hand, giving his drawing the expert once-over.

"That's nice, Hugo," she said appreciatively, as if concluding that his effort met with her approval. "I don't think I can draw these ones." She wrinkled her nose, intimating that all his other drawings were within her capability, but this one just slightly escaped her. Hugo turned his attention to the little girl by his side.

"Who drew this?" he asked in a raspy whisper. Natalie eyed him curiously, her eyes traveling over the drawing and back to him again. He seemed very tired all of a sudden and leaned forward to place his head on his arms. She appeared to be contemplating an important matter, unaware that the grown men were staring at her and waiting for her reply with great anticipation. Then she straightened and put a protective hand on Hugo's arm. He had fallen asleep at the table and it was to Steve that she now directed her attention. There was a strange quality about the blonde six-year-old as she spoke slowly, deliberately.

"Sakhota did. He knows about the stars and he knows the meaning of all these shapes. He said so when we were in the Meadow."

"I'm glad you called your parents to help out with the children. I let Caroline know that I will be here for the night, just in case Hugo needs me." Brad held the glass of brandy in his hands and swirled it around, not looking at Steve. "Eva must be quite a woman."

Steve nodded his head slowly, not trusting himself to speak. Eva's abduction gnawed away at his very soul and he couldn't stop thinking about her. He wished he could be alone somewhere just to gain some clarity to deal with the terrible nagging feeling that she had been taken from him before. The mere thought of it made his body ache in a dull way, as though he couldn't bear to recall the terrible anguish of being without her. It was only the circumstances that eluded his anxious mind and he took a deep breath to steady himself.

"No contact for forty eight hours. That must be to guarantee the getaway." He heard Brad's voice and he looked up to meet his old friend's concerned stare.

"He is taking her out of the country." His voice was devoid of all emotion. "Every moment we cannot act to find her, it becomes more hopeless. You heard what her brother had to say when he called a few minutes ago."

"Do you know him?"

"No. His name is Uri and Eva had called him only once since she's been on the farm. He had been contacted by a dissident on Goldberg's team who wants a way out of this mess of deception and killing. According to him, Goldberg has no respect for life and has paid a sharp shooter who will kill Eva's mother and sister in Tel Aviv if they are apprehended within forty eight hours. The caller, who is still unidentified, is a telecommunications expert and he had intercepted a few of Goldberg's calls. Uri says he sounds legitimate and he is looking for someone to stand guarantor for him. He claims he is not a killer and wants out."

"Well, that is good then, isn't it?"

"Every second Goldberg is getting further away with her. I cannot stand the thought of her distress. It is eating me alive."

"Where is he taking her? Perhaps there is a way in which I can help?"

"We're not sure. But according to the informant, all indications point to Pakistan. He said he would be able to confirm it when he calls back. That is all I know."

"Christ! That is a big country with an even bigger mountain range. Why there?"

"I don't know. Uri thinks her husband is there. But I know this to be true from contact that she has had with a monk who lives in that area. I didn't go into details with her brother."

"She's married?"

"Technically, yes. But he's asked her for a divorce. They're on amicable terms as far as I understand, but drifted apart years ago. Tom Norman, her husband, is somehow involved with Goldberg. I'm not sure how. It is all very complicated and Hugo is at the heart of it all. He is exceptionally gifted; don't know if I mentioned that to you?"

"No. But from his unusual behavior today, I can tell something is afoot. The kid had a seizure and the next minute he got up and made those strange drawings. I've never seen anything like that before. And yet he doesn't seem to remember that he drew those sketches."

"He's certainly unusual and very talented. And he has a very strong bond with his mother. I think her abduction set him off today and I am convinced that Hugo knew before I got her note explaining that she was gone. He felt it before anyone else. And those sketches mean something important. Right now he is not talking, but maybe later he will." He looked at Brad and shook his head. "I don't know where to go from here."

"Maybe I do." Brad smiled. "Now I know your rational mind wants to think everything through, looking for logical explanations, but perhaps this is one occasion where Caroline's varied interests in the esoteric world may be of service to you." Steve waited.

"Go ahead."

"Mark Watson lives in this area. He is a reputable psychic and a medium, and in the past he has been very successful at locating missing objects and people." For a long time Steve said nothing, and the silence between him and his old friend stretched. Then he stood.

"I'll go."

That evening, Steve prepared his room to accommodate Hugo and Natalie and brought in some bunk beds from one of the spare rooms. Hugo was virtually unreachable and had withdrawn almost completely into his own world. Steve could tell the boy was deeply traumatized and he hoped that if he kept the two children close to him, it would help in some way. Eva's absence had upset Hugo's regime of routine and absolute order, and because he had never been without his mother, his point of reference was suddenly devastatingly missing. He was thrown into a state of utter confusion and interpreted her absence as permanent, something with which he was not equipped to deal.

To help settle the children, Steve suggested to his mother that he would take Hugo and Natalie to the stables to visit Quah Dreamer and Razzle before bedtime. Janet and George had arrived just before dinner and although there were no definite plans of where to go from here, Steve knew that he would have to go after Eva alone. One way or the other he needed to find her, or lose his sanity. It was that simple.

Quah Dreamer stood tall and erect when they entered his stable. He appeared to have been waiting for them and seemed highly alert. Brad had finished his check-up and had moved on. The horse held his head high whilst letting out anxious little snorts as they approached.

"Steady, boy. We've just come to say hello." Steve reached a calming hand toward the big animal and patted him gently on the neck. "Shall I fetch Razzle for you, Natalie?"

"No." She climbed onto a bale of hay and began stroking Quah Dreamer's nose, staring intently at the animal. Hugo stood off to the side of the stable and watched her dispassionately. It was not hard to get him to accompany them, but the disconnection the boy felt was very obvious and he followed them around mechanically. Steve stepped back and again noticed the unmistakable communication between Natalie and Quah Dreamer, wondering if he dared to interrupt.

"Is he talking to you, Natalie?" he asked quietly. But she was humming softly and appeared not to have heard him; she too was lost in her own world. Then finally she spoke, still stroking Quah Dreamer's face and not looking at Steve or Hugo.

"Bullet, Quah Dreamer has many names; and many coats. I don't know them all but he likes the black one best because it is the same as Spethla's and he says—" She caught Steve's eye, but the rest of her words disappeared into a playful giggle as she turned her head away.

"*Spethla?*" Another shock jolted violently through his body, rooting him to the ground. The child looked innocently at him.

"Yes, Spethla," she whispered. "Do you know him?" His heart contracted painfully as he took an involuntary step backwards and looked over to where Hugo was standing. But the boy's gaze was strangely fixed on him as if he too had been waiting on an answer.

"I don't know." Then he looked at Quah Dreamer, but this time the horse offered no assistance, opting to sniff Natalie's golden curls instead. "Natalie—" His breathing had inexplicably become labored and he reached an uncertain hand toward her, desperate to understand the meaning of her words and anxious to banish the distraught feeling that name evoked in his heart. "Are you making this up?" His mouth was dry and he sounded a hundred years old. But the little girl shook her head and skillfully evaded his touch as she jumped down from the bale of hay.

"Don't worry if you don't remember Spethla." Her attention was on Hugo as she skipped over to him. "Come, Hugo." She took his hand and looked over her shoulder to Steve, smiling sweetly. "Spethla has not forgotten you. And you will remember again. One day when you're back in the Meadow."

The visit with Mark Watson appeared to be a big disappointment. The psychic looked at him and the boy by his side and flatly declared that he couldn't pull a rabbit out of a hat. He refused to take any money for his advice and claimed that, knowing about their impending visit to him, he had had a vision the night before and said that Steve should visit a location in town that would help him to put matters into perspective.

"Where is this place?" He had a hard time hiding his frustration and he felt angry and burdened by the realization that their time to find Eva was running out.

"It is called The Meadow and it is just around the corner from here; walking distance, actually." The name caused another internal jolt but this time Steve didn't move and he kept his eyes on the man in front of him. *The Meadow? Here in town?* He looked at Hugo but the child remained expressionless.

"What is there?" he asked cautiously, curious to know whether this was the place Natalie had spoken of and he wondered how she could know of its existence when she was a virtual stranger to this area.

"Don't know, Professor. It is a small, fairly new housing estate which was originally a market gardener's field annexed to his living quarters. It was built only fifteen or so years ago."

"How will this help me find Eva?" His voice shook. He didn't know if he could handle much more of the mystery talk and uncertainty of the last day. He felt as though he was sinking deeper and deeper into a quagmire where fact and fallacy took turns to masquerade as truth and it was driving him insane.

"Can't answer that. But you won't know until you go there."

Rounding the corner to the estate to which Mark Watson had referred, Steve noticed that it consisted of about twenty houses, each uniquely built and spaced well apart with neatly cultivated and maintained lawns. The houses were in stark contrast with the surrounding dwellings from the 1930s and with a shock, Steve recognized it as the same hunting ground where as children, he and some mischievous friends went raiding for apples in the neighborhood. Or was it?

Following the winding entrance road into the quiet, neatly kept estate, the familiar background of older housing began to fade as it was swallowed by the now unfamiliar terrain that faced him. He wondered how they had never discovered this place. And then he suddenly understood. The original field, called The Meadow, had been surrounded by other older properties that would have kept its existence a secret. Even if they had known, they would have had to trespass through the gardens of those houses to get to this field.

The Meadow. A square white board displaying this name on black poles was unassumingly mounted at the entrance. His heart began to beat faster. Was this it? Was this The Meadow? He looked at the area again and mentally pictured it as the original field; he thought of the name again. It meant nothing to him and he looked around indecisively, at a loss as to exactly what he was supposed to do here. The day was quiet and pleasantly warm but he was only aware of a nauseating empty feeling inside him.

Then he noticed Hugo's strange behavior. As if drawn like a magnet, the boy began walking toward a schoolhouse-type dwelling with a small garden, fenced by a green metal railing. When an elderly woman emerged from the front door to inquire as to their activities, Steve realized for the first time how suspicious their behavior must appear. But she invited them to sit in her garden if they so wished after he explained that they were from the local College of Art, making sketches of unusual dwellings, of which her house was one.

Hugo seemed to be preoccupied with an object in front of him and Steve sat on the grass near the boy and threw his arms around his drawn-up legs. Then he closed his eyes and allowed the sun to soak into every pore of his body. The forty eight hours would be up the next day and he still had no idea of where to start the search for Eva. His mind had given up its frenzied effort to make sense of the chaos her absence had created and he realized that he was powerless until the time restriction was up. He was forced to wait.

He had hoped that the excursion to this unusual place would bring some answers, but there was nothing. A wry smile crept around his mouth and he kept his eyes closed. He had foolishly allowed the fantasies of a little girl to influence him and he had begun to chase phantoms in reality and in his dreams. He had no idea any more of how to make sense of his life since Eva Norman had stepped into it. *Why do I feel I should have known that he would take you from me? Where does this terrible guilt come from?*

The warmth of the sun penetrated his tired body and for a short while he half-heartedly resisted the desire to drift off into oblivion. But soon the tension of the last two days got the upper hand and Steve blissfully lost track of his surroundings as time and space was erased and he crossed the invisible line between illusion and reality. He recognized his surroundings immediately and his heart expanded with anticipation and excitement. At first he thought he was alone but then he heard the familiar gallop behind a nearby hill. *Spethla!* A wondrous smile spread over his face and he looked around him, waiting patiently on the graceful approach of his ancient friend.

He took a deep breath and filled his lungs with the peace and tranquility that this celestial resting place offered. Oh, God! Was the Meadow ever more beautiful than on this day? How many times had he been here and yet the beauty of this heavenly halfway house still filled him with such awe and wonder. Of course he knew the Meadow! His heart was suddenly infused with indescribable joy. Anacaona! She was here, he could *feel* her presence. This is where they always met. Sometimes he arrived in the Meadow before her and every so often she showed up first. But they always waited on one another. And over many thousands of years, their commitment and love had grown into an indestructible bond that impelled them toward each other, life after life. How many desperate lives had they lived?

He didn't know. He only knew that the Meadow opened its arms to two of its cosmic children at the end of each life and allowed them a short union, a brief respite before they were swept away into the illusion of yet another earthly adventure. But it was to the Meadow that they always returned, exhausted and aching to be together. He had never forgotten and neither had she. How could they? They were released into the Cosmos for a purpose, a reason that they were still unraveling and it drew them together like powerful magnets, time after time. Their mission was not yet over; both knew that.

"Teuch." Her voice was soft and gentle behind him and his heart swelled with joy. He felt her as she kneeled and wove her arms lovingly around him, burying her face tenderly in the warmth of his neck. He put his head back and relaxed into her feminine embrace, feeling the sun on his face. No matter the trials and tribulations they had lived through together or separately, it was to this, to her, that he was impelled to return until the end of time.

"Anacaona, my love..." In his dream he reached fervently for her but the vision disappeared as quickly as it had come. His attention shifted and he was at once captivated by the clear, joyful laugh of a child. "Natalie?" he asked, surprised. He felt the stir of a light breeze over his body and remembered this was a sign of the energy changing. His gaze roamed over the wide expanse of the Meadow, but the playful laugh was lost in the dance of the wind as it streaked its wispy fingers through the grass and carried the giggle away into the rustling leaves of the trees. Could it have been his imagination? But his ancient memory was suddenly fully awake and active and he waited patiently for the secret to be revealed.

His eye caught movement on a nearby hill and he squinted into the sun to identify the two figures quietly watching him. He smiled. The tall erect figure of Sakhota in his tribal gear was unmistakable as he proudly gripped the lance in his right hand and raised it in respectful greeting. But it was the little girl standing close by his side that caught his attention and he frowned in confusion. The gorgeous child with the blonde curls blowing in the wind could only be Natalie!

"Professor!" Steve awoke abruptly and stared at Hugo in confusion. The boy was on his haunches in front of him. "Please come." He gave Steve a curious look and then he got up and walked away. Steve struggled to his feet and followed, noticing immediately that the old Hugo had somehow returned. He wondered what had caused the sudden transformation but decided not to ask any questions before he could process the magnitude of what he had experienced in his short, but vivid visit to the real Meadow. *The Meadow*. It all fit so perfectly. Anacaona, Spethla, Sakhota…but, *Natalie?* Where did she fit into this celestial puzzle? She looked exactly the same! He was left speechless; overcome with the experience. "There it is." Hugo pointed to an object perched on a pedestal slightly hidden behind a low wall. Steve went down on his haunches to examine it. Like a treasured artifact dating back to another time, it appeared to be very old and did not fit into the modern surroundings where it had been placed. Stretched wide open from wingtip to wingtip, the stone eagle was perched on its powerful legs and appeared ready to rise from the cold cement base where it had been anchored for untold years. Steve looked from the eagle to the page in Hugo's hand.

"Numbers, Hugo?"

"These represent an eagle," the boy said quietly. "Everything has a numerical base."

"Is that what you drew when your mum was taken?"

"I do not know; I think so." Hugo carried on talking about the sketches and how the measurements were important, but Steve's experience in the Meadow called him back for one final revelation about the name of his horse. He closed his eyes.

In the Meadow, he sat atop Spethla, the emblem of an eagle proudly emblazoned on his body armor. The eagle! The brown feather—*her* feather. Anacaona! *Quah Atowahl* is what she had called him. It meant *my Eagle Man,* a term of endearment. But she was a storyteller and a romantic. It was slowly coming back to him. Steve strained to remember the name he had had for her. Something about dreams drifted to the surface of his conscious mind. And then it suddenly broke through. She wove beautiful dreams. *Dream Catcher!* That is what he had called her. He was mesmerized with ties to the past that he did not yet fully comprehend. How had the original Arabian owners chosen Quah Dreamer as a name for this magnificent horse, when it was a composite of their ancient names of times gone by? He simply had no answers. Hugo's voice brought him back.

"We can go now, Professor. I made the sketches, and I have the measurements." The boy looked strangely at Steve. "We will find my mum." He picked up the satchel that held his drawings. "But only if *you* go. We must leave now." Then the boy started walking away.

He wanted to take Quah Dreamer out for a vigorous run so he could clear his mind and he didn't expect to find Natalie in the stable. She sat high on a bale of hay near Quah Dreamer and stopped humming when he entered. They looked at each other and neither spoke. The horse flared his nostrils in recognition but held still, waiting. Then Steve walked up to the little girl and looked her level in the eye from where he stood.

"I saw you today." His voice was soft, like one who was making conversation with an equal. She returned his gaze, but remained quiet. "I also saw Sakhota."

"You found the Meadow," she whispered, a tiny smile creeping around her mouth. "And Spethla?" He nodded his head slowly, watching her closely.

"But there is something I don't understand, Natalie." He hoped he could engage her attention long enough for her to answer but she extended a hand to be helped down from the bale of hay. As he reached for her she threw her arms briefly around his neck and pressed her mouth close to his ear.

"Hugo found the eagle, too?" Her excitement was accompanied by a delightful little laugh, the same one he had heard in the Meadow earlier that day.

"You *know*, Natalie?" He let her slide down to the floor of the stable but kept his eyes on her, hoping that she would be more forthcoming. But she appeared not to have heard his question and tugged absentmindedly at a wild curl as she made her way to the door. There she hesitated and then turned back as if she had forgotten something important.

"He is taking her to where the eagle lives. You must take both feathers with you when you go. They will protect you." And with that she was gone.

Chapter 25
The Way Of The Eagle

"Is this the place?" Appleyard ignored the question from the man next to him, and pushed his sunglasses onto his forehead, peering through the windshield at the dilapidated building that was once painted white, but now was only a dull muddy brown color.

"No wonder they called this the rural outskirts, Naidoo. They weren't kidding!" He slid his sunglasses back over his eyes. "Tracing this phone line was not easy. Let's go." Appleyard slammed the car door shut and crossed the dirt road without looking back. "We'll have a clearer picture once we're inside the store. I know your Punjabi is rusty, but I trust you can follow a conversation well enough so no detail will be lost. We need to track down Chong-ba as soon as possible, and every little bit of information counts."

But half an hour later Appleyard realized that they had made no progress whatsoever. The man in the long white caftan had pursed his lips and backed away, shaking his head, clasping his hands together as if in prayer.

"What the hell does that mean, Naidoo?" Although Appleyard already knew the answer.

"He's not talking, Colonel."

"Really. We'll see about that." Appleyard pushed his way brusquely in behind the counter and ripped away the beaded bamboo curtain, which separated the front of the store from the back. It revealed a frightened woman and four young children huddled together. The entire room was filled with the aroma of strong curry simmering on a stove tucked away in a corner; the overpowering smell made his eyes water. "Bobby!" he yelled over his shoulder. *Jesus!* He coughed loudly, not bothering to hold a hand to his mouth. *You eat enough of this crap and embalmment will be a waste of good money when the time comes.*

"Get in here!" When he heard Bobby Naidoo behind him, he turned and looked at the store owner, but spoke to his subordinate.

"Yes, he'll take me to a guide," he said as he reached inside his jacket and pulled out a pistol, handing it to Naidoo. "You'll be watching over his family while *this man* shows me the way. Now, I don't speak Punjabi but I bet the lanky bastard understands what is happening here." Appleyard met the anxious stare of the store owner, who confirmed his assumption with an imperceptible nod. "Very good then; we're on the same page. This man will wait for me to come back in one piece before he will see his family again." He looked around the store. "Naidoo, put a sign on the front door that this place is temporarily closed for business. I know it has been a long time but you're not so bloody English now that you can't write in Punjabi anymore! Or are you?" He didn't wait for a response and made his way to the front entrance with the store owner in tow. Just as he reached the rental, his cell phone rang in his breast pocket. He waved his unwilling passenger into the front seat while he stood outside to take the call.

"Stanway? This must be important—" He frowned heavily as he listened to his colleague on the other end. Then his face lost all color. "He grabbed her *two days ago* despite our efforts?" Colonel Appleyard wiped the sweat from his forehead. "They found her passport—*where*? What was that—Wagah?" He squeezed his eyes shut in an effort to concentrate. "You know what this means, don't you? We are now in a race against time! We have just lost the advantage of tracing Chong-ba's call to this godforsaken place and I'm not sure we can still surprise the monk and Tom because we might not get there first. *Jesus!*" He listened impatiently for a few more minutes. "Do what you have to do, James. But my guess is that he is going after Tom and I don't have to remind you how high those stakes are. Goldberg is becoming a real threat and you and I cannot afford for Tom to speak to anyone before we do. And he just very well might if Goldberg threatens to harm his wife. I'm counting on you to make sure no one else follows us and I want you to put a stop to this fucking exodus into the mountains! They don't call you the Silver Fox for nothing."

Two minutes later the shopkeeper was sitting erect and uncomfortable in the front seat next to Appleyard, now refusing to make eye contact with him. He kept his head down and waved that the way was straight ahead toward the Grand Trunk Road. Appleyard didn't care that there was no conversation. He had only one purpose. He needed to reach Tom before anyone else.

Despite her physical exhaustion, Eva's senses were highly alert as she discreetly watched her two captors. Josh Goldberg was a formidable opponent and she had ruled out escaping from these two madmen as soon as the ferry docked in Amsterdam. The relative ease with which they moved through border checkpoints and airports convinced her that Goldberg's influence was not to be underestimated. Their journey seemed flawlessly planned although she realized that some of the arrangements must have been made on the fly. He seemed very sure of himself and taking advantage of her Middle Eastern appearance, she purposely remained in the background, keeping her head down, and endeavored to minimize eye contact as much as possible.

In an effort to throw pursuers off their trail, Josh swept them on an erratic journey from Ijmuiden, the port of Amsterdam, into the city center where they left the car in a parking lot and hastily boarded a train for Paris, France. At Charles De Gaulle Airport they had three hours to kill before catching the Air India flight to Amritsar in the northern part of India. During the waiting period Josh forced Eva to eat a full meal for the first time in over twenty four hours. Knowing that he was watching her like a hawk, Eva made an effort not to do anything out of the ordinary. She almost gagged on the airport food, but managed to get some of it down and drank lots of water.

She only spoke when spoken to and then only to Josh, completely ignoring Dmitri Anchov. Josh noticed her dismissal of his accomplice, but chose not to comment. Instead, he almost reveled in the big Russian's inability to retaliate while in his presence. Josh was convinced that if he wanted the pleasure of punishing Eva personally, he could no longer afford to leave her in Dmitri's company for any length of time. The brooding gaze of this killing machine was constantly fixed on Eva. Josh knew that Dmitri felt her disdain and that would make him very dangerous. Thus he kept a close watch, realizing that the Russian had become a liability and that he would have to take care of him very soon.

An evil air surrounded both her captors, but Eva sensed a barbaric trait in Dmitri which she found utterly unnerving and impossible to face. On the long flight to Amritsar she was seated between the two men and kept her eyes closed most of the time, endeavoring to block them out of her psyche. She tried to think of Steve and Hugo but the malevolence she sensed in her immediate company was overpowering and she retreated into a blank space where she was only aware of her own shallow breathing. The time to signal for help was fast running out.

Beneath her abaya, she clung desperately to her passport which had been oddly left unattended by Josh and his CIA cohort after making comparisons with the new fraudulent one. She had taken it instinctively and hid it unobtrusively beneath her clothing, nervously expecting him to ask for it. But he never did, surprising her with this apparent blatant oversight. She had no idea what to do, but frantically held onto it, convinced that any attempt to reveal her true identity in public would swiftly result in her death.

At the army outpost of Wagah, the Indo-Pak border between Amritsar and Lahore, Eva knew she would have to create an opportunity to leave a message before they crossed into Pakistan, or face the ultimate punishment that Josh had planned for her with no hope of Steve ever finding her.

"Welcome to Amritsar. The bus terminal to Attari is just over there." The guard at the airport exit smiled broadly and respectfully waved them through the revolving door, pointing to a bus about two hundred meters away. Josh nodded his head curtly and for once stood back for Eva to exit first, but then followed directly after her and took firmly hold of her elbow as he propelled her through the glass panels. They had arrived in the Sikh holy city and her heart fell like a stone into the pit of her stomach.

She had overheard Josh and Dmitri discussing the remainder of their journey to enter into Pakistan. Wagah was twenty eight kilometers away. The bus would take them to Attari and from there they would have to take a rickshaw for the last two kilometers. Once they had passed through customs on the Indian side, the final two hundred meters of their journey would have to be completed on foot until they passed into Pakistani territory. Time was running out.

"Look at me." His voice was ice cold. Eva reluctantly halted her stride and didn't turn around, but he held mercilessly onto her elbow and she was forced to obey. She kept her head down.

"I'm listening," she said softly.

"*Look* at me!" He hadn't moved and his black eyes were fixed on her like a snake watching its prey. She shuddered inwardly but met his stare with as much courage as she could muster. He kept his gaze on her, but spoke to Dmitri. "Pay the bus fares and stay there." He waited until Dmitri had shuffled out of earshot before he spoke again. "Are you afraid yet, Eva?" He didn't wait for a reply, knowing that none would be forthcoming. Then he pulled her closer and put his mouth to her ear. "What's your price? I'm wondering if you are ready to negotiate." She closed her eyes, choked and nauseated by his malice but strained to keep her voice even.

"What have I to bargain with?" For a moment he was taken aback with her reply, but then he gathered himself.

"How could I have underestimated you so badly?" He hissed under his breath as he let go of her arm and put both his hands on her shoulders, forcing her to face him squarely. Josh studied the beautiful face so close to him and remembered how startlingly attractive he had found her when they met all those years ago. No one knew better than he that a normal relationship with any woman was out of the question, but his psychotic nature invented endless scenarios of conquering her quiet and composed exterior to punish her for making him feel so insignificant.

Her biggest sin was her disregard for him as a man and he had been constantly plagued with insane desires to create havoc in her life through some form of physical violence, tempered only by the desperate need to hold onto Hugo. Before she stole the child and his chance to greatness, harming her had remained a cherished fantasy, although never a real option. But not anymore.

"Oh!" His laugh was soft and menacing as he leaned closer to her, deliberately aiming for her mouth. "Have you *forgotten* what I want?" Eva instinctively turned her face away, willing to suffer his wrath rather than have him touch her in such a personal manner. Josh straightened away from her, staring bleakly at her averted profile. "I think I can wait." He was completely devoid of emotion and dropped his voice so low that she could hardly hear him. "Of course, I can wait. A skillful hunter can wait for its prey to come to him. And I have been waiting for a very long time."

"What do you really want?" She could barely breathe, but she nonetheless faced him bravely again.

"To plead for mercy." He didn't blink. "I want you to plead for *goddamned mercy!* And before I'm done with you, believe me, *you will*. That is my unmitigated promise to you." He suddenly let go of her and began walking away. "One more thing," he said over his shoulder. "I'll be watching you closely as we cross the border into Pakistan. Don't tempt the devil in me. You have no idea what I am capable of." Her blood ran cold. The danger was palpable but she knew that this would be her only chance to leave any evidence of where she was. *Oh, God. Steve!*

The border outpost was an elaborate complex of buildings, roads and barriers on both sides of Pakistan and India. Eva spoke to Josh of her own accord for the first time inside the customs office, as they were finally waved through.

"I need to use the bathroom." He looked at her beseechingly, but realized that neither he nor Dmitri could insist on accompanying her.

"You have two minutes. I'll wait for you here." She nodded and kept her head down as she disappeared into the ladies' washroom. Inside the bathroom she waited nervously and noticed that two stalls were occupied. Then one of the doors opened and a young woman, dressed in tight fitting jeans and a bright pink T-shirt with a print of the Golden Temple of Amritsar, exited and headed for a basin. She caught Eva's uncertain glance and smiled.

"Howdy!" *An Australian tourist.* From the many Australians who visited the Embassy in Tel Aviv, she would know that accent anywhere. Eva purposely stared at her feet and held her passport out to the woman, and faking broken English, explained that she had found the document on the floor of the bathroom stall. "Who does it belong to?" The woman looked at the passport without taking it whilst drying her hands, noticing the European Union stamp on the outside. It was clearly a British document. Eva pulled her shoulders up and turned to the door.

"Please…you give it to officials?" Her hand was on the door. "I'm sorry, my husband is waiting." The Australian girl looked at her and then at the passport. She assessed the situation in the blink of an eye and realized that the poor woman was not allowed to speak to other men.

"Sure thing! No problem. I'll hand it in. Whoever this belongs to will come back for it, or they will be in this country for a very long time." But before she could finish her sentence, the door had closed behind the Middle Eastern woman. She shrugged and stuck the document in the back pocket of her jeans. She would have to hurry if she still wanted to get a good seat for the spectacle of lowering of the flags later in the day.

Wagah was famous, not only for the smart drill of the soldiers on either side of the border, but for their attempts to outperform each other in a display of mutual contempt. Later on as the show reached a crescendo, spectators would cheer the soldiers on as if they were gladiators, but Eva did not witness this magnificent demonstration as she crossed the border on foot with her two male companions. She kept her head slightly averted but tried to scan the crowds in the pavilion, who were waiting to watch the daily spectacle that drew tourists from all over the world. Then she noticed the Australian woman in her outrageous pink T-shirt. Their eyes met briefly; the woman waved and then Eva knew she hadn't failed. Her passport had been handed in. Tears of relief stung behind her eyes. She didn't know if that was enough, but it was all she could do.

They had to catch another bus from Wagah on the Pakistani side to Lahore, in a journey that would take them just over an hour to complete. Eva was suddenly very tired. Although he had never said as much, she suspected this madman was heading into the Himalayas to reunite her with Tom for some bizarre, unknown reason. It was impossible to know what Josh was really planning. He seemed hell-bent on acting out some injustice in which he was the self-appointed judge and executioner and Eva knew that he was very dangerous. In the last day he had vacillated precariously between the persona of Josh Goldberg and someone he called Bahar. The first time he referred to himself as Bahar, Eva's bones turned to water and at the sound of that name, she began shaking uncontrollably. Dmitri was not in the immediate vicinity and Josh scrutinized her through narrow slits of eyes.

"Ah! You remember!" It was the only time she looked around to see if Dmitri was near, but Josh was clever enough not to show his unstable side in the presence of an accomplice whose brutality matched his own insanity. "He can't help you, Eva!" he laughed, not taking his eyes off her for a second. "Dmitri is just a dim-witted goon who does as he is told. He was too dangerous, even for the KGB, which is why I hired him. Before that he had been a beggar and a thief for most of his existence. And *he* was not there when that arrogant leader of the Lembas refused my gracious offer to protect his people."

Eva stared transfixed at him. She opened her mouth to speak but no sound would come out. The confusing experience she had had on the ferry, when she saw the man in Eastern garb, came into clear focus and was alarmingly amplified by his identification as Bahar. She *knew* the name and shrunk back in panic. She saw a magnificent river with many natural inlets and the stone walls of a craftily erected compound on one of the banks. *Oh, God!* She was stricken with paralyzing fear when her life as a member of the legendary Lemba tribe in ancient Africa agonizingly began to drift back into her memory. Josh noticed the chord he had struck and he continued slowly, deliberately.

"The kindness offered so generously by the great Bahar was thrown back in his face, and he had no choice but to demonstrate that he could not be dismissed so easily." He took a step closer. "So he ravaged and killed the leader's only child!"

"No!" The scream tore hoarsely from somewhere deep inside her and she clasped a hand anxiously over her mouth as helpless tears began to blur the monster in front of her.

"Yes," he whispered cruelly, leaning closer to her. Dmitri had been sent to collect the rental for their journey to the foot of the Himalayas and where they waited outside the bus station in Lahore, raw anguish was etched on her face. He sneered and relentlessly pursued the source of her pain. "Tell me, what did those feathers mean? Your fucking father killed me before I had a chance to ask him about the witch-thing—"

"*Sekayi!*" Across hundreds of years his name rose to the surface of her conscious mind and spilled uncontrollably from her trembling lips. "Oh, God! *Sekayi*!" In what felt like an eternity, she glimpsed the tall, lissome stature and felt his deep love for her, his only offspring, reverberating through her body. When she had the courage to open her eyes again, she was left with a lasting impression of the unspeakable pain in which Sekayi, her father in the African life, had lived out the remainder of his days. She began to cry softly. Neither Eva nor Josh questioned the authenticity of what was happening. Deep down she sensed the veracity of a very old cosmic drama nearing its conclusion in which she and this man were from opposing polarities. And whilst she felt an unmistakable commitment to a mysterious mission which she still did not fully comprehend; Josh Goldberg was obsessively plagued only with retribution.

And in that very instant, she clearly saw the trap he had laid for her and she understood how remarkably cunning her captor was. The door to the memory vault of the past was blown wide open and Eva stared in horror at him as she slowly wiped away her tears. It was the *very same* trap he had laid for them when he grabbed her from her horse on the plains of Africa. He knew that Sekayi would come after them, just like he didn't doubt that Steve would follow her this time. And he *knew* about the passport, she could see it in his eyes. What she foolishly thought was an oversight, instead was a deliberate plot to lure her and Steve into a crafty ambush. Sekayi and Bahar were destined to meet again. Josh expertly read every emotion and feeling on her expressive face.

"Of course." He wore a look of scorn; his voice, ugly and hoarse. "How else would he know where to find us?" He didn't need her confirmation, but her alarm at having fallen for his conniving plan was very rewarding. "And Sekayi *will* come, just like before. Only this time the tables are turned, but I am sure you know this." He observed her dispassionately, frowning. "What was your name then? I don't remember bothering to find out." That is when Eva knew what she had to do. The beast had to be played at his own game. Fear in his victims enhanced his cruelty, but facing him as an equal exposed his insecurity and encouraged him to brag and show off; the only time he made mistakes.

"Nyasha," she said softly as another clear vision of her life as Sekayi's beloved daughter flashed across the screen of her mind. "My name was

Nyasha." Eva held his gaze and stood her ground, remembering the revulsion she had felt for him inside that stinking tent where he had raped and killed her hundreds of years before. At the time she had only glimpsed fragments of the mission, but it was enough to tear the precious feathers from his coarse hands with her dying strength. He took her life, but her cosmic journey was far from completion, and the feathers had to be carried forward. Josh watched the play of emotion on her face and had trouble hiding his surprise.

"Well, well!" He put his hands together and applauded her daring display of courage. Over her shoulder he saw Dmitri approaching but he had one last message for her and leaned forward. "Gorgeous Eva," he whispered in her ear, "for all your sins, past and present, I look forward to taking you apart once again. I find a good fight extremely stimulating and if your efforts match the look I see in your eye, I will not be disappointed. Only this time we will have an audience, won't we? The gods are smiling on me and history is about to come full circle. I can't wait."

He waved Dmitri off with one hand, indicating he should wait at the car and watching her like a hawk, he pulled his cell phone from his pocket. Then he hit a programmed number and waited patiently for the connection to Tel Aviv. When his call was finally answered, he made sure that Eva heard every word.

"We've reached our destination. The money was wired to your account an hour ago. The mother and sister are off the hook for now. Get away from there, but lie low. I might need you again." Josh snapped his phone shut and he suddenly appeared somewhat disconnected and self absorbed as he ambled toward Dmitri, talking loudly to himself. "Josh, the merciful savior…and Bahar, the vengeful warrior. I wonder who will win." Eva watched him walk away and touched a hand to her heart. Had Stanway fulfilled his promise to protect her mother and sister? And what about Steve? *Oh, God, Steve! Be careful, please!*

"What do we know so far?" They were at the kitchen table and Brad watched as Steve meticulously jotted down some important facts. It was 8pm and the phone had been ringing constantly as Eva's brother, Uri, filled them in on developments. The informant had finally identified himself as Tomer Mendel, after written assurances from Steve had been emailed to Uri in Tel Aviv.

"We know Tomer Mendel is an electronics expert and that he was involved in the original surveillance operation on Eva and Hugo before they left Israel. We also know he was responsible for tracking the movements of Chong-ba Chong, the Tibetan monk with whom Eva had contact here in England. And he was the one who identified Eva's cell number in the UK." Steve shook his head in amazement and continued. "He appears to be very resourceful and there is seemingly no system that he is not capable of breaching." He stood and walked to the window. It was already dusk outside. "But today he intercepted a phone call made by Goldberg close to the Indo-Pakistani border, near some military outpost, which confirmed our earlier suspicions of their whereabouts."

"They're in Pakistan then?"

"Yes." Steve ran his fingers through his hair. He didn't want to admit it, but he was feeling the strain of the last forty eight hours. "Mendel says that he has no doubt they are heading into the Himalayas. No one knows what he is planning, but her husband and the monk are there at an unknown location. The monk has a high profile with the CIA. They have been tracking his activities for years since he began to disclose the differences between the Dalai Lama and the real spiritual leader of the Tibetan people. According to Mendel, Goldberg borders on insanity, and God alone knows if he will equip them sufficiently for the trip into the mountains."

"That's all we know?"

"Mendel was also able to trace the number of the sharp shooter Goldberg had paid to kill Eva's mother and sister in case we chased after them within the restricted time. Mendel passed this information to Stanway at the British Embassy—the man who was involved with springing Eva and Hugo from Israel. He said that the villain would be picked up immediately."

"That's good then, isn't it? One down, two to go."

"No, Brad. Mendel cautioned Uri that Goldberg would have had Eva listen in on the conversation. He has seen the man in action many times and psychological games are his style. He said there would be another body in Soho, a prostitute whom he deliberately allowed to use his stolen credit card to provide her with a false sense of security. Then he sent an assailant in after her, the same one he has in tow with him and Eva."

"Good God!"

"Yes. According to Mendel, Goldberg is at his most dangerous when he is engaged in mental warfare."

"But why use it on Eva? And surely, she's no match for his physical strength?" Brad could hardly believe that Steve was involved in any of the intrigue he had been witnessing since he showed up for Quah Dreamer's check-up.

"It's an old trick, Brad, but a dirty one. First he lifts her up by pretending to save her mother and sister, but at just the right moment the bastard will drop her like a stone. The purpose is to keep the victim on unsure footing all the time. Eva is intelligent and so he is wearing her out psychologically *and* taxing her physical strength by taking her into the mountains."

"I see." But Brad didn't really understand any of it. He had no idea who Goldberg was or how it all hung together, but Steve was his friend and he wanted to help where he could. "Shouldn't the chase be left to the authorities?"

"Absolutely not! Goldberg took Eva from under their noses. You saw their reaction when I let them in on her abduction. They didn't even have the decency to look embarrassed. They must know how vulnerable Eva's mother and sister are but with these idiots and Goldberg's cunning, who knows what could happen." The set lines around his mouth told Brad not to argue, but concern for his safety made him try one more time.

"Let's not kid ourselves here, Steve. This is England. We're not exactly famous for high mountain ranges. What do you know about climbing the Himalayas?"

"Nothing. But according to Mendel, neither does Goldberg." Then he stood. "I have to do some packing and look in on the children before I go." He smiled. "I appreciate your concern but I want to be on the first flight out of here tomorrow for Heathrow. Mendel has an opportunity to show his true colors. He told Uri that he would call in a few markers in order to get me a visa and flight ticket into Pakistan at short notice." He caught the look on Brad's face.

"No, I don't know the logistics of the operation and neither do I care how he does it. The relevant documents will be at the Air India information booth and nothing will stop me from going. Once I arrive in Lahore, Mendel will contact me again with further directions of how to proceed."

"You are going to get my mother." Hugo was standing in his doorway, watching him pack and his words were a statement, rather than a question. There was a remarkable difference in the boy after the unfortunate incident two days before, of which Steve did not comprehend much. Despite his anxious watch over Hugo, the boy's eyes seemed remarkably clear and he conversed in quite normal terms. The only one who did not seem particularly fazed with his new behavior was Natalie, who followed him around everywhere with a sweet smile on her face.

"Hello, Hugo. I was just coming to say good night. Where is Natalie?"

"Sleeping." He looked at the light backpack on Steve's bed. "You must be careful. He wants to kill you." Steve looked at him curiously, and then asked softly.

"Josh Goldberg, you mean?" Hugo studied him for a second and then came into the room.

"I could not see his colors until after I got sick. He tricked me and my mum and we could not see him as he is."

"Can you see him now?" Hugo nodded and then Steve noticed the blank piece of paper in the boy's hand. "What is that for?"

"Can I trace your right hand? I have a tracing of my mother's left hand," he said softly. "Hands unlock mysteries because there is so much energy in them." Steve nodded, but didn't understand at all. There were many things about the boy's mind he couldn't fathom, and although this wasn't the time to ask questions, he did so anyway.

"Is it because I am going to look for her?"

"Yes." Steve put his hand down on the desk. "You know martial arts, Professor?" he asked as he carefully traced Steve's hand.

"I do. I specialize in Ba Gua, but I know a lot of other disciplines. How do you know this?"

"In recent visions I have seen many animals around you as you defended yourself in combat. Because of these visions I know the hands are important." Steve smiled. He was relieved that his protégé was thinking more rationally and, more importantly, it appeared he was using those special mental skills again.

"My style is the Yin Bagua Zhang and it is a combat stance that represents the natural offense and defense positions all animals have. There are many stances that I can adopt, depending on my enemy. I usually practice a few evenings during the week in the stables, with Quah Dreamer looking on, and combine it with fencing whenever I get the chance." He laughed and ran a playful hand through Hugo's hair. "The horse seems to know what I'm doing. But my regular opponent is Mike Burley, whom you know from the science lab." He was suddenly serious again, intrigued by the maturity of the boy's behavior. "What exactly are you trying to tell me Hugo?"

"To defend yourself and my mother, you will need the wisdom of an owl and the stealth of an eagle. The man who wants to kill you is like the wild dog that lives on the open plains of Africa. It never loses the scent of its prey. He found my mother and now he has found you. That is why I asked about martial arts. This time, you will need more than strength and skill. That is why I need this outline; and the numbers." He walked to the door and lifted his hand in greeting, the same way Sakhota had done in his visit to the Meadow. "Look for the way of the eagle as it soars. It has all the answers."

That night at a few minutes before twelve, the phone rang beside his bed and Steve woke instantly. The voice on the other end identified himself as James Stanway, who had returned to the British Embassy in Tel Aviv after his meeting with Eva. It was Steve's first opportunity to speak personally with the man behind the scenes who had dealings with her.

"I apologize for calling at this hour, Professor Ballantire, but I have some news for you."

"Eva?" His heart began to race wildly.

"Well, no. But we at least have a definite lead. Her passport had been handed in by a tourist at Wagah on the Indo-Pakistani border. The officials waited until seven o'clock their time to make sure no one came to claim it, and then contacted the offices of the British High Commissioner in Lahore who, in turn, notified us. I'm sorry for the delay but I just got off the phone with them." Steve listened with a heavy heart to the diplomat on the other end, not sure whether he should reveal his hand. He already knew what Stanway was confirming.

"Thank you, Mr. Stanway. May I ask what your plans are?"

"We will have a meeting first thing in the morning and then make a decision on how to proceed."

"Eva's life is at stake, and you can afford to wait until the morning before you string the resources together to go after this madman?" He was suddenly furious. "Or am I witnessing the usual incompetence of the establishment when it comes to the personal safety of their citizens?"

Stanway remained quiet. He was an experienced negotiator and there was more to this conversation than Ballantire was letting on. He was surprised to hear that Eva had chosen to move to the farm with him when Goldberg's presence became known in the UK, instead of taking advantage of the safe shelter they offered. This arrangement, of course, suited their agenda perfectly. But now he was concerned and he hoped the man was not planning to go after her himself. The last thing they needed was another body in the mountains chasing after Tom.

"Pakistan is a dangerous place, Professor, especially if you don't know your way around. I would not advise following Eva. We will do what we can to apprehend Josh Goldberg and bring her back. Please give us the opportunity to find her." What he did not say, was that they were more anxious to apprehend the stray husband, and if they managed to save Eva, it would be killing two birds with one stone.

Sleep evaded him after the phone call. He had never been so unprepared for anything. He was leaving on a mission to find the woman he loved in a country where he had never been. And yet, the feeling that the journey was inevitable and was destined to take place, would not leave him. His mind kept going back to the experiences in the vision he had had the day before when he visited the estate to where Mark Watson had directed him, unbelievably also called The Meadow.

The images were still fresh and he no longer doubted that this heavenly halfway house truly existed as a world invisible to the naked eye. It required insight and understanding to become discernible. Although he knew some rather big pieces of the puzzle were still missing, he had begun to understand that time does not really exist. The Meadow kept all secrets of the past craftily hidden, until cosmic travelers stumbled upon it in a semi conscious state and willingly entered, as had happened to him.

He could not explain Natalie's presence, but recognized Sakhota as a familiar figure from a distant past, even though he was yet unable to place him. But regardless of the confusion, he was all the same convinced that he would gain clarity on this trip and that many of the mysteries would be solved. Or so he hoped.

But Steve had no idea that besides Josh Goldberg and his small group, another person was already making his way into the mountains. Neither did he know that soon the Himalayas would stage a cosmic drama of epic proportions, for which all the heavens had been waiting and watching to witness the final outcome.

Josh stopped the rental about forty kilometers into their rough ride to Gujrat. Once they had hit the main highway out of Lahore on their eighty five kilometer trip, it wasn't long before the tarmac changed into a dirt track and everything was soon covered in dust. It caused Dmitri to have a coughing fit and Josh stopped, trying to find a signal on his cell phone. He needed to make contact with the individual group that would find the guide who was to lead them to their destination.

Eva watched the two men quietly and then turned her attention to admire the magnificent landscape. They had allowed her to discard the abaya and head scarf. She was wearing the clothes she had on when Josh managed to snatch her away, in what now felt like ages ago. As she got out of the car to stretch her legs, she caught sight of a large bird silhouetted beautifully against the clear blue sky. As it slowly circled, Eva closed her eyes in reverence. It was unmistakably the majestic presence of an eagle.

For a very short time she forgot about her two captors as the bird filled her inner vision. And then without warning, it suddenly transformed into that familiar shape that she had seen so often, followed by a procession of all the shapes that she had experienced over the course of her life. She was witnessing them in a full conscious state.

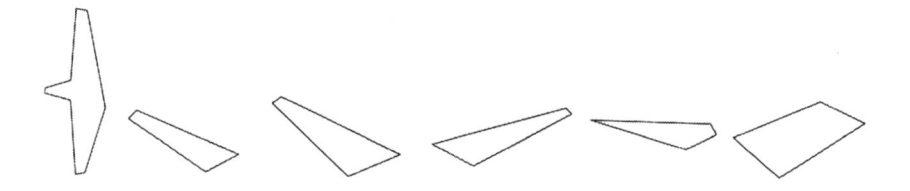

She opened her eyes and looked at the circling eagle. It seemed to linger in the sky as if conveying a message, but the meaning eluded her. Then she thought of Steve and the eagle's feather that she had left with him, and her heart instantly filled with warmth. *Was there ever a time that I did not love you?* But something else extraordinary was happening and she could feel it as she suddenly recalled Hugo's words when he was only a little boy.

"I know the secrets of the shapes and the colors." He was very young then and she thought his words to be fantasy. And yet, where she stood she could feel her son's presence, and the bird in the sky appeared to confirm that. Or was that her imagination?

Was it time for the mystery to be revealed?

Chapter 26
THE GREAT GAME

When the small shadow passed over his head for the second time, Chong-ba halted his steady climb and looked up into the blue sky. He spotted the eagle immediately and smiled, lifting his hand in salutation.

"Greetings, friend." His lips barely moved. He reduced his eyes to mere slits to keep sight of the circling bird. "You are not hunting?" he inquired softly. The eagle seemed to hang suspended in the cold mountain air for a long time. "Another message then?" Without warning the bird suddenly swooped down and passed over Chong-ba's head, exposing its lean torso and tucked talons, as it caught a thermal cushion and headed to a spot higher up the mountain. Chong-ba followed its flight and felt his heart warm; he knew where the bird was heading. They were going to the same place.

The monk drew his blanket closer about his thin body; he would have preferred to remain close to the fire where Tom was, but his sleep had been restless and fraught with dreams and visions that alerted him to the presence of strange energies. When the sun finally rose, he stood at the door of the cabin and looked at the sleeping face of Tom Norman and noticed the concern etched on his brow, even in sleep. Chong-ba added more wood to the dying embers and left quietly. He understood the whispering of his inner voice and honored the guidance. Waking in the small hours of the morning he felt an urgent need to be alone and wasn't surprised when the eagle showed; the signs were becoming all too clear. Chong-ba's restlessness increased as he ascended the steep slope, arching his body slightly forward. Colonel Appleyard's face had appeared in his dreams during the night, but he could not understand why it kept disappearing behind veils of fog every time he endeavored to enter the scene to communicate through lucid dreaming. Something very strange was going on.

His thoughts went back to the day he spoke to the Colonel on the phone on Tom's behalf. The physical appearance of the man when he met him at the airport was no surprise. They had got the measure of each other on the phone that first day and knew that despite the obvious physical discrepancies, both were soldiers in their own right and they were evenly matched in tenacity. When Appleyard asked if he had a passport, the monk knew that the militarist on the other end of the line had already made the connection. If he didn't know about Chong-ba's past, he was at least highly suspicious. The mere fact that Appleyard had allowed the UK trip to proceed was enough proof that the Colonel's primary interest was not in him, but in Tom. And Tom was a very troubled man on all fronts.

The shallow cave where he regularly spent time in deep meditation was ingeniously hidden from the prying eyes of any stray souls who could be traversing this dangerous terrain. The cave itself did not reach far into the belly of the mountain and could easily be mistaken as just a crevice in the rock face. The entrance was partially covered with sparse vegetation which hid the narrow opening effectively, although the monk knew exactly where he was going. The eagle would be sitting on a ridge high above the cave.

As he finally approached the opening, he looked up to the ledge jutting out above the entrance. An untrained eye could easily miss the presence of the bird, masterfully camouflaged against the backdrop of the dull rocks and sparse vegetation, but Chong-ba knew where to look. He smiled and bowed his head in acknowledgment before entering the shallow cave.

The bird didn't move. Their silent allegiance had begun when the mountains became his home some years ago and throughout this time any unusual behavior of the eagle became very significant. Chong-ba knew that this day would be no different; it had started with those strange dreams and when the eagle showed up, his notion was confirmed. Something big was afoot.

The cave had a narrow sloping floor leading to a highly energized stream that sprung much higher up from the center of the mountain. In the semi darkness he could hear the water and he followed the sound of it as far back as the cave would allow him to go. Then he found the flat rock on which he always sat. Before taking his seat, Chong-ba went down on his haunches and then stretched out on his stomach to scoop some of the water into his mouth. When he was seated on the rock he took a few deep nasal breaths to clear his mind and airways, and closed his eyes to begin concentrating. But instead of gradually leaving the material world behind, he found himself drawn even deeper into it. The parallel between what he was forced to endure here in the mountains and what happened to the Penchen Lama in 1923 was, on this day, very hard to ignore.

He kept his eyes closed and waited. Everything he needed to know was not always revealed through the meditative state, or in dreams and visions. There were times when the boundaries between his conscious and subconscious mind were subtly erased and it became possible to see ties that were otherwise obscured, without going into a trance. He knew that the energy at work was very delicate and could easily be disturbed if he tried to impose his own will on the unfolding message.

He disciplined himself to remain the observer, and after almost an hour of dedicated quietude, he saw the face. Chong-ba bowed his head in solemn acknowledgment. It was the ancient and wise face of the Penchen Lama, the true spiritual leader of the Buddhists, the one who had been forced to flee for his life from Tibet so many years ago. Chong-ba had not encountered him often in this manner, but marveled at how his ancient eyes always held a glimmer of hope that justice would be done and that truth would some day triumph. Few in the West knew the real story of the Tibetan people and their leader. It was mostly those who read Nicholas Roerich's famous book, *Shambala*, who were aware of the difference between the Penchen Lama, and the Dalai Lama, who essentially is the political leader. Lacking adequate research, the information in this book could easily be construed as fanciful.

Chong-ba didn't move as the laughing, wrinkled face faded into the background and was replaced with Colonel Appleyard's, wearing a scowl. That broke the delicate spell and the monk was immediately uneasy and highly alert, although he instinctively knew that the vision had served its purpose. It was now up to him to draw the loose ends together. He opened his eyes slowly. What did this mean? What was the link between the Penchen Lama and this man from the West who was so anxious to talk to Tom?

Chong-ba stared into the distance. In Tibet he was considered a seditious man; a non-conforming dissident, because he openly taught the principles of the Tashi Lama, the colloquial term the West had for Tsang Penchen Rimpoche, the Penchen Lama. In the orphanage where he was raised, Chong-ba had learned that this humble man was not only educated, but enlightened and free-thinking. He was a pacifist, opposed to increasing taxes of the poorest villagers, supporting the expensive army that the British had encouraged.

And, contrary to the disinformation spread deliberately by the West, this co-regent of Tibet was forced to flee from the 13th Dalai Lama, who had sent soldiers to take his life in the middle of the night. This paved the path for authentic Buddhism to be replaced by carefully engineered Lamaism, and with that Tibet officially joined the Great Game.

The interests of the West in Chong-ba's activities were not spiritual in nature. They could care precious little what any monk did as long as he stayed out of the political arena. But in the orphanage, Chong-ba had learned from the wise old woman, who was mother to the few children who had lost their parents through natural disasters like avalanches or floods, that even as far back as 1901 the Tibetan Lamas were implicated as players in the Great Game.

It was the Opium War of 1840 that finally put the issue of Tibet's independence on the table and Chong-ba understood that this was the time when the British began their efforts to separate Tibet from China in order to keep a foothold in this region. The Great Game, involving the Indo-Himalayan region, officially ensued when the People's Republic of China was established, and the British required fortification against further advancement in Asia by a communist nation.

At the time of his exile, the Penchen Lama, who was not interested in political gain or material matters, automatically caused the segregation between himself and the Dalai Lama, who identified great opportunities for personal power, shrewdly disguised as piety and spiritual zeal. But Chong-ba was educated in Nichirren Daishonin Buddhism, a practice based on the highest of Sakyamuni's teachings. Thus, he was raised to honor purity, simplicity and detachment.

When he began to teach these principles to others, he enlightened them about the differences between the Penchen Lama and the jumble of indigenous pagan and shamanistic practices. The small ripple of discontent amongst the people of Tibet soon grew to a more significant wave and inevitably attracted the attention of the local police. However, the disquiet amongst the people of Tibet was also echoed by the media in Germany who, in Munich of May 2000, openly accused the Dalai Lama of falsifying the history of Tibet. Chong-ba's life was in peril when he confirmed to his followers that the allegations made by the German press were true. Their revered leader was guilty of an undemocratic and autocratic leadership style, suppression of political opposition and religious minorities.

In short order, the slight monk, whose only goal was to spread the truth, grew in stature and importance and attracted the attention of international vultures and bullies, in particular the CIA, who kept a watchful eye on this region after having ousted the Brits as the global power. When he began to travel after receiving invitations to speak at conventions around the world on subjects of freedom of religious expression, his international file grew in thickness and MI6 also began keeping tabs.

His thoughts returned to his immediate situation. Appleyard's appearance in his dream was significant and Chong-ba waited quietly for the information to unfold. He focused all his attention on his rhythmic breathing, completely overriding the biting cold that was even more pronounced in the belly of the mountain. He was certain that Appleyard would not agree to Tom's withdrawal from the material world without a struggle.

Then he heard chanting and while he thought he recognized the voice, he couldn't be sure. Experienced as a listener and observer, he remained motionless, with eyes closed, as a strange landscape slowly drifted into his inner vision. The chanting came from behind a tent, and then he saw the old man sitting on his haunches, awkwardly holding a big stick in his left hand. The hand that held the stick had only three fingers and he increased the volume of his chanting to override the screams that emanated from inside the tent. Chong-ba had only once before heard screams like that in the village where he grew up, but a midwife carrying a big jug of steaming water had ushered him away swiftly, scolding him at the same time for wandering too close to a woman who was giving birth. That day he had had no time to explain that he thought someone was dying and only came to help, because the midwife slammed the door shut before he could open his mouth.

Chong-ba watched and listened; mesmerized, not understanding any of what he was witnessing or hearing. Then another scream came from within the tent; it was the first cry of an infant being born. The old man behind the tent at once ceased his chanting; he stood and walked around to the opening where he waited, still holding the stick in his left hand. Then the flap opened and an older woman came out, covered in blood.

"It is a girl." She sounded impatient. "Now be gone!"

"I know." The old man looked at her, nodding slowly. "Name her Tiva. A daughter gifted with great enlightenment and wisdom has been given to the Kawahi people." He began walking away, muttering softly. "She is born enlightened and wise, but in this life she will need sufficient love to support the difficult journey that leads through the stars. In the far distant future there will be many tears." He scratched his head. "Wrap her in love. One day her soul will need to remember."

Beads of sweat were running down the side of Colonel Appleyard's face; his breathing was extremely labored and he wondered how much more of this torture his heart could stand. With every painful breath he took, it seemed as though his lungs would collapse from the strain. Then suddenly the guide halted and pointed to a wisp of smoke rising from over the next hill.

"Chong-ba?" The Colonel could barely get the words out. The guide nodded, looking at him strangely. He regretted bringing the big man to this point up the mountain, but he was more upset that he hadn't managed to let the other base camps know, as was their custom, that a Westerner had gone to see Chong-ba. Even more disconcerting was the fact that the store owner, whom they all knew, had refused to speak, except to urge him not to return without this man. But no one knew that Chong-ba had left his cabin at sunrise to meditate in his cave and wasn't around to receive guests.

"You wait here?" Appleyard didn't know if the guide understood, but hoped that hand gestures would convey the order. The Sherpa kept staring at him and didn't blink. Then he nodded slowly, watching as Appleyard caught his breath, and began the final climb toward the summit of the hill in front of them. When the Colonel disappeared from sight, the guide went down on his knees and put his hands together in prayer. Not being one of the regular Sherpas, something didn't feel right and he couldn't ignore his anxiety in leading this Westerner to their spiritual teacher. However, he trusted the store owner implicitly when he said it was imperative that Chong-ba met with this man.

The cabin was completely unassuming and appeared to be fairly small from where he stood. There was no one in sight and for a terrifying moment David Appleyard feared the treacherous journey up this godforsaken mountain had been in vain. Then his militaristic training took over and he approached the cabin to check on its contents before he came to such drastic conclusions. In front of the wooden door he hesitated, then he lifted the catch and the door creaked open softly to reveal a figure silhouetted against the bright light streaming in from the window. He couldn't see the face immediately, but noticed the robe and assumed it to be the monk.

"Chong-ba?" His voice sounded uncertain.

"Hello, Colonel." Tom turned around from the window and looked David Appleyard directly in the eye. The older man's sight had adjusted to the light and he caught his breath slowly as a shock ran through his body. He took in the long orange outfit, the bare feet and the shaven head. He didn't comment immediately but the expression on his face evidenced his surprise and his momentary inability to know how to address his subordinate. Finally, he spoke.

"It has been a very long time, Tom."

"Yes, Colonel."

"You're saved—holy or something, now that you are wearing that ridiculous orange frock?" He took a step closer, consumed by sudden anger. "Have you lost your marbles, man?"

"You're not here to discuss my sanity, Colonel. You and I know that you would not have come after me this way, if it were not a case of the utmost urgency." He held Appleyard's eye with just a glint of humor beginning to show. "Or is the cavalry waiting outside?" Appleyard didn't reply, but he watched Tom closely. He looked harmless enough and there were no weapons anywhere in sight.

"The work you were doing for us was very important, Tom. I trusted no one else with your responsibilities. I went out of my way to accommodate you and your family in every respect. Don't you think I deserve better?"

"No, Colonel. What we were busy with is positively evil. I know that now." Appleyard remained silent as he stared at Tom, realizing that he found himself in unknown territory, in more ways than one.

"Where is the little monk?" he finally asked softly.

"Around, I guess. Chong-ba has his own schedule, his own time. He comes and goes as the spirit takes him."

"As the spirit takes him?" Appleyard asked snidely. "And what about you? Who do you answer to?" Tom smiled.

"I realize this is hard for you to take in, Colonel, but I have made up my mind. I'm staying here on the mountain and I'm going to learn from Chong-ba what I should have learned a long time ago." He folded his arms across his chest and spoke softly. "You needn't have made the trip up the mountain, Colonel. Your secrets are safe with me. And I no longer have any of the equipment you gave me. The mountain has many hidden crevices willing to swallow evidence for a very long time."

"Have you gone completely insane?" Appleyard was beginning to lose his composure. He was physically exhausted from the strenuous climb up the mountain, and he was entirely frustrated with Tom's physical appearance and his air of non-compliance. "You still work for me, in case you've lost your memory while becoming so bloody pious all of a sudden. Holy mother of God! I've seen turncoats and other traitors, but none endeavored to step up the ladder to heaven as vigorously as you are apparently hell bent on doing. It's quite sickening!"

"Colonel, let me repeat again. Your secrets are safe with me."

"My bloody secrets are safe? Screw you, Norman! Don't give me that! I need those contact names and I need to know how far you got with those people you were paid to negotiate with!"

"You call plotting the deaths of innocent people, *negotiating*?"

"*Jesus Christ!* What has happened to you? You know we must steer events in the world. And whether you decide to become goddamned holy and no longer participate won't change a bloody thing. We create wars because we have to." Tom didn't blink.

"Correct. It is about greed and power. The audacity of the game we play negates the sovereignty of other countries to do with their natural resources as they see fit. I haven't seen you for a while, David, but the President of Venezuela laughed me out of his office. He was never for sale." The older man refrained from comment; Tom continued. "And then there is Africa."

"Don't be fucking ridiculous! And spare me the lecture on morals. *Please*. I'm not interested. How arrogant to attempt crossing those who pull the strings. I never thought you'd be that stupid! Do you really think that your refusal to give me what I want will make any difference? For God's sake, Norman, wipe that holy shit from your eyes! Why assist Africa when we *pay* the warlords to keep these regions unstable!" Tom nodded.

"You will have to continue without me."

"You owe me, Tom." Appleyard's voice was ice cold. "Have you forgotten that we are watching over your wife and child?"

"A threat, Colonel?" Tom barely moved his lips. "It has not escaped me that MI6 is still in charge of the case that should by now have been in the hands of MI5. But we both understand the reasons, don't we? And what are you threatening me with? If you don't get the answers from me, you will not get them from Eva. You know she doesn't know anything."

"I want the information. Then you can go off and be as holy as you want."

"Colonel, you and I know the ending will not be that simple. We've been in this game long enough. You want to know who is contributing to the destabilization of Iran, and how you can use those people, *and* you want their contacts in Tehran. You came all this way because common thugs can be found anywhere, but sophisticated terrorists capable of using military equipment are prized commodities. You're here because you suspect I have netted some big fish. But I won't divulge anything." When he continued, Tom's voice was devoid of all emotion. "You don't really want the information, do you? Because, once you have it I will remain as big a threat as before. I am the only one who knows how deeply you are involved in this mess; you and Stanway." They measured each other eye to eye. "You are here to silence me, David. Getting your information will simply be a bonus. It won't take you long to make new contacts. You have already written me off. You just want to make sure that I don't have a change of heart and spill the beans in some newspaper, if there is still free press in our world."

The Colonel seemed at a loss for words. He didn't know what to expect, but it sure as hell wasn't this composed figure of Tom Norman, who was still an impressive man, even in the ludicrous attire of a monk. He wondered vaguely what could have made his prize soldier snap in such a dramatic way, but he was well aware that he would have to stay alert. Tom was one of his best and he couldn't make the mistake of assuming that he suffered from complete amnesia and would not remember how to defend himself.

"The holiness of the monk has rubbed off, it seems. Either that, or you are just as brilliant a student as you have always been because my presence here doesn't seem to bother you in the least."

"I am not armed, David." Tom held the Colonel's gaze. "That is what you are really asking of me. But I expect you to be and I know you are. We both know that you are waiting for the opportune moment to reveal your hand." He smiled. "No pun intended, of course." His eyes caught the Colonel's hand straying toward the inside of his jacket. "Don't!" He didn't raise his voice, but the soft warning was unmistakable. "I won't go down without a fight, David. But I am hoping we can reach a sensible compromise that will satisfy us both. There is always that possibility, although I suspect you have not given it consideration."

Colonel Appleyard listened to the calm voice of Tom Norman and knew he had been outplayed and it infuriated him so much that he was ready to choke. Strictly speaking, he held the upper hand; he was after all the one with a loaded gun. But Tom's equanimity unnerved him and he involuntarily reverted back to what he had done as a child when he thought he was about to lose a fight, and that was to get personal.

"If this whole charade is to impress Eva, I have news for you, Tom." Only the slight flicker in Tom's eyes revealed that he had hit the right spot; the rest of his body remained relaxed as he carefully watched the older man.

"Eva has nothing to do with this, David."

"No? I hear she is quite the woman. I haven't met her, but I've seen pictures in your file. And I imagine that men—"

"David, I am warning you to not take Eva's name in vain." But Appleyard saw he had opened up an emotional artery and that Tom was beginning to bleed. Some perverse part of him actually enjoyed it.

"With you gone so often don't you wonder how or where she had her needs satisfied? I know where the likes of you and I went, but a woman with her physical attributes…" He recklessly took a step closer to Tom, who looked as though he had stopped breathing; his face had turned to stone. "Or did you marry a saint who was beyond sexual needs?" But the movement in his direction was enough to set Tom off. He reached with both hands for the thick jacket David Appleyard was wearing and immediately felt the gun as he yanked the older man toward him.

"The one thing you will never know, Appleyard, is what it feels like to be loved by a real woman," he hissed in his ear, while each struggled ferociously to gain control of the weapon. "I always knew that you couldn't be with a woman who was your equal, therefore you had to be derogative and demeaning to all women. You could only stand those who submitted to your domination. You dragged your top dog phobia into all your relationships, including those with women. You have been an insecure big boy all of your life, and then you have the temerity to question the conduct of a woman whom you have never met!" When the gun dropped from underneath Appleyard's jacket onto the floor, the Colonel knew this was his only chance and he dove for it. Rolling over, he grabbed the gun and aimed it securely at Tom, who curiously stood still and just looked at him. "Still the street fighter, David?"

"Oh, shut up! I've had enough of your preaching. I'd rather keep company with the devil than have to listen to this holier-than-thou drivel. And get the fuck away from that door!" But Tom knew this was his only chance and he lunged for it just as Appleyard fired the first shot, hitting him just below the shoulder. The impact of the bullet stunned him for a second, but he wrenched the door open and stumbled outside, not immediately feeling the pain, and headed for the cover of rocks that formed the backdrop to a deep chasm behind the cabin. The second bullet hit him in the thigh just as he climbed onto the nearest rock, and Tom knew that the only way to draw Appleyard to him was to feign that he was mortally wounded.

"Look at you now, your holiness." David Appleyard stood a meter away from him, the gun pointing to the ground as he surveyed the trail of blood Tom had left on the rocks. His eyes were closed and his body appeared limp. "This could have turned out so differently for us all, Tom. It's not such a bad thing to be paid for the service we were delivering. There will always be expendable, stupid people in the world, and those are the only ones we need to get rid of." He sounded genuinely sad in the midst of his self righteous delivery.

But the next second Tom lifted himself off the rocks and threw his arms around Appleyard's torso, dragging him toward the precipice. His body registered no pain as he locked the older man in a vice grip and dragged him even closer toward the edge. He heard Appleyard gag as he desperately fought for air but Tom only tightened his grip. Balancing precariously on the ledge, he was acting on instinct. But on some very deep level he knew that a favorable resolution to their struggle for the upper hand was no longer an option.

Yet, it was David Appleyard that made the final choice. With his lungs bursting from lack of air, he felt the gun still in his grip and locked his fingers around the trigger as he deftly pushed it into Tom's side and fired. For one impossibly clear moment, Tom's eyes widened as he recognized the end. As he began to topple backwards into the abyss, his locked arms held on to his executioner and they plunged together into the chasm toward certain death.

The echo of the first shot reached Chong-ba's ears in the cave. He immediately gathered his blanket around his shoulders and made his way toward the entrance. And then the reason for Appleyard's presence in his vision clearly dawned on him. Colonel Appleyard was on the mountain and he had come armed. As he set foot onto the faintly distinguishable path outside the cave, his eye fell on the tail feather. He bent down to pick it up and looked toward the ledge above. The eagle was gone and he hurried down the mountain toward his cabin.

Appleyard's Sherpa babbled incoherently as he pointed to the bloodied rocks and gestured frantically toward the edge. The scrawny man was sick to his stomach. He knew that his gut feeling of earlier that day was right and, shaking violently, he waited for Chong-ba to signal the next move. The monk put his hands together and bowed his head to the guide, acknowledging his co-operation and thanking him for his assistance. Then he avoided the blood stains as he climbed to the top and peered over the edge. Fifty feet below, Appleyard's body was grotesquely impaled on a jagged branch which had broken his fall. Even from where the monk stood, he knew the Colonel's journey had ended. Tom's body was caught between two rocks and Chong-ba couldn't tell whether there was still hope for his friend.

He instructed the guide to wait at the cave where he had been meditating, and with a heavy heart, began the arduous descent toward Tom. To his astonishment, he heard faint gasping sounds when he neared his friend's body and realized that he would have to find a way to free him from where he was wedged between the boulders.

Unable to help him, the monk reached for a branch, broken during the dreadful fall of the victims. Using it as a lever, the slight man began to pry the rocks slowly apart, wondering how to free Tom without assistance. Then he leaned his shoulder against the branch and, hearing what sounded like a last gasping breath, Chong-ba reached desperately toward the trapped body, but lost his footing and caught his hand between the rocks as they mercilessly closed. The monk let out a wail that echoed through the mountains as he pried his left hand free in an almost superhuman effort. Then he stared at it in absolute horror. The two little fingers were completely crushed, barely attached by skin.

Chong-ba did not hesitate. He reached for his pocket knife, tied by a cord to his waist and, with a few quick cuts, he severed the fingers completely. Then he took the knife to Tom's orange robe and cut off a huge piece to make a tourniquet. His mind was utterly blank as he began to wrap his badly mangled hand. He knew he had to get help and that he had to sterilize the wound in clean water as soon as possible. He stood in front of Tom's lifeless body and put his hands gingerly together in prayer, taking care not to touch the blood-soaked tourniquet.

"Good-bye, my friend. Until we meet again." Climbing to the top with only one hand was going to be an almost impossible task. As he slowly ascended the rock face, he became aware of the presence of the eagle; he felt comforted by this but didn't look up. Instead, he fervently began mumbling to himself in an effort to divert his attention from his injured hand.

"Pain and hardship mean nothing to my people! We live with it every day!" he frantically called out through his pain, holding up his bloodied hand for the eagle to see. "And let this be a display of our resolve! The truth will triumph in the end!" He had no idea yet that those words had been spoken before, only under different circumstances.

Chong-ba could barely hold himself upright as he reached for the final ledge. He could not remain at the cabin. The constant presence of the eagle had warned him that more people were coming and he was in no shape to defend himself. He would have to return to the cave where there was fresh water but he would have to ask the guide to collect herbs to tend his wound. He was suffering from considerable loss of blood and he felt very weak.

Hours later, after drinking some of the cold broth he had brought with him from the cabin, Chong-ba sat ashen-faced on his rock beside the stream inside the cave and this time there were neither dreams nor visions. Immersed in a sea of pain, he floated in and out of consciousness as the mountain herbs began to ward off infection and close up the open arteries. He shook violently as he lifted his left hand and stared at the remaining three fingers. He barely noticed the stoic face of the guide huddling nearby. Then he clearly saw Eva Norman's bright smile, and was stunned as his subconscious mind effortlessly made the connection. Tears streaked silently down the little monk's face. His bond with the eagle was finally beginning to make sense.

"Name her Tiva." He repeated the words he had heard earlier that day and he smiled through his pain. That was in fact his ancient phrase of hundreds of years ago. The cry of the baby girl in his vision was still fresh in his mind. Only he hadn't understood then that he was not observing the birth from a distance, but that he was actually attending it. Chong-ba, the monk, had to lose his own two fingers to remember his life as Nahiossi. He closed his eyes and drifted away in feverish sleep as Eva's beautiful face again appeared in his mind's eye.

Tiva, have you remembered your gifts in this life? Do you still move with the same ease between the boundaries of illusion and reality? And have you found Chaska, the only man you ever loved, in another world? Everyone yearns to love and be loved like that...everyone.

Chapter 27
From Dreams To Reality

Hugo watched Natalie surreptitiously from the corner of his eye where she sat opposite him on the ground. He found the way she communicated with her hands and eyes immensely intriguing. To him she represented his favorite symbol, a shining star, and he associated her with the number five. Her engaging mannerisms absorbed his normally calculating mind and opened doors for interacting that he never knew existed.

She looked as though she was going to keel over any minute and fall asleep right where she was. That would not surprise him at all. He had never seen anyone who could doze off on her feet, sitting up in a chair or on a hard uncomfortable surface like a floor. But Natalie did this all the time. On this day her typical bubbly and sunny nature had curiously been replaced by a quietness that he did not understand at all. He wondered if it was the discussion of the number six that had caused her to withdraw. He was at a loss of explaining to her why that particular number mathematically represented a horse. Hugo's comprehension and interpretation of colors, numbers and shapes far outstripped his ability to verbalize any of it to others and the only one who could read him fairly accurately was his mother.

George and Janet Ballantire, who had been left in charge of the children and the farm when Steve had left for Pakistan, had given them permission to take the horse for a walk into the woods. Natalie insisted they were going to visit her winged friends, the fairies, but when George raised his eyebrows to check this statement with Hugo, he was met with a blank stare pleading ignorance to such outlandish claims.

She was his friend, but he had not seen or met any of her fanciful companions and while she took off and played in the foliage with her imaginary playmates, he spread the piece of canvas on the ground that

Steve had given him to protect his drawings on outdoor adventures. For a while he only watched her from a distance, wondering at the carefree way in which she interacted with seemingly no one at all. He never tried to see her friends. He understood that they had different perceptions and he had no interest in analyzing any of it, and in fact wouldn't know where to begin. It was when she came to sit opposite him and they began tucking into Janet's delicious homemade sandwiches and lemonade that she asked the question about Quah Dreamer.

"He is the most beautiful horse I have ever seen! Don't you think so, Hugo?" She looked over to where Quah Dreamer stood staring off into the distance. As the leaves moved lazily in the light breeze, splotches of sunlight randomly shining through the trees, reflected brilliantly on his coat as the horse rippled his muscles. When he didn't answer, she looked at him. "Hugo?"

"Quah Dreamer is a six." He spoke calmly, narrowing his eyes into slits as he brought the horse into focus. The more he concentrated, the more convinced he was that Quah Dreamer was the most perfect six he had ever seen.

"The number six? *Why?*" she cried a little frustrated. "Quah Dreamer is a horse, Hugo!" They were only children but the irritation they felt between them was suddenly palpable. She plopped over onto her side and rested her head on her arm, not looking at him. Then she began to hum like she always did when she wanted to be left alone or withdraw from her immediate surroundings.

Hugo watched as she began drawing patterns in the dry loose soil with the index finger of her free hand and knew that Natalie would not speak another word until she was ready. He began unpacking his drawings and only looked up when the humming had died down and the pattern-making in the soil stopped. Her face was completely hidden behind her golden curls but from the gentle rise and fall of her small body, he knew she was fast asleep. Natalie had done it again; the hard ground of the woods had become her bed.

"Hello, child." She stood quite still and didn't turn around. She didn't think he would come so soon, but his presence was unmistakable.

The Meadow was peaceful and quiet and her little heart was filled with immeasurable happiness. This was her home! "You came to ask about your friend and his love of numbers?"

"Um…Hugo?" She turned her head only slightly and caught a glimpse of him in her peripheral vision. The sunlight flashed brilliantly, if only briefly, on his lance and a tiny smile crept around her lips. She knew many of the permanent dwellers of the Meadow but she thought him to be a transient, which meant he would move on to another place at a given time. Only a few were privy to Natalie's special role and function in the Meadow, but she didn't know if he knew. She only remembered it herself when she came here to visit in dreams.

"Ah, yes, Hugo." Moving quietly, he suddenly stood next to her. He held out his hand and she took it without hesitation. Sakhota smiled. "I will tell you, but will you remember when you return to where Hugo is?" She wrinkled her nose at him and then smiled secretively.

"Does Hugo remember he is you?" Sakhota chuckled and let go of her hand to hold up two fingers.

"Only when he thinks of the number two and combines it with a zero. The number two represents duality to him—or two things, child. In this case he can see his present life and other lives too. This he accomplishes by adding a zero and that opens the gateway to the past and the future; an easy and natural thing for him to do when he enters the Zen state."

"When he becomes very quiet and he looks like he is not breathing?" He stared intently at her and nodded his head slowly, but she pressed on regardless, even though she did not quite know what the next question should be. "But zero means nothing, Sakhota?"

"Not to Hugo. To him it is the beginning of everything. Zero opens the door to infinity and every other number he couples with a zero has a lot of meaning. Combining it under special circumstances with the number two, will lead him to remember that he and I are two expressions of the same soul energy."

"Oh." She considered his answer and then looked directly at him. "Are all people like that?" Sakhota smiled and put his arm around her shoulders.

"No. Hugo is different. You have seen his pictures and sketches, have you not?" She nodded.

"I can't make pictures like that."

"I know." He hugged her lightly. "And you are not supposed to. But all his drawings have numbers written all over them. Is that right?"

"Yes."

"That is because Hugo sees beneath the surface of everything before he can see what is outside."

"What does that mean?" She looked at Sakhota, a little frown furrowing her forehead.

"Hugo sees the mathematical blueprint of everything before he sees the object, or the thing." He heard her draw in her breath and anticipated the confusion, but continued nevertheless. "Everything has a number as you call it, child, or a combination of different numbers. A tree is a tree because of the numbers in its makeup, or molecular structure, as the learned people say. And it is the same with people, animals and everything else. Hugo can only recognize feelings and emotions once he recognizes and understands the numerical structure."

"Isn't that very hard to do?" She stared wide eyed at him, only catching the gist of his words.

"Not if that is the only way you can communicate with the outside world."

"Oh. Why does he say a horse is a six?" Sakhota considered her question and then began to speak in a subdued tone as he took her hand and they walked side by side through the Meadow.

"Does Hugo see your fairies?"

"He says he can't."

"That is because he does not have a number for them and they belong to another dimension. When you play in the shrubs and see your friends, he sees the complex numbers of the plants, nothing else. His mind is brilliant but in a special way, it is also locked. And the keys he needs to open it are hidden in mathematical equations. But, Natalie, being locked away like this has made some very strange things possible for him." He looked sideways at her as she frowned in concentration. "His mathematical reasoning faculty is very well developed and he can overcome barriers and analyze complicated data as a result. Few people can accomplish this." Natalie sighed dramatically, notifying him that her perception was being stretched way beyond its limits on this matter. She nevertheless held on tightly to his hand, concentrating hard.

"Steve says Hugo is very clever. Is that what you mean?" Sakhota laughed, realizing that most of his terminology had escaped her, but she at least had caught the essence of it and he conceded.

"Yes, child. Hugo is very clever." Sakhota felt the ripple of energy pass over them as the wind suddenly changed direction. He pulled her down to sit on the soft grass beside him and looked earnestly at her. "Hugo has a special task to fulfill. Do you know that, Natalie?" She nodded her head slowly and whispered.

"Eva?"

"Eva *and* Steve." Sakhota dropped his voice and spoke softly. "That is why you are there, to make sure they get it right this time, but they do not know that. Am I right, Natalie?" She shook her head slowly from side to side.

"When I'm with them, I don't remember any of that, Sakhota. I only remember when I am here. This is my home."

"I know, child," he murmured soothingly, resting his hand for a moment on her head to brush a stray curl away. "I know."

"Did you know Steve and Eva before?"

"Yes. A long, long time ago Eva was called Nathaniel and I was there to give her the feathers of an owl and an eagle to remind her of the mission." She stared mesmerized into the eyes resting kindly on her, not moving a muscle. "I gave her the feathers, just the same way you and the horse found the feather of the owl to give to Steve."

"Do you know Quah Dreamer too?" She could barely contain her excitement.

"Yes, Natalie. A long time ago I gave Wyomah to Nathaniel when he came to visit our village with his father. Quah Dreamer was a beautiful black dog then." She suddenly burst out laughing and rolled away in the grass, indicating that she had heard about as much as she could handle.

"What is Hugo's favorite number, Sakhota?" She lay on her back a few feet away from him with her eyes closed.

"Eight!" He too fell onto his back and watched the lazy clouds float by, although his attention was focused on the child nearby.

"Why?" She giggled behind her hand.

"It gives him the freedom to express himself in any way he chooses."

"What does number one mean?"

"Feeling good or positive. This number reminds him of new beginnings." He looked sideways at her and smiled broadly. "You now know the meanings of zero, one, two, six and eight. Next!" She rolled onto her stomach and pillowed her head on her arms again.

"Three?" He could barely hear the soft whisper.

"That number reminds him of the three primary colors of red, yellow and blue. Each color in its own right will give him a specific insight. If he thinks of the number first and then adds blue, he will feel sad and depressed. If he combines the three primary colors and gets brown, it heightens the feeling of being rooted to the earth. The combinations are endless and when other numbers are added, all manner of experiences and feelings will enter his consciousness."

"He loves his mum very much. What is Eva's color?" Her voice slurred ever so slightly and he wondered if she was drifting off to sleep. Sakhota smiled at the face hidden behind the golden curls.

"She has more than one." Describing how Eva's colors changed with her emotions was too complicated for the little girl's perception, and he let it slide.

"Tell me about the others."

"Four is a cube and it symbolizes his specific genius or talent. His mind projects him inside the walls of the cube when he sees the number four. He feels isolated here but the seclusion acts like a personal laboratory, where he can figure out very difficult equations others have trouble unraveling." He looked at the little girl but she didn't move, and he continued. "Five is a star, Natalie. You are a five to him. Five holds heavenly proportions and this is where he keeps and holds his affections for those who are most dear to him.

"Seven is his least favorite number because he associates it with negativity and when he sees a seven he always tries to find a way to combine it with a zero, so it will mean something else. And nine represents a point of no return. It is closest to the magical number of ten—one, which is *possibility*, combined with zero, *infinity*—to make a ten. Do you understand that, child?"

She was very quiet. Sakhota stood silently and took a few steps to her side. Holding the lance securely in his left hand, he bent down and lightly stroked her shining hair.

"One more thing." He didn't bother to simplify his words any longer for Natalie had fallen asleep and he knew she was already beginning to leave the Meadow. Soon she would disappear from his sight. "Hugo took out the drawing of the stone eagle before you came to visit today. He saw the number nine very clearly. There are endless possibilities to what Hugo can do with numbers and their combinations. But the secret to his quest is to understand the dimensions of the stone eagle and get that right. Remember that, little one," he whispered earnestly. "The secret is in the eagle." Then he straightened and walked away into the sun. His journey had been long, but the end of his mission was in sight.

"Are you finishing the eagle?" She slowly sat up and leaned forward to see what he was doing.

"How did you know?" Hugo looked surprised but was glad that she was awake. He enjoyed having her around. She reminded him of a happy twinkling star, and of course, thoughts of Natalie always were preceded by the number five, one of his favorite numbers. She was much like his mother in some ways.

"I'm hungry. Can I have another sandwich, please?" Hugo handed her one and while she tucked in, he began taking measurements of the eagle. "The eagle hides the secret." She wiped her mouth with the back of her hand, staring closely at his sketch. He had measured the angle between the shoulder and right wing at forty two degrees. When he looked up at her, Natalie remembered that Sakhota had said the number two helped him to remember past existences and the number four put him inside his own cube where he could figure things out. She smiled sweetly, recognizing the numbers, but didn't quite know what he would do with them.

"Who says?" Hugo concentrated on the sketch in front of him, barely aware of her presence, or that his mind had made a leap, of which he was not immediately aware. "Did you talk to Sakhota?" She sat up, stunned, and then called out excitedly.

"Hugo, you remember!"

"Maybe," he whispered and smiled shyly; clearly not anxious to discuss something he did not yet understand and for which he had no numerical reference. He leaned forward to continue his work and measured the angle between the head and the shoulders at eighty five degrees. Then he drew in his breath slowly as a clear vision of his mother flashed onto the screen of his mind, and temporarily excluding Natalie, Hugo purposely closed his eyes and waited.

Accessing the Zen state was a skill at which he had become a master, but his mother was so real to him that he could reach out and touch her, and yet he understood that he had to resist the temptation of focusing on Eva or any numbers at this time. But his conscious mind persisted in its effort to engross him in the object of his admiration and love. Eighty five…Eva smiled at him and as the vision grew clearer he felt the sting of tears behind his closed eyes. Her expression was filled with love for him.

From the very beginning she was his guiding star. His mother was the perfect symbol of a five, just like Quah Dreamer was a perfect six. Through the haziness and fog of other worlds swirling slowly into focus, his mind tried in vain to process this new information that he could not yet place or access unless he entered the stillness and remained quiet and receptive. Natalie had said the secret was in the eagle.

The smiling face of his mother faded into the background and Hugo's conscious mind registered that his body temperature had started to drop. A shiver ran down his spine but he kept completely still as he slowly began to drift into the stark white landscape of Zen, an inhospitable barren place that discouraged the presence of any who came for selfish reasons. The quietness grew in intensity and he slipped effortlessly through the first obstacle of feeling lonely and deserted.

He had been taught that many don't make it past the first barrier because of their need to feel connected to other beings, but Hugo's inborn isolation helped him to easily overcome this complication. He waited patiently for the revelation, unaware that today it was the number eight, his favorite number, in the combination of eighty five. It drew him into this bleak and desolate landscape where universal mind opened its doors to earnest seekers.

His breathing had become very deep and slow and his heart rate had dropped considerably as the young boy's vibrations began to match the answer he was looking for. Soon it would reveal itself and he would know, but when it happened, he was caught completely off guard. He had great difficulty maintaining his role of observer as the magnificent bird rose quietly from the far horizon and flew soundlessly into his inner vision. From wingtip to wingtip the eagle was glorious and majestic in its direct approach.

Hugo didn't move. The meaning was surprising but unmistakable and he felt its significance in numbers long before his mind was able to convert any of it into language. He also realized with great certainty that a real eagle existed somewhere near to his mother, and that it could act as a conduit of energy, a transmitter that could send information to her. An ancient promise, symbolized through the feather the monk had brought to Eva as evidence of her bond with the eagle, was being fulfilled.

And even though most of the information still came to him as complex numerical equations, Hugo sensed he had been afforded a brief glimpse of the interconnectedness of everything and he began to shiver violently. The physical reaction of his body brought him out of the Zen state and he opened his eyes and looked into Natalie's concerned stare.

"Are you going to be sick again, Hugo?" She sat cross-legged in front of him. Her bottom lip quivered, looking as though she was going to cry.

"No, Natalie." His voice was hoarse and barely audible as he stumbled to his feet. "Let us go to where your fairies are." Even as he spoke the words, he realized that he was intuitively drawn to the place where he and Natalie had had extraordinary but very different experiences of energy.

"Thorp Pelkington?" she whispered, wide-eyed.

"Yes." He held a spontaneous hand out to her and as she reached for it, their fingertips barely touching, Hugo froze, staring at their hands. Then he went down on his haunches and lightly linked his fingers with hers, gazing intently at the pattern their interlocked hands formed.

"Hugo? What are you looking at?"

"I think I see the eagle, Natalie." He touched the tip of his thumb to hers and smiled at her. "Yes, I do see it."

"Where is the eagle? I don't see anything!" They were whispering to each other but neither knew why. They were only vaguely cognizant of treading an almost sacred path, unraveling a secret together of which they saw only parts. Hugo sat down again and reached for the tracings of his mother's and Steve's hands and brought the two sketches out, placing them alongside on the canvas. He didn't look at Natalie, but kept staring at the sketches. Hugo had disappeared into his think tank again and his mind was consumed with numbers and mathematical equations.

He was convinced that if he completed all the measurements of the stone eagle and interlinked Steve's hand with Eva's, these dimensions would correspond to that of the stone eagle. Then it dawned on him that the purpose of the statue was to confirm the significance of the hands. He laid one sketch over the other in an interlocking position, and began to trace over them.

Hugo's breathing imperceptibly began to slow down again. He was intensely aware of profound feelings that instantly transported him to the same place from which he had seen the eagle approaching earlier when he went into the stillness. This was the key he had been trying to find. The blueprint was complete and all he had to do was use the figures that represented the angles between the joined symbolic fingers and he would find the answers that he was seeking.

It took a while for him to come to terms with what had just been revealed. But soon his mind produced a myriad of different images, decoding mathematical equations, leading to incredible possibilities, yet undiscovered. The combination of numbers corresponding to the angles of his sketches had unexpectedly opened the door to cosmic communication. Some were simply visions that had always represented the figures he recognized as feelings, shapes, or colors, but others were completely new to him.

Eventually, a whole new genre of thoughts entered his consciousness and he understood the meaning of the symbolic hands—they were a gateway which linked his mind consciously to unsolved mysteries. This was what the testing in the Azvaalder laboratories was all about, which he now understood for the first time. Hugo realized that Josh Goldberg had been aware of star gates; he just didn't know how to find them. And now Hugo did.

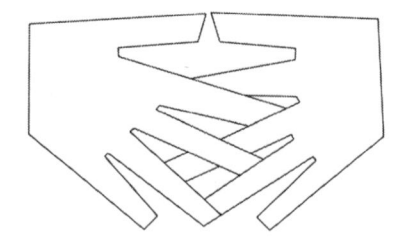

All he had to do was to use the numbers that represented each angle within the symbolic hand. Each different set would act as a catalyst for channeling different energy, which meant information would be available to him and when combined would produce further channels. The permutations were endless, and to him this was even greater than had he found the Holy Grail. Only a mind like Hugo's was capable of locating a unique star gate such as this with which to interpret information about the Universe. Not only could he understand it, but he had also recently acquired the ability to communicate his findings in words.

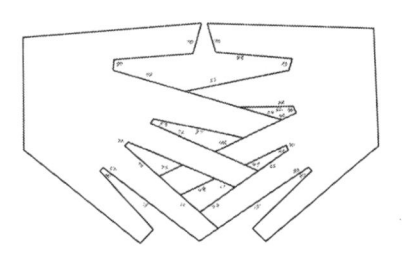

With a single glance he suddenly recognized all the individual patterns with which he and his mother had been so familiar, as each one came separately to him from the interlocked hands. The eagle shape stood out above all the other patterns and he was deeply under the impression of its power to act as a communicative device that could help him to reach her. He did not yet know how that would come about, or that the eagle had already made contact with her and that it was restlessly circling the cold blue skies just below the peaks of the Himalayan Mountains, waiting patiently for all the players to take their places on the final field of battle.

"That is it," he whispered, putting his pencil down. Hugo locked the fingers of his own hands above his head and brought his thumbs together. "See that, Natalie?" He smiled at her. "I think my mum has been trying to find Steve for a very long time." The tracings of the hands were symbolic of his mother and Steve and his words to Natalie reflected the truth of the energy encrypted in the physical contours. She crept closer to him and wiggled her way under his outstretched arms to look up at his hands.

"Oh!" She drew in her breath. "I see it! It is flying!" Then she leaned even closer to him and cupped her hand over his ear. "Now send the eagle a message to give to Eva." She didn't know why she said that but when he didn't move, she dropped her voice and whispered softly. "Let's go to Thorp Pelkington, I'm sure you'll find the right numbers there." She rolled her eyes playfully. "I know you're looking for more numbers!"

Steve did not anticipate any trouble passing through customs in Lahore, but he fully expected to be met by a reception committee at the other end. He was not disappointed and immediately noticed two men purposefully approaching, each wearing a determined expression. He couldn't help wondering at the complexity of the case to warrant this level of interference. Steve unhooked his backpack and dropped it to the floor, waiting for the small delegation to reach him. The older man was quite a bit shorter than Steve and to compensate for the disadvantage, he kept his voice very official and curt as he looked up at him.

"Professor Ballantire?"

"I'm sure you are fully aware of my identity, sir. What can I do for you?"

"I'm agent Foster. Can you step aside with us, please?" He tilted his head toward his partner, and briefly held out an MI6 badge before slipping it back inside his pocket. Steve hardly looked at it; the badge confirmed that Stanway had sent in the troops.

"What is the nature of your business?" He kept his voice even.

"May I see your travel documents, Professor?" Foster no longer feigned courtesy. Steve held his gaze, unwavering.

"I'm under no obligation to show you anything, and let me remind you that you have no authority over me in this country. The Pakistani establishment had no problem with my documentation, so I must assume you have an agenda you would rather keep under wraps. I notice also that you are not accompanied by a Pakistani official and therefore must be acting on the orders of Mr. Stanway."

"Professor, we are here for your protection and that of Mrs. Norman. We don't believe you know what you're getting into." Derek Cook, the younger of the two officers, had taken over the task of addressing him in lieu of Foster, who was red in the face and obviously had trouble controlling his temper. Steve noticed his discomfort but didn't take his eyes off him, barely acknowledging Cook.

"You are here to stop me," he said deliberately. "My protection and that of Mrs. Norman has no bearing on your presence here. I know that and so do you." He allowed his words to sink in and then continued. "Now, I am willing to report to your offices in London when I return to the United Kingdom so we may clarify issues around travel documents and where I obtained them, but for now, you will have to excuse me. Good day, gentlemen." And with that he picked up his backpack and strode purposefully past both MI6 agents toward the terminal hall, not looking back at them. He didn't doubt for a moment that he would be followed, and his first task would be to lose the tail once he was able to identify it. His cell phone rang just as he was heading out and he remained inside the building to ensure better reception and reduce the noise of aircraft.

"Professor Ballantire?"

"The name is Steve." He was expecting this call. "Tomer?"

"I assume you made it alright through customs?" Steve turned back and gave the arrival hall a quick once-over, and noticed the two agents hanging around out of earshot.

"I'm impressed, Tomer. That could not have been easy to do, but I am willing to wait for an explanation at another time. Right now—"

"I intercepted another of Josh's calls, Steve."

"You have a location?" He dropped his voice down low and strained to hear the response.

"Not exactly, but there cannot be too many Sherpa camps in the vicinity of Gujrat." He paused briefly. "Do not endeavor to go up the mountain without help. I did a bit of research on your behalf, and besides appropriate clothing, which you can purchase anywhere in Lahore, you will need a Sherpa to guide you up the mountain. My information is that there is a devout group of Chong-ba's followers who live about two miles north of Gujrat in one of the villages. They are not traditional Sherpas but they know the mountain well and, according to some of my CIA informants, they are fiercely protective of him. In the last few years the authorities have largely left him alone, since he rarely comes down the mountain. But to get to his dwelling, you will need help from his supporters."

"What about Goldberg? Is he on his way there?"

"Unfortunately, that is my guess." He hesitated briefly. "I delved into his records to determine how he originally contacted Chong-ba and that is how I found out about this place. Do you know anything about their connection?"

"I don't. And right now, that is not important. I need to get to this camp and up the mountain as soon as I can."

"Then I suggest you get to Gujrat quickly and ask around in the town how to get to this camp. The town is fairly large, but you want to reach the villages on the outskirts on the northern side. Ask specifically for Chong-ba. I believe he is renowned in that particular area and someone there will know how to direct you. Then you will know that you have hit on the right village."

"Thank you for your help so far. We'll settle the matter of your protection as soon as Eva and I return safely to England. Is there anything else I should know?"

"Yes, there is." The ensuing silence made Steve wonder if their connection had been broken.

"Tomer?"

"Be very careful, Professor Ballantire. Josh Goldberg is an unpredictable and dangerous man. He has killed without reason or cause in the past. I don't know what his grudge is against you, but in his warped estimation, Eva had crossed him by taking Hugo away from him. He intends to make her pay for that. "

"But surely he knows that Hugo is useless to his cause without his mother's blessing?"

"You don't understand. Goldberg had grandiose dreams of importance and he and Hugo achieved a breakthrough no one expected shortly before Eva took her child away from him."

"Do you know what the breakthrough was?"

"It's not my field and I cannot state this as fact, but it has something to do with Hugo breaking through conscious levels of human communication and interacting with intelligence in other dimensions." A shiver ran down Steve's spine. He didn't know much about this topic, but his observation of Hugo's ability to map the stars and unravel highly complicated mathematical equations left him in no doubt that Josh recognized Eva's child as his ticket to greatness. But his rational mind nevertheless needed some form of proof.

"How do you know this, Tomer?"

"I had to repair a computer software problem for Goldberg one day and saw the graphs Hugo's brain activity had produced during some of these experiments. When I asked what those were, Josh replied that neither he nor the two scientists working with him could tell yet, since activity of that nature had never been mapped before."

"Can you see them, Hugo?" Natalie's eyes were dancing as she pointed to her winged friends waving from the low growing shrubs and foliage on the ground. But Hugo was remote. The boy appeared very withdrawn and somber as he slowly retracted into his own world again and even though it wasn't cold, he shivered visibly.

Sitting at the exact spot where he had identified the underground stream flowing beneath him, his eyes were closed and he was adrift in a sea of mathematical computations. His particular talent had evolved to grasp physics in more than one dimension and he was adept at using and developing partial derivatives and differential equations. Hugo was a past master and easily grasped the linear, separable ones derived and solved in the 18th and 19th Centuries by people like Laplace, Green, Fourier, Legendre, and Bessel.

It was Josh Goldberg who had first noticed that the boy's seclusion from the outside world had enhanced his perception and insight tremendously and moved him past this point some time ago. But now, as he drifted deeper and deeper into the stillness, he was in search of a sound, a color or a shape alien to the world he had come from. He waited patiently, convinced that when it presented itself, it would inevitably be an otherworldly mathematical equation.

He shook visibly from the cold as his body temperature began to drop rapidly, but his mind remained highly alert and primed. The answer, the revelation was tangible and within reach—he could feel it, but he consciously disallowed the excitement to materialize; he knew that any show of emotion could spoil it all. Then in a split second it was there and the boy's mouth opened in astonishment as the information flashed like lightning across the screen of his mind. Incredulous, he tried to capture it again, but was met with a vacuum as the equations pointing to the star gate were instantly erased; leaving him staring into a white desolate landscape. But he had recognized the channel opened by the star gate, making it possible to communicate with the eagle directly. A closely guarded secret, the interconnectedness of the Universe had been demonstrated. If the channel hidden by the star gate could be identified, communication on all levels was possible. He opened his eyes slowly. It didn't matter that it had lasted so briefly; he understood and he now knew what to do. Natalie was sitting on her haunches in front of him, drawing patterns in the soil with her index finger.

"Did you talk to your friends, Natalie?" He had difficulty finding his voice but needed to say something, anything, just to integrate the incredible insight he had just had. But the little girl also behaved strangely. She looked like she was going to cry. She didn't answer his question.

"Steve doesn't know where to find your mum, Hugo." Her eyes were filled with tears. "My friends say the mountain is very big and he might get lost." Then, for the first time in his existence, Hugo reached toward another human being, other than his mother, to display physical affection and touched her cheek softly with the back of his hand.

"Do not cry, Natalie," he whispered, "Steve will know where to go."

"How?" She was also whispering.

"The eagle will show him. I found a way to communicate with the bird. It will take Steve to my mum."

"Did you use your numbers?" Her voice was almost inaudible, but Hugo only smiled at her gaping mouth and pulled her to her feet.

"Let us go home, Natalie."

Steve spotted the tail that was put on him without any difficulty. The two men who met him at the airport dallied around until they saw him get into a taxi and then followed him in another one to the Holiday Inn in central Lahore. He didn't care and pretended not to notice them at all. Physically he was exhausted from the long flight and he needed to get some rest before the next day. His plans were already made and he would give them the slip when they least expected it.

After an energizing shower he ordered refreshments to his room.

He was waiting for dinner to see if his cab driver had come up with a solution regarding his short stay at the hotel. For the first time since he had left Ocean View, Steve retrieved the feathers of the owl and the eagle and placed them on the bed; they looked odd and out of place. He remembered Natalie's words that these would protect him and Eva and his heart lurched at the thought of the dark-haired woman who had so completely taken hold of his heart and his life. He ran his fingers lightly over the feathers and then returned them to his backpack.

He needed to remain sharp and alert, knowing that the next few days would dramatically impact his life and that of the woman he loved so much. Tomer had cautioned him that he couldn't afford a single mistake and he had every reason to believe him. The slightest misstep would result in victory for his opponent and somehow Steve sensed that the battle had been fought and lost many times before, but that this was a rare opportunity for them to be delivered from the past completely. He didn't know from whence the thought came, but intended to make good on it, realizing that for the first time his rational mind didn't demand an explanation for a fantastic notion.

He smiled crookedly. Hugo's quirkiness seemed to be rubbing off, but he was happy with it. He cared for the boy as much as he loved his mother. And that alone was a wonderful thought.

Chapter 28
Into The Darkness

Josh pushed a plate of food in front of Eva and then sat down opposite her before he unceremoniously got stuck into his breakfast, not giving her so much as a glance. Eva choked at the sight of the traditional breakfast of Halva Puri. What she was expected to eat consisted of two separate dishes. There was Halva—a sweet, made from semolina and Aloo Cholay, and a spicy chick-pea and potato curry, eaten with Puri, both served with deep-fried flat bread.

The seating in the restaurant consisted of narrow wooden tables and chairs placed in close proximity, and the air was heavily infused with the suffocating smell of curry, coriander, cumin, ginger and other conventional spices. She could barely breathe. The presence of Josh Goldberg was so overpowering that she had to put a tentative hand to her mouth, nauseated by his constant and overbearing company. She didn't look at the man sitting across from her and made no attempt to eat.

"You had better get some sustenance. The day will be long and hard." He didn't bother to look at her while he ate and she remained frozen. Eva felt weighed down with the magnitude of what faced her, and her mind was strangely blank. She felt unusually lethargic and was convinced that if she made the decision to get up and tried to flee, she would not have the strength to do so; after all, where would she go? No matter how hard she tried, it was impossible to determine Josh's ultimate motive for dragging her with him and Anchov into the mountains.

Although he barely mentioned Tom, she knew her husband was somehow part of Josh's equation. She suspected that in a bizarre way he wanted to reveal to Tom her relationship with Steve; branding her as a scarlet woman. But in the back of her mind the fear had started to grow that what Josh was scheming also involved Steve, and his diabolical plan would rival and surpass the most evil mind in wickedness. She stared at the food in front of her without touching it and shuddered involuntarily at what the future could hold.

"God, Eva! Don't test me." He dropped his voice deliberately and she closed her eyes, not wanting to meet his stare. "You should be grateful to me because last night was hard enough." There was a strange quality in his voice that she had not heard before but she kept her head bowed, listening against her will. "It would have been so easy to punish you. Don't you know that?"

He remembered the elegant curve of her back which she turned to him as soon as she went to bed in the clean but sparsely furnished room. The facility was advertised as the Mountain Gateway Motel, but it was a lot more primitive than its description suggested. Consisting of three modest separate single story buildings constructed mainly of timber, it was reputed to be an established watering hole for serious mountaineers and day tourists alike.

Their room had two narrow single beds and as soon as she had had a chance to wash in one of the two communal bathrooms all the guests had to use, she returned to the room while Josh constantly shadowed her and went straight to bed, facing the wall. He stared at her still form for a long time, deeply frustrated and angry as he deliberated his limited options, constantly mindful of his own shortcomings. Finally he begrudgingly resigned himself not to go near her. But where she sat opposite him, he was intensely aware of her withdrawn posture and in a disturbed way he suddenly wanted her gratitude for the mercy he thought he had shown her.

"I watched you sleep last night and wondered if you knew that at any moment I could have—"

"You're lying." She didn't raise her voice but when she lifted her head to look at him, the dispassionate stare surveying her captor was very cool. "You could have harmed me so many times since you abducted me, but you haven't." She held his gaze and didn't blink, not stopping to question the wisdom of taking on Josh in earshot of others and especially Dmitri sitting at the next table over from them. "What does punishment mean, Josh?" she asked deliberately, unaware of the source of her courage, enabling her to talk to him like this. And then she purposely leaned forward and whispered into his face. "You cannot afford to injure me, because then I will be a liability to you and you will run the risk of blowing your cover. I'm sure you want me in one piece, or at least for now. What else could you do to me?"

She noticed that he had stopped eating and had become very quiet. His head had dropped like a bull contemplating the right moment to charge and he looked as though he could erupt at any moment into a violent outburst, even strike her, and yet she was unable to stop herself.

"Should I be grateful that you haven't raped me yet?" She raised her voice slightly and straightened her back, waiting for his response. Josh Goldberg lifted his head slowly and fixed his gaze on her while Eva watched his glare transform into the fixed stare of a snake, but she didn't balk. Acting on pure instinct and spurred on by an ancient dread, she recognized him as the serpent that had been dogging her footsteps eternally, and coiled himself about her life in so many existences. It filled her with exhaustion more intense than the physical tiredness she felt in this moment, and she sensed it was time to face him head-on, regardless of the consequences. "I know you *can't*, which is why you haven't touched me." Ignoring him deliberately, she leaned back in her chair and took the bread between her slender fingers and delicately broke it in half, watching her own actions.

"Have you lost your mind?" The astonished whisper escaped hoarsely from his parched mouth. Her words had caught him completely off guard and he was temporarily at a loss as to how to respond. But while her thundering heart threatened to drown out her voice, Eva pretended to be oblivious that she was publicly embarrassing him—a mortal sin by his book, and continued her relentless appraisal of him.

"You forget, Josh, that I know what you need to stimulate your most basic desires and cravings. And I will not provide that for you. If your warped need of sexual gratification or your compulsion for killing drives you mad, you won't get any help from me." She looked at him again; her face expressionless. "That is why you have devised this diabolical plan of dragging me into the mountains with you. You hope Steve is going to show up so you will have yet another opportunity to punish us both for the failings of your putrid and petrified soul, a weakness for which you somehow hold us responsible. Yes, you and

I are aware that although not many know how to do this, your mind has found a way to access the indistinguishable and obscure pathways leading into antiquity—from where Steve and I emerged. But so did you, unfortunately." He opened his mouth to speak, but she ignored him and continued solemnly.

"You have also discovered how deep and old our love for one another is and you are beside yourself with anger and jealousy. You, Josh, loathe the possibility that beauty, passion and true love have the power to cross all physical boundaries and shine, despite your repeated efforts to eradicate them. Your envy and hatred has been festering for eons and now the poison of it will kill you, or you will have to kill us." Her stomach was in a tight knot but she leveled her gaze with his, determined to soldier on; knowing with great certainty that the only way to force him to lose control and commit blunders was to play his game even harder than he could.

"*Jesus!*" The curse strangled in his throat and he seemed to have difficulty breathing. "You *have* gone fucking mad! Have you no idea what I can—" But she ignored his attempt to stop her and leaned across the table, her eyes boring into his while, to his utter bewilderment, her voice was suddenly soft and sweet.

"You have never heard a woman cry your name in the act of lovemaking because she couldn't bare the thought of you leaving her. *Have you, Josh?* You have never known the closeness, the warmth and intimacy of a female's body enveloping your own and felt the desperate need to remain with her; be part of her." She dropped her voice to barely a whisper. "And you have no idea of the glory of simultaneous fusion where the sensation is *so* exquisite that you no longer can tell the difference between your body and hers. *Have you, Josh?*" They stared across the table at each other and neither moved as her carefully crafted scorn found its target and mercilessly exposed the shame of his most cherished façade; his horrendous inability to be with any woman, let alone initiate or maintain meaningful physical contact.

"Shut your mouth!" He forced the incensed hiss through clenched teeth; not caring if anyone else was listening. He was momentarily naked and speechless as her words compelled him to look into the black void that was his childhood. He saw his father's merciless fist crashing against his mother's jaw; and for the thousandth time he was transported back into his six-year-old body and winced as the big hands closed over her large, maternal breasts before he felled her in loathing and utter disgust to the floor. He didn't know when exactly he had become an appreciative spectator, but he never missed a single opportunity to watch. Then he began to look forward to it.

He detested his mother's pathetic failure to defend herself, and even felt she deserved her punishment. Unbeknownst to anyone, he tracked down the man who sired him many years later and without a single word, shot him at point blank range between the eyes. He left Abe Goldberg's body for the rats to feast on and didn't look back as he casually strolled out of the gutted factory behind Ballard's rundown funeral parlor in the back streets of the Bronx.

He didn't settle the score on his mother's behalf; for her he felt only contempt. Killing his father was self aggrandizement of the highest order, an act of brutal and cold sadism to thank and outdo the man who had initiated him in the way of violence. That is when Josh discovered that delivering what he deemed to be justice, is what made killing easy and very, very sweet. After that he never again needed a reason to kill; he self righteously concluded that his own suffering had earned him the right to lord over the life and death of others.

But now, temporarily exposed by the worthlessness of his childhood that insanely spurred him on to seek self importance and recognition in any way possible, he was filled with uncontrollable rage and an unintelligible ugly growl escaped from the rot that was his terrified soul. Although he was incapable of feeling remorse or regret for anything he had done in the past, he was all the same very annoyed that she was able to see through him the way she did.

"For this you will pay dearly," he croaked hoarsely; aggrieved humiliation etched on his face. "I'm going to destroy you and enjoy every moment of it." At the adjacent table Dmitri ceased the frantic shoving of food into his mouth and looked over to them, but Josh paid him no heed.

"You'll need Steve for that. And perhaps Tom too." She resumed picking at the heavy breakfast, apparently unaffected by his threat. "Or you will have to throw me to the dogs," she nodded her head in Dmitri's direction, "and I know you want the pleasure of me suffering at your own hands. But that won't happen unless you can incite some significant violence which will only occur if you can also involve Steve." Looking past Dmitri and ignoring him as she always did, she stole a glance through the window at the busy street outside the café. "You seem very convinced that he is following us, but I'm not so sure."

"Oh, he is coming, Eva. You can be sure of that!" An ugly snarl spread across his face and he sat back in his chair, feeling confident again for the first time since she had so skillfully exposed his Achilles' heel. His mind was simultaneously razor sharp and deliciously confused as he looked at the beautiful woman across the table. He was in no doubt that he could keep his wits about him when needed. "I have only one small dilemma, gorgeous Eva. Do you want to know what that is?" He didn't wait for her reply, knowing none would be forthcoming anyway. "I cannot decide who to punish first. Should I teach Teuch a lesson for having taken my sister and caretaker as a bride and turning her against me? Or should I remind Sekayi of the torture of finding his only child ravaged and murdered by the great Bahar?" Her eyes were on him and although she tried to hide her fear, he saw it creeping back into her expression. The past and the present had merged into one continuous event, and she was acutely aware of all their prior incarnations.

He watched the play of emotion on her face and felt immensely powerful and pleased that she was finally at his mercy. He didn't tell her that their ancient names often escaped him. His sanity was slipping dangerously, but it was important to keep her believing that he was in full control. The thrill and anticipation of his planned retribution was almost enough to stir him sexually, but he forced himself to stay focused on her and the immediate task at hand.

"You're not so brave after all, are you Eva?" He leaned across the table and laid his hand against her cheek, but she flinched and turned away from him. He sneered at her obvious aversion and dropped his hand to take hers, forcing her to pay attention. "Or tell me; is it that horribly deformed child and his haughty mother I should make pay for spreading profane lies in my community? I planned to have Ann ravished by all my loyal henchmen, but that was before the cohorts of that fucking half naked witchdoctor showed up. I separated his head from the rest of his body for the insolence of fraternizing with people in my town without my permission." His voice took on a hollow, peculiar quality. "You remember that don't you, *Nathaniel*? Because I made you watch!" He noticed with glee how her mouth dropped open slightly as the shock of Sakhota's decapitation so many centuries ago instantly flooded her conscious mind. And it pleased him even more when he saw how the horror of the memory translated into visible tremors that she was incapable of controlling.

Josh coldly watched her and then he began to shake with suppressed laughter; appearing decidedly mad. Punishing this woman for past and present transgressions against him was going to be a sheer delight, for she remembered *everything*, and nothing could make his mission any more exciting or rewarding than that. His fanatical mind concluded sanctimoniously that he had clearly conquered the succession to godliness that escaped other lesser human beings. The power he felt was intoxicating and he was certain his spiritual superiority was plainly visible to all.

"It is never too late, Eva." He spoke solemnly. "Not for punishment and neither for payback." Josh Goldberg was completely at the mercy of his own greatness and generously allowed a touch of reverence to creep into his voice. "But justice demands that all sinners must pay. And I have been so patient. I've been waiting for such a long time." Then he suddenly stood as if nothing had happened. "Let's go." The spell was broken and he looked over to Dmitri. "Get to the car, Anchov. And take her with you." He kept his eyes on Eva, but it was Dmitri whom he addressed. "The rules have just changed. Teach her a lesson if she shows the slightest sign of resistance." The look he gave her was entirely devoid of any emotion. Then he purposely leaned forward and took her face between his hands, staring at her sensual mouth and whispered softly.

"You have overplayed your hand, Eva. You are no longer safe from the Russian. I have no doubt that he will enjoy having his way with you, which I will allow at your slightest provocation." Caught between his big hands, she watched in revulsion as he drew his mouth nearer and held his lips a fraction away from hers, breathing heavily into her face. "I think I will let you teach me the art of making love, Eva. *After* of course, I have disposed of your unreliable husband and slaughtered the knight in shining armor who is tracking us as we speak." He smiled maliciously and without warning pressed his lips coldly over hers before withdrawing just far enough for her to hear his faint mutter. "I assure you that you will cry my name, you *bitch*! But it won't be in ecstasy, I don't think. Your plea will be for the mercy of death. You can count on that."

Josh obtained directions from the café assistant to locate the nearest mountaineering store which could supply all the clothing and equipment needed for the journey ahead. He emerged with loose warm clothing and provisions plus a few extra packages which puzzled Dmitri. His boss had been inside the store for an inordinately long time, but he knew better than to ask questions about anything which did not concern him. He eyed the packages as Josh stashed them into the trunk of the vehicle, clueless as to their content, but he let the matter drop as his attention was once again drawn to Eva.

Since Josh had declared her free game, Dmitri had been struggling with finding an excuse to exact punishment on her. It infuriated him that despite what Josh had said, she still stubbornly refused to acknowledge him with as much as a glance, which only served to stoke his smoldering hatred of women, whom he collectively blamed for his feelings of insignificance. Since they had left the restaurant, he had been trying fruitlessly to attract her attention to let her know how excited he was about his latest assignment to keep her in line, but she steadfastly ignored him.

The inferno erupting inside him was all consuming and the big Russian knew that given the right set of circumstances, not even Josh would be able to stop him. Unlike Goldberg, who needed physical violence for sexual stimulation, the fear of his victim was enough to launch him into a frenzy of brutal rape and inevitable killing. His satisfaction did not come from the rape; the killing was the lure and ultimate reward. Snuffing the life from another human being, confirmed his personal worth and established superiority over them. After all, who in their right mind could argue the finality of death?

"Chong-ba?" The elderly man spoke softly. His eyes wandered wistfully to the car with the two other occupants and back to the tall man with the dark hair standing in front of him. He steepled his long bony fingers and kept looking at Josh over his hands before he slowly brought his palms together as if in prayer, and began making strange clicking sounds with his tongue.

Josh got the impression he was trying to see right through him and he made a real effort to keep his composure, knowing his mission could fail right here, and that it would be game over. He could not afford for that to happen, and gave the old man what he hoped was a reverent smile and put his hands together, bowing his head. *Hurry up, you ancient bastard! We haven't got all day; we have to get up this fucking mountain before the sun sets.*

It had been hard enough to track down the right camp with guides who knew enough about Chong-ba, and he was sent on a wild goose chase from the store where he bought their supplies until he finally met with an information center on the outskirts of Gujrat. Here he learned that all Sherpas were registered and it wasn't until he recalled the name of the guide that had put him in touch with Chong-ba originally, that he started making headway. The camp to which he was directed was the most remote of them all and he was annoyingly aware that it was already near midday when he pulled up in a cloud of dust to what seemed like a circle of mud huts.

Josh was conscious of the change in Dmitri Anchov since he had casually committed Eva to the Russian's altar. He couldn't help remembering the graphic descriptions of how he had disposed of Justine, and understood implicitly that he and Anchov had become rivals as he frequently caught his brooding stare on Eva's averted face. Inwardly he was seething with pent-up frustration but he forced himself to control his breathing, keeping his eyes on his shoes.

The old man shook his head slowly from side to side and then called something incomprehensible over his shoulder, keeping Josh in his sight all the time. Almost immediately more scrawny and stern-faced people crept like shadows out of the woodwork to form a circle around him. Goldberg didn't look up until he heard the gentle voice of a man standing to his right.

"You know Chong-ba, sir?" Josh carefully raised his head to meet the clear soft eyes of the younger man and, without missing a beat, smoothly added a Middle Eastern accent to his speech.

"I do. He came to England not so long ago to meet with Mrs. Norman, whose husband I believe is still with him here in the mountains?" The imperceptible nod of the guide was only the slightest acknowledgment, and Josh continued in a subdued voice. "My wife and I promised to make a journey into his world on our scheduled visit to Pakistan. That is why we are here." He smiled. "Chong-ba didn't leave an address. He indicated that someone would show us the way."

"You follow his teachings, sir?" Da-nu wondered at the unusual number of visitors to Chong-ba in the recent past and contemplated if this was an indication that their revered spiritual teacher might be leaving them soon. Everyone knew of the tall Westerner, living and studying with Chong-ba, especially after a robe had been acquired for him. However he was still mindful of Chong-ba's request not to allow different parties to ascend the mountain at the same time.

"Not yet, but we are most intrigued with his point of view." Josh was aware that everyone in the circle was listening, although he wasn't sure how many of them followed English. "My name is Ishmael Khaznawi." He pulled the forged passport from his breast pocket and held it out. "I am the Jordanian Cultural Attaché and I'm here with my wife and personal secretary." The man ignored the passport, waving his hand in polite dismissal and looked over to the vehicle, raising his eyebrows quizzically.

"They are in the car?"

"Yes, sir. I wanted to make sure we had come to the right place first, but as you can see we are already dressed appropriately for the climb." He looked around him at the remote location of the camp and the obvious absence of other tourists. "I hope that our efforts are not in vain." The dwellings were humble rural homes built in close proximity to each other, where speckled chickens scratched around in the dirt and a few long tailed dogs of indistinguishable breed, lazed about in the sun. Josh realized these people did not receive a lot of visitors and everyone was subjected to a healthy dose of suspicion.

"Chong-ba does not come down the mountain often, sir. He invited you?" Josh immediately recognized his opportunity, remembering the name of the guide he was told would accompany Tom to the monk.

"I was told to ask for Da-nu?" He allowed time for his words to sink in. "The Normans are old friends of ours." He pointed to the vehicle where Eva had wound the window down and was listening to Josh spinning his fantastical yarn. He glared, warning her not to contradict him. "And my wife and I are most anxious to learn more about his special way of meditation. We all are. Perhaps he will consider bringing his wisdom to my country?"

"I am Da-nu." The speaker's voice remained gentle.

Eva contemplated making a break for it by just opening the door and running toward these strangers to alert them to the looming danger. But she remembered this madman's threat to have her mother and sister killed. She couldn't take the gamble that he could reach them despite any protection that had been offered by Stanway, and restrained herself as hope sprang eternally in her bosom; there was always the chance that Steve would find her. Josh was certain he was on his way, and she hoped that he was right since he had demonstrated a few times that he was capable of accessing all kinds of information. She knew Goldberg was a madman, but his special brilliance was to hide his instability and access more than one reality, which gave him an unfair advantage over anyone who dared to cross him.

The journey up the mountain began in earnest a half-hour later and soon the enclosed camp disappeared from sight. They struck out in single file after a mule had been packed with all their belongings as well as the mysterious packages Josh had bought in Gujrat. He couldn't care less that the young man who did all the talking and who was leading them along an almost indistinguishable pathway, expressed his concerns that the cabin in the mountain was too small for so many visitors. He overcame that objection by assuring him that they were not staying that long and would endure discomfort for a short while in order to benefit from the monk's presence and wisdom.

They maintained a fairly good pace, traversing along the foot of the mountain, but soon they left the even terrain behind and began to gain altitude. Eva looked back over her shoulder to see if she could make out where the base camp was, but if it was still visible, the landscape had swallowed it completely. Then she looked up at the snow-capped peaks and wondered how far they were going to climb. She also knew with dreadful certainty that her abductor planned to become her executioner. Even though she could never match him physically, she had to rely on all her mental strength to beat him at his own game. She had no idea how she would accomplish that, but for the first time saw value in the overweight Russian who was trudging laboriously behind the mule. As soon as the rugged slopes became more of a challenge, he had started to breathe very heavily and began to hang back. Eva welcomed anything that slowed down their steady climb, for she too felt pangs of breathlessness.

Perhaps there was a way in which she could play the two men off against one another, and remove herself from Josh's immediate firing range. She was also counting heavily on the possibility of forming a united front with Chong-ba and Tom. She was unsure of how Tom would react to seeing her after such a long time, but she also knew that the meeting was inevitable and that it was perhaps for the best.

Then she noticed the eagle that had been circling around them the previous day. It soared directly above them, riding the thermal cushions, as if watching and waiting. And then, amidst the incredible uncertainty of what lay ahead, she was nevertheless momentarily filled with new hope. She remembered Hugo's promise as a small child that one day he would help reveal the real meaning behind the shapes and colors. Was the eagle a sign of anything? She hoped so but just didn't know anymore.

She almost missed the feather lying unobtrusively in the short, sparse grass and stopped to pick it up just in time. She didn't know what bird it belonged to but its presence increased her optimism. She carefully stuck it into an elastic band that held her hair in a ponytail, knowing that Josh would notice and that it would incense him. He was aware of the significant presence of two specific feathers over many centuries, and just the sight of any feather in her possession would anger him. As she expected, he did notice and the cold stare he gave her convinced her that he understood the meaning of her action, but she also knew that he wouldn't dare to cause a scene before they reached their destination. Everything was dependent on Da-nu remaining oblivious to the nature of their mission.

Eva wondered at the ability of the mule to navigate some of the difficult slopes they were scaling, but soon realized that it was trained to ascend these tricky heights. It seemed completely at ease despite the dangerous environment, and although the guide switched positions to take charge of the animal as they approached a narrow and hazardous rock ledge, it seemed completely trusting of its handler. The guide explained that this ledge was the only pathway that led to Chong-ba and cautioned everyone not to look at the sheer drop as they carefully shuffled their way along the jagged, unsafe pathway leading to the seclusion of the monk's home.

Da-nu insisted that no one could walk behind the mule at this point, except him. He indicated that Eva take up position in front of him as the two bigger men would need all their skill and attention to focus on the path. As she watched Josh and Dmitri cautiously begin to move forward, Eva suddenly knew with great certainty that Josh was right and that Steve was in pursuit of them. But she also remembered from the conversation at base camp that this guide, Da-nu, was only one of a few who accompanied strangers to the monk, and she hoped that at least one of them would be around to show Steve the way.

There was no hesitation as she pulled the feather out of her hair and while she and the guide waited for the other two men to make significant headway before they followed, she turned carefully around and stuck the feather upright in a soft patch of soil on the side of the mountain, right where the dangerous pathway began. Then she gathered a few loose pebbles and dry sticks and packed these around the base. It wasn't very obvious at all, but she hoped that Steve would see it.

When she had finished, she caught the guide's puzzled stare on her. If ever there was an opportunity to cry for help, this would be it, but Eva knew the guide couldn't assist in settling a score that was countless centuries old. The kind man watching her had no part in this encounter and she didn't plan to hook him innocently into it. Events over millennia had led her, Steve and Josh to this point and she knew with great certainty that they were all about to take their place on the final battlefield. She smiled at the guide and turned away quickly.

"It's for good luck," she said. He nodded slowly, not taking his eyes off her. Eva knew the guide was aware of the lie, but it couldn't be helped. After navigating the rock ledge, Josh reclaimed his position behind Eva but was forced to focus on the steady and difficult climb toward the monk's cabin in the sky. Eva was constantly in his sight. He knew his control was slipping, but he didn't need to speak. As of yet, no one could plainly discern his mounting madness as her physical form appeared to interchange relentlessly with that of the striking young woman who was sister to Mautotl in ancient times.

He did not see her beauty; he saw a thief, a witch who stole his pot of lentil soup by being born first, thereby denying his right to become the natural successor to his father's rule. *She* was the one who had robbed him of future glory and the chance to showcase his inborn brilliance. It was *her* fault that he had to keep the company of shadows and demons. Ironically, in this life a remote chance existed to redeem himself through the unique talents of her son whose magnificence *he* had discovered, but she had even torn that from his hands. And for that he would make her pay dearly. Watching her narrow hips move as she labored to keep pace with them, her name came to him again, for it kept slipping through the holes in his consciousness. *Anacaona!* He suppressed an angry shriek as his sanity partially returned. He had sent henchmen to take her life then, but this pleasure would be all his. The anticipation of it was almost unbearable.

Although Dmitri was sweating and breathing heavily, he noticed his boss's wavering stability and felt his chance approaching ever closer to teach this haughty bitch her final lesson in life. His only obstacle was Josh, but he reckoned he could outsmart the crazy bastard when he lost his wits again, the signs of which the Russian read very accurately. Having never been a planner in his entire life, the dilemma of what to do with Tom and the monk didn't cross his mind. He was too enthralled with punishing Eva Norman, a long overdue task, and he was growing very impatient. Dmitri was not capable of understanding his compulsion. Killing was undoubtedly the most nefarious of all addictions.

"This is far enough, sir." Josh almost didn't hear the guide. He forced his mind back to reality and pretended to listen politely. The guide indicated that the cabin was no further than three levels of winding and twisting turns above them and he would only take them to the second last level from the cabin. From there on they would have to make their own way. This suited Josh as the guide would be going back to his village with information that the journey had gone without a hitch and that would ensure that none of the elders would sense any danger and be eager to reach Chong-ba. He held his excitement in check.

At the penultimate level, Da-nu told him that Chong-ba would signal with smoke when it was time for them to be led down the mountain again. The mule was relieved of the packing and the weight of it distributed between Josh and Dmitri. Then the guide was gone, taking the mule with him. The landscape had thinned out considerably and there was no substantial foliage or shrubbery to be seen. The only visible trees were near a formation of rocks at the foot of a steep cliff. Josh slowly approached the trees and the sight that met his eyes as he peered between the cluster of rocks sent a shock through his body, but he didn't make a sound.

It took a few seconds before he recognized Tom Norman although the twisted orange robe and shaven head surprised him somewhat. The other man's identity was a mystery and it didn't take a genius to know that a scuffle of some sort had sent these two to their rather brutal ends. He looked up toward the cliff top from where they had obviously fallen and realized that the cabin would be very near. Without a word, he quickly made his way back to his waiting party and waved them on to their final destination.

They saw the cabin simultaneously. It looked quiet and deserted and all three knew instinctively no one was inside. There was no faint smoke rising from the chimney to indicate that the home fires were burning. *Where is Tom?* Eva panicked and hung back nervously, watching as Josh called Dmitri over to a steep precipice behind the cabin. They appeared to be in deep conversation, pointing down toward the bottom of the ravine.

"Are you sure it's him?" she heard Dmitri ask. The Russian leaned a little further over to take a closer look and without warning, Josh skillfully crashed a clenched fist into the side of Dmitri's temple. Anchov was instantly stunned and robbed of the ability to scream as Goldberg shoved him hard over the precipice to join the small ensemble of corpses at the foot of the cliff. Eva was too shocked to utter a sound for it all happened so fast, but she clasped a hand in horror over her mouth, backing instinctively away from another cold blooded killing. But Josh looked at her and spoke as if nothing had happened.

"Not to worry, Eva," he said, waving her over to his side. "Anchov is in good company. Come look for yourself." She had no choice but to do his bidding and edged her way closer to him, shaking uncontrollably. She had to play for time until Tom and Chong-ba showed up. But Josh grabbed her impatiently by the hair and dragged her so she could see where he was pointing. Peering over the side while he held her, her heart stopped in her throat at the gruesome sight. Three men were sprawled out, one impaled on a branch and another caught in the crevice of two big rocks; the third was obviously Dmitri.

"Who are those people?" The bodies were too far down for her to identify, but Josh seemed to know. Gripped by an enormous fear she desperately tried to pull away from him, terrified at the sight of the mangled bodies and incapable of letting her mind consider the horrific possibility of what she was seeing.

"Take a good look, Eva. Don't tell me you don't recognize him? Does the shaven head and monk's outfit really fool you?" He held her head in position and forced her to keep looking. "It's *Tom*, Eva!" He began laughing, enjoying the consternation on her face. "The quasi monk caught between the rocks is your beloved husband whom you have been cheating on!"

"You're lying!"

"No, Eva. That is Tom. Who the other unlucky bastard is, I don't know. But that is Tom." His voice was suddenly ice cold. She turned her eyes slowly from his expressionless face and stared down at the body again. And then she knew with dreadful certainty that he was right and she screamed her husband's name over and over.

"Tom! Oh my God, Tom!" Blinded by tears, she clasped a shaky hand to her mouth as her stomach violently began heaving. How could this have happened and who was the other man? "Tom!" The stare Josh fixed on her was neutral and dispassionate.

"You're upset that Tom is dead, Eva? Now that surprises me! Don't you have a boyfriend? Besides, *your* fun has not been spoiled. Mine has! I would have loved to have sent Tom Norman to his end, but now I shall have to concentrate on my two arch rivals." His voice took on an eerie quality and he looked feverish as he pulled her face closer to him, still holding her. "Remind me of your ancient names again," he demanded menacingly. "I forget all the time what you and Steve were called, but I know that you know. I want you to tell me the names and then I will let you confess your sins. The names, Eva!"

"Let go of me! You are hurting me!" But Josh had slipped back into the murkiness of his iniquitous past where there was no reason, and mercy was never discussed, for no one knew the meaning of it.

"*Teuch and Anacaona!*" He yelled at the top of his voice, making the breakthrough once again. "Jesus Christ! My day has finally arrived!" Then he pulled her away from the cliff's edge and dragged her to the cabin. If the monk was waiting and watching, he didn't care, for he would break his goddamned neck like a twig! He felt every bit as mighty and unstoppable as any deserving god should. But when he kicked the door open, he was greeted by the cold embers of a dead fire and two thin mattresses with neatly folded blankets, a few pots and pans, and a hand carved wooden box that served as a small pantry. Eva hadn't stopped shaking and she was sobbing openly. She didn't know what she had expected, but she was completely unprepared for the horror at the foot of the cliff. In denial and in complete shock at the sight of Tom's twisted body, she angrily turned on Josh and fiercely wrenched free of him.

"Get away from me, you monster!" she screamed at the top of her voice. "Take your filthy hands off me!" His sudden release of her caused her to lose her balance and she stumbled backwards against the wall of the cabin and leaned exhausted against it, letting out desperate dry sobs. "Don't you dare lay a hand on me, Goldberg! Not now or ever again!" Her words sounded like the forlorn howl of a lost soul, but she didn't care. She was too overwhelmed with the magnitude of Tom's death *and* being in Josh's evil presence. *Steve! Chong-ba! Who can help me?* She knew she had to play for time, but her mind was frozen and devoid of its characteristic common sense. Eva felt completely powerless as she and Josh Goldberg stared at each other for what felt like an eternity. Then a strange light came into his eyes and he took a step closer, disregarding her feeble warning not to come near.

"Ah, but you are doing this all the wrong way, Eva!" He sounded almost disappointed. "Don't you see that? Your opposition of me will bring on my desire, which will end in killing you! And death cannot come too soon!" He turned angrily away. "It is too merciful and too easy! We must wait for Steve!"

"No!" she screamed at the top of her voice. "I won't let you do that to him!" Through the tears she tried desperately to bring him into focus. "You will have to kill me first!"

"You won't let me do this?" he asked softly, walking right up to her and taking her face between his hands again. "You think you are in a position to dictate anything?" He stared at her tear-stained face without any compassion. "You think you can force my hand by resisting me so I will lose control?" He squeezed her face harder. "Not in a million years will I let you thwart my plans." Then he let go of her and left the cabin abruptly. Eva reached a tentative hand to where he had bruised her cheeks but before she could contemplate her next move, he strolled back carrying some of the packages they had brought with them. "For one thing," he said without looking at her as he ripped the paper off the first parcel, "we're going to tie you up and shut that busy mouth of yours. And then we will organize a welcoming party for our honored guest."

Much later that night, while he snored away, she sat uncomfortably on the other mattress with her hands firmly bound behind her back and her mouth tightly gagged. He had succeeded in stopping her from provoking him. She didn't know what she had thought earlier that day when she saw him undoing the parcel and noticed the rope and the knife. She only knew instinctively that she had to get away from him and took off from where she leaned against the wall and made a wild dash for the door. But just as she had done centuries ago in Africa, she misjudged the size of the man and his agility, as he caught her in flight and spun her around. He laughed and took pleasure in subduing her wildly thrashing body before he drew her to his chest and brutally forced her hands behind her back.

"Where do you think are you going, little sister? Off to join Tom perhaps?" he breathed into her face. "Your day of reckoning is here, but I will decide when to snuff your light out. *Not you!*" By the time she was tied and gagged, Eva knew Josh had lost all touch with reality. He had begun muttering to himself and didn't make eye contact with her at all. It was as though she wasn't even there. A few times he got up and walked out, looking in all directions, but returned without saying a word. He was waiting for Steve. He and she both knew that he was on his way. When dusk began to fall he came inside to sleep, knowing Steve could not come during the night. Eva sat quietly staring at the slowly darkening landscape through the door that had been left ajar.

It was as though a widow's veil had been drawn across the Himalayas as, one by one, the shadows diffused to melt into the greater darkness of the night and she was left with nothing but loneliness and despair.

They were faced with an evil that had started with Mautotl, but lived again in Bahar and William, to finally manifest in the wicked persona of Josh Goldberg. It appeared as though the forces of darkness were determined to eradicate the bond that existed between her and the man she had loved for so long. Eva closed her eyes and waited desolately for daylight. It was still a long way off, but with the coming of the dawn, she knew with dreadful certainty that all the players of this incredible cosmic drama of love and devastation would be present.

The battlefield had been prepared and as the darkness of the night intensified under the heavy cloud cover, hiding a bejeweled night sky, the mountain seemed to wait quietly with her. Over millions of years it had witnessed many accidents and deaths, but it sensed a special kind of danger in the form of the one who slept and an infinite sadness in the tears of the woman who wept.

But of course it couldn't help. It was only a mountain.

Chapter 29
Code Of Honor

The bed was lumpy and too small for his tall frame, but Steve knew that even if he were not cramped into this tiny room, he would not have slept anyway. His mind was weighed down with the enormity of his mission and the uncertainty of it. Most of all he could not escape Eva's image which haunted him during his waking hours and followed him into his dreams. Once or twice he blindly reached for her in his sleep, but came up empty handed, realizing that his need of her had begun to erase the subtle lines between reality and illusion.

Steve lifted himself off the uncomfortable bed and walked over to the window where he peered through the grimy curtain, noticing the taxi parked about two hundred meters away from the rear of the Holiday Inn. He surveyed the entire street carefully, but there was no movement. Assuming that everything was going according to plan, he pushed away some of the dirty clothing belonging to the room occupants and scooped some water onto his face from a bowl he found in the tiny kitchen area. Under different circumstances he would have been very irritated in such clutter, but he barely noticed the mess around him and focused all his attention on the day ahead. He wondered if he would manage to get to his final destination and if he would be successful in finding the woman of his dreams.

Steve questioned the man who had delivered him to the hotel about the availability of a very early morning collection for the following day. When asked to be taken to Gujrat, the driver looked at him in the rear view mirror and immediately smelled a hefty tip. Despite the casual clothing, his experienced eye summed up a distinguished looking man with plenty of money, and since he bartered his way through life, he knew he had to play it cool and not seem overanxious. He kept his eyes casually on the road and looked back to make eye contact with his passenger only briefly to confirm his interest in the discussion.

"Gujrat is far. One hundred and twenty kilometers." He said it solemnly and slowly, allowing the words to sink in.

"One hundred British Pounds." Steve caught the quick movement as the driver's eyes darted back to him, but he pretended not to notice and dropped his voice a little. "That is around twelve thousand Rupees. Is that right?" He said it softly and it was not as much a question as it was confirmation of the small fortune being offered. Bartering flew right out of the window, but just for effect the driver put a little frown between his bushy gray eyebrows as he realized the money equaled two months of work. He kept his face expressionless and began to hum some incomprehensible Hindi song, knowing that his passenger was aware that he had already taken the bait. Steve waited patiently, knowing that the driver would move heaven and earth to accommodate his every need. And he needed an enthusiastic assistant who could help him give the slip to the pursuing MI6 agents. He also had to get to Gujrat in the shortest possible time.

"One more thing," he kept his voice even but realized that he could virtually ask anything of this man, who was already in his pocket. "I have people following me and I need to throw them off my track. The details are irrelevant; I will book into the hotel, but I want to switch rooms unobtrusively with someone who works and sleeps there. Can you help with this?" The driver immediately thought of the porter, a tall thin man who occupied a small room at the back of the hotel together with his wife, who worked as a room maid. They had come from the mountains some two years ago and mostly kept to themselves.

"How much?"

"Twenty five British Pounds."

During dinner that evening, a lanky man dressed in a porter's uniform approached his table and put his hand to his ear indicating that there was a call waiting and that he needed to follow him. But instead of going into the foyer, he veered off into a narrow passageway leading to the back of the hotel. At the end of the corridor he stopped to unlock a tiny room and stood aside for Steve. The dark-skinned porter was about his height and although he smiled constantly, he never made eye contact. Then he respectfully held out his hand for Steve's room access card.

As Steve placed the card in his hand, he also counted thirteen Pounds from his wallet. As agreed, he would leave the rest of the money in the room to be collected the next day and he couldn't help but marvel at the creativity of people where money was involved. Then the door closed behind him and the only thing he could do was to lie down on the uncomfortable bed and wait as the evening dragged slowly by. He kept his eyes closed but was still awake at the first streaks of daylight.

Steve knew that MI6 would have his position pinned down in no time, and that they would either be staying at the same hotel or be keeping surveillance from a respectable distance. On foreign soil, they would not have the eavesdropping facilities at their disposal; so easy to install when the right infrastructure was in place. On such short notice he suspected that they probably had some activity device focused directly at his room, which would be picking up the movements of the porter as he enjoyed the luxury that it offered.

At 5am Steve quietly closed the door of the porter's quarters behind him. Dressed somewhat awkwardly in the hotel uniform of his accomplice, he strolled casually down the corridor and made for the back entrance. He was not convinced the disguise was quite necessary, but decided not to take any chances, as he tucked the packet, containing his own clothes, under his arm. Once outside, he crossed the street leisurely and headed toward the waiting taxi. If all were still going according to plan, it would be around breakfast time before the bloodhounds would realize that they had lost his scent.

The rest of the beehive that was Lahore seemed unnaturally quiet at this time of day, but the street vendors were already drifting in slowly as they began to prepare for a busy day of commerce. For the locals, the smell of the city never changed and the pungent aromas only varied in intensity from the quiet of the night, to when food was being prepared in makeshift sidewalk kitchens. Inside the taxi, Steve turned to his driver.

"Did you get my jacket and thick sweater?" The driver had his arm along the back of his seat as he quietly surveyed his passenger's attire. The man in the turban pointed to the package beside his customer. Steve lifted his hand in acknowledgment.

"Can we go?" The driver didn't wait for a reply. He knew this man was in a hurry and with the first half of his hundred pounds already in his pocket, he was anxious to deliver him to his destination and collect the balance. Then he planned to take a whole month off to enjoy his good fortune. For all he cared, his bearded brethren could serve the whims and wants of the countless Westerners who constantly swarmed across their borders, while he took a well deserved break.

As soon as they hit the Trunk Road, Steve leaned back and closed his eyes and, as always, she was immediately before him. *Eva, don't let him lay a hand on you. Hold on!* Gujrat is an ancient district of Pakistan located between two famous rivers, the River Jehlum and the River Chenab. Because of its proximity to water, the land lends itself exquisitely to cultivation of rice and sugar cane, but Steve hardly noticed. It was just after six thirty in the morning when they approached the outskirts of the town, which was already about its day. Gujrat is known for its clay with which the Gujratis have produced quality pottery for many ages. At the outskirts of the town the taxi driver stopped at the stall of a clay vendor to ask directions to the camp of the Chong-ba supporters.

"Luck must be on your side," said the driver shifting in behind the wheel again. "The woman who mixes the clay here is one of the monk's most devoted followers. She explained the way."

The cluster of unassuming huts was located at the foot of the mountain and they appeared dull and uninviting. Except for the thin wisp of smoke trailing from one or two roofs into the bleak morning air, there didn't seem to be much activity at all. The taxi driver was eager to get back to Lahore. The gods had smiled on him thus far and he wanted nothing at all to spoil his good fortune. As soon as he had confirmed that they were at the right location, he dropped Steve off and with the other half of his money in hand, quickly disappeared in a dust cloud down the dirt road.

The thin figure in the doorway of the hut didn't move as he surveyed yet another stranger to enter into their sacred circle in the span of only two days. Something very odd was going on. His eyes were expressionless as he waited for Steve to notice him. When he finally did and lifted his hand respectfully in greeting, the man in the doorway responded by disappearing into the shadows of the interior and reappeared with three other people. All wore solemn expressions.

Twenty minutes later, Steve realized that the magnitude of the problem he faced was almost as big as the mountain he needed to ascend. In the circle of curious onlookers who had all crept from their houses to stand around him, no one was fluent enough in English to converse. They all seemed to recognize Chong-ba's name but instead of assisting him, they closed ranks and just looked at each other, shaking their heads. Steve tried to hide his frustration. Despite the fact that no discernible communication had been exchanged, he was sure that he had arrived at the right place but, looking at the vastness of the mountain in front him, he knew that any attempt to find Chong-ba's dwelling without knowing where he was going would be insanity.

"Sir?" Steve turned to find a much younger man standing quietly behind him. He had no idea where he had come from but he was much more interested in his apparent command of the English language.

"Hello." He smiled at the man, who looked him straight in the eye. "My name is Steve Ballantire and I hope you can assist me?"

"How, sir?" He didn't move or take his eyes off Steve. "We are simple people. What do you need?"

"I must find Chong-ba." The young man's eyes narrowed, but he kept himself composed.

"I'm afraid that is not possible."

"Why?"

"Chong-ba does not want different parties visiting him at the same time. He is very strict about that. There is a small group with him now." Steve's heart lurched in his chest.

"When did these people arrive?" The young man ignored Steve's question.

"I am Da-nu. I showed the visitors the way to Chong-ba's hut. You must wait until they return." Steve nodded his head slowly.

"Was there a dark-haired woman in the group?" Again Da-nu did not answer the question directly.

"The latest visitors said they were invited by our teacher when he went to England. And they knew my name." He pointed toward a rental parked under a nearby tree. "That is their car."

"I can't wait, Da-nu." Steve spoke softly but kept his eyes on the guide. "My business is urgent. Can someone else show me the way?" Da-nu watched as Steve began to pull a sweater over his shirt, staring openly at the emblem on his chest.

"You follow the way of the eagle, sir?" he asked softly. Then Steve noticed the crest of an eagle in full flight emblazoned on the front of his sweater. For a few seconds he remained speechless, aware that all eyes were on him. He had not seen the design until a few seconds ago. Steve ran a tentative hand over the front of the sweater and felt strangely moved by something he could not explain. Could this all be just a coincidence? He had no way of knowing just yet. Then he reached into his backpack and pulled out the feathers and held them for the Sherpa to inspect, vividly recalling Natalie's advice to take them with him for protection. Da-nu made no effort to take them, but instead lifted his hand and beckoned Steve to follow. When they were well out of earshot, the Sherpa stopped abruptly and turned to look at Steve.

"I am bound by my word not to mix visiting parties. I must honor that promise. The slight man had to look up at Steve as he spoke, but his expression remained unperturbed. "Chong-ba taught me to listen to my sixth sense, the same way we read the danger of the mountain when there are high winds or lots of snow. We can smell disaster long before it hits us because we have been taught to be at one with nature. That also means we know people." He looked at Steve's sweater again, focusing on the crested eagle. "But yesterday I could not read the guests and that has never happened before. The tall dark man was very convincing, but the woman kept her head down. The other man remained silent; he was not the decision maker." He looked Steve directly in the eye. "I trust you, sir. And if you cannot wait, I will tell you where to start, but you will have to make the journey yourself."

"I understand." Steve spoke the words slowly, overwhelmingly aware of the heavy beat of his heart as if he was about to participate in an important contest or dangerous game. At the same time, extraordinary emotion rushed through him and although he looked at Da-nu, his subconscious suddenly flashed a vivid image across his mind, instantly transporting him back thousands of years. He was riding a black stallion behind a caravan hauling salt down the dusty road of a very old world. Then he noticed the eagle crest carved into the hilt of his sword. His ancient persona had come alive.

Still staring at Da-nu, Steve felt the stirrings of a hunter and a warrior coarse through his blood. He calmly scanned his surroundings and his breathing became somewhat labored. Where he stood at the foot of this magnificent mountain, he didn't doubt that there was a hunter out there waiting and watching and that he would need all wits about him to win this battle. In this highly alerted state, all his senses became acutely primed and he smelled the grass beneath his feet and tasted the air. Looking into the blue sky, he spotted the circling flight of a bird. It could only be an eagle. The memory chest of the past had begun to open, and in a semi dark sky, he glimpsed two birds of prey facing off with each other. An eagle and an owl. Steve put the feathers in his shirt pocket and spoke determinedly.

"Show me which way to go, Da-nu. I will find it." In the long silence that followed, the Sherpa finally looked away from Steve and turned his gaze on the mountain.

"I believe you will." Without looking back, he began walking again. "I will take you over the first rise and from there you must pay attention to the voice of the mountain. If you listen with all your senses, you will hear it." A half hour later Da-nu stopped again and pointed toward a faint path. "Chong-ba's cabin is this way. He too honors the eagle, sir. Follow the path least taken." He put his hands together, bowed his head and then looked up to fasten his eyes on the crested emblem of the eagle. "But above all, follow your heart. The journey will take at least five hours, but you must set out now." And with those words he turned on his heel and started down the path toward the village.

Steve watched him leave with a feeling of indescribable desolation. He was at the foot of the Himalayas in search of the woman he loved and left to his own devices to find a cabin in this godforsaken mountain. Unable to move in any direction, he stood rooted to the ground for a few minutes as if waiting for something to happen. But even the wind had settled down and he watched as it ran its long wispy fingers in every direction through the grass and shrubs, confusing him about which way to go.

James Stanway took the call at breakfast the next morning and swore profusely when he learned that Steve Ballantire had slipped the net. He screamed and yelled about the gross incompetence he had to deal with, but soon realized that the steam he was letting off would not alter a thing. He hadn't heard from Colonel Appleyard for two days and not since he had learned about Eva's capture by Josh Goldberg. Stanway had no further use for Foster and Cook in Lahore, but told them nevertheless to stand by and await further instructions. He was hoping that the store on the outskirts of Lahore would shed some light on what the hell was going on with his boss. He knew it was also David Appleyard's reference point, and decided to head there as soon as possible.

With Steve gone, the bond between Natalie and Hugo seemed to be more pronounced than ever. Both children were huddled in Quah Dreamer's stable for their daily visit and they sat together on a bale of hay watching the movements of the horse as he kept stamping his hooves and snorted endlessly, shaking his head.

"What's he saying?" Natalie didn't look at Hugo. Her averted face was hidden by her golden curls and he only saw her hand movements as she lazily picked at loose strands of hay.

"Are you not the one who speaks horse language?" There was no trace of sarcasm in his voice, only slight surprise.

"I don't know what he is saying today. He is not talking to me; he is talking to you! He keeps looking at you." Hugo noticed that the state of distress of the horse seemed to increase, and Razzle was also clearly becoming unsettled in the next stable. Then he made up his mind and in his usual quiet way, stood and looked at the horse, but spoke to Natalie.

"Let us go to Thorp Pelkington and take Quah Dreamer with us. That is where he wants to be."

"Oh! Is *that* what he said?" Natalie smiled sweetly.

"Untie his tether, Natalie, and wait for me. I am going to fetch my charts." And with that he started back for the farmhouse in his usual unperturbed manner.

On the short journey back into the woods, Hugo's mind was heavily impressed with the number six which, under normal circumstances, could have been because the horse was right there, walking between himself and Natalie. But on this day he sensed there was much more to this number and he allowed the impression of it to fill his consciousness.

"It is trying to tell me something."

"*What* is, Hugo?" Natalie was used to her friend's mental explorations, and constantly asked questions, unaware that her innocent querying helped him to gain clarity.

"The number six. It is a key to something, but I do not know what."

"A key that opens something?" When she looked at him and saw him nodding, she was suddenly all excited. "Oh! Like a treasure chest?" She looked up at the magnificent animal walking between them and frowned. "You said six is a horse, Hugo!" But the boy had already entered into another world and his reply seemed to reach her from afar.

"Not today, Natalie. I did not know that sixes could unlock mysteries." His voice trailed off and he absentmindedly put his hand on Quah Dreamer's shining coat. "But somehow this horse has something to do with it."

"Oh!" She sounded as though she fully understood when in fact, even though she didn't know this, she was just giving him the opportunity to find his way through the labyrinth of energy strings he always talked about. She had never seen any of the things he spoke of, but always vigorously nodded her head. As soon as they reached the spot with the underground stream, Hugo felt the energy increasing. The horse became extremely restless and hung around the children as if it was also waiting for something to happen. The boy had his charts all lain out in front of him, and although he stared intently at them, nothing new would open up.

"Natalie…" He sounded as though he was speaking to her from inside a dream. Quah Dreamer stood in front of him rippling his muscles and showing signs of nervousness. And yet, when he concentrated on the horse, its unique number of six interchanged with another name he had not heard before.

"Natalie—who is *Spethla*?"

"A friend from the Meadow." There was no hesitation at all. She stared closely at him and her eyes took on a dreamy quality as she whispered. "His other name is Quah Dreamer." And then she smiled her most angelic smile. "Quah means eagle. Sakhota told me that. Don't you remember?"

He didn't answer, but for the first time Hugo clearly saw the treasure chest which bore the crest of a lance and a black stallion, and that is also when he realized the chest was symbolic. The first breakthrough was readily followed by the second, and he recognized the lance as that of Sakhota—*his* lance! He imagined opening the lid carefully, finding some charts inside—*his* charts! But there were a few special numbers that he had not seen before. Hugo waited patiently for the meaning to be revealed, and then a smile crept around his mouth and he knew. The secret was in the charts he had drawn himself and he would have to consult those! Something was not right.

Natalie didn't once take her eyes off him. She had noticed the gathering of her little friends under the shrubs who had come to observe, but it was to Hugo that she gave all her attention. She watched as he laid out his charts again and quietly slipped into his own world as the stillness became tangible around them. He stared at them intently, concentrating hard to find the flaw, but the answer escaped him, even though he knew the adjustment would be a simple one. Natalie leaned forward to see if she could see what he was looking at, but to no avail. He was engrossed in the sketches he had made of the interlocking hands of Steve and Eva and she had no idea what could be so fascinating about that.

"Give me your hand," he whispered.

"Are we going to do it again, Hugo?" She gave him her hand, clearly recalling the breakthrough he had made the last time he had studied their hands together. But as he linked his fingers with hers, Quah Dreamer let out a loud neigh which scared a skittish owl to rise from one of the trees and head back into the woods. Natalie closed her eyes and cringed a little in fright, but Hugo knew that despite the eeriness of the occurrence, the energy had intensified and he was moving in the right direction. An energy string had been touched and a domino effect had begun. All he had to do was to follow the direction of the flow.

He looked at his and Natalie's hands and back again to the sketch of Steve and Eva's. Something unique, extraordinary was happening. In the interconnectedness of all, the horse seemed to have registered something, but what? Hugo's own consciousness was wide open and he waited patiently without judgment or expectation for the information to reveal itself. And then slowly, he began to see possibilities that had previously escaped him.

"Whose horse is Spethla, Natalie?" His lips barely moved.

"He belongs to the warrior; the man with the eagle on his chest." For a long while he remained completely silent and then finally he spoke.

"Could this be *Steve?*" She stared wide-eyed at him, holding her breath. And then she nodded her head slowly as big tears began to form in the corners of her eyes. She didn't normally remember these things, but today, here at Thorp Pelkington where the energy is so vibrant, she suddenly knew. Steve needed help and only Hugo could possibly reach him, although she had no idea how he would do that. "Thank you, Natalie. Now I know why Quah Dreamer was so upset. He recognized his master." Sitting on the grass along with his charts, Hugo allowed himself to be still again, as the eagle gracefully glided into his inner vision. The image was even more magnificent than previously. As the bird soared above him in his mind, he remembered the strange sequence of numbers on the charts in the treasure chest. There were two—0 and 9.

They appeared in that order, and suddenly were accompanied by the three primary colors of red, yellow and blue along with their carrier number of three. Hugo kept perfectly still and waited for the revelation. The energy strings were moving, and the general flow would reveal itself in time. The figures of 0 and 9 kept drifting in and out of his consciousness until he again recalled the joined hands of Steve and his mother. And then he saw the tiny space between two symbolic fingers that represented a triangle—or so he thought.

The 09 was not an extra equation at all, but simply a symbolic minus instruction that needed to be applied to the small shape that *should* have represented a triangle. Instead of having three sides, albeit asymmetrical in shape, there were four sides, and four apexes. The zero symbolized infinity and the nine represented the point of no return—

and put together, these numbers presented a paradox. Something had to be removed; taken out of the equation! What was it?

Finally, in silence and utmost concentration, Hugo understood the significance of this monumental error and deleted the shortest, fourth side of the shape. The three primary colors immediately filled his whole being again, accompanied by the figure three, only this time the figure represented a true three-sided triangle—symbolically signifying father, mother and son. And for the first time in Hugo's existence, he too felt the physical stirrings of emotion as the tears began to flow. The triangle was a symbolic representation of himself, his mother and Steve.

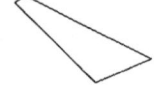

Under normal circumstances, Hugo would not have been able to cope with such a shift in mathematical reference, but today was different. He understood perfectly. A connection had finally been made. On a cosmic scale, no matter how bizarre the whole thing appeared, Hugo had found the ability to communicate between his mother and Steve. The eagle in flight represented the inside formation of their locked hands, transformed into a three-way connection, and a real eagle would lead Steve to his mother. The groundwork had been done by the children when they had visited Thorp Pelkington. It prepared the road for unfolding energies to pre-empt the boy's conscious ability—just like the bird made its presence known by circling Eva a few days earlier.

Then Hugo understood that all he had to do was to have clear purpose and wait for the eagle to rise above the horizon of his subconscious mind. Beyond the state of the intellect, in a space where it was understood, the bird could act as a go-between. He knew the pre-requisite was laser sharp intention. Then the bird would lead Steve to his mother. But it would unfortunately do more than that. It would take Steve to Eva's side, but also lead him right into the trap of his nemesis.

Steve looked at the faint mountain path Da-nu had pointed out and approached it cautiously; staring intently at the ground and the way the grass had been flattened. What was he looking for? His heart beat heavily in his chest as he went down on his haunches and closed his eyes, waiting. Then his ancient mind opened even further and he heard a familiar laugh, and every hair on his body stood on end. He recognized it instantly.

Holding onto the spell, he allowed the feeling and the memory to wash over him until his subconscious flashed a vision of her across his mind as she tore across the plains of Africa holding onto the mane of a golden stallion; her joyful laugh trailing in the wind. *Nyasha!* Every muscle in his body strained in agony and he slowly opened his eyes, feeling momentarily sick to his stomach. *Oh, my God, Eva.* It was the same laugh he had heard that first day when she stood on the steps of the administrative building. His mouth was completely dry and he had difficulty swallowing. *Anacaona, Nyasha, Eva…* How many more lives were there?

And then he knew the context *and* what he was looking for. Tracks! He was Sekayi of so many hundreds of years ago and like him, he was trying to read the markings left behind by four people, one of whom was his beloved Eva. Completely lost in reverie of the past, he didn't hear the first shriek but as the magnificent bird circled lower, he looked up and clearly heard the second call. Steve watched mesmerized, as it descended gracefully, riding the thermal cushions, coming closer and closer to the ground. He wondered if it was hunting but the bird glided silently in to perch itself atop a tree along the path Da-nu had pointed out as the one to follow.

Pure instinct drove him to cautiously move forward, but when he was within fifty meters, the bird suddenly took off and flew a short distance to perch itself in another tree. Again Steve followed vigilantly and when the same routine repeated itself for the third time, he realized that they were treading up the unclear and overgrown path to which the guide had pointed. As unbelievable as it seemed, the eagle appeared to be leading him toward a destination of some sort.

He looked down again at the crest on his chest and in that moment, ancient memories came flooding back. The eagle crest represented his father's code of honor of times gone by. His hands began to tingle as he held the feathers separately and they felt like mighty weapons of peace. He seemed to know exactly what to do with them as he placed them safely back in his pocket.

The eagle faced away from him where he sat quietly scanning some far off location. Was it possible that this was really happening? Was the bird leading the way? Then he thought of Hugo and how, despite his limitation, Eva's brilliant son seemed to have the mathematical answers to the interconnectedness of all that exists. If the bird was truly guiding him, then Hugo had accomplished a monumental breakthrough between physical consciousness and the ether. Realizing that he was trembling with excitement, Steve knew that in the given circumstances, he had to follow his instincts and trust in what he felt stirring so deeply within him. The final player was on his way, while on the battlefield, his executioner was waiting. He too, had sensed his approach and knew with great certainty that the cosmic drama was nearing its end.

Where he stood waiting and carefully scanning the area around Chong-ba's hut, Josh Goldberg took a deep breath and then began to laugh softly. Death was in the air and he could smell it!

The eagle sometimes took off and flew into the blue yonder before returning unexpectedly from a surprise angle to land on a tree top high enough for Steve to see. Regardless of the astounding magnificence of what was occurring, he was steadily making progress along a path that he knew he would never have found by himself. Three hours into his journey he spotted the bird perched high on a cliff and he questioned his own sanity.

Undecided as to what the next step should be, he remembered the children's words when Natalie had remarked that Eva's captor was taking her to "where the eagle lives" and that he should take both feathers with him for protection. But it was Hugo's words that rang in his ears as he observed the still silhouette of the bird against the blue sky. "Look for the way of the eagle as it soars, Professor. It has all the answers you are looking for."

Then Steve noticed the narrow ledge a few hundred meters beneath the cliff on which the eagle was perched and slowly walked toward its dangerous beginning. That's when he saw the feather planted in the side of the mountain supported by a few rocks, and overwhelming emotion coursed through his body as he bent down to retrieve it. She had left him a sign! He didn't doubt its purpose. And with that he set foot on the narrow ledge and began to edge his way painfully, slowly along the treacherous path.

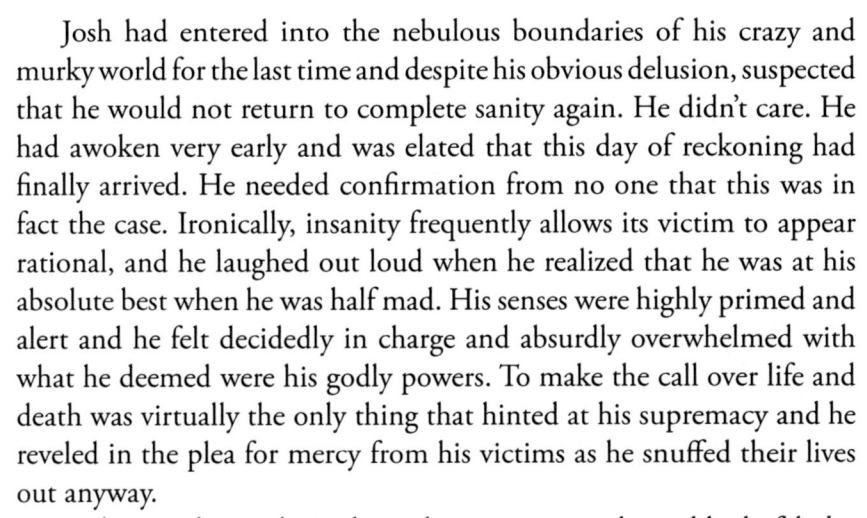

Josh had entered into the nebulous boundaries of his crazy and murky world for the last time and despite his obvious delusion, suspected that he would not return to complete sanity again. He didn't care. He had awoken very early and was elated that this day of reckoning had finally arrived. He needed confirmation from no one that this was in fact the case. Ironically, insanity frequently allows its victim to appear rational, and he laughed out loud when he realized that he was at his absolute best when he was half mad. His senses were highly primed and alert and he felt decidedly in charge and absurdly overwhelmed with what he deemed were his godly powers. To make the call over life and death was virtually the only thing that hinted at his supremacy and he reveled in the plea for mercy from his victims as he snuffed their lives out anyway.

As he stood outside in the early morning sun he suddenly felt *her* presence again and responded instantly to the fear her image always invoked. Josh began to shake uncontrollably when he turned to find the woman who had been his constant shadow for eternity. But as always, the bloodied apron of Mary, his wife of the 17th Century, disappeared just in time from his peripheral vision to drive him even crazier.

"You fucking bitch! I should have killed you long before you could take an axe to me!" He yelled at the top of his voice as he groped blindly at the ghost that had dogged his footsteps for so long, yet always escaped his murderous hands. Then he began to laugh hysterically. "Hold on, Mary! You just wait! I will be sending you that haughty snob and her deformed abomination of a son as companions before the end of this day, and perhaps then you will leave me alone, once and for all!" Breathing heavily, he looked around him and suddenly wasn't sure anymore who *he* was.

But then he remembered the woman in the cabin and stomped back to kick the door open. Eva was awake but still gagged and tied up as she stared at her captor with fearful eyes. Josh walked purposefully toward her and then bent down to unceremoniously rip the duct tape off her mouth.

"Can you feel him coming, Eva?" His sanity had briefly returned.

"Our hero is making his way here. And he is not far now. Not far at all." His voice dropped to a dangerous whisper and she had to strain to hear what he was saying. "Eva?"

"Josh, please…no one has to get hurt. Can we discuss this as—"

"Are you *insane?*" His voice was ice cold and Eva knew that his detached state was ten times more dangerous compared with him ranting and raving. "Centuries ago when you were that horribly deformed brat, I hung you and your mother because she didn't know when to show respect. She tried to *negotiate* with me when she had nothing of value to offer in return." Then he grabbed hold of her face and yanked her mercilessly closer to him, holding her centimeters away and pressed his mouth to her ear. "What do you have that I might be interested in?"

"Josh, please—"

"Answer me! What do you have that I cannot take without you or your lover's permission?" He didn't wait for a reply and pulled her brusquely to her feet, dragging her outside into the sunlight. "I've been waiting for so long. How many centuries have you humiliated me, or made me the lesser one?" He sounded as though he was going to cry.

She looked at him almost with pity in her heart and knew that there was no place for reason or mercy. Josh Goldberg had gone stark raving mad; he was a man possessed and he needed to see her and Steve suffer, for nothing else would satisfy him. She wondered forlornly what had happened to Chong-ba, but guessed that he had met his end somewhere else; their executioner had cleared the deck and systematically removed the opposition one by one. He was determined to have his day and he wanted blood.

Eva had no idea what he had in mind and she tried not to anticipate the next move for fear of facing so much evil. She wondered if Steve was really on his way and looking into the sky, noticed the absence of the eagle. Could she have been wrong about everything? All seemed lost and hopeless. And then she began to cry softly. At first he ignored her quiet sobbing while he fiddled with some of the packages they had laboriously carried with them up the mountain. Her body began to shake as grief for Tom tore through her. She was paralyzed with fear at what Josh could still do to her and Steve if he showed up.

"Shut up!" he yelled, almost completely out of control. "It is too late for tears and they won't move me! You should have considered the consequences of stealing Hugo from me before we got this far. Quit the sniveling or you'll spoil the surprise I have in store for your lover!" Then Eva knew that the only chance she had, albeit a slim one, was to co-operate as much as possible. If Steve was on his way, then perhaps they could catch this madman off guard and overpower him together. But her hope was short lived, for the next moment he grabbed hold of her and dragged her to the only tree near the cabin and, standing right in front of him, Eva stared into his black hate-filled eyes. "Does this bring back fond memories?" he asked as he flung a rope around a high branch, expertly catching and looping it tightly around her neck. In a state of complete shock, her mind froze and her blood ran ice-cold as the terror of that night near the Charles River vividly came into focus. The monster standing in front of her was no longer Josh Goldberg but had transformed into William Wainthorp. And once again she stared death in the face. She was incapable of speaking. "Now of course, we are not going to have any fun if *he* is not present. So we will wait." Then he suddenly turned away from her and picked up a bow and arrow that he had been putting together in the early morning hours while she was in fitful sleep.

Then she knew without a doubt what his plan was. He had bought this in Lahore while she and Dmitri were forced to wait outside, and it was frightfully clear that Josh Goldberg planned to re-enact all the lives that they had experienced together. He was going to make her and Steve pay for all his shortcomings in the most horrible way his twisted mind could conceive. The past and the present had merged into one and there were no more secrets. There was only waiting and hoping for the end to come quickly.

When the eagle suddenly took off and flew away, Steve realized that he was very near his destination. He stood quite still and listened carefully. It was eerily quiet. Just ahead of him there was a small cluster of rocks that drew him like a magnet, but when he came close enough, he immediately spotted the three mangled bodies and reeled back in shock. The first arrow pegged into the ground right at his feet before he had had any time to wonder who these people could be. It came like a bolt from the blue, but it was plainly aimed to warn, not to harm. There was only one direction from which the arrow could have come, and that was from the cliff above him. Steve had no doubt that he had reached the end of his journey and that he was about to meet the man he had been chasing half way around the world.

"Would you like to know who the dead are, Sir Galahad?" Steve looked up to see the silhouette of a tall man, aiming a loaded bow at him. Josh Goldberg! He was staring the enemy and death right in the face. He froze and waited without saying a word.

"One of them, looking like a dead monk, is your whore's husband, Professor. And who cares about the others?" Josh sounded almost jovial. "But you are not here for them, are you? Come on up here, and join us! I caution you to be careful though. One wrong move and I will put an arrow straight through your woman's heart."

Chapter 30
Honoring The Pact

The meaning of the arrow boring deeply into the ground was sinister and unmistakable. A heavy stillness descended upon the mountain and Steve remained immobile and guarded as, bit by bit, the familiarity of the situation enveloped his consciousness. But there was a difference this time. Thousands of years before, Teuch had been unsuspecting of the ambush, but the arrow at Steve's feet was a threat and an invitation to do battle. The man waiting at the top of the cliff wanted much more than just a cold blooded killing. He wanted to settle a score.

In those days Teuch had the crest of an eagle emblazoned on his armory and today a similar crest was displayed on Steve's sweater. His eyes narrowed in concentration. The same executioner of antiquity was present and waiting for the right moment to fire the fatal arrow. Keeping his body perfectly still, Steve had no doubt that this was indeed the day of reckoning; the ending of an epic cosmic drama, in which death appeared to be an inescapable conclusion. The boundaries of time had been eerily erased, and hundreds of years of suffering, indescribable joy and unspeakable violence were laid bare before them. None questioned the certainty of their ancient personas or the reasons for meeting on the mountain. It was equally understood.

The target was composed and calm as he slowly raised his eyes to fix upon the figure clearly etched against the blue sky with a loaded bow trained on his chest. The executioner gripped the ancient weapon with zeal and grit in an effort to belie his frantic state of mind. Still deadly accurate in his aim, he was nevertheless disappointed that his mental clarity had become so erratic. The familiar euphoria of a prospective kill lingered just below the surface, while the distracting stir in his groin threatened to throw him off balance. He forced himself to ignore the signs. His unstable mind realized that history had come full circle and that his chance would come but once. What had been set in motion so long ago demanded a conclusion, a final outcome. It was time.

"Come on, Professor! What are you waiting for?" The veiled note of hysteria in his voice did not escape his target, who still had not made a move. "Or do you want me to draw you a map? She's up here waiting for you!" He drew the bowstring tighter and an uncontrolled snigger escaped from his mouth. The thrill he felt was immense and, despite his best efforts to contain himself, his erection was growing. Swept away by the incredible power trip a killing brought on, his mind teetered precariously on the verge of a very deep black hole and while he managed to hold his hands steady, his intestines had begun quivering. *Oh, Josh, you fucking master of the Universe!* He couldn't resist the congratulatory smile; it was so well deserved! But just as he began to revel in his own greatness, he was suddenly jolted by a nagging and whining voice that had lately so unnerved him.

Who the hell is Josh? It was Mautotl of his life in early Mexica times, screaming loudly in his head. Josh grimaced inwardly. Of course, this snickering little bastard had only recently started showing up when he was sure that he, Josh, had begun to lose his grip on reality. He seemed to know when there was a bounty or a prize to be had. Mautotl wanted to claim ownership of the killing. *Like hell! I will never allow that! Fucking brat!* Josh feared the presence of this little horror, for it reminded him continually of his inadequacies and was the source of a huge power struggle within him.

Who are you swearing at, you incompetent fool? Mautotl again. *Look at who you have in your cross hairs, and you have the temerity to question my presence! You should let me take over! I know where to hit him! I did it once before and I will do it again.* Josh refocused his attention on the chest of the quiet figure below and muttered out loud.

"Shut up! I don't need your help!" Mautotl had reminded him that this was *Teuch*, the fearless warrior and tradesman who had married his sister. That was who he had the arrow aimed at! But in the next instant, Josh capitulated and leaned forward to let Mautotl take over. In the murky world of hate and retribution in which he now permanently resided since Hugo had been taken from him, he had long since lost his ability to enter the Zen state. He had become a dangerous spiritual rambler who traversed the inner worlds in an effort to punish and maim those responsible for his demise, and one by one he had systematically taken them down. In some of his lucid moments he remembered that these two, whom he had lured into the mountains, were responsible for the loss of his sanity. And for that they had to pay.

Irrationally convinced of his godly powers, he was intensely annoyed by the unsavory characters that lurked in his netherworld. The trade-off for losing his sanity was the insight he gained into the characters of his dangerous spiritual alter egos of a far distant past. In an absurd way he felt superior to them although he also feared their presence. Subconsciously, he endeavored to disassociate from the pathetic whining of Mautotl and the brutality of Bahar when Josh was in charge.

William Wainthorp hovered in the deeper recesses of his mind, ominously wielding a deadly axe. Josh was inexplicably terrified of him and while he had not yet accessed William's particular evil, he suspected that his reluctance had something to do with Hugo. His black heart managed to contract for only a second. The boy had been his ticket to freedom. But that was before his selfish mother had stolen him away. Coming out of his trance, his anger suddenly returned. The time of reckoning was here and he did not want to waste one second longer.

"Teuch!" He yelled at the top of his voice. "You turned into a pillar of salt or something? What is keeping you? There are no plans to make, warrior! You are cornered and you have nowhere to go, except here. Get up this cliff so that the games can begin!" Steve listened as Josh uttered Mautotl's pathetic high pitched laugh, but didn't respond. He knew that this was ultimately a waiting game, and the one with the most patience had the best chance of winning. Mautotl needed to show off and wanted to be recognized for his genius at trapping them both here in the mountains and, even though he was a coward, in reality, he wanted his victims to admire him. Steve realized this and chose his words carefully.

"Is she still alive, *Mautotl*?" The gentle wind carried the words to his would-be executioner. "The last time, your henchman bravely slaughtered a defenseless woman in her sleep. How do I know that you have not succumbed to your characteristic spinelessness?"

Oh, how brilliant! He is trying to upset me. Josh Goldberg was impressed with Steve's words, but it was Mautotl who felt the effects of the innuendo. The former would have shrugged it off, but Mautotl was instantly incensed. Cursed by the gods for being born second to his sister, not only had she inherited physical beauty and wisdom, but they had lavished upon her a sense of honor and respect that he had always envied and hated. People had recognized her natural grace without any effort while they had always frowned upon him, mystified at the blood bond. For him, the gods had had no mercy. They had cursed him with a short and squat body, but as an afterthought, had left him with a sharp mind. And that was a mistake, for his only talent became a cunning streak that stood down for nothing, not even his own father. Indeed! He almost saw the humor in it all. Her lover and husband of times gone by was actually trying to distract him by angering him.

"You have another chance to execute me now, Mautotl." Steve calmly pulled his parka open to reveal the crest of the eagle on his chest. "I know you can't see it from there, but today the eagle's crest is over my heart and you, Mautotl, are holding a loaded bow. This is where you aimed your arrow after you had slain my father and my steed. Come on, Mautotl, why don't you crown your cowardice by killing me again?" The stillness stretched out and became tangible, like an impenetrable mist, while both men waited for the other to make the first move. Finally the man on the cliff spoke.

"Ah, I see you remember." Mautotl nodded his head in appreciation. "But this time it will get you nowhere, *Teuch*." His voice was deadly calm. "Anacaona is here—right behind me. And if you knew the manner in which I am holding her captive, you would not prolong her agony by playing word games with me."

"Where is she, Goldberg?" Addressing his present day persona was an effort to force the situation back to reality. An ice-cold hand gripped Steve's heart and a sudden sobering thought crossed his mind. "There is another alternative, of course. We could bury the hatchet and let bygones be bygones." But Josh wasn't listening anymore, for William Wainthorp's imposing character had swiftly emerged from the shadows of his troubled mind, fiercely gripping his axe and forcing him to scamper off without any protest.

"On what basis are you negotiating with me, *Ann?*" he roared. You are *not* in a position to offer anything of value. *I,* on the other hand, can take anything I want. We are *not* equals. You live or die at the mercy of my good graces. In hundreds of years have you not figured that out?"

Ann? Steve's mind reeled. *Jesus!* His opponent was no longer Mautotl but had flipped into the body of William Wainthorp. Even Josh was taken aback at the ease with which this dark alter ego claimed possession of him. He bared his teeth in rage as he threw the bow and arrow down and suddenly disappeared from sight. William needed to get to his victim at the tree right away. Plagued by hideous spasms of inadequacy, inherent to all his murderous personas, his psyche was riled into a frenzy that forced him to lash out and punish, and he reached Eva in a few huge strides. He frantically grabbed the end of the rope, which he had earlier looped around her neck from the branch above, and yelled feverishly over his shoulder.

"Your whore is still alive, Professor! But she might not be for much longer!" Eva was ecstatic to learn that Steve was so close by, but Josh's sudden outburst caught her by surprise and momentarily paralyzed her. She tried to scream his name to warn him of the maniac holding her captive, but only managed a hoarse whisper before Josh's big hand clasped hard over her mouth. *"Steve?"* he echoed softly, incredulous at her defiance of him. Bound by hand and foot and with the noose around her neck, she stared back at him, oblivious that her fear failed to mask the contempt she felt. Filling him with boundless anger, it amplified the grudge he had been nurturing for centuries. Unable to fathom how she dared to show disdain in the face of certain death, he lashed out blindly. Intending to hurt her, he viciously yanked at the rope and felt immense pleasure when she helplessly began gasping for breath.

In desperation she tried one more time to alert the man she loved by calling his name. But what escaped from her lips was a muffled gurgle as the rope tightened around her neck and she partially blacked out. William had hoisted her just far enough into the air for the tips of her toes to touch the ground, and dispassionately watched her body swing in pathetic half circles, while frantically trying to find her footing. Keeping a close watch on her, he yelled loudly to Steve.

"I am tired of waiting for you, Ann! Quit making speeches down there when your audience is up here. Now get the fuck up this cliff!" The shock of hearing Ann's name halted Eva's gradual surrender to the darkness and, with extraordinary effort, she ceased struggling and forced her eyes open to look in terror at the madman choking her to death. Then the true horror of what was happening hit her. *William Wainthorp* was hanging her for the second time and Steve would ascend the cliff only to come upon her hung body. Unbearable anguish tore through her stricken heart and she inwardly cried out for this agony not to be put upon him.

"Josh, William…*Please*!" She laid her pitiful plea at his heart of stone. "I beg of you…" Visibly excited by her suffering and eager to prolong it, her captor reached a lazy hand toward the rope.

"You're finally begging, Eva?" It was Josh speaking, with blatant pleasure in his voice. But her eyes had closed again and he stared frustrated at the swollen veins on her forehead and temples before he realized the magnitude of his mistake. "Oh no, you don't!" He gritted his teeth, suddenly bewildered. This was not the outcome he had planned. "You won't steal this pleasure from me! I want at least one of you to witness the demise of the other." And then he rapidly released the rope and dropped her hard to the ground, where her body fell into a wretched heap.

The man who walked away from her without looking back to see if she was breathing, was decidedly confused and agitated. Below the cliff, his arch enemy was waiting for the right moment to kill him, but up here he was surrounded by a host of phantom thugs who all lived somewhere within his crippled mind and were at war with each other. Each one of them wanted to claim credit for the imminent kill, when he, Josh Goldberg, wanted to be recognized as the mastermind.

In England, the unusual bond between the children had intensified. They were together constantly, and Natalie had even taken to camping out on the floor in Hugo's room, something that he allowed, to the surprise of Janet and George. They spent much of their time in the woods and, knowing that they were safe, the older Ballantires just let them be.

A gentle breeze chased the first leaves that had begun to fall around the woods that were known as Thorp Pelkington. Natalie spoke very little as she snuggled into Hugo's shoulder. Her legs were drawn up to her chin and, with her eyes closed, she appeared to be sleeping again. Hugo looked absentmindedly at her and then continued staring at his charts and drawings, intensely aware of a strange energy around them. Then he felt her move.

"Natalie?" A light shudder ran through her and, catching a few shallow breaths, her body sagged with its full weight against him; she was fast asleep. Hugo smiled, this time he had been waiting for her to doze off; he knew where she would be heading. And true enough, soon the golden-haired girl stood in the waving grass of the Meadow smiling broadly at Sakhota.

"You called me, Sakhota?" His frame was silhouetted against the blue sky, his face hidden in the shadows. She couldn't read his expression.

"Hello, child." His voice was somber. Her bubbly nature released the giggle before she caught onto his mood.

"What's wrong, Sakhota? Are you sad?"

"It is time, Natalie." She looked away from him and let her eyes wander over the expanse of the Meadow. The energy was moving fast and the quick ripples over the grass were an indication of the rapid change. She nodded her head slowly.

"Did Steve find Eva?" He stepped closer to her and held out his hand.

"Come, let us walk. I want to tell you a story."

"I love stories!" she beamed, slipping her small hand into his as they strolled away into the sun.

"Then you will love this one, child."

"Why?"

"Because I want you to help write its ending."

"Really?" She laughed out loud. "Is this an old story or are we making one up, Sakhota?"

"Oh, it is a very old story, Natalie. It started thousands of years ago, when you first came across the warrior and his horse. It was his first visit to the Meadow and they were looking for someone." The little girl smiled and lightly pressed her head against his arm as they walked.

"The beautiful lady with the long black hair; she came before them and was always very quiet," she whispered in admiration.

"Anacaona."

"Oh, yes! And Teuch and his big strong horse, Spethla!" She looked up to find his eyes. "What about them, Sakhota?"

"Well, they returned here many times. Not always together, but they never stopped looking for each other. Because you were sometimes playing in other parts of the Meadow, you did not always see them, but they returned again as Chaska and Tiva and brought the white horse, Nwaptoah, with them."

"I know about the horse." Natalie wore her angelic smile. "Spethla has many coats, but he loves the shiny black one best," she said softly. "I know all the animals." Sakhota nodded. "What's the story about?" She was eager to assist in the task he had in mind.

"It is a story of love between two souls."

"Who is writing it, Sakhota? And why do they need me for the ending?"

"Hugo needs you." She stopped and pulled at his hand, frowning.

"Is Hugo writing the story?" Her frown deepened. "But you are Hugo! Are *you* writing the story, Sakhota?"

"No, child. The Great Spirit is recording an expression of his love and how it manifests in many different ways through these souls." She nodded her head but didn't understand at all.

"Teuch and Anacaona became Chaska and Tiva?" Sakhota waited patiently and then she continued. "Where are they now and what must I do?"

"You have to know the rest of the story before you can help, Natalie." He pointed at the soft grass. "Let us sit." When she sat cross-legged in front of him, he touched his hand to her hair and continued patiently. "There were two more very significant lives for these souls and in both they were born as children to each other. Nyasha was Sekayi's beloved daughter and then Nathaniel was born to Ann."

She had closed her eyes and was listening intently, but he knew she would soon drift off to sleep; she always made the transition during sleep. When Natalie came to visit the Meadow, she never stayed for long; he knew he would have to get the information across to her quickly.

"I am part of the story also." He said it quietly, but she had heard him and responded without opening her eyes.

"How?" It was barely a whisper.

"I gave the dog, Wyomah, to Nathaniel. Wyomah means Spirit Wind. Before that he was the horse with the different names—Spethla, Nwaptoah and Zuka in the African life. But when the son of his real master came for him, I had to let him go. And I had to make sure the feathers were given to the root personalities of Teuch and Anacaona."

"Is this because Ann was the real master, Sakhota?" The proud young brave acknowledged Natalie's sharp insights into the confusion surrounding the changes in gender around the reincarnated lives of Teuch and Anacaona. "The feathers?" She seemed to stop breathing. "When I am in the Meadow, Sakhota, I can remember that Steve and Eva are Teuch and Anacaona." Sakhota waited. He didn't want to interrupt her, but realized that on a few occasions her knowledge and insights had carried through into her earthly existence; however she was not aware of it. "And Bullet, Quah Dreamer…is Spethla."

"Yes, child. That is right."

"What must I do, Sakhota?" Her eyes were still closed but her smile was innocent. She didn't see him lean forward. She only felt a light pressure where he placed two fingers in the center of her forehead.

"Speak up, Natalie," he urged. "You will have to talk in your sleep so Hugo can hear your words. Tell him there is one nearby in the mountains who can help Steve and Eva. Tell Hugo to send the eagle to alert him. We have to make sure the evil one does not trick them again, as before. That is how you can help write the end of this story."

Hugo watched her mouth move and heard every word as he waited quietly for her to wake up. He knew what to do now, but he was surprised to learn through Natalie that the eagle could be directed to someone else besides Eva or Steve. He was glad that Natalie didn't ask him why his ancient form of Sakhota was still in the Meadow. He didn't know how to explain that his special talent was also closely shared with Sakhota's gifts, but that he needed a connection to that source of information. And that Natalie was his link.

Once he knew how to use the constellations and nearby stars as a means of calculating, multitudes of patterns and designs had become accessible. To him these heavenly designs were simply the conduit for receiving energy and information. Because of his condition, his brain frequencies were diverse and it was only a matter of time before his multi-dimensional awareness would bring him to the Meadow. But Natalie's intervention had sped up the process, and he wondered if she was supposed to be his guiding star. He smiled and liked the idea. He was unaware that it meant that he needed her and that it represented a radical departure from autism where social contact is avoided.

The innocence and ease with which the little strip of a girl traversed universal playgrounds, unavailable to those steeped in dogma, encouraged Hugo to reach beyond his fascination with mathematics and venture into the inner levels of his own ancient mind. As he disappeared into the familiar silence, he became aware of a change in appearance and when he looked down at his body, Hugo saw himself as Sakhota for the first time as the two personalities merged. He smiled, not sure if what showed on his face was Hugo's shyness or Sakhota's broad grin. There was no one around to confirm either way, and he just enjoyed the exhilaration of the experience; noticing also that the landscape was rapidly changing as he navigated a breathtaking path along parallel universes. He sensed that he was on his way somewhere specific, and his excitement mounted in leaps and bounds.

With Sakhota's mind and vision, he recognized a myriad of characters from his far distant past. However, he didn't feel the desire to interact with anyone until he unexpectedly found himself in a rural community full of fellow braves. He thought he recognized them as friends from the time when he was the son of the village chief. Yet, upon closer scrutiny, he realized that the traditions and culture of the people surrounding him didn't relate to the life he had known as Sakhota. And then he understood that he was with a different race of people, *and* in a different time.

Drawn to an old man tending to some of the sick in the village, he sensed a special purpose to his presence in these strange surroundings, and waited respectfully in the background to be noticed. Finally the old man lifted his head and looked directly at him, a slow smile of recognition creeping around his mouth as he straightened. Then he lifted his left hand in greeting, and that is when Sakhota noticed there were only three fingers on that hand. Filled with the wonder of what was happening, he raised his lance to salute one of his oldest and most trusted companions. With the vital mental connection established, Sakhota's attention was almost immediately redirected, as he felt himself drawn into a powerful energy vortex where his own mind instantly fused with the controlling spirit which embraced all the personas that were Hugo.

In amazement, he allowed himself to be transported even further back in time to a place beyond antiquity, of which no earthly records existed, except in dreams and visions of those who could calibrate these very fine vibrations and interpret their meaning. Taking in his surroundings, he noticed the magnificent garment covering his body—the one he had worn as *T'nabi,* scribe to the kings. Then he recognized the crystal cave where his mentor and guardian, *Suklus,* had educated him in the ways of the Universe. This signaled the beginning of a great bond and friendship. It would be carried over many lives into multiple futures that they could only sense. But they didn't doubt that it would also materialize into myriad realities from which they could freely choose. T'nabi bowed his head in reverence to the past incarnations of his old companion. *Suklus…Nahiossi.* The vision disappeared as quickly as it had come as he slipped back into the body of Sakhota. He had returned, and was again in the presence of the old man and the other braves.

"Hello, old friend," Sakhota smiled, holding his lance high at the medicine man of the Kawahi people, but honoring Suklus of ancient times.

"Nehanupti, my young warrior." The left hand with three fingers was still in the air. Sakhota acknowledged the ancient greeting with a nod. "We meet again." The smile around Nahiossi's mouth reached deep into his eyes.

"Yes, my friend. We have been drawn together once more to serve, as the darkness endeavors to shut out the light." The old medicine man heard the young brave out and then beckoned him to enter the circle of the fire; the smile had not left his face.

"The evil one has moved further into the shadows."

"Yes." Infused with the wonder of reconnecting in this magnificent way, Sakhota's eyes burned like coals in his head, but he waited respectfully for Nahiossi to take the lead.

"You brought me a message this time?" Nahiossi stared into the fire, speaking very quietly. But Sakhota didn't answer immediately and, honoring the ancient bond between them, for a while they simply enjoyed being in each other's presence. The tremendous energy that existed between them transcended any need for verbal communication. Just being was more than enough. Then, without a word, the sacred pipe was lit and they passed it back and forth, sharing the essence of peace and tranquility while they stared at each other through the blue wisps of smoke snaking lazily about them. Finally Sakhota responded in a low whisper.

"The eagle must take flight one more time." He recalled the words he had spoken to Natalie and repeated them once more to the ancient form of the one who was waiting in the cave in the Himalayas. "The one in the mountains can help Steve and Eva. Hugo can stir the energy strings to alert the eagle, but he needs you." Nahiossi's nod was almost imperceptible.

"The one in the cave will soon remember. He too loves the eagle and its untamed ways. He recognized a mission the first day he picked up a tail feather, and he has not forgotten. Fear not, my young warrior, he knows what to do. The symbolic significance of the feathers is an unwritten law."

When Hugo opened his eyes, he looked right into Natalie's curious stare.

"How did you do that? I have never been *there*!" She had been watching him all the time and her eyes shone with admiration.

"That is because your home is the Meadow." He was Hugo again and looked at his charts as he spoke under his breath. "The eagle will know soon, Natalie."

"How?" A tiny frown appeared on her brow. He contemplated a reasonable answer, but knew that whatever he said would not really mean much to her. She had sensed the energy around him and knew he had had an extraordinary experience, but she was in essence a child of the Meadow and she would return there again. Hugo suddenly looked at her with different eyes, feeling the strangest pangs of loss. *What if I never see her again after this life?*

His response was to take her with him to where the two streams crossed in the woods at Thorp Pelkington. Natalie followed him around like a little puppy, in awe of everything he did. She could see the vibrant energy enveloping him. To her he seemed to be glowing like a bright star and she didn't understand anything about the plume of negative ions emanating from the two streams, forming a concentration of cosmic fluid and static electricity around him. Neither could she tell that this greatly increased the conductivity of the Universe or that all of nature's laws were apparent to him in this state; especially because of his advanced understanding of the mathematical processes that give structure to the material world.

His task was to reconnect with the eagle and this would soon become an energy chord that would reverberate throughout the mountain. Chong-ba would soon feel the effect of it somewhere inside him and realize the true significance of the eagle's presence. Hugo knew that not only would this powerful energy influence the eagle, but the little monk in the cave would also recall his bond with Sakhota. And perhaps he would mentally and spiritually reach as far back as Suklus to that place in history, now lost far beyond the annals of antiquity, when crystals were commonly known for their brilliant conductivity of energy.

The shriek sounded as though it had come from inside the cave, but Chong-ba knew that was not possible; the eagle would never venture inside a confined area like this. Neither was the bird hunting, because it would not advertise its whereabouts if it was hungry. Chong-ba rose slowly from the flat rock where he had spent most of his time after the injury to his hand; he barely looked at the huddled figure of the guide pressed up against the wall of the cave. Neither did he doubt the call of the eagle or the meaning of it. He knew exactly what he had to do.

At first he thought it was a dream, a hallucination due to the intense pain in his hand, but when he heard the eagle's call, he realized that the meeting with Nahiossi in the elevated levels of the astral had been real and, despite the searing pain in his hand, he felt a mighty energy surge coursing through his entire body. As an experienced traveler of the astral worlds, he marveled at how pieces of the universal puzzle, as they came together, constantly surprised him. Realizing earlier that he in fact was the old medicine man, was quite a revelation to him, but his connection with Eva's gifted son, Hugo, explained why he had been attracted to the eagle so long ago. He had a role to play in this universal drama between light and dark, and it had all started with the eagle. But his unexpected bond with Hugo had brought it full circle, enabling him to complete what the boy had started. He thought of the bird again as he remembered it perched high in the treetop near his cabin and how the first feather had been dropped, foretelling the arrival of a visitor—Tom. Now it was time to communicate directly with the bird through the channel created by Hugo.

"We must ward off the darkness and stop the evil one." He imagined it to be a thought, but mouthed the words out loud, attracting the attention of the guide, who concluded that his master was hallucinating.

"Master?" The man half rose to his feet, but Chong-ba waved him down.

"I will call for you later. Wait here." Then he directed all his attention to the eagle, which he knew was now sitting on the ledge high above the cave. "You must deter the evil one." His lips barely moved. "We need your help." Then he began his slow decline toward the bottom of the cliff below his cabin. He didn't know why he was heading there, but thought that his spirit was directing him. Chong-ba smiled as he silently made his descent and noticed the eagle take off from the ledge to fly in the direction of his dwelling.

"If I did not know any better, I would have said that I had been on this mountain for too long," he mumbled to himself. As Chong-ba, he was not aware of Hugo's brilliant mathematical mind and how his efforts were finally bearing fruit. He was only happy at having discovered the ancient bond as Nahiossi with Sakhota. But he was even happier to see the bird in the air and didn't doubt for a second where it was heading.

As Josh strode away from his hapless victim under the tree, his eye caught the glint of the two swords lying in the sun just outside the cabin where he had left them earlier that day. He hesitated for only a second but once again was pushed aside as the furtive character of Bahar barged in and let out an insane belly laugh at the sight of the weapons. *What genius to bring the swords up the mountain! It is time to set the record straight and repay Sekayi for the mortal sin of pinning me to a tree with my own sword.* He looked around carefully, but there was no sign of the lissome leader of the Lemba tribe. *Where the hell is the arrogant bastard?*

But while Bahar waited for Sekayi to show himself, Josh zealously managed to put in an appearance again. The swords were *his* trump card—his piece de resistance—with which he planned to slay his enemy in style. He recalled with glee how he had made this incredible find at the mountaineering store in Gujrat. He had noticed the swords when he had asked for a few simple tools and some length of rope as the assistant had gone to the back of the store to fill his order.

Two replica historical Pakistani swords were magnificently encased in a glass frame just behind the counter. A plaque beneath them explained their history but Josh couldn't care less. His eyes fastened on the thirty seven inch scimitar with its stainless steel blade, snuggling in a black leather sheath. Though Pakistani in origin, it closely resembled the lethal Arabian scimitar with which he had sent many souls to their death in his colorful but brutal life as Bahar. Then he felt the excitement stir and was convinced that the gods were for once smiling on him. This was too good to be true!

The second sword looked more ancient and appeared to require a higher level of skill to handle effectively. A Pakistani St Michaels sword, it was thirty three inches overall in length, with a twenty four inch stainless steel sharpened double edged blade, sporting a brown wood spiral handle. Each weapon in its own right was lethal, but he was nevertheless thrilled at the sight of both, and as always, was able to overcome the owner's objections to selling them with the help of the almighty dollar. His mission took on a whole new meaning after adding the swords as part of the equipment to take on their journey. He took pains to have them wrapped carefully to obscure their identity and particularly enjoyed making Dmitri carry them most of the way, without letting on what the contents of the packages were.

The persona of Bahar carefully and ceremoniously laid the swords cross-wise on the ground near to where Eva was, when he noticed that she had regained consciousness and was watching him from a distance. To his amazement she spoke again.

"Josh, please don't do this. Won't you listen to me? Josh, please…"

But Josh had become firmly rooted in the sadistic persona of the ancient Arab. His eyes rolled back and forth in their sockets and he could smell the scent of his enemy below the cliff. Bahar had no patience for Josh and he was admiring the blades as they shone brightly in the afternoon sun. If anything, he found the woman irritating; it was Sekayi who interested him, not his daughter. Ordinary killing was not on his mind; he planned to have a bone chilling bloodbath in which he would slaughter his adversaries of hundreds and hundreds of years, and finally be rid of his inadequacies. He meant to redeem himself once and for all, and no one would stand in his way this time.

"Steve! Turn back and save yourself! Please!" Her voice did not carry very far and Bahar turned a perplexed look at her.

"Sekayi can't hear you, Nyasha." His voice sounded gruff and detached. "He can't get up this cliff without me taking his head off. And he knows it." He smiled broadly in her direction but she could tell he had lost touch with reality. "I am invincible." He had picked up the bow again and tilted his head sideways, contemplating his words solemnly. "Just like God." Eva nodded her head slowly, comprehending for the first time the vastness of the confusion within his madness.

"I see. That must be true then, Bahar?" She was the first to notice the eagle as it appeared once more, rising silently above the cabin. She looked toward the blue sky and the bird of prey with its massive wingspan as it swiftly approached from behind him. Then she smiled sweetly at her captor. "God has sent you a sign. Look, there!"

When he turned to see what she was looking at, the bird was almost upon him as it swooped down low, aiming its powerful claws directly at his head. Bahar let out a fearful cry at the sight of the sharp talons and rolled away while frantically trying to regain his grip on the bow as it fell from his hand. Unnerved and shaken, he grabbed it and fired an arrow in the direction of the eagle, but missed by a wide berth, realizing that the opportunity to kill it was lost. Halted by the confusion in his mind, he stared at the disappearing bird until it was only a speck in the blue sky and then fixed his attention upon Eva; his face contorting with rage. From the sludge of his murky past, a clear memory drifted to the surface and he vividly remembered that day in the tent on the plains of Africa.

"You!" he yelled furiously. "You brought this on! You have lured that goddamned bird here!" Then another sickening thought entered his panic-stricken mind and he reached her side in a few huge strides. "Did you bring the feathers this time, Nyasha?" Josh's mouth was bone dry but his memory banks, in overdrive, were churning up detailed images from a far distant past. He recalled reports from his henchmen of two feathers they had found beside the bed of Anacaona on the night he had ordered her life ended. On the plains of Africa, they fell from Nyasha's bosom before he suffocated the defiant little bitch. And he took two feathers off Nathaniel before beheading Sakhota and hanging mother and son together. He began to tremble uncontrollably as fear gripped his black heart. "What do they mean? *Tell me*!" Eva was petrified and incapable of speaking. The man breathing into her face was extremely dangerous and she realized there were no right answers to give. In his insanity nothing would make sense, and everything would be turned against her. "Did you bring the feathers to the mountain?" He reached a hand to her bosom and brusquely grabbed hold of her shirt. "Where are you hiding them?" A note of desperation had crept into his voice and suddenly he sounded as though he was going to cry.

"She does not have them, Goldberg." Standing on the edge of the cliff, Steve spoke calmly behind him. "I do." He held the feathers for him to see, but Josh didn't move and stared stoically ahead of him without turning around. Steve remained calm. "Take your hands off her. This is between you and me."

Eva was unable to speak. Tears of joy filled her eyes and she bit down hard on her lower lip, forcing herself not to call out his name, for it was Josh Goldberg's ominous quiet that demanded her immediate attention. He had not moved nor blinked and remained crouched forward, still holding her. Then his entire body began to shake with soundless laughter and he tightened his grip on her shirt, still refusing to turn and face his enemy. When it appeared that he would lose complete control, he opened his mouth and hollered through the mountains.

"Professor, Professor!" He could barely speak through his fits of laughter. "You finally came to rescue your damsel in distress! Just when we were beginning to think we would have to kill her without the privilege of you watching." Then suddenly he let go of her shirt and in one swift movement he stood behind her, holding a knife to her throat that he had stealthily drawn from the sheath hidden on his calf.

"All of you step closer!" He yelled at the top of his voice, nodding his head at Steve. "It is time for all of you to die! We will rid the world of Teuch, Ann, Sekayi and the brilliant Professor, in one fell swoop!" He nodded his head toward Eva. "Then we'll get to the whores who pained me so over thousands of years." Josh suddenly became quiet and the color drained from his face. He stared solemnly at the man opposite him and then his expression twisted into an ugly sneer. "I see you were not lying about the emblem on your sweater. What is this unholy alliance you and she have with the eagle?" Steve didn't answer. His eyes were on Eva and the terrified look on her face; she appeared exhausted and on the verge of collapse.

"Glad you brought the feathers, Professor," the madman continued, watching him carefully. "After thousands of years, I have figured out how to break the spell and divide you *forever*. We'll have to burn those feathers while you watch. Then you and *she* have to die together. Today is that day."

Chapter 31
Full Circle

Despite a highly sophisticated intellect, Josh Goldberg was driven by the intolerance of a severely fragmented spirit; a direct result of the unwillingness to make wise choices over lifetimes. His biggest illusion, that all humans had free will in the absence of conscious choice-making, had brought him to a very dark place of imagined greatness and pseudo power. Here he skulked around in the shadows like a wounded animal, ready to strike and punish the two souls from whom he had a real opportunity to learn. He knew nothing of the powerful cosmic alliance that existed between Steve, Eva and Hugo.

Goldberg's gradual but consistent move away from the Light over thousands of years resulted in an obsession with personal importance. This unswerving rejection eventually tore his psyche open, to allow free reign to each spiteful, jealous and murderous character in whom he had masqueraded over millennia. The bell was tolling and yet, he could not hear it, for he had driven himself mad. He had never recognized polarities and adversity as a tool for spiritual growth and understanding and, enveloped in complete darkness, his comprehension of eternity was drenched in unspeakable fear; one that put him into a frenzy to kill his challenger at any cost.

Steve caught the eagle in his peripheral vision as it soared into the blue sky toward the sun and understood at once that its mission was complete. Now it was only he and Josh Goldberg and the ancient grudge of his opponent. The time for negotiation was over, only death would satisfy Josh. He quietly assessed the scene in front of him, astonished at the depth of Goldberg's hatred and the elaborate scheme he had devised to bring him and Eva to this place in the Himalaya Mountains to exact his warped version of retribution on them. His eyes were drawn to the crossed swords that lay between him and his opponent, and he understood their meaning instantly. In his madness, Josh had carefully planned this meeting. He seemingly imagined that re-enactment of some of their past experiences would provide the satisfaction his tortured soul was crying out for.

Time froze as he stared at the swords; the chilling similarity of the weapons displayed on the ground to those used in antiquity by and against him, was unmistakable. It was as obvious as the madness of the man who had brought these weapons to their final showdown. The sight of the first sword transported him back to Amustopl in ancient Mexica where, as Captain to the Royal Guard, he had used it. But as his skill had increased, the hatred and jealousy of Mautotl had grown in leaps and bounds. Soon Anacaona's envious sibling began to plot Teuch's demise. Unable to face him as an equal on the battlefield, Mautotl had planned the ambush carefully and, as an accomplished archer, waited for the right moment to end his adversary's life with a poisonous arrow.

The second weapon, a Scimitar, brought into vivid focus the painful life he had had in Africa. The evil Arab had used a weapon such as this one to kill so many of Sekayi's people as he hacked his way toward stealing his precious Nyasha. His eyes rested briefly on Eva and for a moment the intensity of the pain he had felt when he had discovered Nyasha's lifeless body, seared through him again. The power of the memory surprised him. And, in that moment, Steve realized that not only were their past lives laid bare in their entirety, but the whole gamut of emotions that they had lived through was also available to them.

But now, for the first time in many hundreds of years, two opponents stood eye to eye to conclude what had begun such a long time ago, whilst quietly in the background, the forces of Light and Dark watched and waited to record the final outcome. Like thousands of years before, history would follow a new course if the balance of power was changed significantly.

"This is ridiculous Goldberg; two grown men using ancient swords. These weapons belong in a museum."

"Pretty, aren't they, Professor?" Josh held the knife to Eva's throat as he began to shuffle his way over to the weapons, ignoring Steve. The next minute, without warning, he was sucked into one of his ancient personas. "Don't even think about it, Sekayi!" He yelled out loudly, gesturing wildly with his head in the direction of the weapons. "If you make one move toward the swords, I will run this knife through her neck. And as you probably know by now, once she's dead, there is no undoing dead. Now stand back!"

Steve didn't move. He knew Josh wanted a sword fight and although he was anxious about the knife against Eva's throat, he was convinced that Josh was using her as his shield to get to the weapons first. He knew that if there was ever a moment to be patient, this was it. The frequency at which his opponent changed his own persona, suggested a high degree of instability. He waited for Josh to make a mistake; in his confused madness, Goldberg had addressed him as Sekayi. Yet, Steve knew that the madman was extremely dangerous. His most important objective was to make sure that Eva was safe before he engaged in a face-off with Josh, and he took a step back to show compliance. Within striking range of the swords, Josh brusquely shoved Eva inside the cabin and dove down onto the ground, grabbing the scimitar.

"If you move from there, you witch," he yelled over his shoulder, keeping an eye on Steve, "I will take an arm or a leg off your father before I kill him!"

When Steve saw Eva stumble into the cabin, he took off in the direction of his opponent, but Josh was on his feet before he could reach him, swinging the sword wildly in the direction of Steve's head and narrowly missing his jugular vein. Then he stood back, crazily wielding the weapon and laughed out loud, sounding more insane by the minute. He held his other arm horizontal to the ground, poorly mimicking an ancient sword dance, taunting the man who was watching him like a hawk.

"Pick up the other weapon, Sekayi." It sounded like a polite invitation. "We have a score to settle." He smiled and pointed with the scimitar to the sword on the ground. But when Steve remained motionless, his opponent exploded in uncontrollable rage and hysteria. "You think I have forgotten the humiliation? The nerve of it! You refused the protection of the great Bahar—and in the presence of others!" His voice rolled loudly through the mountains. "No one ever dared to do that! No one!"

"You were a slave trader and bandit." Steve maintained eye contact and his voice was calm. "Do you want a fair fight, Bahar, or do I have to overpower you with my bare hands?" The other sword was at his feet, but he made no effort yet to bend and pick it up, and continued his casual conversation. "Tell me. Which demon is before me?" Then he dropped his voice, forcing his opponent to lean slightly forward to catch his words. "I know that Bahar would like to demonstrate his skill because he was quite a swordsman, from what I recall, but I know Mautotl is a sniveling little rat who simply wants to win at any cost. He might take my head off as I bend to pick up this weapon. He's not a very brave man, you know. He had so much opportunity to make something of his life, but—"

"Shut up!" Josh was suddenly back. "Who are you lecturing, Professor? I lured you into the mountains, didn't I? And that is nothing short of brilliant. Admit it! I am a fucking genius!" Steve surveyed the demented man with feigned interest and nodded his head in agreement.

"Yes, you are brilliant. Who can miss greatness like this?" Josh smiled in acknowledgment; the short distraction in his persona from Bahar to Josh was all that Steve needed. Josh was not a swordsman, and he was nowhere near as alert as Bahar in combat. Steve felt the weapon at the tip of his shoe and swiftly bent down to pick it up. Then he stepped back immediately and straightened, while raising the sword vertically to the right of his body. "Ready when you are, Bahar." He caught the movement from the cabin at the same time as his opponent. "No, Eva! Don't!" He and Bahar took off simultaneously. Bahar raised his scimitar and aimed for her where she stood frozen and petrified outside the cabin wall. As it came swooping down toward Eva's shoulder, it was met by Steve's double edged sword. He had reached her with superhuman effort, deflecting an impact, vicious enough to have severed a limb. "Stay inside, Eva. Please! Let me deal with this!" he called out, keeping his gaze on the crazy man in front of him.

But as she edged back into the cabin, Josh Goldberg's confusion had become complete and he remembered the searing pain as the leader of the Lemba tribe pinned Bahar to the tree and stood back dispassionately to watch him die. And then he remembered something else. With blood gurgling from his mouth and a clear knowledge that he would surely die against the tree where Sekayi had run his sword through him, he noticed the tears in his executioner's eyes. He appeared to be in more pain than *he* was. It confused him only briefly until the veil dropped away and Bahar realized the true identities of Sekayi and his daughter. Despite the agony of his dying, a great satisfaction enveloped him.

"It was all worth it," he had spluttered in Arabic. Sekayi didn't understand his words that day, but had picked up on the meaning and his face contorted as he stepped forward one more time and pushed the sword in deeper. With his heart and soul drenched in pain, not a single word reached his lips as the tears ran freely down his face. Numb to the bone, there was nothing else to do but to disappear into a chasm of incredible loss and loneliness as he watched the filthy Arab die. Only his mortally wounded heart silently cried her name over and over. "*Nyasha, Nyasha…*" But Nyasha was gone and already waiting in the Meadow.

In cold fury, and incensed by the past and the present, Bahar struck again. Steve managed to pull back from the full blow, but not before the scimitar brushed against his left arm, slicing through the bulging surface vein running along his biceps, causing profuse bleeding. From the door of the cabin, Eva shrieked in horror at the gushing wound, but the sight of blood stimulated Bahar immensely and a mighty surge of adrenalin coursed through his body as he prepared to lunge again.

Aware that he had become slightly handicapped, Steve knew there was not much time and that he would have to move swiftly. Focusing on his opponent, he gripped his sword tightly and, ignoring the wound on his arm, kept his body relaxed. The two men glared, waiting for the other to make the first move. Then Steve's left hand wandered to his sweater, and without taking his eyes off his opponent, he touched the eagle emblem.

"Reminiscing, are we, Professor?" Josh had put in an appearance again. "I see you have me figured out and you are trying to confuse me with all the different personas, and so far it has been working. But no more of that!" Steve ignored his words.

"There's still time to end all of this, Goldberg." But Josh wasn't listening either.

"I will not kill you straight away, Professor; that is just too easy. I want you to watch as your whore dies slowly whilst I violate her, much the way I disposed of her when she was your precious little girl. I have decided that she will go first and then it is your turn." Steve nodded in solemn understanding.

"Then make sure you get Bahar to assist, Goldberg. You don't have the skills needed to execute both of us if you remain in charge. I don't know a great deal about you, but if you hold the sword *that* way, you don't have much of a chance." He smiled, but didn't blink. "This is quite the challenge, I must admit. I follow a madman into the mountains to find Eva, and get to fight a whole army of thugs. What a pity that none of them had learned to forgive and just move on. Then none of this would have been necessary. And you would have had a chance to evolve from the sad and misguided soul that you are."

Natalie was standing on the small wooden bridge that crossed the babbling brook. Directly beneath her and below ground, the hidden stream flowed diagonally to the one above. Hugo was using the powerful energy of this watery intersection to amplify his thoughts. Then he looked at the horse and saw that its nostrils were flared and every muscle in its body was rippling. He whistled softly, the way he had heard Steve communicate with Quah Dreamer many times before. Natalie smiled and cocked her head at him and then looked up at the horse; there was wonder in her voice.

"He knows, Hugo! He knows you have sent a message to the eagle!" The boy nodded his head, smiling broadly.

"Quah Dreamer has been with Steve and my mum for a very long time. He knows a lot of things, Natalie. Remember how he helped you to find the owl's feather in the grass?" She giggled, nodding vigorously; her pixie face disappearing behind golden curls. "Then he knows about the eagle! Animals are like that. They understand."

Eva stood breathlessly in the doorway to the cabin and stared in alarm at the tall man bleeding from his left arm. The full impact of his role through all the centuries, beginning with their lives together as

Teuch and Anacaona, was highlighted by the emblem on his sweater, and she remembered their sacred pact of so long ago as the tears streaked down her face. Past and present flowed into one continuum, and everything was revealed.

"I remember it all, Teuch!" Her shaky whisper was lost in a sob, but she hoped the words would reach him and give him strength. The two men were still facing each other. Without taking his eyes off Josh, Steve acknowledged her words with a slight nod and took a deep breath. As he had done so often in antiquity, he raised his sword and crossed it over his chest, to acknowledge the eagle before engaging in battle. Deeply cognizant of his prime directive to favor defense instead of offense, he beckoned Josh with his raised sword to do his will.

"To consummate your pact with the devil you will have to kill me first, Goldberg. This will be your only opportunity. Don't waste it." But Josh was done talking and he was suddenly eager to end it all as quickly as possible. The imposing man in front of him was unnerving, but the dark characters within him were becoming impossible to contain, and he feared that any one of them could suddenly burst out and railroad his cleverly devised plan. Noticing that blood was still flowing from Steve's open wound, he lunged toward him with blatant hatred in his eyes, swinging his sword wildly.

But Steve recognized the desperation in his opponent and moved aside just in time to avoid the blow, allowing Josh's momentum to carry him onwards. As his body fell forward, Steve clenched his fist and threw a mighty punch into the back of his neck. With Josh caught off balance, Steve turned quickly and threw another hard punch into his back, instantly rupturing his kidneys. His martial arts skills were razor sharp as he aimed to injure and disarm his opponent. Josh was oblivious to his handicap and rose to face Steve again, reeling in pain as the blood and bile began to leak into his other organs.

"Nice move, Professor!" he coughed, filled with the bravado of his own illusory greatness. "But now you die!" Josh flicked the blade of his sword into his hand and threw it like a large dagger with all his might straight at his opponent. But Steve had noticed Josh's disadvantage and raised his sword to deflect the weapon and it fell harmlessly to the ground. With his rival defenseless, and in fair gamesmanship, he threw his sword alongside the scimitar. If necessary, he was prepared to overcome his adversary with brute force.

"It is all over for you, Goldberg. Let me tend to your injuries and we'll sort this out once we're off the mountain." But Steve had underestimated Josh, who flung himself to the ground to retrieve his weapon while attempting to knock the other one out of Steve's reach. Steve had expected some underhanded move and he dove horizontally at Josh, endeavoring to pin him to the ground. Whilst both were off balance, it was Josh, now filled with the urgency of winning, who scrambled to his feet first and immediately ran toward the cabin and Eva. On his way he grabbed Steve's sword and reached frenetically for her. He thrust her back hard against his chest, holding the tip of the sword to her throat. His breathing was labored and his eyes shone with a feverish glow.

"Stop right where you are, Professor!" In the back of his confused mind he heard William Wainthorp's sarcastic laugh, while Mautotl whined perpetually about being left out of all the action, and Bahar bellowed like the animal he was. He wanted to close his eyes and ears to the maddening voices screaming in his head, but he didn't dare. If he wanted to win, it was important that the Josh persona remained in charge.

Steve froze, realizing that Goldberg now held the upper hand. Time stood still and a bleak sadness filled him as he once again recognized the place where they had been so often—a place where someone had to die. If the madman threatening Eva's life responded to the recklessness of his own insanity, the cycle would have to perpetuate itself in another incarnation.

Eva held her body perfectly still and kept her eyes closed; she too knew that they had reached the end of this road. She felt the tip of the sword pierce her skin and a thin trickle of blood began to run down the side of her neck and yet she didn't move. An eternity slowly passed between them, and then she finally opened her eyes. She looked desolately at Steve. His love for her was clearly visible on his face, marred only by a deep sadness at the unfortunate turn of events.

Then she noticed his slight nod, and at once understood his message. He was guiding her to make the first move to break free. She closed her eyes again and remembered where Steve had thrown the second punch, and recalled how the impact had registered on Josh's face. There was no time to waste, and there were no further decisions to make as she pushed her elbow hard into Josh's injured side. Eva freed herself in the instant that it took for him to recover. Ducking under his arm she let out a frightened scream and ran toward the relative safety of the edge of the cliff.

An equal distance away from her, both Steve and Josh realized that whoever got to Eva first would have the upper hand. Steve had picked up Josh's discarded scimitar, and each understood that the time, the place and history demanded a re-enactment of what had previously gone between them. Josh was the first to speak, although with far less bravado this time.

"Do you think you can handle that scimitar, Professor? It needs a special skill, whilst I, on the other hand, can handle this sword." He looked down at the double edged blade and then swung it through the air. "After all, I am Bahar, the great swordsman. Am I not?" He sounded extremely confused. Steve held the scimitar down by his side and said nothing, realizing that his opponent was exceptionally dangerous and very unpredictable.

Then, without warning, Josh lunged at Steve. As he raised the scimitar to meet Goldberg's sword, Steve knew that his challenger was once again fighting with the skill and speed of Bahar and that ultimately only one of them could survive. The weapons met and flashed in the sunlight as they moved and clanked to block each other's blows, steadily inching their way toward Eva, who watched the battle with her heart caught in her throat.

Looking into his opponent's eyes, the cowardice of Mautotl suddenly returned and Josh realized that he was up against a very skillful man. Without warning, he abruptly threw down his sword in a desperate attempt to grab Eva and force her to the edge of the cliff. But Steve saw through his plan and lunged at his heels just as Eva anxiously sidestepped her captor's hands. With her safely out of the way, there was nothing to break his momentum, causing Steve to lose his grip as his opponent slid helplessly over the loose gravel toward the edge of the cliff. Goldberg let out a terrified scream as the dry soil and brittle rock began to give, paving the way toward certain death. But no man, with an ancient unsettled score, surrenders that easily and he desperately grabbed hold of some foliage, clinging frantically to it.

Steve cautiously approached the edge and held up his hand to Eva, gesturing for her not to come any closer. Peering over the cliff, he met with the hateful glare of thousands of years that came from Mautotl, Bahar, William Wainthorp and ultimately Josh Goldberg.

"When will this end for you?" He sounded very tired. "What will it take to forgive, forget and move on with your own journey? Here let me help you." Steve extended a hand toward his nemesis of old to pull him to safety. But the complicated persona of Josh Goldberg was riddled with hate, jealousy and envy and, pretending to accept the offer of help, he reached for Steve and with his free hand gripped on to his wrist. Then he let go of the foliage and grabbed Steve's shoulder, but only managed to take hold of his sweater. Their stares locked. Then the life seemed to vanish from Josh's eyes completely. Finding his footing against the rock face, he suddenly pulled back with all his power and bodyweight, endeavoring to take them both to a rocky end.

"You are going to die, Professor!" he screamed. "This time I am taking you to hell!" Steve had to use all his strength in anchoring his body to counter the frenzied tugging of his rival. But despite his efforts, the sweater in Goldberg's grip began to slide over his head. At the same time he turned his wrist in Josh's strong hand and, loosening the hold, realized that his opponent had nothing more to grasp onto.

"Not this time, Goldberg," he said as he hung back with all his might, feeling the inevitable slide of the garment. And then suddenly there was nothing to stop the madman's fall any longer as the sweater with the eagle emblem came off completely and Josh fell toward the rocks below, just as Eva's terrified scream echoed through the mountains. She stared transfixed at the man tumbling through the air with naked shock and fear in his eyes, realizing that he was heading for the same horrible death that he had meted out to those at the foot of the cliff.

Exhausted and spent, Eva crawled into Steve's embrace and in the sudden eerie silence that descended upon the mountain, they simply held on to each other, listening to their labored breathing. Then they heard the faint laugh coming from the rocks below. It could only be Goldberg. The devil was obviously looking after his own.

The madman wasn't dead yet.

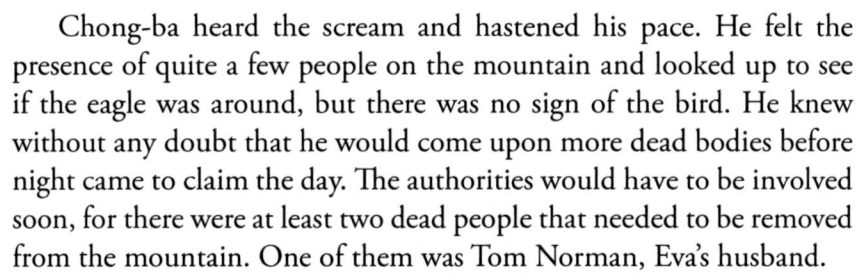

Chong-ba heard the scream and hastened his pace. He felt the presence of quite a few people on the mountain and looked up to see if the eagle was around, but there was no sign of the bird. He knew without any doubt that he would come upon more dead bodies before night came to claim the day. The authorities would have to be involved soon, for there were at least two dead people that needed to be removed from the mountain. One of them was Tom Norman, Eva's husband.

When he arrived at the rocky foot of the cliff, he stopped dead in his tracks and stared in horror at the grotesque ensemble of death before him. No less than four bodies were draped over the sharp rocks and, besides the hapless form of Tom Norman caught in a crevice and David Appleyard, impaled on a branch, he had no idea who the others were. Then he noticed that at least one person was not yet dead. He approached slowly, sensing the evil as he came closer. He stood quietly at the side of the man, whose eyes were closed, but his belabored breathing gave away the severity of his injuries. The expression on his face changed from contorted pain to something that resembled an effort to laugh. Then he opened his eyes and, turning his head slowly sideways, he noticed the monk.

"Oh, look who is here!" He coughed weakly and tried to spit the blood from his mouth.

"Let me help you, sir." The monk took a step closer, but kept his hands folded lightly in front of him.

"Keep your fucking holy hands to yourself, you righteous bastard! You're God or something?" He wheezed painfully and closed his eyes, but when he felt Chong-ba's hand on him, he furiously turned his head to the monk and with a mighty effort, spat blood in his face. "Leave me alone!"

Chong-ba stepped back and then noticed two figures at the top of the cliff. One was a woman, and the other was a rather tall man. He smiled to himself and thought about the eagle feather and its history. Could that be Eva? Had it all come full circle? He turned his gaze on the man, sprawled and bleeding on the rocks. Goldberg's blurred vision was fixed on the people looking down on him.

"Curse you all!" He coughed more blood. His eyes had a distinctly glazed look, but he continued staring at them. "You haven't heard the last of me…I swear." Chong-ba turned to the gravely injured man.

"It is done now, sir. It is over. You never understood, did you?" Josh gurgled noisily.

"The feathers…?" The dying man feverishly remembered that he had not had the chance to make good on his promise to burn them. But Chong-ba didn't answer, for he felt the presence of another being even before Josh Goldberg's body suddenly went rigid with fear. The monk was perplexed at such terror. It seemed more imposing than even the man's fear of dying. When Josh recognized the silhouette approaching from his inner world, he desperately tried to lift himself from the depths of the black hole into which he was sinking, and began cursing every living soul that had crossed his path.

"Hello, William."

"You!" He barely moved his mouth as the blood ran freely into his lungs, slowly beginning to block his airways. He coughed and rasped in agony.

"Are you happy to see me?" Her voice sounded hollow.

"Mary, why don't you ever leave me alone?" His dread of her was many hundreds of years old, and Chong-ba stood back to let the forces of darkness deal with their own. Josh Goldberg tried one more time to feebly lift himself up. "Oh, Mary, you cow!"

"Save the compliments, William," she said as she lifted the axe high above her head. "They have sent me to fetch you, and I know how much you enjoyed dying this way before." The blood curdling scream that came from very deep within his rotten core sent a horrendous echo through the mountains. The desperate holler was reminiscent of his fragmented soul as the dark forces each claimed a piece, and his body finally went limp. Mary Wainthorp smiled forlornly as she dropped the axe and trundled aimlessly off into the shadows. She too had not learnt how to forgive, but as yet had nowhere else to go.

Chong-ba put his hands together and bowed his head. These two souls were still enveloped in darkness; it would be some time before the Light could reach them. And then he lifted his head and looked toward the couple on the top of the cliff, locked in a warm embrace. He smiled. They had finally reached the end of this road. For the first time in so many lives they could be together without having to wait to unite in the Meadow. They were safe and they were home.

"What will happen to Stanway?" She lay in his arms in the dark. His eyes were closed but she knew he was listening. They were back in the Holiday Inn in Lahore, waiting to make the connection to England the following day. Their first night together had been a rediscovery and confirmation of their ancient love, and was filled with tenderness and care for each other. The passion they felt, burned just under the surface, but for the moment, had been tempered by the trauma of the final face-off and the subsequent involvement of the Pakistani government, as well as MI6. Steve pressed his lips to her forehead and held her tighter.

"I don't know, Eva. I'm sure he will find a way to explain himself and lie his way out of this conundrum." He drew his head back to look into her eyes. "I don't want to talk about the intricacies of the establishment and their deception. As it is, the average person cannot see through the illusion and, until a considerable number of people awaken to the truth and we reach a critical mass, the status quo will be maintained. The only thing that will change is that another villain will take Stanway's place to create the false impression of having cleaned up. But enough of that. Tell me about the shapes and colors. I know Hugo sees colors, and that these are all interlinked with the eagle." He stroked her hair softly as he waited for her response.

"The shapes started showing up when I was expecting Hugo. My boy has some explaining to do when we get back to England. Why don't we leave this for him to unravel when we return?" He nodded in the dark.

"It is not too late for us this time, is it Eva?" She understood his question. Parenthood was a privilege denied to them in their previous lives.

"No, it is not too late. And I think Hugo will enjoy having a sibling." She smiled and hid her face in his neck, secure in his embrace and loving every aspect of his nearness.

Outside the boundaries of the Meadow, Teuch and Anacaona had found each other at last.

───

On a wooden bridge above two ancient streams, Hugo and Natalie watched as an owl swooped down one more time before heading back to its wooded home that was once Thorp Pelkington. Quah Dreamer snorted in recognition and pushed away some of the soft soil. His hoof didn't hurt any more.

Chapter 32
The Eternal Dance Of Life

It was overcast and dreary outside, but Jake Fletcher hardly noticed; his troubled mood had nothing to do with the disappointing lukewarm English summer. More than two excruciating years had gone by since they had finished editing their novel, but he remained as haunted as the day he had parted with Rachel D'Angelo in Spain.

His journey with the book started at sixteen in Mr. Borthwick's barn when he was convinced the nesting owls in the roof rafters were prompting him to tell the story that so mysteriously took root in his mind at that tender age. But of course, he didn't write it then. Years later he learned of Rachel's captivating experience with brooding eagles on the cliffs of Cape Breton in Canada, and her dream to write a love story. What a mighty coincidence that worlds apart, two young children each had had an extraordinary experience with wild birds, *and* nurtured a dream to write! Yet, neither was prepared for the exorbitant price of realizing that dream. The bitter irony and incomprehensible turn of events still filled him with anguish.

At the outset of the venture, it was impossible to know that the powerful tale of the feathers would not end with Steve and Eva. His gaze wandered back to the answering machine on his desk, and his melancholy deepened a shade. Since returning from a fourteen day business trip, he had been trying to reach Rachel at her private number for more than a week, but to no avail. He listened to her message one more time.

"Jake, there is an important matter I want to share with you…" Her soft clear voice trailed off, followed by an uncertain pause. "Call me back as soon as you can." It disturbed him that his efforts to contact her were now met with no response; even emails went unanswered. A rather large package with a foreboding quality had arrived earlier that day from her by means of an overnight courier. It was yet unopened.

The last time they had seen each other was at the book launch in Los Angeles three months previous. And before that—there was Spain, a small piece of history already more than two years behind them. *Spain.* Through his office window he noticed gray clouds packing in tightly over the horizon and it darkened his somber mood. Soon the rain would come. At last, troubled and anxious with his inability to reach her, he relented and opened the forbidden door to the past. When Spain came rushing back, he relived every moment of the agonizing parting and it was like it had all happened the day before…

Jake hadn't moved from the patio, from where he had watched her leave. He knew that he was going to miss his flight to England, but it didn't matter anymore. The subtle chill of the Spanish winter was getting to him, and he stuck his hands deep into his pockets. His mind was frozen; stunned by the events that had unfolded during their two week stay here in Spain. He had no idea what the next step should be. He smiled ruefully. *That* was the dilemma. There *was* no next step. Coming face to face with Rachel D'Angelo had caught him on his back foot. The vibrancy of the dark-haired woman with the beautiful laugh surpassed any of the family pictures they had exchanged once in a while, during the time that they were writing *The Meadow*. The meeting at the airport would be etched into his memory forever.

Rachel was not a traditional beauty, but there was something very unusual about the oval shaped face, framed by shoulder length chestnut hair. Shaking her hand that day, Jake was shocked by the strange familiarity she invoked as he looked into her striking hazel eyes. The feeling unnerved him. She lived just outside of Toronto in Canada with her husband and two sons, while he had made his home in North East England with Ruth; they had no children. *The Meadow* was no longer a dream, and the purpose of the meeting, their first since inception of the book three years before, was to edit their epic novel. *This* was the story he had nurtured since boyhood that Rachel had helped him to tell.

First contact between them was the consequence of a friend's recommendation about a book by an unknown author. That was Rachel and his natural interest in esoteric matters prompted him to visit her web site. Then he bought her book.

A slight wind had picked up where Jake stood anchored to the patio, sending a shiver down his spine. Yet, he was barely conscious of his surroundings. His mind was filled with Rachel. She would be at the airport by now, waiting to board the flight back to Canada. He tried to force his thoughts away from her, but soon gave up; she could not be forgotten. He understood that better than ever before.

At first he was convinced of the hand of providence in the unfolding of events, but didn't spend much time analyzing his good fortune. Nothing else could explain why an author, who lived on another continent, would take an interest in *his* untold story and then help him to write it. When she learned how long he had been nurturing the idea for the book, she overruled all his objections and encouraged him to take the leap in committing it to manuscript. He had nothing to lose and, at the very least, was thrilled at her offer to assist. There was a rabbit hole waiting, but neither could see it.

When he finally penned the first chapter and sent it off to her, Rachel not only evaluated his work, but to his surprise, completely rewrote it. When Jake had finished reading her version, he was inwardly stunned. He stared at his computer screen and read it repeatedly, amazed at her ability to pick up on his thoughts and feelings and her detailed description of events. It left him with an eerie feeling, like one slowly descending in very deep water, not knowing when your feet would touch solid ground again. That was when he extended the offer to co-author, and instead of merely helping him, Rachel became an integral part of the project. Three years later it led to their meeting in Spain—and the inevitable parting.

Upon his invitation she had agreed to come to Sitges near Barcelona, where he and Ruth owned a quaint villa along a strip of golden sand. Rachel's husband, Ben, was involved in a building project in Toronto and couldn't afford the time away, while Ruth seized the opportunity to attend a long overdue gardening convention in Japan. It was an unusual arrangement, but both spouses liked the story very much, and editing the book in person just seemed like the natural next step. Jake remembered the slender woman who came through the swinging doors of customs at the airport in Barcelona. The flesh and blood experience of Rachel was something he would never forget.

For the thirty five kilometers between Barcelona and the town of Sitges, they maintained a lively conversation and he looked forward to completing the book and spending time with the woman he had only known through email and phone conversations. He had no idea that destiny had been waiting to play one last card.

En route to the villa he took her to lunch to afford them a chance to become better acquainted. From the terrace where they were seated, Jake's eye caught the impressive outline of the parish church of Sitges, L'església de Sant Bartomeu i Santa Tecla, perched perilously on rocks at the beach. It completely dominated the skyline and was as impossible to overlook as the woman across the table.

"I am a storyteller," she blurted out spontaneously, laughing.

"Really?" He smiled at her. "Is that still a closely guarded secret after the five hundred page novel we have written?" She pulled a face at him but didn't answer his question.

"Do you remember your dreams, Jake?" They were each sipping at a glass of cold, crisp Viura, a popular Spanish white wine. He shook his head slightly.

"Rarely. Do you?" He watched her unobtrusively and noticed how she communicated with her hands and her eyes. She had a great sense of humor and her quick wit was evidence of a sharp mind. The nagging familiarity he had felt at the airport resurfaced and this time it was more distinct. It was a disturbing feeling for which he had no explanation, and for the very first time since inviting her to edit the book at his villa, Jake questioned the wisdom of his decision. When she had begun coaxing the details of the story from the secret corners of his subconscious mind more than three years before, it had revealed a powerful yearning for emotional fulfillment. It made him wonder where such a desire fitted into the life of a happily married man. Her voice drew him back to their discussion.

"I remember them vividly and as a little girl I had a recurring dream of being aboard a wooden galleon."

"If it kept coming back, it must have been significant." He studied her expressive face as she spoke. She was very animated and laughed easily.

"Oh! I must have read too many books as a child, Jake. And I must like happy endings because in this dream a member of the crew was brutally flogged by a foreman and I came to his rescue." She laughed again and a little shock ran through his body. Her laugh triggered something that he couldn't identify. He tried to hide his impatience with himself. What was the matter with him? He turned his attention to her.

"Let me guess, Rachel." She looked up, surprised at his suggestion. "You were a man, a captain or some high ranking officer and rescuing this poor soul put him eternally in your debt. Then he became your personal assistant so you could keep him out of harm's way." Suddenly her smile was gone and she stared at him, a little confused.

"How do you know this?"

"I am not sure I *know* this, Rachel." He spoke softly, watching her closely. "I simply imagined myself in the poor fellow's shoes and what I said, felt right." Rachel held his gaze for a few moments and then averted her eyes to the glass in her hand.

"We had better start the editing, Jake. We have a mammoth task ahead of us." Her dream would not be mentioned again until the day before she left.

Only a half hour from Barcelona, Sitges is a renowned tourist destination with a strong community of English speaking residents who make their permanent homes here. The specific time of year for her visit was perfect since the Spanish winter meant that the normally overcrowded beaches would be quiet. The cocktail bars, the sarong and souvenirs shops would no longer take center stage and he had been optimistic that, time permitting, he could interest Rachel in some of the town's more hidden charms. He enjoyed museums tremendously and hoped that she could be enticed into taking a break from their grueling editing schedule to visit Museu Cau Ferrat which featured not only Picasso and El Greco, but also a fine collection of Sitges artists. His instincts had been right; she loved museums.

"Of course! How can you know where you are going if you don't know from whence you came?" The exact phrase struck a chord. It was one he used frequently to entice Ruth to visit historical places, but she was rarely interested.

"It is settled then. We'll go to the museum when we need a breather."

Where he stood in his office at home, Jake tried to stem the flow of memories, but every small detail of that day relentlessly thrust the past back into the present. He recalled the palpable chill in the air as he slowly made his way back into the villa. He realized that he would have to re-book his flight, but couldn't muster the motivation. Inside the house it was very quiet; even eerie. His gaze roamed over the table in the dining room where they had worked side by side for two weeks. Even if he could turn back the clock, Jake knew that he would never do so. Some memories are worth the pain and confusion it would cause for a lifetime. This was one.

He walked over to the music center and, flicking the switch, the room immediately filled with the soft classical music that had constantly played in the background as they worked on their book. The clear soprano tone of Angela Gheorghiu, an old-timer, drifted gently through the room. "O mio Babbino caro" was one of Rachel's favorites, but he tried not to think of that as he sat in his usual chair. To avoid mistakes, they had chosen to work off one computer; his. It was still open, but had gone into hibernation and the screen was blank. He looked around the room. Everything was very much the same, except her chair was vacant. Rachel was gone.

Fourteen glorious days in Spain. His mouth felt dry. The magnitude of what had occurred was beginning to sink in, but he no longer knew how to plot a course for the future. His mind stubbornly wandered back to the harmonious confluence of their energies and the creative environment in which they had worked. Like two very old friends, they perfectly understood the needs and shortcomings of the other. They laughed frequently and finished each other's sentences, to the amusement of the one who had been quipped. Their time was drawing to an end and they had almost completed the editing when it happened. They were seated in the bay window of a local restaurant after a hard day's work, watching the flow of local pedestrians, when he caught her look.

"That is quite a penetrating stare, Rachel. Is something the matter?" She didn't answer his question immediately and looked away.

"Remember when I told you about my recurring dream?" He nodded, suspecting what she wanted to know. "How did you know what had happened?" She watched him closely. His tall frame was relaxed but his expression was pensive as he stared earnestly back at her. There was no recognition, nor remembrance—only curiosity.

"I wish I knew the answer. Perhaps it was just a good guess. Who knows?" Then he leaned forward and said quietly. "But there's another matter, Rachel." He hesitated, appearing slightly apprehensive. "It's about the first chapter of our book. It might not seem important to you, but I have been plagued with a thought that sometimes seems rather absurd, but I can't get rid of it." She looked inquiringly at him. "Remember when Anacaona was thrown from her horse and Teuch thought that something terrible had happened?" Rachel smiled coyly and raised a hesitant hand to interrupt him. Her heartbeat increased slightly, overwhelmed with the specific scene that he had chosen from the story.

"She wasn't unconscious, Jake." Her voice had dropped to a whisper. "She only pretended." Rachel's eyes shone brightly. "She did that because she wanted him to come closer." Her calm delivery shook him; the insecurity he noticed before in her was suddenly gone. For a few moments he just stared at her without moving. None of this was in the story or had ever been discussed, but her words perturbed him greatly and he needed to hear more.

"How do you know?" he asked hoarsely. "Are you guessing?" But she didn't waver.

"She told him on their wedding night," Rachel said simply. His eyes bored into hers and she stared back, unblinking. "She confessed while he was helping her to remove the red feathers she had worn for the wedding ceremony; *that* was when she told him." At last she looked away, this time shaking visibly. "Then they made love," she whispered, avoiding his eyes. She had no idea that he also knew.

"Jesus!" The color drained from his face and his voice sounded raspy as he struggled to regain his composure. The enormous implication of her words had driven his thoughts into complete chaos. "How can we both know that she had been pretending? We have never discussed

this. I don't understand, Rachel!" He hesitated, incapable of finding the right words, *any words*. "Do you?" he finally managed to ask. She didn't answer. They hadn't placed an order yet, but their appetites had evaporated. "Is this why I knew about your dream?" he asked barely audibly. She nodded slowly, but kept her eyes on the ocean, answering softly.

"Yes, Jake. You *remembered*. You just didn't realize it." He leaned forward and took hold of her hand, needing to touch her. His world was in total disarray, but he wanted more confirmation. He wondered if they took the time to discuss each of the past lives, more would be revealed. But his conscious mind resisted the information; it was too much to take in. It all sounded fantastical and impossible. Yet his pounding heart suggested otherwise and impelled the burning question that had plagued him since the beginning.

"Is the Meadow a real place, Rachel?" He strained to get the words out. "We have written about it as though it exists, but I always thought that it was only a figment of my imagination. I fantasized about its existence when I was a child, but had no certainty." Jake hesitated, confused. "*Is it real?*"

"I don't know." There were tears in her eyes. "I would like to believe it is. How else can we explain any of this? For years I have visited a place in my dreams similar to the one we have described in our story. That is where the images of the waving grass and changing winds originate; they come from my experiences in dreams and visions." She looked away. "Everything we can imagine exists somewhere in the Universe; or so I believe."

"Let's get out of here." He had seen the tears but he didn't know how to deal with what had just happened, and he was suddenly afraid to touch her. A myriad of confusing thoughts flooded his mind and he needed to find his way through a labyrinth where truth and imagination randomly intertwined, seemingly with no rhyme or reason. "Do you think we will be able to walk this off?" He smiled at her, not sure anymore of the right thing to say. She nodded, not trusting herself to speak, but felt a tremendous relief that he finally shared her knowledge.

They spoke very little as they walked slowly through the streets of Sitges, peering into shop windows or just admiring the bustling activity. She hadn't told him how closely he resembled Teuch and how surprised she had been when they came face to face at the airport in Barcelona. That was when she realized that the description of Teuch must have originated from memory and that the tall dark-haired man walking beside her shockingly resembled the character in the book. More so, the distinctive gait of Jake Fletcher was unmistakably that of Teuch.

He couldn't remember how they ended up at the Museu Cau Ferrat in town. They must have driven there, but his memory was fuzzy about the details. The museum was the home and studio of the painter and collector Santiago Rusinol who had bought two 16th Century fisherman's cottages and renovated them, later adding Gothic features. The ground floor of the house was filled with beautiful ceramics and neither of them spoke as they wandered around admiring the paintings, some by Rusinol and a few by Picasso and El Greco. Deeply affected by the startling detour they had taken into a far distant past, they were curiously suspended in a place where the boundaries of time were erased, incapable of addressing the overwhelming implication of what was before them. Yet, each took pains to avoid the only thing they wanted to talk about.

Back on the street, they were drawn to a small gathering of people on the sidewalk. Sitges was famous for the variety of artists it attracted from all over the world, and in the bright sunlight they sauntered over to watch a stoic-faced mime attempt escape from an illusory glass box. A few enthusiastic street musicians formed an impromptu ensemble and more onlookers joined the small street party. Then Rachel noticed the painter seated against an outer wall of the museum that they had just visited, and the array of artwork displayed casually around him. As she approached, a painting propped up against the whitewashed wall immediately grabbed her attention and she caught her breath. The leather-faced native Indian from South America looked out of place. He had heard the gasp, but did not look up. She was staring at what seemed to be an ancient town square dating back to the Aztec period, or even much earlier. She felt Jake beside her and pointed at two rather small feathers in the bottom corner of the painting. The word "Leyenda" was written underneath and Jake's heart lurched.

"Are these meant to be the feathers of an eagle and an owl?" he asked incredulously, turning his attention to the artist. It was a wild, improbable guess, too far fetched to even consider. But the imperceptible nod from the wrinkled faced man with the silver braid snaking down his back came as a shock.

"Leyenda," the old artist mumbled softly, and continued painting. Jake looked at Rachel, shaken.

"My Spanish is not very good but I know that 'leyenda' means 'legend.' There is a restaurant by that name in the next town. He caught her outstretched hand, still pointing at the feathers. She was clearly as stunned as he was. "Rachel...*Oh, God.* What is this native Indian doing in Sitges with a painting about two feathers and a legend? Can this be a coincidence?" His face was etched in disbelief. "Is there something we need to realize?" He paused, his lips scarcely moving. Then he pulled her urgently aside.

"Is it possible that we have written our *own* story?" Incapable of speaking, she nodded her head slowly, and watched in wonder as he lifted her hand to his mouth, unlocking the passion that had been ignited thousands of years before. She didn't resist when he deliberately pulled her into his embrace. She slid her arms around his neck easily, as if she had done it a thousand times, not caring if anyone was watching. Her mind went blank. Nothing else existed; nothing else was real. There was only Jake. She wanted to remember this moment for the rest of her life. She felt the warmth of his skin through his shirt where her face pressed into his chest but neither could find the right words. The fragile breakthrough barred any attempt at rationalization, but finally he managed a soft whisper over her head.

"What forces have drawn us together, Rachel?" He held her away and looked into her eyes. "It seems so impossible but I think I've been waiting all my life for you." His voice echoed dully in her heart. The reality of their lives could never accommodate this discovery; there was no future for them. "What will tomorrow bring?"

The poignant question hung unanswered between them, but they were still in Spain and Rachel's feminine body was pressed softly into his. At that moment nothing else seemed to matter, and throwing caution to the wind, Jake's mouth closed warmly over hers. He didn't want to think of the next day, and drawing the full length of her body tightly against his, he deepened the kiss. How could love like this be forgotten? The ancient dream had awakened into the twenty first century. Like a thin wisp of smoke it had risen from the smoldering embers of antiquity and snaked a path through centuries of unspeakable violence, impossible sacrifice and incredible passion to find its way back into their lives.

Afterwards he bought the painting for her without quibbling about the exorbitant price. He would have paid twice as much. He only wanted her to have it; he had nothing else to give her.

Jake couldn't remember how long he had remained seated at the dining table that day, but recalled that his body felt stiff and that he had lost all track of time as soft classical tones drifted through the air. Music had been such an important part of their closeness, but that day it bared his anguish because it reminded him of her. He had closed his eyes and concentrated on the beautiful voice control of Earnest Young and Nicolai Gedda singing the Temple Duet of Bizet. It was another of Rachel's favorites and it was the same melody that had opened the doors to paradise that night.

When they returned from the museum, they were famished and he joined her in the kitchen. His culinary skills were nothing to write home about, but what was between them was palpable and real and impelled closeness. However, in the confined space of the kitchen, the growing intimacy between them strained their movements and stilted communication, and they were both relieved to get away.

On an uncharacteristically warm night for that time of year, they had dinner on the patio with only a single candle between them. The salt of the ocean was in the air and while the Temple Duet played softly in the background, they ate in silence. Their hearts and minds overflowed with unasked questions, craving reassurance of what they felt, but for which words were hopelessly inadequate to fill the blank spaces left by thousands of years of separation and loss. Thus they remained quiet; warily avoiding the topic of her leaving the next day. They simply relied on each other's nearness for confirmation of a bond and a love that was ancient, but unmistakable. Finally she made the first move and stood, gathering their plates.

"I have a long day ahead of me tomorrow. I think we should get some sleep, Jake." But when she walked past him, he held out his arm to prevent her from leaving. She trembled as she put the plates back on the table and addressed him softly. "Perhaps tomorrow we will see it all in a different light. This sultry night, the wine, the painting we have found—us; it has all been so overwhelming and…intoxicating." But as she spoke those words, she knew they were meaningless. Ending the night was not what either of them wanted and he rose as if he hadn't heard her.

"Don't go, Rachel." He laid his hands tenderly on either side of her face and, leaning in closer, whispered softly. "Come with me." She felt his warm breath on the side of her face and wanted more.

"Jake…" Rachel recognized the tidal wave of emotion as it approached, but his gentle plea tore at her heart. Thousands of years before, they were Teuch's words to Anacaona, luring her to the forest. Enchanted with a moment anchored so securely in an ancient past, she whispered against his mouth. "Where to?" At first he didn't answer. This was the crossroad, but he no longer hesitated. Her dark eyes shone in the flickering light of the candle and he knew that she understood. He dropped his hands to her shoulders and spoke thickly just as the wave swept over them.

"To paradise," he murmured as he gathered her to him. Did he carry her to the bedroom or did they walk? He thought he might have carried her, but the details were lost; time had ceased to exist. All he could remember was her quivering body as they stood face to face in the semi-dark of the bedroom where she slept, and then he knew with blinding clarity why she had seemed so familiar to him at the airport in Barcelona. She was not quite as tall, but Rachel physically resembled Anacaona. He put his arms around her waist and drew her close, burying his face in her hair. "How long have you known?" He sounded lost. She closed her eyes as she descended with him into forbidden ecstasy. She too was lost.

"I discovered parallel universes during meditation when we were working on chapter three, our life in Africa. When I realized that we were writing our own story, it came as an enormous shock. But I didn't know how to tell you." He listened to the soft tone of her voice and held her tighter. He never wanted to let her go. "I knew that you would have to discover this in your own way, Jake."

"You didn't have to trick me when you fell from your horse, you know," he reprimanded tenderly. The sensual combination of her femininity and agile mind was enormously attractive, but Rachel was so much more than that. And then he understood the inexplicable longing for emotional fulfillment he had felt for so many years. It was explained in the flesh and blood woman he held in his arms.

"I was so afraid that you would never come any closer," she said with a shy smile. The reality of their respective responsibilities loomed large in his mind and feebly raised a red flag, but her closeness negated any coherent thought and he deliberately ignored it.

"Oh, God, Rachel…" An ancient dream had come alive to resurrect them as Jake and Rachel in Spain. Together at last, yet still apart. But he was willing to take that, if only for one night. Tomorrow was another day that he'd rather not think about while the image of the first night with his bride of antiquity burned so feverishly in his mind. "Do you remember the final part of the marriage ritual before we united as man and woman?" Her answer was to gently loosen his grip around her waist. Then she reached for the top button on his shirt and, keeping her eyes on her hands, she spoke softly.

"We had to undress ourselves. In our culture it signaled parting with a single life for the last time." A tiny smile played around her lips. "You were *so* impatient, Jake." He could barely breathe. His head was filled with her softness, the magic and beauty of her sensual seduction and the wild anticipation of being gifted with a piece of history that had sustained him through eons to be with her again in this way. He reached for her blouse, fumbling to find the buttons.

"Shouldn't we be doing this ourselves?" He sounded tortured.

"We were married then, Jake." Her lips barely moved, but he heard every word. There was no hesitation on her part; only a mature acceptance of what the moment offered. She wanted it as much as he did. "That bond has never been broken."

The intensity of their love threatened to destroy him, yet he had never known such utter joy and fulfillment. Rachel's mind and body intertwined with his in an act of such complete abandonment that it left him breathless. In the heightened state of each union, he realized that they were compensating for the intense pain and frustration of the ancient lives which they so vividly remembered. Jake marveled at how she moved with him and instinctively followed his lead, and how peacefully she drifted in and out of slumber. Yet he fought sleep, afraid that it would hurry along the hours to daybreak when he wanted to hold her for as long as he could. The desire to touch her was constant. When she slept in between their lovemaking, he watched her in the dark and gently traced the outline of her body with his hands, comforting her and etching upon his mind forever the wonder of her closeness and warmth.

"Have you not slept at all?" It was a soft whisper in the dark. She put her hands over his where they rested on the full curve of her breasts. He brushed his lips gently to her ear, before kissing her softly.

"I can't bear to sleep when I know what tomorrow holds." He sounded very tired. "How will we live after Spain?" She turned her head to meet his mouth. She had no answer.

"You need to get some rest, Jake. Let me help you." He watched spellbound as she placed two pillows against the headboard and then leaned her back against it. "Come here." It was the most beautiful invitation he had ever received. Lying on his back between her legs, she tenderly pulled his head onto her chest. Then she locked her legs over his groin and sensuously ran her fingers over his face and into his hair. He listened to her soft breathing and felt every muscle in her body move, as she worked her way gently around his temples and the contours of his features with excruciating tenderness in a deed that was unbearably erotic. Finally, exhausted, he closed his eyes, and in the small hours of the morning they both drifted off to sleep.

When he looked again he was in a place that was eerily familiar with Rachel by his side.

"The Meadow?" he asked in wonder, looking around at the waving grass and babbling brook. The sweet smell of wild vegetation filled the air. Rachel nodded, enchanted.

"It is the same place, Jake. This is the Meadow of my dreams," she said simply. "And we are here together; it must be real." Then she stared off into the distance at the shimmering horizon. "Someone is coming." The figure emerged from the haze and slowly approached to stand before them. They had no idea who she was.

"Hello, Jake. Hello, Rachel." Her long blonde hair blew gently in the wind and the expression on her face was serene. "It has been some time. You have questions for me." They looked at her, mystified. Then

Rachel frowned. *Is this possible?* She stared intently at the young woman with the tranquil expression. Then she heard a familiar laugh bubble up.

"*Natalie?*" she ventured with caution, thinking that she couldn't be right. Natalie was a little girl in the story that they had created; this beautiful young woman was probably in her mid twenties.

"Athenae." She smiled at them. "Natalie is the character Jake had subconsciously created for you because you always wanted a girl, where you have only two boys with Ben in your life as Rachel." In the shocked silence that followed, she continued. "You have already discovered that you have written your own story. You are Teuch and Anacaona, just as you were each of the lead characters in subsequent chapters of your book."

"How do you know this?" Jake had found his voice, astonished.

"You came here to the Meadow after every life, Jake. This is the halfway station for souls who are progressing on a spiritual path and you and Rachel met in this beautiful place at the end of each earthly existence." She smiled at them. "Come, let us walk and I will try to explain."

"There is something that doesn't make any sense at all." Jake had his arm around Rachel. It was the most natural thing for him to do and she leaned into his body as though they had never been apart. Athenae noticed, but didn't comment. After all, she knew their whole history.

"The story of Steve and Eva?" She pre-empted him and laughed at his surprise.

"Yes. Their lives overlap with Rachel's life and mine. How can that be?"

"Well, of course they do! They are complete figments of your imagination, Jake. You created these two characters because you so desperately wanted to find a way to be together and have that happy ending that has eluded you for so long. In fact the seed for the book had been planted in your consciousness before you incarnated this time. We had talked about it here, and *that* was what niggled at you in the barn when you were just a boy." She smiled broadly. "But of course, you needed Rachel to help you tell the story. The eagles reminded her of the same mission when she was but a girl on the cliffs of Cape Breton." Jake stared at her and frowned.

"The shapes were present in the chapters about our ancient lives, but the theme carried through into the fictional existences of Steve and Eva. How could we have known to expand on the idea the way we did?"

"The purpose of the book you have written was to demonstrate the interconnectedness of the Universe. You were subconsciously aware of this and therefore brought the true meaning full circle by introducing the shapes as a symbol of the bond that existed between Steve and Eva, as it does between you. Hugo had to be included at some stage, as he would help unravel the mystery. And although the eagle appeared to dominate these various shapes, it is the triangle that has the deepest esoteric meaning. It represents the true origin of the Universe." Their faces shone with wonderment.

"We must have felt the influence from somewhere, Athenae." Rachel's voice was soft, almost reverent. "How did we get it right?"

"The prompts came from here." Athenae smiled. "One more thing," she continued, not missing a beat. "Hugo used the colors of red, yellow and blue, remember?" They nodded. "This was his combination number of *three*, representing the three sides of the triangle, from where he could add any other number or color to create the desired experience. In essence *one* represents force; *two* signifies the opening and *three* becomes the birthing of true wisdom. The tie between Steve, Eva and Hugo is a demonstration of this triangle and the immense possibilities for accessing knowledge from Source, if the intention is pure. There really are no secrets. If you can match the frequency or vibration of what you want to know—then by design, the answer will be revealed. Hugo demonstrated that brilliantly in your story, but it is true for everyone." Athenae allowed sufficient time for the information to be absorbed and then turned to Rachel.

"You are curious about me?"

"Are you really Natalie?" The young woman seemed more familiar by the minute, but she couldn't comprehend how she could be the same sweet elfin child in the story.

"I am Athenae. But you enlisted my help subconsciously and were able to access my child form to assist Hugo. Therefore yes, I am Natalie. That is the name you have given me."

"Is Hugo also a fictional character?" Athenae shook her head.

"With the exception of Steve and Eva, some of your characters are actually based in reality because they are linked to your past." She looked at them somberly. "But before we get to them, there is another matter of importance." She got right to the point. "Life on earth was never meant to be ideal because perfection stands in the way of spiritual progress. Time and again, those who had contributed most to the advancement of the race had suffered terribly. However," her gaze wandered to the shimmering horizon, "*mindless suffering* makes no sense. It is just more ignorance." Then she turned her gaze directly upon them. "Insight into pain and misery is the basis of self-empowerment which could potentially end the cycle of rebirth and elevate you to adventures elsewhere in the Universe." She smiled sweetly. "When have you learned enough? *You decide.*" The soft spoken wisdom was beguiling. Jake suspected it was a personal message of some kind, but it was Rachel who asked the question.

"We decide when we've learned enough? I'm not sure I understand that." Athenae looked from Rachel to Jake and hesitated only briefly.

"You will." She began walking away, beckoning them to follow. "Let us clear up some mysteries; we do not have much time. Remember your interlude with the owl, Jake?" He nodded, smiling. How could he forget that? It was what had motivated him to write. "When you return to England, pay the Borthwick farm a visit. The old man is long gone, but his son keeps a shining ebony stud who will be overjoyed to see you. Spethla has followed you through many lives and this one is no exception. You subconsciously knew this, which is why you created a role for him in Steve's life. But Spethla is real." Athenae smiled at the expression on Jake's face and continued.

"Hugo lives on the island of Cape Breton where you were raised, Rachel. He is a recluse with a brilliant mind who rarely agrees to receive visitors. He is also an expert in the Mayan Calendar and its spiritual meaning, and a genius when it comes to mathematics. But he also studies birds, in particular eagles. He regularly goes to the same cliff where you made your acquaintance with Mrs. Eagle when you were just a girl. He is of course, Sakhota, dating back to your lives as Ann and Nathaniel and as Weayaya, your beloved brother in the life as Tiva. His spiritual name is Sathwa. Sathwa is a transient, like yourselves, but he is about to move on and will not incarnate in the earth sphere after this life. His learning there is complete. He has made the decision to move on to adventures elsewhere." She smiled.

"What is your role in the Meadow, Athenae?" Rachel was captivated. "And is this recluse's name Hugo?" Athenae looked from Rachel to Jake and nodded her head slowly.

"This has been my home for eons where I act as a spiritual guide. But to answer your second question, Jake chose all the names for your characters and his imagination lead him to choose appropriate ones. Hugo's name on the earth is Simon Gregory, and Chong-ba's is simply Xzan. He is still a monk and his real spiritual name is Mantohl. Xzan is quite old and he lives in the Sumela Monastery high in the mountains of Trabzon in Turkey where he keeps busy as a tourist guide. Xzan, alias Chong-ba, is also Three Fingers, the medicine man who announced your birth to the world when you were born as Tiva." She looked at them closely. "That was the only life in which the evil one could not find you."

"You mean Josh Goldberg, in all his grotesque incarnations?" Jake sounded astonished. "Is *his* name real? This sounds so incredible, Athenae." He took Rachel's hand and squeezed it. "Can you tell us where he is?" She looked curiously at them and didn't answer his question immediately.

"I am glad that you came to the Meadow together as Jake and Rachel. In the past you were always in the inter-life phase. This is why you don't remember me as such."

"Are we dreaming, Athenae?" Rachel was filled with wonder.

"Not really. Rather, your deep love for each other and a mutual desire to visit the Meadow has made this journey possible. This is a good example of the Law of Intention." She smiled secretively. "But in reality, it is a combination of lucid dreaming and astral traveling that brought you here. You will remember everything when you awaken."

"Who is Josh Goldberg? If he is real then it would be important for us to know." Jake felt a slight impatience. He was aware that the energy in the Meadow was changing and that time was running out.

"Right now he resides in Germany and his real name is Stefan Kröll." She stared off into the distance and dropped her voice. "He has no spiritual name here as he does not belong with us yet. Don't be fooled. He is still real and very dangerous; another reason why you instinctively included him in your story. He represents the negative aspects of humanity as he turns his back against the Light, casting his own dark shadow, but providing the contrast so crucial for spiritual growth." Jake gathered Rachel close to him.

"Will this end some time, Athenae?"

"I do not know. Kröll is a prominent member of your establishment. He will soon know about your book. He wants the masses remaining oblivious to the interconnectedness of their world; it is the first requirement of manipulation. His mission is far from being over, but you must remain focused on your journey, not his. Attention to his path will force you to return again and again. Remember that you decide when you have learned enough." Then she looked up into the sky and whispered. "The wind is changing direction and the energy has shifted. It is time for you to go." She lifted an arm in greeting. "Until we meet again." In her role as a keeper in the Meadow, Athenae never meddled with destiny. A great deal would depend on how Jake and Rachel exercised their free will.

Rachel reached a hand towards Athenae, but she disappeared into the shimmering light the same way that she had come; rippling away in the wind. Then she felt Jake's strong arms around her and woke up in his embrace. For the longest time they just held each other and allowed the overwhelming experience of the Meadow to wash over them in full consciousness. Neither had the courage to mention the parting scheduled for that same day. She had to return to her life in Canada and he had to go home to England. Instead, he cupped her face in his hands and whispered with reverence.

"I am so relieved to know that the Meadow is a real place." She nodded slowly, smiling through her tears. No words could describe the depth of the love that they felt for each other. Neither was there any question that they would return to their respective families. It was the only thing to do. Just like so many times before, they had come together, only to part again. Neither he nor she mentioned it.

She didn't want him to drive her to the airport and he would never forget the expression in her eyes when he kissed her for the last time as she got into the taxi. She didn't look back and he remained rooted to the patio for more than an hour after she had left. And then, as an overwhelming sadness filled his entire being, he finally spoke softly to himself.

"I will pray for us, Rachel. There is nothing else to do."

But she was long gone. Spain had come to an end.

When he had finally awakened from his reverie, he noticed that the rain was coming down hard. How long had he been sitting there? He didn't know, but decided to open the patio door to his office. He seldom subjected himself to remembering Spain in such detail, but when he did, it fatigued him. He needed the fresh air. Standing on the patio listening to the rain beating down, Jake almost did not hear the phone ringing. He reached it with a few long strides.

"Jake? This is Ben D'Angelo." The connection between England and Eastern Canada wasn't very good. Jake was puzzled.

"Ben?" He had met her husband only once at the book launch in Los Angeles.

"Rachel's husband." He sounded faint.

"Oh! My apologies, Ben. I wasn't expecting to hear from you. I've been trying to contact Rachel for over a week and—"

"That is why I am calling, Jake." The raw tension in Ben's voice reached him through the telephone line.

"Is everything alright?" He suddenly had trouble breathing, but didn't know why.

"Our worlds have been shaken up… I am at a loss for words, Jake."

"What is wrong, Ben?" A cold hand closed over his heart.

"She had such a bright future ahead of her…especially after your book."

"What are you talking about?" His heart raced wildly, in vehement denial of the terrible thing he already sensed.

"She's dead, Jake!" There it was. The unspeakable, spoken; the ghastly suspicion, manifest. He reeled in shock; his mind refusing to process the news. He waited anxiously to awake from the nightmare, but Ben's words hung resolutely in the air. Then everything came to a slow halt, and the light went out of the world. There was no sound.

Jake tried to speak, but couldn't move, nor hear anything. "Rachel died last night."

"Died...?" He mouthed the words mechanically, but his mind rejected its meaning as incomprehensible and impossible. *"What?"* A dry whisper reached his lips. Ben was still speaking but Jake was standing in a wind tunnel where a mighty force threatened to end his existence. He had no lifeline and his world careened dangerously out of control. Then his legs gave way to the chair at his desk. *"How?"* he rasped with a frozen mind. A part of him managed to ask questions, but the answers disappeared into a void of denial. He closed his eyes, but saw her laughing image at the airport in Barcelona where they met for the first time. *Rachel!* The silent cry smothered in anguish.

Jake didn't remember much from the rest of the conversation. His heart had dropped into his stomach and his voice echoed dully, as he backed into a black hole of irreversible loss. He tried to express his condolences, but saw the light in her eyes and heard that beautiful laugh. His heart faltered. Ben said something about a fast growing inoperable brain tumor discovered shortly after the launch of their book, preceded by a series of blackouts. She didn't want anyone to know. *That is why she called! She changed her mind. She wanted to tell me!* His heart expanded and contracted frantically, as if weighing the decision to live or to die. The hand holding the phone shook visibly while Ben's voice droned on in the background.

"I found the package addressed to you still sitting on the desk in her office. I sent it with a courier yesterday, Jake. I thought she had done it already, but obviously—"

"It is here, Ben." Her husband rambled on as if he hadn't heard. "It came today—"

"Rachel went to quite a bit of trouble to get it for you, but a week ago she prematurely slipped into a coma. No one expected it would happen so fast—" But Jake couldn't listen any more; it was excruciating to think of her as incapacitated. They were back in the town of Sitges again after he had bought the painting for her. The sun was on her hair and her eyes were full of love for him. That was when he kissed her soft mouth and held the woman he had loved for so long for the first time. He didn't tell Ben that the package was yet unopened. He forced himself to look at it, unaware that tears were streaming down his face. The rest of the conversation blurred. He heard something about funeral arrangements to be posted on her web site before it would be taken down for good. Then the phone call was over and Jake sat staring at the package.

Infinity passed before he finally stood and opened it with trembling hands. He couldn't think. The news about Rachel was impossible to take in and he fumbled clumsily through the layers of bubble wrap protection. Then at last he pulled a large silver frame from a box and held it at arm's length. Jake stopped breathing. In his hands he held the tail feathers of an eagle and an owl, wonderfully framed together. He stared dry-mouthed at her magnificent gift and understood for the first time how a heart could break. Then he felt the envelope taped to the back.

It was still pouring with rain when he noticed the patio door ajar. He slowly walked over to stand in its opening. Her letter was in his pocket but he didn't have the courage to read it. His heart beat with a dull aching thud. As long as he didn't read the letter, it felt as though he could stall the finality of her death; ward off the terrible pain of living in this world without her. She didn't belong to him, but somehow it was enough to know that she was around somewhere, breathing, laughing, and thinking of him.

"Come with me…" he said softly, imagining her in front of him.

"Where to?" The whisper that reached him blew away in the wind but it was enough to jolt him back to reality. He felt like a very old man when he pulled the letter from his pocket. She must have still been able to write; the short note was in her handwriting. In the fading light Jake mustered the strength to read Rachel's letter.

My dearest Jake

The Legend promises that he who finds the feathers will live eternally with the one that he loves. I have found them for you.

In the endless dance of Life, I will forever meet you in the Meadow.

Rachel

When he had finished reading, he folded the note and slipped it into his breast pocket. Then he stepped out into the rain and began walking.

It was a solemn, mechanical walk and every step he took heightened the grief of his enormous loss. The path led through mud pools and loose gravel on the side of the road, but his mind labored back to a time before the dream awakened from the swirling mist of antiquity. And while relentless rain poured from the heavens, Jake ambled along in a void of pain, trying to grasp the meaning of their history; mulling over each life they had shared, searching for the thread that held the tapestry of the past and the present together. But to no avail. His hand strayed to the breast pocket containing the note, but it fell helplessly to his side. He couldn't bear to think of her letter or her gift.

Hours later he recognized the field in front of him, but Mr Borthwick's barn was no longer there. It had been replaced with a modern stable dimly identifiable in the distance through a gray curtain of rain. Yet, it was the same spot where he had begun his writing career years before under the auspices of the barn owls. He turned his face to the darkened skies.

"Where does our history leave me—*without you*, Rachel?" He did not expect an answer, but expressing his anguish comforted him in a strange way. "What is the point if you are taken from me every time? And what am I to learn *this time*?" In the constant rain he continued his heartbreaking monologue, but the solemn conversation with Rachel, who wasn't there to listen to him and love him, heightened his despair. His voice dropped to a whisper. "What is the missing piece, Rachel? What don't I understand?" In the distance a light had gone on in one of the stables and he heard voices calling, but was only momentarily distracted. "What force keeps us apart?" He leaned his arms on the fence surrounding the field and his thoughts drifted back to their wondrous visit to the Meadow. He closed his eyes and waited, and for the longest time, heard and felt only the rain. Then suddenly, she was there.

"It is *knowing*, Jake." Her breath was warm and sweet against his cheek. "Knowing is so much more than faith. We cannot die." He kept his eyes closed, willing the moment to continue forever. "We are already immortal and physical death is simply a door to the next adventure. Loss is what teaches us to love more deeply, which is why we love each other as we do." He thought he felt her soft and feminine embrace. For one excruciating moment he held onto the idea that her presence was real, but it was only his imagination. Rachel was no longer here. In his hour of need the answer was effortlessly revealed, just like Athenae had promised. And this provided the means to carry on without her.

However, the soft snort in the twilight just ahead was beyond question, and he opened his eyes in shock to the horse standing on the other side of the fence. He hadn't heard its approach, but in the semi-darkness, the ebony coat was unmistakable, glistening brilliantly in the rain.

"*Spethla?*" he whispered incredulously. The muscles of the proud and regal animal rippled in nervous anticipation and he neighed softly, anxiously. Jake's heart almost exploded as he reached with trembling hands for the strong, familiar face. And then, in the drenching rain, Spethla stepped closer and sniffed his ancient master's hand, his face, his hair in a deeply emotional reunion. They both heard the soft whistle from afar, but neither moved. Finally Jake spoke and, while he reverently stroked the strong neck of his faithful friend, he wondered what name had been chosen for the horse in *this* life.

"She is already in the Meadow, Spethla." He laid his open palm on the head of the horse in a signature greeting which the animal, flaring his nostrils, instantly recognized. "And she's waiting for us," he whispered softly, smiling through joyful tears. "This time we came to write the book. But I wonder what we will do next. What adventures lie beyond the earth plane?" The whistle grew louder. "You had better run along, Spethla. But I will be back." Long after the horse had taken off and disappeared into the mist, Jake stood anchored to the spot where his old friend had come to console him. His heart still ached, but a shift had occurred.

When he began the long walk home it was still raining hard, but the final piece had slipped into place. The pact they had made thousands of years before was still intact and would never be broken. They had discovered the real Meadow—and that life is eternal.

And now the story of "The Meadow" has been told.

The Meadow 481

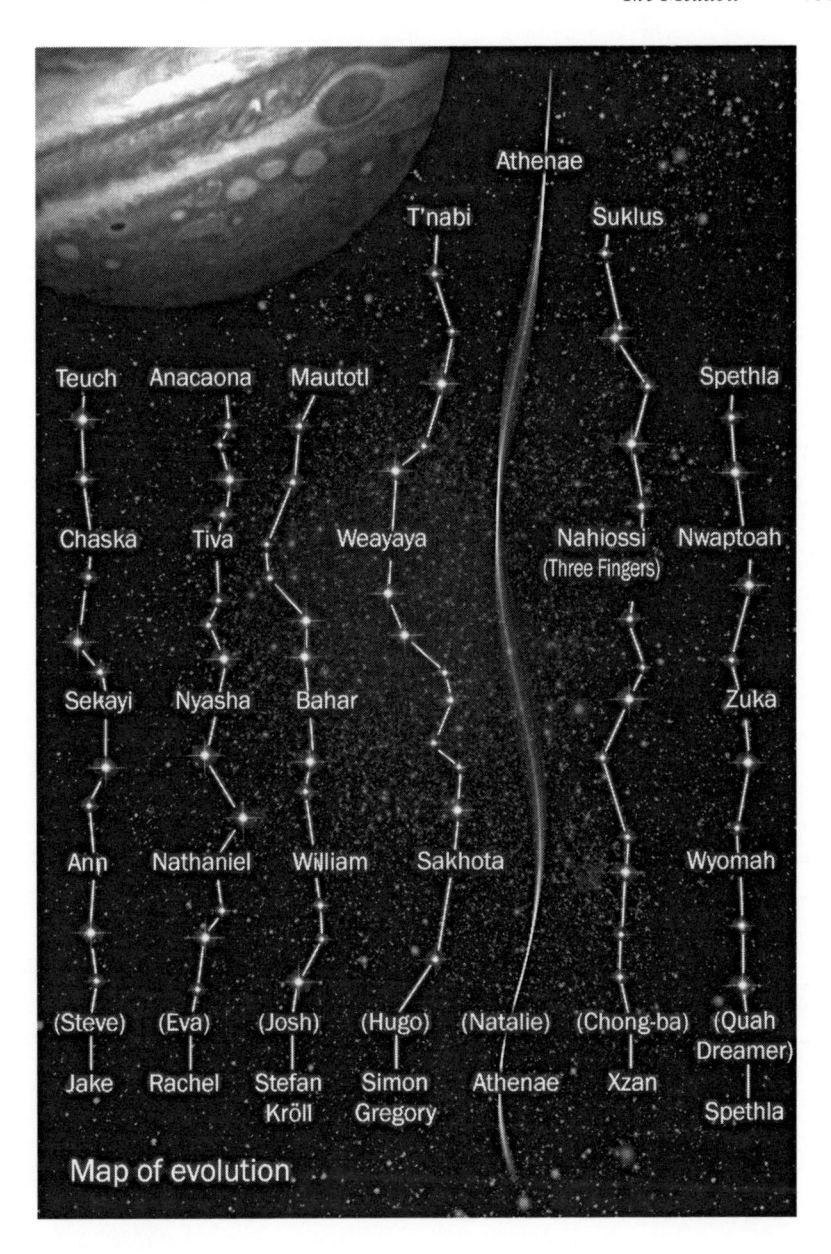

Map of evolution.

Perseus Cluster: A. Fujii
Jupiter: Reta Beebe, Amy Simon (New Mexico State Univ.), and NASA/ESA
Creative application of these images as per: http://creativecommons.org/licenses/by/3.0/ does not imply
endorsement of the story or its philosophy.

ABOUT THE AUTHORS

A remarkable aspect of *The Meadow* is that the authors hail from separate continents and for most of their lives knew nothing about each other's existence. By the time they had completed their mega manuscript they had still not laid eyes on one another and, given their life circumstances and vocations, even a chance meeting was a most unlikely possibility. Yet, with Mike O'Hare who is from North East England and Elfreda Pretorius, who resides in Canada, an interesting but powerful force was at work which would dictate almost three years of their lives. In 2005 an unusual meeting of minds set the scene for an ambitious project that neither author could have foretold, even if they had had a crystal ball.

Mike O'Hare began his career as a compositor in the newspaper industry but with an inherent love of writing, the pen always lay alongside the setting stick/Linotype keyboard and he soon began contributing short editorials for his local paper. In 1969 when Neil Armstrong stepped off his moon ladder, "one short step for mankind" became the foundation for Mike's article, which set a trend for years to follow, during which time he wrote a series of short pieces for magazines and newspapers.

In later years he lost heart for his trade as it evolved into the electronic era and transferred from the production side of printing to the excitement and trappings that sales offered. Eventually he brokered his way to a comfortable existence and retired early to nurture his love of writing and concentrate his creative efforts on an idea that had taken root in his mind when he was in his late teens. Fearful of ridicule, the idea remained a closely guarded secret, but an unusual meeting with a stranger would soon lead to its blossoming into *The Meadow*.

Elfreda Pretorius's field of expertise is communication, expressed in writing, coaching and teaching. As a best selling author in the self-help industry *(Stop Struggling and Start Living – Rules of the Game)*, she demonstrated her grasp of the human psyche through authoring this book which has become a powerful tool to help change the games of others along with its companion workbook, *Ten Truths from the Top of Table Mountain*. Due to popular demand, a self coaching program based on the book will soon be available for download from her personal web site: www.elfredapretorius.com.

Similar to Mike, she is intensely interested in the world, the dissemination of accurate information and the evolution of man as he is subjected to various schools of thought. They became acquainted via the Internet, on a web site where just such a meeting of minds was in progress and very soon slipped into a wonderful friendship, as comfortably as one would slip into an old pair of jeans. She learned of his wonderful idea for a book, and spontaneously offered to help him dip pen in ink. Due to a pressing workload, her plan was not to linger for too long, but she never left the project. Through the confluence of their combined creativity *The Meadow* developed into a narrative neither could have imagined in their wildest dreams. And that is the book you are now holding.

The entire novel was written via the Internet, through an exchange of ideas and thoughts that defies accurate description. Both authors were aware of a creative force at work in the two and half years that it took to complete a project of which they feel very privileged to have been a part.